MW01134354

Oh Ye Mighty

THE TWO CHURCHES

SHANE MICHAEL JONES

iUniverse

OH YE MIGHTY
THE TWO CHURCHES

iUniverse books may be ordered through booksellers or by contacting:

iUniverse
1663 Liberty Drive
Bloomington, IN 47403
www.iuniverse.com
844-349-9409

ISBN: 978-1-5320-5446-4 (sc)
ISBN: 978-1-5320-5447-1 (e)

Library of Congress Control Number: 2021904518

Print information available on the last page.

iUniverse rev. date: 02/27/2021

*There are so many people who deserve this book dedication.
My loving mother who's compassionate hand steadied me when
tempest whirled through my skull. My stalwart father who
taught me virtue even when it was difficult to be virtuous.*

*Susan Crawford, Uncle Michael, and Pat Mcasilin who
encouraged me to pursue what I'd already given up as lost.*

*Parker, Tanner, Taylor, Brad, Woolley, Preston, and the
other friends who loved me despite my difficult nature.*

*To my training partners and teammates at Vida
who gave me purpose when I needed it most.*

*However, I swore my first work would belong to the
one who never got to see it put to print...*

*Joey, you were brave, headstrong, fiercely independent, and we
loved you for it. All of us wish your story had been a little longer,
but I think it was a beautiful story all the same. Your name has
become a holy thing in the time since. A battle cry to give us
courage when we face the vicious demons of our own life.*

*As we face our times of trying, and the world weighs heavy against
us... As our will is broken and our cunning run out... We reach for
strength not our own and courage we never had. We find your spirit
in our breast, and it is enough to continue on for a moment more.*

*We wish to have known you longer, but perhaps
it is enough that we knew you.*

Ozymandias
By Percy Shelly

I met a traveller from an antique land,
Who said—"Two vast and trunkless legs of stone
Stand in the desert. . . . Near them, on the sand,
Half sunk a shattered visage lies, whose frown,
And wrinkled lip, and sneer of cold command,
Tell that its sculptor well those passions read
Which yet survive, stamped on these lifeless things,
The hand that mocked them, and the heart that fed;
And on the pedestal, these words appear:
My name is Ozymandias, King of Kings;
Look on my Works, ye Mighty, and despair!
Nothing beside remains. Round the decay
Of that colossal Wreck, boundless and bare
The lone and level sands stretch far away."

The Fires of Sterling

The blast blew a hole in the wall, and I was the first man through the breach. My army was a hundred meters behind me, but I couldn't wait for them. If someone didn't capitalize on the chaos, then the defenders would have a chance to form up. Not that it mattered. They were fighting me. Everyone in the world had heard the name Thomas Belson spoke in hushed awe. Belson the Blessed they called me.

I stood atop the rubble for the briefest of moments. I wasn't wearing the uniform of the New Church, the tattoos on my arm that marked me for a Constable were covered in mud, and they'd probably heard I was a giant built of muscle and steel. There was no reason for them to know who I was, but they did. I could read the fear on their faces. Only one man was fool enough to stand alone in the wreckage. Only one man was powerful enough to bring the great wall to the ground. Only one man could hold the fire I had in my eyes without it tearing him apart. They knew they were dead men. The bullets from my sixshooter were just a formality.

I'd only known terror second hand. I'd seen it in the eyes of my victims, but it was a strange phenomenon to me. Some called it self-preservation, but there was no self to preserve outside of battle. Sometimes men met me in peculiar lulls of peace and were disappointed in what they found. They were right to be. I was a shell, meant to be filled with hellfire and gunpowder. The real Thomas Belson could be found on the battlefield and nowhere else. He had come today.

For a heartbeat, I stood upon the rubble of the wall. For a heartbeat, the soldiers of the Mojack dynasty looked upon me helpless. For a heartbeat I counted them, thirty men scrambling for their muskets with more on the way. I smiled at that. For a heartbeat, the world froze. It waited to see what I would do. Then I moved.

Six bullets shot so fast it sounded like one. Every piece of lead found a home in a Mojack skull. I pulled my second gun, but this time I chose my targets. One soldier leveled a rifle at me and dropped it when I put him down. One officer tried to give an order to his troops. He found himself missing the requisite face to do so. I picked the men who presented any threat. Every shot I moved closer. Finally, my second revolver went dry. I was on them with tomahawk in hand. The slaughter was begun.

I was buried in the Battle Mind. Pain, doubt, and remorse couldn't touch me. I saw men load their rifles. I felt the bayonets being stabbed at me. I sensed their weak points. It was all part of an old calculation. A calculation of how many would die. I attacked the first soldier I saw. He thrust at me with his bayonet, but he put too much behind it. I stepped by him and buried my ax in his neck. The next man fumbled his weapon, and I put a knife in his chest. I left it there. I had plenty of knives.

I was surrounded. Outnumbered. There were no formations. The blast from the wall had disrupted them, but finally, they realized I was just a man, alone in a hostile city. Surely all the rumors about me couldn't be true! I showed them that they were.

I spun, ducked, and dodged as they tried to kill me. It would have been easier to catch smoke in their hands. I used the corpses I made as obstructions. I weaved through them, all the while laying waste to those around me. It was as if Death himself touched my enemies and they fell lifeless.

Many soldiers spoke of battle as if weathering a storm. Those men weren't me. I was the storm. I was vengeance, rage, and justice released upon those the Three found wanting. I was fire, blood, and death incarnate, sent to fill the earth with men. I was the gods' mistake, and now that they realized their folly, it was too late. I was too powerful to be killed.

Women, drink, wealth. They were all pale distractions from my true love. Now that I saw her again, I wondered how anything less than her could satisfy me. Perhaps, men weren't meant to take such delight in carnage, but I had long since surpassed the natural law. If the world took issue with my wicked ways, it kept its peace. I served the New Church, but my heart belonged to war.

My soldiers had begun to stream in through the breach. They provided a useful distraction, but these were my enemies to kill.

I felt necks crack beneath my iron arms. I felt ribs shatter, puncturing lungs leaving the victim coughing blood, waiting for death. I felt skulls fracture as I slammed them against whatever surface I could find. I felt shoulders dislocate, bones snap, and eyes pop as I moved through the enemies like a tide through stone. Men with bullets in their muskets tried to shoot me, but I was too quick. Most didn't even have time to pull the trigger before I put my clever hands on them. I exploited weak spots they never knew they had. I hit nerve bundles that left half their bodies useless. I taught them what their bodies were. They were clay to be molded into corpses. It was a mix of the precise martial training I'd received at God's Rest and the fury of a wild animal I'd learned on the battlefield. It was effective, and none could stand against me.

Some men spoke of battle as a blur. I'd always found that strange. I could give an accounting of every move I made. An artist does not mindlessly paint, and I do not mindlessly kill. I slaughtered ten, twenty, fifty, a hundred. I knew they would break soon. The only thing that stopped them was that reinforcements were still rushing in. The ones at the back hadn't seen my work.

Ten years of my life, I had worn the Constable's mark. The first five I had spent battling a titan across all of Thyro. The last five I had spent searching for a man worthy of replacing the one I beat. I would not find him here.

Then, I felt the tattoos on my arm burn like white fire. It was a *Warning*. My tattoos held a separate sort of magic. The kind that let me feel where the Old Religion was being practiced. It wasn't the dull throb to signal that somewhere close a Priest was dabbling in things best left alone. It was a stabbing pain, to let me know Demons were being called to strike me down.

The din of battle died out immediately. Soldiers on both sides went to their knees and prayed. I looked up to see a regal Priest of the Old Religion dressed in the flowing robes, colored red by men's blood. He chanted in a booming voice that seemed to come from the earth itself and reverberate through men's souls. He had the same face as all Priests. The face that was so beautiful it had to be evil. Then I felt the winds pick up and heard the familiar popping and cracking of a man touching something that gods couldn't handle.

Men like him were my sworn enemy. My New Church and their

Old Religion had been circling each other since time had gone. The New Church preached reason and empathy, which put them directly at odds with anyone wearing a blood-colored cloak. My church taught a message of logic, compassion, and optimism, given to them by the Three. However, logic, compassion, and optimism weren't enough to defend the world from the Demons Below and those that called upon them. When virtue failed, the Constable appeared.

I took a step towards the Priest, slow and full of grim purpose. I knew this Priest was weak. Despite his showmanship, he was a poor imitation of the Imorans who engulfed the world in fire two millennia ago. I had already killed any Priest powerful enough to stand against me. He was what was left, hardly worth my time and certainly not worth the prayers the soldiers sent to their gods.

I walked towards the blood cloaked man, violence oozing off my every step. A gust of wind blew a wooden crate beside me to pieces. I walked on. A blast of fire landed just before my feet. I walked on. A bolt of lightning flashed so close to my face I smelled the hairs on my beard burn. I walked on.

The Priest's will faltered. He back peddled away from me. I saw the fear seep into his handsome face. He probably forgot what it meant to be human, to feel afraid. The Demons abandoned him. They judged him too pathetic to deserve their power. The crackling stopped, and the world returned to normal. That was his mistake. He trusted in strength not his own. It had made him weak.

"Please." He went to his knees in front of me. "Mercy." He called out again.

I reached out and took his head in my hands. I placed my fingers in the spots I knew, then I squeezed. He would find no mercy from me. I knew what he'd done to earn that cloak and handsome face. I knew how many innocents he'd tortured. I knew how he'd chased children through their dreams and into madness. He was too far gone to be considered human. That was enough to kill him, but I picked the most painful way to do it because he'd offended me. I was insulted he thought wind, fire, and lightning could defeat me. I killed the soldiers quick because I took no pleasure in their suffering. They were beaten, and that was enough. However, this Priest needed to learn.

I put pressure into his head. My thumbs pressed into his eyes, and my fingers into the soft spot between his skull. He screamed like a pig being roasted alive. I'd never been the strongest man. Ten years of war had made my muscles harder than most, but my frame would never allow me to be huge. However, I knew where to hurt a man better than any alive. I squeezed and squeezed until I felt his body go limp beneath my hands. The screaming stopped, and he was dead.

I turned back to the men still on their knees. "This is our city now!" I screamed. "Take it!"

Those fighting against me ran. Those fighting for me hunted them down. Sterling was large. There was still battle to be done, but it was all a foregone conclusion. I looked down at the body of the Priest, then around at the carnage. I heard the moans of the men I hadn't had time to end properly. They called out for mercy. I wasn't sure if they wanted me to spare them or finish the job. I didn't kill the wounded. I wasn't a child with a magnifying glass. I was a lion looking for a challenge. I wouldn't find one with them. I'd given orders for those men to be spared. Officially, I was just an advisor to the Burbo Republic, and they didn't have to obey me. Unofficially, they would.

There were two sides in the world, the New Church and the Old Religion. One wore robes stained in human blood. One released Demons from worlds below and spoke with the voice of evils older than time itself. The other side had Thomas Belson. Men who survived both in their full glory had nightmares of tattooed arms and prayed to the Three.

I straightened my hat and moved on to the heart of Sterling.

I smoked calmly in the temple of the Old Religion. I was still holding onto my Battle Mind, but I was only splashing in the shallows, not the deep engulfment that caught me in the heat of combat. She was like a lover I wasn't quite ready to part with. Just enough to keep the weariness away. Just enough to keep the hunger at bay. Just enough to escape the pain for one moment more.

I felt the tattoos in my arm burn dull. It was a *Warning* but not the sort that screamed danger. It let me know there was a job to finish. I looked up at the ten Priests I had rounded up. They were beaten, bruised, and bound like cattle. Each one had the handsome face and blood colored robes, but the Priests didn't look quite as regal now. To be fair, though, it was hard to look regal standing on a chair with a noose around your neck. Some Constables preferred the guillotine, but even though I worked for the New Church, I was rather old-fashioned.

I surveyed the room one last time. The walls were covered with lavish paintings. Each picture must have taken the artist a lifetime. I could see the care of every brush stroke. Each artist had slaved away, telling his story the best way he knew how. This was but one room in a cathedral that spanned wider than some towns, and each room was decorated the same. So much history could be gleaned from these walls. This Cathedral had survived two thousand years, but it would not survive me. It would not survive Belson the Blessed.

I was a Constable of the New Church, sworn to rid the world of the Old Religion. I existed to break the shackles the Priests had put on mankind. I was sent to inspire men to heights never dreamed of before. However, to build a better world, sometimes the old one had to die.

"Best to get this over with." It was Brother Seiford. If I stood in iron, he was forged from copper. One was strong but brittle. The other was weak but flexible. Both were needed to make steel, and steel has ever been the only thing that changes the world.

He was as handsome a man as I'd ever run into. His hazel-green eyes struck a chord with his dancing blond curls and played to the rhythm of his noble, well-defined bone structure. His constitution would never allow him a heavily muscled frame, but five years of road hardships had turned him from a sickly thin to a wiry sort of strength. One could almost imagine him in a painting surrounded by nymphs and satyrs.

The New Church teaches that the Three are just. However, Brother Seiford provided a strong argument against that. If a man happens to be as handsome as my friend was, you should at least be able to console yourself with the fact that he probably can't tie his shoes as he takes the woman you've been buying drinks for all night.

There was no such consolation to be had there. Seiford was one of the most talented intellectuals the world over. His fields of expertise when he'd been studying at Harfow were engineering, mathematics, and physics. People hailed me as a master of siege warfare, and there was some truth to that. However, a good bit of my perceived prowess was that Seiford could turn dirt, rocks, and mud into a fortress so long as he had some paper and charcoal to do the equations. Sometimes, he didn't even need to paper... or the dirt, rocks, and mud come to think of it.

That had been his area of expertise, and he'd been better at it than any professor at the most famous universities. If it had stayed that way, he'd have been a useful man. A mind like Seiford's gets bored though. He'd become more than proficient in law, history, and diplomacy. Half the legislation, treaties, and contracts signed over the past five years bore Seiford's fingerprints, even if the signers didn't know it.

Still, I needed him with me for a deeper reason. Seiford's girlish good looks and regal stature made some men think the monk lacked a strong stomach. They were wrong. He was just a moral man in a world where people considered that a weakness. His brother had been like that too. In the end, it had cost him. I wouldn't let the younger Seiford fall prey to that.

I'd hated him once. I'd looked for the first chance to be free of his idealism. It wasn't his fault really. The Thaniel Wars had left me broken and alone, and I was resigned to living out my days that way. It was hard to point to one moment where that had changed. However, five years later, maybe I was still broken, but I wasn't alone.

Seiford put a hand on my shoulder to release me from my thoughts. "Best get this over with." He repeated. That was his way. The monk understood that sometimes a man needed to be hung, but the hangman should never have a smile on his face when he did it.

"Aye." I looked at my friend and nodded grimly. I didn't like this sort of work any more than he did. Killing Priests was my life's duty, but standing as an executioner never suited me. It echoed of a dark past I'd prefer forgotten. It made me feel too much like the leaders I overthrew. Worse yet, it made me feel like the leaders I sometimes served.

I walked up to the first Priest and kicked the chair out from under him. The crimson bastard twisted and struggled as the rope drained his life. I moved to the next one and did the same to him. "Wait!" One would scream. "Fuck you!" Another would hiss. I moved down the line slow and full of purpose. A week ago men would have fallen at these Priests' feet and given their own children if it was asked of them. Belson the Blessed had brought them low. Well, technically the nooses were tied rather high, but philosophers could argue the semantics.

It wasn't long before I reached the last Priest. I expected the bastard to curse or beg like the rest of them, but instead, he laughed. "You think you've won don't you?"

"Well," I gestured to the other Priests doing the hanged man's dance, "I don't think your people will be singing songs about this day."

"Pieces on the board," the Priest smiled maliciously, "sacrificed for a greater cause."

I stared up doubtfully at the crimson cloaked devil. "Whoever's playing the game has sure been biding their time well." I gave Seiford and upraised eye. "They've waited through Thaniel, Westbrook, and Theron's Field." I counted them off on my fingers, "Honestly, it seems your master fell asleep ten years ago and hasn't woken up yet," I took a long drag on my cigarette, "but I'm sure when he's ready, he'll tan my hide good."

"*She*." The Priest kept that ridiculous smile on his face. "She will show you what fury truly means."

"I'm sure she will." I nodded in mock acquiescence.

"You will rue-" The Priest started, but was cut off by having his chair kicked out from under him. I imagined he wasn't going to say anything terribly creative anyway.

"Until she does though, this rope will show you how little I care." I blew smoke into the man's face. That's what he was, after all, just a man. He wasn't the godly powers he channeled. Just a man. Gods can't be killed with a noose. I knew that first hand.

"Demons... never... die..." He managed to choke out.

"Now, now," I wagged my finger, "if I've proven anything, it's that Demons do, in fact, die." I turned around and walked out of the lavish room, leaving the Priests to their fate.

"You didn't have to taunt him." Seiford muttered as we walked out of the Cathedral.

"I didn't have to box Gregory the Big," I puffed on the shortening cigarette. "but they were both asking for it."

"As your advisor, I'm glad we won this battle, and those Priests are dead." Seiford paused. "As your friend, I'm afraid what it will cost you."

I stopped in my tracks. "Those Priests have caused nothing but pain." I took the monk's shoulder. I remembered the children who couldn't tell nightmares from reality, the elderly who had been tortured to insanity, and even the good men turned to evil purpose. I felt no remorse for anything that wore a crimson cloak. "Their sins have set all of Thyro ablaze. Excuse me if I don't weep at what I have to do to put out the fire."

"That might be true, but the Three teach mercy." Seiford stared into my eyes. "When you stand before them, saying, 'I did what I had to,' might not be enough."

I nodded. The monk didn't give sermons often, but when he did, they hit hard. I had learned that, despite the monk's sometimes childish demeanor, he was a man I should listen to. There was so much of his brother in him. "Let's get back to the city." I gestured towards the exit.

"Aye, we should." Seiford agreed. "How long have you been in your Battle Mind?"

"Two days." I lied, but my friend's disapproving hazel eyes made me tell the truth. "A week I think, maybe more. It was a hard battle."

"You need to pace yourself." Seiford gave me a concerned look. "Other Constables have died staying in it for less than that."

"I'm the greatest who ever was." I used to say it with a twinge of arrogance before it had been proven beyond doubt. Now I just said it as fact. "I've done three weeks before and came out alive."

"You almost didn't." Seiford remembered my battles well. "The world isn't so incompetent that it can't go without you for a three-hour nap."

"These soldiers were." I nodded to the door. It was true the army I'd let into Sterling couldn't have taken a brothel without me kicking down the front door. "Besides I haven't taken any serious injuries."

"How would you know? You can't feel them?" Seiford shook his head. "That shot in your shoulder looks bad to me."

"I'll let you treat it when we get a chance." I finally relented. "After the celebrations of course." I smiled at my friend and started walking to the door.

Seiford smiled back and followed me. The thought of merrymaking dismissed his uncharacteristic gloom. "No doubt they're already setting up their victory parades." The monk chuckled. "I'm sure the women of Sterling will give us a special sort of confession tonight."

"I'm sure they will." I smiled as we reached the end of the hallway. The fuse still lined the ground ending where I'd set it earlier. I lit the end and watched the sparks dance across the floor. The charges were set to bring the chapel toppling in on itself. There'd be no damage to the surrounding structure. "It's a shame all this has to go up in flames." I threw my cigarette on the ground and stamped it out. "Say what you will about these Priests, they have style."

"That they do." Seiford said mournfully. He was Anthanii nobility and used to a particular lifestyle before I had dragged him across half the world.

We walked out of the cathedral, and any elation I had at winning the battle was gone. I'd taken more cities than I could remember. Sometimes it ended with liberation parades. Sometimes it ended with forced smiles and strained reconciliation. Sometimes it ended with fire and bands of soldiers going house to house taking their revenge on anything they could find. This was the later. Black billowing clouds touched the horizon as everything people build the honest way went up in flames. The collective screams of a city in pain reached my ears in a nonsensical harmony. A thousand tragedies played out as I watched from atop the temple. The landscape seemed to exist only in shades of blood.

I took precautions not to let this happen again, but the army I'd led weren't disciplined professionals or determined militiamen. They weren't even mercenaries who would take their loot and leave. They were the worst sort I'd run into during my long tenure of fighting other people's wars. They were revolutionaries drunk on righteous anger.

I hadn't thought it through. Usually, my name and orders were enough to keep the peace. If that failed, the six-shooter at my side could keep them on the straight and narrow. These were possessed by something far more dangerous than greed or bloodlust. They believed what they did was right proper justice.

"Three above." I whispered to myself.

"What's going on?" Seiford stared aghast.

"The bad sort of victory." I gritted my teeth in anger. "We need to stop this." I took off running towards the city. Sterling's clean streets and rich history were being consumed by fire and blood. One of the greatest cities in Thyro was dying, and I had led the killers inside.

I sprinted down the streets until I found a group of Burbo soldiers drinking and screaming about revolution. "Ho, your eminence," an older man with sergeant stripes on his shoulder shouted, "come to take part in our glorious revolution?"

"Where are your officers?" I shouted. "They should be stopping this madness!"

"They're celebrating in the main hall." The sergeant looked

confused. "They told us to show these bastards what happens when you stand in the way of progress." He smiled back at his men.

Seiford finally caught up. "Thomas," he got out through labored breathing, "this city is tearing itself apart."

"I know." I said to the monk then turned back to the sergeant. "Gather whatever soldiers you can find and end this madness!" I gestured to the rifle the man was carrying. "Shoot anyone who disobeys."

The sergeant straightened himself. "On whose authority?" He narrowed his eyes.

I put a hand on my six-shooter as the cold threat entered my eyes. "On mine." He'd have never talked to me that way if he was sober. The drink makes fools of us all.

"We serve the Burbo Republic," the sergeant spit on the ground, "not the New Church."

I hung my head. I felt the hopelessness settle on my shoulders. These men were too far gone.

The sergeant's face softened. "I'm sorry your eminence." He did look genuinely sorry. "We might not have won if it weren't for you, but things like this-"

I pulled my weapon and shot him through the face. Blood and brains splattered his kinsmen. Discipline would be restored by whatever means necessary. These barbarians needed to be reminded why I was called Belson the Blessed.

Looking at these soldiers it was hard to believe they had taken a city. Not one of them tried to take vengeance on me for killing their compatriot. They stood their sobered from the shock of watching me kill the sergeant. I cocked my pistol again and they moved to a rigid attention. I wouldn't be questioned again.

"You!" I shouted at a terrified corporal. "Do as I say, or I swear by the Three, I'll have you strung up."

"Yes, your eminence!" He jumped to attention.

"Now!"

"Aye, your eminence!" He screamed back, gesturing for the men to follow him. The corporal spared a glance at his unconscious sergeant before running off into the heart of the city.

"What now?" Seiford asked, looking around helplessly.

"We need to get the officers off their asses." I watched the group of soldiers hurry towards somewhere. They might help to stem the violence a bit, but they wouldn't be nearly enough. "Damn them!" I shouted. "They were meant to control their men!"

"Whatever you're going to do, do it quick!" Seiford was frantic. "This city can't handle much more."

I saw a pair of terrified horses and ran to them. I hopped onto one's back and spent a moment consoling it. I looked behind me and saw Seiford doing the same. "We need to get to the main hall." As soon as the horse was placated enough to run, I put the heels to the beast. It was faster than I thought but not fast enough.

As I sped down the city streets, I watched the horror unfold. I saw soldiers taking turns on screaming women. I saw a boy who couldn't be older than twelve hanging from a window ledge. I saw a group of angry Burbo's stomp an elderly man's head into the street. I couldn't spare the time to save anyone. I needed to get to the main hall, and every second I was delayed, countless innocents died. I couldn't pause to protect one while I felt the world burn.

I was finally at the hall. It was an impressive building by anyone's standards. Statues to Sterling's heroes stood as if guarding the heart of the city. I had imagined they'd put one of me in the walkway, but after everything I'd seen, I wondered if the city would still exist come morning. The actual hall stood on a hill overlooking the fires. Once it might have seemed to protect its citizens, now it stood only to watch the carnage. The stones of the building had been set two thousand years ago, the columns that held the roof were ageless. This building was the perfect melding of what had been and what could be. Perhaps the Three should have asked the architect's advice when they forged man. Man had seen the perfection of the building painted in blood.

I dismounted and ran through the doorway flanked by Seiford. What I saw inside turned my stomach more than even the senseless violence outside. The officers sat around the main table looking drunk and merry as the people they claimed to serve were slaughtered in the street. The paintings that had once stood proudly on the walls were defaced and cast aside, to be more thoroughly destroyed later. The officers should have done the same with the wine they were drinking.

"Ah, the conquering hero!" First Citizen Nicholo said, raising a cup in my direction. "We were just drinking to your feats at the wall." Nicholo was a handsome man, too handsome for my taste. His sharp cheekbones and piercing eyes had helped him form the army he'd used to sack Sterling. He was a charismatic and regal looking leader.

When the peasants looked on his face and heard his promises, they had rallied behind him. His blue uniform was pristine, not a sign of wear on the thing. He wore medals of bravery on his chest, but I had found him curiously absent on the battlefield.

"This city is being sacked, and you're sitting here drinking toasts!" I screamed. It can be said that I was the exact opposite of Nicholo. Ten years of constant war had left its mark on me. I was still wearing blood from the battle and a bullet wound in my shoulder that desperately needed attention. My uniform was simple and black, adorned only with the Tree of Faith on the front. I wore my courage on my face and the well-worn handles of my six shooters. The only thing that separated me from a beggar with poor fashion was the missing right sleeve and the intertwining tattoos on my arm. "Go!" I screamed at the confused officers. "Restrain your men!" No one moved.

"My men are showing these people what happens when they stand in the way of progress." Nicholo answered calmly. He echoed the same words of the sergeant.

"If progress raped women in the streets the way your soldiers do, then I'd stand in its way too." I hissed angrily.

That got a rise out of the First Citizen. "These people need to know that we Burbos are every bit as convicted as the Mojack king we ousted." Nicholo smiled towards a corpse in the corner of the room. It was the old king clutching a knife in his chest. Apparently, he'd rather die than see his city sacked.

"These people have known tyrants with conviction!" I screamed around the room. The officers seemed just as unbloodied as their leader. Most were lawyers and scholars who'd decided they'd attract more women in a uniform. There were no true soldiers among them. "They need to know they are protected under a wise leader."

Nicholo took the statement as flattery. "A wise leader knows when to let his men off the leash."

That sent me into a shaking rage. "Your 'wisdom' couldn't get these men past the first wall!" I screamed at him. "I didn't give you this city so you could sit here and drink!"

"Take care who you're talking too." Nicholo narrowed his eyes in anger.

"I should have taken care who I was serving." I shot back.

"I will not be spoken to this way." Nicholo stood and leveled a sneering glare my way.

I stopped screaming and turned my anger to something far more terrifying. "Neither will I."

I whispered to the room through my cold fury. "I turned the Rose Petal Throne to ash while you were harassing whores at University." I took another step forward. "I brought Thaniel to his knees while you spoke of fashionable rebellion." The ice in my voice grew. "By the time you finished your lessons, I had changed this world." I paused. "Do not test me. Better men than you have tried."

Nicholo sneered down his nose. "I rule here, not you." He spat into the ground. "If I order my men to murder every child in the street, all I want you to do is nod quietly." He gestured to the door. "Leave this city. You're no longer welcome here."

I drew my gun, and every man in the room jumped terrified. A good many of the officers fell out of their seats.

"No!" Seiford screamed and moved between Nicholo and the six-shooter. "Not like this." The monk pushed the weapon down. "This isn't our way." It was true. When I'd met him five years earlier, it had been, but I'd been trying to be better. There was one rule a Constable couldn't break. He couldn't kill the man who requested the assistance of the New Church. If my order gained a reputation for killing leaders who had asked our intervention, the whole system would fall apart.

I nodded and holstered the gun "It's not our way." I said to my friend. "Let's leave." I had made my mistake. The best thing to do was let it play out. What was done couldn't be reversed, but leaderless, the violence would only grow. No good could come out of the end of my six-shooter that day.

"Leave boy!" Nicholo had finally found his courage. "Sterling is mine now, and I renounce the New Church."

I stopped mid-stride. Seiford knew the look on my face. "Thomas, don't!" He whispered. I drew and fired before anyone had a chance to move. The bullet took Nicholo between the eyes. At least the uniform finally had some blood on it.

I lowered my weapon. "Restrain your men." I said it barely a whisper, but they all heard me through the silence. There were a hundred officers present. They were all armed, but they knew that even all of them together were no match for Belson the Blessed. They ran out the door tumbling over one another in a drunken stupor.

"Thomas..." Seiford was at a loss for words.

I let myself fall to the floor when the last of them had left. I knew the officers wouldn't do any good. They couldn't have ordered a man to march across the street, much less stop an army with a taste for blood. I looked at the body of Nicholo. Even though the man was a coward, his charisma was the only thing that could have held the city together. I felt the shadow of the man I'd been five years ago. The shadow lapped at my ankles, and now I felt it trying to retake me. Sterling was dead and Belson the Blessed had killed it. The fires might be put out in time, but the city would burn forever.

Five Years Later
Present Day

J smoked my cigarette trying to wipe the travel dust off a poor map of Cechzno to little success. I twisted and turned the damn thing, but it still seemed more like a child's first art project than a rendering of a far eastern Thyran city. I squinted my eyes one last time and took a drag on my smoke.

I was standing in the middle of the small but important city we'd taken the day before. All around us soldiers and workmen were going about their business. It was a relatively swift and decisive victory not a drawn out siege, so there weren't many repairs to be done, but still, it was good to keep the lads busy. Meanwhile, I tried to figure how to hold such a city.

"Is this really the best the Council could provide?" I turned to face Lieutenant Cassov. He was my adjunct from Captain-General Mustero, the military leader appointed by the Council of Sixteen. Cassov was a tall, straight-backed man who looked every bit the picture of martial virtue. His pressed green uniform and broad shoulders were only eclipsed by his exceptionally impressive mustache.

"What's that your eminence?" The man's eyes went wide, as if I had looked over his people and found them wanting. The thought of my disapproval hung over the lieutenant like the headsman's axe.

"If there is anything your eminence finds substandard, I will be sure to improve the situation immediately." He moved to rigid attention.

I walked towards him. "It's this map." I put out the cigarette. "It must have been drawn by someone who's never been to Cechzno." I handed it to him. "For all I know, the cartographer never stepped outside his home."

Cassov relaxed a bit, perhaps relieved that my displeasure was not a direct reflection on his people. "It's not so bad, your eminence." His approval was made only slightly less meaningful by the fact that he was reading it upside down.

I took the paper out of his hand. "According to this map there's a centaur fighting a troll in the woods three miles south." I pointed to the drawing. It wasn't a very good rendering of a centaur either. The troll wasn't bad though.

Cassov shrugged his broad shoulders. "That is probably what you would call a metaphor, your eminence." He said through his thick accent.

"So should I metaphorically deploy troops there or should I be too worried they'll be caught in the metaphorical crossfire?" Actually I was already making plans for Seiford, Ayn-Tuk, and I to go through the forest before we left. If there was a centaur fighting a troll, I wanted to see it.

"The Children of Gusov were made for fighting, not drawing lines on maps." Lieutenant Cassov invoked the mythological patriarch of the Gusovan people.

"A big part of war is drawing lines on maps." I screwed up my face in confusion. "One might say it's the purpose of the endeavor even."

"The point of this war is to honor our-" The Lieutenant was in danger of going on a patriotic speech, so I cut him off with a wave.

"Sorry, your eminence." He said meekly.

"How do you even know where you're fighting if you don't have a map?" I looked around the forested landscape of Cechzno. "Do you just see a pretty tree and decide it's a fine place to have two armies meet?"

Cassov straightened his already rigid back. "The blood of Gusov tells us where to fight."

I blinked away the coming headache. "Listen lieutenant…"

"Hold just one second your eminence." Cassov uttered as he went for the notepad and pencil he had in his jacket pocket. He pulled out a pocket watch and checked the time, writing it down.

"Are you quite ready?" This was the more annoying parts of my job. The people I fought for often took meticulous records of my every uttering like I was a prophet sent from above. I tried to entertain myself by interspersing my "sermons" with random swear words and rude comments about the chronicler's mother. However,

I'd stopped the practice when I realized those rude comments actually got written down.

"Almost, your eminence." He stopped writing to look up at me. "What's the date?"

"Does it matter?" I asked.

I was answered by a blank stare.

"It's the twenty-fourth." I finally uttered to move things along. I had no idea if it was the twenty-fourth, but it sounded right and Cassov didn't object.

Finally the man stopped writing and looked at me to continue.

"Listen lieutenant, your people fought well yesterday." I took a step forward. "*You* fought well yesterday. You'll make a fine officer."

"Thank you, your eminence!" The man wiped what I hoped wasn't a tear out of his eyes. "My late grandfather always knew I was destined for greatness. I told my fiancé I was so nervous to serve under Thomas Belson, but she said-"

I held up my hand to cut him off.

"Sorry, your eminence." He seemed embarrassed. "You were saying?"

"Your people fight well." I repeated. "The natural forest of Gusovia means your people are accustomed to the hardships of being on the march. Every lad knows their way around a rifle from hunting. Most importantly you have a certain toughness conducive to soldering." I smiled. "It's not unlike my own homeland."

"Conducive?" Cassov questioned.

"Have someone define it for you." I was running out of patience.

"Your land is more full of natural resources than anyone's aware of, and the Council's modernization campaign seems to be working." I pulled another cigarette out and lit it. "In time, Gusovia could be a real player in politics, not just a pawn on the board for proxy wars between larger nations."

"That's all we've ever wanted." The Lieutenant's face went stony as he stopped writing for a moment. He knew better than me the troubles of his people. "It's what I will give my life for."

"It requires more than the deaths of good men." I put my hand on his shoulder. "You need to be teaching mapmaking in your universities. It would have made this campaign much easier."

"Noted, your eminence." He blushed at the compliment, but refrained from a monologue like before as he finished his notes.

"It's not just for warfare." I kept smoking. I knew I should quit the nasty habit I'd picked up some years ago, but I had too much to worry about already. Besides, even if I wouldn't admit it, smoking made me feel closer to my native Confederacy across the ocean. It helped me remember the tobacco plantation I'd grown up on, and the family I hadn't seen in fifteen years.

I finally came out of that thought. "It's not just for warfare." I repeated. "The Council will need to know where to build roads and infrastructure." I'd found early in my campaign the tracks of Gusovia were not conducive to armies. "Businessmen will need to know where to build factories. You cannot compete with the powers of Western Thyro without these maps."

"Understood, your eminence." Cassov caught up to me with his notes.

"You need to be collecting population data as well." I pointed at him with my cigarette. "How can you manage your people if you don't know how many there are." I paused as he wrote down what I said. "There's a great many foolish and arrogant practices that countries like Kran and Anthanii engage in. Map making and censuses are not among them."

"Yes, your eminence." He kept writing.

I poked the notepad. "I strongly recommend that the Council of Sixteen make cartography a required discipline in all military colleges. There's a few people I could recommend to teach the class. They won't be cheap, but they will be worth it." I paused again. "I would also encourage them to start collecting population data. Those are both major steps to becoming a real nation state."

"Constable Belson," I heard a voice call behind me, "I need to talk to you."

I turned around to see Constable Julius behind me. He looked to be just over twenty and a few inches taller than me. The man was of Rhorri decent from his dark complexion and black hair. Most of all, he was much better looking than me, even before my face was scared and beaten from a decade and a half of war. He wore his Constable's uniform well, and the tattoos on his arm were striking even on his dark skin.

"One moment, Constable Julius." I said as I turned back to Lieutenant Cassov. "Until the Council does invest in those reforms, we'll have to work with what we have."

"What are your orders, your eminence?" Cassov looked back to me.

"Well, the map says there's a mountain that reaches above the clouds about three miles east." I paused. "That's probably an exaggeration because I'd be able to see it from here, and there are no mountains in Gusovia to speak of." I pointed at the part of the map the mountain was supposed to be. "I am willing to bet that there's a little hill locals used to sacrifice on in their pagan days."

"Why do you say that?" Cassov asked me with thinly veiled indignation. "We may not have factories or world famous universities, but we pray to the Three here."

"If you go back far enough, everyone's got a pagan past, and there's always a little of it left over, no matter how many factories or world famous universities you build." I said without looking up from the map.

"Oh." Cassov realized I hadn't actually given his people offense.

"I'm willing to bet this is one of them because of the description." I took another drag. "Everyone wants to believe they're sacrificing as close as they can get to their gods, and no one in ancient Chechzno had actually seen a real mountain, so they were willing to believe it." I paused. "In my experience these holy places look over roads and natural ways of approach."

"That's quite a deduction from a map as useless as that one." Constable Julius crossed his arms.

"You think I'm wrong, Julius?" I turned back to the Rhorri youth. The lad had been pushing back on all my orders since I'd gotten to Gusovia. He was a competent young man and a good soldier to have at one's side, but he didn't take well to being under my command.

"I think it's just what I said," the Constable shrugged, "quite a deduction."

"Constable Belson is right, your eminence." A sergeant who was clearly eavesdropping and trying not to look like he was eavesdropping stepped forward from his men.

"Of course he is." I heard Constable Julius mumble under his breath.

I ignored that and continued at the sergeant. It was a problem better faced without prying eyes. "How do you know?" I asked.

"My paw was a candle maker, your eminence." The sergeant's eyes roved over all of us, somewhat nervous. "He set up shop here for five years when I was a lad."

"And are my deductions correct, sergeant?" I smoked some more.

"They are, startlingly so, your eminence." He paused as if embarrassed. "They said it was an old pagan gathering place in the old days. Cursed they said." He gave a little smile. "Me and some of the lads used to dare each other to climb up it at night. Paw whipped me good when he found out."

"Good Father." I smiled back and gestured for him to continue.

"If it was cursed we didn't find any ghosts up there, but it had one hell of a view on the two roads into town." The sergeant glanced at Constable Julius who was clearly annoyed. "We used to camp up there during festival week and watch the people come in."

I gave him the piece of paper in my hand. "Is it where this map says it is?"

"Is that a centaur fighting a troll?" The man asked.

"Focus, sergeant." I tapped the place the hill should be.

"Kind-of-sort-of but not really." He said. "Maybe a mile to the south of that."

I turned back to Lieutenant Cassov. "Take this man and find out where this hill is." I put my cigarette out on my boot and tossed it. "When you find it, place the twelve pounder artillery there. Place a regiments here and another one here." I pointed to a place on the map. "The lighter cannons can cover the infantry's north flank. Push the scouts down the road, and place the heavy cavalry behind that to act as a quick reaction force."

"It'll get done." Cassov nodded.

"Give copies of my orders to Captain-General Mustero. I don't want confusion." I paused. "I'm not expecting Razca and his lot to counter-attack. We whipped them pretty good here, but we should be ready for something. Chechzno is too important for him to just limp away. If we hold this city, Razca's army will fold eventually, and he knows it." I thought for a moment. "Also make all the officers draw maps, they probably won't be worth much, but it'll give them practice."

I nodded one last time. "Dismissed, soldiers."

"Yes, your eminence."

I watched them go and turned to Constable Julius. "We should speak in private."

"I think that would be best." He responded.

We walked behind an alley where we wouldn't be easily overheard.

"We're not supposed to to take over the whole army, Thomas." Julius hissed. "We train and advise. We fight with the men and lead attachments when we're asked to." He paused. "We do not assume command from military leaders lawfully appointed by sovereign governments."

"How long ago did you get your tattoos, Julius? Four years? Five years?" I narrowed my eyes.

"Three." Julius clenched his jaw.

"Fifteen years I've worn these marks." I pointed a finger at him. "I fought-"

"I know what you've done, Thomas." Julius shook his head. "Every lad round the world had their paw telling them stories about Belson the Blessed." He looked me in the eyes. "If there's a heavier name than yours, I've never heard it, and those stories are half the reason I joined the Constabulary." He paused. "I know who I'm speaking to. You're the man who beat Thaniel."

"Then you know better than to tell me what my duties are." It wasn't the argument I was expecting to have.

"Maybe." He paused. "Then again, maybe all those years of having people look up at you makes a man think he's above the rules."

"Captain-General Mustero listens to my advice. My authority comes from him." I paused. "He's free to veto any of my orders."

"Does he know that?" Julius took a step forward. "Do the men know that?"

I narrowed my eyes. "What are you getting at?"

"I think maybe he's too afraid to veto you." The young man shrugged. "I think he knows well what happened when First-Citizen Niccolo did the same." He kept his gaze on me. "I know the other stories. The ones they don't sing about in taverns."

"You weren't there!" I hissed back at the boy. "You didn't see what that monster was doing to his own people." My teeth were clenched. "What I did was right!"

"Who decides what's right?" Julius didn't flinch. The boy had bones to speak to me this way. I'd give him that.

"Sometimes you just know it when you see it." I spat on the ground.

"For all our power we are servants to the Testament and the

Nameless Man who wrote it." Julius shook his head. "There's times I think you've forgotten that."

I eyed him up dangerously. "I've seen things, boy. I know more about the Three than anyone in the New Church."

"You've become so great you've slipped the little book all us lesser men must concern ourselves with." He spit back.

The boy was closer to the truth than I'd care to admit, so I didn't let him keep on it. "Let's be honest, you're not angry I broke some tradition. You're angry this was your assignment, and I finished it." I gave Julius a viscous smile. "You're angry they worship my advice and treat you like an afterthought."

"They're right to." Julius admitted. "We may wear the same marks, but I'm not fool enough to think that means our names hold equal weight." Julius nodded. "What I do think is that you've done amazing things. I think you were the only one who could've torn Thaniel down. I think you're still the best soldier the world over, and we would all be well served to listen to your advice and follow your example."

He gave a heavy sigh. "I also think the Order needs a future. I think that one day, when you're gone the people need to be able to trust that other Constables can continue your good work." He put his hand on a six-shooter like mine. "You won the people's faith in the New Church, but if it's only in your name then it'll be gone before your body's cold."

"So you're saying I should have stayed away." I lit up again. "I should have let you do your job here, and maybe then people would start to associate my accomplishments with the Order and not the other way around."

"Maybe."

"You're missing something." I shot back.

"What's that?"

"Before I turned the tide on Thaniel and his Kranish legions, there were twenty Constables trying to win that war." I tapped the six-shooter at my side. "They all died. I beat the Emperor of Kran alone." I leaned towards the Constable. "Maybe people don't associate my victories with the Order because they're smarter than you give them credit for."

"You shouldn't disparage our fallen brothers that way." Julius straightened up. "Constables are the greatest warriors the Three make, even if they're not named Thomas Belson."

"You're right." I bit my lip. "They were all clever, brave, and talented fighters…" I paused as I puffed on my smoke. "They all lost anyway. It wasn't because they weren't good enough. It was because they were too good." The memories of those wars would be seared into my brain till the day I died. "They wouldn't walk the path it took to beat Thaniel."

"You mean they couldn't have done what you did at the Pillars." Julius spoke of the moment that had defined my life for a decade. My last action in the Thaniel Wars that left me broken beyond all mortal kin. It bit deep.

"Aye, they couldn't have done that." I stared at him in cold fury.

"Maybe you shouldn't have done it either then." The lad didn't back down.

I broke off my stare and looked down. "Aye, maybe I shouldn't have." I paused. "Not a day goes by I don't think about what happened, but I did it." The echo of their screaming rung in my ear. "No one knows how many millions died in that war." I pointed a finger at him. "You don't know how many friends I lost to burn that damn Rose Petal throne." I stared up at the sky. "I hope you never learn what I stopped with those pillars…" I paused as I took a drag on the cigarette. "I'll pay for what I did every day till I die, and when I do, I'll pay in the afterlife, but the world is a safer place for those pillars."

I shook the memories off me. "The long and short of it is that if you didn't want me to win this war, you should have won it first."

Julius let some of his guilt show. "There were complications."

I gave a huff of laughter. "Well, I'm sure you'll do great things in the next war when everything goes according to plan." I threw up my hands at the ridiculousness of it all. "There's always complications!"

"Not like this." Julius muttered, though he was clearly embarrassed he couldn't deal with them on his own.

That got my attention. "What kind of complications?"

"An agent was working against us." Julius shook his head. "Factories refused to take our orders or wanted ungodly prices. The Council of Sixteen couldn't even vote on a war tax, much less elect a Captain-General. Besides that every major trading partner of Gusovia threatened to cut ties if we fought Razca." The Constable clenched his fist. "I wasn't even sure we could go to war."

Julius gave me a reluctant nod of respect. "When you showed up most of those problems ended. Some of the men that owned those factories fought with you. They sold us weapons and equipment for cost, practically gave them away." He gave a little laugh. "The Council levied the war tax and elected Mustero Captain-General. Even the trading partners backed off their threats."

"I have that effect from time to time." I put my hand on my tomahawk. "Did you ever find out who this agent worked for?"

Julius shook his head. "It could've been anyone. The great nations of Thyro would rather Gusovia remain a divided prize to fight over and exploit with one sided trade deals." The young man crossed his arms. "Beating Razca was the last thing standing between a backwater and a united player in the game. There's plenty of reasons to not want that."

"So you think it was Anthanii, Kran, or their like." I took a step forward.

"Maybe." Julius shrugged. "It would make sense." He looked up at me. "Then again maybe it was banking interests or one of the trading companies." The Constable blew a deep breath out his nose. "I may not be you, but I'm pretty good at getting information. No one could tell me who she was. I doubt if even the factories knew her real name."

"So it was a she?" I asked.

Julius cocked his head to the side. "Women can be spies too."

I had to chuckle at that. "No one knows better than me how good a spymaster women make." I paused. "I was wrong to blame you for not being able to end this war." I eyed up the Constable. "Was she pretty?"

"By all accounts she was beautiful." Julius cocked his eyebrow up. "You know this woman."

"About as well as you do." I spat again. "Still, she's done similar things to me. That fiasco at Hunthu had her fingerprints all over it." I paused. "There was a Priest at Sterling who said something as well." *She.*

"You don't want to know who she is?" Julius took a step back.

"Of course I do." I had to laugh at that. "I've spent the past five years trying to organize an investigation."

"Why haven't you had one?" The Constable asked.

"They say I'm being paranoid." I shrugged. "The populace may still see me as a hero, but there are powerful people that think I've outlived my use."

"Maybe she got to them too." Julius echoed my thoughts over the past half decade.

"I wouldn't doubt it." I licked my lips.

A moment of silence stretched between us. "Listen Julius, I spoke out of turn. You seem a good Constable. You'll do fine for yourself."

"That means something from you." Julius leaned against a wall. "I wouldn't want you thinking I don't respect the past. You've always been a hero of mine, but I needed to voice my concerns." He gave a half smile. "When I went off to God's Rest, it was always your boots I was trying to fill."

"I don't think you'd like the way my boots fit much." I said it half to myself.

The lad cocked his head in confusion. "What's that mean?"

"It's nothing really." I waved it off. "You'll do well for yourself, but there's some paths men weren't meant to walk."

Julius shrugged. "If you say so." He gestured out the alley. "We better get back to the rest."

"We better." I stomped on the cigarette, and we walked out to our duties.

Before I turned the corner I heard a tenor voice telling the sort of story a monk shouldn't tell. "So then I said to the lady, 'it's my divine duty in fact!'" This got a chorus of laughter.

I reached the alley to see most of the soldiers in the square were gathered around my monk, Seiford. With his high cheekbones, striking eyes, and blond hair he cut a handsome figure even through his church uniform. He was a natural showman. Something about the man made people want to listen to him.

He was leading my horse, Shaggy Cow, and even she seemed to be laughing at the joke. I'd let the monk take my steed to tend to a minor scrape she'd suffered in the battle.

I was unreasonably fond of the horse. She had been given to me by a grateful chieftain four years ago. Everyone in the world knew her by some ridiculous name or another like *Constables Fury* or *Moon's Stead*. They probably had a different idea of what Shaggy looked like too. The Eastern horse stood just a bit higher than most ponies and was covered in a fluffy tan fur that gave her the name Shaggy. She was rather unimpressive to look at, but then they saw her run. She could match most horse's top speed and hold it for the whole day, she had a keen sense on how to move in the thick of battle, and she was the smartest animal I'd ever met. I had a sinking suspicion she was more intelligent than some humans. She certainly seemed to understand what I said. In truth, I wasn't even fully aware of her limits. In the four years I'd ridden her, I'd never had to stop for her sake, and I'd never pushed her to a place she couldn't go faster from

Ayn-Tuk was sitting on a box, cradling his gilded quarter staff. The five feet of ashen wood which depicted golden serpents dueling across the length, was the only weapon he'd use. He was damn good with it though. Knocked me down more than a few times in the practice square even. That was a boast few men could make honestly. Still, he refused to kill the men he beat in battle. It was a strange way for a warrior, but then, I wasn't sure he was a warrior. At the very least that wasn't all he was.

Ayn-Tuk was a Souren, black as night, and had joined our band three years ago after my adventures on the continent. If I wrote down everything that man said in the time he'd followed me, I might have enough to fill a page, maybe two. His black skin, height, muscular build, and stoic demeanor gave him the appearance of a chiseled statue.

Ayn-Tuk was a strange sort. He didn't drink, rarely talked, and seemed to avoid all modern technology. The black bastard didn't even wear a shirt! Some people saw him and decided his mannerisms were just a part of the Souren culture, but I'd fought on the continent long enough to know that wasn't the case. The Sourens I met weren't so different from Thyrans. They could be talkative, heavy drinking, and as appreciative of industrialization as anyone else. Both continents were huge places, and you'd find every taste of man there, from moral to evil. Sure, the culture differed. When it comes to societies, laws, and custom that sort of thing matters, but when it comes to individuals, I've always found that culture is a sheet we throw on people we don't know. Humans around the world respect heroism, want to feed their families, and dance on a moon-lit night. Their version of heroism changes. What they fed their families changes. The music they dance to changes. However, underneath it all, we're far more alike than different.

Ayn-Tuk was different because his soul was different. It had almost nothing to do with his skin. I had never really discovered why he followed me. Every time I asked he'd just say, "because you need it." When people approached me about my strange companion, I'd respond with something suitably exotic about how he owed me a life debt or his family had been slain. That seemed appropriate. In truth, I hadn't even realized he was going to accompany me until he stepped on our ship, much less why he had. He was a strange breed, but he was just as strange in Souren as he would be anywhere else.

"That's not the best part though." Seiford went on. "Her sister comes up the stairs-"

"Seif, please refrain from corrupting the good men of Gusovia." I said as me and Julius walked towards him. "There's still a tribe in Souren that thinks you're a fertility god."

"Ho, Constables Julius and Thomas! I was just looking for the pair of you before I started regaling these men with stories of our travels." Seiford hopped up from the brick wall he was sitting on with a flourish. "As I spread the good word of the Three to different cultures, I must find new ways to reach the faithful." The monk turned to see the soldiers that had been his audience trying to hide their laughter.

I shook my head and smiled at my old friend. "Aye, I'm sure you did it all for the Three."

The corner of Seiford's lip curled up in a smile. "I certainly made a few women call out to our gods." That got another round of laughter from the soldiers.

"Don't be to hard on him, your eminence." A grizzled corporal said through a grin. "He's just raising our spirits is all."

Constable Julius cocked an eyebrow up. "I thought monks were supposed to lift men's souls not their spirits." There was no bite to the rebuke though.

Seiford shrugged. "I find where one goes the other follows." He handed over the Shaggy's lead rope. "She's fine. Barely more than a scratch, but I patched it up."

I rubbed her nose and produced a dried apple for the beast. "Good Shaggy."

"Smarter than the man who rides her." He poked at a cut on my side an officer had given me during the battle.

"It's nothing." I waved it off. "How stand the casualty reports."

"The battle went well for us." Seiford scratched the back of his head. "Still a battle though."

"Two hundred and twenty-six who will heal." Ayn-Tuk stood to walk towards us. "fifty-four who won't."

Julius put his hands on his hips. "I've got some letters to write then." He paused. "What of the enemy?" The Constable had given orders for Razca's men to receive equal treatment.

"Still getting a handle on those, I'm afraid." Seiford looked back at the soldiers for a moment. "They're more spread out, and a few of them are still hiding in the forest."

"I expected as much." Julius kicked a pebble. "Anything you can tell me?"

"The number's already more than ours, but probably not that much more." Seiford crossed his arms. "Razca realized pretty quick he was losing and ordered the retreat."

"Those are still some mothers who'll never forget what happened to their sons." The Constable glanced around at the city. "Our goal here was to bring Razca into the fold."

I glanced at my younger counterpart. "Whatever your goal was, the means were war." I paused. "Casualties are a part of that. We knew it, and they knew it."

"Aye, suppose you're right." Julius put his hand on his gun belt, then turned to Seiford. "Whatever your faults as an evangelizer are, this battle would've gone a lot less smoothly if you hadn't spotted that weak point in their fortification."

Seiford put a hand on his heart. "Good sir, you do me too much praise."

I laughed as I turned to Ayn-Tuk. "The leader of that artillery battery you took out sends his personal gratitude for sparing his men and himself."

The black man shrugged.

I went on. "Said he'd name his first born son in your honor."

Seiford cocked an eyebrow up. "You don't think a Gusovian boy named Ayn-Tuk might be subject to bullying." He said. "Children can be rather cruel."

"My thoughts exactly." I responded. "Which is why I told the officer our black friend's name is John."

Constable Julius cut in. "As clever as that is, we should probably discuss how to press our advantage." He nodded for the gaggle of soldiers to get back to work. "Cechzno is the last piece to breaking Razca."

"Aye, and we should just to be safe." I turned to the young man. "I don't think it'll be necessary though."

"How do you mean?" Julius cocked an eyebrow up.

"I told you earlier, with Cechzno in our hands Razca will fold quickly and he knows it." I tapped the tomahawk at my side. "I sent terms to the man, I'm willing to bet he'll accept."

"You sent terms?" The Constable turned to me, clearly more than a little angry. "Without consulting anyone?"

"They were previously agreed upon by the Council of Sixteen." I shrugged. "Well, Council of Seventeen once Razca accepts."

"That's not the point!" Julius hissed. "It isn't your position to offer or accept terms. That privilege belongs to Captain-General Mustero alone."

"Careful lad." I turned to face him.

"You really think you're the one to be lecturing on caution." Julius shot back.

I waved my hands in the air. "What does it matter who sent those terms?" I asked. "They would have been the same anyway. Soon it'll be the Council of Seventeen, and the Gusovians will have their united nation to build into a global contender."

"It matters." The boy insisted. "It matters who's name is on the bottom of that letter. It can't be any of us that forced them together. The history books need to read that the Gusovians were able to build their own nation, or else this whole thing could fall apart." The Constable huffed. "Maybe not in our lifetime, but eventually this will matter."

Seiford took the both of us. "Now's not the time to be having this argument." The monk gestured over his shoulder to the men who were pretending to work.

"Aye." My friend had a keen eye for propriety. "There's still a chance he might not accept the terms anyway." I paused. "You should prepare the follow-up force, Constable Julius."

He shook his head. "Are you sure you trust me to do that all by myself, your eminence."

"Yes, Constable Julius I do." I caught the sarcasm in his voice. "Despite your evident snark, you've proven yourself competent."

"I'll get on it." The boy turned around and stormed off to his duties. He clearly wasn't mollified by the responsibility.

"I can almost see the chip on that boy's shoulder from here." I muttered under my breath.

Seiford gave a huff of laughter. "Remind you of anyone?"

Maybe he expected me to tell him it wasn't the same or laugh it off. I didn't. "Aye." I responded as the boy stalked off. "Do you think I was well served by it though."

"I think that's a hard question to answer." The monk kicked a pebble on the ground. "I think you'd sleep better if you could get it off though."

"I don't think there's any good night's sleep for men like me." I sighed, and a long moment of silence stretched between us.

"Gentlemen!" We heard someone scream behind us. I turned to see Captain-General Mustero in his glittering armor a century too old to be of any use. He was tall and well built like most Gusovians with the typical mustache they all seemed to fancy, but his was waxed into a curl at the end of his lips.

I smiled to see him. "Captain-General!" I responded. He was a likable fellow, honorable and charismatic as they came. The men seemed to love him for that, and that was a good bit of the business of soldering. Still, he'd probably been appointed to his position to avoid ruffling any feathers. It wasn't that he was bad at his job exactly, but the best commander in Gusovia was Razca. The only reason Mustero had won was because Razca had turned to the Old Religion, and the New Church had taken an interest. Namely, I had taken an interest.

"That was some battle!" The Gusovian said as he walked towards us.

"Your men fought well, Captain-General." Seiford nodded his respect to the man.

"That they did, and I'm proud to have marched with them." Mustero bowed humbly. "Soon Gusovia will be one."

"Perhaps sooner than you thought." I put in. "I sent terms to Razca, the ones the Council agreed upon."

"You sent terms?" Mustero seemed taken aback. "Without consulting me?"

I cursed myself and turned to Seiford. He just shrugged. I scratched the back of my head. "Well..." I started.

Mustero saved me by waving it off. "It doesn't matter now." His face went back to that same jovial grin. "What matters is my homeland will be as one, as it hasn't since the days of Gusov."

I nodded. "My thoughts exactly."

The Captain-General gave a warm smile. "And I have you and your young friend to thank for that." He squinted his eyes. "Where is Constable Julius anyhow?"

"He's getting the army ready to march." I tapped my six-shooter. "Just in case Razca's got some fight left in him."

Mustero laughed. "I reckon that old goat will never be without some fight." He let out a deep breath. "In a perfect world, he'd be leading this army of ours." The Captain-General gave a mournful frown. "He was a good friend of mine."

"Hopefully, he will be again and soon." Seiford put in.

"Hopefully." Mustero nodded. "I think he'll accept our terms. Like I said, he's a good man, and he sticks by his convictions, but he won't lead his people to devastation when he realizes the game is over." The Captain-General crossed his arms. "Razca's a conservative. He's cautious of this nationalization business, thinks that the old ways should stand, and the Council should stay out of the doings of the provinces."

The Gusovian spat out a large glob. "In some ways he's right, but our people can't compete with Kran or Anthanii like that. He'll come around eventually." Mustero gave a chuckle. "If a bartender brings Razca the wrong brew, he'll remember it till the day he dies, but he doesn't keep grudges over war. Knows it's just business." The Captain-General eyed me up. "So long as that business is conducted honorably."

I matched his stare. "I'm sure it has been."

"Aye it was, this time." Mustero turned away to look at the sun. "You know the Council was all giggles and smiles when they heard you were coming. How could we not win with the great Thomas Belson leading our armies."

"And you Captain-General?" I knew what he was getting at.

"I knew we'd win, but..." He trailed off. "I had my concerns."

"They weren't enough to make you refuse my help though." I lit up another cigarette.

"And a fool I'd be to refuse the help of Belson the Blessed." Mustero put his hands on his hips. "Everyone the world over has heard your stories, but there's some stories that aren't sung of quite so loudly."

"That a fact?" I couldn't show this man my underbelly.

"I think you know quite well it is." The Captain-General eyed me up. "I don't mean to give you the wrong idea, your eminence. I'm grateful for everything you've done for us, but I'll breath a sigh of relief when you leave Gusovia."

"Breathe whatever type of sigh you want." I blew out a cloud of smoke to illustrate the point. "You'll do it in a peaceful homeland."

"Suppose I will." He turned to walk away. "Before I do though you have a visitor, Mother Vestia. Says she'll meet you in the church."

Seiford and I looked at each other in confusion. The Matriarch of the New Church rarely left God's Rest.

"Says she's in charge of you." Mustero said as he made his way to the army. "Everyone answers to someone it seems."

———◆◈◆———

Seiford, Ayn-Tuk, and I were waiting in a church of the Three on the outskirts of town. Razca had accepted support from the Old Religion, but he hadn't taken to the common practice of burning the place down, despite the advice I was sure he'd got from those Demon-mongers.

It was a simple building, made of stone in the old ways. Pews lined down parallel from each other all the way to the back, with the front being adorned by a sparse altar with the Tree of Faith.

"Why do you imagine she's here?" I asked Seiford.

The Monk shrugged. "Maybe she just wants to see you." He marched down the pews. "You two have always held a special connection."

I smiled to myself. "Come halfway across the world to see me?" It wasn't as ridiculous a proposition as I made it though. I had a mother and a good one at that, but I hadn't seen her in fifteen years. Mother Vestia had put her arm around me, seen the man I could become before anyone else. I'd always treasure her for that. "We'll know soon enough."

Finally, I found what I was looking for. It was the little black piano in the corner. It wasn't an expensive piece, and I reckoned it was probably all sorts of out of tune. I smiled to see the instrument all the same.

"Go ahead." Seiford urged me on.

Ayn-Tuk looked up from his prayer and nodded for me to play.

"If you insist." I tried to make it sound like they were forcing me to entertain them. In reality I wanted nothing more than to sit at those black and white keys.

I lifted the cover and tested out the notes. A few were sour, but it would serve. I sat down and began playing the song my mother had taught me.

In the valley lost to time
There did lie a castle's crime
For all men do fear to speak
The stories of prince Death once meek

I started to sing. My voice wasn't terribly good, but I could carry a tune. My fingers remembered the notes, and I played the mournful song with growing conviction. I could have been a great pianist once, but my life hadn't left much time for practice. Even still, the notes were carved into me deep.

For it was not always so
This castle was not a place of woe
Once did joy run down these halls
Till the Serpent paid his call

On the night of Mid Winters day
A prophet came from far away
He looked upon the King's consort and said
"One year hence plague will strike you dead."

The queen resigned to death's fate
But her good husband fell to hate
"Build me a mask of dark ebony!" He cried
"We shall turn back this pestilence tide"

"We shall forge an image to scare both God and man
So as our father's did with blood of lamb
Death shall pass o'er my keep next Mid Winters night
Let this dark beast pause for fright"

But to wear mask alone would not work
The Death would continue to lurk
Around every corner and every bend
Death did move, sure as the wind

So the good king did study Death
He watched it's every move and breath
This king did darken his ways
To save his queen her final days

But Death could tell between man and God
Pestilence thinks with different thoughts

So the good king became black in thought and deed
And his castle was done with merry and mead

Finally death did leave their house
But so did our kings most unfortunate spouse.
For if death could not tell between,
How could the King's poor mortal queen

And our king found that Mask and man were one
So too did the queen before Midwinter's night was done
The new Death would not let her pass
And our king felt her grow cold in his grasp

He found that death came with his kiss
And in the end learned the truth is this
Man is Man and tree is tree
But we all do become what he pretend to be

I ended the song with a crashing minor chord, but I wasn't satisfied. That song had been old for more than a century. It was a good one, and I'd have liked to speak to the man who wrote it, but it wasn't my song. It could have been written about me. I put Death's mask upon my face fifteen years ago. The song that played across my quiet moments had forged me, and yet part of me was still human. I wouldn't admit it to anyone, least of all myself. Seiford saw it occasionally. In my most desperate moments, he saw what the mask I wore had done to the man beneath.

Those moments were fleeting, though. I think Ayn-Tuk also knew that dark strings tugged on my soul though he never mentioned it. The only thing I truly showed myself to were the black and white keys. Listen to me play. Some part of you will understand the man I've become.

The song of Death's mask came easy to me. Every time I sat at a piano some part of me dragged it out, but it wasn't my song. I could have sat an illiterate peasant boy at a piano, and taught him the words and notes. He wouldn't understand what they really meant or play them as well, but the song would come. I needed to play a song that could only come from me. I needed some tangible proof that I was more than my weapons. Seiford liked to hear me play, so did Ayn-Tuk though he wouldn't admit it. I decided to indulge them.

Slowly I played the keys of a major chord. It whispered *happy*. Then I hammered down on a minor chord. It screamed *sad*. That was the way of the world. Triumph and tragedy. You tell your story in the space between.

I started slowly, playing octaves in my left hand and hammering out a simple melody in my right. I picked it up as the music came back to me. It wasn't a song anyone had ever heard. It hadn't been written down by one of the great composers for cheering crowds. It was my work. Clumsy though it might have been, it meant something more to me.

I wasn't the pianist my mother said I could've been as a child. My hands were battered and callused from years of war. My mind had never spent years learning the theory and scales needed to make an instrument truly sing. Still, there was a time men thought I would be a great musician. I tried to pretend that potential was a bit brighter than the dim disappointment it had become.

I played my song. It was one of victory, edged with sorrow. It was one of glory, tempered with loss. I showed simplicity disguised as complexity. I showed complexity masquerading as simplicity. There were many better pianist around the world. Men who could play me to shame, but none of them could make this music. This music belonged to me alone.

I played until I felt the six shooters fall from my soul. I played until the tomahawk was just a distant piece of wood and steel. I played until the dead retreated to the recesses of my mind. They always nagged on me. I played until I felt the man I had chosen to be change. The Thomas Belson who walked this earth was one of peace and music. The Thomas Belson who shattered empires and brought kings to their knees, the Thomas Belson who had become a hero to any that believed Man was greater than what lay beneath, the Thomas Belson who's pride had cost more lives than plague or winter, existed only in the song. While he lived in the black and white keys of the piano, I was free to be whatever I wanted.

I could have lost myself in that music. I could have let the hero live on in song. I could have risen from that stool a different man. The kind of man mothers want their children to be. I could have set my hunger aside and been clean. Thaniel, the Golden Fort,

Sterling, they could have just been names that meant something to another man.

It was a pretty song, a delicate thing, and I was not trained in the way of delicacy. Soon my finger hit a note that sounded sour. I tried to adjust and hit a pair of keys that just didn't quite fit. I retreated to the recesses of simplicity, an octave in my left hand and a simple melody in my right, just as I had started. Soon even that was too trying for me to keep pace with. I ended with a chord and let the song sing out a little longer, not willing to part with who I was at the piano quite yet.

Then I closed the cover and stood. The Thomas of peace and music ceased to be. There was no turning back for the likes of Belson the Blessed. Too much blood between him and an innocent man. Too many sins to touch the divine once more. I had become what I'd set out to be all those years ago. Men spoke my name in hushed awe, and if they heard me play a sour note well… Heroes aren't allowed to make those mistakes. The tattoos on my skin spoke of a different story cast in white and black but told in shades of gray.

I rose from the stool the same man who sat down. My weapons seemed to weigh heavier on me though. The dead flashed behind my eyes. If the world was going to stop me, then it wouldn't be with a piano. It would have to be steel.

I heard clapping from the door. It was First Priestess, Mother Vestia. "Don't stop on my account." She smiled. "You know I've always enjoyed when you play." It was true. She'd had a piano brought into her office when I was a boy training fifteen years ago.

"Afraid I'm all played out, Mother Vestia." I stood from the piano stool and took a knee in front of her. I'd had emperors tell me to prostrate myself in their presence. I never listened. I kneeled to Mother Vestia though.

"We're not in public Thomas." She waved me up. "You can greet me as a friend, not a High Priestess."

"How about I greet you as a mother." I walked over to her and gave her a sincere hug. Finally, I released it, and looked the woman up and down. Mother Vestia was old, but the years had treated her well. She held a shadow of the beauty that had once been hers. Her face had more wrinkles, and her hair had gone from blonde to gray, but her eyes still held a twinkle of youth.

She was dressed in grey sackcloth. It should have looked plain, but nothing could look plain on a woman such as her. There were precisely two leaders I respected in the world. One, I'd led to the chopping block, the other stood before me. Mother Vestia, was gentle as a lamb and cunning as a snake. She epitomized the Three virtues of Wisdom, Honor, and Love. It was why she had been chosen for the highest position in the New Church. I would have marched into the sea with lead in my pockets if that's what she asked of me. Vestia had been the first kind face I'd seen when I arrived at God's Rest fifteen years ago, and even after all the countries I'd fought for, she was the woman I served.

"How long's it been?" I asked. "Three years? Four?

She looked away somewhat awkwardly. "Five." She shook her head. "Not since that business with Sterling."

"Right, that." I took a step back. After that day she'd been forced to give me a reprimand. I'd done the one thing I could never do, kill the leader who had requested the service of a Constable. I'd been brought to God's Rest and tried. Sometimes a mistake like that would cost a man his head. I'd gotten five lashes for it. Mother Vestia called it extenuating circumstances during the sentencing. First Citizen Niccolo was not a good man, and I was the one who'd saved the New Church and maybe the rest of the world from Thaniel's legions. However, there were those that thought she'd gone soft. There were those that thought I should've payed the old price for that sin. Above all, there were those that quietly believed I'd outlived my use.

Seiford saved me from having to respond. "Your holiness." He walked forward with a bow and folded the Matriarch in a hug.

Mother Vestia smiled as they separated. "Oh Seiford," she sighed looking at the monk, "if it weren't for our vow of celibacy, I would have married you years ago." Mother Vestia smiled. "I still might. The Three know that vow hasn't stopped you."

"All I can do is atone." Seiford smiled back.

"Well, you could just stop sinning." The First Priestess said playfully. "However, that's like asking my dog to stop licking his balls..."

"It's not in our nature." Seiford responded coyly.

"No, it's not." Mother Vestia chuckled, then turned to Ayn-Tuk. "I've heard much about you."

The black man bowed. "And I you." It was as deep a sign of respect as I'd seen from him.

"Not that I don't enjoy your company," I leaned against a pew watching the woman, "but I'm curious as to why you're here."

"You mean besides watching the Gusovian's quest for self-determination." She shrugged.

"Aye, besides that." I cocked my head to one side.

Mother Vestia produced a letter from the folds of her sackcloth.

I took the paper and read it aloud. "After fifteen years of honorable service, I, First Priestess Vestia, do hereby relieve Thomas Belson of all duties and responsibilities of Constable." I looked from the paper to her face, there was more about my *honorable* service, but the first part was the only bit that mattered to me. "What is this?" I asked, more shocked than I should have been.

"It's good news." She reached out and put her hand over mine. "Your duty to the New Church and me is fulfilled." Mother Vestia stared at me with those kind eyes. "Go live in the peace you've forged for us all."

I shook my head. "Peace never suited me well." I tossed the paper back to her. "If it's all the same to you, I'd rather stay on." Then I touched the six-shooter at my side. "Unless, it's an order, not an offer."

Mother Vestia's face dropped. "I was hoping I wouldn't have to make it one."

"So it's that kind of paper is it?" I sighed. "What did you expect, exactly?"

"I expected this." She placed the paper behind her. "I hoped you'd see sense though."

"Aye, you hoped you'd get all the benefits with none of the dirty work." The anger in me was growing. I expected better from her. "Fifteen years I've been fighting. Fifteen years I've been killing for your church."

"*Our* church, Thomas." Vestia chided me softly, but I didn't listen.

"Fifteen years!" I screamed back at her.

"Thomas…" Seiford put a hand on my shoulder.

"I've lost more friends than most men have to begin with!" The rage was bubbling up. "I've sacrificed everything to win wars no one else could. I turned away the only woman I ever loved! I led the greatest ruler Thyro ever knew to the chopping block and took his head!" I pointed an accusing finger at Mother Vestia. "I did it all on the New Church's order."

"You did." She said meekly. That was harder. I could have stayed angry at defiance. Humble acceptance was a harder medicine to swallow. "You deserve to know more than that, though."

I leaned back against the pew. "The things I've done..." I hung my head. "The man I've become..." I tried to shake off the memories. "There's no going back for me." I wiped what could have been a tear from my eye. "If you ever cared about me, don't give me that piece of paper." I'd have walked into a lake with lead in my pockets for her, but this was one sacrifice too many.

"Thomas..." She shook her head. "I should've done this ten years ago."

"When I was the greatest warrior the world had ever known." I narrowed my eyes at her. "When I started winning the war you've been losing for five hundred years."

"When you became the man people warned me you might." She didn't flinch away.

"The same people who were losing?" I smashed a fist against the wood. "We're winning now because of me!"

"We're not just winning, Thomas." Mother Vestia eyed me up. "We've won."

"There's still Priests out there." I touched the tattoos on my arm. "They may not be what Thaniel set loose, but they're out there."

Mother Vestia shook her head. "This war was never about hunting down Priests."

"Then why are any of us here?" I held up my hands gesturing to the city I'd just taken.

"To prove that we don't need them!" Mother Vestia took a step forward. "You proved that when you tore Thaniel down from his Rose Petal throne." She paused. "Men today want good government and the liberty to choose their own path. They want rights and a say in how things are done. More than anything, they want to raise brave and virtuous children to live better lives than they had a chance at. They don't see mysticism and tyranny as the only way anymore." She took another step forward. "Belson the Blessed proved that. He proved that Man is greater than the Demons Below."

"Then why send me away?" I crossed my arms. "If I proved all that why cast me to the shadows."

"I love you more than I can remember loving anyone since I took my holy orders." Mother Vestia shook her head. "All those things they say about you are true. You were strong, cunning, and brave as they come. You saw hope when the world around you despaired." She looked at me and I saw she spoke true. The truth rarely made things easier. "You were great. Maybe more importantly, behind that greatness, you were a good man."

I shook my head. "A good man doesn't have dreams like I do."

Ayn-Tuk looked up from his staff for the first time since I stopped playing my song. "A good man makes mistakes and has the sense to regret them."

"Well said." Mother Vestia smiled at the man before turning back to me. "Maybe there was a time when that fiery boy at God's Rest wanted nothing but glory and a name." She put a hand on my shoulder. "However, you came to care about the people you led to greatness."

"Those are all pretty good reasons to keep me on." I stared at the paper. "Why aren't you?"

"Because there's more to you than a good man or even a great one." Mother Vestia took a step back. "I'll be the first one to sing your praises, they're worth singing about." She took a deep breath. "You're not just the man in those stories though."

I leveled a finger at the woman I respected more than any other. "You're fucking right, I'm not the man in those stories! The man in those stories could have used his magic sword to cut through Thaniel's legions." I pulled the six-shooter out of its holster to show her. "I used gunpowder and bullets to win my wars. Only fools use swords." I sighed. "I've made hard choices. I've knowingly sent good men to their deaths." I thought for a brief moment of Seiford's brother.

A silence stretched out as I worked up the courage to say what came next. "I've killed children..." It came out as barely a whisper. "I did what I had to..." I composed myself once more. "I did what I did, and the world is a better place for it.

"Like the Massacre of the Golden Fort?" She asked.

"Yes."

"The Pillars of the Kranish?"

"That too."

She sighed as if not wanting to say what came next. "The Fires of Sterling?"

That put me on the back foot. I knew it was coming, but expecting it and hearing it were two different things. "It wasn't supposed to happen like that." I said it almost too myself.

"But it did," Mother Vestia paused, "and you haven't become more tempered for it." She looked up to the altar of the Three. "What happens when you do something the people can't forgive? That will be the day that mankind stops trusting in man altogether." She pulled a flask out and took a sip from it. "If the best falls, what chance do the rest of us have?" The woman locked my eyes with hers. "If they see their hero fail, it would have been better if that hero never existed at all."

"I never fail." I hissed at her.

"You never lose." She cut back. "There's a difference between the two."

"And how did you think I was going to beat Thaniel? Hugs and kisses?" I threw my hands up at the ridiculousness of it. "You knew exactly the kind of man I'd need to become!"

"Maybe I did." Mother Vestia admitted. "Maybe somewhere deep down I knew." She took another draught from her flask. "You think I don't see the cruelty in this? We set you on an impossible task with only one way to win. We made you into the very thing we condemn."

"Aye, you did." I glanced at Seiford.

. "The truth is, we're not desperate anymore." Mother Vestia whispered. "Thaniel's dead and he's not coming back."

"You'd be a fool to think all the threats are gone." I remembered the last words of that Priest in Sterling.

"You're still chasing that ghost, *she* or whatever it is you called her." Mother Vestia rolled her eyes. "This is what I mean. You forged yourself to fight emperors, and now that there's no emperors, you see an apocalypse behind every shadow."

"Constable Julius has heard of her too." I shrugged.

"You want me to say it?" Mother Vestia threw up her hands again. "There probably is some woman playing with things she shouldn't. That doesn't mean there's some grand conspiracy afoot."

There was a tense moment of silence that stretched for too long. "What if you're wrong?" I asked. "What happens if when I'm gone, the Old Religion isn't quite as dead as you thought it was?" I took the flask from her hand and drank deep. "What happens if all that greatness you speak of comes under attack, and I'm not there to stop it?" I remembered the Priest's words at Sterling. I remembered his ominous warning of *she*. At the time, I had thought it unimportant, but *she*, whoever she was, had left a dark shadow on my soul as the years wore on. A subtle hint that I might not be as knowing as I thought I was. Even by the bizarre standards I set, strange things had been happening over the past five years.

"There are other Constables." Mother Vestia cocked her head one way.

"There were other Constables when Thaniel waged his war." I narrowed my eyes. "It didn't matter then, it might not next time." I meant that. "You know as well as I do, there's none who wear the tattooed arm as good as I am."

"No, there aren't," she admitted. "but now we've seen Priests fail. We know they can be beaten." She paused. "Now we've seen men succeed, and that can be done as well." Mother Vestia was pleading. "Do not see your legacy tarnished for bloodlust!"

"What am I supposed to do?" I threw the flask across the church. "Go farm?"

Seiford spoke up again. "I've always known you were the man to follow." He felt me relenting. "My brother died believing the same," the monk looked down at the mention of his brother, "but he didn't do it so you could fight endlessly." Seiford held my gaze again. "He did it for a day when your weapons might not be needed. Maybe that day has come."

"Thomas," it was Ayn-Tuk speaking, "it's time." He said in that deep ashy voice

"I-I-" What could someone possibly say to having their world torn apart. "What am I supposed to do?" I repeated more hopeless than angry this time.

"Thomas, there's a great many political reasons to let you go." Mother Vestia took a step forward. "There's another more important reason to do it."

"And what's that?" I knew I was defeated. I wasn't walking out of that church a Constable.

"I want you to know peace and happiness." She said it barely a whisper. "I love you like my own son. I will not see you die knowing nothing but war."

"It's too late for that." I shook my head.

Mother Vestia rolled her eyes. "Three above, you're thirty years old. Make it to sixty, and you'll realize how foolish 'it's too late,' sounds to me."

"Thirty's twice as long as anyone thought I'd live." I gave a sad little smile.

"So that's it?" Mother Vestia grabbed both my shoulders. "You don't think you deserve a ripe old age surrounded by good friends and a loving family?"

I met the woman's eyes. "After the things I've done..." I paused. "I don't know." The truth was I did know. It wasn't an answer Mother Vestia wanted to hear.

"After the things you've done no one deserves it more." She folded me into a gentle hug.

I took a step back. "You still haven't answered my question." I folded my arms. "What am I supposed to do?"

"Thomas, there's problems in this world that won't be solved at the end of a gun." Mother Vestia glanced back at the altar. "Just because you won't be in battle anymore doesn't mean you have to stop fighting. Your name will always hold weight. Your words can change the world just as your tomahawk did."

"I didn't argue Thaniel into submission." I reminded the Matriarch of the New Church.

"The world is a different place than it was fifteen years ago." Mother Vestia looked at Brother Seiford for a moment then back to me. "The battle ground now is one of ideas. No one in human history has ever held your wealth of knowledge. From the nation states of Thyro, to the plainsmen of the Mong, to the tribes of Souren, you've seen them all."

She went on. "You can write treatises on conflict, save the next generation of soldiers from catastrophes because the generals don't understand modern warfare." The Matriarch went on. "Of all the political systems you've helped create, you don't think you have something to say about good government."

I chuckled at that. "Seiford did the lion's share of the work."

The monk shrugged his shoulders. "We complimented each other well."

Mother Vestia gave a wry smile. "Like Seiford isn't going wherever you go."

It was actually something that had been troubling me. "Despite his many failings as a human being," Seiford rolled his eyes, but he knew it was meant as a joke, "he's one of the cleverest men the world over. I figured the New Church might have more need of him than offering companionship to a former Constable."

The Matriarch gave a heavy sigh. "I know the decision to release you from the Order may seem cold, but in time I promise you'll see it's for the best, not just for the world but for you." She paused. "Separating you from your closest friend would just be cruel."

"That so?" I glanced at the monk who gave me a comforting look.

"You're not just a former Constable, anyway." Mother Vestia went to pick up the flask I'd thrown. "You're the greatest warrior who ever wore a tattooed arm. You're the man the whole world looks to as an example." She took another sip from it. "Personal feelings aside, I have a vested interest in your well being."

"You think I'm a good influence, your Holiness?" Seiford snagged the flask from her.

"There's been many, pure as the driven snow, who've tried to temper our fiery friend." She cocked an eyebrow up. "You're the only one who's managed to make him put his gun down though. It makes no sense to me, but you're the only one who could guide him to the better path."

"Got tired of his yapping is all." I shrugged, but everyone in that room knew that Seiford had been the only thing standing between me and madness the past decade.

"Still can't get him to bathe regularly." The monk shot back, but everyone in that room knew, for all his complaining, the monk wouldn't have spent the past decade with anyone else.

Mother Vestia crossed her arms. "Besides, I've learned some things being High Priestess all these years." She wagged a finger. "Don't give an order you can't enforce." She turned to the monk. "Brother Seiford, if I ordered you back to God's Rest to teach history, engineering, or some other subject who's name I don't even know, how long would you stay there?"

The monk gave a look of feigned guilt. "I probably wouldn't even get on the ship." The corner of his lip curled up. "God's Rest is all sorts of cold."

Mother Vestia turned to Ayn-Tuk. "Mr. Tuk, what will you do now that Thomas is relieved of his duties?"

The shirtless black man looked up from cradling his ornate staff. "Our paths are linked." He gave a solemn nod. "I will walk it to the end."

"What is your path exactly?" I asked. It was one mystery I was never able to uncover.

"Atoning for the thing I could never do." Ayn-Tuk went back to his staff. "That is all I can say for now."

"Well that explains exactly nothing." I looked up to the altar of the Three.

"Don't you see?" Mother Vestia stepped forward. "This isn't an ungrateful world casting you out. This is the people that care about you trying to help their friend love the thing he spent so long saving."

"I don't even know who I am…" It was perhaps the most honest thing I'd ever said.

"That's the question at every man's core." She hugged me one last time. "I'm giving you the freedom to find the answer for yourself."

"I won't thank you for this." I said but didn't pull away.

"I didn't do it for your gratitude." She tightened her grip on me. "I did it because I want the best for you. If that means you hate me, then so be it. That's what love is."

"I won't thank you for this, but I don't hate you." I pulled away and looked her up and down. "You were the first person who looked at a runt from the Confederacy and saw something more." A tear ran down my cheek despite all attempts to keep it in. "You loved Thomas before I was ever Belson the Blessed."

"And I've never regretted it." She patted my shoulder before releasing me one last time.

I looked around the room into the eyes of the people around me. "When people ask what became of Thomas Belson…" I didn't know how my story should end. There were so many things I'd put off till tomorrow. I never really imagined I'd outlive my duty, but things seldom turn out the way we expect them to.

Then there were the secrets no one but me knew. What I'd seen in Imor, the city gods feared to walk through. The last words Thaniel had whispered to me with his head on the chopping block. The dark works of desperate Priests I'd found in the Rose Petal throne room. The fear it had struck in me so deep I nailed children to pillars. The secrets I swore would die with me. The secrets that could tear the world apart.

"When people ask what became of Thomas Belson…" I repeated. "Tell them something suitable." It was the best I could come up with. My secrets would stay with me.

She nodded back. "I'll tell them that Thomas Belson watches from the shadows." The Matriarch of the New Church wiped a tear from her eye. "I'll tell them that Thomas Belson smiles as we build our better world, and I'll tell them we better not disappoint the man who gave us the canvas to paint it." Mother Vestia's gaze made me feel fifteen years old again. "I'll tell them, Belson the Blessed deserves our level best."

"We better leave." I gestured to the door. Seiford gave the woman a hug and Ayn-Tuk nodded his respects. Both walked out leaving Mother Vestia and me alone. Perhaps they hoped I'd say some last tender words, but I was all out of those.

"Thomas..." She started.

"I hope you're right." I bit my lip. "I hope the Old Religion is beaten, and warriors won't be the only thing standing between liberty and tyranny. I hope the people are ready to reach for this bright new future you want for us." I touched the six-shooter at my side. "I don't think it is though." I turned to leave the church. "Hope is a fine good thing, but it doesn't often keep the monsters away."

I stared at the door. I was afraid of trying to be just a man. It hadn't gone well for me thus far. Sometimes it was easier to be a hero than human. A hero belongs in stories where things make sense. A human belongs in the real world where things get tricky. I'd never let fear stay my hand though. I stepped outside.

I walked out and met Seiford and Ayn-Tuk. The monk turned to me. "Thomas-" He was cut off as someone grabbed me in a crushing hug. I almost stabbed the body in the ribs before I saw it was Lieutenant Cassov.

"Um, Lieutenant..." I managed to squeak out. Finally, he separated from me. The young Constable Julius was over his shoulder.

"Razca has surrendered! He will join the council and expel the foul Priests he's kept with him." Cassov released me and I saw he'd been crying tears of joy. "We're finally free! We've accomplished everything my people have fought generations for. Today will be celebrated by Gusovia for a thousand generations." He wiped his eyes. "We have you to thank."

Constable Julius took a step forward and nodded respect. "You were right."

"I usually am." I glanced back at the church where Mother Vestia was still sitting. Mother Vestia thought the Old Religion was desperate and the New Church was safe. Safe enough to send her greatest warrior away. I thought something different.

What really bothered me about her assessment was more of a feeling than fact. Still, the truth was that desperate didn't mean gone, and safe rarely meant ready. I had walked the streets of Imor.

I knew what Priests could do when they got desperate. There was a time Thaniel had considered himself safe too. I didn't know much about *Her*, but I had a feeling she was in a better position than anyone thought.

I touched the tattoos on my arm. No matter what I became they would stay with me. "I usually am."

Present Day

he moon twinkled over the field. The bodies laid twisted in their last attempts to escape death. I looked upon them all. My men and their's framed grotesquely in the night. They would be buried tomorrow, forgotten later. *Is this what hell is?* I asked myself. Was hell an eternity looking over the men who'd died, in my quest for greatness? I walked through the corpses. Each step unveiled a new terror.

The dog was there, sniffing at the bodies. That's how I knew it to be a dream. The dog always followed me in my sleep. Black, mangy, and starving. I could never remember the soldier who owned the animal, but that beast was never far from my thoughts.

I walked through the forest of corpses I had made. The wounded had already been given mercy, be it medicine or a last bullet. This was a place of the dead. I couldn't tell which battlefield it was. Before the fighting starts, every landscape seems different, new tools to use, new obstacles to smash. Afterward, they're all the same. A dozen corpses or a hundred thousand, they all look up at you.

Suddenly I felt a hand grab my leg. I spun around, prepared to kill whatever touched me, but it was already dead. "You've killed me!" The body screamed. It was just a boy really. His face was streaked with dirt, the black hair on his head was matted with blood, but the blue eyes shown true. His uniform was ruined, not including the red spot on his chest where his heart might have been.

"I was going to open a shoe store one day." The corpse's face twisted and contorted with each word. "I was going to move to the Confederacy, and be a cobbler. You killed me!" The other hand of the corpse reached out for my leg. "I had a woman back home I was going to marry. You killed me!" The body released my leg and slammed its fist on the ground. "YOU KILLED ME! YOU KILLED ME! YOU KILLED ME!"

"Aye." I took a step back.

"Why?" The boy whispered up at me.

"For the greater good." It sounded like a shit excuse even to myself.

The body stood up and grabbed a rifle. "Why have you killed me?"

I fell into my fighting stance. "The greater good." I eyed up the rifle thoughtfully.

"You lie!" The boy screamed and made a weak poke with the bayonet. "You cannot lie to the dead, Thomas Belson!" He swung the rifle like a club at me. It was a pathetic attack.

"It needed to be done!" I screamed back, growing angry.

"Why have you killed me?" The boy screamed and took another swing.

"For the Three!" I felt the fury well up inside him

"You cannot lie to the dead!" The boy charged one more time, and I was on him.

"I killed you because it fed my legend!" I shouted as I threw the boy to the ground. "I killed you because the only way to build glory is with skulls and blood." I jumped on top of the corpse and tried to choke the life out of it. "Most of all, I killed you because I am the better fighter." The boy's neck was clammy and cold. I broke it, but the body kept moving. "You stood in the way of Thomas Belson! That is why you died!"

"You killed me!" The body said one more time.

"Aye, now I'll kill you again and think no more of it!" I screamed, and the body went limp.

"What have you become, my child?" I heard a voice say. Though, to call it a voice wasn't quite doing it justice. It seemed to resonate through the earth and inside my own soul.

"I've spent my life serving you!" I stood up and looked at the man who spoke with the voice of all the earth and sky. It was one of the Three, Wisdom, come to chide me. "Is it too much to ask that my dreams remain my own?"

"Your dreams have not been yours since you took your first life, but it isn't us that gives them to you." Wisdom walked to me. He was always impossible to describe after the dream. Even looking at him then, I couldn't quite put a finger on the god. He looked like every wise man who ever lived. In one shade he was elderly with a long beard. In another light, he was a child, fresh-faced and young. Somehow he was all these things at once. Well, I referred to him as he, but I'd seen shades of female on his face. In my dreams, he never showed himself as he did in life. "Your dreams belong to the dead now."

"And what does that say about me?" I shot back.

"That you need help." Wisdom glided ever closer. "That you need to try a different path." I'd met the Three before. Maybe it was just my head playing tricks. Maybe it really was the divine. I had killed gods though or as close as makes no difference. I figured the Three ought to speak to me with more respect. After all, I'd won their damn wars.

"Haven't you heard?" I sneered. "I'm retired. It's all leisurely afternoons and sipping mint juleps from here on."

"Changing one's circumstances is a far cry from changing one's heart." Wisdom moved ever closer. "Your heart is still the same, so you will choose the same path."

"What do you know about my heart?" I realized as I was saying it, the arrogance of calling a god named Wisdom ignorant.

"We formed you, Thomas." Wisdom was in front of me. "We placed the darkness in your heart."

"You could have made me a bit better looking," I thought for a moment, "and taller."

"We made you as we make all men," Wisdom was in front of my face now. "perfectly flawed."

"You couldn't have given me that dragon," I turned, "or a magic sword."

That set Wisdom to chuckling. "When we sent the Demons to the world below, and the Earth was formless, there was some talk on whether to include dragons and magic swords."

"Why didn't you?" I cocked an eyebrow up. "I think the world would have liked to see both."

"Because if we did, you would have bent both of them to your will." Wisdom was all business now. "You relying on strength not your own would have made you weak. You would never have become the man we needed you to be." The god paused. "You're more interesting than dragons and magic swords anyway."

I wouldn't admit it, but the thought that the Three considered me when they formed the world, fed my pride a bit too much. "So you chastise me for the man I've become, but you made me become that man?" I scratched my chin in mock thought. "That seems a bit ruthless, even for the divine."

"We knew what you would have to become to defeat Thaniel." Wisdom admitted. There was sorrow on his divine face. "However, that man was like another step on the ladder to something better."

"I've spent my whole life serving you!" I screamed back angrily. "All I want now is a thank you and to wish me on my way."

"You've spent your whole life serving the hunger inside of you." Wisdom was unaffected by my rage. "That hunger has served you well. It has made you great, but now you face a fork in the road we have set you on." He put a hand on my shoulder. "Leave your hunger behind or cling to it. The whole world will feel what you choose." Just like that Wisdom was gone.

I looked around myself. I wasn't on the battlefield anymore. I was floating over an armada of ships. They surrounded an enormous, ironclad beast. I dropped towards that one. I didn't know how I knew it, but the ship was named *The Thaniel*. I fell through the deck and stopped.

There was another Thomas Belson there, only he looked older. The tattoos on his right were gone. They appeared to have been burned away. He stood in front of a hooded man. The other Thomas pulled away the hood and what I saw sent a shiver up my spine.

It was Seiford. He looked older too, but there was more to it. His once handsome face was scarred, and his eyes held the bearing of a warrior. "Thomas, what have you become?"

The other Thomas didn't answer. He reached down with his two strong arms, my arms, and broke the monk's neck. "What I needed to be."

———◆◆◆———

I woke screaming. I reached around the room forgetting where I was.

Seiford jumped on top of me doing his best to restrain my flailing arms. "Thomas stop!" He screamed. "Thomas you're in Suffix." He was used to the things that haunt my dreams. He knew how to handle them. "Thomas we're in the Two River's Tavern."

"I... I..." I shook my head. "I'm fine now." I lied. "Thank you." I took a look around the room, trying to get my grip on reality again. The room was small with two beds. I looked to the right and saw whiskey. I drank some of it to calm my nerves.

"Where are we?" Seiford repeated keeping my eyes locked on his.

"We're in Suffix?" I scratched my head. Finally, I was back to Earth. We had paid for passage to the Confederacy. Ayn-Tuk was probably somewhere around. "We're in Suffix sleeping at the Two River's Tavern." I said more surely.

"You dreamt about them again, didn't you?" Seiford got off me and sat down on the bed. "Why should seeing our gods leave you like this?"

"I'm not sure they are our gods." I took another drink. "Might be, it's just my mind playing tricks on me." Now I was lying to myself. I knew just what those dreams meant.

"Thomas, I think maybe these dreams mean more than you let on." Seiford looked me up and down.

"No!" I screamed with more violence than I meant and lowered my voice. "They can't."

"Why not?" The monk asked genuinely confused.

I thought about telling Seiford of the dream. I never kept anything from him. I thought about telling him how I'd watched a future version of myself break his neck. "I'm hardly the holiest individual around." I settled on. "I don't think the Three would show themselves to a man with enough sin to stain a brown cloak black."

"I don't think the Three need to show themselves to the holy." Seiford was still unconvinced. "I think they need to show themselves to broken men on a bad path."

"I thought the whole point of this retirement was to try and set me on the right path." I shot back.

"Do you feel like you're on the right path?" Seiford answered softly. "We don't even know what path we're on."

"Aye." My mouth had the sour taste that always came from a night spent drinking, and my head was pounding in a way it hadn't quite in my youth. Besides that, fifteen years at war had taken their toll. Not a part of me didn't ache when I woke up in the morning.

After Mother Vestia cut me loose, we made our way to the closest port we could find, Suffix. There wasn't a place in the world you couldn't buy passage to from Suffix. It seemed the perfect place to make a decision about where to go, but I hadn't been doing much deciding. It was mostly Ayn-Tuk pulling Seiford and I out of our own vomit and carrying us to our rooms.

"So where are we going, Thomas." Seiford slapped my leg.

I shrugged off the pain in my shoulder. "Where does a man like me go?"

"Wherever you want." The monk gave a toothy grin. "Anywhere that has girls with a monk fetish preferably."

I had to laugh at that. "All girls have a monk fetish when you're involved." I took another swig of whiskey for the pain. "Who was that young lady from last night?"

Seiford scratched his head trying to think through the drunken haze that was last night. "Bertha!" He finally said.

"She was pretty." I said with a hint of jealousy. "Throw a woman my way, next time."

"I tried you daft bastard!" He said through a snort of laughter. "You would've had her friend if you hadn't spent the whole night ranting about how Foucal's philosophy is ruining university."

Ayn-Tuk finally looked up from his staff. "Three above that man's writing is stupid!"

"My thoughts precisely." I chirped happily. "Besides, I wasn't that bad."

Seiford rolled his eyes. "At one point she asked how her breasts looked, and you said 'according to Foucal they're irrelevant'."

"I did?" I put my head in my hands. "I'm sure I meant it sarcastically."

"Sarcastically or not," Ayn-Tuk cut in, "calling a woman's breasts irrelevant, is poor form."

"Thank you for the sage wisdom." I picked my head up.

"So where are we going?" Seiford repeated the question. "You've already driven away all the women in Suffix."

"What about Viverent?" I shrugged. "He likes us well enough." I was referring to the famed intellectual, historian, and scientist Seiford and I had run ragged for a year. He was good company, and he even sent us letters from time to time. However, they usually ended with him asking if Seiford had bedded his sister.

"Aye, he likes us a bit too much." Seiford rolled his eyes. "Viverent is working on things that could change the shape of this world. I don't think he needs us dragging him around every tavern we can find." The monk chuckled. "Let the poor man live in peace. He probably still hasn't recovered from that last hangover."

"Don't want to see his sister, is what you mean." I muttered.

"Two things can be true at once." The monk smiled.

I paused to take a drink. "I could always try my hand at mercenary work." As soon as I said it Seiford's jaw dropped. Even Ayn-Tuk's disposition visibly changed.

"What?" Their reaction caught me off guard. "There's a lot of people out there who would pay our weight in gold to put me at the head of their army."

"You took an oath, Thomas." Seiford had a sternness to him that let me know I crossed an important line. "You swore to never fight for personal gain."

"Aye, I took an oath to do no wrong, pray every night, and even keep my damn uniform pressed." I rolled my eyes. "You also took an oath of celibacy. I assume you didn't have stimulating conversation with Bertha all night." I scoffed at it all. "We all break one oath or another."

"Not that one." Seiford shook his head. "We don't break that one." He let some of his pain show. "If you become a mercenary, the New Church won't stand for it."

I laughed at that. "And who exactly would they send to stop me."

"No one, that's the point." I could see in his eyes, this was what the monk feared. "Thaniel was a mercenary once." He finally said.

"You think I'll be like him?" I narrowed my eyes

He didn't answer that. "I won't let you break that oath, Thomas." Seiford said again. "You'll have to kill me."

"Well, Mother Vestia also swore an oath to me too." I let more of the wounded child show than I intended. "She swore she'd always guide me to the right path, and as soon as I'm not useful anymore, she sends me away."

"It didn't happen like that, and you know it." Seiford sighed. "She let you go to turn you away from a dark path." The monk gave me a hard look. "She let you go because she wanted you to know something besides war."

"She let me go because it suited her agenda." I hissed back. "I am done listening to Mother Vestia. The New Church has abandoned me."

Seiford laughed at that.

"What?" I narrowed my eyes.

Seiford composed himself. "I've watched you spit in the face of emperors because you found them wanting." He shook his head. "I've watched you nod your respect to a farmhand because he had fire." The handsome monk looked me in the eyes. "You didn't listen to Mother Vestia. You listened to your mother, Vestia."

"What are you getting at?" I tried to seem angry, but I was more confused than anything.

"You never kneeled to her because of the robe she wore." Seiford went on. "You kneeled to her because she showed you compassion when no one else would. Mother Vestia saw what you could be before anyone else did. Her faith in you probably saved us all." The monk paused. "You've spent your life inspiring respect, hope, and sometimes fear. The people loved the idea of Belson the Blessed, but she loved Thomas."

Seiford smiled in his special way. "You loved her back for that. You followed her because she followed you." He glanced at my tattoos. "In war men fight for you because they don't have a choice. Without you, their homeland would have been turned to ash." He took a deep breath. "Mother Vestia had a choice, and she chose you, same as me, same as Ayn-Tuk, same as Shaggy Cow. You love that woman."

It took me a minute to take it all in. He was right, of course. Seiford usually was in matters of the heart. In my own way, I'd always known it, but the monk simply had the words to let me see clearer.

"Do you think that makes this easier?" I asked him.

"No, I don't." Seiford nodded. "I think if some distant king had released you, we'd already be composing a drinking song about how much of an ass he was." The monk went serious. "This hurts you because you love her, and she loves you back."

"You're damn right it hurts!" I hit the table.

"And now you want to make the world feel it too." Seiford cocked his head to the side. "You want to take the worst path just to spite her."

"I-" I started to protest, but realized he was right. I could always look into a man and tell what he wanted. It was the source of my prowess. There was a time I could do it to myself also, but I'd gotten what I wanted, and the water had grown muddy. "Maybe." I finally said.

"It hurts now." Seiford went on. "Right now, you're ready to tear the world apart because you think it wronged you," he paused, "but one day you'll realize she was right." The monk surveyed the room as if drawing inspiration. "One day, the fact that she did it for love will mean more than the fact that she did it." The monk paused. "Don't go down a path you can't come back from before then."

"So you think she's right?" I scoffed at him. "You think I've grown too dangerous." Everything he was saying made sense, but I wanted to be angry. Anger is the greatest climber that ever was. It can cleave to any foothold no matter how small when a man's inclined to it.

Seiford answered me levelly. "I think a wise woman who cares gave you a warning." The monk said. "I think we'd be fools not to listen."

"I'm not itching to take up the mercenary trade." I said. "I'm just saying it's an option."

"Not a good one." Ayn-Tuk held me with his dark eyes.

"And what should I do? Learn barrel making?" I huffed. "All I know is war."

"I know you don't want to hear this," The monk gave a heavy sigh knowing we'd hashed this out a thousand times and none of them ended well, "but you do have family west of the ocean." Seiford took another sip of his drink. "You'll want to see them before it's too late."

"It's already too late." I bit my lip.

"Thomas, they're your family." Seiford reached across the table. "There's nothing in the world they'd want more than to see you again."

"You don't understand." I shook my head.

"You're right I don't understand." Seiford narrowed his eyes. "You have a family that loves you. I've read the letters even though you won't. If my brother were still alive, there's not a thing in the world that could keep us apart."

"They've moved on." I leaned back in my chair.

"Three above," Seiford rolled his eyes, "you're not a woman they had a fling with. You're their family. You're right. They probably have built a life without you, but they don't have to choose between one or the other." He said it like he was talking to a child. "If they were watching this conversation, do you think they'd be rooting for you to stay away."

"I would if I were them." I took another drink.

"What did you do that was so horrible?" Seiford asked. "I've roamed with you for ten years, and every time I ask you about them, you say that's a story for another day." He paused. "Well, today's the day."

"I told them they were a weakness." I tried to smother the guilt, but that only made it worse. "I told them I'd be better off free of their love." I hung my head. "I told my brother I'd come back the day he died."

"A fifteen-year-old said some mean things once upon a time." Seiford mocked surprise. "Should I go out and check to make sure the world is still turning?"

"We're not going to the Confederacy!" I slapped the bed post and realized I was screaming. "We're not going to the Confederacy." I repeated more softly. "That's the end of it."

"Thomas-" Seiford started but I cut him off as I stood up.

"I need a smoke and some fresh air." I grabbed my dusty leather coat and went to the door.

"Thomas, we need to talk about this." Seiford grabbed my arm as I left.

"Aye, but later." I shook off his hand. "I need to clear my head for a moment."

"No, not later." He held me.

In that moment I needed a solitary smoke more than anything, so I played an underhanded trick. "We'll go to the Thro'ncat wall."

Seiford's eyes twisted in rage then settled into acceptance knowing he'd been beat, at least for a time. "You're a right bastard you know?"

"I do." Then I gestured to the bed. He dutifully sat down.

"Thro'ncat." He repeated to himself dreamily, and I knew I could have my smoke in peace.

I walked down through the full bar ignoring the veiled looks and hushed whispers. I made my way to a bench, and sat down to take out a cigarette.

It was later than I thought, maybe noon. I never slept that long. The docks were abuzz with workers as I tried to light my smoke against the sea wind.

I felt a presence sit down next to me and assumed it was my monk. "Damn Seiford, I usually get half a day out of thro'ncat." I turned to see Ayn-Tuk sitting next to me, black and shirtless looking almost a shadow. That was strange. He usually seemed to enjoy his alone time.

Ayn-Tuk took the cigarette and had it smoking in a moment.

"Here." He handed it back to me. "It takes some practice doing it in the ocean wind."

I took it from him. "Didn't know you smoked." I said after I'd had a drag.

"Back when I rowed with the Norsi, pipe tobacco was the only thing to keep a man warm." He cradled the staff in his arms.

"How is it a Souren found himself rowing in the frozen north?" I asked. This was beyond strange. The black man never talked about his past.

"I was looking for a name." He said quietly. I instinctively knew that was all I'd learn of my companions adventures with the Norsi.

We sat quietly on the bench for a moment while I smoked.

"When is the last time you woke up too late to watch the sun rise?" Ayn-Tuk's deep voice penetrated my thoughts.

"During the Thaniel Wars I spent a month comatose." I puffed some more. "Besides that, I can't remember." We watched the dock workers bent to their tasks. "Even when I got piss drunk, there was always some task that couldn't wait till the cock crows." I slumped back into the bench. "I guess this is retirement."

Ayn-Tuk shrugged his well muscled shoulders. "Some men might look forward to a good nights sleep."

"You heard me this morning and every morning before that." I gave a sad little chuckle. "I think a good night's sleep is beyond me, retired or not."

"Perhaps, that's a sign Mother Vestia was right." Ayn-Tuk tapped his staff against the dirt.

"I know she's right." I muttered. "Or at least close enough as makes no difference."

"Yet you rage against her?" I could tell by the way the man spoke, he already knew the answer. "Yet you are hurt by her words?"

"Lies can irritate, make things harder than they need to be." I watched the docks. "Only truth cuts deep enough to hurt." I chuckled remembering days when I believed myself blessed. "When I finally beat Kran, the rumors King John and his wife spread made me laugh." The chuckling gave way to grim memory. "Thaniel spoke his last words where only I could hear them." I paused. "I was never the same after that."

"Yet, you do think she was wrong about something." Ayn-Tuk saw through me. "Something important."

"She's right about the politics. I'm not such a fool I can't see that." I smoked on the shortening cigarette. "She's right to fear what I could become. There's few who know how close I came to those fears."

"But…" Ayn-Tuk prodded me.

"She's wrong to believe I might be saved." I tossed the smoke away. "This is who I am. This is who I will always be."

"I once thought the same." Ayn-Tuk held me with those dark eyes.

"What changed?" I asked almost as a joke.

"Acceptance." He said it softly. It would have sounded like a cliche from anyone else.

"Acceptance?" I tried to make it sound ridiculous, but it didn't.

"That is the central objective of man's time on Earth…" Ayn-Tuk cast his gaze upon the crowds of people. "The only objective. Accept the things you did. Accept the things you didn't. Accept the things you couldn't achieve. Accept the things you could have done but failed." He traced the tree of fate in the dirt with his staff. "Accept the parts of yourself you refuse to admit even exist."

It was something pulled straight from the Testament, the book I was supposed to serve. "So you're the Nameless man now?" It was another joke meant to throw him off the scent.

"I am Ayn-Tuk, but once I was more." He ignored the joke, or perhaps didn't see it as one. "Once I was less."

Something in his voice made me take stock of the black man. I knew he was telling me more than he was saying. I'd wondered who Ayn-Tuk was a thousand times. Seiford and I would often pass time on the road by loudly speculating his back story while he pretended not to hear.

He's a holy man on a mission to find god.

No, he's an adventurer meant to bring the secret of civilization back to his people.

No, he's a sorcerer who's lost his voice.

No, he's a poet searching for the perfect verse.

Surly, the answer must be a dark mystery. That's how the stories went anyway, but I'd been in those stories, mysteries were just things you didn't know yet. Mysteries are more valuable lusted over than when you hold them in your hand. This was true of all currencies but doubly so for mysteries.

Fifteen years I'd roamed the world. Fifteen years I'd led armies down paths others had refused to walk. I had seen many questions answered. Only twice was the answer more valuable than the question.

The first answer I had sworn to take with me to the grave. I swore it not on the Three Above or the Demon's below. Oaths said to such things are always broken. I swore it on nothing because no man can break nothing. This answer would die with me, and the world would be better for it.

The second was the Thru'ncat. The thing that had set Seiford to pondering. I spoke of this often because there was wisdom in it, but I was not wise enough to know what it was.

I stared at Ayn-Tuk. Often we wondered about his story but never really wanting to hear the truth. It would ruin the fun. However, perhaps this man was more than fun. Perhaps, he was a third secret. The first I did not want to understand but did. The second I could not understand though I wanted little more.

Fifteen years of sacrifices and regrets. Fifteen years of a life given to a cause I'd never really believed in. Fifteen years of doubts that reached up to swallow me whole. Two secrets was my payment. Maybe there would be a third. The third time pays for all, as the stories say.

A child's ball smacked my leg taking me away from my thoughts.

"Can we have the ball back?" A boy about eleven ran up.

I stood up and tossed it at the wall behind me. It took a bad bounce and rebounded awkwardly landing in the water.

"Damn." I turned back to the lad. "Sorry I was aiming for something else."

The boy was clearly irritated, but to well raised to be impolite. "What were you aiming at, sir?"

"The truth of all things." I muttered to myself.

"You ever hit it?" The boy humored me. Maybe he just thought I was insane. He was probably smart enough not to provoke a man with two loaded pistols and a face that anvils would feel sorry for. Even though I had my tattoos covered, I'd been fighting for fifteen years, and every bit of it showed.

"No but I once met a man who couldn't miss." I reached into my purse and pulled out a silver coin to hand the lad. "For a new ball."

He was dumbstruck by the coin. "That's worth more than a ball, sir."

"Then buy a ball and some sweets."

The boy gave a toothy grin. "I'm gonna buy a book!"

"I don't want to live in a world where children buy books." I shook my head in as I fished another coin out of my pocket and handed it to him. "You are only to use this money for opium and whores. If you buy anything so sinful as books, the Three will know and they will punish you."

The boy's face lit up with recognition. "You're Thomas Belson!" He whispered loud enough that the whole city could hear.

"Damnit." I muttered again and tossed the boy a third silver. "This is for your secrecy. You may use this on books but know that I do not approve."

"Are you on a secret mission?" The boy gave a conspiratorial whisper.

"Something like that." I gave the lad a wink. "Now go spend your money. Remember one silver for whores, one for opium, and one for books if you must."

"You're my favorite! My dad tells me your stories every night!" He chirped. "I'll never read books again!"

"Good lad." I nodded my approval.

"I'm not sure what opium is." The boy's face dropped in confusion as he surveyed the docks. "Where do I find it?"

"You know that uncle who always rants about the government and the banks?"

He nodded. "Uncle Taylor."

"He'll know." I gave him a last nod to send the lad along.

"You love reading." Ayn-Tuk muttered.

"You want him to wind up like me?" I gave a huff of laughter. "Opium and whores are expensive habits. He'll need a well paying job to support it, and saving the world from the Old Religion just won't cut it."

I tried to trace back my train of thought before I got distracted by the boy. It took me a minute. "So accept myself?"

The black man nodded.

I gave a snort of laughter. "Should I love myself too?" I gave a wry smile. No matter how wisely said, a cliche was a cliche. The only greater sin in conversation was talking about the weather. Neither were forgivable.

Ayn-Tuk didn't see the joke I was playing. "Acceptance requires understanding. When one understands a thing, he is compelled to love it."

I chuckled when I saw his game. I was hoping he wouldn't stoop to that. It was like watching a lion eat rotting meat. "So that's your solution to my dilemma?" I asked. "Quote the Testament?"

"And why not?" Ayn-Tuk gave me an appraising look.

"After everything I've been through..." I trailed off. "Accept thyself seems a bit pedestrian."

"You've become too great for basic wisdoms then?" Ayn-Tuk said it like he wasn't losing the argument.

"If simple folk find comfort in those pages, I won't begrudge them that." I tried to light another cigarette and actually managed it this time.

"Is Mother Vestia simple folk to you?" The black man asked.

"I'm not saying you're simple for believing it." I shot back. "I believe parts of it. I've seen too much to not believe in the Three, but there's a point a man has to move past the Testament. The whole world doesn't fit in that damn book." I puffed a bit more. "Pretend it does and you'll make mistakes there's no coming back from."

"Such as..." Ayn-Tuk prodded me.

"When I first became a Constable, I had a monk named Brother Keys." I paused. "Not a day went by he didn't read that fucking book and quote it back to me, telling me all the ways I came up short."

Ayn-Tuk listened patiently.

"I found it irritating but harmless." I took a deep puff of the smoke, not wanting to relive what came next. "Then one day I faced the hardest decision of my career." I bit my lip and watched the workers go by. "I was still a boy. Despite all I'd done, I was still a boy."

The feeling of that day came back in waves. "I was alone and scared with the weight of empire on my back because no one else could carry it!" I took another puff on the cigarette to steady myself. "I looked to the man who was supposed to guide me, and you know what he said?"

I looked at him, not expecting a response but he surprised me. "Kill them all." Ayn-Tuk whispered. "Kill them all and make them suffer." He tapped his staff on the ground. "I've heard you say it many times in the nightmares."

"Kill them all and make them suffer." I repeated. "I still don't know what the right answer was that day. Things got so messy at the end of it." The smoke filled my lungs. "I know that was the wrong one for a monk though."

"So a monk failed, now you throw away the whole book." Ayn-Tuk cut to his point.

"No, I'm just saying I've read the Testament. Everyone's read the Testament." I said with the smugness that comes with certainty. "If that's the treatment then the diagnosis is wrong."

Maybe Ayn-Tuk wasn't as wise as I'd thought him all these years. Sure he said things that left me off balance, but so could a barmaid worth her salt. The bastard never really talked much, so how would I know anyway. Maybe his deep voice just veiled the fact that he was full of shit. That argument was too easy to smack down.

Ayn-Tuk waited a moment before he began his response. "There was a time when those words were uttered, and the greatest fell to their knees for the beauty of them. Many years later, when they realized what they meant, they wept as men had never wept before. By their tears they were made clean. Awakened in them was a truth that slumbered until they heard it spoken.

"This knowledge was too precious to die with them, so they passed it on to their children. After all, what father would not wish to save his most beloved from years of torment and blindness. Their children learned well, and so to did their children's children. Generations past until none had heard the words spoken from the original lips. None remembered the moment when they first became aware of their own souls. It had always been so to them. This was enough for a time.

"But then the weight of antiquity settled upon them. From their first moment they remember a teaching that brought fire to man's heart. These lessons are ignored with repetition. They are made meaningless because all insist that they have meaning. Familiarity is the enemy of beauty.

"Where men once pondered and questioned the teachings, came to understand the words that made life worth living, now they are taught that it is truth. One cannot question and ponder because he fears what he will find in doing so. With one thread pulled, he fears the fabric will fall apart. The works of countless generation all wasted.

"He is told what is true and he pretends to believe. However, one cannot be told what is true. He must find it for himself or it means nothing. He wields a toy sword because steel can bite. He pretends it is real, but secretly he feels a fool when he draws it, even if all those around him also pretend the sword is real. They are held to the companionship of isolation. The words that once made men realize they were more, now only serve to make them feel less.

"They become even less than their forefathers who stumbled blindly through a petulant existence. Men who do not believe are easy to save, and in some ways are saved already. The greatest poverty lies in denying you are poor. None is more damned than those who pretend to believe even in the privacy of his own thoughts. Wisdom will only remind him of a lost inheritance.

"When wisdom is spoken, the scions will not fall to their knees for the beauty of it. They will not feel the sleeper awaken. They will be moved to resentment and tear apart that which makes them face the loneliness they pretend is not there. They will tear apart the first who speaks, and who will be brave enough to speak second?

"Perhaps it was a mistake to dictate our wisdom with paper and pen. Perhaps we should have hidden our wisdom on the tallest mountains or beneath the desert sun. Perhaps then men would know that the wisdom they found was venerable, but if it is a mistake, it cannot be unmade now."

Ayn-Tuk nodded to indicate he was done.

I was right, Ayn-Tuk wasn't as wise as I thought. He was more than I'd ever suspected. I wasn't quite sure what he'd said, but he said something. I felt it in the same way the people of his story had.

"You must cast the toy sword away then." I finally managed to respond.

Ayn-Tuk shrugged. "Perhaps that is the only choice left, but I would prefer a better one. There was a time the sword was real. In losing one we may lose both, and behind the facade there was something beautiful."

The black man took my shoulder in a firm grip. "You are one who cannot abide wearing a toy, but let's see if you can find the sword." He tapped me with the staff. "Forget that it is cliche. Forget that the people who tried to teach this lesson did not understand it themselves. Forget that you feel a fool for saying it." He paused. "Acceptance of self is all. Even the parts that you refuse to admit exist.

I thought for a moment before answering. "The whole damn thing is a paradox." Ayn-Tuk nodded for me to continue. "I need to love myself, accept myself, but also go to war with my worser demons, which I'm also supposed to love mind you." I took out another cigarette growing more sure. "There's not a damn bit of sense to it."

"That is certainly an objection," The black man tapped his staff on the ground, "but it is an especially clumsy objection for one such as yourself."

"How do you figure?" I shot back.

"You loved Thaniel."

That one hit hard. "For a merciful man you're rather ruthless." I finally got out.

"It's been said before." He nodded.

"So what must I do?" I gestured to the wide world around me. "Where should I go?"

"Seiford was right." Ayn-Tuk said. "You must go back to the Confederacy."

I shook my head. "That's not an answer I'm willing to accept."

He tapped his staff some more. "That is how you know it is the right one."

"I realize riddles might make you seem awfully powerful and mysterious," I shot back, "but they are of very little use to me now."

"You must go there because it is the only place you fear to go." He didn't rise to my tone. "The things that make us whole are in the last place we want to look." For the first time since I'd known him, Ayn-Tuk smiled. "Wisdom hidden on mountain tops if you will."

I hung my head. "What if it breaks me?" There was desperation in my voice.

"It will," he did not try to brush away my fears, "but you may be made whole from your brokenness."

I gave the black man a nod of respect. "You are truly wise Ayn-Tuk." It was true. "Any man would do well to listen to your council."

"Thank-" He started.

"Because of your wisdom I'll say this one time." I turned to the man. "I'm not going to the fucking Confederacy." I sat back on the bench. "Let's go to Inte. I've never been there."

Ayn-Tuk shrugged as if it made no difference. "You truly are an unpleasant man."

That made me laugh. "It's been said before."

"THOMAS!" I heard Seiford scream from the door as I cursed under my breath. "I think I figured it out!" He rushed towards me.

"No you didn't." I shook my head in irritation. "The Thro'ncat is beyond mortal knowledge." I nodded to the people of the dock whispering amongst themselves and pretending not to stare. "What you have done is ruin my afternoon."

"Oh..." The monk finally realized his mistake.

The people on the dock had been glancing at me out the side of their eye since I first sat down. They saw the resemblance between me, and a hero who's picture had appeared in the paper. However, the greatest disguise a hero can wear is his own fame. Men never imagine they'll meet such a man in person. Such things just do not happen.

Still, there's no disguise so good it can survive a name screamed in broad daylight. A small crowd had started to gather.

"Is that him?" One old man with a greying beard asked to no one in particular.

"Can't be. He's too little." A large woman carrying a basket of eggs responded. "He's supposed to be seven feet tall."

"I heard he was little." I couldn't see who said that, lucky for him.

"Where's his dragon?"

"He ain't got a dragon. That's a rumor."

"Don't get too close to the monk. I hear he's got foreign diseases."

"Three be damned, I do not have the Kranish drip!" Seiford screamed into the crowd.

"Aye, that's them." A portly man in the front nodded. "I heard the monk has the Kranish drip."

"He just said he didn't have it." A pretty girl shot at the man.

"That's what he'd say if he had the Kranish drip."

Seiford shook his head in dismay. "We should go back in side." He said to me.

That gave me a chuckle. "What and you think they'll just forget about it if they can't see us." The monk knew I was right. "They're not pigs Seif."

"Then what'll you do?" My friend asked.

"Play the part of the generous hero." I shrugged. "We'll be going to Inte soon anyway."

"Inte?" Seiford asked.

"Aye, Inte." Ayn-Tuk said with more than a little reproach.

I stood up to address the crowd. There was no hiding from them, now. "My name is Thomas Belson." I said it in the voice that carried. "I'm not here on business, so you have nothing to-"

"Monster!" I was cut off by someone in the back screaming.

"Wait, what?" I had never gotten that reaction.

"He's a damn hero, you jackass!"

"I'm afraid I missed something..." I whispered to Seiford.

"Won his name by stepping on people like us!"

Before I could even begin to grasp the situation, the crowd erupted into loud yelling and then violent shoving. The topic of the disagreement seemed to be whether I was, in fact, a monster.

"Calm down!" I screamed, but no one listened. I wasn't used to being ignored. Even before I'd won my name, the tattoos on my arm entitled my opinion to be heard. "Be quiet!" I shouted again to the same effect. I pulled out my six-shooter and fired once into the air. The gunshot rang for a moment, and silence descended on the crowd. "Shut your fucking mouths!" They all turned to stare at me.

"You're a monster who does nothing but push us common folk back in the dirt!" One particularly brave boy in the front leveled a finger at me.

"I don't know what in the Three's name you're talking about," I holstered my weapon. "But I'm quite sure I'm too hungover to sit here and learn."

"My daddy told me you're a monster, with not a lick of honor in you at all." The boy punctuated the point by poking his finger in an accusing fashion. He couldn't have been older than ten. "He said Thaniel was the real hero."

I went to one knee so I could be at eye level. "Your daddy should have taught you not to insult a Constable of the New Church to his face."

"You threatening my boy!" I heard a deep rumble from the back of the crowd. I saw his head poking up through the press of people. It was an ugly head, bald and scarred from years of bar fights, and it looked as if the body it was attached to was almost seven feet tall. The big, ugly man finally made his way to the front. He stood head and shoulders over me, and every inch of him was covered in heaping slabs of muscle. "I'll beat you bloody if'n you threaten my boy."

"I wasn't threatening him." I said with a sigh. "I was informing your son that his father is a bit slow in the head, and maybe he shouldn't take after your social graces."

"You calling me stupid?" The big man screwed up his already damaged face. He no doubt only understood every other word, as it wasn't spoken in his moron vernacular.

"Yes," I admitted, "but I was doing it politely."

"Three above Thomas, let's just leave." Seiford implored over my shoulder. "We don't need to prove anything to these people."

"Stay out of it you pillow biter." The big man spat a glob of something disgusting in front of me.

I stood to face the man, but Seiford grabbed my shoulder. "His son's watching."

"Thomas, don't." Ayn-Tuk said to me.

"He's yeller Paw!" The boy screamed with pride at his father intimidating Thomas Belson.

"Maybe you didn't catch what I told your boy." I said through clenched teeth. "I've killed more men than you've ever met."

"Aye, you have." The big man spat again, just as disgusting the second time. "I think you ought to be punished for it."

"Better men than you have tried." I hissed back.

Seiford tried to restrain me. "Whatever, the issue is we can get it sorted out later, but not if you beat a man to death in the street."

"You're next." The big man leveled a finger at the monk. "I don't want you spreading whatever cock-rot you have to good folk!"

Seiford squeezed my shoulder. "He doesn't know what he's saying." That was the monk's way. He didn't want to see anyone hurt for some snide comment, but I had a different way.

"I don't know what you think of me, and I don't care," I tried to control the rage building up, "but I'd rather not do this in front of your boy."

"He ought to know what happens to bastards like you." The big man gathered his saliva for another disgusting spit, this time headed at my face. He never got to release it though. He was on his left knee screaming in pain before he knew what happened.

There was a way to hit small men and a way to beat big men. A small man you'd punch in the ribs. It'd knock the wind out of him and put enough hurt into his body that he couldn't react to the next strike. Realistically if you were as strong as a Constable of the New Church tended to be, you could hit him anywhere and have an adequate response. The man who was standing before me, who I'd taken to calling Mangle-Face in my head, was a big sort, and that required a tad more precision. They had too much muscle and fat to do any real damage. You had to know precisely where to place your punch in his stomach. Even still, big men didn't go down easy. They needed to be helped to the ground. I put my heel into the space just below his right kneecap. I felt the sickening tear of sinew and Mangle-Face went to his good knee screaming like a baby taken from the tit.

"Fuck!" Mangle-Face let out.

I could have stopped right there. The fight was over, but I couldn't help myself. Once you had a man on his knees, there was really only one of two things to do. You could help him up and possibly make a good friend, but I wasn't really in that kind of mood. That left only the second option. The second option was to ram your knee into whatever stupid face had managed to offend you until the bastard got the idea and rolled over.

When you had a man in that position, you really didn't need to take big or small into account, it's just a matter of how long it takes to get your message across adequately. Everyone reacts pretty much the same to being kneed in the face. Big or small didn't matter. Lord or peasant didn't even matter. Everyone was equal before the knee.

One, two, three, and Mangle Face went limp. That surprised me. I figured the big man had at least five in him.

The whole crowd was silent as the grave for a few precious seconds. I stared out at the people, waiting for the surprised gasps and applause at my strength and prowess. They never came. "Paw…" was all I heard then louder. "Paw!" I looked down at the boy frantically shaking his father.

I felt a pang of guilt in my gut but smothered it with anger. "That'll teach him to call me…" I looked around at the crowd for support, but none came, not even from the ones who had defended me before. "He was asking for it!" I said more to myself than anyone. I saw Ayn-Tuk shake his head.

"Three above, Thomas!" Seiford pulled me behind him. "Get out of here!" The monk screamed at the crowd who dispersed immediately. "Here," he pressed a few coins into the boy's hand, "go get a doctor! I'll treat him until you get back."

The boy ran off without protest. I thought that was strange. If the companion of the man who'd just beaten my father had given me an order, I probably wouldn't have obeyed. "What?" I looked at the monk even though I knew exactly what. "He'll live. He just won't speak to me like that again."

"And you think you proved him wrong!" Seiford turned to me filled with true rage. "You think beating him into a bloody pulp in front of his son shows people you're a true hero?"

"He was going to spit on me." It sounded weak even to myself.

"So you almost killed him!" Seiford shook his head.

"He'll live." I repeated as if saying it again made it more likely.

"Probably he will," Seiford bent down to check Mangle-Face, "unless that blow to his stomach ruptured his bowels, in which case he'll die painfully in about two days." The monk furiously ran his hand over the man's body looking for something. "Or maybe those blows to his head could have caused internal bleeding in the brain, in which case he'll never wake up from this nap." Seiford opened his eyes to check the pupils. "He could die in the thousands of ways a man's body can stop working when you beat him like you just did, but you're right. He'll never call you monster again." Seiford stood up to face me.

"Good," I spit into the ground, "he learned his lesson."

That made the monk even angrier. "But the people who saw will." There was sorrow mixed with rage in him. "They'll call you a mad dog, and none who were here will say otherwise." He stared at me. "Him and everyone else who watched will call you a tyrant, who casually ruins men's lives."

"Don't be dramatic." I rolled my eyes. "I'll bet he's been in countless fights."

"That knee you hit will never be the same, even after he spends months recovering." Seiford's face went to pure stone. "Look at him! He's a dockworker. If he can't work, he can't feed his family."

I pulled out a few gold coins and threw them on the man. "That's more than a year's salary for him, right there."

"And the boy?" Seiford narrowed his eyes.

"Learned not to pick a fight with me." I said it with defiance.

"Aye, he did." Seiford nodded in mock agreement. "He also just watched his father beat halfway to death for a remark he made." He gestured to the unconscious Mangle-Face. "Do you really think he's the tender love type? I don't. I think he's the beat his child for making him look like less of a man type." Seiford shook his head. "There are better ways to teach people not to insult you."

"Like what?" I spit into the dirt.

"Like being better, Thomas!" He screamed. "Like being better..." He said it softly like he was pleading. "We could have walked away!"

"I did what any other man would do." I kicked the ground.

"You're not any other man!" Seiford grabbed my shoulder. "You're Thomas Belson. You've won more battles than most people can name. Do you really need to beat a dockworker to feel like it?" The monk looked back at Mangle-Face. "You can't act like any other man because people look to you for a better way."

I finally admitted defeat. "You're right I shouldn't have beat him the way I did." I hoped that would end the argument.

"It's not just about him." Seiford turned his gaze back to me. "You're getting worse. You're having those dreams almost every night. This is why Mother Vestia let you go."

"I'm fine." I answered shortly. I didn't want to have this argument. People were staring at us.

"You're not fine!" Seiford said it quietly, but with force.

"You're fucking right I'm not fine!" I hissed back. "I'm the greatest warrior to ever walk this earth, and I'm being cast off like an old shirt!"

"I didn't think she was right, but after this…" Seiford gestured to Mangle-Face. "Maybe she was." He shook his head. "What happens if you take a city, and you decide to finish that like you did here?"

"That won't happen again." I said firmly.

"What if it does?" Seiford wouldn't let up. "How many thousands could die?"

"So that's it?" I gripped my fist tightly. "You think I'm a mad dog, who can't be controlled anymore."

"No, I think you're the greatest man to ever walk this earth." That took the wind out of me. "I believed that when I met you, I believed that after Sterling, and I believe it now. I believe that when you become the man you're destined to be, the world will never be the same," Seiford took a step forward, "but that man needs to be more than just a warrior."

"It's what I am." I bit my lip. "It's what they needed me to become." I shook my head. "I won't go apologizing for that."

"No, it's not." Seiford hung his head. "You've pretended to be that for so long you can't tell where the act ends and you begin." Seiford put his hand on my shoulder as if comforting me. "I know why. If you're just a warrior, you're not responsible for your mistakes. You're just a gun who had the misfortune of being pointed the wrong way, but you're not a gun. You can choose when to stop. You can say when enough is enough."

There was one boy still there, watching around the corner with three silver pieces in his hand. It was a fortune to a lad that age. He was meant to spend them on whores and opium.

I watched the boy drop his coins and run off crying. Crying because he'd seen Belson the Blessed. It's hard to think yourself the hero after something like that. He wouldn't understand the subtle hardships that brought me here. He wouldn't hear all the excuses I played in my head.

All he'd know was that there was a man he respected.

All he'd know is that he didn't respect that man anymore.

"I'm sorry..." I said to no one in particular.

"I know." Seiford put a hand on my back. "I know."

"Things'll get better when we get to Inte." I whispered.

"Yeah." Seiford said, but I knew he didn't believe it. "Yeah, they will."

That was worse than anything else. That moment broke me in ways that fifteen years of war never could. Seiford was my greatest friend in the world, and he was starting to lose hope in me. Doctors tell the truth to the patients they think they can save. They only lie to the doomed.

"Or we could go to the Confederacy." Ayn-Tuk said calmly.

Seiford cringed, but I nodded. "If that's what you think is best." There was no more fight in me.

The monk gave a sad little smile. "That's a real good idea, Thomas." He put a hand on my back and we walked to find a boat. "That's a real good idea."

Seiford couldn't hide the sorrow in his voice, though. It was like he was mourning something that wasn't dead yet. Part of me wanted to tell him something more. Something that wouldn't make his voice heavy with pain.

I was so tired though. It was like the eyelids of my soul were closing. Every thought found an edge to cut me with, so I just wanted to stop thinking. Maybe I wouldn't feel this way in the morning.

Maybe I'd be able to ignore it in the morning is what I meant. For a decade this was what crept in my shadow. Since Thaniel's last words... Since the Pillars...

I'd done heroic things in that time. Good things. Things a man can be proud of. I hadn't done them for the right reasons though.

I had done these things because for ten years, I'd been looking for an excuse to die.

For this men called me hero.

Fourteen Years Earlier The Thaniel Wars

The door opened without knocking. "Two hundred and one." I finished my pushups, using whatever reserves of strength I could find.

I rolled over massaging my aching muscles. I looked up at whoever had interrupted me. It was Captain Bradly Seiford. He was everything a soldier should be, tall, strong, and handsome. His bright, green eyes and wavy, blond hair would have gotten just about any maid to bed with him. That was if he was unchivalrous enough to let them. I'd seen a hundred women try and open their legs to the man, but he just shut them back. He was older than I was, maybe approaching thirty.

Perhaps, we learn temperance in our later years. I wouldn't have turned away those women, but then again, I was sixteen. The trouble was that none of them ever offered it. I wore the marks of a Constable of the New Church. The New Church was losing, and the losing uniform seldom attracted women. Captain Seiford wore the uniform of Anthanii. They were losing too, but patriotism would always get the girls.

Constables have no country, only an obscure religion that no one really followed to the letter. Obscure religions don't attract women. That's what I told myself at least. I tried to blame his successes on the uniforms we wore, but the truth was, if he had a tattooed arm and I had a red coat, girls would still flock to him. However, they might have turned to me after he said "no."

"You really think it's wise?" Bradley looked at me like the enigma I was. "Doing two hundred pushups on the eve of battle."

"Two hundred and one." I corrected him smugly.

"Same question." He kept his steady gaze on me as I laid on the floor.

"Wisdom is for farmers and hermits." I took a sip of water from my skin. "A warrior needs cunning and strength."

"Not very cunning then." The captain wouldn't let me win.

I eyed him up. "I did two hundred pushups before Milhire, and I did alright there." I rubbed the feeling into my arms. "Your men are calling me Belson the Blessed because of that day."

"Still lost."

"Aye, that's why I did two hundred and one this time." I tapped the tomahawk at my side.

"Besides I think you misunderstand the point of that name." Bradly cocked an eyebrow up. "It was supposed to be a joke."

"It won't be tomorrow." I said it mostly to myself then looked up at him. "I assume you didn't come to talk about my name though.

"The assembly is assembled." It was a cleverer pun then I thought the stoic man capable of. Everyone thought a large vocabulary was a mark of intelligence. In some ways it was, but the real way to show your mind was by using the same word in two different ways. *The assembly is assembled.* I mused to myself. Captain Seiford was a deep, clever man. It was probably why he was still a captain, despite his noble blood, wealthy parents, and five years in service. He was everything a soldier should be, reliable, loyal, and dashing. He was also a few things that generals thought a captain didn't have a right to, intelligent, imaginative, and his worse sin was being stationed under me.

"Let me get dressed." I hopped to my feet.

"Best wash up a bit too." Captain Seiford wrinkled his nose. "You smell like you did two hundred and one pushups."

I smelled myself and realized he was right. "Just so." I went to the wash bowl.

"I got those damn medals you had me mint." Captain Seiford rubbed his chest, self-conscious. "I bet they'll look pretty on our corpses."

"I don't plan on pinning the dead." I rubbed the water over my sweaty self. "It lessens the meaning of the award."

"Why make those medals then?" The Captain scratched his head. "The whole thing seems like a waste."

"Those medals are key to my plans." I scraped off the sweat.

"I'd rather artillery be key to your plan." He scoffed at it all.

"So would I." I responded shortly. "If you find any lying around, do let me know." I turned back to the water. "All I have is thread and a bit of copper, so I do what I can."

Captain Seiford nodded. He would often doubt my actions. That was what a good second in command did, but he would never doubt me. He was with me at Milhire. Before that day he hated me because I was young and foreign. Not just foreign but not even from the same continent. After that day, he saw something in me. I respected him too. It wasn't easy overcoming one's station at birth. Men with noble blood and wealthy parents were seldom worth anything. Even more so he had years of university nonsense to unlearn. Despite that education, he had actually managed to become quite learned.

"How many men are assembled." I put on a white flannel shirt and went to button it up. I'd asked for every man capable of carrying a rifle to meet in the town square. I'd hoped three thousand. I suspected it would be twenty-five hundred.

"Not enough." Captain Seiford said it as much to himself as anyone else.

"You know phrases like that might be fun to quote in two hundred years, but they do very little to help me prepare for battle." I stopped buttoning to give the man a suitably reproachful look.

"What, in the Three, are you planning?" He finally let go of his bearing. "You've had my men gather up every scarecrow in Wuntsville, appropriate seventy-five donkeys, and now we're minting medals?" Captain Seiford raised his hands in defeat.

"My thoughts exactly." A woman said as she walked into the room. She was Lady Gerate, the noble in charge of Wuntsville since her husband died in some battle against Thaniel a few years back. Lady Gerate was beautiful by anyone's definition of the word. Her long dark hair and sharp figures made me want her. She was too young to be a widow and too talented to be a figurehead to any noble's family. She was younger than twenty, but she didn't act it. She was probably the only reason Wuntsville hadn't already torn itself apart.

Her brown eyes always seemed to be assessing me. Her grace could have belonged to a woman three times her age or a man four.

I was jealous of that. Despite the tattoos on my arm I often acted younger than I was. Her dress was simple and black, not the fine thing ladies usually wear. People who understood fashion would have called it unstylish, but I knew nothing of fashion, and the way the dress hugged her curves was definitely stylish to me.

"Lady Gerate." I nodded my head in respect. I always tried to treat her well. I knew it was a fool's hope, but at sixteen, I was hoping she'd want me back.

"I would also like to know what your plan is. My people are angry over your acquisition of their property." She stood straight-shouldered and elegant. "I don't know what the peasants use scarecrows for. They don't seem to actually scare crows, but they like them." Lady Gerate took a step further into the room. "As for the donkeys, they're the pride of our city. Wuntsville is famous for our fine donkeys." She sighed. "And those medals… No one really seems to care about them, and that's its own problem isn't it?" She had a way of making me feel like a child.

"I'll make them care, damnit!" I stopped dressing to face both of my detractors. "By the way, I hate to be the one to tell you, but calling this place a city is a bit of a stretch, and anywhere that's famous for its donkeys, isn't really famous!" The optimal word in always trying to treat Lady Gerate well was trying, but sixteen-year-olds can be intemperate. Even where pretty girls are involved. *Especially where pretty girls are involved.*

"Famous donkeys or not, these are my people." She said it firmly against my tempest. "Whatever you're planning seems a lot like a fool's parade. If it's hopeless, let me know now so I can discuss terms. No Kranish army has been beaten in the field since Thaniel became emperor" Lady Gerate stepped to the side of Captain Seiford. "I know you're searching for glory, but I will not see my city set ablaze for the ego of a prideful child."

"I'm not a damn child." I had however at that point tried and failed many times to button the collar of my shirt. It did appear quite childish.

"Here." Lady Gerate came to my aide to help with the last button.

"Thank you." I grumbled despite myself. "As for your city being sacked on account of my vanity, do you know who leads the Kranish armies at your doorstep?"

"General Gostfeld." She took a step back. I wish she hadn't. Even with her being as difficult as she was, I liked her close to me.

"General Gostfeld is one of Thaniel's best generals." I said as I buckled on my gun belt. "He's also one of his most bloodthirsty. He was at Milhire, and I saw what he did there."

"All the more reason to consider terms." Lady Gerate would have rolled her eyes, but she had too much class for that.

"You don't understand." I shook my head. "Why send a man like that to accept a meek surrender? He'd have sent some buffoon he owed a favor to." I checked to make sure both of my revolvers were full. They were of course, but it helped ease my mind to know for sure. "He wants to make a statement here. You wouldn't open your gates to him immediately, and now he's going to level your whole damn city. He wants to show people what happens when they pick the wrong side."

I narrowed my eyes at the woman. "Thaniel doesn't need this city for strategic purposes, and he sure as shit doesn't need your world famous donkeys. The only way this place has any value to Kran is if it's wiped off the map." I rolled my eyes. I didn't have too much class for that. "Sure, officially Thaniel will chastise Gostfeld for raping your donkeys and killing the womenfolk. That goes against his man of the people image, but unofficially, everyone in Thyro will know exactly why he did it, to send a message." I paused. "Nothing sends a message quite like a burned out city."

"So it's hopeless." Lady Gerate looked at her feet. For a moment she seemed the person she was, not the one she pretended to be. She wasn't even twenty years old and she was the lady of a city about to be under siege. I didn't envy her that. I was responsible for just myself really, and Captain Seiford only had two hundred men who probably would have died in battle anyhow the way the war was going. Every horrible thing that happened to her people, she felt herself. I should have been less blunt.

The moment left her quick though, then it was back to the mask. "If it is hopeless, then we need to start getting the women and children out immediately." Still, I saw the weight hang on her shoulders. I knew by women and children she didn't count herself, even though she qualified as both. I wanted to help lift that weight.

"It's not hopeless." I stepped forward to her. "I'm here, and while Thomas Belson is in the fight, it's never hopeless."

"Milhire was hopeless." She pinched her face into a scowl. I try to be nice to people, and they bite the hand. That's why I so rarely do nice things.

"Three be damned," I turned to Captain Seiford, "you've seen me fight. Tell her it's not hopeless while Thomas Belson stands here."

"It probably is hopeless." He said to Lady Gerate. I wanted to strangle the bastard right there.

"Damnit, Bradly!" I shouted as I stowed my other pistol away into a holster near my chest.

"Still, I have seen him fight." He gave me a look almost bordering on respect. "Despite his ridiculous penchant for referring to himself in the third person, Thomas Belson is probably our best hope." He gave the girl a compassionate look. "None of us are going to leave Wuntsville until it's safe. I promise you that."

"Thank you, Captain." Lady Gerate laid a tender hand on his shoulder that lingered for too long. That seemed unfair. After all, it was my plan. She should have been laying tender hands on my shoulder that lingered too long!

I rolled my eyes at the absurdity of it all. "If the women and children leave, the men won't fight as hard, and they'll all die anyway." I paused. "Even if they leave this instant, which they won't because it takes hours to prepare evacuation, they can't outrun Gostfeld's cavalry."

"Then tell us what your plan is." Lady Gerate implored me. "What possible reason could you have for donkeys and scarecrows?"

"Well, that depends." I nodded to Captain Seiford. "How many men have answered our call?" I said as I stowed some throwing knives into my bandolier. "And if you give me an answer that sounds even a little poetic, I swear to the Three you'll fight the coming battle naked." I crossed my fingers for three thousand but prepared for twenty-five hundred.

"Just under two thousand." Damn, not even twenty-five hundred.

"Congratulations Captain! That wasn't poetic at all." I stopped getting dressed and sat down on the bed, and beckoned them to do the same. They sat in chairs facing me. I explained the plan in its entirety. It took a while because it was complicated. Any plan that involves donkeys and scarecrows tends to be. Generally speaking, it's not good to have too many steps in a battle. It just gives you more of a chance to fuck it all up, but there were five thousand Kranish soldiers led by General Gostfeld out there. The odds were against us, and when the odds were as bad as they were in Wuntsville, you needed more steps. I finally finished explaining my plan and held up my hands waiting for the praise that was sure to be mine.

"You're sure he's our best chance?" Lady Gerate looked to the Captain in pure horror.

"Well, we did only fight one battle together," he considered it, "and we lost."

"What's wrong with my plan?" I said not a little insulted.

"Well, as I feared, it hinges on donkeys and scarecrows." Lady Gerate looked around the room as if the world itself knew how foolish I was.

"Thomas, it's just that it seems rather complicated and far-fetched." Captain Seiford was trying to look diplomatic. "Battles aren't won by ridiculous stunts. They're won with artillery, cavalry, and men." He looked up at the sky as if praying. "You're breaking every rule in the book. We're splitting our forces, relying on levies, and risking our leader."

"He's insane." Lady Gerate said as if I wasn't even there. "Start the evacuation, now!"

"I'm not insane!" I stood up. It was at that moment I realized my zipper was down, and I must confess, I looked rather insane. "Those books you're talking about were written by men with armies, cannons, and disciplined troops. We don't have any of those, so we can't follow their rules." I looked around the room. "If we had better infantry we'd rely on that. If we had better cavalry, we'd rely on that. Three above, if we had a prayer, I'd be on my knees already, but we don't."

I caressed the six-shooter at my side. "What we do have are donkeys, scarecrows, and, thanks to my foresight, medals. We have shadows and stealth. I can use that. We have our desperation and their arrogance. I'd rather cannon, but that'll have to do." I looked out the window for a moment. "We have me, and I don't intend to go to waste." I scratched the tattoos on my arm. "We have nothing so our plan must rely on our enemy. I can give us a chance, but only if everyone knows that it's victory or death."

"We have a wall," Lady Gerate said it like she was trying to talk herself out of agreeing with me, "a strong wall."

"That might have mattered a hundred years ago, but it doesn't now." I tried to look endearing. I really did. "Their cannons can blow it away, and I doubt they'll even have to reload."

Lady Gerate took a moment to gather the courage to ask what came next. "What about the Old Religion?" She knew that the answer to that question could end any hopes we had.

"It's bad." I tapped the tattoos on our arms. "That's an easy philosophical question to answer." I smiled at her, which was completely inappropriate.

"You know what I mean!" She didn't like me making jokes at her expense.

"Aye, I know what you mean." I sighed. "You want to know if there's a Priest ready to call fire and lightning upon our god-fearing heads."

"I think that's important to know." Lady Gerate crossed her arms.

"Yes, it is, but I don't know for certain." I rubbed my arm. It wasn't burning, that was a good sign. "I don't have the best intelligence despite being wildly intelligent."

"So there's half a chance they have a Priest, and we're all dead regardless of your donkeys and scarecrows." Lady Gerate tried to keep the fear out of her voice. It reflected well on her that she even tried to hide it. The people of Thyro had an ingrained fear of the blood-colored cloak. To them it was like being scared of storms or an earthquake, it just made sense. I had already vowed to change that, but I vowed again.

"I don't like the idea of fighting one of them." Captain Seiford touched the sword at his side. He was ever a stoic man, but even after all the horrors he'd seen in battle, the Old Religion hit a nerve.

"I do." I said it mostly to myself. I was going to teach Thyro what the Priests were, just men. Men could be killed. "I love the idea of killing those fuckers but not here with this army, with your city as the battleground." I finally turned my attention back to the company. "It doesn't matter though. I don't think they brought any Priests with them."

"Why not?" Captain Seiford looked at me.

"Because for all its power, public opinion is against the Old Religion." I worked on my clothes. "Thaniel is trying to change that. He's trying to sell some damn fool notion that those Priests are a force for good."

I looked from Lady Gerate to Captain Seiford but didn't see the realization on their face. Sometimes I forgot that everyone else's mind didn't work the same way mine did. It wasn't that they were stupid. Captain Seiford spoke five languages and had mastered some idiocy called calculus. Lady Gerate was brilliant enough to run a city as a woman. If you put the three of us in a classroom, I would rank in the bottom third. The thing that separated me is that people put rules about everything they do. They see things one way and refuse to step away from their biases even in the privacy of their own mind. I learned young that understanding could not be had from one view.

I could see the stories men wrote on their souls. I knew what they wanted. When you know what your enemy wants, and you know what you want, you can always win. "Thaniel wants this city destroyed, and he wants to be able to say he didn't want it. If the Priests are at all associated with the slaughter he's planning, then it could drive public opinion even further down. Thaniel's fate is tied to the Old Religion. If a Priest is here when the city burns, then it's like he was giving the orders." Thaniel was made in my own mold. I knew him well. "I'd bet the life of everyone in this city, we'll find only soldiers in that army."

Lady Gerate nodded. "You've got cunning. I'll give you that." I was about to make some pithy response, but she stopped me with a look. "However, if I'm going to let you lead my people into the teeth of Thaniel's legions, I need to know you really believe we can win."

"I already told you my plan will-"

She stopped me with her hand. "I'm not just talking about this battle. I'm talking about Thaniel as a whole." She eyes Seiford up than me. "Anthanii brought the greatest army she's ever mustered to Milhire." Lady Gerate let a sombre pause ring through. "We lost there, and one battle over a town famous for it's donkeys won't change that."

I sat back down considering this question. Finally, I looked back up at her. "If we win here, it'll get me noticed." I paused. "The court won't be able to ignore me once I beat Gostfeld."

"So it is all about the legend of Thomas Belson." She shook her head and went to leave.

"I won't lie to you and say I'm here for altruism because I'm not." That stopped her. Candor always makes people stay a moment more. "Still, there's more at stake than my legend."

Captain Seiford cut in knowing my thoughts. "We do a lot of things wrong in Anthanii. Make mistakes Thaniel doesn't." He nodded to me. "The Constable here can change these things, but he's not a popular man with the king and his court." He took a pause. "If we win here, he'll have that chance."

Lady Gerate took a moment to digest that. "He's as good as that, you think?" She finally asked.

"Yes," the Captain nodded, "I do."

"I can win this battle." I hardened my look to show her who I was. I was the man you didn't bet against. "And after that I can win this war." I would find a way to win if all I had was a dog and a wooden sword. I didn't think she wanted to see any more of my certainty. I think she mistook it for arrogance. People often made that mistake.

"I think he's our only chance." Captain Seiford said to the Lady.

"I think you're right." She finally gave in.

"Of course, I'm right!" I finally smiled at the both of them. "Now, someone help me with this damn button!"

"Three help us." I heard Gerate say she helped me with the button.

<hr />

"It's suicide!" A man near the front screamed.

"Belson the Blessed strikes again!" A man in the back screamed to the chagrin of those around him. He was lucky I couldn't see who he was.

The town square was filled with the men who had answered the call to arms. I'd just told them we were going to attack at dawn tomorrow. They were taking the news better than I expected.

"We want our donkeys back!" An older gentleman who looked like he could barely walk shouted.

"Thomas Belson can win this battle." Lady Gerate calmed the crowd with her hand. They respected her far more than they did me. "He killed two thousand men at Milhire, and almost turned the day." In truth, I hadn't killed two thousand men, and nothing could have turned Milhire around, but the townsfolk seemed to accept the lie from their trusted leader's mouth.

"My lady we should sue for peace." A noble looking man tried his best not to seem cowardly.

"We can't." I finally tried to get my word in. "I received a letter this morning from General Gostfeld saying he will level this city with us inside." That was a lie too, but I didn't think they'd understand the delicate politics of it all. Regardless of how I knew it, the city would burn if I didn't do something, and everyone in it would suffer the price of my disobedience.

The town hall erupted at that revelation. "We should run!" The same man who said it was suicide shouted. I was really beginning to get annoyed with him.

I was about to explain why running was futile, but Lady Gerate spoke first. "Run if it's in your hearts." The crowd calmed to hear her speak again. "I will be on the battlefield fighting for our city. If we fail, then the Kranish will overrun you in short time." I wanted to stop her and tell her to take that back. I didn't want her fighting. I looked at her beautiful as she was. She wasn't meant for war. She was tough, but things happened in battle. I wanted to make her take it back, but it was already said. "I do not plan on letting our city be taken by Thaniel's hoards."

To their credit, no one ran. They didn't look particularly eager, but they didn't run.

I finally got my senses back after her revelation that she would fight. "I'll need two groups of volunteers." I stared over the crowd daring them to be brave. "Three hundred will be sitting in the woods waiting for the signal. It'll be dangerous, but this is a dangerous situation." No one raised their hands.

"That is the group I will be leading." Lady Gerate said over the crowd. *Three be damned*. Couldn't the girl have shared that with me first, so I could talk her out of it? "We will be close to the fray."

The men in the crowd grumbled as if considering it, but still ultimately no one raised their hands.

"The second group will be with me. I'll need a dozen of you're bravest men to ride at my side, causing havoc." I knew no one would raise their hands for this bit. "Has anyone here soldiered before?" I asked of them.

One elderly man with half a leg raised his hand.

I sighed. "Has anyone here hunted before? It's kind of like hunting." It wasn't like hunting at all, but I saw no reason to stop lying.

A few more raised their hands.

"Good, now how many of you will volunteer to fight with me?" The hands went down rather quickly.

I sighed again. I was only sixteen, but even I knew that in earlier years men wouldn't need to be convinced to defend what was theirs, no matter the odds. Thaniel had made cowards of the world.

"I'll say what we're all thinking." A well-dressed man pushed his way to the front of the crowd. He was tall, handsome, and young, maybe only a few years my senior. He had the bone structure of a noble. They all looked the same to some degree or another. He held himself like a man used to being respected. I'd have bet my life that respect was unearned. Lady Gerate had pointed him out to me earlier. He had been trying to court her for some time. His name was Alexander ve Holsen. I learned that ve was just a pretentious way to tell people where you're from.

"If you knew what I was thinking, you'd already be running." I didn't want to hear from that brat.

He ignored me. "Thaniel puts a high price on a Constable's head." Alexander walked up to the platform and gestured to the crowd. "If we give this man to the Kranish," he pointed to me, and I tried not to break the offending finger, "maybe they'll forgive us our transgressions."

"I think you'll find my head rather hard to remove." I took a step towards him.

"This foreigner wants to risk our lives for what?" Alexander raised his hands out as if to invoke the crowd. "For pride." He said it barely a whisper. The boy had a gift for oration. If words won battles, Wuntsville would stand for a thousand years.

"Careful." I gave him one more warning than I was accustomed to giving.

"What? I might speak the truth." Alexander turned to face me. That was a mistake.

"He's just a boy!" Someone in the back screamed. I knew they were talking about me.

"The Constables can't save anyone from Thaniel!" Another voice thought to put in.

Alexander was emboldened by this "My friends at court tell me what they call him." He pointed a finger into my chest. "Timid Thomas."

I didn't think, I just reached out and took his hand in the way I knew caused pain. "It's a shame your friends at court were more concerned with sharing rumors than soldiers." I pushed hard and drove him to his knees.

"Argh." Alexander didn't have any clever words left.

I kicked him in the head, and he flew back unconscious. No one moved to help him, a small victory. I turned back to the crowd, and they had a new look in their eyes. It was almost bordering on respect. Regardless of a man's other qualities, if he could fight he was afforded some level of admiration. If only because they hoped he wouldn't fight them. "Even if Thaniel would have forgiven you, is that the sort of men you are?" I surveyed the crowd. "Are you the sort of men who beg forgiveness for not rolling over? Is that the age we live in? Is morality so great a sin as that?"

The crowd grumbled again. Somewhere deep inside them, they hated giving in to any foreign power. They weren't cowards. If it were just the men standing in front of me whose lives were at risk, most wouldn't have thought twice. The issue was that their families lived here. It wouldn't just be them that paid the price of fighting back. It wasn't fear of death that paralyzed them, it was fear of failure. I needed to show them there was hope. I needed to show them their families were safer behind me.

Perhaps they'd be better off if I let Alexander take my head, but it wasn't in my nature. I was going to win here. No one else had any say in the matter, not the townspeople, not the enemy at our gates, not even the gods, whoever they might be. I had decided to win, and so it would be. The size of my army mattered, and planning was even more critical, but conviction could make an empire tremble. I planned to make one tremble, and it began at Wuntsville. A master swordsman carrying a spoon was more dangerous than a fool carrying a halberd. I would win regardless, but it would be easier if I had the halberd, so I set about convincing them once more.

"Your fathers wouldn't have stood for this." I kept on the same note. "Thirty years ago you wouldn't have listened to a man like this." I gestured to the unconscious Alexander. "Thaniel has turned brave citizens into cowards on their own land."

"Thaniel can't be beaten!" Someone screamed.

"No, he hasn't been beaten!" I screamed right back. "I was at Milhire, and it's true we lost there."

"He killed a hundred thousand men in one day!" A man in the front shouted. He looked like he'd been in a few wars himself. "What chance do we have?"

"I addressed the man directly. "That's what he wants you to think." I touched the revolver at my side. "When we faced Thaniel at Milhire the day was lost before the first shot was fired. Of a hundred thousand soldiers, not one of them believed we had a chance to win. The battle itself was a formality." In truth, poor planning, training, and leadership played their part as well, but even if we'd had competent commanders and a veteran army, the outcome would have been the same. It would have been less of a slaughter, but Thaniel would have won. The man knew his business, no one could deny him that. "Kran cannot be beaten because no one believes it can be. I plan on breaking that illusion. I plan on showing the world he can be defeated. We will build our own legend. Tomorrow we place the first stone, and when, a thousand years from now, scholars study how Thaniel fell, let them say it began at Wuntsville. Let them remember that you stood while the rest kneeled."

Their grumbling assent grew louder. I had preyed on their fear, but pride was ever the better motivator. I knew I almost had them.

Captain Seiford walked over with his box of medals and set them on a table next to me. "That was a decent speech." He whispered. "Just don't mention the donkeys or scarecrows."

I reached in and pulled out a copper boggle with a red ribbon. "King John and the Parliament of Anthanii have authorized me to create three new medals." I held it up so they could see. "This is the Anthanii Service medal. It will be given to all those who participate in the coming battle. It marks you as a brave man who stands with your king, no matter the cost."

That peaked their interest. Every man wanted something to let the world know he was a hero, a little piece to remind them of their finest hour. They wanted to be able to show their children concrete proof they were people worth looking up to. What I held in my hand wasn't just ribbons and copper. It was respect given form.

I set the first medal back and picked up another one that looked much the same but a bit more silvery. "This is the Anthanii Bravery medal. It will be given to all those who fight with Lady Gerate in the woods. It entitles the wearer to free drinks anywhere in the nation. It is reserved only for the bravest of the King's subjects."

I could almost feel their desire to reach out and grab one.

I set that one back into the box and pulled out another one, almost exactly the same as the first two, but it had a slight gold tinge to it. "This is the King's Medal of Valor. It will be given to the men who accompany me personally. It is one of the highest decorations a non-regular can receive, and possessing one entitles the owner to personally hold council with the King whenever they so choose."

They were crowding in now. They wanted that medal more than life itself, which was good, considering it would probably cost them just that.

"Now, do I have any volunteers?" I asked the men assembled.

Every hand in the room shot up, accompanied by the screams of "choose me." Peasants often complained about the ruling class, but for some reason, they'd die for a man who would never know their name. Perhaps, that was their wish, that in dying for him, the king would look upon their corpses and see that they were noble in death if not life. If any of them actually knew King John, they'd realize how foolish that wish was. He'd squash a hundred commoners if they stood between him and a good game of tennis, regardless of what medals they earned. Thaniel might appreciate their sacrifice though. He was ever the better of the two.

"Good." I took a step back. "Captain Seiford will choose who those volunteers will be."

I turned to go back to my room and plan, but the Captain stopped me before I could make my escape. "That's a clever trick. They'll fight to the death for those pieces of copper." He gave me one of his rare smiles. "Did King John actually give you permission to mint those medals?"

I shrugged. "He didn't tell me not to."

"What happens when those peasants show up at court demanding to see the King?" He cocked an eyebrow up.

I turned to look at the crowd of men pressing their way to the front, all hoping to be chosen for the most daring mission. "You know as well as I do," I said, "none of those men are going to survive."

The Thaniel Wars

I looked around the hallway and took a deep breath. I knew where her room was, but something in me was afraid to enter it. I have never been paralyzed by fear, and yet as I stood before that door, I was paralyzed. Perhaps, it was wrong to call it fear then, but fear is a broad word. In that base emotion lies a thousand shades. Fear of death could not touch me, but fear of obscurity kept me awake at night. Fear of failure was something I knew only of in the second hand, but fear of losing crept upon me in my most private moments. *What type of fear holds me now?* I wondered. What was it I was expecting to find through those doors?

I don't like being afraid, so I knocked on the door and awaited an answer. "Come in." Lady Gerate said through the door. I obeyed. She was dressed strangely. She'd never been one to strictly follow the fashions of Thyro's elite. Lady Gerate usually wore well-fitting dresses, far more practical than the puffy things the other noble wives preferred. At first, I thought it was some kind of statement to her people that she could rule as well as her husband. However, it soon dawned on me that even those who wore the puffy dresses hated the custom. Lady Gerate was just beautiful enough to get away with such things. Now she wore a loose-fitting pair of pants, that she had likely pilfered from her husband's chest, her shirt was made in what was probably the most innocuous color she owned, and her boots looked like they were made for riding but worn down enough to be useful for walking as well. She still looked beautiful but also mildly ridiculous. I had to remind myself that despite her impressive qualities, she wasn't a warrior. In better times her seeing combat would have seemed like a plot in a bad play, but times didn't get any worse than these.

"Oh, it's you." Lady Gerate looked mildly disappointed.

"It is me." I surveyed the room. I'd never been in a noble's private quarters. I was a Constable. Surely, a useful tool but hardly proper company. I was also from the Confederacy, which put me somewhere between a beggar and a dog. Try as I might to hide my accent, it still showed through.

"Who were you expecting?" I asked. She had two ladies in waiting attending her. They were both old and dutiful. As far as the room, it was exactly what I expected a noble's bedchamber to look like. That was disappointing. I expected it to look more austere than that. Instead, it was tastefully decorated with paintings and a nice bed. It was all completely appropriate. People as competent as Lady Gerate were rarely appropriate.

She sighed and gestured for the two ladies in waiting to leave. If they thought it was inappropriate, they didn't say anything. They either trusted their Lady enough to not do anything unbecoming with me or loved her enough to not care. It was probably somewhere in between. Most things are. When they were gone, she sighed again and sat down on the bed. "You know I was married to Lord Gerate at fifteen."

"I do." I nodded for her to continue.

"Fifteen is too young to truly love someone." She bit her lip at that. "He told me to call him Theo, short for Theodore, and he called me Abby, not my lady." I'd never even considered calling her anything, but Lady Gerate. Even in my fantasies with her, it was always my lady. "He was a handsome man in his own way, but no man ever lives up to a girls fantasy."

"I know that." Girls expected more from a hero than was reasonable.

"When the war drum finally beat, he didn't try to get out of it like other nobles did." I could see the sorrow in Lady Gerate's eyes. "He didn't try to send men in his stead. He fought." She wiped something away from her eyes. I knew it was a tear, but I didn't judge her that. "Some part of me hoped he wouldn't make it through. Some part of me wanted to roll the dice again and see what turned up." She held my eyes. It was her moment of defiance. Even in her sorrow, she wouldn't accept my pity. "Now, every time I hear that door knock a part of me hopes it's Theo returned." She stared at her feet. "I know he's dead. They never found his body, but he's dead. Still, things like that happen sometimes. I've never actually known someone who returned after being presumed dead, but I've known people who've known someone who returned."

"It's better to go on living." It was all I could say. That hope she held only caused her pain, but I didn't have the heart to tell the woman her husband was dead, even if we both knew it.

"I know." Lady Gerate shook her head. "It just seems too cruel. It seems unfair that a girl should be given a husband who's brave, honorable, and good, only to have him taken from me." She stared at me again. "If I seem disappointed at you coming through the door, don't be offended. I'm just waiting on the man worthy of my love, who never fully got it."

It was strange that she'd speak to me like that. I'd seen her armor crack from time to time, but I'd never seen indisputable proof that she was human. Now, she showed me the scar and told me it hurt like hell. I had my own scars too. I often wondered if who we were was chosen by our triumphs or failures. Probably a mixture of both, but most had more failures than they'd like to admit. "You've done as good a job as anyone could here. He'd be proud of you." I said.

Lady Gerate laughed at that. "Pride is a poor substitute for love."

"Then live to wait for the next knock!" I took a step toward her. "You don't need to fight tomorrow. A battlefield is no place for a woman."

She scoffed at me. "A battlefield is no place for a man either. We become queer things when necessity demands it." Lady Gerate went back to lacing up her boots. "I do need to fight, and you know it. They need to know I believe we can win."

She was right on all accounts, but I didn't like it. "Have you ever even worn pants before?" I asked in desperation.

"I'm sure I have." She smiled up at me. "I just can't remember when."

"Stay safe." I implored her. "Live to lead your people."

"If we don't win tomorrow then I won't have a people to lead." Lady Gerate leaned back on her bed. "I may have failed my husband in life but I won't in death."

"Do you think he'd have wanted this?" I narrowed my eyes at her.

"You don't know my Theo." She smiled with some sorrow in her, remembering the man she could only love when he was gone. "He'd have charged into the mouth of a demon if he heard a rumor one of his people was trapped there."

"I don't think he'd have risked you, though." I tried to return the smile, but I've never laid claim to a natural charm. *I wouldn't.* I thought to myself.

"Probably not," she agreed, "but I'm the leader now, and I need to act like one." She looked around her noble room as if she regretted it. "I would have liked to be a painter, I think."

I nodded at that. You had to not want to rule to do it right.

"What did you want to do?" Lady Gerate cocked her head to the side as if trying to understand the man who represented her people's hope. "If you didn't wear those tattoos on your arm, if you had stayed on your side of the ocean, what kind of man would you have become?"

It took me a moment to realize what she asked. I was what I was. The tattoos on my arm weren't something I was thrust into. "I would have always become a warrior, still. It's in my nature." I finally said. "The army I fought with might have changed, but there's something in me that calls out for violence. I'd have found it too."

"So you don't really care who you fight?" Lady Gerate narrowed her eyes at me. "Thaniel's just the man who stands before you."

"No." I said it with a certainty that surprised me. "Logically, I want to see Thaniel defeated. Rationally, I believe his goal of world domination should never be achieved, but in my quiet moments..." I thought for a moment more. "I want to beat Thaniel because he's strong. I want to beat him because no one else can. He calls out to me across the world. He wants a worthy man to defeat him, I think."

"A man of two parts." She said it mostly to herself.

I smiled at her. "If I could change the engine that drove me though, maybe I would. I play the piano sometimes." I sighed. "People tell me I'm good. I think a part of me would have liked to be a musician."

"I'd like to hear it someday." She gave me a compassionate look. Her green eyes sparkled as if to say, she needs me broken as I am today, but tomorrow, I hope you can be whole. I have only been whole on the battlefield, though. That was who I was. Still, I respected her for hoping.

"I'd like to play for you someday." I returned her stare. For a moment, the tattoos fell away from my arm, and the crown fell from her head. I wondered if maybe I could be whole tomorrow. We were two broken creatures with heavy weights on us. We saw each other as people and not Constable or Lady. The moment fell away, and I was glad for it. A man can drown in moments like those. They can trip him up and make him unsure. I was better broken.

"Thomas, do you really think we can win tomorrow?" It was

what she really wanted to ask. It was why Lady Gerate sent her ladies in waiting away. She didn't want them to know she had doubts.

I thought about giving her my pure bravado. I knew I would win and so I would. She didn't need that, though. She believed in me. If she didn't, she'd have already ordered the evacuation. Lady Gerate needed some tangible proof that we had a prayer. "If enough things go according to plan." Things rarely went according to plan, even if the plan was simple, and mine wasn't. "If your men fight as hard as I think they can." Captain Seiford had been drilling them for two weeks, but that hardly made trained soldiers, "If I can make them fear me more than Thaniel." Of hat I had no doubt. "We will win tomorrow."

"If things go according to plan, you'll be in the middle of five thousand enemy soldiers." She gave me another one of those stares. It made me brave.

"I can fight my way through." I took another step forward. "I can make Kran fear me."

"I have a feeling, even if not a man of Wuntsville had decided to serve, you'd find a way to win." She finally stood up.

"Trust that feeling." I stared at her then. "One day that feeling will engulf all of Thyro."

She kissed me then. That surprised me enough that I almost drew and shot on her. Finally, I gave into that feeling. Before I had a chance to kiss her back, she took a step away.

"What was that for?" I asked when I finally got my wits back. "I often get the sense you don't like me much."

Lady Gerate just shrugged. "Sometimes I don't like you much." She smiled at me. "I don't like your arrogance or the way you look at a thing and know its whole story." She stepped forward and stroked the side of my face. "However, that arrogance can one day be earned, and that thing I find unnerving, you can bet the rest of the world does too." She moved her stare down to the tattoos that shown on my arm. "I think one day you might be the man to save us all. I kissed you for luck, hoping you'll survive tomorrow." She sighed. "Besides, I didn't give the last hero a decent goodbye. That's the sort of mistake a girl only makes once."

I went to kiss her again, but she stopped me. "I don't think you need that much luck." She said through a laugh.

"You never know. My plan hinges on donkeys and scarecrows." I smiled back at her.

"No, it hinges on you." She gestured to the door. "Now go get ready."

I left her room smiling. It was good to have something to fight for besides pride.

I had twelve men with me, standing next to the most docile horses in Wuntsville. They were hunters and soldiers all of them. Apparently, after I revealed the medals, we had managed to find some veterans in the woodwork. They were chosen for a purpose. They knew how to stay silent. Even with the woods around us, one unchecked sneeze could end the game.

It was too dark to see. The sun had just started to peak up, but it would be sometime before it would be where I wanted it. I overlooked the enemy camp. The campfires let me see its basic outline. General Gostfeld was good on a battlefield. I'd seen that first hand, but battle is only a small portion of what makes a warrior. The real test was what you did in between. Could you dig latrines after a twenty-mile march? Could you stay vigilant after three sleepless nights? Would you organize a good perimeter even when you were assaulting a defenseless city?

As I looked upon General Gostfeld's army, I knew he was a warrior born. The men in their yellow uniforms going about their business. The way the watch changed like clockwork, the way the cannons faced outward, probably loaded with grapeshot, even the way couriers were always moving, passing some information that was probably unimportant. I knew I'd found a professional. Battle is an art, more to do with feeling the ebb and flow of men than concrete information, but warfare is a science, plain and simple. Gostfeld was both, a scientist and an artist. A dangerous man had come to Wuntsville.

It should have scared me. I should have been shaking at the knees at the thought of fighting a man only a hairsbreadth from Thaniel's skill. I'd planned for this though. I had expected him to do everything exactly the way it should be. He could never have planned for me. If I had attacked him with a regiment of the hardest cavalrymen in Thyro, he'd have known how to react. He'd make me pay. There was no right answer for scarecrows riding donkeys, though. If you read every book on war ever written, you probably wouldn't find a single chapter on such things. Except, maybe not to do it. Damn the books though! I wouldn't be hamstrung by what had been done before. I repeated my mantra inside my head. *Play the game, not the pieces.* When you couldn't win the game though, best to flip the board and shoot your opponent in the face.

It wasn't just certainty I felt. It was excitement, bordering on longing. In my earliest time fighting Thaniel and his Kranish, I'd been scouting and skirmishing. It was dangerous work, but at most, it was a few dozen against another few dozen. Victory was a loose term in engagements like that. The best possible outcome was for my side to come out with their hides intact. I held a few scars from the times we didn't. I had slowly gained a reputation for being resourceful and reckless. After that came Milhire. That battle was doomed from the start, even so, it grated on me. This was my plan, my battle, and my army, though army was being generous. Even still, I would win today because I was in charge.

I didn't want my first real victory to be against some auxiliary force. I wanted to fight professionals. I wanted to build my name here, upon the woods of Wuntsville. When I won, there would be no doubt it was me. If some divine force offered me an extra ten thousand soldiers, I would have spit in their eye. Glory was taken, not given.

I pulled out my six-shooters one by one and checked that they were all loaded. I tested the lubrication on the firing mechanisms. I made sure I could draw them quick if I needed to. I knew I would. I'd checked them more than a dozen times, but when I died, it wouldn't be because my gun jammed. These weapons were new, invented by a man named Calt in my homeland some five years ago. Most Constables shunned them. They preferred the sword, a real hero's weapon. Some of the Constables recruited from Souren preferred their native spears, but the sword was more common, and the six-shooter laughed at. We'd been using the sword since my order was founded five hundred years ago, and we'd been losing those five hundred years. The equation needed to change.

After that, I checked the tomahawk at my side. It was another gift from my homeland. The native Huego's had been using this weapon for longer than history had been recorded. The settlers of the Confederacy had adopted it after they'd felt it used on them. The original version of the weapon was made of hardened stones, but I'd had mine forged by a master swordsmith. Old weapons built in new ways. I'd turned away from the sword for the same reason my people had. The sword was made for elegant killing, timed slashes and perfect thrusts. It was a good weapon for one noble in a circle with another, and if I ever found myself facing such a fight, maybe I'd lament my ways. I'd never found myself in such a situation though. Few true soldiers ever did.

The sword was too long to be used in the melee, It bent if you hit someone hard, no matter how well it was made, and it was easy to block. Above all, outside of combat, it was just a glaring reminder that you were in command, very obvious to sharpshooters. If an officer was genuinely enterprising, he could use it to peel potatoes, but I'd never seen it used like that before. That is the full list of a sword's utility.

The tomahawk could be used however you want. Short enough to hit a man no matter how close he was, It never broke, unless you did something truly foolish, and if you put enough force behind it, you'd find flesh even if someone tried to block. You could hook, chop, and smash with the small ax. You could pull and manhandle men with it. Make them go where you wanted them to. Make them obstructions on the battlefield. A man hit with a tomahawk dies slow and screams a lot. It was the perfect sort of chaos. The least elegant weapon that could be found and by far the most effective. The balance let you throw it if you decided the reward worth losing your best weapon. Off the battlefield, it was even more useful. You could hunt, chop down wood, and use it to build your camp. You could even use it to break stubborn ground for a trench. If I had my way, the whole army would wield one. I'd prove its use today.

"When are we going?" A man whispered in my ear. His name was William. He was taller than me and had more than a few scars from his time in the wars. I tried not to know him too well. I knew what his chances of surviving were, but he seemed a decent man.

"We're waiting for the sun to be in their eyes." I whispered back. "We're waiting for our distraction."

I heard the thunder of a cavalry charge. "Mount up." I whispered to the dozen next to me. I stepped onto my horse. It was a good big one. Lady Gerate had given it to me. I hadn't wanted to hear its name. I knew its chances of surviving were even less than the men that would ride with me. I'd never liked watching horses die, but I wouldn't lose to save the mare some pain.

On top of my steed, I could see the "cavalry charge." It was a group of donkeys with scarecrows strapped to their backs. I'd even had the foresight to put a carrot on their heads to drive them forward. I'd tested for the optimal length between carrot and donkey. Three feet and another donkey would just come and steal it. Six inches and they might be able to buck their way to the treat. I'd found that one for was optimal. Not perfect but optimal. I had a bruise on my ribs owing to this experimentation. *Fucking donkeys.*

From where I was standing it seemed like a poor charade. Donkeys were notoriously poor at following orders. It was quite likely that they would devolve into kicking each other. Even if they didn't, it wasn't so impossible that some officer with good eyes would see how ridiculous it was. The donkeys kept their mettle though. They chased the carrots strapped to their heads directly toward the enemy lines. The sun was in the enemy's eyes too. Perhaps, it made them look slightly more majestic. I waved for us to start moving. We walked our horses to the edge of the forest.

The glorious donkeys charged. The scarecrows stayed firm. I moved to a trot as we edged the forest. They seemed surprised, but they were professionals.

My glorious battle-donkeys bravely galloped into the mouths of their guns. I heard the boom as the grapeshot went through the mass of almost-horses. I hoped the courageous battle-donkeys would find donkey heaven to their liking. I hoped they found many mares to harass. I hoped there were many stable boys to kick. I also hoped scarecrow heaven was much the same. I hoped in that paradise crows would actually be afraid of them. My brave battle-donkeys and war-hardened scarecrows. They'd earned as much.

Despite my prayers to the brave donkeys, I knew it was necessary. That charge made Gostfeld deploy his cannon where my attacks weren't. It made him try and form up his men in the wrong direction. Most importantly, if everything went according to plan, it would make the enemy army feel they were surrounded. Sew division and doubt amongst in the ranks. "Maybe this town wasn't quite as unassuming as we thought it was." They'd say to themselves.

I pushed my horse into a full gallop and drew two of my six-shooters. Then I fell into the Battle Mind. I felt pain fall away from me like shedding a skin. I felt the ability to calculate run through me. It was like being dunked in ice cold water and then struck by lightning. I stopped seeing the world as an abstract thing. It was my world. I understood it, and I would take it.

We reached the end of the forest and were in the open. One hundred yards between the enemy and us. They were forming up now, reaching for muskets and looking to officers. They felt danger approaching. It wasn't the frantic running of scared men but the trained movement of veterans. The men in their yellow uniforms and white pants looked like cogs in a machine. I would break that machine.

Seventy-five yards. A private saw us through the suns rays. He pointed at us. I dug my heels into the horse. This was the most important stretch she'd ever take.

Fifty yards. An officer finally took note. I heard him trying to give orders. I shot him in the chest with my six-shooter. The fifty soldiers that had been looking to him widened their eyes.

Twenty-five yards. A sergeant tried to take up the command, but I shot him too. This time in the head. It was close enough to risk that.

Ten yards. Some enterprising men tried to load their weapons. It was too late. I saw their faces then. Even the young ones looked seasoned enough, but they were afraid. I don't know whether they saw a young Constable leading a dozen peasant militiamen or a god of war leading a thousand horses, but they felt the chill in their spine.

No yards and the hammer hit the anvil.

They were retreating when I hit them. Not routing but trying to find better ground. I trampled them all. I liked this ground. I'd kill them here. Officers and sergeants tried to make order out of the chaos, but I wouldn't let them. I shot them all one by one. Quick but never hurried. I wheeled my horse to the real target. The men following me knew their jobs well. One of my soldiers had already fallen. I felt it rather than saw it. Eleven men were left. I could conquer a nation with eleven men.

We galloped through men as they tried to run away. I shot the ones that made to stop me. The artillery was where I wanted to be, and no man would stop me. I heard a volley of musket fire from the other side of the army. Lady Gerate had joined the fray, but she was too early. She was supposed to be the final strike, not an alert.

I looked at the cannons and saw their operators trying to load more and rolling it around to the east. Captain Seiford must have started to advance with the rest of our forces. One shot of canister rounds could break them. I couldn't let that happen.

I calculated all of this immediately. My mind was moving faster and faster. I could get there. The plan could still hold together if I just got to the damn cannon. I was fifty yards away. Two more of my men had fallen. I could win a war with nine men, though.

I was twenty-five yards away. My six-shooters ran dry, so I drew two more. I started shooting artillery officers and working my way down.

Ten yards. They saw the danger. Sometimes when you charge a cannon position, they run. If they have more mettle to them, they fight. I saw men reaching for rifles, and I knew I had the latter. The Anthanii at Milhire had run, but Thaniel had trained a different breed of soldier.

Five yards. I was almost there. I felt the joy of it running through me. My plan was working. Then I felt the horse beneath me give way, and I went flying. I twisted myself, so I wouldn't break anything when I hit the ground. It would still have hurt like a bad love if I wasn't in my Battle Mind, though.

My yellow-clad enemies had finally found their courage. They tried to circle me. I came up shooting. Five more of my men had gone down, but I could take a city with four men.

I twisted and dodged away from their bayonets and musket butts. I put my revolver in one man's mouth and pulled the trigger. Whatever was inside a man's skull exploded right into the face of his comrades. It blinded some, and to the rest, it had a certain psychological effect. That was my opening. My chance! No matter how many grisly battles a soldier had seen, being covered in your friend's brain had a way of giving men pause. I'd stunned the yellow coats around me, if only for a heartbeat. They recoiled, and I struck. I'd used up my last bullet and went to my tomahawk. I feinted up and went low taking the man between the legs.

The charade was up. However, many men they thought they were facing with the sun in their eyes, they only saw a dozen now, and most had fallen. I wasn't riding a big horse with momentum anymore, I was on my feet with trained soldiers bearing down on me. I was outnumbered and hopelessly so. When you find yourself outnumbered and surrounded, retreat isn't an option. The only thing left to do is attack viciously. Retreat was never an option for me though.

I moved towards the cannons in a flurry of strikes with my tomahawk. I went to work against the Kranish. I dived and shook. Jamming my small hatchet wherever it could find purchase. I threw the wounded into their comrades, letting their death throes do my work for me. Men near me hurried to get away. Men away rushed to get towards me. It was a field for slaughter, but I couldn't revel in it the way I wanted to. I had an objective. The fucking cannons!

I fought my way to the artillery pieces and did my work there. A couple of the men I had brought with me had managed to get away from their horses unharmed. They were fighting for their lives next to me. I was fighting to live. I moved like a snake trying to bite a cat. I was fury and war. I ran around the large weapons using them for cover when I could, and platforms to squash men's heads when I couldn't. Everything around me had stopped being what it was intended for. They were tools for me to make corpses of. I don't remember how many I killed, but it was enough to give me a moment's peace.

I saw Captain Seiford and his contingent moving forward. They were already firing in line. I'd put too much chaos into the Kranish army for them to form their own defense, so it was a one sided affair. The confusion I heard from the other side of the battle told me Lady Gerate had been far more effective than I thought she'd be. Still, they hadn't routed yet.

Somewhere, someone was giving orders and good ones. The Kranish army had started forming ranks. If they could do that, it would be a real battle. Eventually, numbers and discipline would tell. I'd put a lot of casualties into their army while avoiding many of my own. Still, if it came to army against army, they'd win. I'd played all my tricks. The punch had been spent. They weathered it.

I knew what I had to do. I had to kill the general giving the orders. I had to kill Gostfeld. If the men watched him fall, they'd run. There were too many soldiers between him and me though. Then I stared at the loaded cannon next to me and decided I had a perfect tool for punching through an army.

I gleaned all this in a few heartbeats time, while I slammed a man's head into the brass of a cannon. A moment's peace in a battle is really just the time it takes between killing one soldier and choosing another target. Men were still attacking, but in their ones and twos, not the waves they had previously approached me in. They were trying to form up and decided they'd rather face me as a unit rather than individually.

As I killed the last artilleryman, I put my shoulder to the cannon and turned it around. I found the wick still burning and touched it to the gun. In the space, before it shot off, I saw men trying to get away, but they weren't fast enough. "BOOM!" The cannon exploded into the ranks of Kranish. I thought it was loaded with round shot, but the carnage I saw could have only been from a canister round. The sort made of a dozen little steel balls to shred through tightly packed infantry, which by pure dumb luck, was what I aimed at. Ask any infantryman his deepest fear. He'll tell you wet feet and canister shot.

As the smoke cleared the lines in front had simply ceased to be. They were obliterated, and men were running. Not enough to cause a route, but enough to make my path to Gostfeld just a bit easier. I looked around to see if I had any of my own men left. No horses were running around, but I saw William about to be stuck by a bayonet. I considered throwing the tomahawk at his assailant. It would have bought him some time. He'd probably die anyway though, and I needed the weapon. He gave me a queer look as he fell. It was almost like he expected me to save him. I ran.

I ran through the carnage, ignoring the screams of the wounded. I was deep inside the joy of battle. This was what I lived for. As I made my way farther from the cannon blast, more soldiers tried to block my way. I threw my knives at the ones that presented the most threat and laid waste with my tomahawk where I could. I moved quick. To stay still for a moment when you're in the middle of the enemy is certain death. Being in the middle of a five thousand man army is usually death as well, but at least it's harder for them to pin you down when you're moving.

These were trained soldiers and used to fighting hand to hand, but every asset had its disadvantage. Trained soldiers knew not to shoot amongst their own ranks, in the same way a child knows not to touch fire. They could kill each other after all. They should have shot me. I was worth the risk.

I fought, clawed, and beat my way to the center of the army. That was where Gostfeld would be. I did well to avoid getting killed, but still, every once in a while I felt the dull pressure that meant a wound in the battle mind.

Finally, I made it to the General's personal guard. They were the best soldiers in the army and were marked as such by a silly hat. They stood firm against me. I threw myself against them and their silly fucking hats.

I cut into the knee of one man and stabbed the one to my left with the knife in my hand. I saw the sword too late and tried to move my face out of its path. I partially succeeded, but I felt the cut from my forehead to my nose. The blood blinded my left eye, and to take my revenge, I grabbed the offending swordsman and bit viciously at his throat. I saw the horror on his face as I ripped an artery out of him. He fell screaming.

The damage had already been done, though. I was half blind. That idiot guard might have signed my death warrant. I looked up, and through my good eye, I saw him. General Gostfeld.

His staff took a step back, wide-eyed, at me. I must have looked quite mad. Blood covered from head to tow. I'd cut a bloody swathe through his army all on my own. They'd even watched me bite out a man's throat. Who does that? In their defense, I was quite mad.

General Gostefeld took a step forward, sword raised. He was probably a head taller than me and with muscles to match. His blue eyes showed only rage at what I'd done to his army, none of the fear that had struck his staff. The gray that was slowly showing on his sideburns spoke of age. Not the kind that made a man weak, but the kind that made a man clever.

He was an old soldier, one of the few Thaniel hadn't killed in the revolution that made him emperor. If the rumors were true, he was amongst the best fencers in Thyro. I knew they were true. I'd watched him kill at Milhire. I would have been hard-pressed to beat him in a square, healthy and properly armed. Standing before him with a tomahawk, in the middle of an enemy army, not to mention half blind, I didn't stand a chance. Even though I couldn't yet feel the pain, my body had taken a beating through the battle. It wasn't working quite the way it should. My pride often got me into situations like this one. I vowed that if I survived, I'd learn temperance.

If I fought fairly, I'd be dead in three strokes. Even if I had three strokes to fight back. I didn't. I'd be swarmed if the fight took more than a heartbeat. I had to do what wasn't expected. I couldn't fight fairly.

I probably should have screamed, *For Milhire!* Maybe, some invocation of my gods like, *For The Three!* Instead, I shouted, "Fuck you!" It probably wasn't something that would be quoted for the next thousand years, but it captured my emotional state quite well.

Gotsfeld lunged at me with his sword. It wasn't the sort of lunge that you actually used to finish someone. It was the kind he expected me to block, so he could turn back and strike me somewhere else.

I didn't block it. I let him run me through the shoulder. He watched me do it, for the first time every bit as terrified as his men. I imagined he'd never faced an enemy who would impale himself for a killing stroke. That wasn't the sort of thing fencing masters taught you to defend against.

I hit him in the throat with my tomahawk. Then, I hit him again. Then I smashed his head with it. His body fell to the ground lifeless. *Fuck!* I thought. I should have thrown the ax at him. Still, there was little I could do now with the sword sticking out of me. I've always prided myself on finding a way, but sometimes after I found a way, I became blind to a better course of action. Still, it worked.

It took a moment for the enemy to realize their leader was dead. Most armies would have already routed after the hell I'd put them through. The only reason they stood firm was the blind belief that General Gostfeld would save them. I had just proved he wouldn't.

For one cursed second, I thought they might stand and fight. I'd be dead then. Wuntsville would fall, and the only legacy I'd leave was as the crazy bastard who bit out a man's throat and took a sword through his shoulder on purpose.

Still, there is magic in this world of ours. Some of the intellectual types try to say magic is just what we don't have the science to explain. There's some truth to that as well, but it's not all truth. There is magic in this world of ours. It wasn't the Old Religion, and it wasn't the tattoos on my arm. You won't find it in a circus filled with fire breathers and soothsayers. Magic, after all, is a subtle thing. We may know what it does, but we'll never know how or why.

It was in a horrible rogue, who one day devotes himself to charity. It was in the greedy mercenary who hears a speech and finds something to die for besides money. It was in a people who would lay their lives down for bolts of copper and ribbon. It was when peasant militiamen were compelled to face an army their king couldn't stop.

Magic is when you push a man too far, and he becomes something else entirely. Magic is when you think you can't do anymore, but you do.

On that field in Wuntsville, there was magic about us. Those Kranish soldiers had fought more battles than I had. They were hardened warriors. If they attacked me, they would win. All the facades I'd set up would be for nothing. All my clever tricks would be seen through. They would kill me.

Magic can go both ways. It can make us more than we were, or it makes us less. Would they give all for their leader who had sacrificed himself in the end? Would they decide they'd had enough of Thomas Belson and run? It was a roll of the dice, but I thought I had them all loaded up.

For a horrible moment, they stared at me.

Then they ran.

It wasn't a retreat or a falling back. It was a blind route to get away from me. Routes spread quick, and soon the whole army was following suit. I killed any who came my way, but I was somewhat hampered by the three-foot sword sticking out of me.

"The General is dead!" One soldier would scream

"The day is lost!" Another would chime in.

"Their Constable's gone battle mad!" It was hard to argue with that one, looking as I did.

I was still smashing away at a corpse when my allies found me. "Three above." I heard someone say and saw Captain Seiford ward himself against evil with the sign on the Three.

Lady Gerate finally pushed her way through. "Three above." She echoed the Captain's sentiment.

A group had started to gather around me, staring in awe. In the beginning, no one thought we could win the battle, but looking at me then, they wondered how they imagined we could have lost.

"What happened to Gostfeld?" Captain Seiford tried to mask his horror.

"He's over there if you want to talk to him." I gestured to one of the piles of corpses. "You might find it hard though. I ripped off his jaw."

"Oh." Captain Seiford's eyes widened.

"Oh." Lady Gerate echoed him again.

"Will someone take this fucking sword out my damn chest?" I screamed at them, but no one moved to help me.

"I saw him blow a hole through their whole army." One man toward the back spoke softly, but through the silence, everyone heard him.

"I saw him turn into a lion during the battle." Another spoke more surely, even though it was far more ridiculous. No one contradicted him though.

"He killed Gostfeld with his bare hands." A man closer to me whispered. They all knew Gostfeld's reputation, and I'd destroyed his entire army almost on my own. They had known I was dangerous, but no one expected this.

"Pull the fucking sword out!" I screamed. Even Captain Seiford, who'd known me for half a year was too afraid to approach.

"Belson the Blessed…" One man whispered.

"Belson the Blessed." Another joined in.

"Belson the Blessed!" The militia all took up the cry. They didn't mean it as a joke.

They surged forward and lifted me onto their shoulders, screaming the whole way. I had saved their city. I had built a name on the forests of Wuntsville. It was everything I ever wanted, and it tasted sweet.

"The fucking sword!" I screamed at anyone who was listening. Despite my protest, I enjoyed it all. I would have enjoyed it more if I didn't have a three-foot piece of steel sticking out of my chest, but it was a good moment all the same.

The pain would come later. The men I'd sacrificed… The men I'd killed…

I built my name upon the forests of Wuntsville. I built my name on enough corpses to make a hard winter blush. I didn't care about those things then. I was sixteen, filled with hunger and fire. I'd heard soldiers regret the things they did as they approached middle age, but what boy plans for middle age? Certainly not a boy fighting the greatest war in living memory. Thomas Belson making it to thirty was a fool's hope. I'd broken five thousand men, but it would take more to break the hundreds of thousands more.

For now, I would smile as they called me Belson the Blessed. I'd wanted a name so heavy only I could lift it. It never occurred to me what that name might do to the man who carried it.

The Thaniel Wars

After being hoisted around for a good half an hour. Captain Seiford and Lady Gerate finally managed to negotiate with the crowd to let me down. I was led to the town doctor, who specialized in donkeys, but due to my heroics, he'd probably have to shift into another field. Wuntsville did certainly take pride in its donkeys.

The doctor's office was clean and sterile. Despite how small Wuntsville was, it appeared they subscribed to a modern view of medicine. The office was roomy, and the tools seemed to be cleaned well. I probably did a number on the germ population in the room, covered as I was in dirt and the blood of no less than a hundred men.

Doctor Quarrels, as he was called, was a chubby old man with a round face and beady eyes. It was the type of air that made children less likely to cry when they broke their arm. He had a merry way about him, not at all impaired by the recent case of sword-through-the-chest-itis I had contracted. Captain Seiford had convinced me that it was best to have a professional rip it out.

"Do you have a mirror?" I asked him as he sat down to treat me.

"Dear, that's a strange request." He produced a small shaving mirror anyway.

I looked at myself. I was cut in about a dozen places. The blood on my head had matted, but that didn't make it any easier to look at. Also, as I expected, the sword in my chest still looked a lot like a sword in my chest. I cocked my eyebrow to try to make myself look more roguish. It didn't work though. I still looked like a boy who'd hid under a bunch of dead bodies. I didn't mind it all that much. It was a queer vanity I have. "Damn, I've been through it ain't I?"

"Yes, you have my boy." He didn't look up from the rag he was cleaning

"Stop calling me boy!" I leveled a finger at him. "I'm a damn Constable of the New Church."

"Of course, you're a great warrior. The hero of Wuntsville." Doctor Quarrels said like I was child afraid of his tweezers. "Do you want a sweet?"

I should have been indignant about him trying to shut me up with treats, but I did like candy. "Yes." I mumbled under my breath.

He produced a piece of hard candy. "Here." Doctor Quarrels smiled in a way that would have been infuriating if it wasn't comforting.

"Thank you." I replied as I sucked on the treat. I was sixteen after all. I felt old, and maybe it was because I was old in my own way. Still, it was nice to feel the world wasn't in your hands for a moment. I had fought battles, led men, but in that doctor's office, I was a patient hoping he could heal me. It should have infuriated me, but it didn't. "Have you ever seen a patient with wounds like mine?" I asked him. Nothing seemed fatal to me, but of all the contraptions men had built in the past century of science, we'd never outdone the human body for complexity. A simple toy breaks when you drop it down the stairs. I'd done a hell of a lot worse than drop myself downtime stairs. Who knew what might have gotten knocked lose.

He chuckled at that. "You underestimate the trouble boys can get into." He began to wipe the blood off my head. "I've seen children with head wounds like this, cuts as deep as yours, and even pitchforks through their chests." He clucked at it all. "I've never seen a boy with it all put together though."

"I told you, I'm not a boy." I narrowed my eyes at him. Though I must admit sucking on candy in front of a doctor, I felt like a boy.

"Oh really, you must be older than you look then." He started feeling me, seeing what worked right and what didn't. "I took you for not a day over sixteen."

"I am sixteen." I put an edge on my voice.

"Dear, dear, then it appears my original diagnosis was right." He said with a smile as he poked the flesh around the sword.

"I'm a great warrior." It seemed a childish thing to say, even to me. "I've killed men. I am a man."

"I suppose you've raised a family then?" Doctor Quarrels stopped for a moment.

"Constables can't have families." What was this doctor getting at?

"Well, then you've watched your parents grow old?" He looked into me.

"Don't talk about my parents." I was growing to dislike him.

"Well, you've at least loved a woman haven't you?" He gave me another one of those smiles.

"I'm working on that." I was getting angrier.

"Killing doesn't make a man." Doctor Quarrels shook his head. "Living does."

"Take the sword out." I said it short as I could. He hit a note, though, this doctor did. As much as I didn't want to hear it. There wasn't a man alive brave enough to call me a boy. Maybe it was just because he thought I couldn't kill him while he treated me. He was a fool to believe that. Maybe he had my best interest at heart. Whatever his reasons were, this was my life, and I'd sought it out.

"Right away." Doctor Quarrels nodded at me. "This may hurt if you want me to give you something for the pain." He nodded to a flask at the desk.

"It won't hurt me." I was still in the Battle Mind. It didn't seem prudent to let go yet. Besides, I still had the sweet in my mouth. Alcohol mixes poorly with candy.

He pulled out the sword. True to my word I didn't move. "It doesn't seem to have struck anything important."

"That was the idea." I snarled at him.

"Then well done." Doctor Quarrels admired the sword for a moment. "It will be sore for a while though." Then he started to look over my body. He made me get naked for that bit. It only felt mildly uncomfortable. He stitched up what he could, and bandaged what was too small for that. I didn't even realize I took half those wounds until he started working on them. Riding headfirst into five thousand men was decidedly bad for one's health.

We didn't talk as he treated me. Most people in town would be wondering about the things I'd done. However, he acted as if I was any other patient. It almost seemed like he pitied me. I'd felt scorn, envy, and condescension all leveled my way. I didn't care. I could prove them wrong. Pity bit deep, though. It was half the reason I'd left the Confederacy, to escape the looks I'd sometimes feel on the back of my neck. Then, in our private moments, Mother Vestia had shown me that emotion. Our relationship had suffered for that. I didn't know if I hated it because it was unwarranted or because it was justified. Did they just not understand me, or did they know me too well? It didn't bode well that the ones who showed pity to me were all people I recognized as wise. I even suspected the jolly Doctor Quarrels had a philosopher's streak in him.

Regardless of why I hated it, I did. When I felt people mourn for me, I also felt my fist bunch up. I wanted to hit something. I wanted to beat the good doctor halfway to death's door, and show him that pity should be reserved for the weak. I was to be loved or hated. One or the other! Don't mourn me. Fear me!

I would have done it too. I would have struck him down with one blow. I didn't care that he was working to heal me. It wasn't gratitude that stopped me. I figured, he threw a few stitches my way, and I saved everything he loved. As far as I was concerned, he owed me a mountain of sweets. I could find another doctor, but he'd have a rough time finding another Thomas Belson.

It wasn't him being a defenseless old man that saved the doctor. To me all men were defenseless. Great kings or begging peasant children, all were equally helpless if I made up my mind that they should die. I even had a sinking suspicion that the Three and all their divine power couldn't stand against me. I knew this even before the rest of the world recognized it. It was an instinctual knowledge that I could change the world to fit me.

In the end, what kept my hands at my side and off his throat, was pride. Doctor Quarrels knew I could kill him, and all anyone could do was avert their eyes awkwardly. Beating him would prove I was a creature deserving of pity. I got the impression that no matter what I did to him today, he'd pray for my soul tomorrow. You silence the ignorant with facts, but you silence the wise by slitting their throats. If you want a list of men who all stumbled upon uncomfortable truths, check a list of assassinated people. Chances are someone wanted them dead for a reason, and it probably wasn't because they got drunk and claimed the world was flat. It was because they got smart and decided the world was round, and it suited a powerful man for the world to look more like a table than a marble.

Beating him would show the world he was right. More importantly, it would have shown me he was right. I can wrestle the world into submission, but I'd been fighting myself for sixteen years, and it didn't seem like an armistice was on the horizon. It would have been nice to be a man who listened to his conscience. I've always respected that sort, even if I'd never be one, but they probably couldn't have beaten General Gostfeld, and they wouldn't have a fool's hope of beating Thaniel. Still, I'd like to say it was morality that kept me from killing Doctor Quarrels. I'd like to say I didn't do it because of the lessons my father had taught me on right and wrong. I'd be a liar, though. Pride stayed my hand.

Pride gets a bad reputation. Every religion in the world cautions against it. Even the blood-colored Priest preach a strange sort of humility to the Demon's Below. It should say something about human nature that they all spoke against ego. It should also say something about us that no one ever listens. In my own experiences, I've found that it's as good a motivator for righteousness, honor, and chivalry as anything else. After all, anyone could poison a royal family at dinner, and subvert their kingdom. It took balls to show up with an army and tell them you're taking it. Anyone could subjugate a city by cruelty alone. It took skill to rule effectively with a light touch. The hard way is usually the right way, and pride always makes us take the hard line. My pride had saved Wuntsville. No amount of righteousness could have made a man take a sword through his chest.

If I had to guess, pride gets a bad name because of the way we study history. Great men are imbued with more than their fair share of the stuff. The issue is that when a great man dies still great, historians tend to beatify them. They'll write that they did what they did for the good of the people, piety, or some such nonsense. The most egotistical great men even had a hand in those histories on how kind-hearted they were. It was all bullshit, and I knew it. Three above, the historians probably knew it to some degree, even if they only had second-hand experience of glory. Great men do great things because they want great statues of themselves raised in great cities bearing their own great names. More than that, they don't want to admit to themselves for even a moment that they may not be great.

The flip side of that argument was that when greedy men sin, no one really hears about it. Greedy men don't like to stay in the public view. It affects profits. When lusty men sin, rumors will strike up in whatever town you live in, but on the by and large, it will be forgotten by the next summer. There is, after all, no shortage of lusty people. Lust rarely looses its luster. When slothful men sin they just melt into their beds. Well, I suspected that's what happens. In truth, I've never really understood that vice. Why lie in bed all day when there's so much excellent trouble you can get into. Go outside and swindle peasants out of their money or sleep with the wrong man's wife. Not that I condoned such activities. I do work for the New Church. Still, it has to be more fun than sloth. If you're going down one of the wrong paths, at least go down the ones covered in tits and gold.

Pride is a different beast altogether. A prideful man calls everyone's attention. When a man falls because of his ego, everyone remembers. The whole world is affected by the headstrong warrior who bites off more than he can chew. If the lord of a small village decides to crown himself emperor of all the sun sets on, people remember that. They remember how that plucky lord tried to fight legions of trained soldiers with a handful of starving peasants. "That was the dumbest thing I've ever seen!" They'll say, and they'll have the right of it. It was the dumbest thing in living memory, so historians write it down. Of course, sometimes he succeeds and becomes a legend. Then he's the most cunning man in living memory, but either way, people remember.

It even works on the small scale.

One drunk peasant will say to another drunk peasant. "I bet you can't fuck that alligator."

The second drunk peasant knows he probably can't, but he's prideful. He figures if he does it he'll be the bravest man in the whole village. If he doesn't, well, at least he'll die like the hero he always deserved to be. "I can absolutely fuck that alligator." The second peasant says.

He tries and get's eaten, but for as long as the world turns, they'll tell stories about him. "Don't let your pride lead you to try and fuck an alligator." A mother will warn her children. She won't warn him about getting greedy or lustful. A child can see what happens to men guilty of that. More common sins play out every other day, but only one man ever tried to fuck an alligator.

The problem is that that's precisely the way prideful men want it to happen. He wants to be remembered. If he fails, he'll do it so spectacularly you'll never forget it. The end game, of course, is being great in whatever fashion he chooses, but if he can't do that, you better believe he'll at least make himself a cautionary tale to youngsters the world over.

Pride has ever been my vice and virtue. I'm not devoid of all conscience, though. I can tell the difference between right and wrong if it's obvious. Is it wrong to kill a man for his beer? Absolutely! If you had to kill him anyway, and the beer is still as crisp and refreshing as before, that's a bit of a gray area. I'd lean towards drinking it, but I'd definitely pay for it! Well, unless he's done that already. On second thought, I didn't order the beer, so why should I pay for it? Morality can get tricky sometimes.

I do have a basic knowledge of what unacceptable behavior is. Though I hold the opinion that all are helpless before me, I don't go around seeking to prove it to whoever looks my way. That is a mark of insecurity. A man who feels his impotence weighing on him will rape a woman or beat his wife, just to prove he's stronger than someone. It's pathetic to me. I didn't want to prove I was stronger than someone. I wanted to prove I was stronger than everyone. Doing something like that would make me less of a man, not more. I couldn't stand it when someone else did it either. It made my skin crawl. If some pathetic man wanted to show he was strong by abusing another, I'd show him how insignificant he was to me. Things like that give the strong a bad reputation, and when that happens, people turn to weaklings like the Anthanii king to save them. I'd made a conscious decision that if I ever caught one of my soldiers raping a helpless girl, they'd find themselves missing some equipment below the belt.

Half a year ago, I saw a man beat his wife in the street. No one made a move to help but me. I broke his arm and pissed on him while he cried about it. I told him that if I saw it happen again, he wouldn't survive. I'm sure the people of those streets had purer souls and better intentions than mine. They didn't save her though. I did. I didn't do it for her. I did it because he had the gall to abuse someone in front of me and thought I'd tiptoe by. I'd have done it if he was an eight-foot tall giant. I'd have done it if he were a dwarf using a stepladder to get to her face. I'd have done it if he was emperor of the whole world. The Three better hope I never find them engaging in such behavior, or they'd receive a similar treatment. Might be it was my pride that saved her that day, but quiet morality wasn't getting the job done.

Pride is what drives me. Occasionally, my knowledge of right and wrong can pull the reigns, but my ego is a poor tempered animal. She rarely responds.

Doctor Quarrels finally finished the stitches on my head. He still had that same look of pity in his eyes. I wondered if the fact that I hadn't strangled him mattered to the Three. Was me not doing it enough, or did the reasons I didn't matter? In their eyes had I beat the kindly doctor to a bloody pulp because that's what lay in my heart? Is pride a good enough reason, or did I need to find another? I didn't really know. All I did know, was that if I ever saw a stronger man abusing him, I'd be the one who saved him. Pride may be a poor reason, but it would protect the weak.

"I think that does it." The doctor smiled like he'd just fixed my favorite toy. He was right in a way. My body was my favorite toy.

"Thank you." I mumbled

"Dear, dear, let me just cover that head wound right quick." Doctor Quarrels reached for another bandage, but I stopped him.

"Best not." I told him. "I'll go without the bandage."

He clucked his disapproval at me. "If I don't cover the wound, it could fester."

"I survived a sword through the chest." I narrowed my eyes at him. "I think if I could die I'd have done it by now."

"That makes sense." Doctor Quarrels gave me another one of those knowing smiles. "However, I'm sure many men are lying in graveyards who's tombstones would read, 'here lies a man who said if he could die he'd have done it by now.'"

"I don't like bandages." I shot back at him. "They give me a rash." It seemed like a poor excuse even to myself. I really didn't want to tell him the reason for not wanting a bandage on my face. He made me feel enough like a child already.

"You didn't say anything when I bandaged the rest of your body." He chuckled at my youth. "Should I take those off?"

"No, it's just the forehead." I tapped my noggin. "Gets itchy."

He cocked an eyebrow up. Doctor Quarrels wasn't buying any of what I was selling.

"Its none of your business why I don't want the bandage." I gritted my teeth at him. I realized that poor response probably made me seem more like a child than the actual reason.

"If the Hero of Wuntsville, dies under my care there'll be a mob at my door before your body's cold." He wiped the blood off his tools. "Besides, you're the only man to ever stand up to Thaniel and stay standing when it was over." He looked me in the eyes for that bit. "I have a feeling we'll need more of you in the future." He patted my leg. Even though I was completely naked, it didn't make me flinch away. "Just tell me why you don't want the bandage."

I scratched the tattoos on my arm. It was a subconscious way to remind myself that I was a man of consequence, not the boy I felt like. "I'm trying to impress a girl tonight, and I'd rather not look like a burn victim when I make the attempt."

Doctor Quarrels chuckled again at that. "Dear, dear, if I had a nickel for every time I heard about a boy trying to impress a girl, we could have hired an army one hundred thousand strong to defend our gates." I didn't take insult at being called a boy this time. Sometimes, I forget my age in a mad dash for the glory that lay at the end. I may know myself to be a great man, but I still hadn't managed to grow a full beard. Being sixteen wasn't all bad. I assumed shaving hurt. The doctor had a way of letting me know without making me feel foolish. "Anyway, I'm sure your heroics today have impressed any girl you choose." He shrugged.

"Or they scared her." I said it almost to myself. "Either way, I don't want to take the risk."

"Sometimes girls like the boys who scare them a little bit." He gave me a reassuring smile. "Just show her that she's safe with you."

It seemed like sound advice. "You know much about girls?" It was meant to be an insult, but it came out as a serious question.

"That's the thing about being older than sixteen," he gave a sad little frown that looked strange on him, "you know more than a sixteen-year-old."

"I suppose so." I shook my head. "So do you think I should take the bandage or not?"

"I don't think it really matters, but I'll tell you what," he stood up and put produced a piece of linen, "I'll give you the bandage, and you can put it on after you've impressed this girl."

"Thank you." I took the linen.

He gestured to a pile of clothes on one of his benches. "A captain by the name of Seiford brought you a change of clothes." He packed all his instruments away. "You can wash up here and change if you want. I have to go."

"You're not going to the victory feast?" I asked. I had in fact not heard that there'd be a victory feast, but we'd just beaten the most feared army in the world and saved a town to boot. If this world wouldn't celebrate that, then I didn't want to live in it.

"There's more wounded to treat." He put on his hat.

"I already set people to take care of our fallen soldiers." It was what a good commander would do. "Our casualties weren't very many, so they're probably fixed up by now." I didn't mention that the ones who were dying were probably beyond care

"I meant the Kranish." He picked up some more tools without looking at me.

"Why?" Let them rot for all I cared. "They attacked us." I went to the washbowl and started cleaning the blood and dirt off.

"Yes, and but for a mistake of where you were born, you'd have been in that army." Doctor Quarrels gave me another one of those pitying looks again. It didn't make my blood boil like it had, but I still didn't like it. "Most of the men in that army were barely older than you. Do you think they really had a choice in the matter? Even if they did, if you were Kranish and the recruiter came to your door, would you turn him away?"

"No." However, it struck me that I might not be the moral paragon for men to follow. If someone faced a soul-tearing choice, they should probably ask, *What would Thomas Belson do?* Then they should do the opposite. They would have led a happier life in the end.

"I've lived a long life, Thomas, and when you get to be my age, you realize that borders and uniforms don't really mean that much." Doctor Quarrels sighed. "Sure, patriotism is important, but we're all just men at the end of the day." He walked over to me and put a hand on my shoulder. "I'd like every young buck to find wisdom in their old age." He patted me. "Sometimes wars need to be fought. Sometimes people need to be killed, but every wounded man deserves help, and every dying man deserves a last sip of water." He removed his hand. "Even if Thaniel found his way to my table, I'd do everything in my power to save him."

"Even if it meant more men would die?" I asked him, genuinely curious.

"Men always die in the end." Doctor Quarrels didn't seem all that sad about it though. "If my goal was to stop death, I've failed miserably." He sighed. "My true function is to give men a little more time to save their souls. I think that chance, no matter how slim, is worth whatever the cost is." He met my eyes to be sure I took it all in. "I think you should learn that lesson. It'll make what comes after easier."

"I will." I had no intention of ever trying to understand him. Some men were saviors, others were killers. Most lie somewhere in between, but I was so far to the killing side, it seemed best to just accept my role. I respected the doctor. I was glad he was around, but his wasn't my lot in life.

"Good." He turned to leave, but I had one more thing to ask him.

"Do you pity me?" I wasn't angry about it anymore. I probably wouldn't have beat him even if my pride didn't stop me. I'd been too afraid to ask Mother Vestia and too proud to ask my father. Maybe, it was just that I didn't know him so well. If he gave me an answer I didn't like, I could write him off as a senile old doctor and forget about him entirely.

"In some ways, yes I do." He responded simply.

"I'm as clever as they come, I'm stronger than most, and now I'm a hero." I scoffed at the ridiculousness of it all. "I'll become the greatest name to ever walk this world." I touched the tattoos on my arm. "What is there to pity?" I threw my hands in the air. "Is it because I'm short? I'll grow some more you know. I come from a tall family."

Doctor Quarrels chuckled at that. "It's not because you're short."

"Then why?" I needed to hear it, just once and then I could forget it forever.

"Thomas Belson." He said it to himself. "I do believe your name will be the greatest in living memory." Doctor Quarrels seemed like he was mulling it all over. "I believe you will smash Thaniel and forge a legend like we've never seen before. I believe the world needs you. I believe you will bring back our faith in Man. We've been sorely lacking in that as of late. The true problem in Thyro isn't Thaniel. It's that we have nothing else to hang our hopes on. You can be that hope." He stopped as if not wanting to say what came next.

I nodded for him to continue.

"That is a hard path, though." The doctor hung his head for a second. "It'll cost you, I think. You have too many scars for a sixteen-year-old, and I've learned that scars on the body generally reflect what lies within." He looked up at me. "Those scars will only get deeper. I wouldn't wish that path on anyone. I know what war does to men, and you'll see more of it than anyone." He sighed, and I saw the ghost of his past in those gentle eyes he had. "You will be shaped by nothing but violence, just as I was. I hope you can tell where the legend ends and you begin, but I'm not sure you will."

"You were a soldier?" The way he said it made me think he knew something of my path, even if it was just where the entrance was.

"In a sense." It seemed like it pained him to answer it. "Then, something saved me, and now I'm a healer of men." He forced the pain away with a smile. "Now, I'll see if I can save some of my own."

"I hope you do." I meant it. Not for the Kranish soldiers, but for him. He'd tried hard to save me, and I knew he wouldn't. Doctor Quarrels deserved a victory.

"Thank you." He turned and left. As soon as he was out of sight. I opened the first drawer I saw looking for my prize. He must have had excellent hearing because he called out through the hallway. "The sweets are up top. Take as many as you want."

I didn't respond, but I did take as many sweets as I thought I could carry in my pockets. Even though I couldn't feel it through the Battle Mind, I was probably hungry. I didn't know what kind of meals Wuntsville served at a victory feast, but judging by what they took pride in, it was probably donkey. I'd eaten worse, but it always pays to have a contingency. Besides, pride could make me do almost anything, but it couldn't keep me away from a sugary treat. If I'd heard a rumor that Thaniel was hoarding all the candy in Thyro, I'd have already launched my assault.

⸻◆⸺◆⸻

I got dressed and put all my weapons into their respective holsters. I was sure the victory feast had already started. There was only one thing left to do. I was still in the Battle Mind. Coming out of it was always painful. I'd been in it for longer than that before, but this was probably the worst I'd been hurt in a single day. I knew it would hit me like a galloping horse, the weariness, the hunger, then the pain.

The rumor goes that Constables never fall in battle. That was because of the Battle Mind. It took a shot straight to the heart or head to stop a man with a tattooed arm once he got started. Of course, that rumor had lost a lot of its truth when Thaniel had cut the head off a senior Constable and raised it over Milhire. Still, that was an outlier. In addition to our training at God's Rest, the Battle Mind was part of the reason we hadn't been completely overwhelmed by the Old Religion. Constables did die often, but that usually came because he'd taken too much punishment and his body went into shock. I knew there wasn't a real risk of that happening to me, but it didn't make me any more eager.

I slowly came out of it. Returning to normal was like unclenching a frozen fist, except that fist was being stabbed by a thousand needles, and it was all over your body. It was nothing like unclenching a frozen fist. First, came the weariness that hung on you like a weight, then came the pain. I felt all the cuts I'd suffered during the battle. As I expected my leg was screaming in agony at being thrown off a galloping horse. Also as I expected the sword through my chest felt a lot like a fucking sword through my chest. I had a dozen other injuries I didn't know how I came by, but they all begged for recognition now. Slowly, it all settled into a dull throb. I could deal with that sort of thing. I couldn't remember a time since I got to God's Rest I hadn't been injured in some way or another. I was used to it.

That was it, or so I thought. Then I had memories hit me. That never happened before. I saw the faces of the men I'd killed. I saw the look in their eyes as I took them apart. I even felt a bit of guilt for Gostfeld. I had respected him in my own way. Then I killed him. That wasn't the worst of it though. I saw the faces of the dozen men I'd brought with me, knowing they had no chance of making it home. They probably had families that would mourn them. They knew it would be dangerous, but I never gave them the full information. It was a death sentence. Then I saw William. The man whose life I had judged as worth less than my tomahawk. I saw the way he looked at me. I could have helped him, but I didn't. I'd wanted to win.

It was too much I fell back into the Battle Mind. "Fuck!" I screamed at the top of my lungs. That had never happened before. I'd killed men, and I'd watched my comrades die. Surely, people I knew better than William of Wuntsville. This was the first time I'd ever been hit like that, though. I used the cool logic I'd achieved to think of what had changed. I knew what almost immediately. I'd gotten what I wanted. It had been my plan, my army, my victory, but all the failures were mine too. I'd chosen to kill the Kranish. I'd chosen to sacrifice those men. There was no higher authority to blame it on, except maybe the Three, but cursing at gods rarely helped men feel better about their actions.

I took a deep breath and released my Battle Mind. I felt the weariness fall on me. Then I felt the pain show itself. Right before it faded into a dull ache, I jammed my thumb into the place the sword had run me through. It hurt. It hurt the right way, though. I saw the Kranish I killed. I pushed harder. I saw Gostfeld, one of the greatest leaders in Thyro up until a few hours ago. I pushed harder. I saw the dozen brave men I'd lead to slaughter. I pushed harder. I saw William looking to me for salvation. I pushed until I thought my hand would go through my chest. *Focus on the pain*. I told myself. *Focus on the right pain*. It halfway worked. I pushed until I felt the guilt turn into a dull throb with the rest of my body.

It wasn't like the other pain though. It felt like it was trying to take my soul. When the body gets hurt, it's an honest sort of ache. Our anatomy is, at its core, made for boasting. It loves to tell you how much work it's doing to fix it. Like all braggarts, it's annoying but bearable. At worst it screams at you to stop doing whatever it is you're doing. Even that can be ignored if you've the stomach for it. When the mind gets hurt, it's like a plague. It spreads until you finally do what you should have at the start. Kill the infected and burn the bodies. Kill the part of your mind that hurts you. Cut it away. At the very least, numb it up. I reached for Doctor Quarrel's flask and leaned against a wall. Slowly, I let my body move to the floor.

I drank until I found the bottom of the flask. It helped a bit. I sat there for what must have been quite a while. I ate another candy, but guilt has a way of ruining the taste of everything. I spit it out onto the floor. Why should I eat candy while William was dead in the mud? I'd felt guilt before. I was hardly sinless before my arm was tattooed. Still, this was worse. I'd lied to men. Let a man die I could have saved. If you betray someone and they live, there's always the hope that someday you'll make it right. I had wronged William, and it would stay that way.

Finally, anger took me. I had won! I had scraped out victory where no one else could! It was a battle. Of course, good men died. It took me a while to realize why I was so angry. Knowing what I knew then, lying against the wall, I would have done it all the same. I had won a great victory, morally if not strategically, but there was a long way ahead. More battles to fight. More men to sacrifice. *Play the game, not the pieces*. I told myself. Sometimes the pieces got hurt, though. If you tried to save one, you'd lose the game. It wasn't in me to lose.

I stood up and put another candy in my mouth. I felt the same guilt as before. I was alive to eat sweets, and William, along with so many others, was dead. I pushed it down and sucked on the treat. I picked up the sword General Gostfeld had put into my chest headed to the door. Doctor Quarrels was right. It was a hard path, but I'd chosen it, and I'd make it to the end. If I had to stand upon a mountain of skulls, I would see Thaniel fall. Not because it was the moral thing to do. Not because the world needed me to. I'd do it for pride. Let the historians make up a better reason later.

The Thaniel Wars

J walked out of Doctor Quarrel's office, feeling warm from all the whiskey I drank. I looked around, and the city did seem to be celebrating. Children were waving colored batons in the streets, men were drinking heavily, and the women were fawning over anyone wearing one of my medals.

"I want to be Thomas Belson!" I heard a girl scream. I looked and saw a group of children with wooden swords in hand. None of them could have been older than eight. The little girl had a set of pigtails in her hair.

"You can't be Thomas Belson!" A plump blonde boy hollered back. "You're a girl!"

"You can't be Thomas Belson either!" The little girl shot back, undeterred by how much larger the boy was. "He used an ax, not a sword!" She proudly held up her own makeshift tomahawk. It was a piece of stick with a large rock tied to it. It seemed a bit dangerous for a child to have.

"Everyone knows a hero uses a sword!" The plump boy declared, much to the delight of his friends.

"You're stupid!" She put a finger into his chest.

"No, you're stupid!" He pushed her down into the ground. All eight-year-old arguments usually ended that way.

The little girl tried to stand up, but the plump boy pushed her down again. "Stop!" She cried out. I saw her try to wipe away a tear without anyone noticing, but eight-year-olds tend to be observant. I sighed. Though I may occasionally be cold, I will always come to the defense of eight-year-old girls with pigtails. It's a weakness of mine. If the Kranish ever found a way to use it against me, we'd all be doomed.

"Thomas Belson wouldn't cry!" The plump boy kicked dirt on her.

"This is my favorite dress!" She screamed like someone had pinched her.

"Thomas Belson doesn't wear a dress neither!" He went to kick more dirt on her, but I got there before he could.

"I don't think you know me well enough to assume what I wear on my days off." I reached out a hand to help the girl up. "Here you go, sweetheart."

I gave them all a minute to look at the tattoos on my right arm, then to the gun on my belt, and finally to the tomahawk at my side. "You're Thomas Belson!" The little girl was the first one to recognize me.

"That I am!" I responded in the same cheery voice she used.

"I thought you'd be taller." The plump boy scratched his head. "My Da's bigger than you."

"There's a lot of men bigger than me," I went to one knee so I could be at eye level with them, "but there are precious few men as quick as I am and none quite as clever." I looked around at the group. "So what's this argument all about?"

"She wants to be you, but she can't because she's a girl." He pointed a finger at the girl.

"That is true. I am not a girl." I gave Pigtails a smile. "However, Lady Gerate was there too, and she fought, brave as any man." I was embellishing a little bit. I hadn't actually seen her fight, but she didn't seem like the sort to cower. I picked up her makeshift ax. "Besides, she's the only one that got my weapon right." I tapped my tomahawk.

"Just like yours!" She said excitedly.

"Just like mine." I smiled at that. "Now," I stood up, "I think you'd better let her play me."

"We will." The whole group sounded off at once, except for the little girl who was jumping around in victory. Then, after a second, they all stopped. "Are you going to beat Thaniel?" The girl asked.

"I am." I said it firmly. I had been too drunk with victory to see what everyone else in Thyro saw. They had known heroes before, and they had watched them fall before Thaniel.

"He'll come with a bigger army." The girl looked at the ground. "He'll have Priests too." She kicked the dust. She had seen too much disappointment for a child. She had seen too little optimism. Children weren't meant to think about the future like that.

"And you'll have me." I nodded. "Trust that." I smiled at her. "While I stand between you and Kran no harm will come to you. Do you believe me?" I asked her.

Despite every disappointment she'd ever known, she smiled back. "I do."

"Good." I gave them a roguish sneer. "Now, play safe." I said as I walked off to the town hall. They wouldn't listen to me. Eight-year-olds will never play safe, even if the person they're imitating tells them too.

Wuntsville was the perfect place for a celebration. They'd been mostly untouched by the wars that had been raging in Thyro for two thousand years. They had a wall, of course, but it was more a "please, don't attack us" wall. The town was well built but simple. Above all, the population was low enough that you didn't need to worry about a riot. Though, I suspected Lady Gerate could have governed the capital of Anthanii without incident.

I finally made it to the town hall. Wuntsville didn't have a castle, but a well-kept center where the lord usually lived. It was much like the rest of the town, except bigger. It had the same tint of brown and white as all rural buildings do. I vowed, one day I'd find out why they all look the same, but at that moment, I wasn't much interested in architecture.

I took a deep breath at the door. It reminded me of being outside Lady Gerate's room. I ran a hand through my hair, straightened my coat, and did all the other things men do because they think it makes them look better. Eventually, I realized I was stalling. Before I opened that door, there was a story I could tell about how it would go, but after I did it, there would be no story only truths. If I turned away right then and rode to the Anthanii Court, I could tell myself Lady Gerate would have spent the night with me. I could say, "I'd have liked that, but I had my duty to fulfill." If I walked in that door, I would admit to myself that I wanted her. Any failure would have been put on my shoulders. I couldn't blame it on anything else.

I had already determined that I would beat Thaniel, and I'd gone a long way towards proving it. I told myself, I wasn't interested in anything not related to that. The song that played deep in my heart was a war song. There wasn't enough room for anything else. I wasn't a machine, though. I was a man. My life was defined by a quest for greatness, but it was not made up of that entirely.

Picture me as a castle built to defend an important piece of the map. The hallways, stairs, and walls were all made to ensure an attacker would pay the maximum price to take it. However, it was built by men, and the other parts of humanity would filter through. You'd find in such a castle a stained glass window, put there for no better reason than it was pretty. You'd find the lord's room on the top tower, where he could watch the sunrise, for no better reason than that he wanted to. You'd find a church where men prayed, for no better reason than that men wanted to feel close to their gods. Sure the warrior who built such a structure would say that the stained glass told a picture of heroics to embolden his troops, the height of his tower was so he could see an approaching army, and the church was because men who think their god is on their side fight harder. He might even believe it, and all those things might also make sense, but he built it that way because he wanted to.

There is no such thing as a love, morality, or war story. Every yarn we weave has all of those things put into it. A story has love, morals, and conflict. Some tales have more of one than the others, but they're all there if you look hard enough. No building is created with one thing. Stone may be the most prominent ingredient, but you'll find it also uses nails, wood, and rope. No man is built on one pillar. His destiny may be forged from a single hour of a single day, but if you start to look at the tapestry a little harder, you'll find something else. You'll see he has lost loves, hopes he cleaves to in the night, maybe even a bit of regret at what he's become.

If you want to write a textbook about me, you can know me as a warrior alone. If you want to write a song about me and have it sing true, you'll need the other bits. I wanted victory more than anything else. If I had to sacrifice anything to achieve it, I would, but I was still a man. A thousand desires play out across my soul, a thousand regrets too.

Sometimes, I don't like to admit that. It's easy to be a warrior, hard to be a man. If I walked through that door, I'd admit that there were other things I cared for. I'd admit that there were other things that could hurt me. I took another deep breath and opened the door. I might say later, that it was to extend my legend a bit. The truth is I did it because I wanted to see Lady Gerate. I wanted to be able to call her Abbey not my lady. I wanted to hear her call me Thomas with something more than respect. I wanted her to see the arm, not the tattoos. I wanted her to know me as something more than Belson the Blessed. I knew we wouldn't live happily ever after. I'd be sent to fight somewhere else in a day or two, and she was a noble, too high for a man like me no matter how heroic. Constables don't get married, but perhaps they can be loved for a night.

I walked in and was overpowered by the smell of beer and roasting meat. Men and women were feasting. They all looked to me as soon as the door opened.

"It's him!" One man hollered to the rest.

"Belson the Blessed!" Another chimed in.

"Our hero!" Another announced.

I raised my hand to quite them. "Of course, I played my part," I smiled to the crowd, "but the people of Wuntsville fought brave as lions today."

"He's too humble to admit it!" An older gentleman in the front shouted. "A true hero!" The man raised a drink my way, and the rest joined him in a toast to me.

I nodded at them all. I wasn't sure there was anything I was too humble for. If I were proclaimed king of all creation, I wouldn't have thought it too much. However, going on a rant about how I'd have won with an army of toddlers, wouldn't gain me any friends, even if it might have been true. "Where is Lady Gerate?" I held up the sword in my hand. "I have a present for Wuntsville."

I saw her across the room. She'd changed into something more appropriate than pants and an off-color tunic. She wore a black dress with an elegant neckless. Lady Gerate could have worn cow shit and mud, I'd have still felt the desire well up in me. She smiled at me. It was one of gratitude and respect. I'd earned those emotions, but what I wanted from her couldn't be earned. It had to be given freely.

I walked towards her. The tables where people sat and drank were quite. Everyone in the room wanted to hear me speak. She had people around her, but besides Captain Seiford, I didn't really notice them.

When I finally got to her, I produced the sword ripped out of my own chest. "The blade of General Gostfeld," I said it so the whole room could hear me, "given to the people of Wuntsville as a token of their own valor." I flipped the sword around so she could take it.

Lady Gerate grabbed it by the hilt and held it up for everyone in the room. "It is graciously accepted." She announced.

I turned to face the feasters. "I vowed to you, we would break Thaniel's army." I didn't quite know what to do with my hands, so I pounded one fist into the other. "We have done that and more. Today will be remembered as the day Thaniel's fall began!"

The crowd cheered.

"Now eat and drink. You've earned it." I gave them a nod of respect.

They cheered again, and conversation returned.

I turned to Lady Gerate. "My lady." I nodded.

"Your Eminence." She cocked an eyebrow up at me. Eminence was my official title, but I could count on one hand the times I'd been called that. Bastard was much more common.

"There's no need for such formality." I smiled at her.

"Of course, there is." I heard a familiar voice say in his smug tone. "You have done your king and country a great service." It was Alexander Ve Holsen, the man I'd beaten in front of the whole town because he called me coward. It made me happy to see he had a large bruise on his face. It made me angry to see how close he stood to Lady Gerate.

"I'll remind you I don't have a king or a country." I told him levelly. "I serve the New Church, and this morning I served Wuntsville and her lady." I gave her a sideways smile. "King John never factored into it."

That took Alexander by surprise. Everything I'd said was true, but it was considered impolite to throw it in a nobles face. "All the same," his handsome face quickly regained its composure, "the people of Anthanii thank you." His expression went to something with a bit of an edge to it. "The court will be very grateful indeed, and if you had a friend to help you, all the better for you."

I could see in his eyes, every word was carefully crafted to distract from me beating him in front of a crowd. He saw me as a potential tool to be used for his own elevation. He offered me something in return as well. If I were a tactful man, I'd have nodded my head. "Do you know, I'm starting to doubt you have any friends at court." The words settled amongst the guest about as well as a lit keg of gunpowder. For all the qualities I have that men see as admirable, tact has ever eluded me.

I saw Alexander's face move from insulted, to shock, to attacked. I saw his feelings dance across the set of his jaw and the blush of his cheeks. Finally, I watched them settle in his eyes. Those emotions moved for a second, maybe two. He was as well trained in controlling the subtitles of his feelings, as I was at controlling my guns. In the moment between when a man is threatened and when he realizes it, you can know him. Poke me in the back with a stick when I'm not expecting it. If I don't take your head off, you'll learn a thing or two about me. Did I defend or attack? Know my nature. What part of me did I protect? Know what I value. How quick did I realize it was a stick and not a knife? Know how trusting I am. As a rule, I always assume it's a knife until I break the damn stick in half and sometimes the man who poked me.

The young Alexander ve Holsen was handsome. Handsome people are easier to read. Perhaps that's why we like those characteristics. It's easier to see indignation in a strong chin then a wobbly one, it's easier to see embarrassment in pale skin than scarred tissue, and it's easier to see fear in bright eyes than dull ones. I noticed all on him, indignation, embarrassment, and fear. I learned that I had the truth of him. You only feel threatened if you can be threatened. A man made of stone will sleep even if he's being nibbled on by wolves. A man made of clay will grab his weapon when he hears a leaf fall. If I called Captain Seiford an incompetent coward, he'd laugh and call me an ass right back. He knows his measure. If I called him my bitch, I could expect a fist in my jaw. He knows he follows me, but he doesn't like to be reminded of it.

I knew how Alexander would respond even if I didn't know the words he chose. "I'm sure I didn't understand you right." He spoke with the fake geniality that would have offered me a chance to backstop. The noble offered me a chance to make amends. He didn't want to spar with me. Alexander was a fool. Any opportunity for peace is also a chance to attack. I've always been disposed to aggression. Call it a curse, but a man ought to do what he's good at.

"I'm sorry. I forgot the nobles' language of choice changes so much." I pretended to ponder it for a moment. "Sometimes it's Kranish. Sometimes it's Rhorii. Whatever the most influential lord picks as the most civilized." I turned the full weight of my stare at him. "I always speak the language most confusing to them." I gave him my most wolfish grin. "I always speak plain." I let the grin fall from my face. "I'll say it again so you can digest it. I don't think you have any fucking friends at court." If I had judged him worthy of my partnership, I might have made an excuse for my remarks. I didn't need him, though.

"Thomas!" Lady Gerate tried to cut in before it got worse. I respected her, but my proclivity for making things worse often rivaled that of a hurricane. I vowed to change one day, but it was just so much damn fun.

"I'll have you know, I'm in direct correspondence with Lord Bunderwall of Cornory." Alexander said it like I should have been suitably impressed by the name. I met him once. He was a chubby man, who cut the corn off his cob instead of nibbling at it like everyone else. I've always found that practice unsettling. "He writes me daily!" He seemed to think that made him greater than he was.

"I pray to the Three." I shrugged. "I'm not such an idiot I consider them friends." I caressed the six-shooter at my side. "Neither the Three nor your Lord Whatever answered the call for more soldiers."

"The Holsen name is a great one, with a storied history!" Alexander saw I had the right of it and changed his line of argument.

"I'm sure it is." I took a step forward. I wasn't taller than the noble. Still, I towered over him. "However, I think your names like a bank note without the gold to back it up." I let the wildness in my eyes show. "Something worthless that makes worthless men feel a bit better."

"Thomas, stop!" Lady Gerate tried again.

"I don't have to take this from a provincial savage!" I wasn't sure if he had forgotten the lump I'd given him earlier.

I made like I was going to strike him and laughed when he cringed away from me. "Yes, you do," I chuckled, "because you know if I so choose I could break your neck, and not a damn thing would be done about it."

He tried desperately to compose himself. "Lady Gerate." He nodded to her. "Captain Seiford." He nodded again. He gave me a look that said he wanted to hit me, but his cowardice got the best of him. He walked away. I would have hit me.

"Thomas!" Lady Gerate hissed at me. "You ass!"

"He's a useless tit." I gestured to Alexander, not caring much if he heard me.

"A useless tit who could make governing Wuntsville a hell of a lot harder, if he thinks I disrespect him the way you did." She slapped my arm in one of the places I'd been hurt. "He's trying to court me, you idiot."

That took the wind out of me. "You're going to marry him!" I felt betrayed, even if I had no right to it.

"I wasn't," Lady Gerate clenched her teeth in anger, "but if he thinks I will, then he won't petition the court to subvert my rule."

"Oh." I should have seen that. I was usually more clever. "So you're not going to marry him?" I was too thrilled at that revelation to take proper note of her anger.

"I might have to now!" Lady Gerate shook her head. "I'm going to go mollify him." She nodded in Alexander's direction. "I know it goes against your nature, but try not to antagonize anyone while I'm gone." She pointed at a statue. "Don't worry, its face is just carved that way. It's not challenging your manhood." She followed the young noble, placing the sword I'd given her on a table.

I should have been insulted, but the statue did look a bit too condescending for my taste. I wondered how many times I'd have to hit it with my tomahawk to take it down a peg or two.

"Why, in the Three, did you have to insult him like that?" Captain Seiford took a step towards me. He had that usual disapproving look on his face.

"He's a tit." I scoffed.

"A tit who might have helped us." Captain Seiford wasn't letting me off that easy.

"He couldn't help a dog wrapped around its leash." I glared at him.

"You're probably right," Seiford admitted, "but getting his friendship would have cost us nothing." He looked down at his own dress uniform for a minute. "As it stands he'll write to Lord Bunderwall and tell him how your victory here was a fluke." He put a hand on my shoulder. "That could be the difference between us skirmishing over a provincial town or fighting a battle with real meaning behind it." Captain Seiford held my gaze in those intelligent eyes of his. "We need to play the game."

"Fuck the game." I spit on the ground.

"I agree, but that attitude isn't going to help anyone." He released my shoulder.

I knew he was right. It would have been easy to pay lip service to Alexander, but the same thing that wouldn't let me surrender to the Kranish, wouldn't let me speak kindly to the idiot noble. I've always been called to violence, but violence takes many forms. "You're right." I finally surrendered. "Should I apologize?" I asked.

"Absolutely not!" Captain Seiford chuckled. "I hate that little fucker. I have it on good authority he spent the whole battle cowering in his room." He nodded to the feast. "Now, let's get suitably drunk. It's our victory after all."

I did just that. I drank until I couldn't feel the pain in my body. I drank until the faces of the dead were just a blur. The trouble was that everyone else's face seemed to blur a bit as well. Captain Seiford and I walked around the tables sharing drinks with the men who'd fought with us. A couple pretty girls came and offered me a beer, but I could tell they were offering me more than that. I sent them away with a smile. I knew who I wanted to share my first taste of heroism with. A man can only really choose once at a feast who he wants to spend his night with.

I was sitting at the head of one table watching Captain Seiford talk to a man I knew only as Fletcher. He was a young, good-looking man who'd served with Lady Gerate in her part of the battle. He'd offered to come with me, but he didn't have the skill set for it. Fletcher had light blue eyes and an inviting smile. I wondered when he and the captain had gotten so close. They seemed rather friendly. Seiford always seemed to make friends like that quickly. Every time we were out drinking, I'd find him next to some swashbuckling chap.

I was still scratching my head over it when Lady Gerate finally sat next to me. "My lady." I raised my drink towards her.

"Thomas." She smiled at me.

"I take it Alexander ve Holsen is suitably mollified." I said as she sat down next to me.

"He's not hard to deal with." She chuckled at that. "Just a few compassionate touches, and he'll do whatever I want." I didn't like the idea of her touching him at all. "Well, except be any decent sort of human being."

"That's good to hear." I drank some more.

"I told him the wounds you suffered made you a bit hot-tempered and to not take them personally." Lady Gerate shrugged. "That seemed to calm his temper a bit."

"So he forgives me?" I was foolish enough to ask.

"Three above, no!" She laughed at me. I liked watching her do that. The way her hair moved. The way the dark green of her eyes seemed to change. It was worth charging into the mouth of five thousand men, just to see the weight lift from her shoulders long enough for her to laugh. "You could have had a snake hanging off your ass, and he wouldn't forgive an attack on his pride." She took a drink of beer. "You'll pay for those comments."

"They were funny though." I gave her a knowing stare.

"They were inappropriate." Lady Gerate tried to hide her approval.

"They were funny!" I persisted.

"Fine, they were funny." She laughed again. It had the same effect as before. It took the wind from me. It made my heart quicken. She was meant to live in peace, not stand like a rock against a tide of war. I saw she had a small bandage on her shoulder.

"You were struck?" I touched the wound.

"Oh," it seemed like she realized it for the first time, "yes, I was. I just survived a battle after all." She looked at the cut running along the top of my head. "I think you got the worse end of it."

I ran my finger across it self-consciously. "It was a hard battle."

She slapped my hand away from it. "Don't touch it." Lady Gerate sounded like a mother. "Why isn't there a wrap on it? Wounds like that can fester." She probed at the soon to be scar with her middle finger. It hurt quite a bit, but I liked the way her finger felt through the pain. In that moment, I'd have been willing to stand on a burning pyre just to feel it again.

"The doctor ran out of bandages." I lied to her and made sure the linen I had in my pocket wasn't visible.

"Let me see if I can find some." She stood up, but I stopped her.

"Don't worry about it." I waved her down. "I'll find some in the morning."

She sat down. Something in the way she moved said she really didn't want to leave. "I didn't mean to seem ungrateful before." She looked down shyly. "You saved my city. To me and everyone here you'll always be a hero."

I shifted around uncomfortably. I should have basked in the compliment, but I didn't know how to react to it. That wasn't quite true. I knew how to act. I was a hero. I just didn't know how she wanted me to react. "It's my job." I finally said.

"You're a Constable." She touched the tattoos on my arm. It felt like they were on fire. It felt like a *Warning*. It took me a moment to remember my skin always burned a bit where she touched it. "Your job is to fight the Old Religion. You didn't have to stand against five thousand men, but you did." She leaned back in her chair. "I knew you were the man to save me."

"I don't really think you're the sort who needs saving." I stared at her. She was strong. A thousand lords would have packed up and ran to the closest safe place. One lady stood, though.

"Everyone needs saving from time to time." She smiled at me like she saw something I didn't. "I'm no great warrior. I needed one to help defend this city." She took another drink. "It doesn't make us less that we need someone's help from time to time."

I suppose you're right." I said. I didn't need anyone's help. I would topple Kran with a spoon if no one would give me a damn bullet. Still, you'll find few drunk sixteen-year-olds who will argue with a beautiful woman. Even my pugnacious nature couldn't disagree with her. It made sense on her anyway. I didn't think her a damsel in distress because she couldn't beat Gostfeld on her own. She had her skills, and I had mine.

She tried to change the subject. "I saw a couple, pretty girls come pay homage to our hero." She gave me a stare with a tinge of jealousy on its edges.

"I think they were really more interested in Captain Seiford." I nodded to the man still deep in conversation with Fletcher.

"I don't think they were his type." She chuckled at that. I didn't get the joke, but I chuckled too.

"Well, whether they were his type or not, there are other people I'd rather spend tonight with." It was supposed to sound romantic, but something got stuck in my throat, so it came out less so.

She ignored my blunder. "I'm glad you did." I couldn't really tell what I'd get with her. One minute she'd try to freeze me with icy formality, the next she'd scold me for something. After that, she'd be getting friendly with another man. Then, out of nowhere, she'd start acting like she cared for me. She'd treat me like we were close friends, and then... I thought back to the kiss in her room. I didn't have a lot of experience with being kissed. Maybe it was more common on this side of the ocean. Maybe it didn't mean as much in this part of the world. It didn't feel common, though. It felt like it meant something.

We talked for a while. It didn't feel like long, but soon people started to filter out of the hall or drink so much they passed out. I even saw Captain Seiford walkout followed by Fletcher. The Captain was probably showing him his horse. He'd brought a lot of men to see his horse. It was strange. I never really thought he took that much pride in the animal.

Lady Gerate didn't seem to notice. We spoke of small things at first. Then the conversation changed tone. She seemed to find more excuses to touch me. Eventually, she had to go to her room for some reason and asked me to join. I saw Alexander ve Holsen watching us. I should have just ignored him. I gave the bastard a rude gesture and a smile, though. Lady Gerate didn't see it, thank the Three.

We walked through the halls and up a flight of stairs until she judged us alone enough to take my hand. Then she pulled me into a vicious kiss. We moved to my room hands roaming across every inch of the other's body. It was an awkward movement to my door, but we finally made it in.

As soon as we were inside our clothes fell from our bodies. Between the drink and lust, it was hard to really make a good account of what was happening. It was like the battle almost. I knew what to do instinctively.

She pushed me onto the bed, and I got my first full look at her naked frame. It was exactly what I thought it'd look like. I moved my eyes up her body, starting from her feet than to her legs, up towards her womanhood, and finally her breast with her dark hair curling around it. Her face was still the most beautiful part of her. Her green eyes seemed different somehow. I wanted her.

"Lady Gerate." I said dumbly.

"Call me Abbey." She said as she moved her hips on top of me.

"Abbey." I whispered to myself. I liked the way the name tasted.

———◆———

After it was over, and after it was over again because a woman like her deserves more than once, She placed her head in my shoulder, tracing the bandages on my body and the scars that had already healed. It was a truly sublime moment. "Was that your first time?" She finally asked.

"Was it so obvious?" I felt a bit offended.

"It was." She looked up at me with a smile. "Not that you

did anything wrong. You were just..." She thought for a moment, choosing the right word. "Enthusiastic."

"I can't imagine many men wouldn't be in my position." I tried to defend myself. "I'm sure Alexander has had his fair share of experience." It was probably true. He was a handsome, pompous noble. Girls always seemed to go for that sort of thing.

"Don't be like that." She slapped my chest playfully. "I assure you I enjoyed it quite a bit." She leaned over and kissed me. I decided I didn't want to even make the effort at being angry with her. "Besides," she settled back into my shoulder, "it means something more that I was your first. It makes it special. I wouldn't trade that for some arbitrary experience." She moved her head to look at me. "I'd be remiss not to mention, that you are a quick study." Abby moved her hand a bit lower on my body.

"Well, it's good to know how I stack up against your lovers." I stroked the side of her. I wanted to feel every inch of her.

"It's not like I'm an expert at it." She chuckled. "I was married for a time, and that taught me something." Her face turned a bit more serious. "After my husband was lost," she still couldn't quite say dead, "there was an explorer who came to my court asking for money. He didn't get that, but he helped me forget my grief for a night."

I laughed at that. "I wouldn't really care if all of Kran had run through you." I kissed her again. "You'd have found me just as enthusiastic."

"So why haven't you had a woman yet?" She pinched her face in curiosity. "I don't mean to pry, but heroes are usually considered stylish."

"Up until yesterday no one really knew I was a hero." I shrugged. "Men in the army knew my mettle, but outside of that, I was a laughing stock at court. I might still be. I'm from the Confederacy, and the Anthanii nobles are still a bit sore over our revolution. They consider us to be too provincial to be reasonably respected." I considered it for another moment. "Besides that, I'm brash, pugnacious, and fiercely arrogant. I've never been able to make friends quickly, and after all, courtship is making a friend but with an extra step."

"And what about the common folk?" She asked. "Confederacy men can be quite popular on our side of the pond with farmers' daughters."

"That's just something people say." I scoffed. "When people

ask why they slept with someone, girls like to say it was the accent or the mystery." I looked down again at her naked body. "The truth is they slept with him because he was good looking and charismatic. I've always had a martial sort of magnetism, but it rarely extends to women." For all my bad traits, I like to think I'm self-aware. "I thought about paying for it once, just to see what all the fuss was about. It didn't seem right though."

"Well, I'm glad you chose to spend tonight with me." Abby kissed my neck.

"I'm glad too." I chuckled. "I thought you were partial to Captain Seiford." I frowned as I played with her hair. "Women always like him."

That set her to laughing. "I'm quite sure they do." Abby finally caught her breath. "He's tall, handsome, and clever. That uniform doesn't hurt at all either." She sighed. "I'm quite sure I'm not his type though."

"I think you're everyone's type." I gave her a curious stare.

"Not the good Captain's." She returned the look. "I think he's more of competition than an opportunity."

"Wait," I sat up, "what do you mean?" I couldn't quite put it together in my head.

"You haven't figured it out yet?" Abby sat up too and watched my face. "I've seen you calculate everything about an army with almost no evidence, and you never knew about Captain Seiford."

"What are you talking about?" The beer I'd been drinking had largely run out of my system, but I still couldn't understand what she was saying.

"You didn't see the way he was talking with Fletcher." She screwed up her face, confused at my ignorance. "You didn't see them leave together."

"He was just showing the man his horse." I said dumbly. "He shows that beast to a lot of people. Captain Seiford's quite proud of it."

"I know everyone in my city." She looked for the understanding in my eyes. "Fletcher prefers the company of men."

"So do a lot of people." I scoffed. "Women are confusing." I still had no idea what she was getting at.

"I mean intimately." She put her face in her hands, chuckling at the joke I couldn't see.

"Oh." I said like I knew what she was saying, even though I had no idea. It seemed like a waste of time to talk about Seiford with a beautiful woman naked in my bed, then everything clicked into place. "Ohhhhhhhh." I let the idea sink into my brain. Somehow, it didn't quite go with the image of the Captain in my head. "You mean Bradly wasn't showing those men his horse at all!"

She laughed at the shock on my face. "Does it matter?" She cocked her head to one side in a way that looked quite pretty on her.

"A little bit." I scratched my head. "I'm insulted he never tried anything on me."

She rolled her eyes and went to slap my chest again, but I caught it and pulled her against me. "My poor Constable needs his ego stroked?" She whispered in my ear.

I kissed her, and we rolled back into the bed in a passionate flurry. It was as good a way to spend a night as any I'd ever known. When it was over, she put her head back into my chest.

"So why me?" I asked her.

"You saved my city." She kissed my neck. "It didn't seem right to have you leave unthanked."

"I think there's a bit more than gratitude here." I cocked an eyebrow up. "I'm not saying I don't deserve it, but if you wanted to thank me, you could have just given me one of your famous donkeys."

"You're right." She paused. "It was more than gratitude."

"What was it then?" I rolled over to get a full look at her.

"You were born in the Confederacy, thousands of miles away from here." She touched the tattoos on my arm. "I hear it's a happy place. A place where people are free to reach as high as they want."

"It is." I admitted. "It's a dangerous place, men hang onto the edge of the world by their fingertips. Your people wouldn't call it civilized, but it's a good place as well." I remembered my home for a second. I had been so eager to leave, but now that I had, it seemed the world didn't get much better than my plantation. I was a warrior born and drawn to conflict. Thyro had that conflict, but if I were a different man, the Confederacy would be where I wanted to live. "I don't think I'd trade my frontier for your cities."

"It was like that here once. I remember it from when I was young." Abby's eyes seemed lost in some distant past. "Thyro is old. The nobles dominate the peasants, and we have too much history for it to change all at once." She looked at my six-shooter on the table. "It seemed like we started on the right path, though. Confederacy ideas seemed to make their way across the ocean. We industrialized, built guns to replace knights. For a time, the power of the nobles was waining. Talented men of every stripe and caste started to reach for the stars." She smiled at that. "We started to aspire to great heights. Science, music, agriculture, there was nothing we couldn't master. Men even started to put aside the Old Religion of their own accord. Sure, there were problems, but we were working on them. Men became much more than their king or country."

"I haven't seen that kind of optimism here." I said flatly.

"Thaniel changed all that." I saw the ghost of hope in her. "I was five when he took the throne. At first, he was a beacon of something better. A peasant who overthrew the king of Kran. The people had finally taken control of their country." She laughed at her own naivety. "Then he crowned himself emperor, and started conquering the nations around him." She sighed. "It seemed natural at the time. Usurpers often try to consolidate their reign with conquest, but Thaniel wasn't like any we'd known before. He was insatiable. One nation after another fell. The first armies that tried to stand against him were smashed, and so were the second and third. We tried and failed. Then he brought his Priest to bare against us." She shook her head. "Men lost hope."

"He's a powerful man." I respected Thaniel, even as I plotted to destroy him.

"He is." I felt Abby shudder against my arm. "He was so powerful men stopped thinking he could be beaten. They stopped hoping for a great victory and instead prayed that they'd be the last ones he conquered. They prayed that maybe he wasn't as bad as they say. Any thought of turning him back was gone." She touched the place where the sword had pierced me. "There are two schools of thought when it comes to Thaniel. The commoners grit their teeth and wait for the Kranish armies to ravage their lands. The aristocracy believes it too. The only difference is they're willing to send peasants to die, to make the effort. Ask people if they're afraid of Thaniel. They'll talk brave, but in their hearts, they've already lost." I saw her grit her teeth again. "Even my husband only fought because he believed it was his duty. He marched against Thaniel knowing they'd never win

"That takes honor." I didn't like hearing her talk about her husband, but from what I heard he seemed like a decent man. She deserved a decent man.

"It did, but we need more than honor now." She bit her lip. "In this world of nihilism, where can good people turn?" Abby gave me the full weight of her stare. "Then you rode into my city." She sat up and moved on top of me, resting on my hips. "I expected you to organize an evacuation or try to negotiate a surrender, but you didn't. You trained a militia, prepared a plan, started doing strange things like mint medals and appropriate donkeys."

I smiled at that. "It must have seemed quite odd to you."

"It's what we needed." Abby ran her hands down the length of my stomach. "I had a city to lead. I couldn't let myself be driven by an abstract optimism, yet I found myself placing hope upon you. I had no reason to, and yet I did. It wasn't that you seemed competent or that you acquitted yourself well in battle before." She smiled, not at me exactly but at a distant chance that the world could be made right again. "I placed my hope in you because for the first time, I saw a man who thought he could win. Not only that, you were convinced that you'd beat Thaniel if it were only you standing against all of Kran." She shook her head at the ridiculousness of it all. "It wasn't that you believed some divine power would intervene on your behalf. It was a sheer belief that you could not be stopped. I found myself believing in you too. I found myself wanting to stand next to you." She leaned over and kissed me deeply. "We could have lost today, and that belief would have been worth it all."

"There were times it didn't seem you believed we could win." I cocked an eyebrow up.

"Of course, there were!" She laughed. "The lynchpin in your plan was donkeys and scarecrows." Her face grew serious. "I may have doubted the plan, but I never doubted you." Abby held my face in her hands. "You're wondering why I decided to spend the night with you? I did it because in times as dark as these, where do good people turn? They turn to you."

She went to kiss me again, but I stopped her. Something about what she said made me feel uncomfortable. "I may not be the hero you think I am." I said.

"What do you mean?" She leaned back.

"I'm glad I saved this city. I'm glad I gave you back something you thought lost forever," I bit my lip, "but at the end of the day, I did it for me." I didn't want her to leave me, but she deserved the truth. "I fought Gostfeld because I wanted to be the one to break him."

"I knew that." She laughed. "I never said you were an arbiter of morality." She looked at the six-shooters on the table. "There's a lot of good men in this world. I'd rather a moral hero, but we need you." She paused. "Captain Seiford is a good man, and he follows you. Why do you think that is?"

"Well, after recent revelations, maybe he wants to show me his horse." I reflected upon the Captain's preferences.

She slapped me playfully. "No, you ass!" She calmed down a bit. "He follows you because he believes you're the only one who can end this war and save his country."

"He's a good man and a good officer." I said. "He follows me because it's his duty."

"He volunteered to come here with you. He didn't have to do that." She gave me one of those curious looks. "I asked him about it one day. Do you know what he said?"

"I haven't the faintest." I shrugged.

"He said he wants his younger brother to grow up in the world he thinks you will create." She smiled at me. "He wants his brother to know nothing of the war that has shaped him."

"He has a younger brother?" That surprised me. I don't know why, but it did.

"Captain Seiford's followed you for the better part of a year." She rolled her eyes. "How do you know so little about him?"

"He doesn't talk much about his personal life." I admitted. "Besides, I know what I need to. He's a damn good captain." I didn't tell her the full truth. I had never taken the time to learn much about Seiford because one day I might be forced to sacrifice him like I'd done with that William boy. One day he might need to hold the line for one moment more. The difference was I'd probably tell him he was going to die, and he'd still hold for one moment more.

"I think you've a hard road ahead of you," Abby said almost sadly, "and I don't think a moral man could bear that weight."

"Huh." I thought back to my visit to the doctor. "Doctor Quarrels said something to that effect."

"Who's Doctor Quarrels?" She scrunched up her face.

"The man who patched me up." I gestured to the bandages. "You're the one who sent me to him."

"I know everyone in Wuntsville by name and skill." She shook her head. "There's no Doctor Quarrels."

"Really?" I had thought I remembered her telling me to go to that office. After I thought about it, I don't really remember why I went there. It just seemed right, like I was drawn there.

"Really." She responded. "Now do you want to spend all night talking about doctors." She wiggled around on my hips.

I didn't. That was a mystery for another day. I hadn't slept in more than two days, but some things are worth staying awake for.

———◆·◈·◆———

Captain Seiford and I headed out early the next morning. There was no fanfare, but we left the company we'd brought behind. They were to train the militias of the town in case Thaniel tried to retaliate. I knew he wouldn't. He didn't want to make Wuntsville into a symbol.

Lady Gerate stayed behind too. She had a city to run after all. I assured her I'd tell the Anthanii court of her competence. I knew we'd see each other again, so it wasn't so sad a goodbye.

As we rode towards the Anthanii Capitol, I couldn't control my curiosity any longer. "Why don't you ever ask me to see your horse?" I asked.

That took the Captain off guard. "Would you go with me?" He cocked an eyebrow up.

"No," I admitted, "but it's nice to be offered."

"Then stop asking stupid questions." He turned back to the road.

"Ass." I mumbled to myself.

Present Day

J woke up screaming again. Seiford was on top of me. "It's alright, Thomas!" The monk shouted as he tried to wrestle my arms to my sides.

I hit him in the head hard, and Seiford was thrown against the side of the room. Ayn-Tuk jumped on top of me put his knees in my chest. He didn't like to get involved in my dreams, but sometimes when I went too far, the black man would hold me. After he saw I had control of myself, he released me with a nod.

It took a moment before I realized what I'd done. "Seiford!" I rushed to him. "Seiford, are you alright?"

The monk rubbed the cheek where he'd been struck. There was a cut bleeding across it, and a purple welt would grow soon. Seiford smiled up at me. "Of course I am. It doesn't seem right for you to have all the scars that girls fawn over." He nodded to Ayn-Tuk. "I just like knowing he'll raise a hand to save me."

I cursed myself. This kind of thing happened more often than I liked. The cycle was the same. I would have a nightmare, and Seiford would try desperately to restrain me before I could hurt myself. Sometimes I came to my senses without violence, other times I didn't. The monk would always laugh it off with a witty comment, but it stuck with me. How long before I did something that couldn't be shaken off? I'd killed thousands and maimed countless more. If I did something like that to my closest friend, I couldn't live with myself. I had once attacked Seiford with a knife before I came to. To me, it was hurting the thing I loved most in the world, my friend. If Seiford were smarter, he'd have run as far as he could from me. If I were a better man, I'd make the monk leave, but we needed each other. We were like two different pillars leaning on each other. If one went, the other would fall. I hoped Ayn-Tuk would always be there to stop me.

"I'm so sorry, Seif." I helped my friend to his feet.

"Oh now you're sorry," Seiford chuckled, "but when you told half of Kruntell I had the cock rot, all you did was laugh."

"It was funny." I answered still trying to steady the monk. "This isn't."

"I know." Seiford put a hand on my shoulder. "If this is the price I have to pay to stand next to the greatest of men, I pay it gladly." He smiled. "If the price were higher, I'd pay it still."

I couldn't respond to that. It was Seiford's way. I had just struck him, and here he was, trying to comfort *me*! Not a day went by I didn't wish Seiford had my skills and reputation. He'd have been worthy of them.

"Land hoe!" We all looked up as we heard the call.

"That'll be the Confederacy." Seiford stared into my eyes. "Are you ready?"

"I charged Garrow with fifty men." I grunted. "Of course I'm ready." *I'm terrified*. It's what I really meant but couldn't admit.

Seiford knew I was but had the decency not to say anything. "I never doubt you."

I picked up my gear and shouldered the repeating rifle I carried. I always kept my essential belongings on me. I even rolled up my right sleeve to show the tattoos. "I need to be doubted from time to time." I gave my friend a coy look. "What about you, Ayn-Tuk?" I nodded to the man. "This is a completely different kind of white people."

"Still people." Ayn-Tuk walked out the door. It was mighty philosophic of him.

We walked up through the ship's hold and onto the deck. The sailors were already furiously preparing for the dock. I saw the captain screaming at the crew. The words were Anthanii, but it was in a vernacular I couldn't understand.

I looked around at the sailors working. It was a merchant galley, big and lumbering. Not the sleek war frigates I'd found myself on from time to time. I watched the captain take note and walk over to me. He was a lean man in his mid-thirties with a patch over his eye and some marks on his face that could have only come from war. All in all he had the bearing of a fighter.

His name was Captain Charles Dumas. By all the accounts of his sailors he was a decent fellow. We hadn't spoke much besides what men were obligated to say to each other when locked on a boat for more than a month. Still, I could tell there was something he wanted to bring up but hadn't found the will to yet. Approaching the shore, this was his last chance.

"Mr. Belson." The captain said with respect but not deference.

"Captain Dumas." I responded with much the same demeanor.

"Be at port in an hour." The captain looked at the horizon. "Maybe two."

"You run a good ship." I muttered as I lit up a cigarette. I'd gotten the knack for it on the ride over. "I'd bet on one."

"You mind if we speak?" Charles finally said what he wanted to. "Alone that is." He nodded to Seiford and Ayn-Tuk.

I shrugged as if it meant no difference to me. "Seiford, can you go check on Shaggy Cow for me?"

"I can." The monk gave me a curious look but set out to see the horse anyway.

"Ayn-Tuk," I turned to the black man, "can you go do something strange and incomprehensible to civilized folk?"

"I have some crosswords to keep me busy." He said in his deep ashy voice before disappearing below deck.

"See?" I gestured after Ayn-Tuk. "Strange and incomprehensible to civilized folk." Smoke rolled out of my mouth to dissipate in the sea breeze. "Who the fuck does crosswords?"

"I do." The captain leaned over the railing with an ease that only came from half a life spent at sea.

"Hmmm." I eyed up Charles cautiously. Any man who did crosswords for fun was suspect in my book.

"Helps me sleep."

"So what'd you want to talk to me about?" I really didn't want to speak of crosswords. "You have a loved one who served with me?" The man looked and sounded Kranish, but that was usually how these conversations went. Still there were mixed opinions of me in Kran. Some saw me as a liberator. Others saw me as the man who had ruined their dreams of greatness.

"I suppose it was too much to ask that you'd remember me" Charles looked me up and down.

"Should I?" I turned my gaze from the sea to the captain.

"You did this." Charles pointed to his eye patch. "With that ax of yours, you took my eye."

"You fought for Thaniel?" I cocked an eyebrow up.

"I was in the navy." The captain nodded. "After Fredua, I took up with Colonel Smith and the Hammer Battalion."

"Hard man." I said with the respect he deserved. "Led the hardest unit in Thaniel's army, and that's saying something." I paused to watch the ocean. "He hated me almost as much as the king and queen, but he had an honest reason for it." I took another smoke. "Hard man…" I said mostly to myself. "Almost had me more than once."

"Deserved better than he got anyways." Charles joined me to stare at the horizon.

"Aye, he did." I'd seen too many brave lads killed trying to make the world a little safer than they found it. However, what happened to Colonel Smith was on a list of its own. I never imagined Thaniel would do something like that to his man. I never imagined Colonel Smith would let it be done. "But most men deserved better than they got in those days. Reckon you're on that list."

"If you're talking about this," the captain pointed at his patch, "I had my sins in those days. Who's to say I deserved both eyes." There was a slight chuckle on his lips, but he replaced it with a sad grimace. "Still, that's not all you took from me." The captain shook his head. "I had seven brothers before you invaded my country. Now I have none."

"Seven?" I asked with more shock than I intended to show.

"Remember any of them?" It wasn't an accusation, but it wasn't friendly conversation either.

"Did any of them have dogs?" I was curious.

"Aye, the youngest one." That took Charles aback.

"Was it black and skinny?" I thought I might be close to cracking a mystery that had plagued me for the better part of my life.

"No, it was a terrier." Charles answered back still confused.

"Then I don't remember them either." I puffed on my cigarette, hoping the captain would leave me be. Admittedly it was a vain hope. "Just some more pieces in a game I already won."

I don't know what made me say that. It hurt just coming out of my throat. After everything I'd taken from this man, why couldn't I just give him an apology?

I knew the answer though. I wouldn't mean it. I'd wept upending tears over the things I'd done in the Thaniel Wars. I cried out in the night for my sins. Still, I never apologized for it. I did what I had to, and the world was better for it.

Charles gritted his teeth. "I expect with the dead that follow you, it'd be hard to remember." He paused. "They were my brothers though, so don't speak of them like that in front of me."

"I'm Thomas Belson, greatest Constable of the New Church. The man who turned the Rose Petal Throne to ash." I said shortly. "There's not a whole lot of men who can tell me how to talk."

"I have fifty sailors on this ship loyal to me." The captain took a step forward. "I think you might consider that before you offend me."

"Aye, so you do." I smoked nonchalantly. "I've faced worse odds though, and I'm still standing. Your brothers aren't." I turned my body letting the full brunt of my warriors pose show. "You seem like a good captain, but even Thaniel couldn't get men to charge me at the end." I paused. "That was ten years ago. My reputation has only grown since."

"Aye, I suppose." Charles nodded, but he wasn't cowed, not exactly anyway. "Still, it wasn't a threat."

"What was it then?" I shot back.

He took a moment to respond. "One worn down fighter to another," he wiped away what I hoped wasn't a tear, "saying he misses his brothers, and it hurts to hear them spoken of like that."

That took the wind right out of me. "I'm sure they were good men." It wasn't an apology, but it was better than before.

"They had their virtues and their vices." The captain responded. "Like all men."

"Well, if they died by my hand they were brave at least." I flicked my cigarette. "That's all that really matters in the end."

"Maybe." Charles responded. "You're all sorts of brave, and no one can say you're not." He paused. "You think that's all that matters?"

"Why'd you want to have this conversation, Captain." I turned to him, finally angry. "As far as I can tell it's just made two worn down fighters hurt more than they need to." I gave the man a cold glare that spoke of violence. "What? Were you gonna kill me and lost your nerve?"

"I spent a long time dreaming of killing you," Charles returned the look, "but I realized killing you wouldn't bring back my eye," he hung his head, "or my brothers." He took a moment to compose himself. "This isn't one of those stories where a wronged child grows up to avenge himself. They don't tell stories about the man who tries to piece his life back together after a *hero* tears it apart, but I assure you it's much harder than killing a treacherous uncle."

"What do you want then?" I asked pretending like I didn't really care, but I did.

"Happiness." Charles answered with a nod. "Contentment."

"Well, I wish you the best of luck in that." I stared back to the sea, "That's not much more of a realistic a goal than killing me, though." I pulled out another cigarette. "Not for men like us anyway.

"I think it is." The captain shrugged his shoulders. "Maybe after this, I can put it all behind me where it belongs." He took a deep sigh. "I've mourned my brothers, and I've learned to live with one eye."

"And until then?" I asked.

"I wanted to face you before I've forgotten you." Charles took a step forward. "I wanted to know the man who's taken so much from me." He kept after me. "I wanted to know if you had the same regrets I do."

"I'm not sorry for fighting Thaniel." I answered back coldly.

"I don't ask you to feel sorry for that!" Charles vibrated with fury. "Thaniel was wrong. I know that now." The captain looked at his feet. "I think he only wanted what was best for us, but what Kran did was unforgivable." Every one of his words seemed to hang with regret. "I ask the Three every day to forgive me taking up arms for him. Yes, I even pray to your gods now. I wish I'd been clever enough see what he was, but I couldn't look past the nationalism. I couldn't look past the fear of being a coward, but there are worse things to be in this world I suppose." He stared into my eyes. I knew what he meant by worse things. "I don't want you to apologize. I want you to understand what you did, even if it's all you could do. I want you to know it wasn't pieces on a map you knocked down. It was real men with real dreams."

I saw the man in a new light. "You've heard me screaming in my sleep." I was humble for the first time in ten years. "You know that I don't see the men I've slain as pieces on a board."

"You fight those dreams." Charles shook his head. "Accept them, and they might go away." The Captain looked almost sympathetic. "I may have good reason for wanting you dead, but the world doesn't."

"I've been fighting all my life." I stared at the shore. "I fight whoever has the poor fortune to be on the other side. Don't think that changes just cause it's me I'm fighting."

"It's a fool's hope that you'd turn a peaceful leaf," Charles shrugged, "but then again, it was a fool's hope that a fifteen-year-old boy could beat Thaniel."

"Suppose so." I nodded. "We're getting close to the shore. A captain's got to make things ready, don't he?"

"He does." The captain slapped the railing and took a step back. "There's something else, though."

"Don't know that I can handle much else right now." I flicked the cigarette into the water.

"You should hear this." He got closer and whispered. "A day after I agreed to take you across the ocean, an agent came to me."

I narrowed my eyes at the man. "What'd they want?"

"Real vague on that bit." Charles said. "Maybe it was just information. Maybe it was more."

I shrugged. "Probably just some yellow page tabloid reporter trying to fill out his column."

"I never met a reporter who could offer me a bag of gold heavy as the one he handed over."

That caught my attention. "There's a lot of wealthy people that want to get under my skin." I still wouldn't admit it unnerved me.

"Maybe," the captain agreed, "but after I threw that bag in the water, she offered to bring my brothers back from the dead."

That got a shock out of me. "You believed her?"

"I believed she believed it." Charles responded wisely.

I nodded. "I get you don't want vengeance and good on you for it," I eyed the captain up, "but you didn't owe me a bag of gold."

"I didn't throw it away for you." He looked over his sailors.

"Then why?"

"We fought on different sides ten years ago." The captain said. "There's plenty of regret for both of us, but the thing that turned the noble Thaniel I knew into the man you killed was bags of gold given by shady characters. They're the reason it all turned to shit in the end." He sighed. "I'm not sure who was behind all that, but someone was." Charles shook his head. "I won't be a part of it."

"Thank you for the warning." I nodded to him. "I mean that."

"Watch your back, Thomas Belson." He said and then went back to his sailors.

"Captain Dumas." I hollered after him.

"Mr. Belson..." He turned around waiting.

"What happened to your brothers..." *I'm sorry.* "I wish it hadn't happened like that." Not an apology. Not even close.

"Yeah." Charles let out a deep sigh. "Me too."

I watched the shores of the Confederacy grow closer as I thought about the captain's words.

Eventually, Seiford walked up beside me. "That must've been some conversation."

"Aye." I muttered. "Some conversation."

"Penny for your thoughts."

"They might be worth more these days." I responded dryly. "Retirement adds value, don't you know?"

"There are two things I don't pay for, it's women and thoughts." Seiford chuckled.

"Do you think that the Demon's make men evil, or do they just give them the power to fulfill the evil inside them." I finally tore my eyes away from the ocean.

"I don't know." Seiford looked down at the ground. "Lots of wise people say lots of different things."

"My parents taught me that people were decent enough if you give them half a chance." I sighed. "But I've seen how evil they become when they're pushed."

Seiford looked at me. "I was with you when the emperor of Ruskia burned his children alive so they couldn't oppose him." The monk said. "I was with you when the lord of Wenswill offered his head to save his city from being plundered." He shrugged. "People are strange."

"It doesn't make any sense." I struck the railing. "The Three should have made us all good or the Demons should have corrupted us all."

Seiford thought for a second. "Your assumptions wrong." He said finally. "Good and evil aren't two base elements or different sides of some cosmic coin. Good is what we aspire too, and evil is what happens when we fail."

"It seems the line between the two is thin at best." I muttered.

"Because they are." The monk said. "Thaniel didn't start a war that killed millions because he wanted to kill millions." He paused. "He wanted his people free from Anthanii control. He was tired of his land being invaded by every king with a sizable army. He felt for every peasant who had their houses razed and daughter raped." Seiford put his hand on my shoulder. "He wasn't evil, not at first anyway. He was afraid and angry more than anything."

"And I took his head."

Seiford stared at me with those sad eyes. "That's a greater burden than any man should have to bear, but you did it because, in his fear and rage, he turned to powers he couldn't understand. His high ideals were corrupted by base means."

"What's the difference between them slaughtering men with lightning and fire and me slaughtering them in battle? Who decides what means are base and what are justified." I shook my head and searched the sky. "Is it the Three above or the Demons below?" I gave a chuckle and looked at my hands. "Maybe it's something more powerful than either. Then again, maybe it's just the man who wins."

"Maybe there are no justifiable means. Maybe we'll pay for our actions no matter what king, country, or god we do it for." Seiford smiled a soft smile. "Or maybe there's a difference between the lion who protects and the wolf who preys." He patted my back.

"Were the people I went to war with much helped?" I looked down at my pistols. "Do you think when I destroyed their armies and put them at my mercy, they hailed me as a hero?"

"Did your father ever spank you?" Seiford asked.

"More often than most fathers did, but less than I deserved." I smiled despite myself.

"Did you love him at that instant?" Seiford asked again calmly.

"No."

"How quickly did you forgive him?"

"As soon as it was over." I was still looking at the pistols. "There's a wide gap between a father spanking his child and me killing their sons and conquering their lands."

"You're right in that too." Seiford paused. "The men you led would have liked you more if you hadn't woken them up at the crack of dawn and let them sleep till noon." He nudged me. "It took a while before they realized you didn't make them hike twenty miles up a mountain because you hated them but because you loved them."

"A good many of those men might have been better off if I'd never recruited them." I said sullenly.

"And their mothers would have hated you a good deal less if you hadn't." He waved his hand. "Until the Demon Worshippers tainted their land with evil, and foreign soldiers raped them, at least." Seiford made that sound oddly comforting. "The difference between you and the men we've fought is that no matter what their intentions they did what they did to be loved, and you did it because you loved them."

The monk put a hand on my shoulder again. "But, maybe that's part of being a hero, the part I don't tell stories about, and the part singers will never sing of." He sighed "Perhaps that's the greatest thing a hero can be. It's easy to die for a just cause, but to be hated for their own good…" He trailed off. "It's a heavy thing you've been asked to do."

"Maybe it's time the Three choose a different man to carry their load." I shook my head. "Maybe this man's getting old."

"I don't believe there's anyone else who's strong enough." Seiford said then sighed. "I hope it's in your future to marry a good woman and raise children who never see a battle in their lives. Those were shit times to be a Constable."

"Shit times, indeed." I nodded.

The monk took his hand away. "I also don't believe the reluctant hero act. You became what you are because you did what no one else could do because they weren't strong enough, quick enough, or clever enough. If you wanted a quiet appointment and an easy life you'd have had it. You could have let the world pass you over, but you didn't, because you were too good a man." He stepped in front of me. "You charged it with a bayonet. Great men don't have greatness thrust upon them, they pick up the weight because they're the only ones who can carry it. If there's one man who can see this through, it's you." He looked deep into my eyes. "But don't believe there's no one here to help you carry it."

I took out another cigarette. Maybe I could bear what was to come as long as at least one man knew me truly. "I'll do what I have too."

"No, you'll do what you can, like you always do." He put a hand on me.

"I'm lucky to have you, Seif." I couldn't manage a full smile, but the edges of my mouth twitched up.

"Oh, I'm the lucky one." The monk put on a positively evil face. "I bet your mother's a rare beauty." And he was off as I gave chase to give the man a swift kick in the backside.

Present Day

"**S**o this is your homeland?" Seiford surveyed the city as if he was trying to find the rest of it. "It's quaint." He said trying to sound diplomatic, "Are you sure this is the Capital? I always figured Capitals to be more... Capitaly."

"It's the Capital alright." I took in the sight. I knew what Seiford was referring to. It would seem like a large town to Thyro eyes. It was orderly and clean but lacked the grand architecture of older cities. Men walked about their business, but it wasn't bustling by any means. The buildings were well constructed but small. It had only been around for a century and hadn't had the time to sprawl out like cities tended to do. Besides, the seedy characters that usually gave a city its flavor had elected to try their hand at the frontier instead. Most seedy men were really just restless at heart. There were bigger cities, of course. In the North, they had sprawling industrial complexes. In the South, they had elegant plantation centers. Most countries expect their capital to be the biggest in the nation. To the men of the Confederacy, the government was a mild nuisance. They didn't want the place that governed them to be overly big.

"It has more culture than it seems." I said simply. Still it had seemed larger in my memory.

Seiford chuckled at that. "I bet there's a fascinating show of some man trying to fuck a sheep right around the corner."

"I'm sure the sheep is getting sore if you'd like to stand in for it." I smiled at my friend.

"I don't think I'm ready for that much culture yet." Seiford shot back as we walked down the gangway.

"What about you Ayn-Tuk?" I asked the black man. "You think you'll like this place?"

"I like all things." Ayn-Tuk held his spear in the crook of his arm.

"I'm sorry I can't be as optimistic as our tan friend." Seiford called from the shore.

"Don't dwell on the negatives, Seiford." I shouldered my pack and readjusted the rifle slung over my shoulder. "This is an entirely new frontier for you to spread those diseases you carry around between your legs." I hit solid ground, and it took me a moment to adjust to not swaying constantly. I really did despise ships

"I've never had the Kranish drip!" Seiford gave me a dirty stare, almost as dirty as what was between his legs. "That was a completely false story you told a man in a bar when you were drunk." The monk saw his own pack which had been unloaded by the sailors. He tried to shoulder it the way I had but managed to trip himself up in a truly pathetic fashion. "The story just so happened to spread like wildfire."

"Not unlike the diseases between your legs." I cocked an eyebrow at him.

"I never had the Kranish drip!" Seiford screamed definitively. A few dockworkers heard his scream, and it was becoming more likely that the story of his infamous cock would follow him across the ocean.

"Please," I scoffed, "In some languages, it's called the Seiford drip." I gave Ayn-Tuk a little nudge.

"Cause you keep spreading those damned rumors." The monk shook his head in defeat.

"Well, you tell those damned stories about me." I mocked him gently.

"Yes, you get to be heralded as the greatest hero in living memory, and I'm the man who spread Thyro's most irritating itch to foreign lands." Seiford looked at a group of three men who were whispering to each other and pointing at us. They'd no doubt recognized my tattoos, heard the magnificent stories about Seiford's cock, or were wondering what Ayn-Tuk was doing with his shirt off. "Does that really seem like a fair trade-off to you?"

"Once again stop dwelling on the negative side of things." I set my pack down as I waited. "The countries we've forged will one day be gone, my battlefields will be forgotten in the centuries to come, and one day my name will turn to legend and then to myth. People will start to doubt I even existed. Time makes ghosts of us all," I turned to the monk and gave him a stare full of sincerity and respect, "but the world will never be free of the Seiford Drip, no matter how hard it tries."

The monk sighed. "The only insufferable parasite I've dragged around the world is you."

I managed to keep a straight face despite Seiford's tired stare, which honestly was hilarious. "All men dream of finding their way into history, but we've already done that." I stared up into the sky as if envisioning our legacy. "Now, because of your proclivities, we'll make it into the medical records as well."

"You're an ass." Seiford wasn't actually angry. Well, he had been when the story had first picked up traction, but we'd been having different variations of the same argument for years. It was an amusing way to waste time. Friends who had been together for as long as we had tended to do that. It was the sort of argument we'd been having for the better part of a decade, and neither side had managed to win. The dispute could easily have been settled if Seiford would just let me thoroughly inspect his cock, but the damn monk always refused. He said there were enough unsavory rumors about the two of us already.

We continued to argue about whether or not the content of Seiford's trousers were poisonous to the touch until we heard the angry screaming of sailors and an even angrier horse. "Damn evil donkey!" One man screamed as he struggled with Shaggy Cow's reigns.

"Shaggy!" I shouted, and the horses' ears went up finding her master. She raced down the ramp any fear of water forgotten and in the process threw two of the men into the bay who came up swearing in languages even I didn't speak. She ignored them and ran to be embraced, which I did. The horse even gave Sieford and Ayn-Tuk a few nuzzles and sniffed around both of them until I presented Shaggy with a few dried apples. Satisfied she looked around the city curiously. "Oh, how I've missed you." I hugged her again

"Me too." Seiford patted the horse. Shaggy had always liked the monk and responded accordingly. "Of the two of you I've always found Shaggy the more agreeable."

The Eastern pony gave the monk an affectionate nuzzle.

"When are you going to leave this crabby old Constable and come to me?" Seiford gave me a distasteful stare. "I'd treat you better than him. I would have given you a suitable name like Desert Wind."

"Good cow." Ayn-Tuk patted her face.

The horse seemed to relish the compliments.

"Shaggy Cow is much smarter than the women you take to bed." I said as I threw mine and Seiford's gear over her. "She'd never let your diseased cock anywhere near her back."

The pony shook her mane as if laughing. I had spent many hours wondering if the horse could actually understand the words. She was undoubtedly the smartest animal I'd ever met. I had resolved to speak to her like a human being until she proved me wrong.

"Shaggy is also too wise to believe your slanderous lies." Seiford narrowed his eyes at me. "Aren't you Shaggy?" He said the last bit in the same way you'd speak to a baby. Shaggy must have found it slightly patronizing because she turned away from the monk.

"Ha!" I shouted in triumph. Shaggy was often the final arbiter in our disagreements, and it appeared she'd chosen my side, at least until Seiford managed to produce an apple. Ayn-Tuk also could have broken a tie, but he refused to comment on the state of Seiford's cock.

"I'll never understand why the Khan didn't give me a horse like her." Seiford mumbled in self-pity. "I did my fair share."

"Well, firstly there is no horse like Shaggy, so the correct question is why didn't he give you a horse almost like her." I gestured to my pony. "The answer to that question is he was obviously sore about you spreading the Seiford drip all over his tribe."

"I hate you." Seiford finally admitted defeat.

With our gear and Shaggy all unpacked, Seiford led us around the city. I found it strange that he'd lead the way, but I didn't stop him. The monk peered down every alley shaking his head and then moving on.

"Where are we going?" I finally asked.

"We're looking for an inn called Reginald's." Seiford responded as he looked up at a street sign.

"Oh." I nodded and followed my friend dutifully.

"So do you know where Reginald's is?" Seiford finally turned back on me. "You're from this damn country."

"I haven't been here in fifteen years." I spit at the ground. "Besides, I can't even remember what we ate for breakfast."

"Gruel!" Seiford responded with venom. "We ate gruel for breakfast!"

"I like gruel!" I looked up indignant.

"You like battle, week-long rides, and biting your toenails

off." Seiford rolled his eyes. "The rest of the world stands strongly against you."

"What's so special about Reginald's anyway?" I tried to pick some of the gruel from breakfast out of my teeth. "I saw an inn thirty minutes ago with a lovely picture of a fish on the sign."

"I could smell the rat shit off that place from the street." Seiford kept walking searching for some clue as to Reginald's. "Besides we're meeting someone there."

"Who's that?" I asked following my friend. "Perhaps an agent from Mother Vestia? A secret mission perhaps?" I had a bit too much hope in my voice.

"Your brother." Seiford said without looking back.

"Are you being serious?" I glared at him.

"Serious as the dead." The monk tried to avoid my eyes.

"Why, in the Three's name, are we going to see my brother?" I pulled my friend back. "How did you even set that up?"

"I've been writing him for years." Seiford shrugged.

"Why?" I threw his hands up. "How?"

"Mother Vestia gave me the address." The monk cocked an eyebrow up. "Someone had to tell your family you were alive. Besides, he seems like a kind fellow from what I can gather."

"Oh, he's undoubtedly very personable." I stared up into the sky. "He also has a million good reasons to never want to see me again."

"And one better reason to want to see you again besides." Seiford gave me one of those caring stares. "He's your brother."

"Aye, he's my brother." I admitted. "He's my brother, and when I left, I said everything I could to try and hurt him." I touched the tattoos on my arm absentmindedly.

"Don't you see?" Seiford said like it was so obvious. "You can only be hurt by the people you love."

"Then he deserves to love someone better." I couldn't meet Seiford's gaze.

"Undoubtedly, he does," Seiford nodded, "but we don't choose the ones we love."

"I can't face him." I said it mostly to myself.

"Once he's gone you'll regret that." The monk leaned in. "Trust me I know."

"Your situation was different." I mumbled. I knew how he and his brother were. It compounded my guilt at how the man had died.

"We've talked about this." Seiford rolled his eyes. "You agreed to come to the Confederacy. You were going to have to see your family sooner or later."

It hadn't seemed real being halfway around the world. It hadn't seemed real even on the boat. Now that it did, I felt something creep up my spine I hadn't felt in a decade. It was fear. "I changed my mind." I finally uttered. "Let's find a ship headed for Souren. They've always liked us over there." I turned to Ayn-Tuk. "Isn't that right?"

"They tolerate you." The black man mumbled.

"Tolerate is good enough." I turned back to the monk. "Let's go."

"We're staying." Seiford shook his head.

"I say we're leaving." I dug my heels in.

"Do whatever you will." Seiford turned his back on me and started walking again. "I'm going to visit your brother, and if you do anything except that, know you do it without me."

"Three be damned." I cursed the whole way to Reginald's inn.

After wandering around for an hour, Seiford finally relented and asked an old man for directions. Those directions proved useless, and the monk asked another. Eventually, we found ourselves standing in front of Reginald's inn. It was a nice establishment, painted brown with a picture of a man riding a lion on the sign. It was idiotic. I had once gotten drunk and tried to ride a lion. I still had the scars on my chest.

"I don't like this." I muttered to myself.

"Well, isn't that a shame." Seiford chuckled. "I didn't like the idea of having dinner with Duke Tremin." The monk helped tie Shaggy Cow to a post. She didn't really need to be tied up, but it made everyone around feel more comfortable. "He tried to poison us, and you said the next time I wanted to do something we'd do it."

"That was five years ago." I rolled my eyes. "I'm quite sure I've made up for it by now."

"I'm quite sure you haven't." Seiford cocked an eyebrow at me. "You keep on pulling idiotic stunts like that. As it stands, you owe me a new wardrobe, a new deck of playing cards, and a new damn elephant!"

"We couldn't take the elephant with us!" I shot back. It was another one of our long running arguments.

"I loved Surus!" Seiford was still sore over losing the beast.

"I loved Ventinville." I responded curtly. "I didn't try to take the whole damn city with me when we left."

"Regardless, I'll forgive those debts if we have dinner at this establishment." Seiford thought for a moment. "Except for the playing cards. They had naked women on them."

"Which is why that farmer gave us supplies for them." I shook my head. "The only reason I had to do that, was because you lost all our damn money playing with those cards."

"We didn't trade your gun for clothes when you managed to lose our entire pack in a whorehouse." Seiford narrowed his eyes.

I shrugged my shoulders. "I like my guns."

Seiford gave up arguing. "We're meeting your family here, and that's final."

"Fine." I grumbled. "Just don't try and make me feel guilty about Surus."

All three of us walked into the inn. Ayn-Tuk got some strange looks. The shirtless, statuesque black man cradling a large spear usually did. However, many curious people passed through the Confederacy. After the clientele got over their initial feeling of emasculation, they mostly went back to drinking. I had my sleeve rolled down, and neither Seiford or I were wearing our uniforms. Between the two of us, we'd probably only wore the black robes a dozen times. People did give the rifle on my back a peculiar look. They'd never seen one like it before, but they got over it quickly. The inside of the bar was much like the out. It was brown and simple yet clean. The patron's seemed to vary. Some were working-class men, others more upscale. A few foreign sailors were gambling in the corner, but that was the extent of the customers.

"I don't see my brother." I whispered in my friend's ear. "Maybe we got the wrong bar. We should leave."

"It's the right bar, and we're staying." Seiford said firm as a rock. "Your brother told me he might be out on business, and to enjoy ourselves until we got back."

"Fine." I gritted my teeth. "I'm going to wash up first though. I haven't had a proper bath in more than a month." It was the highest form of luxury to be able to bathe on a ship. Water was precious at sea. Some captains had allowed me to indulge in it, being the hero that I was, but Captain Charles didn't seem like the sort. Besides,

I wasn't nearly so vain to bring it up. "Order me a beer and some food." I told Seiford.

"Will do," The monk nodded, "and if you slip away, I will hunt you to the ends of the earth."

"What'll you do if you catch me?" I had, in fact, considered slipping away.

"Do everything in my power to ensure you catch the Seiford Drip." The monk narrowed in his eyes.

"I'll come back." I said begrudgingly. I wasn't usually one to be threatened, but Seiford's promise had an heir of honesty I found terrifying.

I went to the barkeep and bartered for the use of a bath and soap. We agreed on a fair price, and I went to fetch my spare clothes.

I headed around to the bathhouse. It was small and empty. Some neighborhood boy had probably been paid a copper to keep the water hot, and he had done a reasonable job of it. The bath wasn't steaming like it would be in a noble's house, but it was warm enough not to send a chill up my spine.

I had a phobia of being completely naked. I even tried to leave my socks on when I was with a woman. It was a well-founded fear for a soldier. I had been undressed when the Rochen's had led their final assault on Gurtly. I had been forced to defend the city barefoot and shirtless. It had added to my legend, but it wasn't something I was itching to replicate.

I reminded myself that the days of living by my guns were over, but even when I had finally gotten myself suitable naked, I couldn't fully enjoy the warm water. As I scrubbed my skin, there were subtle reminders of what I'd become.

It was an alloy of all the things that had happened to me since I'd been released by Mother Vestia. It was the fact that I couldn't apologize to Captain Charles. A normal man would have. It was the fact that I felt the need to beat a man in the street. A hero would have shrugged it off. It was the fact that sitting naked in a tub, I was still looking over my shoulder. Mother Vestia had given me my resignation paper, but that hadn't made me a civilian.

I washed the tattoos on my arm. They were the mark of a warrior. They would be with me until my death, just like the memories of battle. It wasn't just that I couldn't be a regular man, it was that I didn't want to. It was true that some nights I had nightmares, but Seiford was mistaken about their nature. The nightmares weren't about the battles. They were about what came after. In truth whenever I was cold or in pain and needed a warm memory to hold onto, it wasn't nights spent with beautiful women or good company and better beer that my mind drifted to. It was always the thick of battle. It was always that one pivotal moment in the fray in which I'd claimed victory over my foes. If I could live eternity in the thick of combat, I would. The great curse of a warrior was that actual war made for a small portion of soldiering. Still, in my own way, I loved all of it. I loved the endless marching, the sleeping in leaky tents, and even the bad food. Sure, I indulged in my fleshy vices from time to time, but war was my passion. What was I without it? Just a man with too many scars.

Something inside me had changed, and I didn't know that I'd ever be the same again. I hoped peace would be an acquired taste, but that was a fools hope. *Then again so was a fifteen-year-old Constable beating Thaniel.* I echoed Captain Charles's words. If I was a saint, then I was the patron saint of lost causes. I was the lord of desperate hopes and futile prayers. My real gift to the world hadn't been my victories or the peace Seiford and I had forged. It was the fact that no matter how horrible something seemed, there was always a chance that Thomas Belson could show up. Nothing was hopeless while I still drew breath. I hadn't been able to save every desperate people looking for salvation. I hadn't even been able to save most of them. I could only be in one place at a time, but at least those people had died with a bit of hope left in them. If Belson the Blessed couldn't save them, at least he'd avenge them, and I had done quite a bit of that. Maybe hoping I could adjust to peace was foolish, but it was worth a try.

I got out of the bath and reached for my pants, until I spotted a full mirror in the corner and went to it naked. I realized I hadn't actually seen myself naked in what could have been months. Could've been years. My body had changed with the rest of me.

The first thing I surveyed were the tattoos on my arm. They marked the day when the boy had died, and the legend had begun. I'd always liked the way the intertwining black lines looked against my muscled arm. Once I'd been so proud to wear the badge of a Constable. Now, Constables were proud to wear the badge of Thomas Belson.

Of course, they held a purpose, to protect me from being touched directly by the Demons I fought. They also served to warn me of the Old Religion before it was too late. I'd felt their warnings burn me deep to the bone, but now they'd burned so often, I couldn't tell what was a Warning and what was in my head.

Now they served a different purpose. Before I'd started my campaign, they were something to be laughed at or pitied depending upon your political beliefs. If a man in a play showed up with a marked arm, you could bet he'd have his head in his ass by the final act. Now when an actor presented his tattoos, he was righteousness incarnate. He would lead the poor, young lovers to get married in the woods. He would stand against a mob for the greater good. Now my arm let people know hope had arrived, and it was something worth clinging too.

The world was a brighter place than it had been. People used to wake up in the morning and wonder what new disappointment the day would bring. Now, they hopped out of bed early as to not miss another great triumph. Music didn't end with crashing melancholy but with a triumphant horn blast. Poets no longer lamented their sad lives but celebrated the glory of being alive. Men worked harder and gave more freely. Women dressed in brighter shades and laughed more. It was a subtle thing that they themselves didn't realize, but it was there. Had I really changed all that? Even as arrogant as I was, I couldn't take all the credit. I had given them the canvas maybe, and they had made of it something beautiful.

Still, as the sun shone brighter than it ever had, I found myself farther in the shadows. I couldn't stop thinking about what I'd done to give them that canvas. Would they sing as loudly if they knew the cost? Maybe that's what a hero was. They carried the sins of the world so people could live free. The sins of the world was were heavy though. *The Pillars...*

I was covered from feet to forehead in scars. Lines of pinkish gray split my body where I'd been struck by swords and bayonets. Little round lumps of flesh dotted my flesh where I'd been shot by men who thought they could stop Belson the Blessed with a well-placed bullet. They always managed to miss the important bits. Maybe I actually was blessed. After all the Three didn't usually appear in the dreams of men they were going to kill off the next day.

Then again, maybe I was just stubborn. Seiford often joked that if I was shot in the head, the organ would probably just consider it a challenge, and there wasn't much there anyway, so it probably wouldn't affect my day to day routine much.

It wasn't just the scars that made my body different than the one from a decade and a half back, it was the build too. I'd been small for my age fifteen years ago. I was short and skinny. Most of the other boys at God's Rest had looked in their prime, despite the fact that they weren't any older than me. I was the runt of the litter, and my instructors had made it clear that they'd see me dead before my first battle, chief amongst them Constable Grenwold. He didn't want the Constabulary profaned by a provincial child. It was only the special attention of Mother Vestia that saved me from being killed outright. Grenwold still beat me for it, but never my face where she could see, or my hands so she couldn't hear me play. No one ever thought I'd be much of anyone.

I'd had a friend there. A black boy from Souren named Huda. He was the best recruit of us all, and our instructor decided he was ready to face Thaniel's hordes early. Huta had been my first friend in Thyro. The first man I'd seen made into a corpse. The stories said Thaniel killed him in single combat. I hadn't believed a Constable could be killed by one man until I'd met the one man who'd done it. I hoped Huda made a good accounting of himself. At the time, that was all anyone could hope for being sent to fight Thaniel's Kran.

Huta was the better recruit by far and he hadn't lasted a battle. What hope was there for the arrogant runt, Thomas Belson? Grenwold hadn't lied when he called me the worst recruit in living memory. I was bad with his pieces, but I didn't play the pieces. I played the game.

Grenwold and everyone else had an idea about Constables five-hundred years too old. Men with the tattooed arm were supposed to behave like the knights of old, and they fought more like them than was sensible to modernity. I'd thrown away the sword and taken up a six-shooter and tomahawk. I'd thrown away stoicism, humility, and chivalry for rage, cunning, and will.

I beat Thaniel because of the rules I broke. It had seemed awfully clever at the time, but looking at the broken thing in the mirror, I couldn't help but wonder if those rules were there for a reason. I should have died in that war, but I hadn't. What had seemed like the essence of heroism ten years haunted my quiet moments.

As I stood naked in front of the mirror, I knew I had changed irreversibly. That shouldn't have shocked me. After all, what man was the same as the boy he'd been fifteen years ago? The difference between me and everyone else in the world was in what I'd become. All children looked at themselves in bathhouses like when they were young. They hoped that the future would see them as heroes with fame and glory. Then one day they'd put such things behind and grow up. They'd plow their fields, fall in love, and raise children. They'd do all the things they swore they never would because they didn't think they'd be any fun. Slowly, they'd start to love the man they became, bit by bit and piece by piece, until they were happy.

I had become the man I'd seen in the mirror at fifteen years old. I didn't regret that, not exactly. It was always the only path. Achieve greatness or die reaching for it. Someone ver important to me once said, "Asking what Thomas Belson would have been like if he was a farmer was like asking what it would be like if fire was wet. It didn't make any sense." Tattooed arm or not, I would have always chosen that path.

I had become the man I'd always dreamed I'd be. I'd become the man the world needed me to become. That kind of man was only needed for one type of story though, a story of blood and glory. Now the story was over, and I wondered how I'd fit into the new one.

Still I wasn't quite so sure as everyone else the story *was* over. I hadn't killed all the Priests, not even close. The Old Religion was even legal in the Confederacy, though various factions would argue over how legal it was.

I didn't care about what those factions had to say. I knew the Old Religion better than any man alive. I knew secrets their highest Priests hadn't even guessed. I'd been to the ruins of the Old Empire. I'd walked the streets of Imor and been the first man to do it in more than two thousand years. I heard ancient truths whispered. I knew the lie behind it all.

However, I also knew the world would never be completely free of the Old Religion. It was in man's nature to seek out powers beyond. It wasn't the remaining Priests that made me feel hollow. At least it wasn't just them.

When I took Thaniel's head, the rest of the world has breathed a heavy sigh of relief. They called me paranoid. They thought I'd been cracked by the wars. Maybe I was. Still, after Thaniel breathed his last, I hadn't felt any safer. Before I killed the dragon, he told me about the vipers in the bushes.

I thought of *Her*, whoever she was, every night. I'd even heard rumors of a beautiful woman turning my great victories against me. I'd never even been able to prove she existed, much less find and kill her. When I'd written Mother Vestia about it, she dismissed it as the meaningless words of a man about to die. She hadn't gone so far as to call it a lie. There probably was some woman playing with dangerous things out there, but it was more likely a Priest, seeing his doom, had tried to put some meaning to his life at the end than it was some girl playing us all like a fiddle. The truth was probably somewhere in the middle of meaningless specter and an evil mastermind. Still, the middle could hurt.

Many thought the tide had shifted too far to the New Church for anything to change it. These were the same people who laughed as an up jumped peasant named Thaniel clambered his way onto the Rose Petal Throne. The same people who took bets on how long it would take to whip the bastards.

Perhaps that was the real difference between a boy and a man. At fifteen, I'd yearned for victory over my foes. At thirty, I was never really sure what shape victory would take. At fifteen, I'd looked forward to entering liberated cities at the head of a magnificent parade. At thirty, I knew one oversight could costs thousands their lives. At fifteen, it had never occurred to me that I might make a mistake at all. At thirty, I knew there was no count on the number of graves my mistakes had filled.

More than anything, a boy I'd been looked forward to the day he could finally rest on his laurels, safe in the knowledge that he'd done enough to be called a hero with no objection. The man I was now knew that the price of heroism was eternal vigilance. A lifetime spent staring at shadows while the rest of the world wonders if you've gone mad. Every once in a while you believe them. What is the paranoia of one old soldier when stacked next to the complaisant masses. The old soldier turns away, and the monsters living in the shadows reach up to swallow him whole.

I was worshipped and believed by thousands. A saint in my own time. Children fought for the privilege of playing me in their little games. When women find themselves in bed with unworthy men, they thought of me on top of them. When the faithful faced a hard choice, they asked, "What would Belson the Blessed do?" They all wanted to be like me, strong, unwavering, brilliant. Yet if I showed them the cost, would they take my path?

Would the wise old man, with a loving wife and many

grandchildren wish to be reborn in my shoes? I walked roads the brave refused to think of. I stood before armies that had made the world quake. I journeyed to the darkest corner of the world to learn a secret that could tear a hole through everything men hold dear. I looked a god in the eye and kept my feet beneath me.

Millions who forgot the meaning of hope had been given it by my hand. Yet my other hand had given something else.

A saint in my own time... Once men had called Thaniel thus.

I remembered the eyes of those I had slain. I wondered on what they could have been with a dash of mercy. I had pushed away the only woman who had ever loved me. How many men had died thinking I would save them?

These thoughts ran beside me, always. I had seen a dog weep next to the corpse of its master. I am stronger than most, and for seeing that, I had wept in my sleep for half a year. If I were any less, it would have driven me mad. Maybe it did. Everything the philosophers had claimed as man's greatest gifts, I had sacrificed to have my name above all. Even my music was leaving me.

Would the wise old man, with a loving wife and many grandchildren wish to be reborn in my shoes? I would tell him to be a musician. Be a dealer in love. Live in a peaceful age. The secrets of yesterday were forgotten for a reason. Leave the book closed. The cities that survived Imor deserve to survive you. Let them stand.

I was meant for this life. Too broken to want anything worth having. *If you can, want something smaller.* I would say. *Want something better.*

You only get one life though. Thinking about what could have been just brings pain.

I dressed in my new clothes, making sure I could grab my weapons in a heartbeat should the need arise. I was retired but fifteen years of habit is hard to break.

I walked out the bathhouse taking one more look at myself in the mirror. I adjusted what I could and handed a boy my clothes with the promise that he'd be paid well if they were washed by morning.

I thought about riding away and finding a good boat to anywhere else. It was getting dark out, but it never got so dark captains turned away paying customers. Then I remembered my monks promise of the Seiford Drip. I didn't want to risk it. Even though the monk swore to the Three he'd never caught any diseases, I was sure there was something not quite right about Seiford's cock.

I sighed and entered the inn. It was fuller than when we arrived. Working people of various professions looking for a warm supper.

I spotted Seiford in a corner table with two men. Ayn-Tuk was sitting beside them, stoic and shirtless as ever. Both of the Monk's new friends stood when he pointed at me.

For a moment I wondered who the two men Seiford befriended were. One was tall, handsome, and blond. He had the bearing of a man who'd seen a bit of war. He was well dressed, like a Southern aristocrat, but he actually cut the figure all elites thought they did. I decided I wouldn't mind drinking with the aristocrat. He seemed like the rare good sort.

The second man was old. He had grey, thinning hair and wrinkles in his face. He stood in the way that let a perceptive person know, the world was starting to take away the gifts it had given him in youth. Still, the man had a broad face filled with compassion. He seemed like a decent sort to drink with as well.

For a moment I forgot why we'd chosen this particular bar. For a moment the two men looking at me were just two men. Then I saw what I'd been missing. Recognizing someone you haven't seen in fifteen years comes in three waves. First, you look at them like they're anyone else. You wonder what kind of man they are, then the realization hits you. After that, you compare the picture you see to the one you have in your memory. You realize that time makes strange things out of everyone.

For a moment it was as if the past fifteen years hadn't happened, and I was a boy again. Then the third wave hit. That only came if the person you didn't recognize at first ever really meant anything to you. For a moment it was as if the fifteen years had been a century. For a moment I saw the man I'd become, and I mourned the boy who died. The third wave was guilt at not recognizing someone who meant so much to you.

The tall, young one made his way through the crowded bar. Men got out of his way and watched him with an awe. They all went silent. He gave me a look like I was the only person in the room. That look was full of too many emotions. Pride, sorrow, guilt, joy, all made their home in the tall man's eyes. They were like my eyes, bright and blue.

Finally, the man reached me with a tear streaking down the side of his handsome face. I had wondered for fifteen years what I'd do in this moment. Sometimes, I hit that handsome face, and doubled down on the hate I'd left with. Sometimes, it was as if the two of us had never parted. I knew what happened would be somewhere in between. I'd been disappointed too many times to hope for more than that.

The tall man stopped for a moment, and in that moment all things were possible in my mind, then he threw his arms around me. "Welcome home, brother." He whispered in my ear. I cried. I tried not to make it too noticeable, but I did. I was sure the people around me saw, but they stayed silent. "Welcome home." *Andrew...*

Most of the time the reality is somewhere in the middle of what you expect it to be. However, too often it can be the worst possible outcome. Any man who's daydreamed about a pretty girl before talking to her understands this. Still, there's a few times when things actually live up to what you hoped they'd be. Then, every once in a while, they're better than you ever dreamed. This was one of those times. I wept, and the crowd cheered.

"I love you, Thomas." Whispered so only I could here.

For the first time since I'd been retired, I didn't think Mother Vestia was so wrong about me.

Present Day
Jessie's Story

"How do you want it, sir?" The Barber asked the man who had just sat down in his chair. *That was the key to a successful business.* He'd learned that many years ago. *Treat every man like they were princes of your store, and women...* He laughed to himself and gave one of the smiles he gave so generously in his own age. *Treat every woman like a princess regardless of if she's a paying customer or not.*

"A bit off the top and a good shave too." The man stroked his beard. "I'm tired of looking like a mangy dog."

"Nonsense sir, you look rugged as every man should." Of course, the man did look like a mangy dog, but there were better ways of letting someone know they needed help. "Although, there's not a soul alive who wouldn't be better for a nice cut and shave." He said as he put the razor to the man's grizzly beard.

"You're a nice old man. Do a good job, and I'll give you a bit extra, something for the wife and kids?" As the mangy man said it, he shrugged his shoulder, a rather unimportant gesture and one that wouldn't have meant anything to another barber. This one, however, had a past, and he recognized the leather strap that held a six-shooter, anywhere. No one carried weapons there. It was one of the few peaceful towns on the frontier. Still, the barber ignored it because now he was any other barber.

"At the age I am, my children are helping me." The barber started with his razor as if he'd seen nothing at all. "Still, I got more than a few grandchildren I'd like to spoil." He kept at it running the metal over his throat trying to keep his mind off what he'd seen.

"Where do you come from sir? It's not often I get a man in my shop I haven't met before."

"I'm more interested in where you're from Mr. Sowwens." The hand stopped.

"The names Smith sir, Aaron Smith. I'm not sure what you're getting at, but I'd thank you kindly to wait till I'm done." It was ruder than the barber should have been to anyone paying for good service, but Sowwens wasn't any sort of name he wanted spoken in his shop. He had to finish his work, even if his client was trying to talk about things he'd rather not.

"Of course, I'm a guest in your establishment." The mangy man smiled as if nothing had been mentioned. "You know most barbers use the two blade now. They say its easier and quicker."

"Well, that's true enough, and I'll admit I used one for a week or so, but the easier way is seldom the right way, you know."

"Admirable." The mangy man grumbled as he bent his head giving the barber a better angle on his neck.

"I tried the easy way when I was a younger man, but it never seemed to work well for anyone in the end." The smooth, easy motion of shaving the man's neck came naturally after thirty years.

"What do you mean sir if you don't mind me asking?" The mangy customer asked

The barber was confused, but he was never rude to a paying customer "Everyone makes a mistake or two in their youth, sir. It's nothing any man would like to speak about, except as a warning to those he loves."

"Wise of you." The barber observed the man's face as he groomed him. It was battered worse than most farm equipment. He was big too, not a hulking mammoth but the sort of corded muscle that truly scared people. It was his eyes that marked him for a dangerous man. Brown, the color of mud and shit staring hard, appraising everything, never comfortable no matter how the body laid.

When he was done, the man looked up and admired himself in the mirror. The barber looked too. It was good work after all. He'd never be handsome, but cut the right way, his hair could give the look of a genial rouge.

"You're better at this than your old job, Mr. Sowwens." He said after he straightened his coat. The weapon under his arm was clear as day now. All the barber could see was the handle but it looked to have seen some heavy use, and he gripped the shaving razor with white knuckles.

"I don't know what you're talking about sir. Please leave my shop now!" He couldn't keep the fear out of his voice, no matter how hard he tried.

"I'm afraid I can't do that, Mr. Sowwens." He reached into his pocket and pulled out a crumpled piece of paper and handed it over.

The barber slowly folded it open. When he saw the picture, his heart nearly stopped. It was a rendering of him or at least of him fifty years ago. The bounty was set at five hundred dollars. Usually, there was an "or alive" after the dead, there wasn't here. In big bold letters Harold Sowwens. It expired in three weeks. "That ain't me mister, I swear." The squeak in his voice gave him away, though.

"Last week you sent money to your sister in Mainstead. I have a deal with the banks. They let me know how to find you." The big man paused "No good deed, huh Mr. Sowwens?"

The barber gave up. Both of them knew his past. "It was fifty years ago mister. I was young. We were trying to make some money after the government took our farms. No one was supposed to get hurt. I didn't even think the guns were loaded." He looked down at his old hands, more ashamed than afraid. "I didn't know..."

The man looked almost sympathetic. It seemed like he understood better than most would. "I believe you didn't mean any harm, but things are as they are."

"Bad luck it was the mayor's son wasn't it." The barber gave a sad little smile, filled with regret.

"Good luck you've had fifty years to make amends for it." He returned the smile in the same kind.

"I've done my best, I suppose." The barber looked up pleadingly "Any chance you'd wait those three weeks, and pretend you'd never seen me?" He knew the answer before he asked the question. Still, a man can hope.

"I'm afraid I need the money, or I'd have tracked down a man who deserved it."

"So you'd kill a man who doesn't deserve it?" Sowwens asked, trying to beat the man in logic, or if nothing else, make him feel sorry for it.

"I'm afraid we all deserve to die. Otherwise, the gods would've made us immortal." The words were soft and sad, unseemly on a man such as him. "If you'd like to say goodbye to your kin, I'd give you that chance."

"I'd rather not." He said sullenly.

"That's a strange choice, but to every man his own." The bounty hunter seemed genuinely puzzled.

"It ain't a hard choice for a good man, I think. If I went to them now, I'd have to explain what I'd done. Honestly, I don't think they'd even believe me." The barber sighed. "Besides my youngest is twenty now and with no children or wife of his own. He's a bit too much of a firebrand for that. He'd try to stop you, and I'm afraid of what would happen if he did."

He nodded at that. "What's his name?"

"Tommy." The barber choked on the name. It was too sad to think he wouldn't see him again.

"Sorry friend. I didn't mean to make this harder than it had to be." He actually did seem sorry for it. "For what it's worth sir." The bounty hunter looked at himself in the mirror admiring the work. "You're the best damn barber I've ever had."

"Thank you, I suppose." He looked at the man again. "It's important to go out on a good note, I think." Sowwens was done fighting. He'd lived a long life and a good one. The truth was he always knew he'd pay for his sin in this life or the next. He'd rather it be this life. At seventy years old there wasn't much more living to be had. In a strange way, he was happy it was over. Always looking over his back, waiting for someone to put a bullet in it. Now that the day had come, it wasn't nearly as bad as he thought. His story had come to an end, and it had been mostly happy. His debt would be paid.

"I'd agree." The bounty hunter pulled out his purse and put four dollars on the counter. It was two more than he'd have charged, a generous tip. "I think it'd be best if we did this somewhere else Mr. Sowwens. I'm assuming one of your children would take over this shop. It'd be hard on him to have to remember that sort of scene with this place."

The barber looked around the store proudly. "I think, you're right." He said thoughtfully "The second one will take it over. The first is a doctor up in Yunta, and the third's a lawyer out in Cooper's

Bay. My youngest is too restless to stay here. I'm afraid he might join the army one day."

"Would you like to write a note, so they won't think you've run off on them?" He nodded towards the pen and paper on the barber's desk.

"Well, my wife died three years back, but I should let my children know not to look for me." He sat down and penned out in shaky handwriting. *I'm gone now. Don't worry after me. Remember to sweep the hair away in the morning. I wouldn't want it to get in the horses' water again.*

"You ready now?" The bounty hunter was getting impatient, but he was polite enough to try and not let it show.

"I'm ready." Politeness deserved politeness back. They walked to the edge of town where the scarred man's camp was.

"I hope you've atoned for your sins." The man pulled out his six-shooter. "I'll make sure they put a white Silesia on your grave."

"I have." Only two men noticed the gunshot. In the end, a gunshot really only mattered to two people.

Jessie Devote looked down at the body. Between the barber and the bounty hunter, he wondered which one of them really deserved to die. "It's for Bo-Bo." He whispered to himself. "It's for Bo-Bo." He kept repeating the chant as he threw the old man on the back of one of his horses. "It's for Bo-Bo."

There were six bodies on four horses. Some had deserved what they got. Some were just desperate men caught in a bad way. Jessie had shot one of his marks in front of his own son. *Who could do a thing like that?* He wondered to himself. He knew the answer, though. A desperate man in a bad way.

Jessie hopped on his own horse. She was a reliable mare. He led the caravan of dead bodies to the nearest town that would warrant a marshal. He tried thinking back to his army days to ignore the corpses he brought. He had marched with his head high back then, but the Puena War was seven years gone. The man who'd won the Iron Circle for bravery and honor was long dead. Necessity had killed him and birthed the hired gun he was now. He tried to remember the way his father had looked at him when the Prime Governor had pinned the Confederacy's highest award on his chest. Jessie had fallen a long way since Puena.

He galloped through the night and into noon the next day until he reached Rory's rest. The town was already bustling with activity. Twenty years ago it had been exactly what its name entailed, a place for some man named Rory to rest his three sheep and too many sons. After more and more people had decided their fortunes lay west, the frontier town had swelled with every sort of person. The beer flowed, and the morals were loose in Rory's Rest. That's what happened when a man hadn't lived in a place long enough to consider it a home. The buildings were thrown together. If the town continued to grow, they'd be reinforced or replaced. If not, they'd be left to fall.

Jesse used the place often because it was close enough to civilization to have the supplies he needed, but it was far enough for the grey sort of law he practiced to be tolerated.

The only structure that would stand the test of time was any buildings associated with the railroad that the town had grown around. John Reard and his company, Union Confederacy, were building the damn trains everywhere in the country. Part of Jessie liked them. They spoke of something new for the world to revel in. Another part of the bounty hunter wanted to cling to the old ways. Besides, John Reard was far too rich for a man as bad off as Jesse to like.

He slowed his horses to a walk when he got to the outskirts of town where the laborers had pitched their tents. The poor mounts had been ridden far too hard in Jessie's attempt to outrun the rot on his victims.

People had started to stare at Jesse. Death always brought a crowd. As miserable as those laborers were, at least they had a life. The bounty hunter had accumulated enough fame from these displays over the years. A few of the more impoverished residents had even tried their own hand at hunting bounties. They hadn't been very successful.

"Serves them right."

"Get em, Jesse!"

Jesse wondered if they'd be half so encouraging had they looked the barber in the eyes when he died. He didn't think they would.

Jesse ignored them and walked deeper into the town. More people looked at him, but their reactions were mixed at best. The only people it didn't seem to bother were the whores. Due to their profession, they'd most likely seen things far worse than Jesse ever wanted to. It wasn't long before he was in front of the small shanty that served as the marshal's office.

He recognized the man sitting out front in his rocking chair, spitting his tobacco into the dirt in front of him. It was Marshal Vernon. They'd served together as sergeants during the Puena War in Andrew Belson's company.

"Well, I'll be damned!" Vernon hopped out of his chair. "Is that Jesse Devote I see?"

"It's me, Vernon." Jessie dismounted his horse and walked to his old friend.

"It's good to see you." Vernon reached his old veiny hand out for the bounty hunter to shake.

"Likewise." Jesse took the hand. He meant it. The gunslinger had always liked Vernon. He couldn't have been under fifty-five and looked every day of it. His hair was greying, and the wrinkles had set in. He still had a lean, wiry strength to him though. Vernon had battled the Puena well and was as tough a bastard as could be found. If Jesse had to fight him, he'd win, but the old fucker would make the bounty hunter remember he'd been in a fight.

"What have we here? Another batch of ne'er-do-wells?" Vernon moved to the corpses, inspecting each of them. "I assume you've got warrants for these unlucky fellows, or I'd have to take you in for murder."

"Here." Jesse reached into his pocket and presented six crumpled pieces of paper.

Vernon took the papers and stared at them for a moment. His eyesight wasn't as good as it had been. "This man can't be younger than seventy years old." He cocked an eyebrow up at the barber's warrant.

"It's still good." Jessie gestured to the papers.

"So it is." He nodded. "How much do I owe you?" Vernon inspected one of the corpse's teeth for some ungodly reason.

"By my count, five thousand." Jesse followed the marshal as he moved from body to body. "Also," he reached into his saddlebag and pulled out a small sack, "I've got these Huego ears. A northeastern tribe tried to get me, but I reckon I'm a bit tougher than they're used to." Jesse raised the sack proudly. "They still sell for fifty each?"

Vernon looked up from his business and checked the warrants. "I'm sorry Jesse." He scratched his scraggly head. "Your count might be five, but the government's is closer three and a half."

Jesse rested his hand on his six-shooter. He did like Vernon, but if he felt the bastard was trying to screw him, there'd be blood all the same. "Now, I know you ain't trying to fuck your good friend." Good friend was a stretch. Jesse didn't have any good friends. They liked each other, but not enough to keep their guns holstered if it came to it. "I know the game." The bounty hunter sneered with menace. "You screw me and pocket the rest."

"Don't do nothing foolish, Jesse." Vernon's hand fell on his own gun. "I ain't trying to do you like that."

"You're an old war buddy," Jesse got ready for his draw, "but if you think I'll take three and a half for this batch and the ears, you ain't as crafty as you were in Puena."

"Half of these bounties only pay full if you take em in alive." Vernon shook the warrants. "As for those ears, I'm supposed to arrest you for having them." He put a hand up to stop Jessie from drawing. "I ain't gonna, but I can't pay you for em neither." The marshal softened his voice. "Three and a half is the old war buddy price."

"I needed that money." Jesse turned around and kicked the dirt.

"I'd have given it to you had you brought these men alive." Vernon took a cautious step forward.

"You know how hard it is to take six prisoners across five hundred miles of hostile ground?" Jesse leveled a finger at the marshal.

"I can't say I've ever been that desperate for money." Vernon finally took his hand off his weapon.

"Well, I am!" Jesse spat into the ground. "They're off the street. Ain't that enough."

"I'm afraid people like a good hanging." Vernon shrugged. "The government's willing to pay more to give it to them."

"And what's this business about you not taking Huego ears?" Jessie narrowed his eyes. "I've been selling you those ears for five years!"

"Haven't you heard?" Vernon spit out a glob of brown spit. "McAllan got elected."

"I've been a bit preoccupied." Jesse shot back sarcastically. "What's that got to do with anything?"

"He outlawed the sale of them." Vernon shook his head. "Some nonsense about making peace with those savages."

Jesse rolled his eyes. "They ain't near as close to savages as you and me."

That made Vernon chuckle. "That's true enough."

"Aye." Jesse rubbed his head.

"You want that three and a half," Vernon held up the warrants, "or do you still think I'm cheating you."

"I don't think you're cheating me," Jesse bit his lip, "but I can't go home with three and a half."

"What kinda trouble are you in?" Vernon took a step forward and put a hand on his friend's shoulder. "You never gambled."

"The kinda trouble I don't want to drag you into." Jesse thought back to his brother, Bo-Bo. "The kinda trouble, makes me wish I hadn't been so hard to kill in Puena."

"Look, I can give you an extra two and a half for the horses." Vernon released his shoulder and looked at the beasts. "They ain't worth that much, you can be sure of that, but it's the government's money." He sighed. "That'll bring you up to six thousand. Is that enough?"

"No, Jesse replied honestly, "but it's better than three and a half."

"I know you don't want to hear it," Vernon looked at him cautiously, "but you could ask Captain Belson for help." He knew the bounty hunter didn't like handouts. The only reason Jesse had taken the exorbitant money for the horses was that he'd felt cheated over the bounties. "Andrew is a good man."

"He is." Jesse wanted nothing more than to write to his old officer for help, but something wouldn't let him. Maybe it was the last bit of pride he held onto. The gunslinger looked at the barber's corpse. How much pride could he honestly have left?

"He's not like those other aristocrats." Vernon seemed prouder, thinking about their leader from the Puena War. "He doesn't see his responsibility as done just cause the war ended." He looked down at his marshal's badge. "He wants to help us build better lives away from the war. He pulled some strings to get me this post, he got Skinny and Hops a job working for John Reard, he even introduced Jimmy to his wife."

"I won't see a good man like him dragged through the mud on my account." Jessie said defiantly. "This is my own business."

"It might not be for long." Vernon cocked an eyebrow up.

"What do you mean by that?" Jessie looked up at the man curiously.

"You really ain't been paying attention, have you?" Vernon chuckled. "The North and South are circling each other like dogs in a ring." He smiled at the thought. "Can't be too long before one of them snaps."

"I don't like the idea of fighting my countrymen. Jesse shook his head. "Even if they are Northerners."

"I'd feel safer with you at my side." Vernon said hopefully. "They'd pay well."

"Not well enough." Jessie shot back.

"If you ever needed honest work, I'm sure they'd make you a marshal too." Vernon knew he wouldn't take the deal, but the old bastard had to try. "You won the Iron Circle. You're one of the heroes, just like Then Ironwill or Andrew's brother, Thomas." Vernon shook his head. "I don't like seeing a hero like you brought to hunting seventy-year-olds for a paycheck."

"Honest work makes honest pay. I can't afford an honest pay." Jesse bit his lip. "Besides, hero means less and less these days."

"I wish you'd let us help you." Vernon said. "We owe you enough."

"I did my duty in Puena, and I'll do it now." Jessie huffed.

"Now, that's that damn pride of yours." Vernon waved his hand hopelessly. "That pride'll kill you one day."

"Pride's all I got left." Jessie took another look at the barber. Even that seemed to be running out.

Vernon went into his shack and came out with the six thousand that was owed "I hope you find your way, Jesse." Vernon handed over the money.

"I think I found it." Jessie pocketed the cash and got on his one remaining horse. "It's just not a path any man should walk."

"Well, I'll be seeing you then." Vernon extended his hand to Jessie which he took. He knew he wasn't going to get much more out Jessie. "Don't be a stranger."

"I won't." Jesse nodded "I'll be back along before winter comes more than likely." A thought struck him before he left. He counted out a few dollars. "Here put a white Silesia on the old man's grave. He deserved that much. The rest can have the usual violet."

"I'll do that." Vernon wasn't particularly honest, but he respected his old friend. Besides, no one was so heartless as to deny a man his flower.

Jesse led his gear and remaining horse to the center of town. He got fewer looks this time due to there being a notable lack of corpses with him. The gunslinger walked up to the inn called the Western Rose. It was where he stayed every time he was in Rory's Rest, which was often.

Jesse tied his stead up to the post outside and walked into the place to be greeted with the smell of cooking meat and decent beer. The proprietor saw him from behind the bar and gave him a welcoming smile. She was a portly woman in her mid-forties, her apron was stained permanently, but the black and white dress underneath was immaculate.

"How are you, Miss Rosy?" He asked politely.

"Same old, same old." Her smile never faltered. "Things don't change much around here you know."

"Well, that's good to hear." He smiled back. 'I'll take whatever's cooking and a stout beer to go with it."

"Good choice." She said and ran off to fetch everything.

While she was gone, he looked around the inn. All the whores pointedly ignored him. They knew he wasn't here for any of them. There were a few miners gambling in the corner, some farmers drank and talked about how things were getting harder, and a small group of soldiers was sitting around telling old war stories that were probably half true. All in all, everything was normal in the Western Rose. It was a place that suited him just fine. It was nice enough that he didn't have to pick rat tails out of his meat, but it wasn't snobby either. There were a few bar fights sometimes when people got too drunk, but Rosy put an end to them pretty quick. People knew each other here, in passing if nothing else. It was a comfortable place to spend his time in a life that was far from easy.

Rosy came back in no time at all with the food and beer. The dinner was a nice beefy stew with a good helping of potatoes, and the beer was fine as it always was. He ate in silence enjoying the meal after weeks of hard rations and whatever whiskey he could pack with him.

When he was finished, Rosy came and collected the dishes. "Is Mary in?" He asked trying to keep the excitement out his voice.

"Oh, she's upstairs." Jessie was thankful she was polite enough not to say she was fucking someone else. "I'll send her down whenever she's ready."

Jessie ordered another beer and waited for a while, then another when he was done with that one. All in all, it was about half an hour before she came down the stairs. She was followed by a handsome, young soldier with a happy grin on his face. Jessie hated him immediately but wasn't petty enough to start a brawl over some unsuspecting soldier spending time with what he probably thought was a common whore.

Maybe it was just wishful thinking, but Jesse liked to think her face lit up a bit when she saw him. "Jesse!" She hurried down the steps. The soldier looked a bit upset at having been forgotten so quickly, but after a glance at Jesse's scarred face and the six-shooter at his side, he thought better of saying anything.

"Hello, Mary." He responded. The girl may have been a whore, but to Jessie's eyes... Well, he wasn't a poet after all, and it would be improper to say he loved her. Still, she was more than a whore to the gunslinger.

She hurried him into the room she came out of and sat him down on the bed. They looked at each other for a second before either of them talked. Jessie knew she was twenty-five because of a series of careful questions he'd asked, and she looked it too. She didn't like to talk about anything too closely related to her past, but he knew how to ask her after a few months of them meeting together, and age seemed a safe thing to inquire over. She was small too, even for a woman, not tiny exactly, but obviously not overly useful for anything farm related. Her long brown hair was well groomed so that it circled her face like a little heart. Her eyes were so dark you, couldn't really tell where the pupils started, and her tan skin meant she might have had a bit of Puena in her or maybe Huego.

She was beautiful simply put, not in the classical sense. She wasn't pampered enough for that. Most men would have said she was cute as a button or some such nonsense. Everyone found her attractive, as she claimed the highest price of any woman in Rory's Rest. However, most men were fools, and Jesse had a special place in his heart for things like her. Things who'd gotten less than they deserved.

She smiled her broad smile at him. Jessie had been around long enough to tell when a smile was real. She was happy to see him, and that made him smile too, though he doubted it looked nearly as pretty. There was a sadness in her, too small and far away for anyone not looking to notice, but it was there. It made him want to make her happy. "I brought you something." He reached into his pack and brought out a book and a white cloth carefully packed away so as not to be damaged.

Her eyes went wide. "What is it!"

He gave her the book. "It's one of Viverent's poem books." He said suddenly embarrassed. "I know you're learning to read, and I liked it, so I thought you might too."

"I love it." She said softly. Then kissed him. "What's this?" She put her hand on the white wrapping.

Jessie's face went red as he unfolded it. "It seems stupid now, but at the time it seemed all sorts of romantic." He pulled out a red rose pressed so it wouldn't go bad. "I traded some things for it up in Huego country." He tried not to make it sound like he'd gone through too much trouble, when in fact he'd almost been burned alive by two dozen Huego's getting the damn flower. "They don't like it much over there anyway. They say it's bad luck."

She chuckled a bit. "You brought me a flower that means bad luck?" She asked playfully.

"No, not that exactly." The gunslinger said defensively, the smile and hand she put on his leg let him know she wasn't serious, but he still cursed his clumsy tongue

"Don't worry I know you'd never give me anything like that." She looked at him maybe not entirely lovingly but affectionately. It warmed his heart. "So why give it to me then?"

"Well, it doesn't mean that to me." He said calming down a bit knowing she hadn't taken any offense by it. "My mother used to say give it to someone good but with bad luck." If it seemed odd to talk about his mother in the presence of a whore, neither of them noticed.

She smiled sadly and ran a hand through his hair. "I don't feel so unlucky right now." She kissed him again softly and undid the buttons on his blouse with a practiced hand. They laid down on the bed. The world around them meant nothing in that moment. Jesse forgot about his debts, he forgot about the barber's family, even about his brother for a moment. Mary forgot about whatever it was she needed to forget. They undressed quickly but not rushed, never rushed. It wasn't the typical mechanical grunting and thrusting that usually accompanied a bounty hunter and a whore.

It was different, gentler but with passion. The passion of two people who needed each other if only for a day. Jessie had had his share of whores and the rare women who wanted to spend a night with a dangerous man. This was different though. While it was happening, he wondered how he ever felt solace in another woman's arms. Later he was sure when another girl gave him a seductive stare or a whore who was reasonably priced came his way, he'd take her for a tumble and regret it after, but at the moment, he couldn't think of any storybook princess or aristocrat beauty he'd rather be with.

They moved together in the way only two people who knew each other could. Some married men claimed that sex lost its luster after you'd done it too long with the same person. With Mary, it didn't. Every time it was better than before like he was coming closer to loving her. That's not to say he knew every little fact about her. Judging by her dark complexion he doubted he even knew her real name, but, Jesse knew everything important about her, even if he didn't know where she was born or if she came from a good family. *I know enough for this.* He thought as he felt her body slide along his and the arch of her back.

After they were finished, they laid together, neither one wanting to move. Usually Rosy would be pounding away at the door saying the time was up, but she knew the two of them were different. They could spend the night together under her roof.

Her head was on the nape of his shoulder, and her finger made little circles on his chest. It felt just as good as the sex had been, in a different way. When they were in the middle of it all, it was like eating a good meal. With her resting on his arm, it was like having enough food in your pack so you knew you could eat well the next day. While that may have sounded less romantic to a poet, a soldier would understand what he meant. It didn't even mean that he could have her as many times as he wanted, with her in the same bed. It was knowing she was there. It felt the same as having enough food.

No matter what happened, the world couldn't hurt him when they were together.

She sighed softly, and it brought him out of his trance. "I want you to come with me to Pentsville." He said as much to himself as to her.

She lifted her head a bit to look at his face. She looked at his eyes in a way that made him think she didn't see the scars as everyone else did. Sure, she saw them. They were as much a part of him as his own name. However, instead of abject horror or admiration for his imagined toughness, she understood what they really were. They were what had made him, as much as the medals he had. She saw a beautiful painting where others just saw lumps of hard flesh. "Usually when a man offers me something like that there's a few strings attached." She looked at him even deeper than before. "I don't think there is with you though."

Most men would look at her and think she was a silly whore because she was always smiling and kind. Some would even think she was stupid. She wasn't. She was kind because not many had been kind to her, and she knew the value of it. She smiled because showing too much of how she felt was painful. She'd recently started showing more to Jessie, though. He liked what he saw for the most part. She was intelligent in her own way. She'd picked up reading faster than anyone he'd seen, and she knew more about the world than she let on. There were other things there though that made him sad, even angry. Nothing as good as Mary deserved to be treated the way he knew she had, even if she wouldn't admit it.

"I just want you to come with me is all." He said regretting he said anything at all. "Maybe when I pay my debts and I make some extra money…"

"Would you marry me then?" She asked. "Would you make an honest woman of me?"

He looked at her. This time he didn't see her looks, profession, or anything else that didn't say anything about her. "You are an honest woman." He kissed her softly. "In every way that matters to the Three or me."

"Good." She kissed him and settled back onto his shoulder. "I'd like that."

"Good." He said not knowing what else he could say. "I'll do it you know. I keep my word you can ask anyone."

"No one who lives by that thing," she gestured to the pistol on the dresser, "can really promise anything about tomorrow, I think."

"I'm the best at it you know." He didn't say it to impress her or brag, it was a fact,

"I've heard the stories about you. I know you are." She sighed sadly. "But the graveyard is full of great fighters with bad luck."

"I don't feel unlucky." He said and kissed her head gently. "I'll always come back to you. I promise, and once I get the money, I'll put that gun away for good."

"What will you do then?" She twisted her body to look at him.

"Try to be a good man I think." He said stroking her hair.

She smiled at that. "Oh Jessie Devote, you are a good man." She kissed him again. "In every way that matters to God and me."

He smiled back. "I like hearing that even if it's not true." Jessie sighed. "I'd like to be a carpenter. I'm good with my hands, and it's safe."

"You'd make a fine carpenter." She said with a smile "But even if you leave this bar and get shot the second your feet hit honest dirt, if you leave here and find a woman who deserves you, and you never come back to me, you've done right by me, and I'll be happy to have known you." She said, and he actually believed it.

"If you find some aristocrat who knows a damn thing about good women and gives you everything the Three intended you to have," he kissed her again, "you're better than anything I deserve." That sad little look in her eye that seemed small and far away when he'd first seen her seemed smaller and farther away, and he thought she believed it. Mary didn't believe anything that wasn't true.

They settled back into each other and sat happily. At first, they were simply patron and whore, but Jessie knew a good thing when he found one. He'd passed up enough in his youth to recognize it in his older age. They'd met six months ago when she first came to town. He'd come to visit her because she was pretty and not overly expensive. After a while, though they'd started to talk in small ways at first then larger ones. Then talking about the weather or asking him to tell her war stories had changed. She'd forgotten to ask him for the money enough times to let him know she hadn't actually forgotten, and he'd started giving her more without telling her. Then she started to look genuinely happy when he came to Rosy's, and he'd started bringing her presents. Then they talked about each other. Never anything personal about each other's past, but their future which was more important anyway. It wasn't close to something that belonged in a storybook love, but Jessie and Mary didn't belong in storybooks. She was the first good thing that had happened to him in a long time, and if she was the last, he'd count himself a lucky man. They fell asleep, he could only really sleep when they were together.

———◆•◆•◆———

When they woke up in the morning, they had each other again. It wasn't as happy as it had been before. It was more like they were both holding onto each other desperately not wanting to part ways.

"When are you going to come back?" She asked trying to keep the desperation out of her voice as he laced up his boots.

"As soon as I can." He said looking back at her. "I have some business in Pentsville to attend to."

"You didn't answer the question?" She said obviously a bit annoyed.

"Because I don't want to lie to you." He looked back at his boots. "I don't know when, but with luck, I might have enough to do what we talked about."

"I hope you do." She smiled at him happily. "But I don't think I should hold my breath."

"Maybe you shouldn't." He said as he buttoned up his shirt. "But I'll do it as soon as I can. I hope you know that."

"Good." She said, but there was a bit of doubt in her. She'd been hurt too often to trust in a happy future.

He finished getting dressed quicker than he'd have liked to, and as he holstered his pistol. He put some money on the dresser, so she wouldn't see him do it. It was more than a man in his position should have left, but then again, she was much better than a man in his position deserved. She didn't like it when he gave her money, but she needed it. She wouldn't even accept it until he told her to save it for the day he came back for good. Still, he didn't like her seeing him do it.

They parted with a kiss. The bounty hunter walked downstairs and left some money for Rosy to thank her for the room. Then he walked out the porch and took his first step onto honest dirt without being shot. Jesse looked up at her window and saw her looking at him. He smiled up at her happy for the first time in too long.

Then he saw a young farmer stare up at her too and count the money in his hand. After all, it wasn't a storybook.

Present Day
McAllan's Story

"**A**re you trying to start a war, Coleson?" Prime Governor of the Confederacy McAllan slammed his fist against his desk. "A fight like this won't end well for anyone. The Southern senators stood in a semi-circle around the executive desk, smug and self-satisfied.

They were helmed by their leader Senator Matthew Coleson. Why anyone would choose to follow a slimy weasel like Coleson, was beyond McAllan. The senator took his cue. "It's not as though we want conflict Prime Governor," he mocked regret, "but certain demands are not being met. We wish to ease you to this decision." The sneer never left his face. It had the same demeanor as a cat pawing at a cornered mouse. "If the Northerners wish to stop the flow of manufactured goods to the South, it is completely within your rights." Coleson might have cut an impressive figure. He was a handsome, tall man, with a decent chin and cheekbones. However, his greased down black hair and green eyes, that always seemed to hold mild distaste, made him slightly unlikeable.

"You can't eat textiles and steel." McAllan growled the words. He was old now, but there was still the fire of his youth deep down, and men remembered what he was capable of in his youth. A good many of them had watched his boxing matches. Even if they hadn't, McAllan was well over six feet and muscled like an ox. The Prime Governor's tone, matched with his reputation and stature, was enough to sufficiently cur the uppity senator for one glorious moment.

"No, you can't, more's the shame." Coleson regained his posture and sneer quick enough, to his credit.

"This isn't about politics or power anymore." McAllan stared down at his desk, desperate. "This is about lives." He turned his gaze back to the senators. "How many men will starve? How many women and children?"

"Then they can remember who feeds them." Coleson sneered.

"Three above Coleson, this isn't just your south and my north." McAllan desperately tried to reign in his anger. If he lost his cool, there'd be no chance of peace. "This is one country. We are one people!"

"We used to be." Coleson scoffed distastefully.

"What's that supposed to mean?" McAllan narrowed his eyes.

Coleson turned a look to the Prime Governors aide who stood quietly behind the desk. "I think you know what I mean."

McAllan looked back at the boy. His name was Timothy. He'd been his aide for a year. His black skin marked him as an immigrant from the Souren continent. He was a bright lad and fiercely loyal to McAllan. McAllan would not let that loyalty only go one way. "I will forget you said that exactly once." He held up a finger and whispered in white-hot fury. "One more time and I will beat you to death in this office. I swear it by everything I hold holy in this world."

All of the senators took a step back. "Coleson, just leave it." One of the men behind him said. The Prime Governor knew him as Jameson, the most reasonable of the group.

"I'm sorry, Prime Governor." Coleson finally found his words. He wasn't used to such candor.

"Don't apologize to me." McAllan kept the dangerous whisper.

"I think it's inappropriate for a senator to apologize to a-" Coleson started.

"Fucking do it!" McAllan screamed before he had a chance to finish that sentence and the Prime Governor had to keep his oath. People said a lot of things about McAllan, but they knew he kept his word.

"My apologies." He nodded to the black aide.

"It's already forgiven." Timothy smiled back.

"Now may we proceed?" Coleson asked, trying desperately to change the subject.

"Go ahead." McAllan had finally retrieved his calm.

"Here are our demands." Coleson pulled a piece of paper out of his pocket. "We want harsher laws enforced on immigration."

"Who do you think it is that sows and reaps those plantations you're so proud of?" McAllan resisted the urge to call the man an idiot. "It's immigrants from Souren, Inte, Thyro, and anywhere else on the damn earth." He gave the man an appraising look. "Do you even know anything about agriculture?"

"That aside, we believe that they are deluding the greatness we fought the Anthanii to forge." Coleson pushed on unabashed.

"I understand your point." In truth, McAllan didn't. It seemed a horribly outdated worldview. The reality was, that greatness hadn't been forged just because they'd won a war. Then Ironwill had won a chance when he defeated the Anthanii a century ago. A chance that would have meant nothing if farmers, industrialist, and inventors hadn't fought their own war day after day to build something out of that chance and a great many of those men had not been born in the Confederacy. Besides the far west of the Confederacy was empty and waiting to be filled. "If the individual provinces refuse to allow immigrants than I don't know that I have the authority to stop them." He admitted. "However, I also don't have the authority to force provinces not to let them in." Everyone in the room knew that the provinces that allowed the flow of new immigrants would quickly outpace those that did not. The senators understood, despite their racism, they would need to follow suit.

Coleson tried to hide his disgust. It had probably never occurred to the senator that a leader should admit the limit of his power. "Our second demand is that you place heavier restrictions on the northern industrialist, namely John Reard." Coleson read off of his paper, then back up to the Prime Governor. "We believe they have been left unfettered for too long. We fear that John Reard, in particular, will soon grow more powerful than the government."

That made McAllan laugh. "Oh, that's what you fear is it?" He thought back to John. "Then I hate to be the one to tell it to you, but your fears have already come to fruition."

"What are you talking about?" Coleson narrowed his eyes.

"I'm saying that we have soldiers, cannons, and ships." McAllan shrugged. "We could march in and take everything from that man if our government was so disposed." The Prime Governor leaned back in his chair. "Then John Reard could get it all back if he simply threatened to take one day off work." McAllan respected that man more than most. "He has helped build this country more than any warrior ever has. Our navy and armies could never compete with the powers of Thyro, but he has made their economies completely dependent on the goods we produce." He waved his hand to illustrate the point. "Mr. Reard has built railroads that have made transportation safer and easier. He produces half the clothes we wear in his factories. Three above, he even provides the kerosine you use to light your house."

"He can extort us for these things." Coleson seemed indignant at the implication that a northern businessman, born a starving orphan in the streets of Mainstead, was more powerful than he was.

"I suppose he could," McAllan admitted, "but he hasn't, and he won't." The Prime Governor leaned forward in his seat. "Do you know why? It's because he understands it's bad for his profit margins. If he raises them too much, more businesses would appear to move him out." McAllan sighed. "If I can't force the provinces to my will, I assure you, there is no way I could make John Reard cross the street if he wasn't disposed to doing so." He knew the real reason they hated Reard. It was because he didn't play their games or try to get into their aristocrat society. True John Reard wasn't a very likable fellow. He was cold and distant. His gray eyes always seemed to be calculating something, and his lean, hungry look made people uncomfortable, but he was fair. McAllan would not go after a fair man, even if he could.

"Well, we shall see how his profit margins fair when we stop trading our raw material to him." Coleson looked disgusted.

"Hopefully, it won't come to that." McAllan wasn't worried about the cotton or John Reard. He was worried about the precious grain and livestock. John would adapt. He was clever that way. He'd find somewhere else to get cotton or discover something else to spin clothes out of, but the people could not adapt their stomachs to eat rocks.

"It won't if you accept our next two demands." Coleson returned to his list. "We want you to repeal all legislation restricting the Old Religion." He paused. "And swear to pass no more."

That sentence hung in the air for a moment before it hit the ground. This was what they really wanted. "No." McAllan had tried to explain and compromise the rest of the demands. He would not compromise this. Some things required resolve.

"The Ironwill constitution gives us express freedom of religion." Coleson was furious.

"Worship whoever you want." McAllan put an edge on his voice. "I will not let this country be infested with Demons for a moment longer than I have to." He thought of his wife lying in her bed. "Count yourself lucky I have not hung everyone in a crimson cloak."

"You let the New Church practice wherever they want!" Coleson screamed indignantly. There was a truth to his words.

"The New Church never drove a child insane." McAllan growled back.

"The Old Religion has made us powerful." Coleson almost seemed reasonable. "It has let our crops grow round the year. It has stymied disaster."

"Aye," McAllan considered what to say next. "It has given so much you have been blinded to the cost."

"Then there will be no trade from us." Coleson said indignantly.

"You would starve men for Demons?" McAllan stared incredulously.

"We will starve you to save our rights," Coleson shot back angry, "by the law of Then Ironwill."

"He didn't want this." McAllan said almost to himself. "He didn't want us strangling each other like snakes in an overcrowded nest.

"It's a shame we only have his will and not his wants isn't it." Coleson smiled like a cat toying with a mouse.

"It's a shame we only have spoiled children in your offices and not men." McAllan shot back.

"Are you calling us Southerners children?" Coleson's indignity was back.

"No," McAllan pointed to the Southern senators behind him, "I'm calling them children." He turned his gaze back to Coleson. "I'm calling you a girl in a queer type of dress."

"I will not be spoken to like this!" Coleson's face went bright red.

"And I will not sit here and be demanded to do things against this country's best interest." McAllan was slowly losing his temper. "I will not be extorted by the likes of you."

"In case you had forgotten, it was me who won the Puena War." Coleson made it seem like he'd singlehandedly fought off the Puena invaders.

"I hadn't forgotten it." McAllan stood to let his full stature show. Men forgot, from time to time, how large he was when he sat.

Standing helped remind them. "I hadn't forgotten because I never heard anyone say it. To my knowledge, it was General Fennis who organized the campaign, marines who sacked their capital, and Andrew Belson who won the last battle." He counted off the events on his hand. "I seem to have forgotten what battle you fought in."

"Are you questioning my courage." Coleson was seething with rage.

"I do question things from time to time." McAllan admitted. "I question my political views, the nature of life, even the existence of the Three." He sat back in his chair. "There's only two things I always deny, the Old Religion and your courage."

"Those are dueling words!" Coleson screamed.

"They are aren't they." McAllan stood again. He was old, but he could certainly beat Coleson to death. "I've always been more of a boxer though." That suitably frightened the senators. "I know for a fact that you shed no blood against Puena. I also know for a fact it was you who started the damn war."

"Those are slanderous lies." Coleson backpedaled from the conversation.

"We both know they aren't." McAllan smiled. "I've talked to the men on your payroll who raided their farms." That was a bit of an exaggeration. He hadn't talked to them directly, but he trusted the source.

It had the expected effect on Coleson though. "They're liars." *I'll have the'ir tongues.* That's what he really meant. "Well, I can see this conversation is going nowhere profitable." Coleson turned around to walk out the room.

"Before you go, what was your last request?" McAllan was a bit curious.

"You still want to hear it?" Coleson cocked an eyebrow up.

"You came to my office with four requests." McAllan sat back down in his chair. "I only heard three."

"Our last *demand* was that you refuse to let Thomas Belson into our country." Coleson was level. This didn't seem like his other request. He didn't have the same cat-like smile. It seemed like he was scared.

"Why?" McAllan stared up at him. "He's the greatest hero to ever come from the Confederacy. He's even from the South."

"You're right. He is from the Confederacy," Coleson admitted, "but he's not a Confederacy man anymore."

"Once a Confederacy man always a Confederacy man." McAllan didn't dismiss it out of hand though. "He's done great things for Thyro. He could help bring this country together." He squinted his eyes. "This isn't just because he worked for the New Church, is it?"

"No, it's not." Coleson looked around carefully. "You and I rarely agree, but I believe Thomas Belson could destroy this country. You're right, I do have provincial interest for the rest of my demands, but that one was for the good of us all. Thomas Belson is dangerous."

"I don't know that I can keep him out." McAllan shook his head.

"I don't know that anyone can control Thomas Belson." Coleson turned to leave the room. "That's what scares me more than anything." He went out the door, and McAllan was left to think on that.

"Do you think he's right, sir?" Timothy asked when they were alone.

"I don't know," McAllan admitted, "but I do know that if we say he can't return, he'll take our country by force."

"He's one man." Timothy cocked an eyebrow up.

"No, I'm one man." McAllan waved his hand helplessly. "One day, if you keep studying, you'll be one man, as well." He shook his head. "One man can change the course of history. Never forget that," he sighed, "but Thomas Belson is a force of nature. I don't know that I'd bet on an army one hundred thousand strong if he was on the other side with a rusty spoon and a donkey."

"The stories can't all be true." Timothy posited.

"They can't all be false either." McAllan shot back. "If even a fraction of them are, then he's the most dangerous man ever born this side of the ocean, maybe the most dangerous on the other side too."

McAllan looked around his office. It wasn't much for the highest political figure in the country. It wasn't much for a middle-class business owner, either. The room was sparse, with one painting of Then Ironwill on the walls to liven it up. The only piece of furniture was the wooden desk, his chair, and two more on the other side. There was a candle in the corner to help him read when it was dark, and that was it. McAllan was a proud man, but he took pride in deeds not rooms. He'd been spending more and more time in this room. Part of it was the work. The Confederacy was at a pivotal point in its history and McAllan would not be remembered as the captain who slept at the wheel. There was another part he didn't talk about, though. McAllan couldn't even think about it without feeling the cold blade of guilt stab his gut. His wife Toddy needed her husband, but her husband couldn't bear to look at her. To see her caused pain, to ignore her caused pain. She drove his fanatical quest to fix his nation, but in his most private thoughts, he wondered if he was being driven off a cliff.

"How's your wife, sir?" Timothy asked. He was a sharp boy. He knew what his leader was thinking.

"She's doing better." McAllan lied. He didn't want the boy to carry his burden for him.

"I'm happy to hear it." Timothy knew he was lying, but he wouldn't press the issue. The young Souren was smart that way.

"Thank you for defending me to Coleson." The black aide nodded his respect at the Prime Governor. "You didn't have to, though. I've heard worse."

"I imagine you have," McAllan cocked an eyebrow, "but what is shouldn't always be. Besides, an affront to you is an affront to me." The Souren like all immigrants had met racism from those already established in the Confederacy. The difference was their black skin made them much easier to see as the other.

"What's our next item for the day?" Timothy wanted to change the subject. He didn't like talking about race. It wasn't his way. McAllan had chosen the boy as his aide over many more experienced candidates because Timothy was fiercely committed to being judged as Timothy, not a Souren.

"I have some dreary paperwork to do, but I'm expecting a visitor." McAllan reached under his desk and pulled out a bottle of cheap whiskey.

"You mean Samugy." Timothy rolled his eyes.

"Aye." McAllan answered. "I'm assuming from your tone that you're not looking forward to the meeting."

"The man is even more racist than Coleson." The black aide gritted his teeth.

"No, he's not." McAllan poured the whiskey and took a sip. "Coleson says that filth because he actually believes it. Samugy says it because he wants to know your measure." The Prime Governor savored the whiskey for a moment. "Why don't you shoot back at him? He's a Huego, even lower than you on their arbitrary totem pole."

"I'd rather talk about merit than skin tone." Timothy answered coldly. "Besides, he's one of your key advisors, and I'm just an aide. It would be inappropriate."

"You're not just my aide, and you know it." McAllan smiled at his protege. "You have my explicit permission to respond to whatever he throws at you." They both heard Samugy coming before he was in the room. He liked to announce himself with a sarcastic song of his own composition. His horrible voice didn't make it much better.

"Fearless leader what will you do?

I've got a great big mission for you!

We heard you have pluck and we heard you have style!

He'll always go the extra mile!"

Samugy was still humming when he entered the office. "They're letting Souren's drink with white men now?" He clucked disapprovingly. "Be careful, or one day he'll forget to look in the mirror and think he's white. They're not a terribly clever breed." Samugy was spymaster of all the Confederacy, and he looked the part. He was tall, slim, and in a way that made no sense to McAllan, he seemed greasy. In addition, those dark evil eyes didn't make him any more endearing. His jet black hair and almost red complexion made it clear to anyone perceptive he had at least a bit of Huego in him. Still, the man was too cunning by half, and his network of spies made him seem almost omniscient.

Timothy looked back at McAllan who gave the boy a nod. "Would you mind terribly if I borrowed your ears? I have some debts that need to be paid." Timothy turned back to the Huego.

"They're lending to the Souren now?" Samugy shook his head. "Times must be worse than I thought."

"Oh nothing so formal as that," Timothy let his sharp wit show, "I just told them your mother was in town, and I was strapped for

money to pay her. Everyone knows how fun mama Samugy can be."
McAllan tried to hide his laughter, but it was hard. The boy had a
sharp tongue when he let it loose.

"Too much fun for a Souren to know what to do with." Samugy
gave the Prime Governor a disapproving look.

McAllan finally recovered from his laughing fit. "Timothy
you're a clever lad, but few men in the world can match tongues
with Samugy for too long." He smiled at the aide. "Go work on your
studies."

"You let them read too?" Samugy mocked surprise. "You might
as well just give them our womenfolk."

Timothy stopped for a moment at that. McAllan half expected
the boy to lash out angrily, but he surprised him. "If you think
his tongues clever you should meet his mother." Timothy whistled
admiringly. "I'll go back to my studies, but I don't think the memory
of Mama Samugy will let me focus."

McAllan didn't even try to hide his laughter this time. Samugy
scowled at the boy. "Go read your books." It was a rare defeat for
the Huego. No doubt he'd be better prepared next time, but this
exchange went to Timothy. The Souren boy left the room with a
smile.

McAllan nodded at the Huego. "Do you want a drink?"

Samugy shook his head. "I don't drink."

"Really?" McAllan didn't know why that surprised him, but it
did. Samugy seemed like the drinking sort.

"Really." The Huego nodded. "My wife doesn't like it."

"You have a wife?" That was also news to McAllan. He couldn't
see the Huego as a family man.

"I do," Samugy replied, "She's pregnant with our first child."

"Why have I never heard about this?" McAllan scratched his
head.

"You never ask." Samugy smiled. "I try not to give any
information when I don't have too. It helps cultivate my enigma."

"Anything else I should know about my most trusted advisor?"
McAllan chuckled.

"I have a dog." Samugy smiled back. "Also, I shouldn't be your
most trusted anything."

"I fear I am in a curious spot." McAllan cocked an eyebrow up.
"I could listen to a less competent more trustworthy fellow or you."

The Prime Governor took another sip of whiskey. "I've never been a man to fear competence. Besides, there's not another politician in power who would hold a Huego so close."

"It's true. We're an untrustworthy breed." Samugy loved their little sparring matches before the real talk of politics began.

"On the contrary, I've always found the Huego's to be rigidly honorable." McAllan leaned back in his chair. "If anything, you're an exception to the rule."

"I'm adaptable." Samugy tapped the desk. "I can become more white than the white man. I can become more Souren than the Souren. Some men view everything as an opponent to beat. I see the pieces on the board as assets to use." Samugy sighed. "You're right my people are honorable. Honor seems to oppose progress though, so I left to find a better side."

"You don't think me honorable?" McAllan asked.

"It would be better to say I don't think you opposed to progress." Samugy leaned in. "I think honor lies at your core, but it has been mixed with cunning and purpose to forge an alloy that oft escapes the rigid."

"Then tell me what you know." McAllan needed the information sorely. He'd been warned about the canceling of trade by the Huego. Even if he pretended he didn't to Coleson, the warning had probably saved lives.

"I know a certain group of senators left calling you an up jumped boxer." Samugy started. "I know they had a list of demands that you wouldn't accept. I know last night you met with your minister of war and commerce. I know they are two the three people you'd need to speak with if you're about to start a war." Samugy gave a large wry smile. "I know the third sits before you now."

"I know these things too." McAllan waved his hands in dismissal. "I pay you to tell me what I don't know."

Samugy rolled his eyes. "I know that pro-war propaganda has already been spread amongst the South, but you're probably aware of that."

"I am." McAllan responded.

"I know of a Treibian girl who works for a certain retired southern general." Samugy leaned in closer like he was speaking the ultimate truth. "I know she says he's had his uniforms tailored again. I know she says he's been polishing his swords more often."

"I'm assuming you speak of General Fennis." McAllan narrowed his eyes.

"That'd be the one." Samugy lowered his voice to a whisper.

"An old veteran gaining some weight and getting nostalgic doesn't prove anything." McAllan shook his head.

"No, I suppose it doesn't," Samugy mocked agreement, "but another trusted servant tells a more damning story." He sat back in his chair. The Huego always seemed comfortable. "He tells that Fennis sent his daughters off to Anthanii under strict orders to stay there until it's safe again." Samugy paused for dramatic effect. "He tells that Fennis has been giving more sermons to his sons about how a man must do what he thinks is right, no matter the cost."

"It sounds like this trusted servant should be less trusted." McAllan mused.

"Absolutely not! Fennis inspires fanatical loyalty from all around him." Samugy shook his head at the foolishness of it. "They know he is a good man and none would betray him." The Huego chuckled a bit. "However, that trusted servant has a trusted drinking companion who he speaks to about his master's erratic behavior." Samugy wagged his finger. "That trusted drinking companion should be less trusted."

"Well, we know that he's been meeting with Coleson." McAllan scratched his head. "All these things alone would prove nothing, but..." He trailed off.

"But together they paint a clearer picture." Samugy finished for him.

"He's the greatest general since Then Ironwill." McAllan gritted his teeth. "If he goes to war against us, it won't be an easy fight."

"Fennis could make things difficult for us. If you want me to, I can..." Samugy trailed off, miming a noose. When he saw the look of horror on McAllan's face, he added, "They can make it look like an accident. They're very good."

"And can you promise me that there isn't chance your man won't botch the job?" McAllan completely forgot about the whiskey for the first time.

"Oh he'll die, that's for sure." Samugy shifted a bit under McAllan's gaze. "and it wouldn't trace directly back to you." The Huego paused as if calculating something. "But..."

"But there's a chance people would talk." McAllan finished for him and rubbed his temples.

"Precisely!" The spy exclaimed a bit too loudly and a bit too enthusiastically for McAllan's taste.

"Better not." McAllan shook his head. "That could end any hope for peace. The man is a hero after all." He put his hand in his head and looked up. "I haven't given up on peace yet." He sighed again. "Besides, for all his faults Fennis is a good man, and I'm not in the business of killing good men, or anyone else without due process." The Prime Governor frowned. "If I can convince him to give up this war, others will follow."

"That's a slim hope." Samugy grimaced.

"I've lived my entire life hanging onto slim hopes." McAllan chuckled and drank more. "From the boxing ring, to law school, to this office, slim hopes have served me well."

"That could mean you're due to fail." Samugy shrugged.

"Let's not jinx it," McAllan frowned, "but while we're on the subject of slim hopes, what do you know of Thomas Belson?

That stopped Samugy in his tracks. "I've heard the stories…"

"Everyone's heard the stories." McAllan waved dismissively. "I want to hear the truth."

"My reach doesn't extend quite so well in Thyro," Samugy admitted, "but I think it's safe to say he didn't fly a dragon to take off Thaniel's head." The Huego almost seemed scared. "Also, the king of Ragtow probably didn't give him his twelve virgin daughters, considering he's only got two, and ones far from a virgin and there's a reason the other one is."

"So the stories are false." McAllan cocked his head to one side.

"Some of them are," Samugy bit his lip, "but they're false in the most terrifying way."

"What do you mean?" McAllan asked even though he thought he already knew the answer.

"I mean Thomas Belson did take Thaniel's head." Samugy surveyed the room as if searching for help. "He beat the greatest leader Thyro's seen since Imor fell. One Constable, not even twenty years old, with one regiment, did what six nations and ten more experienced men from his order couldn't. Thomas Belson turned the Rose Petal Throne to ash and broke Kran over his knee." The Huego paused. "People couldn't understand how he did it, so they made up a story about a dragon." Samugy looked the Prime Governor in the eyes again. "The truth is far more unsettling. Thomas Belson didn't need a dragon. People find it easier to believe in a mythical, fire-breathing creature than his actual deeds. If that doesn't scare you then, you've lost your sense."

"He had help." McAllan implored the man. "He had Anthanii backing him, along with their allies." McAllan thought for a moment. "Also there were other Constables there."

Samugy laughed at that. "When he finally got to the war most of the other Constable had been killed, the rest wouldn't survive long after. Anthanii and her allies were almost at the negotiating table." The Huego seemed uncomfortable. That was rare. "Thomas Belson was an afterthought at the time. A desperate play to send a fifteen-year-old Confederacy boy to defend the rest of Thyro." Samugy paused. "He won all the same. Mark my words, he would have won that war with a rusty spoon and a donkey if that's all they'd given him."

"I think that's a bit of an exaggeration." McAllan narrowed his eyes.

"It's not." Samugy swallowed nervously. "But the story about Ragtow and her kings twelve virgin daughters is even more terrifying."

"I can't imagine anything more terrifying than Thomas Belson with a rusty spoon but continue." McAllan waved his hand.

"Ragtow was a small, unimportant city surrounded by more than ten thousand men." Samugy started and then stopped to think for a moment on how to say it. "He wasn't under orders to defend it. Some neighboring lord gave him five hundred untrained peasants on a whim." The Huego rubbed his head. "He beat them anyway, but why did he beat them?" Samugy reached across the table and drank the whiskey straight from the bottle to calm himself. Evidently, he was more scared of Thomas Belson than his wife. That was terrifying. "Every man alive can empathize with a hero valiantly defending a city to spend a night with twelve beautiful virgins. That story was added later because it made sense, so I'll ask you again, why did he do it?"

"Perhaps he was a moral man who wanted to see a peaceful city stay free." McAllan suggested.

Samugy laughed coldly at that. "Calling anyone who lives under the Lord of Ragtow free, is a bigger lie than dragons. As for a peaceful city, as soon as the ten thousand men were eliminated, and they were eliminated, Ragtow started oppressing all it's neighbors too." The Huego sighed. "He won the battle because other men told him he couldn't."

"That is a terrifying prospect." McAllan admitted.

"Exactly!" Samugy was happy the Prime Governor finally saw the truth of it all. "You trust me because you know what moves me. I follow you because I know what drives you." The Huego paused for a moment. "Politics is the game of knowing with what currency to buy a man. When you know what a man wants at his core, he belongs to you. Sex, gold, honor, even purpose we can give a man to do our will. On the matter of Thomas Belson, they all seem to be momentary distractions for what he really wants."

McAllan nodded. "And what is it that Thomas Belson wants?"

"When you die and meet the Three ask them for me, will you?" Samugy smiled with no humor in him. "They might be the only ones that know. I don't even think Thomas himself really understands what he's seeking."

"The question remains, if it comes to war will he fight," McAllan poured another drink and sipped on it, "and if so, who will he fight for?"

"He has family in the South." Samugy answered as best he could. "His brother is Andrew Belson, a hero in his own right. Andrew is wise for his age, and he sits squarely in the anti-war camp, but if it comes to war he won't fight against his own people. We'll find Andrew in Fennis's army."

"You think Thomas will follow his brother's lead?" McAllan asked worried about the prospect.

"I don't think Thomas follows anyone's lead, but fighting against his own family may be too much, even for him." Samugy frowned. "The letter we received says he retired, but he's not the sort to sit idle during a war." The Huego thought for a moment. "Behind all the shit about immigrants, Reard, and provincial rights, what's the root cause of the rift between North and South?"

"The Old Religion." McAllan answered softly. "Thomas Belson's a Constable. He's sworn to fight against the Demons and the Old Priest. If he follows his creed, he'll fight for us."

"Fifteen years of war can do strange things to people." Samugy shrugged. "You remember those boys who fought in the Pepin conflict out of patriotism and then bombed their own capital?"

"I do, but I don't think that's applicable." McAllan took another drink.

"Why not?" Samugy asked. "In the last five years, there's been other stories about Thomas Belson. They're not told quite so loud, but they exist. They say that after Sterling the good Constable got a bit of a mean streak."

"How mean?" McAllan narrowed his eyes.

"Have you heard of the Golden Fort Massacre?" Samugy looked up.

"It's just rumors that he was involved in that." The Prime Governor shook his head.

"No, they weren't." Samugy said level as a table. "Those rumors didn't even scratch the surface of what happened either."

"Damn." McAllan said almost a whisper.

"Those are just the rumors everyone hears but dismisses out of hand because they can't imagine Thomas Belson's not the hero they think he is." Samugy stopped for a moment. "There are other stories, known only to a few circles, spoken of quietly in secret rooms."

"What do those stories say?" McAllan said it barely a whisper.

"That he went into the heart of the Old Empire." Samugy matched his tone. "That he walked the streets of Imor as no one has done in two thousand years. They say Thomas Belson touched Dark Forces there, and they say the Dark Forces touched him back."

"That is unsettling." McAllan didn't want to talk about Thomas Belson anymore. The man was beyond his control. "I'll speak to him. Until then we worry about the problem at hand."

"Right you are." Samugy apparently didn't want to talk about him either. "Is there anything else you need to know?"

"I need to know a thousand things, but they're questions I don't think you can answer." McAllan tapped a report on his desk. "I've read your report on the battle readiness of Southern troops, but I'll reread it."

"You plan on sleeping in your office again, don't you?" Samugy gave a disapproving look.

"I feared I might have to, yes." McAllan answered coldly. "Do you have an issue with that?"

"It's a rare, beautiful thing to see a politician work so hard, but I think you should go home tonight." The Huego shrugged.

"I have too much work." McAllan knew where the conversation was heading.

"We both know it can wait till tomorrow morning." Samugy gave a rare friendly smile.

"Maybe it can, but tomorrow there will be even more work." McAllan nodded to the mountain of papers on his desk.

"Let Timothy help you with it." Samugy bit his lip. "He's a smart lad, and you need to give him more responsibility." The Huego may have dogged continuously on the Souren aide, but even though he'd never admit it to Timothy's face, he liked the boy.

"You're right most of this paperwork is inconsequential," McAllan admitted, "but what if lying in the middle of this stack is a report that a family is starving with no one to feed them? What if it's a scouting report about Anthanii ships at our door? What if because I went home early, someone dies I could have saved?"

"That is an admirable rationalization," Samugy smiled again, "but we both know that's not the reason you're afraid to go home."

"I don't want to talk about this." McAllan gritted his teeth.

"We've known each other for many years, and as much as I hate to admit it, I think we've become friends." Samugy sighed. "You take my advice on matters that put the whole country at stake. Take my advice now." The Huego paused. "If you ignore your wife for too long, you will regret it."

"She's not the woman I married, Samugy." McAllan finally let his guard down. "She's an empty shell filled with things I can't recognize anymore."

"She is the woman you married." Samugy refused to let the issue die. "She's the woman you married, and she needs the help of the man she loves."

"I can't help her." McAllan said it almost to himself.

"You can't save her, but you can be there for her." Samugy stood from his chair. "That will help her, and you know it." The Huego left out the door, presumably to be with his own wife. It was strange to think that the greasy spymaster was in a way more moral than him.

McAllan tried to turn back to his paperwork, but Samugy was right. He sighed and put on his large coat and took his hat with him. He walked down the corridors of the Capitol. Even though he was leaving earlier than usual, it was still later than most, and he didn't see many people in the halls. He nodded his head to the few guards that manned the building.

He walked outside and put his hat on. It was an old dusty thing and surely not befitting the leader of the nation. McAllan took one last look at the Capitol building. It wasn't much compared to the palaces and fortresses that dotted Thyro. It looked more like the office building of a business doing moderately well. If he was supposed to govern for the people, the Capitol reminded him of who the people were.

He walked through the streets and bought a few limes from a vendor. She recognized who he was and tried to refuse payment, but McAllan insisted. He didn't like to take from the common man. In the past Prime Governors had brought guards with them to ensure their safety. McAllan chose to forego that privilege. He may have been old, but not so old he didn't remember the tricks of the ring. Besides the sixshooter under his coat would be enough to deter most, and if it wasn't, he was probably going to die anyway. No sense in making a good soldier die with him.

It was dark out by the time he got to his house. It was a simple one, well built but small. It could have housed any middle-class family really. McAllan sighed one last time before he entered, preparing himself. He tried to open the door, but it was locked. He realized he'd lost the key some time ago. How long had it been since he was last at home?

He knocked on the door and heard scurrying. "Who is it?" The familiar voice asked from behind the door.

"It's me, Cathy." McAllan answered.

The door opened immediately, and Cathy stood before him. She was an old woman going gray. She'd been with him for some time, and when his wife had started her decent, it'd been Cathy who'd done the lion's share of the work. "I'm sorry Prime Governor. You can never be too careful these days."

"It's fine," McAllan waved it off.

"Well, my apologies." Cathy curtsied, but McAllan could see her knees weren't what they used to be and the simple movement hurt her. "What happened to your key?"

"I must have lost it." McAllan walked into the house and took off his coat. "Would you mind making another for me and dropping it by the office?"

"I'd rather you come here again and pick it up yourself." Cathy wasn't the type to scold her patron outright, but she had a way of making her displeasure known.

"I'm sorry it's just that..." McAllan trailed off. He thought of saying *I'm very busy*, or *I'm dealing with a lot at the Capitol*. He realized that was what every man who neglected his wife would say. He finally settled on, "I'll try and do better." That was probably what a lot of those horrible husbands said too.

"It's fine sir." Cathy answered in that understanding tone she had. "It's just that she's been asking about you more often."

"What do you tell her?" McAllan tried to hide his shame.

"That you'll be home soon." Cathy smiled sadly. "At least today it wasn't a lie."

"How is she?" McAllan surveyed the house. It was the same as it had been for a while, but an implacable sadness had seemed to fall on the place.

"There's a reason I've been able to get away with that lie for so long."

"I know." McAllan gestured to the door. "Well, you can have the night off. I'll be with her."

"Thank you Prime Governor." Cathy hurried through the door.

McAllan walked up the stairs and into their room. His wife was lying on the bed seeming strangely thoughtful. Toddy was looking out the window at something. "Toddy?" McAllan said it cautiously. He almost hoped she wouldn't hear him, and he could slip away without her knowing he'd ever been there.

"James!" Toddy looked to her husband with a ridiculous smile on her face. For a moment he saw her as she used to be. He saw her bright eyes trying to take in everything in the world. He saw her dark brown hair that framed her beautiful face. He felt the passion she had loved him with at night. He remembered her razor-sharp wit. In their youth, she had been the stronger of them. She had been the smarter. McAllan wished a woman could run for public office back then. She would have been the better of the two. He wished that she was tall and big enough to step into the ring. She would have made the better boxer. Then the mirage fell from the moment. He saw how dull her eyes had become. He saw how even perching on an elbow cost her too much strength. He knew the brilliant mind he had loved her for was blowing away in the wind. *Could you love the ghost of someone?* He wondered to himself. "It's so nice to see you again." Toddy smiled at him.

"It's nice to see you again too." McAllan lied. "What are you looking at?"

Toddy pointed to a lamp post lighting up the night. It was another of Hank Reard's innovations. The gas lamps were half the cost of pitch and twice as safe. "Where does the fire go during the day?"

"It goes into the hearts of men, so we might do right by those we love." McAllan sat down on the bed. He had tried explaining the science of it to her every night. Five years ago she would have been explaining it to him. Now all the technical talk only confused her. She seemed content with his nonsensical answer. "Do you need anything?" He asked.

"I just want you to sleep next to me tonight." She turned and stroked his scarred face. "The nightmares aren't as bad when you're near."

"I'll have our bodies linked with steel then." McAllan kissed her forehead.

He undressed and got into bed next to her. Toddy clung to him like a drowning man clinging to a piece of wood. She fell asleep long before he did, though. *I will make them pay for her.* It was his silent prayer he said every night since the Demons had seeped into her mind. Love was a powerful thing. It could drive men to great deeds, but when love turned sour so too did the man. *I will make them pay for her. I will make them pay for her. I WILL MAKE THEM PAY FOR ME!*

The Thaniel Wars

"Please, just don't be belligerent." Captain Seiford said half to me and half to the Three.

"I'm not such an ass, I'd be rude to the king of Anthanii." We were outside the royal palace in Harfow, the Anthanii capitol. It was indeed a magnificent building, teaming with red banners and the royal stag. I could almost feel the pomposity from within.

"If there was ever such an ass who would be rude to one of the greatest monarchs in Thyro," Captain Seiford leveled an appraising stare my way, "that ass is you."

I shrugged. "It's in my nature." I conceded. "It's part of the package. If you want a man who's going to be polite, there's many gentlemen in there," I nodded to the palace of Harfow, "but none of them could have saved Wuntville."

"I know." Seiford sighed. "Just, try and go through the motion. I don't like it any more than you, but It'll be better for us if they think we agree blindly." He grabbed my shoulder. "Try and act the part of a humble soldier."

"You remember Constable Ferdinand?" I asked. "He was as humble as they come." I scoffed at the memory. "He kneeled when he was told to. He charged when they screamed charge." I looked up at the palace. "He died when it was appropriate too."

"Constable Ferdinand was a good soldier." Seiford shrugged.

"Aye, there were many good soldiers at Milhire." I stared back at him. "Good soldiers won't win this war. I will, and I can't do that if I pretend to be anything except me."

"So we soldiers are just useless cogs." Indignity was not becoming on Captain Seiford. "If you believe that, you're no better than them." He bit his lip. I knew what he was talking about. I knew in his mind, for the first time, he was comparing me to the nobles. The men who saw ordinary soldiers as nothing but cannon fodder.

I was not those men. I would sacrifice to win. I had sacrificed to win. The image of William still burned against me, but I was not those men.

I grabbed the Captain and forced him to face me. "I will need a great many good soldiers to win this war." I told him. "I've never seen soldiers as useless cogs. They're good men who took up the sword because they couldn't stand to let evil trample what they love." I took a step back. "What they do in the coming years will echo against the histories of man." I let my admiration for Seiford show. I didn't tell him enough that he had my respect. "However, there will come a day where the moral can't step forward. There will come a day when honor won't be enough." I looked at a guard, standing rigid with his red uniform. "On that day they'll need me to do what they can't."

"What's that?" Seiford asked.

"I don't know," I answered him honestly, "but it will come. I can feel it in my bones." I spit into the ground. "This war will cost."

"This war has cost." He let the indignity fall from him. "I'll pay what I have to. I'll see it ended." He sighed. "I'm just saying, show a bit of humility here, and it'll make our path easier." Seiford stared up at the banner. "It may even save lives."

"I don't take the easy path." I said as I walked into the palace. "I take the hard line," Seiford followed me, "and if you wanted to save lives, you should have found a doctor to follow. I play to win."

We walked through the sprawling castle. I'd been there a few times. I never liked it, playing at being soldiers while we were losing. I didn't tell Seiford the reason I refused to relent, even to a king, even if it didn't matter. I refused to relent for the same reason I refused to run at Wuntsville. It may have been the smarter option. Historians may wonder over my stupidity, but at the end of it all, I'd know where I stood.

The castle buzzed with life. Curriers delivering messages, bureaucrats grubbing for power, nobles edging for influence. I ignored them, and they ignored me. I was wearing my uniform. A simple black cloak with the Tree of Faith painted on the front in white. The right sleeve was cut off to let my tattoos show. I'd usually be armed to the teeth, but I'd been forced to give up my weapons at the door. I still had a knife strapped to my thigh, but they wouldn't find that. They ignored me because they knew who I was. They knew the court didn't favor me. They knew my mission was to beat Thaniel. They knew he couldn't be beaten. They knew I would end in disgrace, and they didn't want their name attached to mine. They knew all of this as fact. Some of the bolder politicians had even begun speaking affectionately of the Kranish, in hopes of currying favor when they owned this palace. I knew different truths though, and soon so would they.

"Constable Belson." I heard someone call out in a scratchy voice. I turned and saw Brother Keys hurrying over to me. He had decided to stay in Harfow when I went to Wuntsville. He said his constitution couldn't handle such a hasty retreat. He didn't believe me when I said I had no intention of running. Brother Keys was an old man. His beard and hair had long gone white, and he walked with the limp that comes from living past when you're useful. I always hated him, but not in the way I hated cowardice, losing, or wet feet. Perhaps dislike was a better word to use, but I really disliked Brother Keys. It was something about his pinched faced that always screamed displeasure. Maybe, it had something to do with the fact that he never had a single original thought in his head, just regurgitated doctrine. Perhaps it was the way he read the Testament at me, not to me. Regardless, of why I disliked him, I did. I don't mean to give you the wrong idea. If I saw him drowning, I'd throw him a piece of wood to float on, but I wouldn't get my clothes wet trying to save him. Come to think of it, a good chunk of wood has it's uses. I'd throw him a rope. I could always just roll it back up if his body couldn't take the paddling.

"Brother Keys." I nodded at him. Every Constable had a monk to accompany him, to advise him in matters of the Three. That's what they said at least. The monk was really there because he was trained in rhetoric, engineering, and politics. Those could be useful to a Constable, but Brother Key's wasn't really good at any of them. I had drawn the short straw with that old bastard.

"I hear you won a great victory at Wuntsville." He said as he hobbled next to me.

"I did." I responded without looking at him. "It's a shame you weren't there to see it."

Keys brushed off the insult in my words. "It was a great victory, but I should remind you," he thumped his copy of the Testament, "the Three teach humility."

"Well, Thaniel taught boldness." I stopped. "Which one do you think was more important at Wuntsville?"

Keys bristled at that. "The Three are always the most important."

I shook that off and continued walking. I stopped before we reached the courtroom. It was protected by a door twice my size, carved in dark ebony. I say protected, but I think the door couldn't have stood against a single cannonball. If I were King John, I'd have sold the damn door and used the money to buy arms. The philosophy was, if you walked through a pine door to meet a king, how would you know you were meeting a king? My answer was that he'd be the most powerful man in the room, but I was from the Confederacy, after all. A country that only existed because men had wanted to get as far away from their philosophy as possible. A philosophy where worth was decided by the door, not the man inside. My people were made great because they were great, not because their father had been. I may have left my home country in anger, but I would always be a Confederacy man. People call us impudent, but that's only because we know what actually deserved to be pudented. That was another fallacy of Thyro, make a word that meant disrespectful forget the one that meant respect.

"Constable Belson!" I heard another call out for me. I was about to say something insulting back, but the martial tone stopped me. I turned to see Lord Hannas Corbul walking towards me. He wore his years as well as brother Keys did his poorly. His family was wealthy and powerful but lacking in respect. This was because they weren't quite foreign enough to be openly looked down upon, but they weren't quite native enough to be seen as equal. The Corbul line had more Anthanii than anything, but the jot of Pentol made itself known. Hannas was darker than most, with hawkish brown eyes. His shoulders were broad in a court that found litheness fashionable. If it weren't for his strict military life, he'd have been fat. Lord Corbul was a couple of inches above me, but I'd probably reach him in time. He dressed the right type of austere too. Some men, like Brother Henry, actively tried to look as simple as possible. Men like Captain Seiford just didn't have the time for it. Lord Corbul was the latter. Everything about him was so delightfully unstylish I couldn't help but like him. It takes more than looks to make me like someone, but it certainly gave some a head start.

"Lord Corbul." I nodded my head in respect. He was one of the few nobles I'd do that too. His family hadn't forgotten why they were really called lord. It wasn't because powers above had made it so. It was because they'd taken the title at the end of the sword. He also hadn't forgotten the highborn part of the social contract. Their duty was to protect. Being able to govern was their reward. Most nobles got it backwards. As I saw it, Lord Corbul was the most competent general in the Anthanii army. His family was powerful enough that he could have had command at the battle of Milhire. We probably still would have lost, but Thaniel would have paid a price for it, and we may not have been destroyed so thoroughly. King John hated him, though. At least he had a reason to hate me. I was an arrogant little shit who wouldn't kneel. Lord Corbul went through all the motions. He probably had the same distaste for the King I did, but he knew raising a fuss would only hurt his soldiers. Corbul loved his soldiers more than anything. He loved them enough to execute one if they put the rest in danger. He'd write the family though. Other nobles just executed soldiers because they liked to be reminded that they could.

"How fairs the Southern front?" I asked him. He had requested the position after he learned Lord Renton would lead the army at Milhire. He'd been given it because it was seen as an undesirable post. There would be no glory for success, and he'd probably lose anyway. The court didn't understand what me, him, and probably Thaniel saw. The South was where the industry was. Lose that, we lose our ability to make weapons, uniforms, and above all good boots. We may have recruited from the North, but without the South, we'd be marching farmers with pitchforks at Thaniel.

Lord Corbul furrowed his brow. "We're holding." He finally said.

"It doesn't sound like it's going particularly well, my lord." Captain Seiford cocked an eyebrow up.

"It's war, Captain. It never goes particularly well," Lord Corbul nodded, "but we haven't had the same success you two had at Wuntsville." Him and Seiford had grown up together. Seiford was nobility, but his family didn't have lands and wasn't particularly wealthy which left him short of lord. Corbul had lands and wealth, but he was only technically nobility. They were a perfect pair. They competed with their deeds, not their father's. Also, one could put his resources behind the other, Seiford with his name and Corbul with his wealth.

"We still receive equipment, so it can't be that bad." I put in.

"Aye, my soldiers are Anthanii's best." He said proudly. "Kran hasn't broken through yet," he made his face stony, "but I fear it might be a matter of time."

"You don't think your men can hold?" Seiford asked.

"My men can hold onto a mountain in a blizzard if I asked them too." Lord Corbul said defiantly. It was true, the army respected him. It wasn't the awe-inspiring regard they held me in, but they knew Hannas wouldn't do them wrong. He had sent away the arrogant nobles who often populated the officer corps and replaced them with hard-bitten men worthy of the rank. It hadn't won him many favors with the court, but it had with the soldiery. "The trouble isn't the men." He tried to hide the despair in his eyes. "It's that there aren't enough of them." Lord Corbul gave a glance of pure hatred at a passing diplomat. "I have three divisions, and I'm losing more every day. Kran has twice that in the South, and I hear word Thaniel's ordering even more." He shook his head. "I can't convince them that I can hold the South if I only had more men. Demons Below, I can't convince them it's worth holding."

"How's the man leading them?" I asked.

"General Holsten," Lord Corbul bit his lip, "he's competent like they all are, but he's young."

"I'm young." I shrugged. "Captain Seiford's young, even if he won't be for long."

"Ass." Seiford muttered.

I ignored him. "We've done quite a bit of damage." I raised an eyebrow. "I wouldn't underestimate him just because of his age." I gestured to Brother Henry. "After all, he's older than dirt and twice as useless."

"The advice of the Three is never useless!" Brother Henry bristled.

"Even you aren't old enough to claim being the Three." I turned my gaze to him.

"I advise on their behalf!" Brother Henry was absolutely furious. I had mixed disrespect with blasphemy.

"If I ever meet the Three I'll ask them if you're worth listening too." I made sure my distaste was known. If he had found the courage to accompany me to Wuntsville, I might have at least hid it. "Until then, I'll assume your brain is just rattling around in there." I poked him in his old head.

"I don't have to listen to this." Brother Henry did precisely what I hoped he would, and stormed off to a chair and sat to read the Testament.

"You should treat him better." Lord Corbul gave me a disapproving look. "He's not so bad a man. He just wasn't meant for this life like you or me." He sighed. "Besides he's not an idiot. He's just..." Corbul took a second to find the right word, "Orthodox." He finally settled on.

"Orthodox is what they call it when you're too stupid to make up your own ideas." I rolled my eyes. "The point stands. This might be a young man's war."

Lord Corbul chuckled at that. "I won't deny you've done quite a bit to combat my prejudices." Hannas nodded. "Is it true you took a sword in your chest to get that killing stroke on Gostfeld."

I poked my chest. "It's true." My body still ached from all the wounds I'd suffered. I walked like I always did, though. It wouldn't do to show weakness here. The palace of Harfow had too much of it already.

"Impressive." Lord Corbul nodded.

"Don't give him a big head." Captain Seiford scoffed behind me. "He should have saved a bullet for the bastard," Bradly thought for a moment, "or thrown the hatchet at him."

"That wouldn't have made half as good a story." I smiled. However, from the way my shoulder hurt, I had to agree.

"Agreed." Lord Corbul let a smile tug on the edges of his face. "I won't even ask about the donkeys. I know you well enough not to doubt that. You've always been a crazy bastard." Hannas sighed. "That was a good bit of work. General Gostfeld was one of Thaniel's best. I've been tangling with him for the better part of a decade, and you beat him with almost nothing." His face grew more serious. "Young men have their advantages. You won't play by the rules, but the rules are still important. Young men are more prone to attack a weakness, but they're also easier to trick. They also show too much weakness. They forget about digging in and feeding their troops."

"Trust me, if I ever get an army big enough to fight conventionally, I know how to do it." I said back at him.

"You're a rare breed, though." Lord Corbul said. "I have no doubt you'll be one of the best in a few years."

"I am *the* best now." I couldn't hold it against him that he didn't see that already.

"You'll need to prove that." Corbul said.

"I will."

Lord Corbul nodded at that as if agreeing. "Regardless, I won't deny this General Holsten is good. He might be Thaniel's best field general." Hannas's hand went to the sword on his side. Nobility was allowed to be armed. "He's the wrong tool to beat me, though. If I gave him a battle, he'd probably win, especially with the numbers being what they are." He went back to his default setting of stoic calculation. "I won't do that, though. I dig in and make them pay for every inch." He sighed. "The trouble is, that wars of attrition usually go to the side with the better numbers, and they are paying for the inches. I don't have an answer for those Priests yet, either." He looked to a banner of the king as if begging for help. "Besides, what happens if Thaniel gets tired of waiting, and decides to come himself. The Kranish worship him like a god. If he comes, they'll start overtaking me if they have to charge on bloody stumps." Corbul let some of the despair show. "I won't be able to hold."

"I plan on keeping him busy up north." I said with certainty. "That's not the real issue, though." I narrowed my eyes. "Thaniel knows exactly what type of general to send against a dug in enemy. Gostfeld would have been best, but he's got Furot and Tommel too." I scratched my head. "He sent Holsten. Why?"

Lord Corbul narrowed his eyes. "What are you getting at?"

Seiford saw it a bit clearer. "You think..." He trailed off

"He sent Holsten for a reason. Thaniel never does anything without reason." I continued. "He sent a promising, young general against one of our best." Lord Corbul didn't blush at the compliment. "He did it to groom him or maybe even to test him. Perhaps, he's even planning for his successor. As I hear it, Thaniel has no children."

"That's all very fascinating, but I don't see how that's more important than battles right now." Lord Corbul was a shrewd general, but his knowledge of politics was lacking. To be fair that's probably a good thing in a general, but a Constable sees the bigger picture.

"He thinks we've already lost." I said it mostly to myself. "He's already planning for a future where Anthanii is his."

"I can't blame him." Captain Seiford shrugged. "Besides what we just did at Wuntsville, we haven't proved him wrong."

"Speak for yourself." Lord Corbul said with some passion. "Anthanii won't fall while my men defend it."

"It's more than that." I was still calculating it all. "Even for Thaniel, that day is a far off one." I paused. "Unless, he has something we don't know about," I looked from Seiford to Hannas, "Something from the Old Religion."

"We've known about the Old Religion for a while." Lord Corbul said. He didn't like to think about the Priest. It made him feel too powerless.

"We know about the Old Religion." I said. "That's a far cry from knowing it." I rubbed the tattoos on my arm. "The ruins of Imor are in his domain. The Priests today won't even attempt what they did, but if the secret to how they did it still exists, it's there."

"No ones gone into those ruins for more than a thousand years." Captain Seiford tilted his head.

"Kran's never threatened Anthanii before either," I responded, "a peasant has never sat on the Rose Petal throne, and no ones ever won a battle with donkeys and scarecrows." I looked back at my friend. "This is an age for doing things that haven't been done in a thousand years."

"I don't care about an empire that fell a thousand years ago." Lord Corbul said with conviction. "I care about saving my homeland, and to do that I'll need more men."

"The two might be intertwined." I said.

Corbul shook his head. "I'll let the Constables worry about fighting the Old Religion." He nodded to the big ebony doors. "I'm going to go petition the King for more resources. I wish you the best of luck too." A page appeared and beckoned to the Lord.

"Should we tell the King about your theory?" Captain Seiford asked.

"Three above, no!" I looked at the man like he'd lost his sense.

"And why not?" Bradly gave me a curious look. "If Thaniel does have some sort of ancient weapon, that's something we should begin preparing for."

"If I let this get out, it'll ruin any moral we just gained at Wuntsville." I said still scratching my chin. "Besides, King John couldn't prepare for something like that even if he believed me, which he probably won't." I bit my lip, thinking. "We don't even know what it is yet. Maybe, Thaniel is just getting cocky." It was a tricky thing, judging a man like Thaniel. There wasn't a precedent for him. "For now it's just a theory."

"I've never known you to be wrong about these things." Captain Seiford still seemed unsettled at the idea.

"I'm usually not," I said, "but I hope I am now."

"You always seem to understand a man. It's uncanny." He gave me a strange look. "I don't so much as say a name, and you can tell me what he writes in his diary. I bet you're a hell of a card player."

"Not really." I shrugged. "I usually walk away empty handed, get too drunk, you see." He was right, though. I did have an ability to know what men wanted. You can't truly beat someone until you know what to beat them for. Maybe the attack was just a distraction. Maybe they didn't even want that city.

"Regardless, I hear there's this new study called psychology." Seiford chuckled. "If this whole Constable thing doesn't work out, you should try your hand there."

"Please," I waved my hand. "That science will never take root. It's like alchemy, a total waste of time."

"I met a man who could turn lead into gold." Bradly said indignantly.

"You met a man who could paint a rock yellow." I rolled my eyes. "I never took you for the superstitious type."

"Just because you don't understand it, doesn't mean it's not science." He shot back.

We went like that for a while. We would never really run out of things to argue about. To his credit, I had actually met a man who could turn lead into gold. At least I thought I had. The man's hands had moved quite a bit. Still, I needed something to keep my mind off meeting the King again. He'd never liked me. Even though he was a twat, he was still a king. Even though I talked a tough game, I was still scared one day he might have enough of my impudence and send a knife in my sleep. I wasn't scared enough to practice more prudence or even sleep less, but I was mildly worried.

More than that, I didn't want to think about what was under Thaniel's sleeve. That man did make me practice more prudence, and I'd certainly lost sleep over him.

We argued until a page came to beckon us in. I straightened my coat and walked through the door. Captain Seiford followed and so did Brother Henry. I walked straight and proud. I might be a Constable, but before the tattooed arm, I was a Confederacy man. My people had grown famous for the pissing off kings of Anthanii. I wouldn't disappoint my ancestors.

I walked through the long hallway with the king sitting on his throne at the end. I meant to stare straight ahead, but I couldn't help myself. I surveyed the room. I saw ladies of the court shy away from me as if I were a wild animal who could snap his collar at any moment. Nobles watched me with disdain as if they could have done what I did, but saving their own country was beneath them. I saw the guards follow me with their eyes. To be a guard you had to be a good soldier. They didn't break their bearing, but something in them seemed to call out to me. *Lead us.* I could hear them scream out in their minds. They hadn't quite given up yet.

There were tapestries on the walls, beautiful things. Some spoke of the great achievements in battles of kings past. Some spoke of the charity they had given to their people. I knew enough about history to understand that they weren't all lies. There had been some excellent rulers of Anthanii, back before the kingdom had seen it as it's right to exist. Still, if you pick your leader because of who his father was, you're going to get some bad ones

My family in the Confederacy were plantation owners and very rich. My father, Leopold, had seen to it that I had received a good education. My tutor, George, was one of the most respected scholars on my side of the ocean. I loved to read. In another life, I would have made an excellent librarian. I always kept more than a few books in my pack. Something to keep me occupied in my quiet moments. I knew that I probably understood more of Anthanii's history than King John.

I finally reached the steps in front of the king's throne. It was an ornate thing rendered in ebony and gold. It could have bought an armada of ships. It could have armed three divisions. To my mind, Anthanii should have kept the old one, forged in hard iron. It had been replaced three hundred years ago, but that's the sort of seat a leader should have.

King John himself seemed impressive at first glance. He was a handsome man of almost forty. His dark hair had slowly given way to specks of gray, but it seemed dignified. His bright green eyes had a good look to them. However, he was the wrong type of handsome. He seemed to look down on the world. He wasn't like Thaniel, who gave the impression that he had a vision of a better world, and he could lead us there. Still, looks often lied. He was too lithe to do anything even remotely useful with his own two hands, and that quivering chin of his spoke to the darker truth of nobility. I would bet my life, if I looked at King John's genealogy, I'd find more than a couple of his descendants who married first cousins.

Queen Harriot sat at the right side of her husband. She was pretty. Her blue eyes and flowing blond hair would have made me look twice at her. I still didn't like her, though. If I saw her in a bar, I'd certainly offer the woman a drink, but as a queen, she was just another thorn in my side. She looked down on me worse than anyone at court. At least they knew me for a useful tool. If Queen Harriot had her way, she'd send my head to Mother Vestia. There was nothing I could do to convince her I was worthy of standing in her court.

Standing behind them was their first son, Prince Edward. I did like Prince Edward. He had grown to manhood fearing Thaniel. He had seen his people suffer and wanted to stop it. The Prince had the look of the old rulers, the look of defiance. If Thaniel ever did sack the palace of Harfow, Edward would die defending it. He even showed me some respect. He was far too bright to do it publicly, but he had snuck into my room once and asked me to tell him everything I had seen at Milhire. He was a lion surrounded by snakes.

"My King." Captain Seiford went to one knee.

"My King." Brother Henry followed suit and struggled to get his body to the ground.

"King John." I stood.

"When you address the King, you will prostrate yourself and call him 'my king' or 'your highness.'" The herald narrowed his eyes at me. He was a small man with beady eyes and a pretty voice.

"I have no king or highness." I returned the look. "My people kneel to no man."

"Why do we suffer his impudence?" Queen Harriot said to her husband, but really to the whole court. "He's a savage from across the ocean."

"You suffer me because I win." I looked at her next. "The Confederacy has a habit of winning, in case you forgot our revolution."

"Hold your tongue in the presence of my queen." King John seethed at me.

"Father, I don't like his disrespect any more than you do," Prince Edward said diplomatically, "but by the laws of propriety he does not have to kneel or swear allegiance to any monarch, not as a Constable or a Confederacy man."

"Thank you, Prince Edward." I nodded to him.

"Do not thank me." The prince leveled a glare my way. "Though you do not have to prostrate yourself, you should remember you fight with our armies in our land." He took a step forward. "Offering respect does not mean you are subservient to us. Do you understand, Constable Belson?"

"I do, Prince Edward." I nodded to him. There was a leader. I wouldn't have kneeled to him, but I would give him respect.

"If I may," I heard a scratchy voice from the court, "it is custom for Constables to show respect to the leaders they have pledged service to with a knee." I turned and saw Constable Fartow. He had too many scars on him to tell what nationality he was initially. He was the oldest man to wear the tattooed arm. He was a competent soldier, and if we sparred, he'd probably win. However, he was too stuck in his ways to be the man to win this war. I didn't hate him, but he hated me. I had no doubt he had a hand in me being sent to Wuntsville with not but two hundred soldiers.

"It is customary," Prince Edward agreed, "but not law." He paused. "I will not see a victor chastised for breaking tradition." He turned his gaze to me. "Especially, when breaking tradition is what lead to his success." He cocked an eyebrow up. "Is it true about the donkeys and scarecrows?"

"It is." I nodded.

"And the medals and sword through your chest?" Prince Edward chuckled.

"It is." I repeated.

"If I may, my prince," Captain Seiford said still on his knees, "the stories honestly don't do it justice."

"He's still a savage." Queen Harriot rolled her eyes.

"Aye, maybe he is," Prince Edward agreed, "but we have a great many gentlemen fighting this war, and we're still losing."

"Hold your tongue, son." King John gave his son a harsh look. "However, we do need to discuss this victory." He gave me an angry glare. "Wuntsville was a key strategic point." I couldn't tell if he actually believed that foolishness. Did he think we'd ride those famous donkeys to victory? He gestured for Captain Seiford and brother Henry to stand, and so they did.

"It shows your wisdom as a ruler." One noble said.

"It is a turning point in the war." Another said.

I shook my head. "It's just a footnote to history if we don't capitalize on it."

That shocked the harem of generals that stood beside the King. They muttered angrily, but none of them spoke out directly. They knew it was true.

"You offer a problem but no solution." Prince Edward cocked his head to the side. "How do you suggest we act?"

"He doesn't get to decide the fate of our nation." King John scoffed at me.

"No, he doesn't," Prince Edward said meekly, "but Thomas Belson has proven himself useful. I think we should hear what he has to say."

"I'll hear from my trusted generals first." King John turned to the officers. "Advise me."

"I believe we should marshal our forces in Wuntsville and launch an assault from the North." A pompous, over-decorated general named Lord Fertin said. A general placed there because his family wanted it. "We can show Thaniel how Anthanii men truly fight." He smashed his fist into an open hand.

I knew he was absolutely wrong. If we brought an army that large Thaniel would lead the opposing force himself. Even if we could beat him, the roads there weren't good enough to feed us. We'd be whittled down even if everything went right, and it wouldn't.

"We should strengthen our cavalry and ride in hard and fast before they know we're upon him." Lord Gregory took a step forward. Another pompous lord, given command for convenience rather than skill. "After all, artillery and infantry have only ever let us down in the past. Cavalry is where our strength is."

He was wrong too. Thaniel had spies in this court. He'd know about it immediately. Kran would meet us with a full army. The days when knights could break a host on their own were over if they ever existed. The game had changed. What's more, our cavalry wasn't better than Kran's, it was just prettier. Thaniel's cavalry was used for what it should be, scouting, distracting, and quick attacks.

"We need to defend." Lord Corbul finally spoke up. "Thaniel can beat us in open field, but if we dig in, and make him suffer, he'll turn away from us." I could see from the look in his eye, he hadn't gotten the soldiers he'd hoped for.

He was less wrong than the rest, but he was still wrong. We'd lost too much land already for that. Besides, that gave Thaniel the initiative. I'd seen what he could do with that. He'd break through eventually. We needed to choose what happened next. We needed to make him move for us.

I looked up at a map of Thyro, hanging on the wall. Thaniel's army was spread out, but it was in such a way that he could mass it in a week. There was only one spot that gave him trouble, the Cretoin Mountains. They were too dangerous to scale, and savages who had never been tamed made their home there. Perhaps, if a powerful country had really put the effort into it, they could have set their flag on that range, but they wouldn't be able to hold it. Why even try? There was nothing their worth having, except maybe an uninterrupted pass into the heart of Kran. However, those mountains were impassible, everyone knew that. No army had ever gotten over them. Three above, no adventurer had either. Yet, people did live there. Somewhere in those mountains was a way over. I felt my mind tugging on the edges of an idea. I couldn't use it yet, but maybe one day...

I looked around at all the incompetent men. I wondered what a council in Thaniel's court would look like. The Kranish generals were all skilled, so were their colonels, majors, captains, etcetera. Demons below, they probably had more competence in their privates than sat at the entire Anthanii war ministry. It wasn't that men in Kran were of a better quality than Anthanii. They were essentially the same people. They both lived in Thyro, a land that had been tamed three millennia ago. They even spoke the same language. If I had a hundred frontiersmen from my Confederacy across the ocean, the war would be over already. Hard men, born on the edge of the world were generally superior to those bred in captivity. You can usually judge how hard a fight will be by how easy a people are to govern. The ones who balked at the slightest regulation were not the sort you wanted to be tangled up with. Thyro had known war but never tasted the sharp edge of survival. They hunted for sport, not necessity. Let the courts laugh at my provincial ways. My name would outlast theirs.

The reason for Kran's success was that Thaniel had changed everything. Kran had been a country for almost a thousand years. For a thousand years, its army had been as hapless as any other civilized place. Then Thaniel had started to claw his way to the top thirty years ago. From peasant to emperor took more than skill. It took skill in those around as well. Anthanii military academies had more classes on dining edict than the proper use of artillery. Some of the higher-ups even viewed infantry as a necessary evil to make your army look bigger for a rousing cavalry charge.

Thaniel had changed that. In every place, there are competent men. He had simply found them and given them power. Even a leader like the Emperor of Kran couldn't be everywhere. He knew he needed help. I would have to beat them all. I wouldn't find help in this court.

I opened my mouth to speak, but a page burst through the ebony doors before I had a chance. "My apologies your highness," he kneeled, "but I've just received word that Thaniel has approached neutral ground under the banner of peace."

"What is the meaning of this?" King John stood up.

"He says he wants to discuss terms." The page kept his knee.

"We'll discuss this later." King John gave me a distasteful look. "Gather my entourage. We leave at once!" He looked as if he'd been drowning and someone threw him a piece of wood. I had a suspicion that the wood was really painted lead

"My king, Thaniel has sent a list of people he wants you to bring." The page waited for the king to lash out.

"He doesn't choose who I bring!" King John screamed.

"I agree, my King," The page looked terrified, "but he says if you don't bring them he will refuse to consider terms."

"Who is on that list?" King John scowled.

"Your Highness, of course." The page paused. "Also Lord Corbul, a lady by the name of Gerate, and a man named Captain Seiford." He looked around. "Above all, he said bring Thomas Belson."

I smiled at that. It was time I looked the beast in the face.

The Thaniel Wars

King John's entourage approached the place where the two monarchs were set to meet. I had chosen to ride ahead and scout the area, a place that lies equal distance between Kranish and Anthaii control. It was a field level as far as the eye could see with a large tent in the middle. This was to prevent any threats from approaching unseen, and also if a threat did slip through the cracks, it wouldn't get far.

Both parties had brought a company for protection, but neither side was allowed to carry firearms. I had left my six-shooters a distance away and kept my tomahawk. An agent of King John had told me to replace it with the more customary sword. However, I'd told him if he didn't piss off I would bury it in his skull. That had been the end of any issue over my attire.

The King had chosen to bring eight of his most incompetent generals, four of his most insufferable lords, and two men who try though I might, I couldn't discern what their purpose was. Of course, this was in addition to Seiford and me, as Thaniel had demanded.

However, the king had refused to take Lady Gerate and Lord Corbul. "I will not have *him* dictate who will escort me!" He had said. To John, it was just a way for Thaniel to push his buttons. It was the usual way of peace talks. The Emperor of Kran makes a multi-faceted demand of the King of Anthanii. The custom was that however many demands the receiving party obeyed were how far that king was willing to give.

It seemed a foolish tradition to me. Why tell the enemy what you're willing to give? Not only that, it spoke of a fundamental lacking of knowledge in the way the world works. You play for absolutes. You either win, or you lose. You either eat, or you starve.

You either win, or you die. Leave the whole party or bring them all. Giving an inch was the same as giving an empire. The only difference was how long it took them to take it.

King John had disobeyed half the demands in an effort to look stronger than he was. However, I didn't fail to notice the two he had obeyed. One was captain Seiford. His rank was so small it probably seemed too insignificant for King John to worry over. The other was me. Lady Gerate's cunning was well known in the right circles, Lord Corbul's toughness had given a spine to a country that had long lacked one, but I was the prize. I was the man Thaniel wanted to see.

Thaniel's demands showed me more about the emperor. King John and all his noble courtiers had failed to see it. I don't mind if a man chooses a different path in life. We're not all meant to walk along bayonets. Diversity of talent was what made the world go round. After all, you need to give warriors something to fight over. What I couldn't stand was a man being incompetent in their field. Nobles were supposed to be well versed in subtlety, and yet they couldn't see what I saw. An, ever so subtle, showing of his hand.

Thaniel's demands said that he knew the custom but hated it. His orders were by far the simplest in living memory. It also showed what he truly wanted, and it wasn't peace. Since Thaniel had started his conquest, there'd been small moments of ceasefires. One didn't take a country as powerful as Anthanii in one go. However, those waves of peace had always been decided by him. They were a chance to consolidate his gains and train more armies. They were a space to raise more money and find some weakness. There were two kinds of peace in the world. The type meant to hold, and the type meant to fail.

Thaniel didn't need to consolidate his gains. The whole world knew rebellion of any sort was futile. Thaniel didn't need to train more armies. He had enough. Thaniel didn't need to raise more money. His conquest had made Kran the wealthiest country in the world. Thaniel didn't need to probe for weakness. He knew Anthanii was on its knees. He wanted to meet me. He wanted to understand me.

His choices showed he was already well on his way. He knew who I respected. He knew who I laid with. Three above, he probably knew what Captain Seiford meant when he asked a man if he wanted to see his horse! Thaniel had been reading my correspondence, listening to my conversations, and watching me when I slept. His spy network was vast. It was an unsettling thought.

This war was between him and me, and he knew it. When you get two commanders as good as us, the pieces on the board meant nothing. It was about the men moving them. The game would be decided by whoever knew the other better. Whoever was willing to sacrifice more of himself than his opponent. He had the advantage. He could hear what I whispered. He could listen to me talk in my sleep.

Part of me was flattered that he recognized what a threat I was. However, it had only been one battle. One battle and he knew everything about me, but it hadn't been just one battle. It dawned on me that my desperate retreat at Milhire might have caught his eye. Once was a fluke. Twice was a pattern. Usually, it took more than that to see clearly, but he'd done it in the bare minimum. Also for him to already know so much about me, he would've had to be watching me since I lead my seven hundred away from him.

It had occurred to me that he wasn't just a man with an excellent talent for war. Most men were simply born to be something. The successful ones found their field. Some men were different, though. Some men could look at a thing, understand its rules, and master it. Some men were of the type that they could compose a flawless piece of music, solve an impossible equation, make a fistful of gold, and have time to slack off before supper. Men who's chosen field went beyond a job. Their skill was to learn. Men such as those were limited only by ambition. I'd always considered myself such a man, but it appeared Thaniel was one as well. War was a means to an end, but what was the end?

The fate of the world was to be decided by a game of two truths and a lie between us. Thaniel had a network of spies that could be devoted to me. I didn't have the money for that and certainly not the time. Yet every advantage can be used against someone. Spies are a far throw from prophets, and both rarely speak the full truth.

There were other things to take into account, as well. He had a name, and I was as of yet obscure. I had fifteen years of history to study. He had two battles. Still, I'd rather read his letters than his history. It was just like Wuntsville. I had nothing except wits and drive. They'd been enough to beat Gostfeld, but Thaniel was a different beast. Now they had some part of my measure. To win this game, I'd need to be creative. I'd need to use every trick I had.

Finally, the annoying drivel of King John's followers brought me away from my scheming.

"My king, we should kneel but not call him emperor." A fat noble said. "It shows we are willing to negotiate, but not give him claim on more land than Kran."

"The king should kneel?" A preposterous general asked.

"Obviously not the king," The fat noble answered, "but we should."

"If we kneel it says he has a right to our land more than saying he is emperor." The general said.

"We can't do both." One of the useless men interjected. "We should at least keep our sword belts on."

"Sound advice, all." King John said out of his quivering chin. I thought I didn't have to suffer more etiquette talk, but the King egged them on. "I will hear more." And every one of them tried to make their opinion heard.

"We should only respond if asked three times."

"No, three times is too much."

"We should put our elbows on the table."

"We should sit only after they do."

"Half of us should sit before, and half after."

"Which half?"

"Obviously the lowest ranked first."

"Obviously from tallest to shortest."

"No, from shortest to tallest."

I'd had enough. "Are any of you even slightly interested in why he wants peace?" I looked around the crowd. They were all too flabbergasted to answer, and Captain Seiford averted his eyes. "Has anyone given a thought to what we're willing to give up for it."

"You will not forget your station again!" A lord by the name of Gregory started. "We are nobles of the great Kingdom of Anthanii! You are a frontier worm!"

"No, what you are is losing!" I screamed back at him. "When I've won this war for you, go back to wondering about who sits first." I calmed myself as much as I could. "For now, shut your fucking mouths."

The whole company stared at me in shock. Finally, King John came to his senses enough to speak with disdain. "Etiquette is what separates us from Confederacy animals." He eyed me up for the final words. "This will decide who has the royal claim, you impudent worm!" He finally turned his voice to white rage.

They all stared at me in shock, waiting to see how I begged for forgiveness. Even a Constable couldn't invoke the fury of the king without backpedaling. I did the only thing I could do when confronted by this snarling monarch insulting me. I laughed.

"You think that elbows on tables are going to decide history?" I asked him. "This will." I beat my tomahawk. "Thaniel doesn't care about any of this." I bared my teeth at him. "Any royal rules that might have saved you went out the door when a peasant became emperor of Kran." I shook my head. "You should be worrying that he has enough spies in court to know who my friends are. You should be worrying that he doesn't even see you as enough of a threat to assassinate, but you're not." I put a finger in King John's chest. "You're worried about etiquette because it's the only battlefield you can beat him on."

He slapped me. I didn't think about it. I just twisted his hand until he yelped in pain. It was decidedly unbecoming of a king.

"Thomas!" Seiford was the only one who reacted. He pulled me away from the man in a huge bear hug. Despite all my pushups, he was stronger.

Seiford still held me as King John regained his composure. I don't think I've ever seen a man that mad. I should have been scared, but I laughed again.

"One day, boy, you'll have outlived your use." He whispered in cold fury. "On that day, I'll see you hanged."

"Better to outlive a use than never have one." I smiled back at him.

"My king, Confederacy blood runs hot." Seiford said still holding me. "Let me cool him down a bit."

"Let the dog regain his sense." The King said still massaging his wrist. He and his followers continued on to the court.

"You slap like a bitch!" I screamed after him. He stopped but thought better of it. After they were out of earshot, Seiford let me go. "Thanks, Seiford, but I wasn't going to really hurt-" He cut me off with a powerful punch to my gut. "What the fuck!" I managed to gasp out through ragged breaths.

"You fucking idiot!" Captain Seiford hissed at me.

"Everything I said was right." I was still trying to catch my breath.

"Of course it was because you're always right!" He gritted his teeth. "You just have to insult him, don't you? You just have to bring the most powerful man in the room down a notch."

"Well…" I shrugged, and Seiford hit me in the gut again.

"You think so hard about how to win this war, you never thought about who you're winning it for." He shook his head. "Think about this!" He pointed to the company of soldiers who were trying their best not to look at me. "They just saw you make a bitch out of their king!" He put his hand on my soldier. "By next week the whole army will have heard that story. How do you think that'll help morale?"

"He needed to hear it." I mumbled.

"Of course he did!" Captain Seiford crossed his arms. "Do you think he actually heard you, though? Do you really?" He sighed. "You could have used an inch of tact, and maybe he might have thought about it." He huffed some more. "Fine, you proved you're the smartest man in the room again, but have you made the cause better?"

I didn't have an answer for that.

"And here's something else," Captain Seiford went on, "I may not like the man, but he's my king." He brandished his fist. "I serve him not you."

"He'll lead you off a cliff." I spat.

"Then I'll follow. Do you know why?" He asked. "It's because I fight for a cause." He cooled himself off a bit. "You're talented, but you need to shape up soon." He stormed off to follow his king.

I knew he was right. I might have even changed his mind a bit if I'd used some manners. Captain Seiford's anger meant something. I'd never really seen him use it before.

"Fuck." I muttered as I walked off to the tent. Seiford did not hit like a bitch.

I walked to the tent King John's harem was standing in front of. It was simple canvas. I could see the men of Anthanii giving it a disdainful look. I could also see the stares they leveled upon the generals Thaniel had brought. They were all some variation of unfashionable. The men of Kran were soldiers born. I could see it as soon as I set eyes on them. However, a soldier comes in many forms.

There was the sort who hates flare. These men were old and grizzled. They'd worked their way up from lieutenant and sometimes private. They had been told to hold the line, and they'd done it. They spit bile and shit coal. They were the sort of men that would grab you by the belt and put as much hurt in you as possible. They wore their yellow coat simply as if to tell the world, *test me.*

These were the kind of generals you used to train soldiers, hold a ford, or merely terrify the enemy to death. To them soldiering was a science they'd devoted their whole life to. They had a weakness though. Their victories were based on rules, and as soon as you went outside them, you owned the battle. These men couldn't seize the initiative, but they'd make you pay hell for any victory you won. General Gostfeld had been the best of this breed.

Then there were the sort who were all fire and courage. The young men who had won their names quickly by always charging. They'd traveled a beeline from company commander to general. In the middle of battle, they'd seen a whisper of opportunity and seized it. They were the sort of men who you show weakness to for a moment, and you regret it. Their uniforms were garish and plumed as if to tell the world, *test me.*

These were the kind of generals you used to do the impossible. They saw adventure, freedom, and the glory that could be there's. They had a weakness, though. They could be impetuous and too slow to realize a course they'd taken could spell disaster. Offer them a hill, and they'd send the cavalry to it, even if that hill could not be adequately supplied. These men rarely thought about what ifs, but show them a moment of real vulnerability and the game was over.

The leaders Thaniel brought to this tent ran the gauntlet of both extremes, and the Emperor of the Kranish knew how to use every one of them perfectly.

King John's entourage and Thaniel's stared each other down until the tent flaps opened and I saw him.

Thaniel walked into the field. In all my life I had never seen a man who commanded such a magnetism. Sure, I'd seen renderings of him on canvas and stone. However, a picture of a fire and the fire are not the same thing. He was tall enough to seem regal but not so much that he stood over anyone. His eyes were emeralds, his hair dark ebony, and his jaw was stone.

Thaniel stood in that perfect posture a noble would but with a slight bend in his knees, a spine ever so flexible. I knew if I drew my tomahawk and attacked him, his change would be quick. This was the hallmark of a master swordsman. That he could disguise his skill. Beginners scream it out, but an expert knows enough to hide it. At Milhire, I had watched him cut down three Constables on his own. This was unheard of. Sometimes a lucky shot could kill a man with a tattooed arm, sometimes they were overrun with sheer numbers, but you would never find a man who could say he stood sword to sword with an agent of the New Church and had come out alive, at least until Thaniel.

This was the peasant who had forced himself into the aristocracy. The aristocrat who had overthrown a dynasty that had stood a millennia. This was the king who had proclaimed himself emperor of the world, and the world had yet to show him he was wrong.

Part of me wanted to kneel to him, part of me wanted to grit my teeth in defiance, and part of me wanted to attack him then and there. I stood firm, only because it was the hardest thing to do. His eyes met mine. He smiled.

The spell was broken as half of King John's entourage went to their knees, and the other half stood and called him emperor. It was a truly pathetic display.

"Fucking idiots." I muttered under my breath.

Thaniel laughed at that. "Ah, King John," he nodded his head so elegantly, "a pleasure to have you."

"Thaniel," King John said in dismissal as his entourage slowly realized how foolish they all seemed and tried to right it, "I wish I could say the same, but I am not used to engaging with peasants."

Some of the Kranish generals went for their swords, but the Emperor stopped them with a hand. "Every line has to start somewhere doesn't it." He curled his lips in amusement. "I bet if I went far enough back on you, I'd find a few shepherds and farmers."

"The king rules by divine right!" One of the useless men screamed out. I'd never cared enough to find out much about the speaker.

"The king rules because people say he does." Thaniel responded coyly. He waited for someone to challenge him, but no one did. I've never been one to let a challenge go though.

"Did we come to argue over genealogy," I leveled a stare at him, "or did we come to talk about peace?"

Thaniel put his gaze back on me. I'd stared into a battery of cannons before. I'd sooner do it again than have him look at me like that a second time. "Constable Thomas Belson," he rubbed his fingers together as if thinking, "I've heard impressive things about you."

I gave a predatory smile. It probably looked less impressive on my young face than his. "I'm sure you didn't hear them from Gostfeld." I saw Thaniel's gaze grow harder.

"Damnit Thomas shut your mouth!" King John turned to me. "You are out of place you-"

Thaniel silenced him with a hand, and he obeyed meekly. The Emperor turned to me. "*General* Gostfeld was a devoted patriot and a dear friend." He sighed. "I will not hear him spoken of so crassly."

I was about to tell him how crass my tomahawk was when it went into his head until Captain Seiford whispered in my ear. "Apologize."

I gritted my teeth. "I'm sorry." The damn word almost choked me.

Thaniel nodded. "Thank you." He recomposed himself. "That being said, I did not hear it from General Gostfeld."

"No, I expect not." I chuckled. "You heard it from your spies didn't you." King John gave me a mystified look I couldn't quite place.

Thaniel chuckled at that. "I keep my ears open." He nodded back towards the tent. "I believe it's time we begin our dialogue for a lasting and prosperous peace."

"Right you are then." King John said. The entire entourage moved forward, but Thaniel held up a hand to stop them.

"I believe this tent is too small to fit all of our company." The Emperor shrugged. "I suggest you take two dignitaries, and I will do the same."

"This is most uncouth sir." A noble on our side spoke up. He was no doubt worried about being left out.

"It is," Thaniel admitted, "but I believe six men have a better chance at reaching peace than forty."

"Understandable." King John turned around as if deciding who to bring. He pointedly ignored Captain Seiford and me.

"If I may," Thaniel interrupted, "I would request that those two men be Constable Belson and Captain Seiford." He nodded gestured to us. "As I understand it, the Captain is a man of character, and though Belson lacks a filter, I believe his honesty will serve us well."

"You do not decide who I bring!" King John started. "You up jumped-"

The Emperor silenced him with a stare that spoke of violence. "You had better stop before you say something that truly offends me." He calmed himself. "You're right, I cannot choose who you can bring, but I sure can choose who I want to meet with." Thaniel smiled. "If you do not bring them then this meeting is over and my campaign will continue."

I watched as the color drained from King John. He was caught in a compromising position. Deny the request and his kingdom would be taken piecemeal until nothing remained. More importantly to King John, he would lose face. He would be admitting that he had never had a single uninfluenced thought in his little head. However, if he agreed, then he admitted Thaniel held all the power.

I saw these things play over in King John's head. Eventually, he softened. "Come then." He snorted and walked impudently into the tent. Captain Seiford and I followed him. I felt my arm burn slightly. I ignored it. We were close to the border of Thaniel's empire, of course, there was bound to be a Demon or two wandering around.

The tent was completely tasteful on the inside. The only notable decoration was a map lying in the center with figures to denote armies. It wasn't adjusted to show the new bounds of Thaniel's holdings. For that, you'd need a man working night and day. Countries belonged to one king when the sun rose and Thaniel when it set.

I must admit, I was disappointed by the fact that I liked the tent. It wasn't so barren as to scream "humble," which is something a humble person would never do. I'd often found the most egotistical people are those who dress so simply you know they did it on purpose. "Look at how ugly my sackcloth is." They'll imply. "I must be a man who thinks nothing about how I look." Of course, they are in the same breath calling everyone to look at them. Just be honest about it. Go outside naked! That'll get some sideways glances.

However the tent was not so garish as to scream, "I'm better than you." If they were really better than anyone, they wouldn't need a solid gold chain to illustrate that point. Seeing something like that made me want to scream, "We know it's not gold, you idiot! It's copper painted yellow." Use that money to buy a gun. They'd really know not to make fun of you then. Gold chains can't kill anyone. Well, I suppose they could if you pulled it against their neck long enough, but I'd rather use piano wire.

This tent was meant to be ignored entirely while more important matters were discussed. I searched the room for some flaw in Thaniel's character. I wanted a reason to hate him. Sure, he had killed millions, but he was hardly the inventor of war. I wanted something I could truly indite him on. He'd burn down a city and shoot its inhabitants. I couldn't despise him for that, especially when I knew the Anthanii I served would have happily done the same, but did he eat a sandwich with a fork and a knife? Surely, he is a barbarian deserving nothing but contempt. Hate can grow on the most slippery of places, and yet in that tent, I couldn't find a single thing to call him on.

People often called me over critical of those around me, Captain Seiford chief among them. They said I was always looking for some fault in their character. "That woman's wearing a pretty dress." I'd say. "She's probably a whore." Captain Seiford would just shake his head. He knew that some women just liked to wear pretty dresses. I know doubt would have been happier if I could have enjoyed watching a woman in a pretty dress walk down a street.

Chief among my many vices was an inhuman love of conflict. Some men like to drink. I like to call the man at the bar a posh because he sips his ale with a pinky extended. However, keep in mind, if you're going to have a conflict with someone you at least need a reason. In the Confederacy, my tutor had often praised my argumentative skills. Little did he know, I had honed them by starting fights with anyone I judged of proper size. That was probably why I wasn't so popular in my native home.

There was another layer to my hatred as well. Even in my most pugnacious moments, I wasn't so critical of people back home. I was from the Confederacy. People from Thyro thought we were frontier savages, too dumb for civilized society. However, the feeling was mutual. We thought they were city weaklings, too soft to take a piss in the forest without being overpowered by an especially tenacious squirrel. I was willing to admit, I was not above such bigotry.

Of course, I had met a great many people who's spines were made of iron. Actually liking someone who wasn't from my side of the ocean felt vaguely unpatriotic. I reconciled this by telling myself they were really just Confederacy men who'd had the misfortune of being born far away from anyone with the requisite testicular fortitude that could have shown them the proper way.

"And who are they, Thaniel?" King John gestured dismissively to two dark shadows in the tent. I didn't need a reason to hate John. I had a feeling if he'd been born without a crown, he'd have been the sort of person me and my brother used to throw eggs at.

Thaniel didn't bristle at not being called emperor. In public he knew that an emperor no one called emperor was just a man with an expensive chair and hat. However, in private he viewed correction of such slights as a waste of his all important time. Despite myself, I liked that about him. "This is Chancellor Machiev." He gestured to one of the figures.

One of the shadows moved into plain view. Chancellor Machiev was a gaunt man dressed in black and white. His cheeks were hollow, and his thin lips were twisted into a contemplating sneer. His eyes were dark and filled with thinly veiled calculation. His hair was so black he had to have oiled it. I knew he spent hours on his appearance every morning but not because he actually cared about how people saw him. He did it because he needed to control everything. He needed every hair to be in place, every wrinkle to be purged. In another life, Machiev would have made an excellent steward. The man wouldn't rest until every stain on the floor was gone. I could have used a man like him around. I'd always been on the messy side, as Captain Seiford continually pointed out.

"Gentlemen," Chancellor Machiev nodded to Captain Seiford and me, "your highness." He turned to the king without changing his expression. I knew he hated John. Well, only a human can really hate, and I wasn't sure the man sitting in front of me was human. I was sure if I opened up his chest I'd find a heart, but it was probably just there for appearances and not to actually pump blood through his body. In any case, King John and Machiev had a history. Once upon a time, the chancellor had served as the chief advisor to John's father. John had dismissed him from court because Machiev had unsettled him. This was the first in a trend of incompetent governing.

Anyone hated by King John deserved a firm handshake. "Charmed." I said extending my tattooed arm which he didn't take, and I returned dumbly to my side. In fact, I was anything but. The man made me feel like I was on the edge of a precipice only he could see. He made me feel like no matter how much I thought I knew, he controlled the situation. I could have put a six-shooter to his head, and he'd still have given off the air that I wouldn't pull the trigger unless it was according to his plan. Three above, I could have shot him, and I'd want to see his body burned before I judged it some play I wasn't clever enough to understand.

I knew Chancellor Machiev's type well. Men like him were low-level aristocracy. They'd no doubt been mocked all their lives as too common for the nobles and too noble for the commoners. They didn't have the constitution for military service to prove them wrong with medals, they didn't have the charisma to embarrass them by seducing their wives, and they'd been too ambitious to join the clergy and at least condemn their mocker's souls, be it the New Church or the Old Religion. Their vengeance would come from seeing those who mocked them penniless and disgraced.

This type was bred to be politicians. They were perfectly equipped to master the subtle art of power. They had one foot in court and one in the mob. They knew the complexities of noble power grabbing and the economics behind how much a baker would sell a pie to a carpenter. They could flatter a lord and terrify the peasants. These were the type of men who showed up in the shadows of history books, looking over the king's shoulder to make sure he didn't do anything too stupid. Anywhere you read about a great conquerer, have no doubt, he had a man like Chancellor Machiev making sure the wealth flowed to the army.

However, Chancellor Machiev was the greatest and most archetypal of that sort. To compare him to a bureaucrat is like comparing a hurricane to rain. You're in the right area, but you may have underestimated the situation.

The stories about him weren't as popular as Thaniel's, but they were twice as worrisome. Thaniel could be defeated in battle, but a politician as adept as the chancellor would have planned for that and then planned for me to deal with that plan. He'd never had anyone executed, but people feared him. He never screamed, but people listened.

As I heard it, when Machiev worked for Anthanii, he had known where the corruption was, what group could bear what tax, and who needed what assistance. Heartless is a word thrown around far too often, but I was absolutely sure Machiev had no heart, metaphorical or otherwise. However, whatever his reasons were, he had done more to help the people than charity ever would. He had helped them get jobs that paid well. He had almost tripled the number of children receiving an education. He had given beggars and street urchins housing and opportunity to become contributing members to society. He understood that wellbeing was not a finite resource. After all, more income means more taxes, and a man who starves is one less who can take up arms for his country. Still, I had no doubt that if it suited his agenda, he'd have every baby's head dashed against a wall. That sort of thing was rarely called for though.

For all he did, though, you could never point at a responsibility and say, "Oh yes trading policy, that's Machiev's business." In all my time inquiring about the chancellor's duties, I had never gotten anything more informative than a shrug of the shoulder. That was the mark of a truly excellent bureaucrat, you never really knew what their job was until they stopped doing it.

Due to his lack of charisma, he would never be popular with any caste, but everyone knew who buttered their bread, both literally and figuratively. He had done some excellent things for the butter industry. No matter how much you dislike the man, you know you need him. Getting rid of Machiev would be like cutting out your lung because you had a cough. No one was that stupid. Well, I say no one…

When King John had sent Machiev away, the ledgers had gone from every copper accounted for to complete disrepair. The peasants had gone from content to rioting. Even the sewers had backed up. This all happened within the space of a week, and it had taken years and a hundred university graduates to bring it under control. Even still the system didn't work quite as well as it used to.

If anything had opened up Anthanii for conquest, it had been that. Somehow under Machiev, the taxes had seemed like a minor nuisance to the people, and yet the coffers always stayed full. Under King John's new "expert team" the people were being crushed by a new regulatory cost every day, and there was never enough money.

Thaniel attracted men of talent, and so Machiev went from the chief advisor of Anthanii to the chancellor of Kran. They're mostly the same position. If anyone in Kran was worried about a foreigner running their affairs, the river of gold he'd brought into their country had silenced them. The general consensus was that to be a foreigner you had to actually be born somewhere else, and born was the key word. No one could actually imagine a baby Machiev being the result of two people mating. I'm sure he had a mother, but I never wanted to meet her.

When word got out that Machiev had begun serving Thaniel, King John had gone to the streets announcing that all their problems since he left were due to the chief advisor's sabotage. This was an effort to shift the blame that failed miserably. To Machiev, sabotage would have meant doing a bad job. That's roughly the equivalent of a cat learning how to swim. The truth was he'd received the news he'd been sacked and left to go see what Thaniel was about. He'd just stopped working one day. At sunrise, he'd set down his pen for the final time, and by noon the country was in the midst of it's worse economic depression since money was invented. They'd found a half-written note on his table that read, *Send the road reports to-*I would bet my life those road reports never got there.

Now the man who could make money appear from air worked for Thaniel, and that meant Thaniel could make armies appear from air.

"So you brought the traitor." King John sneered at Chancellor Machiev.

Everyone in the room gave the king a befuddled look. I even heard Captain Seiford sigh at the idiocy of it. John had sent Machiev away because he looked strange. How arrogant could someone be? Did he expect men to bury their head in the sand when he had no further use for them?

I was about to say something, but the Chancellor saved me. "Yes, he brought the traitor." Machiev kept his face straight.

"Well," Thaniel clapped his hands together, "I'm glad you're already acquainted."

"I am his second advisor." I heard the second shadow say. It was barely a whisper, but it sang through like a flute through an orchestra. It was like a shattering glass whose shards never hit the floor. I felt the tattoos on my arm burn hotter.

He stepped forward, and I wondered how he stayed hidden. His robes were the sort of red that comes from dried blood. He was adorned in jewels and gold from neck to knees. Yet he could have worn a diamond the size of an egg on his neck, and it wouldn't have been the most magnificent thing about him. His face was utterly flawless. In one moment, I saw a picture of rugged masculinity, in another the elegance of an aristocrat. Every type of beauty made its home on his face. I could never point to any exact change on him, but his essence shifted like the blowing of the wind. It all screamed evil though. It felt like watching a snake rear its head back to strike. He was encircled by four boys covered from head to tow in white. There was no way he could have hidden all of that in a shadow. I smelled Demons in play, and the burning in my arm confirmed it

"I am Bishop Harfeld." He took another step. "Ah, the dutiful captain," he nodded to Seiford, "It is such a pleasure to meet you."

Captain Seiford bared his teeth at the bishop.

Harfeld just laughed and turned to King John. "And the man who thinks power comes from a crown." He looked the king up and down. "Tell me, did that crown do any good at Milhire?"

King John remained silent as the grave. I'm sure he told himself it was quiet dignity. Everyone else saw it for what it was, fear.

"Finally, the hero of Wunstville," Bishop Harfeld turned his gaze to me. "I must admit, I had to consult a map to find where you were the hero of." I saw the ridiculousness of it tug at the corners of his mouth.

"Well, clearly you've never bought a donkey." I gave him a cheery smile. "I hear the Wuntsville donkey is famous throughout the world. After all, a few of them beat one of your best generals." The Priest recoiled as if he'd been attacked. Bishop Harfeld had never been talked to like that. Even Thaniel afforded him a certain deference. I wanted to show him I wasn't afraid though, so I went on. "As for where I'm the hero of, I plan on making it easier on you." I pushed one of his little acolytes to the side on my way to the map in the middle. "Soon I'll be the hero of all this." I gestured to the map of Thyro. "You won't be around for that though." I gave him a wolfish smile. "The Old Religion will be quite out of style when I'm done."

Bishop Harfeld clenched his jaw. "Do you think beating us will be as easy as Wuntsville?"

"Now that you mention it, no." I scratched my head as if thinking. "I can't imagine anything as easy as winning that battle." It was bluster, of course. Fighting through five thousand men on my own was anything but easy. My body was still hurting from the wounds I'd taken. "I tell you this though," I turned my voice hard, "one day you'll see me outside your temple, and it won't be with donkeys and scarecrows."

"Is that a threat?" He stepped towards me.

"I know you were hoping I'd bring donkeys." I matched his step. "I heard that's how Priest's mate."

"I'll forgive you this insolence." Harfeld's voice changed and beat through my soul. "You've never seen us on the field of battle. You don't know enough to fear us the way we should be!"

The very air in the room told me to kneel. It screamed at me to retreat. It whispered treacherous words in my ear. I've never been the best listener though. "You're right I haven't seen you on the field of battle." I tilted my head to one side then the other. "I can understand your absence at Wuntsville but Milhire?" I shrugged. "The biggest battle in living memory, and Thaniel decided he didn't need you." I paused. "That makes me think he doesn't need you." I closed the distance between us. The poor acolytes didn't know what to do when someone invaded their little square. "It makes me think all you're good for is making crops grow a bit higher than usual and talking inordinate amounts of shit."

"That's enough from you two." Thaniel said, but it didn't seem like he really wanted me to stop. It seemed like he wanted to see what I'd do. It was some elaborate test. I didn't know what he expected of me, so I went with my gut.

"You insolent little-" Bishop Harfeld started.

"I promise if I ever start a garden, you're the first person I'll consult." I laughed in his face. "Until then you better leave war to the real players in this game."

"I am older than sin and death, child!" The Priest's scream felt like gunpowder going off in my gut. "I will rain fire and lightning upon-"

He never got a chance to finish his threat. I punched him in the nose and felt it break. The whole room held it's breath. Even the impassive Chancellor Machiev cocked an eyebrow up. It was his equivalent of screaming "The world is round! Money is imaginary!

It was my maw leaving presents under my bed!" The sun could have risen in the West, and no one in the tent would have been more surprised than they were then.

I could have hit the Priest in the jaw and knocked him out. I could have hit him in the gut to set him to huffing. The old Constables who taught me how to fight at God's Rest even showed me some spots on a body you could strike that would cause instant death. I hadn't believed them, but this would have been the perfect time to try it. I hit him in the nose because it felt good. I wanted to watch him whimper in pain. I wanted to watch him bleed.

I smiled at him cradling his face. "I've never been overly scared of lighting and fire. They seem terribly unreliable." I held up my hand which had some blood still on it. "Now a fist goes wherever you tell it to." I took a step forward. "Everyone always talks about Priests like their gods walking among us."

I licked the blood on my hand. "Taste like regular blood to me." In truth, it didn't. It tasted like cinnamon which wasn't bad. That threw me off a bit. If someone put a mug of Priest blood in front of me, I'd probably drink it and not just to prove I would. Still, I imagined I was the only person in history to ever taste the stuff, so I'd probably get away with telling everyone it was just like the normal blood. *Cinnamon! Who'd have thought?* I'd have guessed sulfur and salt if anything. Some part of me wondered if it was poisonous, but I took another lick. I pretended like it was all part of my bravado, but the truth was I hadn't tasted cinnamon in a while.

I was smiling until I watched the broken bones on his nose crack back together. I felt the tattoos on my arm burn like wildfire. Then I saw the Priest's eyes. It was like I could see down into the World Below where Demons lay.

He started to chant, and I felt the danger close in around me. Some people call it the fight or flight instinct. In my mind, flight is for birds. I pulled my tomahawk out and charged at the Priest. I could see him calling on powers beyond. For one blessed moment, we almost met. My ax and his Demons, my skill and his magics. I wanted it more than I'd ever wanted anything. To me, it was like seeing a beautiful woman lying naked in my bed. Some situations need to be acted on. It was like hawk and snake. No, it was like the ocean and the shore. Let us fight!

"Stop!"

I obeyed, and so did Bishop Harfeld. It wasn't the word that quelled us. It was the order behind it. It was Thaniel. If he had said the word in a language I didn't speak, I still would have listened. If a peasant walked up to a king and said, "give me your crown," in a voice like that, the king would have handed it over. It wasn't like the subtle emphasis the Priest used to make their speech worth something. It was a natural thing. When Thaniel spoke, you better listen. I stopped, and so did Bishop Harfeld.

Two soldiers rushed in, and Thaniel waved them off. "Everything's fine." He said, and the soldiers cautiously backed out the tent. They could tell from the bloody Priest on the ground that everything wasn't fine.

Bishop Harfeld got to his feet readjusting his robe while the acolytes helped him. I expected him to make some dramatic swear on the heavens and earth or some such nonsense. He disappointed me. "Fuck you!"

"Leave this tent." Thaniel told the Priest.

Bishop Harfeld looked like he was about to say something, but after darting his eyes between the emperor and me, he thought better of it and headed out the front flap.

"Not out the front." Thaniel said sternly. "I don't want my men to see you like this." He gestured to the back. "Be inconspicuous and clean yourself up."

I imagined even with all those precautions, tomorrow Kran would be ablaze with rumors a Priest of the Old Religion had been accosted with no answer. I made a mental note to start a story that I'd raped him too. That would get the tongues waging.

"Three above." King John stared at me with a mix of awe and fear

"Thomas..." Seiford eyes were as wide as eyes get.

Chancellor Machiev took out a note pad and a little pencil and jotted down some notes. Note pads were expensive, but to a man who fought with paper, I imagined it was as essential as a six-shooter. It seemed like a useful thing to do, write down notes. I had tried to develop that habit when I was thirteen, but I was thirteen. The notepad had been covered with drawings of male genitalia and what I imagined tits looked like, by the end of the day.

Finally, Thaniel spoke up. "Now lets commence with the peace talks." He gestured to the chairs surrounding the maps.

There wasn't a doubt in my mind he had orchestrated the whole situation. However, I also knew something else that brought a smile to my face. He hadn't expected me to react like that.

The Thaniel Wars

All five of us sat around the map. King John, Captain Seiford, and I were on one side, Thaniel and Chancellor Machiev on the other. Bishop Harfeld's seat was conspicuously empty. It left a hole in the room that no amount of peace talks could fix. They started to speak on who get's what, but their minds were on something else. Everyone in the room tried to ignore what they'd just watched me do. It was like when your friend brings home a beautiful woman. You try to keep your eyes off her, but sooner or later you'll find her tits in your gaze.

I had just punched a Priest of the Old Religion and not just any small town Demon talker. Bishop Harfeld had power. His name was spoken in hushed fear by all of Thyro. It was as if the peasants believed if they uttered it too loud the man himself would show up on their door to cause unspeakable havoc. The nobles, on the other hand, knew it as absolute fact that he would.

Thaniel might conquer your home. In the battle, innocents could be killed, and women could be raped. At the end of the day though, The Emperor of Kran would begin governing you much in the same fashion as your previous rulers. Their lives might even be better for it. Intellectuals will talk about liberty and equality being worth dying for, but what the farmer wants more than anything is stability. The unspoken truth of it all was that once Thaniel conquered Thyro, a sort of peace would settle upon the land. If the Emperor came, board up your doors and work on a Kranish accent. There'd be some damage, but people in Thyro were used to being conquered. They knew how to rebuild.

Bishop Harfeld was a different story altogether. If you saw Bishop Harfeld on the horizon, run if you think you can make it. If it's too late, kill your family to save them the pain, then tie a noose for yourself. He was the single most feared man in the world.

Thaniel had the most power, I was the most unpredictable, but Harfeld was pure evil. He used the Demons to make sons kill their fathers, brothers rape their sisters, and much worse. I once asked what could be worse than that. They couldn't say. I don't know if it's because they didn't have the words, or their mouth literally couldn't say it. Apparently, just thinking about it was enough to go mad. If I had seen the words written, I would have disregarded it as the exaggeration of rumors. I knew better than anyone how a story could take on a life of its own. Belson the Blessed they called me now. If the Three blessed me, they had undoubtedly picked a funny method of anointment. I hadn't seen the words written, though. I'd seen the eyes of the men who swore Bishop Harfeld got much worse than forcing a brother to raper his sister. I believed them.

Sure, Constables killed Priests. That was the lion's share of our job, but a lot of Priests killed Constables too. The tattoos on my arm did more than warn me about Demons. Woven into them were wards that protected me from being touched by Powers Below. This meant that a Demon couldn't control my body or wrap their ethereal hands over my throat. However, a Demon could call lightning, and lightning could strike me. I wasn't lightning proof. At least I thought I wasn't. I'd always wanted to fight lightning. I made a mental note that when this business with Thaniel was over, I'd go find a tall metal pole and touch it until the sky answered my challenge. I was willing to bet lightning wasn't that tough.

In God's Rest, we were taught how to deal with the Priests. If you had to slay a man with a bloodstained cloak, shoot him from far away. Sneak up behind him in the dead of night and stab the man in the back. If you're in the middle of a battle, kill him quick. If they have half a chance to respond, you're a dead man. Even for my order, specially trained and equipped to fight Powers Below, we held the Old Religion in a certain respect. My instructors taught me that the one thing you never do is challenge a true Priest to single combat. You may get away with a village Demon Speaker, but it still probably wasn't worth the risk. They never told me not to mock one, punch him in the face, and then mock him again. They probably imagined no one was unhinged enough to try it. I was in the business of surprising people.

To anyone who has not looked in the face of a man from Thyro and asked him about the Old Religion, you cannot understand their fear. Let's say you believe in an almighty God who stands at the edge of the clouds watching us. You believe in him the same way you believe water is wet and fire is hot. You believe he has the power to smite you from the sky and afterward send your soul to unspeakable damnation for eternity. This god appears to you one day, and you punch him in the nose. That is what I just did.

I would hazard that the vast majority of people view the Old Religion as pure evil. Those that don't, view it as a necessary evil. It has advantages to be sure. It makes the crops grow and ends disease. It can be used to strengthen your borders and protect that which you love. If you blind yourself to the child trying to claw his eyes out because the Demons chase him through his dreams, if you look away when your mother can't remember her name long before that thing is supposed to happen to the elderly, one can make a point that the Old Religion has done some good.

That's the message the powerful told those they ruled, but peasants aren't nearly as stupid as nobles like to think they are. They know the grain they're eating was paid for with the souls of their neighbors. They see that it's never those with a certain amount of money who's family is hurt. What can they do though? Rebel? Maybe. It had worked in the past, but that was years ago when governments were local lords with a few loyal knights. It still failed far more than it succeeded though. Now governments spanned untold miles with huge nationalized armies.

Thaniel did it, of course. The peasant who became emperor, but first he had the loyalty of the army, and even then, his revolution would have been cut short if he hadn't been such a shrewd politician. A man like Thaniel came once in a millennium. Hoping for someone like that to save you was like walking into a nunnery hoping to get your cock sucked. You heard stories about it, but it would never actually happen. Besides, even Thaniel had embraced the Old Religion in the end. A man who stood for the people now averted his eyes to their worst oppressors.

If you walked into a city and offered a vote to have the Priests' horrors gone from their land, ninety-nine out of a hundred would vote yes, and the one who voted no had probably been kicked in the head as a boy and didn't really understand what he was voting for. However, if a Priest came to town and said kneel or else. Ninety-nine of a hundred would kneel, and the one who didn't had also probably been kicked in the head. That wouldn't stop the Priest from torturing the poor moron to death. That's the trouble with things like that. Freedom is built upon hope, and oppression is based on fear. In Thyro fear was by far the more plentiful resource.

The men who kneeled weren't cowards. When they failed, it wouldn't just be them that suffered. They had families and friends. Priests enjoyed nothing more than making an example. Even still, all they needed was a hope, however small. All they needed was a fool's chance at victory. If they suspected there was a possibility that things could change, they'd damn the consequences and charge into the mouth of fire and death. I would give them that.

Maybe Bishop Harfeld was right. Maybe I hadn't seen enough to fear them the way they should be. Then again, maybe they hadn't seen enough of me to be afraid. Even now men heard stories about a boy who'd led his men out the slaughter of Milhire. They heard about a boy who had stood against Thaniel's greatest general. They were small victories. They were a ghost wind blowing against a hurricane, but ghost winds can grow, and men looked up to the Three and said, "maybe."

If you asked me why I punched Bishop Harfeld, I could give you an answer based on logic and one not. Both would have been enough to do it. The logical one is I knew the risks, and a small part of me had expected to die in a fiery inferno. However, I had a good guess on why Thaniel called this meeting. It wasn't to forge a lasting peace, but it also wasn't to see me dead. I wagered that Thaniel would view me more valuable than his Priest, and I also wagered that he'd be enough to call off the dogs. It had been risky, but there was a subtle reward in it. A reward that could be worth more than a legion of angles. Thaniel saw it too. It was why he told Harfeld to go out the back, but people would see. Priests could bleed, and the man who made them do it could live to tell of it afterwards. I proved that men had power over Demons. If it was Thaniel or me who made the Priest stop, didn't matter. The rumor would spread. Fear is a good weapon, but if you can manage it, use hope. It was far more dangerous in my eyes.

The illogical answer is different. I'd never been the charitable type. I wasn't the white knight who would right all the wrongs of the world, but I had grown to manhood in a free land. I hadn't thought much of it at the time, but three thousand miles away, you start to see the good of where you came from. In the Confederacy, men did not kneel. There were sects of the Old Religion there. I'd seen a bloodstained cloak in my youth, but they were rare, and men did not fear them. It jaded me to see decent folk forced into obedience. Sure, King John wasn't so much better, but in time his power would slip. I liked to work from the top down anyway. Even more than that, I wanted to show Harfeld that all those people he hurt could hurt him back. I did it because I wanted to see the moment when he realized he wasn't all powerful. I did it because it felt good. I did it because he thought I wouldn't.

To the people in the tent with me and to those who would hear about it from rumors, what I had done was either the bravest thing in living memory or the dumbest. It depended on how the war turned out was the honest answer. I was perfectly fine with that. Spectacular glory or spectacular failure, I would not lie in between. Men would know me. The world would be changed by me.

If you think I'd be content with being named amongst the greatest of heroes, you don't know me. If that was all I wanted, I'd forsake my order and forge an empire. Empires die, though. Ideas become immortal if they're good enough. I wanted to build a new world. In the thousand years to come, when men look down from the ivory towers of their utopia, let them say, "Thomas Belson laid the first stone." Let them give quiet thanks.

If I failed, I would do so where the whole world would watch. No matter how hard the powers that be tried to wipe me into obscurity, my name would never be gone from the minds of the righteous, and those are the only ones that really matter in the end. People would think back to the man who risked it all. They would tell their children the story of one who said "no" for no better reason than because it felt good. In time, another hero would rise, and the path will have been set by me.

If I succeeded, then I would have what I wanted. Emperors thought the highest honor was to be the greatest of men. Certainly, that's better than nothing, but I wanted more. To be the greatest of men meant that others had to be less. They didn't see how that reduced their legacy. The highest honor is to be first among equals. The height of man is not to be obeyed. The height of man is that others have a choice, and they choose you.

These were lofty dreams for a sixteen-year-old Confederacy boy. To not only be great but the greatest…

Then again, what are sixteen-year-olds for if not lofty dreams?

The great tragedy of the human race was that they rarely took that ambition with them into adulthood. By the time I died, every young boy would be named Thomas, or the custom would be outlawed altogether.

"Obviously for any peace to be obtained we will require the-" Chancellor Machiev said. I wasn't really listening. I was still smiling to myself that I had broken a Priest's nose. Also apparently the Priest still had some hard feelings over it too. The tattoos on my arm kept going from white-hot, to normal, to white hot. Bishop Harfeld was smart enough to know calling fire and thunder upon me wouldn't be the best move, especially with his emperor in the room, but that hadn't stopped him from trying to explode my heart or choke me to death.

The tattoos screamed with pride every time they saved me some horrible fate. I just thought it was annoying. You're doing your job, congratulations to you! Now let me give a medal to the blacksmith for making a horseshoe. I'd always had a high tolerance for pain, but the constant white, hot burning was enough to distract me from peace. I scratched the arm vigorously. It didn't make it feel better, but it seemed natural.

I stopped scratching when I realized everyone was staring at me. "What?" I asked.

"Thomas," Captain Seiford started, "maybe during peace talks between the two most powerful countries in the world, isn't the time or place to try and scratch your arm bloody." He still felt out of place amongst such power. It was unheard of to have a captain at a summit like the one we were at, and he was no doubt still running through a list in his mind of potentially better candidates.

"Is there something wrong Constable Belson?" Chancellor Machiev asked, but I got the feeling he didn't really care if something was wrong. I don't even really think the gaunt man actually understood the concept of right and wrong, just orderly and messy.

"Your damn Priest is still trying to kill me." I kept scratching at the tattoos. "It's quite annoying."

"Oh." Thaniel cocked an eyebrow up. "Should I tell him to stop?"

"No, he'll tucker himself out eventually." I said without looking up.

"Perhaps some wine to help get our minds off that unpleasantness." He pulled out a bottle and started filling the goblets in front of us. Thaniel was clearly befuddled at my nonchalance. From the way I said it, you'd imagine I was being attacked by a rather brave fly and not the most dangerous man in the world. In reality, I wanted to bang my arm into a wall until it stopped. I wanted to scream bloody murder. More than anything I wanted to go find that Bishop and put an ax in his head, but I wouldn't show weakness in front of Thaniel.

I took a sip of the wine. It was good stuff. I'd always preferred beer or whiskey, but if you're going to drink wine, get it from the Emperor of Kran. Before they were famous for laying waste to countries, they were known throughout the world by their exceptional vintages.

"And how do I know it's not poisoned?" King John narrowed his eyes across the table.

Thaniel did his best to hide a laugh. "It's not poisoned." He took a sip from his own cup to illustrate the point.

"You could have put it in the cup." King John had probably never eaten food that hadn't been tasted beforehand.

"I could have," Thaniel admitted, "but I didn't."

"Here switch with me." He gestured to Thaniel's cup.

"Absolutely not!" The Emperor seemed disgusted.

"Because it's poisoned!" King John said victoriously.

"No, because I have spent a great deal of money studying how to stop disease in my country." Thaniel shook his head. "The consensus is that invisible animals cause it and are spread when people drink after each other."

"They're hidden by sorcery?" King John was aghast.

"No, they're just really small." Thaniel held two fingers slightly apart to illustrate the point.

"Sounds like sorcery." King John mumbled to himself.

"So did gunpowder once." Thaniel shrugged. "Now the whole world uses cannon and musket." He smiled. "I've found that magic and science ride in separate carts that look the same from far away." The Emperor took a sip of his drink. "Both are just too stubborn to buy a new one." He gave a look like in another life he'd have wanted to be a scientist. I could empathize with that. I would have liked to be a pianist.

"I'm still not sure I trust it's safe to drink." King John circled around to the original point.

"Then don't drink it." Chancellor Machiev stared at him with those dark, inhuman eyes.

"But I'm thirsty, traitor." King John leveled a glare at the man who seemed utterly immune to it.

"I'll try it." I reached a hand for the cup, but the King pulled away from me like I'd put a torch in his face.

"Three above, no!" He exclaimed and then somewhat regained his composure. "What I mean is that it is improper for someone of such low birth to drink from the same cup as a king." It was a bad lie. I knew his food tasters were people so poor they were willing to bet their life against a few coins that no one wanted to poison the king. I could imagine a lot of people wanted King John poisoned. I certainly did, but I'd rather slap him in the face a few times. Even his most loyal followers knew he was a meddling ruler at best, waiting optimistically for Prince Edward's reign.

This, of course, made me curious. I poked at him with my trigger finger. He jumped in his chair to avoid it. "Stop!" He screamed.

"Why?" I asked, poking him again, and he jumped out his chair.

"Because a king will not be-" He started indignantly.

"Why?" I poked him again, but this time he backpedaled away from me.

"Because I am divinely-"

"Why?" I tried to poke him.

"I don't want whatever curse you've brought upon yourself transferred to me!" King John huffed. "Now, will you stop poking me!"

"Oh." I mulled the answer over. It seemed like the truth. Then I tried to poke him again. I did this because before I was ever a Constable, before I was anything really, I was a boy who liked poking things. All my great achievements and all my darkest failings in some way or another hailed from that one fact. I just loved poking things.

"Poke." I said out loud and watched the king of Anthanii backpedal furiously away from my treacherous finger.

"Will you two stop." Chancellor Machieve turned his gaunt face to me. He didn't change his expression, but I felt the anger behind it. I'll admit he scared me more than Bishop Harfeld ever could.

The Priest could drag my soul to the World Below, but Machieve could raise my loan interest rate to sixteen percent! As a rule, I avoid tangling with bankers. I wanted to retire one day, and it wouldn't due to have my credit ruined.

"I'll stop poking you." I really did enjoy poking the King though. I'd probably find an excuse later.

"Good." He sat back down in his chair. "The issue remains though I am still convinced this wine is poisoned, and I will not negotiate while thirsty.

"Well, it appears we'll have to convince you it's not." Thaniel clapped his hands together. "Constable Belson why don't you explain to his grace why I don't want him poisoned." He gave me a look like a tutor gives a student. A subtle challenge to test my wits. We didn't have armies to play with, only foolish kings. "Without poking him." He added at the end. That was probably smart. My finger was already poised.

I heard Captain Seiford sigh. He didn't like my ego being stroked.

It was bad luck for him because I loved having my ego stroked. I also never turned down a challenge. "The first answer is that you could have done it already." I smiled at him. "You have spies all over his court." The look on Thaniel's face told me he didn't know I knew, but he wasn't scared, more impressed than anything. "I'm sure one of them could be convinced to kill a king, for the right price."

"A hefty bag of gold?" Thaniel posited the question. It was another challenge.

"If that is the right price for the right man." I shrugged. "There are other currencies than gold."

"Banknotes you mean?" Thaniel asked though he already knew the answer.

"No." I answered simply. *Nationalism, pride, to keep his family safe.* Those were the unspoken words between us. Gold is a good motivator, but there are other ways to make a man do your bidding. People forget, at the end of the day, gold isn't worth all that much. You can't even forge a decent sword out of the stuff. Thaniel wanted to know if I saw that.

The Emperor nodded for me to continue, so I did. "You could have gotten to him at any point in the last five years, and you would have had plausible deniability." I said. "Of course, people would have suspected, but without proof, suspicions are forgotten by the end of the year." I took a sip of the wine. "Here, in this tent, there would be no question." I cocked my head to one side. "That's the kind of thing that gets put in a history book no matter how hard you try to squash it. It could make governing difficult, even for this one." I nodded to Machiev.

"You have spies in my court!" King John seemed aghast.

Everyone in the room took a moment to marvel at his naivety. Thaniel spoke first. "Well, um…" He pushed his eyebrows together. "We are two nations at war." He thought that explained it, but he overestimated the king's intelligence. "Are you saying you don't?" The Emperor asked the obvious question.

"Of course I don't dabble in such dishonorable activities!" King John bristled at what he saw as an insult. "I should have known better than to expect the same from a peasant upstart."

We all looked at him in absolute wonder, except Captain Seiford. He put his face in his hands. He had too much discipline to cry in dismay. I cherished that moment, though. The exact moment Seiford realized he had sworn undying loyalty to a man who cared so little about the war effort he hadn't even bothered to put an agent in the enemies court. No wonder it seemed like the Anthanii leadership had no idea what Kran was going to do. They didn't.

Thaniel raised his eyebrows in surprise. "I just thought you were terrible at it." He tried his best to feign respect, but even on his face, which made every word land true and genuine, it was painfully obvious he was laughing inside. "I commend your honor." The Emperor raised his cup in a toast.

"Thank you." King John was dumb enough to take it as a compliment. Then he turned to me. "You knew about this and said nothing?"

"I thought you knew." I shrugged. "I figured it out within half an hour of fighting this war."

"Takes a savage to spot a savage I suppose." He snorted in dismissal. There was less bite this time than when he usually called me savage. I thought he was finally starting to realize he should just get out of my way. Besides, I was quite savage.

I was about to respond anyway, but Captain Seiford stopped me. "Can we please move on, gentlemen?" He moaned from behind his hands. He didn't want to focus on his ruler's glaring failures anymore.

"Quite right." King John slapped the table. "Good Anthanii men don't like this cloak and dagger business." He patted Seiford on the back. "That's why I've always liked you, Major Sieben."

"It's Captain Seiford, your highness." To his credit, he really did try to say the "your highness" with respect.

"Right then." Thaniel chuckled. "So if you were the king, you would drink the wine on that assumption?" He asked me.

I almost felt Captain Seiford's dismay. He didn't want to talk about poisoned wine anymore.

"I would drink the wine." I was enjoying the Captain's misery too much. "It's worth the risk for such a vintage, and I don't think there's any risk." I filled my goblet again to show I liked it. "However, the real question is why you haven't killed him yet." I circled my cup a bit. "I bet it would be easy."

"It would," Thaniel admitted, "so why haven't I?"

"In the past couple of years, your strategy has changed." I looked him in the eye. "You conquered six major countries and countless smaller principalities." I shrugged. "I studied each campaign closely. They were perfectly designed for the quickest, least costly victory. I couldn't have done better myself." We eyed each other up. Both of us knew the other was our only true peer in these matters. "Each of those countries had a fraction of the power Anthanii did, but now you're not just fighting to win, you're planning for what comes after." I nodded at him. "Are you content with me knowing this, or do you want to hear how I know this?"

"In the interest of time, I think I believe that you do." Thaniel waved for me to continue.

I did. "You won't kill the king because then you run the risk of dividing Anthanii. It's only been together for a century. The uncontested king is the only thing holding it together." I took a sip of wine. "It's still fragile."

King John scoffed at that. "Everyone knows it's easier to conquer a divided kingdom."

"Easier to conquer," I didn't look at him, just Thaniel, "harder to govern." The Emperor's eyes told me I was right. "You want to take Anthanii whole with its infrastructure intact." I went on. "There's two explanations to that." I held up one finger. "The first is that those countries you conquered were harder to hold onto than they were to take. You're feeling the effects of governing places not used to you, and you're regretting it now." I narrowed my eyes. "You're taking steps to avoid that with a nation as large as Anthanii."

"I have had a bit of trouble." Thaniel admitted. "It was nothing we couldn't handle in good time, but it has been quite an inconvenience." He leaned in. "What's the second reason?"

I put up the second finger. "In your mind, this war is won, the actual fighting is a formality." I leaned in to match him.

"Besides the otherwise insignificant Battle of Wuntsville, you haven't shown me I can be stopped." Thaniel chuckled.

"We can hurt you, though" I smiled. "We can cost you more than you're willing to give, and make whatever further conquest you've planned impossible." I drank some more of the wine. "The fact that you're not worried about that makes me think you have something we don't know about." I curled the corner of my mouth. "It makes me think there's other pieces on the board."

"Men like me and you don't play the pieces," he smiled back, "we play the game." He echoed my most personal motto. It was something I rarely spoke out loud. His spies were closer than I thought.

"If he believes he's already won, why did he call for peace?" King John had yet to realize what this meeting was really about.

"He doesn't want peace." I looked at the king. "He's winning. Why stop now?" I looked back at Thaniel. "He wants to speak with me."

"Thomas, you've been right in the past, but that's a huge leap." Captain Seiford finally spoke up. "Not everything is about you!" Then he saw Thaniel's eyes. When you say something of complete and utter truth, the man you tell it to can't hide what it is.

"Three above, no..." Captain Seiford finally realized the war that had shaped his life wouldn't end today or anytime soon. He was clever as they come, but desperation can cloud even the best judgment. He had wanted peace for so long he was willing to grasp for any straw. Then again maybe he was just pissed my ego was getting more inflated.

Thaniel's gaze went from gracious to cold in a moment. "Leave us." He looked at the King.

"I do not take orders from you!" He rose in anger.

"Not yet you don't, but I only intend to give you one." Thaniel glared at King John's temper tantrum. "That order will read, 'put your head on the block and wait for the axe.'"

King John's face went bright red, but he turned to leave all the same.

"Take the wine. It's a good vintage." He smiled. "I'll get the cup back when I sack Harfow."

King John threw the wine on the floor and stormed out.

"You two as well." Thaniel nodded to Chancellor Machieve and Captain Seiford.

They both rose to leave. Captain Seiford stopped to whisper in my ear. "Remember why we're fighting." He said. "Keep your wits about you." Maybe he finally saw why we'd been brought to this place.

I thought about making a snarky comment, but I just nodded. He was right. These were dangerous waters to swim.

When we were alone, Thaniel and I stared at each other for a long space. "Your Priest won't forgive you for that, you know." I finally said

"I wasn't the one who hit him." Thaniel answered.

"But you told him to antagonize me." I gave him one of my calculating looks.

"I didn't think you'd break his nose." The Emperor didn't even try to deny it. "I thought your friend Captain Seiford deserved a medal of valor for just keeping his pants dry." He chuckled. "I imagine Bishop Harfeld worries about physical violence against his person as much as a desert dweller worries about drowning."

"Whatever you thought I'd do, I punched him." I didn't drop my stare. "In his mind, it's your fault, and he won't soon forget it."

"I suspect you're right." Thaniel seemed like he'd already thought about it but wanted to hear me say it. "That being said I think you're mistaking foolishness for bravery."

"You think I'm a fool." I knew he didn't.

"I think you're sixteen and haven't been here long enough to understand the way things work." Thaniel took a sip of his own wine. "In my comparatively short reign, I have taken six countries. I have never lost a battle, and before Wuntsville, neither had my subordinates." He listed off his accomplishments. "I am the greatest conqueror the world has ever known." He didn't say it like a boast. He said it as the fact it was. "I don't speak to the Old Religion with deference, but I never use disrespect either." He gave me a stare full of rebuke. "No one does."

I shrugged at that. "You are the greatest conquerer to ever live and with the most powerful nation in living memory." I paused. "I don't think I'll win by doing what men have done before." I gave him a wry smile. "I think I'll win by playing the long odds."

"You won't," he sighed, "but I guess you have to try."

After that, another silence settled on us. I waited for him to break it, but he stayed stoic. "There's a third reason." I lost my nerve. It felt like a defeat to speak first, but I bit down the bitterness.

"What?" He asked, apparently not following my train of thought.

"There's a third reason you don't want to poison King John." I drained my wine.

"What is it?" Thaniel cocked an eyebrow up.

"If you do there's a chance Anthanii breaks apart." I filled up the glass again. "I wouldn't bet on it, though."

"What would you bet on?" Thaniel dropped any charade at courtesy. Now it was pure assessment.

"The country unites around Prince Edward." I looked down at my cup. "He's been shaped by this war. Prince Edward has lived his entire life on the edge of a precipice." I reflected on the worthy man I'd had a few deep conversations with. "I've always disliked nobility, but when you corner a rat, it becomes more than a rat." I took a drink. "It becomes a lion. He listens to advisors based on their ideas, not their titles. He cares about Anthanii." I paused. "He's intelligent, brave, and compassionate. He might be worthy of the crown his father wears."

"I've beaten a dozen intelligent, brave, and compassionate men." Thaniel waved his hand in dismissal. "You think he's the one to see me fall?"

"Probably not," I admitted, "but there's a chance. Anthanii hasn't had that in a while." I looked up at him. "Besides, you won't just be fighting him. You'll be fighting me."

"Maybe." He shrugged his shoulders.

"What do you mean, maybe?" I stared down at the wine. "Is my cup poisoned?"

"No." Thaniel answered.

"Why not?" I was a bit insulted. "I think I'm worth killing."

"Anyone worth killing is worth turning." The emperor sipped his own drink.

"So that's your play?" I knew it all along. "You want me to join your army." I sighed. "I'm sorry to say, I don't play second fiddle."

"I want to adopt you." That took the wind out of me. It didn't seem like a joke.

"I'm a bit old to be needing a new family." I chuckled. "Besides, I have a father." For a moment my mind went to the family across the ocean. It hurt too much, so I was brought back to reality.

"I am unmarried and childless." Thaniel went on unabashed. "Even if I had a son, I don't want my throne to become hereditary. I've seen the incompetence that leads to." He stared deep into me. "I need a successor. I have many potential candidates. They're all good men, but none are great." He sighed. "My empire is too fragile to be left with anything other than excellence."

"So this whole meeting was about measuring me for your throne." I was mildly flattered. "Is that why you invaded Wuntsville too?"

"Yes."

"I must have really impressed you at Milhire." I mused to myself.

"I didn't let you retreat because there were other targets." He gritted his teeth. "I didn't *let* you retreat at all." Thaniel paused. "Maybe you didn't see it." He chuckled. "Sometimes it's hard to see when you're just a field officer." He sighed as if remembering an easier time. "It's been ages since I was just a field officer."

"See what?" I asked.

"I sent two regiments to break you." Thaniel took another sip. "I wanted a total victory. I wanted men to know what happens when they go against me." He considered his words carefully. "Fifty thousand getting away or just one, it didn't matter," He stared deep into me, "so I sent two regiments, four thousand men, against your seven hundred." The Emperor leaned in. "You mauled them."

That surprised me, two regiments for my sorry outfit. It seemed like overkill. Of course, it had felt like fighting the high tide, but that was how it always felt when I fought. I liked it that way. "Two regiments or twenty," I said, "that wasn't how I was going to die."

"No, it wasn't." Thaniel admitted. "I wouldn't have thought it possible from a man other than myself, even then it would have been my hardest fight." He had a look of respect in his eyes, not the false thing he had shown to King John. It was the sort you tried to hide but couldn't. It was real. "My men didn't break off because they took too many casualties, they stopped because they were afraid of you." He paused. "Your men didn't keep fighting because they hated me, they kept going because they knew that as long as you stood, the battle wasn't over."

"You should remember that as this war wears on." I gave a wolfish smile.

"I'll never forget it." Thaniel responded. "It's why I'm asking you to join me now."

"I've never really liked the turncoat style." I filled up my wine.

"You owe the Anthanii no loyalty." Thaniel waved his hand. "You can take Captain Seiford with you if that's what you're worried about." Thaniel said. "He seems like a good sort. I'll treat him well."

"He wouldn't come." I said. "I'm not loyal to Anthanii anyway." I raised my tattooed arm. "I took an oath."

"Fuck your oath!" Thaniel hissed. "If I die and there's no one else to take my place, the empire I've built will fall apart." He implored me.

"Maybe it should." I shrugged. "One man wasn't meant to stand over the rest."

"So you've been reading those intellectuals then?" Thaniel leaned back. "Viverent, Howdisa, Merewould?" He paused. "I thought you'd be too busy to read."

I took a sip of my wine. "I'm too busy not to read." I settled more into my chair. "I need to know the way people think over here." I said. "Besides, reading precludes knowledge."

He sighed. "Those thinkers mean well, and they'll have a place in my new empire." Thaniel admitted. "However, look at them." He waved in dismissal. "Wealthy commoners, dejected aristocrats, and pampered intellectuals." He counted them off. "They're smart men, but they've never seen what can happen in the chaos they propose."

"Men can do horrible things when they're free." I shrugged. "They can do great things as well. My people are a tribute to that." My quest for glory had often forced me to think of things from a realist point of view, but if you stick around me long enough, a bit of idealism will shine through. I don't know that I really believed the writings of Viverent, but they were fun to quote.

"Maybe things are different across the ocean." Thaniel admitted. "I hope they are, but maybe reality just hasn't caught up with you there." He paused. "You're from the Confederacy. You don't know what it was like before I took over." He shook his head. "You think you're tough because you lived in what passes for a frontier now?

I've studied you too. Your family was one of the wealthiest plantation owners in the country."

"What does that have to do with anything?" That struck a nerve. I didn't want him talking about my family. "I was trained in the hard edge all the same." I'd spent years learning how to be a soldier. I'd been drilled in hand to hand fighting, marksmanship, tactics, and a dozen other subjects needed to make a first class fighter since I could walk. The Belsons were warriors before they were anything, and my father remembered his ancient duties. Andrew and I were meant to safe guard the Confederacy when he was gone. Without that training I'd never have been accepted by the Constabulary. Those lessons had let me survive Milhire and win at Wuntsville.

"You're right." Thaniel nodded. "I've always respected the way your people cling to the end of the world by their fingertips." His demeanor changed then, like a summer shower gone to a hurricane. "You've never been hit by the hard edge though."

I thought about making a comment about Gostfeld's sword in my chest, but I got the feeling he wasn't talking about sharpened steel.

Thaniel took a moment to collect himself and then moved on. "My parents were serfs to some lord in South Kran." He went on. "One day another lord invaded and burned all our crops." Thaniel tried to keep his face impassive, but I saw the pain. "The lord didn't care, the king didn't care, no one cared." He spat into the ground. "It was just some lost profit to them. No one cared but us." He held one hand in the other. I hadn't noticed it earlier, but I saw now it was scarred over. He was a soldier. He must have had dozens of scars. Why did that one matter? I could see it did though. The one scar on which all the others were lain.

Thaniel went on. "My parents starved because there wasn't enough food to go around." I saw him gripping his hand harder. "I had a brother and a sister too. They died the next year because another lord poisoned the water." He was shaking. "I tried to dig a hole big enough to bury them in." He said. "I was just seven though, and I hadn't eaten in days…" He trailed off. I tried to imagine it, watching your family decompose next to you because you weren't strong enough to do anything about it. It was a horror even I couldn't face.

Thaniel seemed to get himself back a bit. "I couldn't do anything to stop it then, but I swore an oath that I'd see the bloodshed stop. I didn't know how back then, but I knew I would. I managed to make my way to Threspin. I begged, stole, and looted to feed myself. I had my first kill when I was eleven. I stole books and taught myself how to read. My mother always said I was clever. She had no idea how clever. Then one day I got a look at the king. I'd heard he was coming to town, so I waited all day to see him."

Thaniel's face twisted from awe to disgust. "I've never been more disappointed in my life. He was fat and weak. He couldn't save anyone. That's when I knew what I had to do. One Emperor, one rule, one law. Someone strong enough to stop it all."

"Someone strong enough to do it to someone else, you mean." I'd seen what his legions had done. "Would it have made a difference if the man who burned your crops was an emperor instead of a backwater lord." I took a sip of wine. "I expect not."

"You know nothing about why I did what I did!" That hit a nerve on the Emperor. "Thyro stands in the middle of a river of blood, the only way to stop it is to pull them to the other side, by any means necessary!" He finally got a hold over himself. "Children will forgive the suffering of their fathers if they can live in peace. For now, I do what I have to, but I see a future where no one has to live in fear."

"Except for fear of running afoul of the Emperor I suppose." I kept at the nerve. I needed to know him. I needed to understand him. I could only do that if he showed me something real, and this was as much real as I'd expected anyone got out of him since he was a starving orphan boy. "Except for fear of stepping out of line."

"Yes!" Thaniel hissed at me. "Let them fear taking from their neighbor! Let them fear abusing the poor! Let them fear evil."

"Who decides what evil is?" I shot back. "Could it be anyone who thinks differently from you?"

"I-" Thaniel started but couldn't find the right words.

"Let's say that the ends justify the means." I waved my hand. "Let's say that you're right and the world will be better for having you." I stared at him. "Do you know what they hate more than guns and steel?" I asked. "They hate a blood-colored cloak, and you've decided to give them free reign in your Empire."

"They hold the last remnant of the Imoran Empire." Thaniel responded. "They lend legitimacy to my rule," he paused, "and above all, you can't beat them."

"We'll find out about that later." I said. "Have you seen the way the children scream in their sleep?" I paused. "Imor wasn't just built on the Old Religion. It fell on it too."

"When my goals are complete I will see them all hung." Thaniel looked like he meant it. "I will not follow Imor to the grave."

I thought about that for a moment. "You know, I had a cousin back home who's leg was crushed by a horse." I said. "He took up the pipe to ease the pain, and always claimed he'd stop when the pain was gone." I took a sip of the wine. "He died in an opium den two years later." I looked back up at him. "I think you misunderstand addiction."

"Then you can finish it." Thaniel knew I had the truth of it. "When I die, you can see them rounded up. That's half the reason I want you. You can do what's necessary." He paused. "You talk about fulfilling your oath to the New Church, then do it. You can end this chapter of the Old Religion."

For a brief moment. I wanted to take his offer, but it didn't feel right. "I will do what's necessary." I said. "I'll be there defending people from a tyrant."

"I hadn't expected you to relent today, but soon you'll see." He shook his head.

"Don't hold your breath." I said.

"One last question." Thaniel's look changed to just pure curiosity. "I've studied you closely. By all accounts, your parents are good people. You've never been cut the way I have." He paused. "Yet you fight with no fear. You risk it all when others would pack up and leave. There's a fire in you I haven't seen in anyone but myself." Thaniel shook his head. "I've always found that a good upbringing leads to good people, but greatness has to have a dash of terrible. That can only come from true pain. Why are you the way you are?" He asked. "Why are you like me?"

That was a question I hadn't thought to answer anytime soon. "When historians pen our stories it will be about battles and campaigns." I said softly. "If you want to find my true pain, it's in the small moments. They won't be recorded, and no matter how many spies you have, you won't find it." I sighed. "Maybe, when this is all over I'll tell you." There was a savage beating once upon a time. A powerless feeling. The arrogance of a child too far gone to question his path. Small things and poor excuses for the things I'd do, but they would be with me till the day I died. However, I hoped when I did die, they would be gone for good.

"I look forward to that day." Thaniel nodded.

I almost rose to leave, but something stopped me. Perhaps, it was the words of an old doctor. "If you could do it again, would you?" I asked.

"What do you mean?" The Emperor cocked his head to one side.

"Would you have gone down this path, or would you have lived a quieter life?" I paused. "A happier life?"

"This was the only path for me." He answered. "It only brings pain to think about what could have been."

"Oh." I said disappointed and stood to leave.

Thaniel wasn't finished though. "In another life, I'd have liked to be a scientist though." He bit his lip thinking about the pain. "I think that would have been nice." He shrugged. "Maybe I'll get one of those." He looked down for a moment. "In the East, they believe that once you die, you're reborn as someone else." He turned his gaze back up to me. "I hope they're right." He paused. "I'd like to spend my days learning how the world works."

"Pianist." I nodded to him,

"To another life, then." He raised his cup to me

"To another life." I picked mine up and drank.

I walked out of the tent with a slow stride. The gentlemen from Anthanii were staring with fashionable disdain at the Kranish Generals. When I walked out, every eye was on me. At first, I thought it might be that I'd just had a private meeting with the most powerful man in the world. Then I realized that there was fear in their eyes, mixed with admiration. I realized they already knew about Bishop Harfeld.

I walked up to King John. I tried my best to look like I was filled with regret, but I still didn't kneel.

"King John." I said.

"Yes." He answered with a sneer to him.

"I have had time to think about my actions towards you earlier, and I have decided that they were not becoming of a Constable." I nodded my head. "It was a poor decision to lay hands on a king."

"The dog finally learned his place." One of the lords scoffed.

I gave him a dangerous look, and he quieted himself.

"It is forgiven." King John said, but his eyes told me he could carry a grudge.

"I still feel poorly about it." I said. "I would request a private audience now." I hung my head in what I hoped looked like humility.

"Anything you have to say can be said in front of my entourage." He looked down his nose at me.

"I know, but my Confederacy blood is still prideful." I had to bite my lip at that. "I would prefer to do it in private." *We need to talk.* My eyes said.

"Fine then." King John walked to behind a tree. I heard some of the entourage make some jokes about my savage nature, but I ignored it.

"I will hear your apology, now!" The King said.

"No, you won't." I spit out at him. "You won't hear it today or any other." I hissed at him. "I'm affording you the respect of quiet council because a good man asked me to."

King John narrowed his eyes at me. "Listen here you little-"

"No, you listen." I cut him off. "You're not just losing this war," I said, "you've lost."

King John gave me one real moment. For the first time, I saw the weight of a crown on his shoulders. I think somewhere deep down he knew he wasn't meant to be King. He was meant to be a courtier. He was meant to do nothing at all except live on the work of peasants. In peaceful times, he would have gone utterly unremembered to history. If scholars spoke of him at all, it would be of an unremarkable king who was mildly incompetent. These were times of the hard edge, though. He didn't have the strength for it. In his private moments, I knew what he feared. He knew what historians would write about them. We all fear history, whether we admit it or not. Once we're dead, we can't defend ourselves. A man will always find something to hope for. I wondered what he found. Maybe it was that he could live a comfortable life until Thaniel came through his gates. Maybe he put his hope in me and just had too much pride to admit it.

"Should we surrender?" King John finally asked.

"No!" I said it as a fact. It was a fact, and I would make it so. Anthanii would not bow to the Emperor of the Kranish. "What I mean is that this war was lost." I continued. "It was lost before Thaniel beat you at Milhire. It was lost before he took six countries with hardly a fight. It was lost even before he sat upon the throne."

It was lost the day a seven-year-old stood over the rotting corpses of those he loved and swore that he would see the world change. I thought. I wouldn't tell King John that. Thaniel had told it to me in confidence, and though he never said it, I knew I was the only one he had. I wouldn't betray that secret. I would use it to beat him, but when I died so would the memory of that poor child. It was what he wanted, for the world to forget such horrors. I wanted it too.

Maybe our goals weren't so different. I believed that my utopia and his would be indistinguishable from each other. We'd just taken different paths. Hundreds of thousands would die to decide who was right. I knew that. He would scream, "Obey!" I would say, "Choose!" He prayed for equality. I prayed for freedom.

"This war was lost a long time ago." I finished.

"Then what can we do except surrender." King John shook his head.

"We can fight," I said, "because this war *was* lost." I straightened my back. "It was lost until I came to your shores, and decided Anthanii deserved a chance at the future we're building across the ocean."

"There's a chance then?" King John seemed to regain some of his poise.

"There's a future I will see made real," I responded, "but you must agree that from here until the day the Rose Petal throne is burned, what I say goes."

For a moment it seemed King John's pride wouldn't let him agree, but in the end whatever logic he had won out. "What do you say?" He finally answered.

I took a deep breath. "The first thing you'll do is send Lord Corbula the reinforcements he's requesting, then double that and send those too." I knew Corbula was a proud man. The general wouldn't ask for a single soldier more than he needed, but he needed more men than even he knew. "If South Anthanii falls so do we. We'll need those resources badly if we want a chance at victory." I paused. "Marshall every trained soldier you can spare to him, even your personal guard." I paused. "Also start cultivating spies. We'll never have them to the extent Thaniel does, but one eye is better than none." I thought for a moment. "Use Lady Gerate for that." I told him. I knew Gerate didn't have experience in that, but she was smart. She'd learn quick. Above it all I trusted her. The great irony of spy work is that it requires a certain amount of trust in the person who was giving the information.

"I'll see it done." King John answered trying to swallow his indignity. He probably knew that before I said anything. Peasants in their huts prayed the bread basket wouldn't be conquered. They knew starvation too well. King John had to have seen it. It was only his natural distaste for Corbula and the long-held belief that the South was backwards that stopped him. Bigotry by its very definition defied logic. He also had an unnatural aversion to gathering intelligence.

I nodded at him. "The second thing you'll do is, you will go from this place and raise a new army, one hundred thousand strong. They will be trained using modern military doctrines not whatever outdated system you've been using." I kept on. "Infantry will be trained to be infantry not fodder, and artillery will be trained to be artillery, not big guns." I paused. "Prince Edward will oversee all of this and be the leader of this new army." I gave him a mildly sympathetic look. "Whatever your faults as a king are, you raised a good son."

"Thank you." King John nodded.

I went on. "Officers will be selected by merit alone not bloodline." I told him. "We will recruit from the universities, but I doubt even that will be enough. You'll need to raise up talented enlisted men to fill the post." I scratched my chin. "You'll need money for that. Conscription might work in the short run, but we're playing the long game. We need professionals." I looked at the tattoos on my arm. There were less and less Constables who could help me. "Hire mercenaries from wherever you can find them, but preferably from the Confederacy." I stated. "They know a different type of war over there that they can teach your men. We'll never beat Thaniel at his game, but we have a chance if we start a new one with different rules."

"I will not put the fate of my nation into the hands of rebellious savages!" I had finally pushed the King so far he had to say something.

I gave him a stare that said. *It's this way, or we lose.*

"Fine, I'll pay for them." King John finally relented.

"Good." I responded. "After that is done, send word to the navy." I continued. "Thaniel can send his whole force east because he believes his western shores are secured by their warships."

"What should I tell them?" The king asked.

"Tell them to rehearse amphibious raids on port towns." I answered. "With shallow water, and a hostile enemy." I thought for a moment. "Tell them to do it until they can pull off the maneuver without a single hitch in the plan, and then tell them to keep practicing for redundancy."

"Raiding?" King John looked offended and rightfully so. Raiding was a tactic used by backwater countries trying to get some wealth. It surely wasn't behavior appropriate for a nation as strong and old as Anthanii.

"Yes, raiding." I said in a voice that invited no argument.

"Fine." King John finally relented. "Now may I ask a question." I was so surprised he asked permission, I said yes.

"Do you have a plan?" The king asked.

"I do." I answered him. I had a multi-faceted, complicated plan, that might take years to accomplish if everything went right, and it probably wouldn't. They were long odds, but long odds were all I had.

"May I hear it?" King John's indignity returned in force.

"No," I said, "as I've known all along, Thaniel has too many spies in your court." I gave him a measuring look. "You're a gossip. If I tell you now, you'll tell a noble who will tell a spy," I scratched the tattoos on my arm, "if that noble isn't already a spy." I paused. "If Thaniel learns about it than the game is over." I tapped my head. "The only place it's safe is in here.

"I demand to know!" King John declared.

I thought about telling him how foolish he was, but I saw an opportunity. "Fine then." I answered. I told him a multi-faceted, complicated plan that might take years to accomplish if everything went right, and it probably wouldn't. Still, it made sense, and I saw the King grow a newfound spine.

"That is an excellent plan." The king said happily. "I promise this information will stay between us.

"My thanks." I answered. In truth, it was a possible plan at best, with almost no chance of beating Thaniel. I also knew in a week's time the Emperor would know every detail of it, so not a word of it was true. There was a chance Thaniel might smell the deception, but there was also a chance he might believe it. If he did, I had another hand to play.

"I've left detailed instructions with Captain Seiford on what to do in my absence." I doubted King John was actually competent enough to see my orders through. I also hoped this day might come, so I'd taken to penning how someone might begin to win the war. "There's also a list of competent men, and the positions I believe they can hold." I gave him a stare that said this was important. "He is to give those instructions to Prince Edward, upon your return to Harrfow."

"Your absence?" I saw the King's face go pure white in fear. "Where will you be going?"

"There's secrets I need to learn." I said. "There's parts of this calculation I need to solve. Without them, all my plans are just fumbling in the dark." I looked over to the horse I'd rode in on. "I'm going to leave this meeting and go find them."

King John hesitated before he said what came next. "Who will protect Anthanii?' He finally asked.

That brought a smile to my face. King John finally knew who'd win this war for his people. "The same thing that's always protected Anthanii," I answered. "brave men and national spirit." I said. Anthanii still had some fight left in it. "That will hold till winter." I felt the cool winds already blowing. "In a months time the snows will hit, and it'll be impossible to move an army anywhere." I gritted my teeth. "If Thaniel could have taken your kingdom this season, he would have done it by now." I stared back over at the Kranish tent. "He's hunkering down for winter. If we're lucky, we can be ready for him once the thaws start in about four months."

"Oh." King John looked like a child who'd just been schooled that it's inappropriate to put your elbows on a table. "This doesn't change anything."

"What's that?" I didn't really understand him.

"You're still a frontier savage." The king reverted back to his usual arrogance. "I haven't forgotten that you've struck me." He took a step forward. "I'll suffer you now. You've a talent with military science, but soon I won't need you." He spat into the ground. "One day when this is over, I'll have my revenge." He glared down at me. "I'll turn everything you love to ashes. I'll see that Captain who follows you hung for treason. I'll see that whore Gerate, married off to the most brutish man I know." He took another step forward, so we were inches away from each other. "I know you have a family, they'll be killed in their sleep as well." His rage seemed to grow. "I'll see every man, woman, and child from your homeland dead, and see if we can't cultivate a better crop when they're gone." He brought his full height against me. "I hate you, Thomas Belson." He said. I knew he did hate me. It wasn't just disdain. He wanted me punished for showing him how weak he was. It wasn't just me putting my hands on him. I'd shattered his worldview. He wanted me to suffer for it.

It took me a moment to tell he wasn't joking. After all, a few seconds ago he'd just meekly obeyed my orders. In this new science called physics, I heard of a law that said for every action there is an opposite and equal reaction. When you force the ruler of the second most powerful nation in the world to acquiesce, you can bet he'll remember it. It also struck me as odd that a man who considered himself too chivalrous to put spies in a warring nations court, now swore to dance on the graves of women and children. I knew he only used his "honor" as a way to avoid actually governing, but even for a delusional monarch, the hypocrisy was too much.

Once I realized he was serious, I felt my own rage boil up in me. "You can go back to your court and tell them I begged forgiveness on bended knee." I hissed. "They won't believe you, but I quite enjoy you wasting your breath." I gritted my teeth. "I don't care what you tell people, but this is what's going to happen." I held up one finger. "One, you're going to do everything I just told you to do." I brought up a second finger. "Two, I'm going to win this war, and you can go back to being as useless as you were before." I held up a third finger. "Three, if you ever touch anything I love, I will come back to Harrfow and show you all the new ways my people learned from the Huego on how to make a man squeal. Then I'm going to mount your head on a pike for the whole world to see." I put my hand down. "You know that's well within my skill set, and the people of Anthanii might even thank me for it."

I could have left it there. I probably should have, but I knew he'd never change his mind on me. When confronted with a challenge, I always go with my gut. The trouble is it usually tells me to do something stupid. I hit him between the legs with my left hand, directly on his balls. It wasn't the bone-crushing punch I'd learned in God's Rest. It was the light tap, I'd learned years earlier. If you have a brother, you know exactly what I'm talking about. If you don't, chances are someone will do it to you someday. It's the kind of tap that hurts a little bit, then stops, then hurts a lot.

I walked to my horse calmly as the King of Anthanii held onto his genitals for dear life.

Present Day

Andrew and I finally made our way to the table Seiford was at. I waded through a sea of cheers and backslapping until finally, the crowd went back to their business. The old man was George. He had been the Belson family tutor since I was eight. He was a top graduate of LeSalle University and should have gone on to be a respected figure in Academia. For some reason, he'd chosen to stay with my family, and had slipped into obscurity. Still, he'd written quite a few books that were still being studied in universities around the globe.

Without his tutoring, I don't know if I would have been nearly as great. Other teachers taught you the way things were. George taught me to ask why and how, not just what happens but what always happens. His lessons in history had served me well. He had tried to avoid teaching me military theory. It was probably wise of him, me being me and all. He wanted more for his prized student than a soldier. Still, from him, I had learned logic in it's purest form. He taught me to see the world as it was, and I learned to change it. He had saved me the learning curve, and in the wars I fought, that curve was littered with bodies.

He folded me into one of those hugs I remembered from my youth. "Thomas Belson as I live and breath." He looked me up and down appraisingly, and I did the same to him. To any other man he might have looked exactly the same. White hairline receding a bit, maybe a few more wrinkles, the narrow face held the same compassionate glow though, and the eyes still showed a spark that spoke of intelligence. There was something else in that kind face and clever eyes, though. I marked it for sadness.

In my early years, I had thought it a sadness only warriors could know, but George had always hated anything that could kill a man. In the time since I had seen my folly. There are many who try to make ideals concrete. It just never struck me that a tutor might be one of them as well. Yet, I recognized the pain he had in him. I bore it too. It was the sorrow that only comes when an old man sees things changing with no way to stop it.

Sometimes that old man even realizes it's for the better, but the world he grew up in was more than history texts and archaeological records. It was where he grew to manhood, loved his first, and stood for something. I'd seen that look in the eyes of elders from Anthanii to the Mongs. Maybe the world just wasn't what it was, maybe everyone felt that way when they get too old to change.

It was the sort of look a man wore for years. Seeing his former student covered in the scars and sins of two dozen wars, couldn't have helped. I had that look myself, even though I was the one who changed the world. George waited fifteen years to see the man became. He deserved better.

"It's good to see you, George." I said through the hug. I meant it. No one taught by George could ever see him as just a tutor.

I took the rifle off my back and set it against the table. I didn't want anyone trying to steal my prized possesion. I sat down to a nice looking plate of stew and a nicer looking beer. Andrew took his seat across from me, still looking at me like the hero he thought I was.

There was a moment of silence before Seiford broke it. "Anyway, I was telling them the story about how you fended off those twenty men and twelve wolves in the forest of Rustia."

That made me laugh. "It was two farmers and a pleasant looking bulldog." I took a sip of the beer and found it to my liking. "The only reason people like that story is because you keep telling it and what came after."

"Well, what came after?" Andrew gestured to continue.

"Me and Thomas defended their town from rouge bandits." Seiford continued on unabashed. "Well, he did most of the defending, but I definitely laid the traps."

"They were good traps." I went for the bowl of stew next.

"So all those stories about you are true?" Andrew asked taking a sip of his own beer. He wanted to believe I had found some measure of happiness.

"To some extent." I admitted. "They get exaggerated in the

telling," I gave Seiford a reproachful look, "but all the things you read in the history books happened, more or less."

"So you really rode a dragon to Thaniel's castle?" Andrew only seemed like he was half joking. Men will believe strange things where his kin are concerned. "You set him to burning the Rose Petal Throne?"

"I've never seen a dragon," I smiled, "but I was there when the Rose Petal Throne burned." I knew I should have been more humble, but it's hard when you're talking to your brother.

George finally cut in. "I hear they call you Belson the Blessed now."

Andrew smiled at that. "It's a credit to our name."

George nodded. "I'm wondering how that got started." He chuckled. "I called you a lot of things as a boy." He cocked an eyebrow up. "Blessed was not among them."

Seiford snorted. "I believe that."

"I heard one story that says it's from when you convinced a herd of wild stallions to charge a line of cannon." Andrew said excitedly. "Another one says it's from when you called a mighty earthquake at Gertinville."

I laughed at his enthusiasm. Sometimes a brother resented a siblings success. I knew I had. Andrew wasn't that sort though. "That's when it started to mean something." I said. "In the beginning, it was an insult, like calling a short man The Big or Seiford the Chaste."

"Would you stop spreading those lies." Seiford glared at me.

"I would if you started being chaste." I shot back.

"You fucking-" The monk started.

Andrew stopped him. "I want to hear how you became Belson the Blessed." He took a sip of beer. "After all, it's my name too."

I turned back to the table. "You remember me when I left," I responded, "small, skinny, arrogant."

"Oh, I remember that." George chuckled. "Continue."

"My teachers at God's Rest saw it too, but they didn't have your tender hand." I shrugged. "They gave me the name as an insult, and it followed me to Anthanii." I put down my beer. "It made a resurgence after Milhire. I was one of the few survivors, and no one could figure out how." I gritted my teeth. "Those who weren't there called it cowardice." I resisted the urge to spit. "Belson the Blessed was what they called me when I was too close for Thomas the Timid."

"You made them forget it, though." The look Andrew gave me was the one I got when I saved Wuntsville. It meant more from him though. It made me want to stand straighter. It made me want to be the hero he thought I was.

"I did." I smiled back. "I started winning, and the meaning changed." I swallowed a bite of stew. "Those were hard times. They needed someone to believe in, so they chose me." I nodded. "They started to believe maybe I was blessed."

"I don't know about blessed," the edges of George's mouth curled with pride, "but I think they chose right.

Ayn-Tuk looked up from polishing his spear. "Thomas is a blessed man." He went back to his work.

"Really?" I asked the black man. "How so?"

Ayn-Tuk just shrugged. I knew I wasn't getting any more out of him so I returned to the conversation.

"How'd you befriend such a charming fellow?" George gave the shirtless man a queer stare. "I didn't think you knew each other until just now." He shrugged. "I thought he just sat next to us, and I wasn't going to be the one to tell him to move."

"Oh, this is Ayn-Tuk." Seiford gestured to him. "He's not much of a conversationalist."

"Yes, our friend Tuk is a follower of the ancient Stoss mindset." I gave the black man a challenging smile. "He believes that words are one of the underlying issues in our society." It was part of my way into baiting him into saying something. I'd make a grand, often full of shit, statement about his thoughts in the hopes he'd correct me. So far, it had been futile.

Ayn-Tuk surprised me. "Actually I find the philosophy has merit, but there are many flaws in the logic." He looked up. "The thinker Dandrien outlines them fairly well." I think what shocked me the most was the perfect pronunciation. He'd never mispronounced anything before, but usually, his responses were limited to one-word answers with the occasional grunt and nod.

"You learned Stossian philosophy in Souren." George asked.

"No." Ayn-Tuk said without looking up from his meal. "Not in Souren."

"So what part of the Stoic tradition do you disagree with?" George asked as curious as we had.

"Conversation is a blessed thing." The shirtless fellow didn't look up.

"You could have fooled me." I turned back to the table. "He started following us when we left Souren."

Seiford scratched his head. "We never really figured out why, but much like yourself, I wasn't going to be the one to ask him to leave." He nodded to George.

"He probably wanted a share in Thomas's glory." Andrew stated. "He looks like a warrior."

"He was probably curious as to the nature of the white man." George posited. "He sounds like a scholar."

"He could have been looking for treats." I rolled my eyes. "Whatever the reason is the black bastard won't tell me!"

Ayn-Tuk didn't rise to the challenge this time.

"Well I'd love to speak to him more." Andrew paused, considering his next question. "So besides making new friends and changing the world as we know it," he leaned back, "how've you been?"

That seemed like a strange question to ask. Fifteen years of constant warfare and legendary battles, seeing sights so beautiful and horrible I couldn't get them out of my head even when I slept, becoming the greatest hero the world had ever known, and "how've you been?" seemed a bit pedestrian.

"I've been good, I suppose." I finally answered to the pair. I realized the situation was just as strange for Andrew as it was for me.

"Of course you have!" Andrew raised his beer. "You're the hardest bastard the world's ever seen!" We all drank to that.

"I did my part." I shrugged.

A pretty serving girl came over to our table. She had dark black hair and long legs beneath her smock. "Here you go, your eminence." She dropped off another round of drinks.

"Thank you very much." I nodded.

"It's my pleasure." She gave me a smile that said she'd like to meet the Terror of Thyro more intimately later. I returned it. Apparently, Seiford had been singing my praises while I was in the bathhouse. I usually thumped him for it, but the girl was quite pretty.

I turned back to the table. "I've got quite a pension too, so tonight the drinks are on the New Church." I brought up my own beer.

"That won't be necessary." Andrew waved his hand in dismissal.

"I insist." I smiled at my brother. It wasn't nearly as painful as I thought it would be, seeing Andrew again. Of course, we had more to discuss. I hadn't even brought up Sarah yet. Maybe things hadn't worked out. There were other, more awkward, conversations we needed to have later. However, that was for another day. We were talking for the first time in fifteen years. What's more, it felt like talking to a brother. My sibling had always had that gift.

"I don't really pay for drinks here." Andrew scratched his neck as if he was uncomfortable.

"Why not?" I pinched my face. "Did you help the owner out of a jam or some such thing?"

"Andrew doesn't really pay for drinks anywhere." George cut in sensing my brothers distress.

"On account of you being my brother?" I didn't mean it to sound so arrogant, but it came off that way.

"On account of him being a war hero, in his own right." My tutor said sternly. "He won the Iron Circle in the Puena War." The tutor didn't say it to embarrass his old student. He said it because Andrew wouldn't say it himself. Still, it did embarrass me. I should have known, and I shouldn't have been so vain to think Andrew was only known as my brother. Life went on without me, and Andrew had always been capable of great things. The difference was he had the wisdom to seek out good things as well.

"Oh." I took a swallow of beer to regain my composure. "I'm sorry, I had no idea." No one said it, but they were all thinking it. I would have known if I'd bothered to write my family at all.

"Some Puena's that got the jump on us. My company was just the closest. Really that's it." Andrew dismissed the awkwardness in the room. That was why everyone had loved him, even in his youth. He always knew what to say, and he always knew how to treat the man across from him. "It's nothing compared to your adventures."

"I think it certainly is." I was proud of him, and I let it show. "There was a war?" I asked. "How'd we fare?"

"Well, I imagine with all the chaos in Thyro, no one really took notice of a border scuffle halfway across the world." Andrew shrugged. "We won though, gained some territory out west too."

"It was more than a border scuffle." George patted my brother on the back. "It was quite a conflict from what I hear, and the Puena were no mean enemies."

"I believe that." I nodded. The Puena were the only real threat to the Confederacy. They were an empire in their own right, and the two countries had been circling each other for years. The Confederacy had innovation and trade. Puena had numbers and a centralized authority.

"It was nothing compared to the Thaniel wars." Andrew waved his hands. "Our soldiers were just better than theirs." He looked up a bit red in the face. "Besides we had General Fennis," his eyes held all kinds of pride, "the best commander to come out of the Confederacy since Then Ironwill." He smiled. "Present company excluded, of course."

"I remember Fennis." I scratched my chin.

"General Fennis." Andrew corrected me. He may have admired his brother beyond reason, but Andrew clearly held the same emotions for the General.

"Sorry, General," I didn't mind giving another the respect he deserved, "but he was only a colonel when I left." I took a sip of beer. "He won medals for fighting the Huego, didn't he?"

Of course, I was understating it, Fennis had won national fame when he battled the Anthanii forty years ago. Our father had fought with him. That had been a bloody one, but since then, men looking for glory had to slack their thirst on renegade Huego tribes. They were the natives of the Confederacy before Thyro had colonized it. Battle was battle, but I'd wanted the great conflicts I couldn't find in my homeland. Still, I had no doubt Fennis was brilliant. In my early days, I'd cut my teeth on skirmishes and scouting missions. Fennis had only been sixteen when King John's father had tried to regain his predecessors lost lands. From what my father told me, Fennis' intervention was all that saved the fledgling nation.

"He's done more than that." Andrew said. "The man is a genius. He smashed the Puena at every battle they faced him in."

George nodded. "He's an icon around these parts."

"I look forward to meeting him." I smiled.

"He's retired now." Andrew said with some chagrin. "He didn't like the way the country's headed."

"What do you mean?" Seiford cocked his head one way. "In Thyro we have a saying. When business is good, we say it's looking like the Confederacy." The monk chuckled. "Every time we look west it seems like you've changed the world again."

"Aye," I agreed, "I've heard nothing but good from this side of the ocean."

George took a bite of his stew. "You may have forgotten Thomas, but we're a new country that produces too much wealth and not enough warships." He chided me lightly. "If we let the powers of Thyro see a hint of weakness they'll strike."

Andrew nodded. "We breed hard men here." He looked around the bar. "To a certain extent, we've proven the kings of the old world aren't the necessary evil we thought they were," he took another drink, "but we're still figuring things out."

Seiford twisted his face in confusion. "I've read the Ironwill Pact." The monk referred to the charter that governed our country. Written at a convention with the founder, Then Ironwill and the brightest minds of that age. "It's the most brilliant political document I've ever laid eyes on."

"I concur." Ayn-Tuk put in. He was being unreasonably chatty. It wasn't quite our dockside conversation, but it was more than I was accustomed to.

"It is at that Mr. Tuk," George responded, "but think back to all of the history you know." The tutor said in the voice he used to address me with. "You seem like an educated man too," he gestured to Seiford, "and I'll tan your hide if you've forgotten what I've taught you, Thomas." He said it with a smile that let me know I was still his student. "There's been a few documents set as law to govern the governors, and a great many philosophers have written books on how the world ought to work." He shrugged. "The Pact was even influenced by some," George leaned in, "but there's never been one that went half as far as we did." He sat back. "Above all, the idea that rulers rule by the consent of their people has never been written down and accepted as the law of the land." He took a drink. "It was always too dangerous."

"What are you getting at?" I started to see, though. The world wasn't as black and white as this country is good and that one bad. Even the Thaniel Wars were more nuanced than people cared to admit. I'd always regarded he Confederacy as the best of them, but there were always problems in paradise.

"The Ironwill Pact was brilliant, but it was written almost a hundred years ago by men who are all long dead." George sighed. "Now, as the world around us changes, we're left with a much more daunting question." He bit his lip. "What does it all mean?"

George let that sink in before he went on. "Is it a living document to be interpreted? Was it meant to be followed to the letter?" The tutor tapped the table. "What can the legislature promise to the people? What can the Prime Governor do when the legislature goes too far?" He shook his head. "All those questions existed a hundred years ago, but the answers may have changed." He looked around the table. "Above all, the Pact declares two things as the highest virtue, freedom and equality."

"Those seem like worthy goals." I said.

"They are," the tutor agreed, "but sometimes you can't have both, so which is the most important." He leaned in. "Did the founders mean the freedom to choose whatever path they want and suffer the consequences of it, or did they mean we are to be free of oppression even if it's ourselves who are doing it?"

I shifted uncomfortably at that. These were heavy ideas with no right answers. "Poetry is for interpretation." I shrugged. "Law is meant to be followed."

Seiford laughed out loud. "Yes your the man to lecture about following laws."

"I see time hasn't changed my student" George nodded as if he halfway agreed. "However, that is the sentiment of many in the country, and one I don't entirely disagree with." He paused. Powerful people will reinterpret anything to give them an edge." He pointed a finger at me. "Even your legacy as it turns out."

Andrew chimed in. "Above all the Confederacy is growing, but not always in the right ways." He sighed. "The plantation owners in the South sometimes see themselves as the lords of Thyro." My brother took another sip. "In the North, industrialists make amazing things, but sometimes it feels like the workers don't get enough for it." George thought about ideas, but Andrew was a concrete man.

"I think I see it a little clearer." Seiford nodded.

"Me too." I put in.

"Capitalist should be able to keep their wealth so long as it is based upon voluntary transaction." Ayn-Tuk said without looking up. "If the free market is uninterrupted the workers will eventually share in the wealth created to benefit all."

"A man versed in economics, I see." George nodded happily.

"What has gotten into you?" I looked at the Tuk still eating his dinner.

The black man shrugged.

"Well, economic theory aside," Andrew was as confused as I was, "there's some discontent in places that could turn into a powder keg."

"Don't pay his 'voluntary interaction' business much mind." I chuckled. "I once saw a man stab someone for a sausage in Souren." I paused to think about it. "Actually I've seeing some variation of that everywhere else I've been, come to think of it." I turned back to the table. "Theory is all well and good, but things get complicated when you put theory into the real world, and people start getting hungry."

"That's not the biggest issue." Andrew went on. "Who has the final say on governing the individual provinces." He paused. "Does the legislature get to tell the individual what to do?" My brother shook his head. "Back when the South and North were equal it didn't matter, but now new provinces are joining, and they seem to be favoring the North."

"Well, the people who live in a province should be able to say what happens in their home." Seiford said.

"I agree." Andrew smiled.

"To a certain extent I do as well," George nodded. "but if they decide, by a sixty percent vote that the other forty should be executed in the street, should the central government shrug their shoulders and say, 'it's their right.'"

"Well, no!" Seiford said then thought for a second. Then after a knowing look from George. "Maybe..." He shook his head. "That would never happen!" The monk said.

"You're right," George agreed, "something that black and white is unlikely, but shades of gray can strangle a man, and a particular issue has come up."

"What sort of grey?" I narrowed my eyes. I had a feeling I knew what he was talking about, even if I wished I didn't.

George and Andrew stared at each other uncomfortably. Finally, Andrew spoke up. "At the time it was so small people thought it would die on its own, but it's made a resurgence in recent years."

"What are you talking about?" I said it with more force.

My brother went on. "That probably explains why Ironwill never dealt with it." He sighed. "The Old Religion."

"That's not grey morality." I clenched my teeth. "It's evil."

"The crops are growing taller than they never have before!" Andrew said defensively.

"Tall enough to strangle you, brother." I leaned in. "I've seen what it did in Thyro, Souren, and everywhere else." I let my anger show. "The Confederacy is special, but not that special."

Seiford jumped in to stop the argument. "I'm sure it will be decided soon." He forced a smile. "Thomas and I will stand by whatever the elected government decides."

Neither George or Andrew answered.

"It's going to get resolved, isn't it." Seiford repeated.

"This has been boiling over for a while." George said. "History always resolves things, but too often there's a lot of blood when it does."

"You're talking about civil war." I sat back considering it. It was a bittersweet realization. I was a creature of war, and like an addict drawn to a drug, I felt desire well up. However, civil wars were anything but civil. I hadn't seen my family in some time, but they would be touched by the violence, and I didn't want that. Besides, they'd heard my stories, but if they saw them be made with their own eyes, I doubted they'd claim me.

"It's possible." George said. "However, the South won't accept any ruling outlawing the Priests" He sighed. "Besides this new Prime Governor McAllan is one of the most competent men to hold the office, but everyone knows he's got it out for the Old Religion."

"He's right in that." I said flatly.

"Regardless of if he's right," Andrew started, "the common knowledge is that his decisions aren't based on law, but on feeling." My brother went on. "That will discredit him."

I opened my mouth to continue the argument, but Seiford saved me. "So enough about politics," the monk said, "I want to hear about Thomas's family."

"Yes," I smiled at the diversion, "what's been changing for the Belson clan?"

"I'm married now." Andrew chuckled. "I have two children, ones seven and the others barely a year."

"Who'd you wind up hitched to?" I asked. "Did I know her."

"You do." Andrew shifted uncomfortably. "It's Sarah."

"Oh." I tried not to seem hurt.

"What'd you name them?" Seiford saw that something was off, so he changed the subject.

"I named them after the two greatest men on this Earth." Andrew smiled. "Thomas and Leopold." After our father and me. Andrew was as good as they came.

"It's a shame you hadn't met me before you gave one of your boys such a brutish name." Seiford said through a laugh

I smacked him on the arm. "So how's the rest of the family?" I asked. "What about father and mother?" I took another drink. "What about Alexis too? She was barely a year the last time I saw her."

George and Andrew looked at each other curiously. Finally, Andrew spoke up. "Alexis is grown now, and she's as stubborn as you ever were."

"She's a great student, might be even better than you." George said.

I laughed at that. "I'm sure she is."

"She'll be off to LaSalle soon." Andrew smiled.

"I can't wait to see her again." I meant it, even though she'd been little more than a babe when I left. "Why isn't the rascal here?" I asked.

"She had other engagements." George said in a way that let me know he was lying. There was more to discuss, but that could wait.

"What about Mom and Dad?" I asked. "Why aren't they here."

"Mom has had some medical issues." Andrew said after some hesitation. "Her doctor decided it wouldn't be a good idea to travel."

That struck me a bit. "She'll get better though?" When no one said anything, I chimed in again. "Right?"

"It's not the sort of thing that get's better, Thomas." George said. "She's at that age when her mind starts to wander more and more."

"I-" I started but had no idea what to say. "I didn't know." I muttered dumbly.

"It's fine, Thomas." Andrew said. "I'm sure seeing her second favorite son will help her greatly anyway." It was a joke. We used to go back and forth about who our mother loved more all the time and never with any bite to it. It didn't feel like a joke though.

"And Father is there with her?" I asked.

There was a tense moment of silence that could only mean one thing.

"Thomas," My brother shook his head. "I wrote you about it a while ago but…"

"No." It was all I could say. Leopold Belson couldn't die. He was my father, but I knew what conversations like this meant. I'd given plenty in my time.

"He passed a few years ago." Andrew said tactfully.

I gripped the handle of my pistol, trying not to let any emotion out. It was like being hit in the gut. The world wasn't what it had been before those six words were said. It would never be again.

"He was very proud of you." George put his hand over mine.

"I'm sorry, I need a minute." I stood up from the table.

"Take all the time you need, Thomas." Andrew gave me a comforting look.

"Where's our room?" I asked Seiford.

"Fourth door on the left." He stood up with me. "Thomas do you want me to come up-"

"No!" I said firmer than I should have. "No, it's just..." I stumbled for the words. "I need some time alone."

I made my way up the stairs and slipped inside the room. Then I let it all out. In the small time, it had taken me to get to the bed, it felt like I'd been holding a broken dish. I let all the pieces fall to the floor.

I wept. I'd wept before, even if I did it where men couldn't see. This was different. In the past, I'd wept for my sins. I'd wept for Thaniel, the thousands I'd slaughtered, and that fucking dog. Now I wept because a corner of my life had been taken away from me. I'd always known that when the time was right, when my quests were ended, my family would be there. Now, I realized they weren't. Life went on even while I fought half the world.

I had protested when Seiford had told me we were going home to meet my family. Half of it had been genuine, but the other half had been more complicated as these matters tended to be. I wanted to tell my father about my conquest. I wanted to show him that the arrogant little boy who left had become something to make him proud. I wanted to beg forgiveness for my sins, and now I'd never have it.

Part of me had thought that when I came home, I could right my wrongs. Maybe when I went back to the source, I could change the man I was, but the book was closed now. The story was written in stone. I was Belson the Blessed, but I could never be Tommy, my parents' little man again. The paint had dried. The clay had hardened.

I wept for that. My path was becoming ever narrower.

I didn't know how long I wept, but it felt like a while. Seiford had probably purchased his own room for him and Ayn-Tuk. Usually, we only got one. There was something comforting about having my only two friends sleep next to me. One of us would take the bed, the other two would lay on the floor. Comfort had never been comforting to me.

Half of me was angry that Seiford hadn't come to talk to me. I probably needed it, but I had told him to leave me alone for the night. Seiford was a brilliant man, but even he probably needed a night to think of something to say.

———◆———

I decided I didn't want to be alone anymore or at least not sober. I ventured down to the bar and found it empty, except for a serving girl cleaning it. It was the one with the dark hair and long legs who'd given me the eyes earlier.

"Is the bar still open miss?" I asked her.

"No, we have a policy that-" She stopped when she turned around to see me. "Well, for your eminence we can make an exception." She smiled brightly at me.

I walked to the bar and took a seat as she hurried behind it. "You don't have to call me your eminence, you know." I smiled at her.

"Then what should I call you." She gave me a seductive look. "You have many titles. The Terror of Thyro, The Savior of Anthanii," she leaned in a little closer, "Belson the Blessed."

"I always tell pretty girls to call me Thomas." I returned the look. I didn't want to think about my failings as a son or a hero. I just wanted to flirt with a pretty girl.

She blushed at the compliment. "Well, then what will you have, Thomas?"

"It's been a long time since I've had good Confederacy whiskey." I said.

"You've earned it." She poured a glass and went to put it up.

"I'll buy the bottle." I laid a silver coin on the table. "I plan on drinking a lot tonight."

"As you wish." She took the money. "I'm Sally by the way."

"It's nice to meet you, Sally." I raised the glass in her direction and drained it. "You drink whiskey?"

"I do." She nodded.

"Then grab a glass and come to this side of the bar." I gestured to the seat next to me.

"The owner doesn't like when we do that." She looked down. "Besides, I wouldn't want to impose."

"He'll never know." I gestured to the empty bar. "Besides, there's nothing sadder than drinking alone."

I saw her consider it for a moment. She knew what the invitation meant. "I suppose when you put it that way." Sally walked around the bar and sat down next to me, closer than was appropriate. "I was hoping you would come back down." She finally said.

"Why's that?" I asked pouring myself a glass.

"It's not every day a hero walks into this bar." Sally leaned towards me.

"This country is full of heroes." I said filling her glass up too. "I understand my brother's become a bit of one too."

"We are blessed in that." She sighed. "We have a great many brave, honorable, chivalrous men." Sally cocked an eyebrow up. "None of them ever made the world tremble quite like you did though."

"Luck." I said. It was false humility. It was my cunning, strength, and fire that set the world to shivering. It was my desire and pride. It was my sins and steel. It was my conviction that the world would change for me. It was my uncaring on how it changed.

"I don't think it was just luck." She leaned closer.

"No, it wasn't," I smiled back, "but a hero's got to be humble doesn't he."

"I don't want humble." She drained the whiskey and poured us both another. "I want the hero."

"In that case," I turned to her, "I boxed Ballon the Strong and knocked him out cold. I played a game of wits with Viverent and won. I climbed the Cretoin mountains and stood on top of the world."

"What about the battles?" She put a hand on my leg.

"I held Gersten against an army with a hundred men." I pulled at the side of my lip. "I destroyed Gostfeld with donkeys and scarecrows. I broke the Army of the River with nothing but an ax and my wits." I paused. "I faced the greatest leader the world had ever known when I was fifteen. By the time I turned twenty his head rolled at my feet."

"You're really trying to impress me." Sally drank her whiskey.

"Is it working?" I asked.

"I certainly like the effort." The girl nodded at me to continue.

I leaned closer to her. "I've killed thousands with my own hands and millions by my orders." I drained my glass. "If a map of the world is a painting then I'm the artist. Those lines were made by me." She was a pretty girl. The hazel in her eyes, the shape of her body, the curve of her face. It was like a trap meant to ensnare me, and I'd never had qualms about walking into a trap. "Some men say I alone am more powerful than half the world put together." I said. "Those men drastically underestimate me."

Sally was fully entranced. "I heard you saved a dozen maidens from a mob of peasants."

"I did," I shrugged, "but trust me most of them weren't maidens."

"I heard you talked a tyrant into abdicating his throne." Sally asked again.

"Lord Henfrow was pretty drunk when I did that." I drank again to put a dent in the bottle.

"I heard you walked the streets of Imor, and faced forgotten horrors." She was so close I could smell her. "I heard you've spoken with gods."

"I have," I admitted, "but they weren't as forthcoming as I'd like them to be."

"You're surely a dangerous man." Her lips were inches away from mine. "Should I be scared?"

"You should run as fast as your feet can carry you." I said.

Sally took my mouth in hers with an enthusiasm that shocked me. "I like my men a bit scary." She said when she broke it off. "I'm sure I'll be absolutely petrified in your room." She took my hand and the bottle of whiskey and turned to go upstairs. However, when she pulled on me, I didn't go.

"You will be scared." I whispered it almost to myself. "Those lines on the map were peoples homes." I pulled her back. "Those men I killed had families, and even worse, sometimes they had dogs." Sally looked at me confused, but I went on. "I've been wounded a hundred times, and those wounds never really leave you. Every day I wake up and feel the pain run through me."

She didn't know what to say to that.

"Every night I have nightmares and see the people I've killed, the lives I ruined." I kept on at it. "I've never lost, but I've made mistakes, and those mistakes had consequences." I stood up. "Everyone calls me Belson the Blessed, but that's just because they're too afraid to call me my other name, Belson the Butcher." I took a step towards her "I've killed children Sally. One day I may have to again." I looked into her eyes. "Do you still want to share my bed?"

"I don't want a saint, I want a hero." She kissed me again and deeper.

"Then let's go."

We moved up to my room in a hurried rush of kissing and feeling each other. When we were safely inside, we started frantically undressing each other. I finally took my shirt off, and she stopped to look at my scars.

"Three above." She rubbed her hands over them.

"Heroism has its price." I shrugged.

She pulled off her shirt, and we fell onto the bed. I showed her every trick I'd learned from women around the world. I heard her moan. I felt her claw at my back. I tasted her desire.

"Thomas!" She moaned.

I climbed on top of her kissing every part of Sally as I made my way. For a moment I stopped to look at her face twisted in desire. Sally met my gaze with her soft eyes. She bit her lip and nodded.

I entered her. I attacked her like I had every army, country, or king who crossed my path. I became a wild animal tempered by nothing except desire. Any higher thinking, any twisting philosophy I held in my soul was abandoned. I wasn't a man possessed of intellect and reason. I ceased to be a creature governed by my heart and mind. I was a beast of stomach and cock.

"Three above, Thomas!" She moaned. "Don't stop!" Sally dug her claws into my back. "Belson the Blessed!" She shook uncontrollably on the bed. "The Terror of Thyro!" I felt her climax again.

I flipped her over and mounted her like dogs do. I wanted her like I wanted victory. I took her like I took my glory. I looked at her back and saw my legend. I saw Gostfeld at Wuntsville. I saw the thousand men of Yeg come to conquer a city I had claimed. I saw the face of the Anthanii court when I road to them still bloody and let them know I had saved their nation. I saw the battles that no one could win, and I had. I saw the men that no one could kill, and I took their lives.

I wasn't the man who looked up at the stars and wondered at his sins. I wasn't the man who woke up and felt pain rack his entire body. I wasn't the man who screamed in his sleep while the carnage played in his dreams. I was the most powerful man to ever live. I was the hero born with no country or army but had made the world shake. I was the man who screamed at the world "Change!" And the world listened because it was afraid of me.

I looked at the hand that gripped her waist. It was the hand more powerful than armies. I looked at the tattooed arm that shoved her face into a pillow. Those dark marks marked me as the greatest of men and beast. I was he who's will had fought back Powers Below. Don't worship the Demons because they aren't strong enough. Don't worship the Three because they don't care. Worship me! Worship your greatest son because he is here, and he is hungry.

As I drove into her, and she squealed, I became what men saw when they said my name. I saw the mighty kings who prostrated themselves because I told them to. I saw the soldiers who cheered to me because I was their savior. I saw that moment in sacred battle when my enemies threw down their weapons and ran. The moment they realized that they in their thousands were not more than me alone. The moment they realized their country, which had stood a thousand years, would not stand before me.

I thrusted into the girl as she finished again. I didn't see the mistakes and the dead. I didn't see the complicated gray that came after I shattered everything men thought to be true as stone. I saw only victory and glory.

The whole inn could probably hear. She was screaming like I had put her on a torture block. If it wasn't interspersed with the occasional "Don't stop!" I'm sure the police would have broken in expecting a murder scene of the worst type. I didn't care. When Thomas Belson wanted something, he took it. Who was stupid enough to stop me. They could bring a hundred thousand armed troops, and it wouldn't be enough to keep me off this girls ass.

I came deep inside her and pumped a few more times for good measure. We both rolled over covered in a thin sheen of sweat. "Belson the Blessed." She said to herself. "You're worthy of that name. I think I'll be walking bow-legged for the rest of my life." If she was worried about me getting her with child, she didn't show it.

"You're a pretty girl." I laughed. "It brought it out of me." I didn't always give performances like that. If I was too drunk or tired, she'd no doubt already be trying to sneak out. I wanted to feel like a man. Some people beat on their women to get that feeling. When I see that I usually break a few bones to steer them to a better path. Hitting a woman shouldn't make anyone feel powerful. It's like beating a card player in a race, and thinking you're the fastest man alive. Women were meant to be treated well, and the best way to show them you're a man is to hump them till they're bow-legged. When I wanted to feel powerful by force, I went and found the most twisted tyrant around and ripped his kingdom from him. The trouble was the world seemed to be running out of tyrants.

"Men always paw at me in the bar." Sally said. "If I knew it could be like that, I'd have let them." She looked over at me. "Is it usually like that."

"No, it's not." I said over my labored breathing. Then things started to click together in my head. "Wait, was that your first time?"

"It was." She smiled. "First time of many I hope." She turned her face seductive. "I figured a hero was the perfect sort to give myself too."

I flipped over the blanket and saw the little red stain of blood. "Damnit!" I cursed to myself.

"What?" She sat up. "Was it bad? Did I do something wrong?" She asked.

Of course, she'd done nothing wrong. I should have asked. I should have pulled away when I felt it break. Her first time, and she'd been used to cure my regret like a cheap bottle of whiskey. "No, you did nothing wrong." She seemed unsatisfied with that answer. "It was amazing. It really was." I tried to think through the spinning of my head and the residual lust. "I just meant damn the sheets will need to be washed."

"I'll do it." She laughed. "It was worth it, to find a man like you."

I dug into my pocket on the floor and pulled out some money. "Here just buy some new ones."

Her face twisted a bit. "I don't want your money." She stroked her finger along my torso. "I want you."

I cursed myself. Of course, she thought it meant something.

It was her first time. She was probably smart enough to realize a conversation and night of fun didn't constitute a marriage proposal, but she probably thought it meant something at least. Maybe, that I'd take her on an adventure, or share mountain side kisses with her.

It wasn't an entirely new situation for me. I'd bedded more than a few girls who thought me walking into their town was the start of a new life full of glory and travel. I'd been young then, and indulged in their fantasies. Three above, sometimes in my mind before we went to their bed I even believed I would take them with me. Then reality set in. The road was no place to bring women. Usually, I'd lie to them and say I'd be back one day. They'd give me a piece of ribbon to tie around my sword so I'd be safe.

Stupid girls! I'd think to myself. I don't use a sword, and a bright piece of cloth is the last thing you want to carry around when your head is worth a kingdom. But they weren't stupid. I was just wrong. *Teach them to trust less.* I'd tell myself. People should trust each other, though. When I left them weeping, I'd punished them for a virtue.

How many wars had I been forced to intervene in because two kingdoms couldn't trust each other? Thaniel had tried to conquer the entire world because he thought men couldn't be trusted to rule over themselves. The world had been torn apart because everyone thought keeping your word was a relic of another age.

I'd never been of the mind that only a maiden has value, and every other girl is just good for plowing. Anyone who thinks like that has never truly watched a woman. Still, a girl's first time means something. She gives herself to someone. There's a special place in the World Below for a man who takes that gift and leaves.

"How old are you?" I asked her. It was something else I should have inquired about earlier.

"I'm about to be seventeen." She smiled proudly.

I cursed myself again. She looked older, early twenties. She was too young to be taken advantage of by a man in his third decade. She didn't know the true shape of the world yet. She didn't know that heroes sometimes turn out to be less than that.

"You're a bit young to be working at a bar." I said. I was trying to find some excuse to say I didn't know. Something to make my sin just an honest miscommunication.

"My father's the owner, so I help out sometimes." She shrugged.

"He's here?" I asked shocked. "He heard that?" Any innkeeper worth his salt slept in his inn.

She laughed at that. "Well, I'm sure he did."

"Why didn't you tell me?" I asked. I could have covered her mouth at least.

"I thought it might scare you off." She ran a finger down one of my scars. "I forgot that Belson the Blessed isn't afraid of anyone."

She was right. I didn't fear anyone. Except myself of course.

"He always told me he'd beat me blue if he found me whoring around his bar." She chuckled. "I think he'll be fine when I tell him I have Thomas Belson calling for me." Sally moved her hand over my body. "He's the one that used to tell me all those stories about you. How brave and selfless you were." She threw her dark hair back. "I'm sure he won't even be mad about me calling off my engagement."

"You're engaged?" I finally realized the scope of it all.

"I was supposed to marry a young merchant on the other side of town?" She rolled her eyes at the idea. "He's a sweet boy and handsome too, but he's not you." She was right he wasn't me. That man might have treated her right. "I wanted a man with fire." She grabbed my cock. "I'm sure he couldn't do that to me no matter how hard he tried."

I looked at her sitting pretty and naked in my bed. I tried to make up a thousand excuses to make my guilt lighter. *You know what they say about barmaids.* Came to mind. *If she didn't want it, she shouldn't have asked for it.* Was another thought. I wasn't proud of either of them. She seemed like she knew what she was doing though. She knew what was on my mind when I asked to sit with her. She should have known I wasn't that kind of man.

Yet, she'd given me signs. I should have seen them. I could have a three line conversation with someone and know everything about them. Somewhere deep in my bones I knew. I was the most perceptive man in the world, and I couldn't see a red stain on the bed.

This would change Sally. When her father saw her in the morning, he would hit her. That engagement would be called off and not just by her. The boy would hear about it. Stories about me spread like wildfire. How could he marry her when he knew what she'd done? No one else would either. They'd feel too emasculated. Even if she did find a man, the memory of me would sour it.

She'd be left with an abusive father and no prospects for marriage at an age she was supposed to find a man. That wouldn't be the worst of it, though. The worst would be looking for me every time she stared out the window. Little by little she'd realize I wasn't coming. It would turn her cold. It would sour the stories about me. The one man who wasn't supposed to be like the others, and I'd turned out to be the man who used her first. What could she hope for when Belson the Blessed failed her?

She'd become a cynic. She was a pretty girl from a good family. Her life was supposed to be happy. Now, what had I done to her? Another casualty of my campaign. Another body tossed to the side when I was done. Another sin, I thought my soul was too black to be stained any further with.

Of course, I'd done it in the past. I was supposed to be a better man though. Even Seiford, lusty as he was, wouldn't have done this. Most men wouldn't have acted much differently, but I wasn't most men. I was supposed to be the hero.

I felt my sins weigh on me more than they had before. I saw the dead and the dying. I saw the dog. I felt the pain in my body. I saw the dog. *I'm sorry.* I prayed to myself. I was sorry for everything. I'd had enough. I was ready to wake up from my dream a boy again and realize the error of my ways. That's how those stories went, wasn't it? A man gets a taste of what he asks for and spits it out.

It wasn't a dream though. I had asked for it. I had gotten it.

"We can go again if you like." Sally traced my chest with her finger.

"I-" I frenetically tried to think of an answer. "The ride over was rough." I settled on. "Another time."

"Another time." But the girl couldn't keep the self conscious waver out her voice. I rolled over and pretended to sleep, but when I turned to the other side of the bed there were tears in my eyes.

Wisdom was there, watching over me. He shook his head at me.

"I'm sorry." I whispered to them.

"I know my child." Wisdom kneeled down to me. "I know."

"Why am I like this?" I asked.

"Because we needed you." He whispered. "You're not like this though. You're better."

"Take it away from me." I said softly. "Take it all away. Make me a weak coward." I wept a single tear.

"We couldn't if we wanted to. This is your cup. None else can drink from it." He smiled. "Now sleep my child, sweet and dreamless." He put his hand on my forehead. "Sweet and dreamless, fell deeds await tomorrow."

"Thank you." I said as I drifted into oblivion. I slept more soundly than I had in fifteen years.

Present Day
Jesse's Story

By the time Jesse made it to Pentsville his mount was half dead. It was a good horse. He'd had him for almost four months, but Jessie had a tendency to wear them out.

Jesse walked next to his mount. The beast had earned a rest, and he was two hours early to the meeting. The inn the gunslinger was to be at was called the Jon and Lewis tavern. It was in the nice part of town, that was all he knew. He did not, however, know that it was not an inn but a restaurant, and not only just a restaurant but the finest restaurant in the city, because of this Jessie had never heard of the establishment.

By the time he finally located the place he'd squandered most of the two hours he'd bought by exhausting his horse. By his count, there were about thirty minutes before his meeting was set to begin. He looked at the building and sighed. It was an elegant place full of elegant people in elegant clothes. There was not a doubt in his mine the prices would be elegant as well.

He walked into the building much to the distaste of every patron, server, and bartender in the building. "I believe I have a reservation here for the fourth bell." Jesse told the doorman.

"I believe you must be mistaken sir we have no reservations for fourth bell." He said without bothering to look at the book. He did, however, bother to look at the gunslinger's shabby appearance, road-worn clothes, and pistol at his hip. Jessie was also reasonably sure he smelled the fact that he hadn't taken a proper bath in three weeks.

"You haven't asked my name." Jessie said trying to keep his anger in check. It wouldn't do to pull guns in a place like this.

"I'm afraid I don't half too." He smiled in mock politeness. "Perhaps you are thinking of Lewis and John's it's a common mistake, sir, you'll find it right over the river.

"You actually think you're helpful you little fuck-" He caught himself before he went too far. "The reservation isn't under my name its for a man named Bellefellow." The way the blood drained out of his face he knew who Bellefellow was, Demons below, even the cats in the sewer knew who Bellefellow was.

"Yes sir, right away sir." He hurried off to the upstairs balcony setting the corner table for two. "What would you like this afternoon sir. As I'm sure you know, the second day of every week is our special wine day. Today we have a fifty-year-old Kranish white, especially crisp.

"How much would that cost?" Jessie asked even though he already knew the answer was too much.

"Two hundred dollars for the bottle sir." The man said polite as always, but there was a bit of scoff in his voice that he couldn't hide.

"Do you accept payment in Huego ears?"

"Excuse me, sir?" He said pretending like he couldn't hear it

"Huego ears." He said it slowly and distinctly. "They used to be worth quite a bit of money. There's not really much of a market for it now, but they'll bounce back I'm sure of it." Jessie smiled politely.

"I'm afraid we do not accept Huego ears." He paused thoughtfully "We do accept personal checks though."

"Better not." He grumbled. "I'm not much of a wine drinker."

"Of course not sir." He smiled patronizingly.

"Whiskey?"

"We have a lovely Anthanii bourbon, at least thirty years old."

It sounded expensive. "Beer?" Jessie said hopefully.

"I'm afraid not, sir.

"Water then." He said in a low whisper.

"Fine choice, sir." He stalked off clearly cursing the powers that be that he'd been unfortunate enough to have gotten the one well-connected bumpkin in the South. Jessie almost felt bad for the man. Even pompous waiters needed to make a living.

He looked around to make sure no one would notice and took a swig out of the flask every wise man held in his coat pocket. If this meeting was to go anything like his last one had he'd need the alcohol.

The particular spot the waiter had chosen gave Jesse an advantageous look over the whole restaurant. However, this also afforded every man, woman, and even a few pampered children a clear view of him. Most looked on in disgust that an up jumped ravel should receive the best seat in the establishment. A few of the cleverer ones looked curiously wondering what he could be doing up there. One extraordinarily average girl in the company of an extraordinarily dull looking old man gave him a look that might have been an attempt at seduction, or maybe she was slow, chances are if she was interested in him it was both. Besides he hadn't been away from Mary long enough to think about someone else.

He was sitting there trying to figure out how to look least like the unmannered peasant he was when he felt a tugging at his coat. He looked down to see a little boy in a nice set of clothes with playful brown hair who couldn't have been older than ten. "Hello." He said.

"Hello to you too." Jessie said with a nod. He looked at the table across from him and saw a woman clearly a nanny with her plain white and gray dress swaddling what he assumed was an infant. It was hard to tell how old she was due to her dark black skin, but she couldn't have been younger than sixty. Sitting next to her was possibly one of the most beautiful women he'd ever seen. Her hair was black and straight, and her eyes were the most powerful shade of green he'd observed in a while. She was one of those women so far above you, she wasn't even worth dreaming about. Both were clearly horrified at the child's boldness. "What's your name?" He asked politely

"Thomas." The black nanny rose quickly to snatch the child, but Jessie gave her what he hoped was a reassuring smile on his ugly face and shooed her off. She sat down, but kept a careful eye on the bounty hunter.

Jesse extended his bear-like hand and folded the boy's in a firm but gentle grip. "My name's Jesse Devote." He said then let go. "It's a pleasure to meet you."

The boy looked at him in awe. "You were in the Puena war!"

Young Thomas was so excited he couldn't control the volume of his voice.

Jesse chuckled a bit. "I was."

"My dad told me about you." He said this time hushed in awe. "He told me you held the bridge at Chupulte all by yourself." His voice went even softer. "He said you were a hero."

"I wasn't by myself. There were many brave men that day" He thought of Ben barely old enough to grow a beard standing with grim determination. And his friend Easy Bear who fought with white men even after everything they'd done to them. He remembered Captain Belson who was, after all, the only reason they survived that hellish week. Even Vernon wily as an old fox. "Brave men." It was almost to himself.

"But you were the bravest of them all." The boy still had that look of awe on him. It was the same look every boy had when they met someone they considered a hero.

I was the most alive of them all. "I got a medal, and they didn't."

"It was a great battle all the same-"

"Go back to your mother, Thomas." Jesse caught sight of a tall man swaddled in crimson and gold surrounded by four small children in white. He instinctively rocked his hand on his six-shooter and tried to keep his voice calm.

The boy looked hurt. "Well, sir I just wanted to ask if you knew my paw, he was there."

Jesse smiled at the boy. "I'm sure I did, and I'm sure he was a brave man." The gunslinger looked down trying to find the harem, but they were gone from his sight. "But now you need to go to your mother."

Before the boy could move though a man spoke with the sweetest purest voice, Jesse had ever heard. "Don't be so hasty Mr. Devote." The voice was so comforting, and Jesse hated it. Mr. Bellefellow had arrived, and Jesse stood to greet him. "I would love to meet your young friend." The gunslinger had sharp ears. If he didn't, he would have been dead a dozen times over, but no noise came from Mr. Bellefellow that he didn't want to. Jesse suddenly realized the entire restaurant was looking at the two in silence. It wasn't quiet. Quiet was calming. It was silence, the silence that came as a snake reared his head for the ending stroke. The disgust and curiosity of the restaurant had quickly turned to pity.

"Please, sir leave the boy be." He tried to keep the pleading out of his voice. He may have been evil incarnate, but even a desperate bounty hunter had his pride. He looked to the boy's mother and recognized something in her eyes. It was the eyes of someone who's most precious thing in the world was threatened. There wasn't a doubt in his mind she was a moment away from throwing herself at the Old Priest. He dropped all facades of bravado. Jesse held up a calming hand to the poor woman. It didn't seem to do much, but she sat back down. Then he let the pleading loose. "Don't hurt the boy. He doesn't even know me."

Bellefellow was dressed in the traditional blood red crimson with ornate jewels cast in gold. He was accompanied by four children acting in perfect unison forming an imposing square. The children were clothed from head to toe in white silk robes, their heads were covered by a pale cowl, and only the bottom of their mouths were visible. It was what Jesse imagined death itself looked like, He couldn't have been more terrified looking down a cannon. "Nonsense." The Priest said with feigned nonchalance, but his voice still chilled the man to the bones. "I'm a family friend of this young boy."

Even through the fear, some curiosity must have escaped him. "Oh, I believe you may be too." Bellefellow walked to the boy followed by his children in white moving as one entity. He gently placed a hand on the small of Thomas's back. The gesture was slightly less threatening than waving a gun in the boy's face. He steered the child to his mother who folded her son into an embrace with the same desperation a drowning man gasps for air. "Hello, Mrs. Belson." *Mrs. Belson?* It couldn't have been a coincidence.

"Hello, your eminence." She said with a strange mixture of politeness and unadulterated terror, but she never let go of her son.

"I understand you're throwing a party soon for your returning brother-in-law?" He leveled a gaze at the woman. "That could be quite awkward couldn't it."

"I suppose so, your eminence." She said meekly

"I'll be sure to come and pay my respects I never miss an nice awkward moment." He shook his head dismissively."It's a shame the apple fell so far from the tree." He said as if he almost pitied said apple. "Your husband is such good stock." Then gave an exaggerated shrug. "Damn fanatics. They're a drain on society if you ask me."

"Yes, your eminence."

He knelt down to address the son. "Why I'm sure you'd make a better acolyte than any of these buffoon's." He said gesturing to the children around him. The mother instinctively clutched at her son. If the boys around him even understood they'd been insulted, they didn't show it.

"I don't think so, mister." Thomas said clearly not understanding the situation. "My mama won't let me wear white on account of I get it too dirty."

"Well, maybe not." Bellefellow huffed with a bit of disappointment, and Jesse could hear Mrs. Belson release a breath. "Maybe the other one then." He leered at the baby in the black woman's arms, and he heard her suck the breath back up. Without another word, he turned around and stalked towards Jesse. The acolytes spun with him as if they knew his next action instinctively, maybe they did.

Jesse was still standing and pulled out a chair for the Priest to sit in. "Here your eminence."

"Why, thank you." He took his seat. "And they say Southern gentility is dead."

Jesse sat down only after his associate was comfortably seated, and the children assumed there position front two kneeling and the back two standing ominously behind him."So that was-" He began but was cut off quickly.

"Yes, that is Andrew Belson's son, Thomas and his wife, Sarah." Bellefellow gave a smile that was anything but happy as the waiter approached. "We'll have the special of the day please and a bottle of that nice bourbon with two glasses." He said before the waiter had a chance to ask.

"Sir, the gentleman, asked for water." The man stated, politely as possible.

"Do I look like a knight to you?" His tone didn't change from the sweet, pure voice so it took longer than it should have for the terror to set in.

"N-no your eminence."

"And did I ask what my associate ordered."

"N-no your eminence."

"Good, then get going." Jesse almost felt bad for the poor

bastard, but to be fair the man didn't look half so pretentious as he hurried away from the table with a growing wet spot on his pants. "What a tedious man, I may kill him tonight." He looked forward as if forgetting he had company. "Unless you would like to do it. After all, I'm not rude. What were we talking about again?"

"Not killing poor, stupid waiters." Jesse said imploringly.

"Ah I remember, the young Thomas Belson!" Bellefellow said as the waiter brought out the bourbon and poured both with shaky hands. "I think he has some potential in my order." The bastard shrugged. "Who knows, maybe one day he'll wear a crimson robe.

"Please your eminence." Jesse started. "I owe Andrew Bellson my life and more besides." He took a minute to collect his rage. "Don't take his boy."

Bellefellow took a sip of the bourbon. "Terrible stuff I ordered it for your benefit." He squinted his eyes which looked unnatural on his perfect face. "I know how much you ruffians enjoy hard drinks." The gunslinger took a sip and decided the Anthanii bourbon was the softest "hard drink" he'd ever had.

If it was any other man, Jesse would have knocked him in the jaw rather than repeat himself a third time, but instead, he leaned forward so the poor mother wouldn't have to hear it. "Please, he's good stock."

"Well, of course, he is." The Priest was as uncaring as he had been when talking about the waiter. "I wouldn't bother with the bad stock." Jesse didn't know what they did to those boys but looking at the white creatures, he'd rather put a bullet in the child's head than give him over to the Old Religion.

"He doesn't deserve this." Jesse was trying to keep his voice low.

"Ah, it must have been a good outing if you can afford two children." He pushed the glass aside distastefully. "Although I have to warn you, I value little Thomas far more than the favors you're paying for, but if your wallet's a bit heavy, you can make a donation for the child's soul."

"It's not, your eminence." Jesse admitted.

"Well, that's a shame." He smirked. "But you know what they say honest pay for honest work."

Jesse spooned some of the soup and decided it tasted like shit. "It's legal work but a far throw from honest."

"Well, the price is nine thousand." The Priest said feigning empathy.

"Last time it was four." The gunslinger could feel desperation seeping in.

"Well, Mr. Devote I don't expect you to understand the intricacies of Demon speaking." Bellefellow said with a shrug.

"I didn't expect the underworld to be largely affected by inflation." Jessie couldn't keep his anger in much longer.

"Careful now, the price could easily be ten." Jesse shut his mouth immediately. "So I'll take the money and be gone. Hopefully, the economy in Hell finishes its recession by then."

He reached into his pocket and set the money on the table. It was barely half. "This is all I have."

Bellefellow whistled a haunting note that the bounty hunter couldn't imagine came from a man. "I'm no accountant, but that doesn't look like nearly enough Mr. Devote."

"It sixty-five hundred." He put his head in his hands. "I can get the three thousand by tomorrow." Jesse had wanted to avoid going to a money lender. The only type that would lend to him weren't the sort who sent defectors to debtor jail. Still, they were undoubtedly better than the man in front of him.

"Well, I'm afraid Demons are notoriously unfair creditors." The Priest pretended to do some arithmetic in his head. "Tomorrow it couldn't be less than fourteen."

No creditor would lend him that much money, not even the dishonest ones. "In an hour then!" Jessie screamed and saw the whole restaurant turn to stare at them. It was impossible to be at ease when there was a crimson cloak in the room, but it wouldn't do to draw attention to himself in a place like Jon and Lewis, so he lowered his voice. "Please one hour!"

"Well, of course, I would be agreeable to that." He leaned forward as if imparting some wisdom to an old friend. "But as you know it is a terrible sin to do business after five."

"Please-"

He was cut off as Bellefellow leaned to the nearest table and spoke to an elderly gentleman with spectacles thick enough to stop a bullet. "Excuse me, sir."

The man stiffened up at being addressed by the Priest, "Yes your eminence."

"What time is it?"

"Ten till five your eminence," Bellefellow looked over sorrowfully at Jesse and shrugged his shoulders.

"Thank you, sir."

"Any time your eminence."

The Priest erupted in a fit of laughter. "Now that's a good pun." He eventually wheezed out. "There's no way I could kill a man with a sense of humor like that." The old man sensed he was no longer needed and went back to what must have been his lifetime task of readjusting his glasses.

"Please." There was no fire left in him. Jesse had once seen a dogfight as a young man. He had expected it to be more entertaining, but one of the dumb animals just keeled over and let the other one rip its throat out. At the time It had seemed absurdly stupid, but now he couldn't help but empathize with the animal.

He cocked his eyebrows up. "I'm afraid it's for your own good, the immortal soul being what it is."

"Please, don't do this." Jesse grasped at the man's hands and pulled them back almost immediately. Jesse was sure he'd touched something colder, but for the life of him, he couldn't think of anything to compare it too. "Please, you can't."

"And why can't I?" The nonchalance of Bellefellow's voice, the acquiescence to pure evil, and his air of superiority were bearable, but the mocking smile was too much. Jesse went for his gun. He didn't care about Mary in that moment or the reason he'd enslaved himself to this beast. He did, however, give a fleeting moment of sorrow for the whiskey that would undoubtedly be spilled in the commotion, but then he remembered it was bourbon and once again his mind was consumed with the thought of putting a bullet right between the Priest's smug eyes. However, Jesse's hand for some unfathomable reason could not remember how exactly to pull the weapon from its holster.

"Having some trouble there?" Jesse's mind was intact in every other aspect, he could remember how to cock the sixshooter, he could recall the exact amount of pressure it would take for him to pull the trigger, but as soon as he tried to imagine the impossibility of removing the weapon, it was like thinking through a dream. His hand simply flopped limply on his belt, useless.

"Please, you can't..."

"I repeat again why do you assume that I can not?" Bellefellow's smile disappeared completely for the first time in the entire exchange.

"Because I love him." The entirety of the restaurant was now gawking at the pair of men, but Jesse couldn't be bothered to care.

"But I don't love him." He looked genuinely perplexed. "So why can't I?"

"I-"

Bellelfellow waved him off "I know, I know. You love him." He took a second sip of the bourbon and screwed up his face. "Answer the next few questions honestly, and I swear I will not ruin your life until at least five o'clock." He paused "Do you understand?"

"I do." Jessie sputtered through his impossible rage.

"Excuse me sir." Bellefellow gestured to the spectacled gentleman again, who was apparently the only person in the building seemingly paying no attention to the exchange. "The time?"

"Yes, your eminence." The man said once again brandishing his trusty pocket watch, leaving Jesse completely flabbergasted at how he had produced it so quickly. It couldn't be too much more difficult than drawing a gun. "It's three minutes to five."

"Thank you." The Priest said, eyes not leaving his prey.

"Any time your eminence." He said returning to adjusting his spectacles and sipping at his soup.

Bellefellow once again burst into excited laughter. "He's a hoot isn't he?"

"Not really." Jesse said through clenched teeth.

"You don't have to be that honest." He rolled his head from left to right. "But I suppose that means you at least get the point of the game."

"Have you killed good men before?" Bellefellow asked leaning in.
"Yes."

"Have you killed great men before?"
"Yes."

"Innocents?"
"Yes."

"Women and children?"
"Yes."

"How many?"
"I don't know."

"Sorry I should have worded it better." He paused for a second to think. "You don't know how many women and children or just all together?"

"It doesn't matter the answers the same." Jesse was now trying to draw the pistol on his left side but with similar results.

"Well, then now we're getting somewhere." The Priest nodded happily. "Do you feel sorry for these instances at all?"

"Sometimes."

"But not often?"

"But not often." *Every waking moment of my life.* The Priest didn't catch the lie though.

"Tsk Tsk Tsk." Bellefellow clucked. "It seems working after five o'clock is the least your soul has to worry about, wouldn't you say?" The Priest smiled cruelly "I'll bet you've shot a man dead over a five dollar poker game." He leaned even closer.

"No."

"Really?" Bellefellow looked genuinely confused. "It seems like you're telling the truth, but that seems completely within your character."

"There was only three dollars and thirty cents on the table when I caught him cheating."

"That makes more cents." The Priest nodded and then erupted into more laughter. Do you get it Spectacles?" He managed to get through his laughter. "Cents!"

"I do your eminence." The man said still staring at his soup as if it were a book of unparalleled greatness.

"I'm a riot aren't I?"

"Yes, your eminence." The man nodded.

"Not particularly." Jessie managed to squeak out

"You really are abusing the rules of this game aren't you?"

"Yes"

"Well, that aside, you've killed all these people and recognized it as a sin."

"Yes,"

"And you've right now willingly and knowingly put yourself within my power and risk death for a monga-"

"Shut your fucking-" Then all at once, Jesse forgot how to breathe. He didn't gasp for air like one would imagine he'd do. Gasping for air implied that he had any control over his lungs at all. As it was, they seemed just too stupid to pump. His body started vibrating, trying to figure some way to get air into his body. It didn't work. In fact, the only real effect it had was to throw the gunslinger out of his chair as he proceeded to flop around on the floor. He tried to see if he could draw his weapon again but no such luck.

"Well, while that wasn't strictly speaking a lie, it is not exactly the answer to my question either." Then a thought seemed to strike Bellefellow and air flooded back into Jesse's lungs. "Well, actually I suppose you did." He said still sitting calmly in his chair. "You are willing to die for him aren't you?"

"Yes." The gunslinger who at that moment wasn't particularly good at gun slinging, tried to stand but discovered he wasn't much better at that.

"But coming from you that doesn't really mean much." Bellefellow smiled. "Does it?"

"No, it doesn't." Jessie flopped back to the floor defeated.

"I bet at this point in your life you'd be willing to die for a bent penny?"

"You'd win that bet."

Bellefellow sighed. "No, the real sacrifice is that you're willing to put yourself at my mercy, which as I'm sure you've realized isn't a very substantial thing be put at."

"I'm starting to come to terms with it." Jessie gulped at the air.

The Priest laughed. "I'm sure you are." He nodded at the man with the spectacles. "What time is it?"

"Five-o-two your eminence."

The Priest looked genuinely disappointed. "Well, I had a task for you that needs doing, but this game has seemed to eat away all of our time." Jesse's lunges ceased to remember their function again.

"Excuse me, your eminence." The spectacled man implored the Priest, ignoring the man vibrating on the grown with his face turning red.

"Yes?" Bellefellow had also apparently forgotten his dinner companion.

"What is today?" He adjusted his glasses again.

"Wednesday." Jesse wished the Priest would just call down lightning and fire to smite him, at least that way John and Lewis's would be nothing other than a smoking ruin.

"No, the actual date." The bespectacled man asked.

"The fourteenth."

"Damn I forgot to set my watch back. It's actually two after four." Jessie felt air rush back into his lungs and gasped greedily.

Bellefellow let out a hysterical fit of laughter. "I like you." He said to the clock watcher.

"I don't." Jessie squeaked out.

"Oh hush." The Priest turned away from the man who went back to his soup. "Well, it seems we can finally progress back to business." Bellefellow stood up, and his white-clothed acolytes in unison stood to assume their square around the man. Honestly, Jessie had completely forgotten the children were real people and not statues. The Priest set a folded piece of paper on the table. "Read this, complete the task, and your debts will be forgiven." He pocketed the money. "Well, the remainder of the debt."

"It'll get done." Jessie was still flopping helplessly against the ground. "Just don't hurt my brother."

"If it gets done I won't." Bellefellow chuckled "Honestly a little mongaliod child really doesn't interest me half so much as his brother." He smiled condescendingly at the gunslinger, who tried again to reach for his pistol it was still impossible. "Honestly, if you hadn't put it to my attention I wouldn't have even noticed the poor boy." Jessie raged against that. He thought of the boy and his love and nothing else. He unconsciously sent it all at the Priest.

Bellefellow recoiled at that as if bitten and his acolytes looked as if they'd been punched in the stomach. It was the first indication that they were in fact human. "Ah!" Jessie screamed as pain shot through his head."

"Make sure it gets done." The Priest said angrily, but the condescension was gone.

"It'll get done." Jessie assured him again.

"You know I'm inclined to believe you." Bellefellow straightened his robes immaculate as always. "Well, I'll leave the bill to you. I better set out soon. People will wonder where I've gone off too."

After Bellefellow left John and Lewis's establishment, Jessie slowly remembered how his legs worked enough to get to his feet. Then he tested his gun hand and found it worked as well as it ever had. He knew he'd need it. Jessie found it hard to believe the note on the table was a grocery list.

"Excuse me sir." The waiter tapped on his shoulder.

"Yes." Jessie turned around trying to look as dignified as was possible after flopping around on the floor helplessly a moment before.

"There's still the matter of the bill." He said trying to look as sympathetic as he could, which still wasn't much.

"Ah, I won't be paying today." Jessie gestured wildly at the soup he had been pointedly ignoring the whole exchange, except now there was a tattooed ear floating in it. "There is a Huego ear in my soup."

"Sir I beg your apologies." The waiter said in confusion.

"Beg all you want." Jessie straightened up his coat. "If it were a white man's ear I would be complimented greatly." He put his hat on. "If it were a blackies ear even I would be inclined to pay half still." He put on his best angry face, which on his scarred pate was more than a match for a bumbling waiter. "But a Huego ear is too much sir. Too much!" He picked up the note and stalked out. He consoled himself by saying that it was probably the most exciting thing to ever happen at John and Lewis's.

Present Day

I woke up to a knocking on my door. It was still dark outside the window. It must have been early. I was still rubbing the sleep out of my eyes as I went to the door.

"Tell them to go away." Sally said from her bed. "I want to spend more time with my Thomas."

"I will." I opened the door.

It was Seiford clearly still tired. He never woke up before me. "We have an important visitor." He told me. "Get dressed."

"I will." I picked my pants up off the floor.

The monk caught a look at the girl. "You dog, you." He punched my shoulder. "I was wondering what all that commotion was about."

"Shut up." I closed the door in his face then threw on my clothes with a quickness that only comes from years of soldering.

"You're leaving?" Sally asked.

"I have to." I responded. "Duty calls." I thought of something quickly and scribbled a note on the paper beside the bed.

If you lay a hand on her, I'll learn of it.

-Thomas Belson

"Here." I handed it to her. "If your father tries to hurt you hand him this."

"I will." She took the paper. "Will you call on me soon?"

"I'll try." I lied. I turned to walk out the door, but I stopped. "Sally, don't let anyone think any different of you." I told her. "Don't let them call you anything." I said. "You're as good today as you were yesterday."

"I won't." She smiled up at me.

I sighed. "Just remember the world gets complicated at times."

I looked for the words. "There's disappointments, but there's some good to it as well." I clenched my jaw. "Those stories you heard about me, they're all true, but there's more to them as well."

She looked at me curiously. "I'll keep that in mind." She gave me a seductive stare. "Will you kiss me before you go."

"I really shouldn't keep them waiting." I told her.

"Oh." I saw the disappointment in her, the kind that grows. "Maybe next time."

"Maybe next time." I said and walked out the door.

I walked out the door, where Seiford was waiting. "Good night?" He asked me.

"For some." I said curtly as we walked down the stairs.

"I see." Seiford nodded. "Thomas, are you alright?"

"I'm fine." I lied to him.

"Thomas," he pulled on my shoulder to stop me, "I know you."

"We have important visitors." I reminded him.

"That can wait a moment while I look after your well-being." The monk said keeping his hand on my shoulder.

"You're right. I'm not fine." I pushed his hand off me. "I just found out my father is dead, and the last thing he heard me say was meant to hurt him." I shook my head. "My father's dead and I haven't talked to him in fifteen years."

Seiford took a step closer. "George meant it when he said your father died proud of you."

"That doesn't change anything." I gritted my teeth. "If that was all that bothered me, I'd have the lightest soul in heaven." I told him. "I've killed more people than the plague. I abandoned my family. I've sins that go deeper than any man in history." I looked the monk in the eyes. "My father being dead is just the cherry on the cake of why I'm not fine."

"Thomas, it doesn't have to be this way." The monk said.

"It does, and there's nothing you can say to change it." I shook my head. "Every day it feels like I'm dragging half the world on my back." I bit my lip. "You and everyone else seems to think I can be a better man. Maybe I can be." I thought back to Sally. "Maybe I can't," I shook my head, "but my sins are my sins." I told him. "And my fucking back hurts more than usual today, so let's just get on with it."

We walked down the stairs, and I saw two men with six-shooters on their hips, looking mean as all the Demon's Below. One had a nasty scar on his face. The other had a jaw that could have cut diamonds. Both were soldiers from the look of it and not the dishonorable discharge kind that usually found themselves working for seedy characters. They were true warriors straight and proud. They were guarding the curtain to the private room, and whoever they were guarding, they were proud to do it.

I pointed to the room, and the man with the scar nodded.

"Who exactly did you say we're meeting?" I asked Seiford.

"I figured you would know." The monk said, gears working behind those hazel eyes. "Must be important though." He got the same impression I did.

I walked to the curtained off room. The one with the chiseled jaw stopped me. "No weapons." He nodded to my six-shooter, and to a lesser degree the rifle on my back.

"Do you know who I am?" I asked the man.

"I do." The Jaw answered.

"Then fuck off." I told him. "I met the Pontiff of Herchaw with a damn poleax."

"He did." Seiford shrugged in a boyish apology. "It was all kinds of impolite really."

"I don't care if you met him with your dick out." The Jaw said. "You're going in that room with a weapon, over my dead body."

"Really, you like this man that much?" I was genuinely curious. I could count the men who talked to me like that on one finger, and most of those fingers had been cut off.

The jaw shrugged as if the question were of no concern to the soldier. "I voted for him."

"Shut up!" The scared man said. "You're not supposed to tell them who you've voted for."

"Sorry Sergeant." The jaw said

"Voted for?" I stopped in my tracks. "Sergeant?" I asked myself. "Who the fuck is back there?"

"Let him in Corporal." I heard a deep voice say from inside the room. "It's not like he's any safer without a gun."

"Yes, Prime Governor." The Corporal nodded.

"Prime Governor McAllan is in there." I pointed into the room. "I should have drank less."

"When you met the Pontiff of Hershaw you were still coming

down from those mushrooms you found in the forest." Seiford rolled his eyes. "You threw that poleax at an imaginary dragon." The monk was still a little sore over that. "Meeting rulers hungover is just par for the course."

The Corporal opened up the curtain, and both followed me in. Four men were sitting around the table. Apparently, they were all being told an entertaining story. What's more, it was Ayn-Tuk shirtless as ever, who seemed to have told it. It made sense that he was there first. He always got dressed quickly because he was always half naked.

"Thank you for your zeal corporal." The tallest man I'd ever seen stood up from his chair. "It's good to know I have a constituent in you, no matter how low my popularity sinks."

The Corporal nodded.

The tall man turned his face to me. "It's a pleasure to meet you, Thomas Belson." He shook my hand then turned to the monk before I could respond. "By the way Brother Seiford, I do not rule. I lead." He gave a smile that spoke of danger. "I think you'll find that's an important distinction in this country."

"Sorry Prime Governor, force of habit really." Seiford returned the gaze, though it looked different on his boyish face. "Most people like to be called ruler anyhow."

"Most people aren't free," the Prime Governor cast an appraising look my way, "but even that's changing these days.

McAllan was dressed simply in a black suit and a blue undershirt, but even though it was simple, I could tell it was well made. His face said he'd been in more than his fair share of fights, but not a battle per say. The damage looked to have been caused by a fist and likely more than one. No casual brawler could have boasted a face like that. The man had to have been a professional boxer at some point. That's how I knew he was Prime Governor McAllan, but even all that damage couldn't quite smother the wise look in his brown eyes or the proud jaw he held. He had the air of a king, no matter what he said about ruling and leading. It put me on edge. Thaniel had appeared to me the same.

The first story anyone in the Confederacy ever heard about McAllan, was that he boxed three men at a time in Yuntsville up north and won. My father saw him fight once and would tell me and my brother about it whenever the opportunity arose. Some people argued he was the best fighter in the world. That was until I finished the argument by getting drunk and fighting a bear in Gertfeld. When I was first told the story, I thought bear was just a figure of speech for a big man. As it turns out, in my inebriated state, I was sure the bear in the cage behind the bar had given me a dirty look. We'd fought, I'd won, and me and my new furry friend got even drunker until I decided it a good idea to let him go in a nearby forest with a bottle of whiskey tied around his neck for safe keeping. It was one of the strangest stories surrounding my exploits, and Gertfeld was still beset by a bear with a taste for liquor. However, it had cemented my reputation as a first-rate boxer.

The next person to stand up and greet us was a young black boy similarly dressed, simple but well. No ordinary servant could have worn clothes like that. He was respected. Souren people in the South weren't respected that way, but the North was a different story, sometimes at least.

"I'm glad to meet any man who's a friend of Ayn-Tuk the Honorable." The black boy said. "My name is Timothy."

"Good to meet you too." I shook his hand. Then I registered what he said. "Wait, Ayn-Tuk the what?

Before he could answer the last man in the party stood up. "I've heard a lot about you Thomas." He was a Huego man and stood out in stark contrast to the rest. He had on well-worn clothes, the sort you wear when you don't want to be noticed. Besides, he just looked greasy somehow.

Something about him made me think the Huego wasn't just talking about stories. "What did you hear?" I asked.

"I heard about the feather incident with Princess Talyia." He raised an eyebrow.

"What?" I asked. "How?" No one knew about that, only me and Princess Talyia.

"I have my sources." The Huego man said. "My name is Samugy."

"What did you and Talyia do with a feather?" Seiford asked resorting to his childish demeanor that only came from hearing juicy gossip about me.

"Nothing." I said shortly.

"Well, it was surely something." The Huego rolled his eyes. "That must be the dirtiest feather, not attached to a bird, in existence.

"What happened with the feather?" Seiford asked again clearly not put off the hunt.

"Nothing happened with a damn feather!" I said shorter than I meant.

"Oh, it was a damned feather to be sure." Samugy's lips curled up in a predatory grin. "It must have done something truly vile to deserve such cosmic punishment."

"What happened, Thomas?" Seiford kept on at it. I knew no other talking would be done until I told him.

"Talyia put a goose feather in my ass, and part of it broke off midway through." I turned to the monk angrily. "We spent half an hour trying to get it out."

"Oh." The monk said, then his face twisted into delight. "HAHAHAHAHAHAHAHA!" It was a wonder his laugh didn't wake up the entire inn.

"Are you quite done?" I asked, my patience wearing thin.

"Why didn't you stop her?" Seiford was still bent over trying to catch his breath.

"I tried to, but it was too late." I was still sore over it all, not literally of course, but I hadn't been able to sit in my saddle right for a week following the event.

"That's not what I heard." The Huego clucked at me.

"It felt good." I finally admitted.

"Really?" The monk shifted from a boy delighted in his friend's idiocy to an empirical scientist on a turn. "Maybe I should try it."

"Maybe you should, and I'll break off the feather for you." I huffed at him.

Ayn-Tuk finally chimed in, as he was the only one not laughing. "The goose feather is not good for this." He wiggled a finger. "Now, the ostrich feather..." He put his two fingers together to show it was the perfect tool for the job. "Sublime."

"Really Tuk?" Seiford nodded his respect to the man. "I'll keep that in mind." I knew my friend was already wondering where he might procure an ostrich feather.

"Three above, I don't want to talk about this." However, I too was already working out how to get my hands on an ostrich feather.

"Please sit then." McAllan gestured to the seats. Seiford and I sat down in them. "If you're not still sore from the feather that is."

The tall man smiled, and the rest laughed, Seiford louder than all of the rest.

I shook my head dismissively, but the gears were already turning in my mind and not just about ostrich feathers, though a large part of my cognitive ability was focusing on that as well. As I sat, I appraised the room. It had been a while since I'd been forced to analyze something this way, so it was slower than usual. However, my mind was considered the sharpest in the world by some. It didn't take me long to figure out the true nature of the feather story.

That Samugy man was a gatherer of intelligence, a spymaster. Every effective leader had one, and so it didn't surprise me that the Prime Governor had one as well. What did surprise me, was how good he was. With the feather story, he wanted to show me he knew things no one else did. Even Thaniel couldn't find secrets I held that close, and he had possessed the finest network of spies I'd ever encountered. I also knew he didn't have the resources the late Emperor did. The Iron Will pact was explicit that no elected official could use government money for spying. Sure most Prime Governor's twisted that a bit, but it was impossible to get away with too much. I was sure McAllan had backers. No one got to be Prime Governor without them. Still, even if Samugy had full access to the treasury, it wouldn't be a fraction of what Thaniel spent.

With little resources and halfway across the world, this spymaster knew one of my most intimate moments. This Huego was good. Samugy was a dangerous man. What else did he know? Did he know how much the Anthanii King wanted me dead? Did he know how I managed to get into Gestalt? Did he know what I found in Imor?

However, a dangerous man could also be a useful one. Maybe he knew things I didn't. Maybe he knew the true reason I'd been let go by the New Church. Maybe he knew what Thaniel's last words to me meant. Maybe he had even listened to the Priest of Sterling's final threat. *You think you've won?* I heard the words ring in my ears. *"Her."* The words that haunted my sleep. The words that might lead to me standing over a battle-hardened Seiford, in a distant future. The words that made me kill him. Maybe, he knew who she was. I was sure he knew something.

Then was his master, Prime Governor McAllan. He was a competent man to be sure. As I knew it, he'd been born penniless, and now he occupied the top post of the executive branch in the

Confederacy. Of course, being born poor and rising to the top, was a tradition of my people. A good many of the politicians in the land came from humble stock, but it took skill. That didn't mean they were all the right kind of politicians, but when they weren't it was usually because they were too good at their jobs, not too bad. Still, I heard stories that the bills he had pushed through the legislature had all been effective.

On top of that, he was a famed fighter. People often thought that being a good fighter meant you were a dumb brute. There's some truth to that, but to be a great fighter you had to be cunning as well. By all accounts, McAllan was a great fighter. I also saw the loyalty the two guards had. Respect for an office wouldn't be enough to make a man try and deny me entrance into a room. They respected the man.

Of course, there were other reasons to be cautious of McAllan. The post of Prime Governor was a far throw away from the absolute authority of a Thyro monarch. The position was held by strict checks and balances, but when you asked for the leader of the nation, people pointed to the Prime Governor. That meant something.

I also knew that McAllan's popularity was waning. In an elected post when you were voted out you left. He might be getting desperate, and desperate meant dangerous. I didn't think the Prime Governor was the power-hungry sort, but I knew he hated the Old Religion. Righteous anger could force a man to make just as bad a decision as the unrighteous sort. I was a testament to that.

Then I looked at Timothy. He was a black, Souren. They were considered mostly equal under the law, but still, they were looked down upon. This Timothy was an aide to the Prime Governor. The boy must have been truly skilled. McAllan probably hadn't made any friends appointing him to the post over a slew of better-connected candidates. McAllan had seen something in the boy that he wanted far more than political capital.

After an awkward moment of silence, McAllan spoke up. "Your friend Ayn-Tuk here has been keeping us busy with his thoughts on differential calculations, and how they might better be used to explore the stars."

"Really?" Seiford asked. "He's never mentioned those thoughts to me."

"Well, you must have him tell you." The Prime Governor nodded to the shirtless black man. "I've always been firmly in the Chaotic Theory camp, but I think your man has brought me over to the Divine Engineering school of thought." He patted the Souren's shoulder. "Truly, you're a gifted rhetorician." He smiled. "You might even consider running for office."

I turned to Ayn-Tuk "Who are you?" I asked.

He just shrugged his shoulders. "Ayn-Tuk."

"Do you study much astrology, Mr. Belson?" McAllan asked.

"Enough to get me through when I've lost my compass." I was still staring at the black man. "I'm just surprised you got him to leave his spear behind." I looked around for the damn thing. "I've never seen him without it."

"Well, when he heard he couldn't meet the Prime Governor with it, he rushed to put it up." Samugy smiled that greasy smile. "Apparently he read one of McAllan's papers, and he was absolutely giddy to talk to the man that wrote it." He cocked an eyebrow at the young black aide. "It's nice to meet a blackie with something rolling around between his ears."

"I'm sorry." I interjected before the aide could respond. "Did you say giddy?"

"To talk?" Seiford chimed in.

"Grinning ear to ear." The Huego sat back.

"Who are you?" I asked Ayn-Tuk again. I'd seen some things that didn't make sense, then I met Ayn-Tuk. If scholars really wanted a mystery to unravel they should follow him around for a few years.

"Excuse me, your eminence," the young black boy Timothy chimed in, "but do you really not know?"

"I thought he was a warrior looking for glory." I said still looking at Ayn-Tuk.

"My guess was some sort of Souren holy man." Seiford was looking at the man intently as I was.

"We have a wager on the matter so please enlighten us." I said.

"Don't forget Viverent." Seiford wagged a finger. "He surmised that Ayn-Tuk was some kind of Souren token of appreciation." He kept staring at the man. "Said he was meant to enlighten the rest of the world."

"You're both partly right, and partly wrong." Timothy said. "Except for Viverent who was completely wrong."

"Huh, rare for Viverent." Seiford said. "Continue."

"Well," Timothy started. "Ayn-Tuk has become famous amongst our people for-"

"Now, now, Timothy." McAllan cut in. "We've spoken of inconsequential things for long enough." He turned to us. "We did not come here to speak of feathers, astrological theory, or Ayn-Tuk's position, engaging though those topics are."

"No, I don't suppose you did." I said.

"Begs the question, why did you?" Seiford asked.

"As I'm sure you've discovered, the history of the Confederacy is at a crucial point." McAllan said.

"Politicians always say that." I dismissed it.

"This time it might be true." Samugy cut in.

"You don't strike me as a self-important man." Seiford muttered gears still turning. "Might be true, Thomas." He turned to me.

"Might be." I agreed. "My brother told me all about these problems last night." I shrugged. "Provincial rights, the Iron Pact might not be as iron as people thought," I met the Prime Governor's eyes, "the Old Religion."

"Exactly." McAllan said. "Your brother is an honorable man. I was there when he received his medal," he paused, "but I fear he may be a Southerner before he's a Confederacy man."

"What do you mean?" I asked not wanting to hear an insult leveled against my brother.

"I mean if it comes to picking up rifles, your brother may choose to side with the South rather than the country." Samugy nodded.

"You think it'll come to that?" I narrowed my eyes.

"I sincerely hope not." McAllan said. "In normal times, maybe I could manage to hold the Confederacy together until the crisis is resolved, but there's a senator named Coleson." The Prime Governor sighed. "He's a tit, but his name means something in the South, and it seems like he's succeeded in fermenting tension."

"Also he has friends." Samugy cut in.

"What kind of friends?" Seiford asked.

"The powerful kind." The Huego leaned in. If he knew more, he was keeping it to himself.

"Yes, powerful friends." McAllan said. "Coleson managed to cut off trade with the North recently." He said. "He thought he was catching us off guard and planned on weakening my term by starting a famine, but my resourceful man here," he gestured towards Samugy, "let me know months in advance." McAllan looked back at the man. "We were able to make preparations for it, and in the end, it was the South who suffered."

"Sounds like a problem." I said with a shrug. "I'm hardly a merchant though, so I can't see why you bothered me at an ungodly hour."

"Because it's the first step." McAllan shook his head in disgust. "If you want to fight a man in a bar you don't just go up and sock him." He extended his callused knuckles to show he knew what he was talking about. "Well, you do if you're smart, but a man like Coleson is too proud for that."

"So he wants a war?" I leaned forward. "I hate to be the one to tell you, but I'm retired." It sounded strange on my tongue. "I fear my response is the same to you as it was to my brother." I leaned back. "What the fuck, does it have to do with me?" I waved my hand. "We thought we'd enjoy our golden years, sipping mint juleps."

"I've always heard you liked beer." Samugy didn't miss the opportunity to remind the room he knew things. "Dark and bitter if my sources are correct."

I turned to the Huego to let him know exactly where he could shove my drink order, but the Prime Governor spoke first. "It matters because this is your country, no matter how long you've been away." McAllan said. "I know what you did across the ocean." He nodded. "You saved people you had no business saving. You did it because when people call, Belson the Blessed answers." The Prime Governor leaned forward. "Now your homeland needs a hero too, and you want to sit on your hands?" He shook his head. "I don't believe that."

"I know you made some mistakes over there too." Samugy put in. "You did some things you wish you could take back."

"It was war." I turned to the Huego. "What do you know about it?"

"Quite a bit." Samugy gave me a look that spoke true. "I know you can't take back what you did, but you might be able to change what happens." He held my gaze. "Might make you sleep better."

"I'm sure a spymaster sleeps sound as a baby." I sneered at him.

"From sunset to sunrise." Samugy nodded. "Since I started spying for the right people that is."

"If you think going to war against my own people will help me sleep better, you're not half as clever as I thought you were." I shot back. "That's what you're asking isn't it?" I put my hands up. "Wield your armies against the South?"

"A day may come when I ask you for that, but it's not today." The Prime Governor said. "I don't want to fight a war." He paused. "I want you to help me avoid one." McAllan said pleadingly or at least as close to pleadingly as a man like McAllan got. "Coleson picked that fight with the Puena because he knew he could win it, without our help, and before we could mount any forces to help. He also knew that we wouldn't want to because they started that fight all of their own without any democratic approval." He shook his head. "That's not how the Iron Pact works."

"So he wanted to build animosity between the North and South." I said. "I expected as much. I've seen that trick before, but he can't be foolish enough to think he can win. The North has the infrastructure and numbers. Besides, the middle provinces will probably side with you, and the western colonies too. Not to mention the South doesn't have any navy to speak of." I scratched the tattoos on my arm. "The only advantage Coleson would have is the Old Religion. I wouldn't discount them. I've seen what they can do, but the New Church will send another Constable here, seeing as I'm retired." I sat back in my chair as if that solved the problem. "He'll deal with them, and you'll win your war." I smiled. "I've always found the best deterrent to conflict is knowing you'll lose, and he most certainly will." I shrugged. "Unless, I join, but as I never grow weary of saying lately, I'm retired."

"Not quite." McAllan said looking at the ground as if considering it all. I was sure he'd thought it over a thousand times already. "What you've said is true, and we don't need the Southern crops as much as we used too because of monks like brother Seiford showing us how to grow them better." He paused and looked up at me. "But Fennis is damn good. He'll make us bleed for it. Also, we have reports that Anthanii and Kran might lend their support."

"Why would they do that?" Seiford broke in. "They both have good reason to hate the Old Religion."

"They do." McAllan admitted. "But they see it as far away and across the ocean. Far enough not to matter. What does matter is that they're both heavily dependent on Southern cotton and tobacco for their economies."

"That doesn't seem like a good enough reason to fight a war across the world though." I said suspiciously.

"To them economics is." McAllan said sternly. "They'd send soldiers to die to line their pockets, and you know it, but you're right that's not the only reason." He sighed. "The Anthanii are still sore from our revolution. King John see's this as a way to get back at Then Ironwill. Also, a divided Confederacy is easier to return to their influence. He wants us to be his property again in all but name. Also that quasi-democracy you installed in Kran is a bit too enlightened for its own good. Coleson's been sending dignitaries that way to convince them that our 'oppression' goes against the Southerner's rights for free government, and whoever they sent is rather persuasive."

"You should tell him the other reason too." Samugy put in.

"There's been dozens of uprisings in Thyro countries." McAllan said. "People saying they want a government more like ours." He sighed. "So far they've all been defeated, but they see us as the root of the problem."

"And they're afraid one day you might ride in and assist one of those uprisings." Samugy said. "Then the uprising becomes a revolution, and revolutions are how kings die." He sighed. "Plus that tit King John seems to hate anything to do with you. He won't even let the historians put your name in the books."

"Yes, he does hate me quite a bit." Hitting someone in the balls will do that. I didn't mention that I had thought of joining one of those uprisings, just to see what it's all about. "Still they can't send enough soldiers here to completely overrun you." I said. "Thyro's too volatile a place for them to commit too many forces elsewhere. Besides, they both have colonies to abuse."

McAllan shook his head at that. "You're wrong, it was too volatile before you beat half the continent into submission." He said. "Still, the ocean is big. They couldn't supply that large of an army, but they can send enough to do some damage, and I don't fancy going toe to toe with either of their navies." He paused. "Besides, some of those men they'll be sending are the ones you trained. That's a crack lot."

"They are." How it all ended still felt like being betrayed by a lover, even after all the time that had passed. "Still it might not be enough."

"It might not be." McAllan admitted. "But I don't want to take that chance. There are other factors to consider. Coleson may be a tit, but he's put the whole of the South against us. The North and everyone else will wonder why we're even fighting. They can't see the long game like we can. If things get bad, they'll want us to sue for peace on any terms we can get it." He sighed again. "Coleson and Fennis know they don't have to beat our armies, our people could do it for them."

"Well, isn't that the point of democracy." I said with what I hoped looked like nonchalance. "A government run by the people."

"Run by the people, not the mob." McAllan shot back. "If I spent my term trying to appease their every whim, I'd never get anything done, and we wouldn't have a country to speak of." He shook his head. "I'll die defending a man's right to choose his own path, but I don't think that's what Coleson has in mind."

"From what I've heard, I think you're right." I admitted. "But if the South chooses him what gives you the right to overthrow Coleson?"

"Because they're not just the South." McAllan shot back. "They're my people as much as anyone North is. When the shepherd sees his flock following a wolf in sheep clothes, he doesn't say 'well they made their choice.'" The Prime Governor narrowed his eyes. "He pulls back the mask and lets the deception be known."

"I don't think the people would like being compared to sheep." I smiled back.

"You're right they're not sheep, which makes my burden all the greater." McAllan paused. "Our founders had a dream of a land where men were free. That dream means something to me." The way he said it made me believe it. "I will not see it thrown away now because it is easy. Men have choices to make, and that's a hard thing, but the alternative is slavery."

"I understand that," I knew what happened when you chose the easy road, "but what if they choose to be slaves?"

"Then I'll show them a better way." The Prime Governor said levelly. "They can choose whatever they want, but I won't let the slave master take half of this land."

"Then explain that to them, and maybe they'll see." I answered back in turn.

"Ha." McAllan laughed. "I try to explain it every day, but Coleson minces my words. I explain it to the people up north, and they understand now, but if a war starts..." He trailed off. "They won't see how evil the Old Religion is, or that it could spread north. They won't see that we could go back to being Anthanii's slaves in all but name. They won't see the future that Then Ironwill wanted for us and that we can only move towards it together. They'll only see widows, taxes, and death."

"That's what war is." I spoke the truth. "Maybe you don't see that well enough."

"I do, and that's why I'm here." McAllan hissed angrily.

"Here to convince me to win you a quick victory." I shot back. I believed he wanted the best for his country, but I didn't believe he came here to have me hold an olive branch. It was like going to a blacksmith and asking for a sturdy piece of wood. It just wasn't in my skill set.

"I didn't come here to ask you to win a war for us." McAllan looked into my eyes as if he was trying to glean something, anything. "I came here to ask you to stop one before it starts." McAllan was desperate but clearly trying not to let it show. "With Fennis, the Old Religion, and foreign allies, this won't be an easy fight, even if everything goes our way, which it never does." McAllan sighed. "There will be blood if Coleson gets his war. I don't want that for my people north, south, or anywhere else." He looked to me for help. "I want you to convince them to stop. There's other ways to solve this. Make them see that. You're the greatest war hero in living history, probably longer than that. War is an easy response to a problem, at least at first. Then we start to count the dead and battered living, but it's only ever after the first bullets are fired. Once those bullets are fired, you can't take them back. They never see peace again afterwards, I won't let war be my only legacy, and I'm offering you a chance to not to let it be yours."

"I haven't been in the Confederacy for fifteen years." I shook my head. "They won't listen to me."

"You're a hero. The whole world listens to you whether you realize it or not." McAllan could see the man wanted to help. "They might not heed you at first, but they'll listen. If you can make them listen long enough, we have a chance to stop this."

"The public view of me isn't as..." I tried to find the right word. "Monolithic as it used to be."

"No, it's not." McAllan agreed. "Most call you a hero, but there are some who prefer traitor." He sighed. "Your to famous to be completely slandered, but the newspapers have been telling a less flattering story of your exploits as of late."

Samugy cut in. "Not an all together untrue version of events either.

The Huego and I glared at each other, until Seiford sensed things were getting close to boiling over. "You said you had a plan to avert a war." The monk said. "I'd like to hear it."

"While there are some who aren't so fond of you, most still view you as a hero." McAllan sat back a bit. "They see you as the man who put our country on the map." The Prime Governor smiled wryly. "They see you as a prophet for what the Confederacy will one day become, a nation to make the world tremble."

"Most was enough to elect you," I responded, "not enough to avert a war."

Samugy spoke up. "It won't be too hard to turn public opinion towards you." The Huego said. "We'll wage a war of propaganda to sway them. I doubt we'll ever convince most of the aristocrats. They view you as too dangerous and likely will until you're in the ground."

"I've been buried alive before." I smiled. "It'll take more than that to make me less dangerous."

"I've heard that story too," the Huego chuckled, "and I think you're right." His face turned stern. "The common people love heroes, and that's what we're going to give them."

"How do you plan on doing that?" Seiford asked. "All I've heard so far is vague promises of propaganda."

McAllan nodded. "We'll distribute pamphlets about your various successes." He went on. "We'll have newspapers sing your praises to every corner of the country. We'll tell the truth about you." He said defiantly. "You can't just take something like the Old Religion away without giving them something better to hold onto." He paused. "The promise that one day we can embody you without the Priests will be enough."

"You think so?" I put an eyebrow up.

Finally, Timothy spoke up. "You're a savant as far as public relations go." We all stared at the young boy. "I'm sorry, did I speak out of turn?" He shifted awkwardly at the attention.

"No, I'm quite curious as to what you have to say." McAllan smiled at what I assumed was his prodigy.

"Um-" Timothy started but was cut off by McAllan.

"Do not use um." The Prime Governor rebuked the boy. "It makes you sound stupid and detracts from your point." McAllan said. "Now try again."

Timothy nodded. "What I was saying, was that as far as public relations go, we couldn't have gotten a better candidate for the task." He looked around the room, still a bit timid.

Samugy rolled his eyes. "Yes, boy, Thomas Belson is famous." He rolled his eyes. "I heard the sky was blue too. Would you mind doing some investigating for me?" The Huego shook his head. "Idiot blackies." He leaned in towards me. "The worst are the ones who think they're clever."

I didn't know how to respond to that, but to my surprise Timothy did. "Yes, Thomas Belson is famous, but that's not necessarily a good thing."

"Really?" I asked. I was a bit insulted.

"Yes, really." The black boy said. "Everyone in the world already knows his stories, so the narrative is out of our control." He gained more confidence as he went on. "The best bet in a situation like this would be to create our own hero, who embodies the values we wish to preach."

"But you said he was a perfect fit?" McAllan didn't look like he was asking for himself, but rather to test his pupil.

"That's because he is if we use his name correctly." Timothy nodded at us. "He's a southerner who embodies Northern values, that can help close the gap between us." The black boy said.

"It can also be a story about how we're corrupting their finest." McAllan said.

"It can which is why we must put special emphasis on his heritage and martial skill." Timothy answered without missing a beat. "Southerners hold those two things in the highest regard."

"Interesting." McAllan scratched his battered face.

"He's from an old family but has also taken a vow of poverty." Timothy continued. "He is an intellectual and a war hero. He is the man who saved the old monarchies, but also one who encouraged a strong shift in their social structure." The black boy looked at me. "He can appeal to the rich and poor, the artist and warriors, the conservatives and liberals." Timothy smiled self-satisfied. "As long as we don't stretch his image until it rips, we can fit many men under that tent.

"Is that all?" Samugy snorted. "I could have told you that."

"It's not." Timothy responded. "He won his fame across the ocean, mostly in Thyro." He nodded. "We don't have to worry about anyone printing sob stories of killed family members." He turned back to McAllan. "The monarchs of Thyro are public about despising him, but we hold such a disdain for those monarchs, it'll be an asset." He shifted uncomfortably. "However, we do view ourselves as almost Thyran, so it's like he helped a distant cousin." He shook his head. "We'll have to downplay parts of his actions in Souren. My people are still considered too barbaric, and Thomas's image could be hurt by that."

"You think Souren is barbaric?" I asked. The boy had probably been born here and didn't know much of his homeland.

"No more barbaric than anywhere else, but propaganda isn't about what I believe or even what's true." He sighed. "Also, he is followed by a Souren warrior. We can use that to say he's a civilizing force for savages."

"I do not follow Thomas to become civilized." Ayn-Tuk said it with some defiance.

"I've never really thought of Tuk as a savage." I scratched my chin at the black man. Despite him being eerily silent I'd never seen him as anything other than polite. I had once seen the man drape his favorite blanket over a puddle so a woman wouldn't get her shoes wet.

He was the perfect gentleman. Whenever we dined at a court, he always knew which piece of silverware to use. He never ate with his elbows on the table, he always placed a napkin over his lap, and he always waited the appropriate amount of time before signaling for the next dish. I, on the other hand, had been rebuked numerous times for trying to feed dogs underneath the table. I figured why have dogs at dinner if you can't pet them. I had, at one point in a drunken stupor, released a chimpanzee into a certain lord's dining hall. There was also that time with the Viceroy of Vintergout when I had ridden Shaggy cow into a feasting area and demanded the noble give me all his paintings in which breasts were exposed. I had never seen Seiford so mortified. Luckily, I threw up on myself and passed out before I had a chance to further embarrass him. Unluckily, that had been the night I had been buried alive.

In short, Ayn-Tuk was probably the most civilized person I knew. If I had a daughter, I would want her to wind up with a man like him. Well, except for the fact that I'd seen him naked. I'd thought his cock was a snake and almost shot it off.

I finally stopped thinking about my embarrassments for a moment. "No, Ayn-Tuk is not a savage."

"Once again, it doesn't matter what we believe," Timothy continued, "what matters is that we maneuver that narrative to further the cause." He looked at Ayn-Tuk. "I promise we won't put you in a bad light."

For the first time, I saw the shirtless man show an emotion. It was begrudging acceptance. It was shame. He nodded finally.

"No!" I said firm as stone. "Ayn-Tuk is our friend. I will not allow him to be viewed as a savage." That seemed to surprise the black man. I tried not to let it show that I was also surprised.

"Thomas that's an important piece to this narrative." Timothy said cautiously. "If we don't spin it as a positive our enemies will smear you for it."

"I don't care." I said. "I don't know why Tuk follows me, but it wasn't to be used as propaganda." I nodded to the man. "I'm glad he's here. I've seen him give good account of himself on the battlefield, and that's more than I can say for many of the white men I know."

Ayn-Tuk nodded back in what seemed like respect, almost bordering on thanks. I felt Sciford pat me on the back. I could tell he was proud.

"Fine." Timothy nodded, looking a little relieved. "I've drafted up a plan to use your image." He pulled a piece of paper out of his pocket and slid it to me. "First we establish you as a hero of note. A hero in the mold of a Southern Confederacy man."

I skimmed over the piece of paper. It was a story about one of my more pure victories. It was Wuntsville. If my life ever boiled down to good and evil, it was that day. It was remarkably close to the actual story as well, with a drawing at the bottom of me leading a pack of mules against a line of cannon. "It's good." I admitted. "Did you do this?"

"I did." He said.

"I'm wondering where you found the time." McAllan gave the boy a stern look.

"Not at the expense of my studies I assure you." He said then turned to me. "We'll use stories like this and preach unity." He looked around the room. "Slowly we'll turn that story into a warning about the evil of the Old Religion."

"It's better than my plan." Samugy admitted.

"I think it is." McAllan agreed. "Timothy you'll take the lead on this, as long as it doesn't interfere with your studies."

"It won't, sir."

"Who's paying for all this?" I asked.

"We have backers." McAllan said. "Men who don't want to see this country torn apart."

"Of course, your parade will help." Timothy added in.

"I'm not going to any parade." I'd heard the rumors about it. At the time it seemed like great fun. Now it was unbearable.

"Thomas, the people need to see you." Samugy started.

"I don't care." I shot back. "I'm not going to a damn parade."

"You sacrificed life and limb for a people you've never met across the ocean." McAllan screwed up his eyes as if trying to understand. "You won't stand in the sun for an hour to save your own country."

"You can use my image however you want." I bit my lip. "When the time comes, I'll speak out against this damn war." I gave Seiford a knowing look. "For now, I just want to go home."

I didn't say the real reason. Half-truths can get you a long way. It's the other half that can sneak up on you. When Sterling burned, I'd counted it as my first mistake. It wasn't. It was the culmination of a life lived for pride and recklessness. A life that always seemed to pay off, until one day it didn't. When Mother Vestia had told me I needed peace to become the man she thought I could, I didn't listen. I thought her an old woman trying to assuage her guilt. I'd thought she loved me too much to see what I really was. When the Three showed me a vision of the future, even that hadn't been enough. They were gods too distant for me to understand. Maybe I was too distant for them to understand as well.

Small moments like these were the thin handholds in a mountain. To hear masses shout my name, might knock me off and send me back to the man I was. On top of that mountain, there was something though. Something to make me let go of my hunger. A better path, a place to lay down my weapons. Broken as I was, I couldn't even want that, but I wanted to want it.

Humans are complicated things. We're like one of those equations with no answer mathematicians study in universities. Fifteen years ago, I'd seen the world as a sharp line between good an evil. Now, I couldn't think of anyone I'd met who was only one or the other. What side does a man take in a war between shades of gray? Is it the chorus or the verse that forms us? With the surety of youth, I'd deemed the world simple. After I'd seen more of it, I managed to trick myself into pretending I didn't care. Now gods visited me in my sleep, and it was a dog that consumed my dreams.

"I'd like to show up at your parade, but I can't." I finally said. "Masses have been cheering my name for fifteen years, but I'm trying to be a better man than I was yesterday." I paused. "That's the only way I can do what you're asking.

McAllan nodded, realizing he wasn't going to move me today. "I hope you find whatever it is you're looking for."

"If it's anywhere, it's in the land of what could be." I responded. "I'll be in touch."

They all filed out of the room, and when they were gone, I put my face in my hands.

"Thomas…" Seiford started.

"Go wake George and my brother." I turned to look at him. "If we get on the road soon, we can be home in a few days."

"Will do." The monk nodded and left.

Ayn-Tuk patted me on the shoulder as he left. "You're a good man, Thomas."

I was alone again. I put my hand in my head. I thought on Sterling and the fires I'd left. I thought on The Massacre of the Golden Fort and the screams of the dying. I thought on the Thaniel Wars and the things I'd done to end them. *You're a good man.* I'd always been a great man, a man of consequence but a good one…

I'd taken the hard roads. I was the only one who could have walked such a path. Yet, Ayn-Tuk said I was a good man. He was rarely wrong, and his words always meant something. Maybe, it was time I stopped walking my road alone. Maybe, it was time I brought the rest of humanity with me.

The Thaniel Wars

J was sitting on a long dock in Fredua. It was a port city in Western Kran. I was wearing my best bumpkin coat, I had recently traded my Confederacy style hat for the one that Kranish peasants wore. It had probably been invented to keep the rain off a farmers face, but the meaning had changed. Now it served to say, "Oh you have sex with pigs, I also have sex with pigs. We should be friends and make fun of people who can read." My face was covered in a thin coat of dirt. However, most importantly my tattooed arm was completely concealed.

I was desperately trying to keep my face shielded from the driving winds of early winter. I wanted to find a warm alley to lay down in, but I still didn't know everything I needed to.

It was night, but the port was lit up all over by street lights. If I was there at a different time, perhaps with a pretty woman, I'd have liked the view. I may have even called it romantic. As it was, the lights just frayed at my nerves. I wanted to take one of my hidden weapons and shoot out the dock light. I didn't like the way it shined in my face.

I was counting the warships. It would have been easier in daylight, but I couldn't risk being seen by anyone. Even in the dark, with my disguise, I took steps to mask who I was. I walked with the limp only an idiot can truly have. I mumbled incoherent things to myself. I even drooled a bit. There was a boy back home named Jim who'd been kicked by a horse as a child. I decided to adopt his persona. It was a bit troubling how easily I slipped into it, but I tried not to think about that.

Because it was dark, I had to move around to get the real lay of the port. There were always people running around docks, so I wasn't going to get away completely unseen. They taught us covert skills in God's Rest, but no one could match the insight Jim-Jim.

Cloak and dagger is a misnomer. There are very few cloaks or daggers in cloak and dagger work. If I saw a man in a dark hood lurking about, I'd certainly stop him, and ask what his business was. I probably wouldn't even listen to his answer before I arrested the vagrant on principle alone.

Pretending you were kicked by a horse as a boy, brought just the right kind of attention. The kind that made people avert their eyes and say a quiet prayer for my well being. People are generally pretty kind to those not right in the head, but they still don't want to ruin their day by talking to one.

The only people who interacted with me were children, but calling children people was a bit of a stretch, vile little shits that they were. "Look mama it's an idiot." One boy would point at me.

"No, I'm Jim-Jim!" I'd respond in an idiots rage.

"Don't call them that." The mother would hurry the boy along. "They prefer to be called morons." She'd say as she pushed the boy along.

"Idiot!" The boy would scream back.

"Jim-Jim!" I'd return the taunt.

Then a group of boys would throw rocks at me before a kind dock worker chased them off.

"Stop giving me rocks!" I'd scream. "Jim-Jim has enough rocks, and your rocks bite!" I'd holler at them.

Of course, the sailors were just as bad. I couldn't blame them, though. Their lives were worse than anyone's. I'd rather be Jim-Jim than a sailor. Three above, I hated sailors.

If I had a family member who was slow, I'd have no doubt found the whole thing offensive. However, I couldn't very well pass as a prostitute, so Jim-Jim was the next best thing to be just the right type of conspicuous. Besides, I didn't have any slow family members. Well, except for my cousin Ronald, but I was reasonably sure he was just stupid.

Two ships of the line first class, three ships of the line second class. I marked them in my head and where they preferred to dock. I had already counted twenty formidable vessels meant for waging war, not including the sloops and occasional frigate.

It wasn't all that hard to find out what ships docked where. War vessels were too big to stay hidden. The real reason I was here was my fishing rod. Except, that it only looked like a fishing rod. There was no hook at the end, just a large lead weight. The only way I was going to catch a fish on it was if I hit one on the head and jumped in to get it. The line was too long and marked off every five feet. I needed to know how close to the shore a heavy war galleon could sail.

This was my fifth dock, and it was going to be my last one. I had detailed renderings of every possible piece of useful information I could find. Water depth, garrison size, how mean the local children were. When my plan came to fruition, I didn't even want people to say, "Thomas Belson did it." Let Jim-Jim have all the credit. Let it be said that Jim-Jim destroyed the Kranish navy.

"This area is restricted." I heard from over my shoulder.

Fuck. I cursed to myself. Of course, the guards approached me. Technically what I was doing was illegal, but no one would really throw a slow boy away from his one love. They usually just went about their business. Still dealing with guards put me on edge. I pretended not to hear them.

"I'm afraid you'll have to leave." The guard continued. He didn't sound old, but he had an authority to him. In a country as long at war as Kran, boys grew up quick.

"Jim-Jim wants to fish!" I said in my defiant idiot voice.

"Well, Emperor Thaniel requires that you do it somewhere else." The guard said as kindly as he could.

"I like Thaniel." I mumbled. "He's got a pretty pony." I turned to the guards and screwed up my face in such a pathetic way it would send most men to shaking their head and going about their day.

"I'm sure you support the Emperor." The man who spoke was wearing a corporal's stripe. He was young, barely older than me. He had dark hair and kind eyes. "If you really support him, you won't fish so late at night." He was trying to defuse the situation. He didn't want to ruin my day, but he had orders. I also noticed that he was flanked by three other guards.

"Jim-Jim wants to fish." I turned back to the water. *Just leave already.* I wasn't quite done yet, just a little more time.

"Just let him fish." I heard another guard whisper. "I got an uncle like him. He's harmless."

"Yay!" I shouted and went back to my rod.

"We've got orders from the top not to let anyone drop a line in these waters at night." The corporal said. "I don't intend to be the man to break those orders." He took a step closer to me. "Now son, it's too cold for fishing. Come back during the day, and they'll be biting at your hook."

"I heat up my hook, so the fishes come to warm up." I tapped my head. "Fishes is stupid. Jim-Jim is smart."

"I'm sorry, lad, but you can't fish here." The Corporal stepped forward and pulled at the line.

"Stop!" I shouted. "Them's Jim-Jim's fishes."

He did stop, but not because I told him to. Maybe, he felt the weight at the end of it. Maybe, he saw the marks on the line. He knew Jim-Jim wasn't just looking for fish. "Please stand up sir." He said it as levelly as possible.

"Well, only on account of you calling me sir." I stood up. I knew I could kill them all. I knew I could do it before any of them shot off their musket, but that wasn't an ideal situation. People got killed on the docks all the time, but four armed guards meant something serious. Thaniel wouldn't know for sure if he found out at all, but it put the plan at risk. Besides, these men were probably decent folk. I didn't want to hurt them.

"Now, who gave you this rod?" He asked.

I had prepared a story just in case. I didn't want anyone to suspect it was another country spying. There were a lot of seedy people who would want to know how deep the water is, smugglers and the like. "A man gave it to me and let me lick a yeller ball. Made me feel warm and happy all over" I smiled proudly. "He said he'd give me another lick if'n I told him how far it went."

The nice corporal put his hand in his head. I'd perfectly described opium to the guard.

"It's the tar sharks at it again." The guard who tried to leave me alone said. "What's this world coming to, giving an idiot drugs." He shook his head.

"I think they prefer moron." Another guard chimed in.

The corporal ignored them. "Now, I know you didn't mean to, but you did a bad thing Jim-Jim." He said softly. "What did this man look like?" He asked. "Was he missing an eye?"

"No, sir." I answered. "He had a special one, though. It was all white and such." I was going on pure speculation. I'd decided to roll the dice until they stopped coming up sixes.

"Damnit, it's Ziegler again." The Corporal shook his head.

"I thought we got him already." One of the guards said.

"I heard he made bail." Another one chimed in.

"I want a big bale of fish!" I screamed excitedly.

"I'm sure you do." The Corporal smiled at me. "Just tell me where you saw him and I'll get you one."

"Yay!" I shouted in excitement. "He was over by the-" I started to give them directions. As soon as they were gone, I could finish up and leave with no one being the wiser. Then the lighthouse shined on my face.

"I'm sorry, but you look familiar." The Corporal said.

"He does, doesn't he." Another guard chimed in.

"My paw makes barrels down the road." I said it proudly, but on the inside, I was cursing that fucking lighthouse. They'd probably been at Milhire or Wuntsville. I knew I wasn't an easy person to forget. I decided to double down on the idiot act.

"I don't think that's it." He narrowed his eyes at me.

"My sister works at something called a brathel." I kept up the proud act. "My paw calls her a whore. She says that it's someone who's a friend to those who need it." I smiled at them. "She has lots of soldier friends." I looked down at the ground. "She cries a lot. That's why I bring her fish." I smiled up at them. "You think someone with so many friends wouldn't cry so much, but she does." I kept on at it. "I was gonna bring her some of the yeller stuff to make her feel better."

It was without a doubt the most heartbreaking story anyone had ever come up with. I knew that would make the list of sins the Three held against me. Still, I was trying to get out without hurting anyone.

I saw the guards wipe away a couple tears. "That's probably it." The Corporal said. "Where did you see that man?"

"He was over by the-" then the light passed over me again.

This time the guards knew who I was. "Demon's below." I heard one whisper.

"I'm sorry it's really not so big a deal." The Corporal took a step back. "Have fun fishing."

He should have tried to make it less obvious, but I probably couldn't have done any better in his place. I pulled a knife and put it in his chest. He didn't have a chance to scream. The others fumbled with their weapons. I heard one musket click, but of course, they weren't loaded for a simple patrol.

One man stabbed at me as I came at him. I ducked under and wrapped my arm around his neck and jerked. I heard the crack that let me know his life had ended.

I pulled a throwing knife and threw it at one man and watched him fall. The last soldier faced me with his bayonet ready. He should have screamed. He should have run. He didn't. He had the look of a man who knew he was going to die, but didn't care anymore.

He stabbed high with perfect form, then low in a way that made me jump back. He was good, but I was Thomas Belson. I moved quick and put my shoulder into him. We fell to the ground, and I stayed on top. I wrapped my hands around his throat and pushed until his fight went away. When he stopped moving, I rose.

"Oh fuck." I heard a gargled curse.

I looked to my right. One of the men was crawling away with a trail of blood.

"I have a family." He said. "I have a wife."

It was strange. He didn't seem like he was begging for mercy. It seemed like the man was just stating facts.

"I was a cobbler before the war." He said. "I was going to be a cobbler when it was over."

I walked over to him and put my hand around his throat. I killed him quick. He deserved better than quick.

After it was over, I put their bodies in a long sheet of canvas and weighed it down with rocks. I rolled them into the river. No one would find them until they were just bone. Just a few more corpses in the river. It was nothing to change a military strategy over. Even still, I knew it was more than enough to give a boy who fancied himself a hero worse dreams than he already had.

I sat beside the harbor and continued my work. I tried to keep my mind off of what I had just done, but I couldn't. I'd killed many men in combat. They were probably similar to those who had stopped me. Still, my conscience felt black as sin.

"Who goes there?" I heard another voice scream after some time.
"Jim-Jim likes to fish." I hollered back.
"Very well." I heard that person say. They were smart. They left me alone.

I was packing up my horse, and changing my outfit to something more innocuous for riding. It was the clothes of a well to do merchant with my tattoos covered well. Fifteen years ago any man riding the road alone in Kran was surely up to something. The highways themselves had been in disrepair, and the brigands that preyed on them were numerous. Fifteen years ago I would have skirted along the edges of the forest. Now, I would ride the roads, and not be the only one so bold.

This was another mark at how well Thaniel ruled. Now the roads of Kran were the best in the world. What's more, the brigands were all but gone. Of course, part of that was because of the Emperor's campaign to eliminate crime on the road. A campaign that involved the end of a great many nooses. However, there was another more important reason.

Some people chose the life of a highwayman because they loved the thrill of it, but most young men did it because there was no other option. They needed enough food for the winter to feed themselves and their families, so they held up anyone who passed by. They swore that after that they'd be done. Then the next winter was just as bad. Then eventually their name got out, and they became an outlaw. There was no turning back after that.

In Thaniel's Kran, people rarely starved. There was opportunity aplenty to feed yourself legally. For all those scholars who claim men are base animals, if you give a man a chance to make an honest living, he'll take it. In addition to that, most of the young men, who'd be attracted to that sort of life were in the army. When their term was up, they weren't the desperate veterans who usually came home. They were educated and knew a skill. They had respect, and a grateful Kran would not let its heroes beg on the streets.

And I had sworn to see it all destroyed. It was a question that weighed on me more and more. If I had a family, would I rather raise them in Thaniel's Kran or King John's Anthanii? I fought the Old Religion, and Thaniel had given them a place to spread their poison. However, sometimes it seemed we were just two bears who stumbled into the same cave. We had to fight. When this war was over, I knew Kran would not thank me for its liberation.

"Thomas Belson, fancy seeing you here." I heard over my shoulders, just as I finished changing

I whirled around with my six-shooter aimed at the voices head. It was Doctor Quarrels. The one who had patched me up in Wuntsville. He still looked at me with those kind eyes of his. His plump girth was covered by a simple coat.

"Aye, it's fancy indeed." I didn't lower my weapon. "It's pretty fucking fancy that no one in Wuntsville knew your name." I took another step forward. "It's pretty fucking fancy that an Anthanii doctor is deep inside Kranish territory, and it's pretty fucking fancy you knew where to find me." I cocked the lever. "I think fancy is the wrong word, maybe treacherous is better."

"So you'll wrap me up and throw me in the river like you did with those guards down there." His look turned solemn. "I'm a pretty good swimmer you'll find."

"A bullet in your head'll make you a bit slower in the water." I took another step. "How do you know about that!"

"A doctor feels every time a life is taken before it should." Quarrels said. "A doctor knows when a man is in need of guidance."

"Are you a Kranish spy?" I asked pressing the barrel of my gun into his head. I didn't want to kill him, but I didn't want to kill those guards either.

"Yes, Thaniel ordered me under pain of death to tend the wounds of his greatest enemy, and give him counsel when he strays." Doctor Quarrels rolled his eyes. "I'm not a Kranish spy."

"Then who do you work for?" I asked. "King John, Mother

Vestia, the Priests?" There were any number of people who would want eyes watching me.

"I work for them all." He raised his hands to show he was a friend. "Just as I work for you and Thaniel." He smiled. "Just as I work for the small farmer praying for rain." He put his hands at his sides. "All men need their wounds tended."

"Stop with the doctor bullshit." I pressed the barrel farther into his forehead.

"You're not the first to make me try." He smiled insufferably.

I hit him with the butt of my pistol hard, and he fell to the ground. I was overcome with an unexplainable feeling of guilt, but I pushed it down. "Who are you?"

"I am, I am." The doctor said. "Any further explanation, you would not understand." He stood up. "When you finally realize what that means, do not be overcome with guilt or fear." He dusted himself off. "I have been hurt far worse by my patients."

"Oh, I'll test that theory." I pressed the gun into his head. "How did you know I'd be here?" The doctor had to have been following me. Not even Captain Seiford knew where I was.

"I've taken quite the study of you." Quarrels said. "I knew you would scout the Kranish harbor." He smiled. "I know after this you'll be on your way to the Cretoin Mountains." His eyes spoke of a strange sympathy. "I know after that you're heading to a land men haven't walked in two thousand years." He took a step forward despite the gun pressed to his head. "A place where secrets lie."

I holstered my gun. He was right of course, but how? I hadn't told anyone about it. A million men were wondering where I was heading, but none of them could have imagined I'd be insane enough to go where I was actually going. This man was more than he seemed. It probably would have been smarter to kill him, but I was curious.

"You're just a senile old man." I shook my head. "I don't think you're here to spy, so why are you here?"

"Of all the things I've been called, that's the most accurate." He said. "I'm here to warn you."

"You're afraid I'll die?" I shook my head.

"I'm afraid what it might cost you." Doctor Quarrels put a hand on my shoulder. "I'm afraid the Thomas Belson who leaves the mountains won't be the same who goes in." He stared into my eyes.

"I'm afraid the streets of Imor will change you." He looked at the ground. "They changed us."

"Who's us?" I asked.

"It makes no difference." He waved it off. "Some places weren't meant for men."

"You don't want me to go?" I narrowed my eyes.

"I don't." Doctor Quarrels took his hand away.

"Let me ask you this." I spun around. "Thaniel stands at the head of the greatest army in the world." I turned back to him. "He holds more power than any man in living memory. Maybe more power than the emperors of Imor too." I stalked towards him. "And he's the best leader we've ever known." I shook my head. "Is there any other way to beat him besides this path?"

"Ah, Thaniel." Doctor Quarrels looked up at the sky as if he was nostalgic. "What a great man. He could have been the scientist to lead you even further into the future." His face twisted into sadness. "In another life…" He let the words trail off.

"Is there another way to beat him?" I asked again. "Is there another way to stop him from conquering this world?" I didn't really expect an answer. There was no other way to beat Thaniel. Gods would battle over Thyro. Not the Demons and the Three, but the Emperor of Kran and me. After all, we were more powerful anyway.

Doctor Quarrels just shook his head. "There is the flaw in your thinking." He surveyed the world around him. "You only see the duality of victory and defeat. To you, one man's victory must come at the expense of someone else." He held me with his eyes. "The world wasn't made like that. There is room for each to die happy at the end of their days."

"Is there another way to beat him!" I was growing tired of his sermon.

The doctor took another breath. "To beat him? No, there is not." He stared up at the sky. "Thaniel is a child of war and hardship. He's had everything he loved taken from him. Now he holds on to what he cares about with an iron vice." Doctor Quarrels turned himself back to me. "Only the most extreme measures will take them away from him. To beat him, the wrong path must be taken again and again. The hand will not be released until the body is dead." He smiled. "Not unlike yourself."

"Than how do you expect me to do it!" The arrogance of him judging my deeds, seemed so obvious.

"This is how we expected it." He shrugged. "We know you, and you will always choose such paths. "There is another road you could walk, though. The harder one. The right one!"

"And what is it?" Once again I really didn't care about the answer.

"Lay down your arms. Come to him in love, not anger." Doctor Quarrels smiled at how simple it was, how perfect it all seemed to him. "Teach him a better way."

I couldn't help but laugh. "So that's it huh?" I waved off the ridiculousness of it. "That's the missing piece of the puzzle?" I laughed again. "I'll just talk, and Thaniel will listen."

He returned the laugh in turn. "Absolutely not!" He finally managed to regain himself. "As I said, Thaniel is a child of war and hardship. He has only ever known them. Words of love and compassion will fall on him like a language he doesn't speak"

The doctor went on. "He is a great man, and those are the hardest to turn. Always so sure of themselves." He shook his head. "No, it will take more than one child speaking of peace to turn them. Even if it was, you're hardly the man to bring that message to him. You were formed with many great qualities. Humble sermons were not one of them." He shook his head. "That's why you'll meet your new partner soon. He's too young now, not yet sure even if he believes our message, but in time..." Doctor Quarrels had a look like he'd given away too much. "Anyway, no, you telling him of a better way will not be enough." He laughed again. "He'd probably have you killed."

"Than why advocate it?" I was thoroughly perplexed.

"Because that path is not to help him, but you." Doctor Quarrels took a step forward. "The righteous way is never a waste, even if it only touches yourself. Besides, others will follow you." He put a caring hand on my shoulder. "A lone voice whispering will become a trickle of men trying to live right. A trickle will become a flood of men screaming about a better way." He gave me a wry stare. "Even a man as great as him can't ignore that flood, even a man as great as you." He stared at me with those eyes that understood me. "People talk about a better world, a utopia for each man, not every man. That's how it starts."

"Is that what you want me to do?" I wouldn't actually do it, but it might answer a few of my questions. "Is that what's best for this world?"

Doctor Quarrels breathed a great sigh. "That's a difficult question to answer." He returned his gaze to me. "Is better measured by middle class wages? Life expectancy? Crime rates?"

"Will men be free?" I tried to cut through his nonsense. "If I fight Thaniel will men be free."

Doctor Quarrels chuckled at that. "Spoken like a true Confederacy lad." He paused before answering. "A man is free because he has chosen freedom for himself. Whether he wears a slave's collar or a king's crown he will retain his liberty." The doctor patted my shoulder. "I can say this, if you choose to lay down your arms though you'll find peace. We would like that. We would trade everything for that."

"So this is my only chance to know peace?" It was kind of a morbid thought. Well, it should have been morbid. Perhaps, it said something about me that I didn't really care if the answer was no, and it sure as shit wouldn't change my ways.

"Absolutely not!" Doctor Quarrels seemed legitimately offended by that question. "Men can always find peace. You have a chance as long as you draw breath and even after." He calmed his face. "Your best chance to find peace will come when you're older after you see what this path has cost you." He got even closer to me. "In a day when you're wise enough to want such a thing. In a place where the ones you love can't go any farther because they love you too."

"Then why are you here?" It seemed like the only question that still mattered.

That question seemed to shock him. To him, it was like asking what color is the sky. It's too obvious. "Because we love you. Because we love Thaniel. Because we love every one of the soldiers that will die in this war." He gave a sad little smile. "We had to try." He shrugged. "Besides, there's never seen a catalyst quite like you."

"Ah, you're such a humanitarian!" I laid the sarcasm on thick. "You don't want people dying in some senseless war." It always irritated me when I heard it. I don't know if it was because it was stupid or because it was right. "I've heard a lot of perfumed intellectuals give that argument. In their hearts, they really don't want us to stop fighting. We're the men that keep the wolves off their doorstep so they can mutter empty platitudes." I chuckled again. "Senseless war! It's got a lot more sense than their stupid bickering."

"Of course, this war has sense," Doctor Quarrels seemed taken aback, "and if I'm being honest, you're right. Those intellectuals would piss themselves if the army threw down its weapons as they advocate. They don't want peace. They just want to seem better than the men who are actually fighting for something." He paused. "Every war has a certain sense to it. People just want to protect what's important to them. It'd be nice if they could remember that line of reasoning when it's them being marched into someone else's land, but still."

"Well, I-" I scratched my head. "If I'm being honest, I didn't expect you to agree with me."

"We understand you better than you think." He smiled brightly.

"Well, then you'll know what path I'm going to choose." I patted the gun in my holster.

"We do." His smile turned against itself. "It pains us, but we won't try to stop it." He took a step back. "If you could just promise me one thing."

"What is it?" I cocked my head sideways.

"When this is over, when Thaniel's beaten," he paused, "don't beat him any worse." He took another step back. "Help him find his way back to us. Help him know peace in his final hours."

"Even after everything he's done?" I asked.

"Especially after everything he's done." Doctor Quarrels paused. "He'll need help. We never wanted this for him."

"I'll help him." I said, and he was gone. Not disappeared, not faded away. I just blinked, and he wasn't there. I wasn't even sure I blinked.

As I packed up my horse, I remembered the sorrow in his eyes. It was the deepest I'd ever seen. It was the look of a parent whose child was too far gone. It occurred to me that Doctor Quarrels might see Thaniel as just that. He loved the world and all its inhabitants. He wept for their failures and sins. He saw them all not as failings to be punished, but as their individual sorrows to be mourned. It wasn't to seem holy or empathic. It was as simple as he didn't need a reason.

Then there was me. I was prickly, mean, and as sinful as they come. I was so much less than him. I touched the tattoos on my arm. Yet I was so much more. For all his sorrow. For all his righteousness, he couldn't save them. How many better men than me wanted to stop Thaniel because Thaniel was wrong for this world. They couldn't though. Only I could save them. Damn the reasons and damn the way. The world didn't need someone to weep for it. It needed someone to save it.

"Am I going insane?" I asked my horse.

It flicked its tail and let out a neigh. I got the message loud and clear. "You are talking to a horse." Only loons talked to a horse.

I sighed and mounted the beast. Whatever I was, whatever I became. I would never be the man who talks to his horse.

The Thaniel Wars

"I can't emphasize this enough," the man known as Marc the Mountain Climber said, "this is a bad idea." Marc was one of those old fellows who only seemed to get stronger as he aged. His long gray hair, wrinkled face and splotchy arms meant he couldn't have been younger than my grandfather when he died. My grandfather needed help to take a shit at the end. Marc climbed one of the tallest and definitely the most dangerous mountain range in the world regularly. His grey eyes seemed to be constantly watching the world around him, looking for danger, looking for the Cretoin. It amounted to the same thing.

"No, the bad idea is living next to this Three forsaken range." I set my pack down and sprawled onto it in an exhaustion I hadn't felt sense God's Rest. "Why don't you move? I'm sure there's some oceanside city not filling its quota of old men telling young men things are a bad idea." I stared at him, angry at the fact that he wasn't half as tired as I was, even though he was at least four times my age. "Try it with me. 'You little whippersnappers'!"

"This ain't the time for joking." He shook his head as he threw down his pack.

"That's exactly what someone who uses the word whippersnapper would say!" I chirped delighted. "You're a natural! You can even tell children the uphill both ways bit, and it won't be a lie." I paused. "Who taught you what emphasize means anyway?"

"Most o' me customers is nobles who fancy climben." He reverted to his bumpkin style of talking. "They seem a' like it when I try n' talk like 'em."

"Well, word to the wise, they just like to laugh at you for making the effort." I sat up from my pack. "Don't give them the satisfaction! They're pricks you here me!" I rubbed at my sore shoulders. "No matter how hard you try to be like them, you'll always be lower on the pyramid than they are. The best you can hope for from them is to keel over and die while they never knew who you were." I moved to rub my leg. "Fuck them! Talk like you talk. This is your fucking mountain not there's."

"Well, I like the gold more 'an a roasting peg." It took me a while to realize peg was bumpkin for pig. "Besides, you poke fun at the way I talk lots!"

"At least I'm honest about it." I was debating in my head whether I should walk off and relieve myself properly or just piss down my leg. My lower body felt like jelly, and the urine would probably help warm me up anyway.

"I wish'n you wouldn't be." Marc shuffled around uncomfortably. "Me mama always wanted me a' speak proper." He frowned to himself. "It right stings when you poke at me like that."

"Would you rather I lied?" I asked him.

"Well, just a bit." He held up two fingers an inch apart.

"Well, I won't." I spat into the ground.

Just then I saw my most hated enemy appear before me. It wasn't Thaniel, or a horde of Kranish in their yellow uniforms come to vanquish me. It wasn't the Priests in their blood-colored cloak. They were distractions from the true enemy of any civilized people. I would have made common cause with all of them to defeat the real threat. His name was Sir Hoofington. The meanest goat I had ever laid eyes upon.

When we hiked, the animal would make sure to only fart if I was behind it. It constantly kicked me. Every day, I woke to him nibbling on my hair. I had actually watched him piss on my sleeping roll. One day in a fit of anger, when Marc wasn't looking, I kicked him down the side of the mountain. He had returned just minutes later, goat eyes screaming *vengeance will be had!*

Our hatred was mutual. It was a pure thing. Our war would not end until one had been slain in battle. If I'm being honest, I wouldn't bet on me. I had turned back five thousand men at Wuntsville essentially on my own, but that goat was tough. Of all the beings in this world, the goat was the most powerful. One day Thaniel and I would rot six feet under. Demons could be banished to the World Below. Even gods could die. Sir Hoofington would outlast us all.

"Sir Hoofington!" Marc hollered in delight. "You found our way up the mountain?"

Sir Hoofington did not answer. He stared at me, chewing his cud as if to say. *You're still alive?*

My eyes answered right back. *On guard goat. Pick the time and place.* Even if he would win, I would not go quietly. *I will raze your goat churches to the ground. I will take your goat wives as my own. Your goat children will be my slaves.*

"Milord this is still a bad idea." Marc woke me from thoughts of goat battle.

"I'm not a lord!" I hollered back.

"All the same, you people think the Cretoin is just tribes who live up high instead of down low." Marc kept at his constant attempt to dissuade me.

"Well, aren't they?" He had tried to explain the point before, but it had failed to sink in.

"They ain't!" He screamed. "The mountains changed them. They jump off the side of the cliff when they get too old to fight. They marry their own daughters. Wolves won't even eat them cause the meat is too evil."

"They meet with you." I shrugged.

"Aye, after ten years serving as their slave." He shook his head to relieve himself of the memory. "You ain't seen what I seen. They ain't human no more."

"The first rule of anthropology is that the other is never quite as other as you imagined." I parroted off the lesson from my tutor George.

"I don't know nothin bout no Anthrowhoever." He walked over to me. "I know what I seen, though."

I stood up, finally making the decision to piss. "I'm paying you good money to take me there, so you better."

"I tried to refuse it." He shook his head. "Ain't no money that good."

"Use it to buy a new goat." I paused. "Better yet, a cat." Then I walked off to piss.

"Don't listen to him." Marc consoled his goat. "He won't live much longer anyhow."

I took my cock out and began the process of warming it up enough so I could get the urine out. If you ever want to challenge your masculinity, climb up into the mountains. There we are all of us eunuchs.

I started to piss, planning my newest assault on the goat. Slowly

I took stock of what I was peeing on. It looked kind of like a tree, but I'd never seen a tree so hairy. It almost seemed a grotesque parody of a leg. Slowly my gaze traveled upward. Apparently, that leg had a chest, covered in so much fur a grizzly bear would be jealous. My gaze moved farther north, and that chest had a face. A very ugly face. As I looked at it. I decided my earlier point about Anthropology was ill-founded. This time, the other was definitely other.

"Hello, my name's Thomas." I smiled and extended the hand not glued to my cock. "Thomas Belson."

He apparently didn't like being pissed on. He swung his oddly shaped club at me, and I moved inside jamming my elbow into his face. The move was slower than usual. My exhaustion mixed with the cold, and thin air made me sloppy. I was still Thomas Belson though. I was still dangerous. He crumpled up. I didn't even have the time to smile before a blow to my head sent my world black. It was all I could do to put my cock away before I was set upon by five other Cretoins.

I heard the voices around me speak in voices I didn't understand, which was strange because I spoke five. I thought I had all the major languages of Thyro mastered. Of course, there were dozens of different dialects for every language, but even then I was fairly confident I could at least understand the gist of what they were saying. I didn't understand any of what was spoken, except a word that sounded like the Varsantii word for gentle hug. I was reasonably sure Varsantii and Cretoin had never exchanged cultures. I was not expecting a gentle hug. A kick in my side followed by screaming Cretoin reinforced this thought. No, one did not have to be an anthropologist to realize that the wine drinking Varsantii and the piss drinking Cretoin had very little in common.

I felt the burlap sack come off of my head and looked up at the face that had freed me from it. "You are ugly!" I announced to the world. "Marc, how do you say ugly in Cretoin?" The man in front of me certainly was at that. He was old, probably not as old as Marc but still no fresh daisy. He wore a strange crown of bones, but like the rest of his kin, he was naked except for a loincloth and his enormous fur. His limbs looked like gnarled wood. He was a mountain man, pure. His eyes were mismatched, too far away from each other. His jaw was struck out at all kinds of strange angles. His nose was only really half there. All in all, if he gave a whore a chest full of gold, the best she could offer in return was a kiss on the cheek and a bedtime story.

"Thomas, this isn't the time!" Marc was also bound up, but he had the good sense to look down, petrified.

"There is always time for linguistics!" I scolded the man lightly. "Now, how do you say ugly?"

"Be quiet!" The Cretoin kicked me in the chest. "I speak the lowlander tongue." I was surprised that he spoke it so fluently. He managed to get his point across despite his strong earthy accent. Well, a smarter man would have gotten the point. When a tribe of savages ties you up, it's better to go along with their demands, and all in all, be quiet wasn't so hard a request to honor, unless your name happens to be Thomas Belson, of course.

"You do!" I gave him a patronizing smile. "And you do it so well."

He kicked me again. I was glad for that. I wasn't quite sure these people would understand patronization or sarcasm. The only thing more embarrassing than being tied up is having someone not get your joke while you're tied up.

"I am Guther, Chief of the Sky People." He grabbed a handful of my hair and twisted it until our faces were inches apart. "You are lowland scum, not worthy to breathe my air."

I managed to shrug despite my bindings and his twisting of my head. "Well, your air doesn't seem to like me much either." It was true. Every step up the mountain I took my lungs seemed to be able to grab less and less. "I'm afraid you mispronounced my name though."

Guther cocked an eyebrow up. I doubted he'd ever seen a lowlander like myself speak to him this way. I pressed my advantage.

"I am the Constable Thomas Belson," I knew that wouldn't mean anything to him, so I went on, "Master of Donkeys and Scarecrows."

Guther twisted his face in what might pass for the human emotion of confusion. "What are these donkeys and scarecrows you speak of?" He let go of my hair.

I made my face proud and dignified. I saw an opportunity. "Donkeys are great beast, as large as the tip of a mountain, that breathe fire, and have skin like armor. Scarecrows are the brave men that ride them."

"Demons Below, you're a fucking idiot." I heard Marc mumble under his breathe. One of the Sky People saved me the trouble of shutting him up with a savage kick to the ribs.

"Your army of donkeys and scarecrows won't save you now." Guther spit.

"You'd be surprised what donkeys and scarecrows can do." I mused mostly to myself, then looked back at him. "You're right, though. I didn't come here to do battle with you."

Guther grabbed my hair again, but this time he produced a bone knife against my neck. "I've let you live too long already!" He screamed. "You came here to feel my blade."

I turned made a face of being mildly offended. "Chief Guther, I must protest!" I said. "I've seen many impressive beards since I've been here, so many I've decided to grow one of my own." I shrugged. "If you shave me now, It'll take me months to regrow."

Everyone around me stopped to stare at my insolence. Even the ones who couldn't speak Anthanii instinctively knew I had gone a step too far. I saw Marc trembling with terror out of the corner of my eye.

"My Chief, he doesn't mean it!" Marc screamed. "Please we beg-" He was cut off by another kick.

I waited in the silence. Any civilized folk watching would have been dumbfounded by my response. Could I really value my own pride over my life? That's a question I'd been trying to answer since I could think, but it wasn't answered that day. There was a reason I mocked him. Hundreds of lowlanders had come to meet with the Cretoins. Some were statesmen wishing to gain access to a pass. Some were businessmen looking to trade in the area without being harassed. Some were scientist wishing to study them. None had come down from the mountain. Except for a few of the lower mountain dwellers, the Cretoin killed anyone not their own, and those mountain dwellers were generally taken in raids as children to be slaves, let go after a decade of good service. I had no interest in being a slave.

I'd guarantee most of those diplomats, businessmen, and scholars had begged for their lives, probably all of them. They would have done what any intelligent human being would do. They would have offered gold, support, or anything else a civilized person would accept. That was the wise way, but the wise way hadn't worked. I take the path men don't dare travel. I walk a road no one else can see.

When Guther demanded begging, I offered strength. I showed him I had fight in me. I figured a people who made their home in this godforsaken place valued that above all. Of course, it could have thrown him into a furious rage. It could have made him kill me slow. However, I didn't hedge my bets. I didn't play for the middle ground. If you want to win, don't plan for defeat.

After a long, tense silence, Guther reared his head back and let out an enormous laugh. "You've got Skyblood in you." He turned to Marc. "Why did you bring him here?"

"I told him it was a bad idea!" Marc had the begging in his eyes. "I told him he shouldn't come!"

"I didn't ask what you told him!" Guther glared with those mismatched eyes of his. "I asked why you brought him here."

"Calm down, Marc." I said as levelly as I could. "Just breathe."

The guide listened to my advice and took a deep breath. "He wouldn't tell me why he wanted to see you." He said. "He's a Constable, though. They're a respected order. It's considered a sin amongst my people to deny one." That was technically true, but people didn't really hold to it. I'd been denied many times in my short stint. "He's a great warrior in the lowlands. People say he'll be the man to beat Thaniel." Marc said. "That emperor has brought a lot of pain to my country." I noticed he didn't mention the money I gave him, but I wasn't about to correct that. Marc was a Frederlander, one of the first countries to fall to the Kranish.

"Really?" Guther cocked a misshapen eyebrow up. "This one's a great warrior?" He stroked his beard. "Seems young." He said. "And short."

"Hey!" I protested in a manner that made me seem both young and short.

"It's true, Chief Guther." Marc bowed his head.

He turned back to me. "How great of a warrior are you?"

I stared up into his eyes. "I charged five thousand men and routed them on my own." Now was not the time for humility. "I stood at Milhire against Thaniel's hordes, and was the only man to come out alive."

Guther nodded. "I believe you." He shrugged. "I'll probably still kill you, but you've earned the right to speak." He went down and cut the ropes from me, and waved for his men to do the same with Marc.

"My thanks." I rubbed my sore wrist.

"Why are you here?" Guther asked.

I stood up. "I'm doing battle with an emperor named Thaniel. He's the most powerful man this worlds ever known." I paused. "He's good too. I'll need a way to attack him, but he's blocked every pass into Kran," I surveyed the mountains, "except this one."

"You want to march an army through here?" Guther crossed his arms. "It can't be done. I've seen your armies, they number tens of thousands."

"I'm not talking about an army. I know it's impossible." I said. "I want to march a thousand picked men over this mountain, maybe two." I stared up at him. This Chief wasn't as dumb as I thought. "Can it be done?"

"Aye, it can be done." He nodded. "If we show you the way and choose not to kill you." He stepped closer. "You're still a lowlander. We don't do deals with lowlanders."

"I can offer you modern weapons, sticks that shoot fire and death." I nodded around him. "With those, you can conquer all the tribes on this mountain."

"It's been offered to us before." Guther shrugged. "We don't use the craven weapons. Only weapons blessed by the Sky Man can shed blood."

I went on. "What about gold?"

"The yellow steel?" He shrugged. "It's pretty, but we have no use for it."

I smiled. I'd anticipated this. "What do your women look like?"

Guther jutted a thumb at one of the people standing over Marc. When I'd first got there, I'd taken her for an ugly man. Apparently, she was an exceptionally ugly woman, though I doubted it was exceptional by her people's standards.

"Really?" I asked. "You mate with them?"

Guther cracked a smile. "We have to make Skybabies don't we." He chuckled. "Sometimes we take a lowland woman in a raid." He shrugged. "They're pretty, but they don't last long."

"Right." I tried not to think about that comment. Dark times call for dark allies. "Bring me my pack, and I'll show you what I have to offer."

He sent one of his men, or maybe women, to fetch my bag.

When he laid it at my feet, I started rummaging through it. Finally, I found what I was looking for. *Please don't be broken. Please don't be broken.* I unwrapped the stone statue I'd put in a cloth to keep safe. Blessedly, it was still in one piece.

It was a small statue sculpted by Teron, the best artist in Anthanii. I'd pilfered it before I left Harfow. It was a beautiful rendering the size of my arm. The piece was done in honor of Queen Harriot, though the artist had taken a few liberties, making the breasts a bit bigger, the legs a bit more slender. It was a perfect rendering of the female form. Nobles in Anthanii simply looked at it as an excellent piece of culture, but to a people like the Cretoins, who had never seen a beautiful woman, it might mean more.

I was right. Every eye in the tribe turned to look at *The Harriot*. Even the one previously identified as a woman. Their faces dripped with lust. They wanted to touch it, to know it. They probably wanted to do more than that with the sculpture, but I didn't want to think about it.

Chief Guther grabbed it out of my hands, cradling it like a child, gently brushing the breasts, moving his hands down to the legs. "You have brought me a goddess." The mix of awe and gratitude caught me off guard.

I thought back to the woman it was made after. The shrill, angry queen who wanted nothing more than my head on a platter. "You could say that." Goddesses could be first rate cunts, after all.

Guther finally tore his eyes away. "This is what you offer us?" He seemed to like it.

"That and more." I answered him. "When I come back I'll bring dozens of other women, captured in canvas and stone." I took a step forward. "They'll be so real you can taste the tits. You can feel the warmth." I held his gaze. "Women more beautiful than you've ever imagined. Women that last forever."

Guther spat in his hand and extended it to me. I took it. Some gestures are universal. "We will show you the pass," he took a step back, "so long as you accept the trials."

"The trials?" I asked.

"Fuck…" I heard Marc mumble.

"Three things you ask of us, so three warriors you must fight." Guther looked back at the woman. "To make sure this union is blessed by the Sky Man."

"Three things?" I thought it was just the one.

Guther counted them off on his fingers. "You ask us to show you the pass." He held up one finger. "You ask us not to attack you." He put the second finger.

"That's two!" I said with indignity.

"I think your men need more to eat than stone and snow." He smiled.

"That's true." I shrugged. "I still think all those can count as one."

"It is three!" Guther was adamant.

"Well, I'm glad I didn't ask to take a piss." I shrugged. "Can I get my weapons back?"

Guther shook his head. "Only weapons blessed by the Sky Man may enter the circle." He said. "You have none, and so you will fight with nothing."

"Damn." I muttered to myself. "Right now?" I asked.

"Yes, while the deal has not yet had time to harden." The Chief answered.

"I can't have some food?" I cocked an eyebrow up. "Some water? Maybe an hour or two to rest." I raised my hands. "The track up here wasn't easy."

"You can," he had a wry smile on his ugly face, "but then it will be six."

"I'll do it now." These Sky People drove a hard bargain.

Guther nodded and lead Marc and me to his village if it could be counted as such. It was really just a bunch of pelts extended over sticks and rocks. A small crowd emerged to welcome us. I fell into the Battle Mind. The aches in my body rolled off me like water. I felt the lightning run through my bones. I felt the joy bubble up in my heart.

Guther began to speak in his Cretoin language. As he went on the people cheered. I assume he told them about the fight. Everyone loves to see a foreigner beat to death in a ring. He kept talking, and a number of his warriors started smacking their chest and howling. I assumed he was asking for volunteers. Everyone's a hero when them and two of their friends get to fight an unarmed man. Eventually, Guther picked three of the biggest, meanest ones he could find. They were practically licking their lips at the thought.

A crowd of Sky People pushed me into a ring outlined with

stones. I tried to ignore the fact that most of those stones were bloodstained. The three men stepped into it as well. They were all large, hairy, and scarred. If I closed my eyes and they changed their position. I probably wouldn't be able to tell who was who.

They were all brandishing bone knives in both hands. I wondered what blessed by the Sky Man actually meant. However, judging by the little interaction I'd had with their culture, I probably didn't want to know. If a bystander was standing nearby, and he didn't know shit about who I was, he'd have put his life savings on me getting killed in a few heartbeats.

"You will fight now." Guther said.

"No ceremony or ritual? I asked. "Just fight.

"Yes." He answered back.

"One more question." I cracked my knuckles. "I assume this fight isn't till first blood."

Guther shook his head. "Death."

I smiled back at him. "I expected nothing less." I turned to the three warriors. "Come on. Let's get this over with." As I waited for the signal, I surveyed the crowd. Every face seemed to blur together, except one. A mean-spirited goat had muscled its way to the front of the group. I'd recognize that goat anywhere. It was Sir Huffington, no doubt come to enjoy my death.

"BAAAA!" He bleated so loud I could hear him over the screaming of the crowd. I was fluent in goat, so I translated it easily. "Die you worthless scum!" The goat meant. "Die like the coward you are."

I was renewed with purpose. I would not be embarrassed in front of my mortal enemy. *You shall be disappointed Sir Hoofington.*

I was wondering in my mind whether it'd be worth it to face another fighter for the goat's head, but Guther cut me off before I made my decision. It was probably a good thing. I was leaning towards adding a fourth. "Begin!" He screamed. Well, I imagine he said begin. The word was Cretoin.

The three warriors didn't waste any time thinking about strategy. Each just wanted to be the man who killed me. All they saw was an unarmed lowlander. I waited the painful second till the fastest one was close enough. He reared up both knives. Just before he was close enough to hit me, I kicked him in the chest with a vicious force that sent him sprawling backwards.

I didn't have time to celebrate that small victory. The next man was already on me. He swung his knife at my throat with blinding speed. I caught the arm and struck him hard in the throat, doubling him over gasping for air. The third one stabbed at me from behind. I twisted to get away from the blade, but still holding on to the second man, all I managed to do was take the knife just below the shoulder. In the battle mind, it only felt like a dull pinch. Still, it annoyed me. I jammed my elbow into his face and heard his nose pop.

It gave me a minute to deal with the man I still held. He swung again at me, but this time not half as strong. I twisted him around in my arms till I was wrapped around his throat. I jerked violently and felt the bone break. He fell to the ground lifeless. The other two were treating me with a bit more caution. I reached down and picked up the knives of the dead man, so I wasn't unarmed.

"No!" I heard Guther scream. "You are not blessed by the Sky Man!" He shouted. "Put them down!"

I huffed and threw the knives away. "Come on then." I gestured to the warriors.

They did come, this time as a team. One moved to my left while the other held me to face him. At once they both charged. I fainted at the man in front of me then when he flinched, darted back. I dodged the attack to my left and moved to put my knee in his stomach. He doubled over, and I struck him in the back of the head, sending him to the ground.

The one who flinched finally regained his courage and attacked me. He struck up and then down. I moved back to dodge them, then I saw him overextend himself and grabbed his throat. I knocked the feet out from under him and slammed him on his back. I took his head in both hands and pounded it against the floor of the circle. It was a hard floor, but so was his head. It took me three times before I felt his skull break.

I stood up and turned to the last one. He was trying to get his feet under him. I could see him struggling for air. That blow to the stomach probably knocked the wind out of him. He also seemed to be shaking the stars out of his head from the strike I'd landed on it. He was still on one knee when I reached him.

I kicked his chin, and he fell back against the ground. I walked over to him calmly. In an instant, he changed from the snarling warrior to a scared child. He tried to crawl on his back away from me, throwing his knives away. I put my foot on his chest to stop him. He started mumbling in his language. I didn't speak it, but I recognized the gesture. He was pleading with me. He was begging.

"I think this one wants mercy." I called out to the Chief.

"Aye, he does," Guther said, "but he knows the rules of the ring." He nodded to me. "Finish it."

"I don't kill beaten men." I thought back to the guard at the docks. I did kill beaten men. I thought back to Doctor Quarrels's words. "I don't kill beaten men." This time it was to myself.

"Then your army will never pass these mountains," Guther said, "and you won't leave this place alive."

"I could kill every one of you if I wanted!" I screamed back at him. "Find another tribe to let me through."

"Aye, maybe you could," Guther nodded, "but their laws will be the same as ours." He looked at the man begging on his back and said something in Cretoin. Then he turned back to me and repeated it in Anthanii. "Shouldn't have been a coward."

I stood there with my foot on his chest. I needed this mountain. There wasn't another way to beat Thaniel. I bit my lip and kneeled down on his chest. I took his throat in both hands and squeezed. First, he clawed at my hands, then when he realized they wouldn't give, clawed at my face. I didn't stop. I watched him squirm, face turning purple.

You shouldn't have picked this fight! I thought. *You should have let one of the other dumb boys in the ring!* It didn't help. *You would have done the same to me!* It's a dark day when you need to look to the Cretoins for moral superiority. Finally, I felt life leave his body. I was thankful for that much at least.

I stood up and faced Guther. "It's done?" I asked.

"Aye, it's done." He nodded. "Come back with your gifts when you're ready."

I nodded. The ring had grown quiet after my first kill, but now the silence seemed a new thing altogether. Three women rushed to the corpses. They must have been the mothers. They wept over the dead, trying to shake life back into their sons. Sitting there crying over the children, it was easy to tell they were women. I wished I could go back to seeing faceless savages.

You should have raised smarter children! I screamed inside my head. *When they asked for volunteers, you should have hidden them away! You should have… Done something different.* It wasn't honest, though. For all my faults, I've always tried to be honest. The truth was they shouldn't have been so eager to kill an unarmed foreigner. The truth was it didn't make my actions any better. The truth is usually complicated, and it always cuts both ways.

If I had a son who got into a bad business, I wouldn't want the man who fixed it to say. "You should have raised a better child." No, I'd want him to say. "Your boy made a mistake, but I chose the right path, and here he is safe and sound."

If a thousand people were in my position, nine hundred and ninety-nine would have done the same! I screamed in my head again. I remembered the words that told me how wrong I was. It wasn't a mystical doctor. It wasn't an honorable officer. It was my father, across the ocean. "Do you really want to be the nine hundred and ninety-nine," he'd told me, "or do you want to be the one."

Many great men had tried to show me the right path, some greater than I knew. There was something strange with that doctor. They all paled in comparison to the first, to the greatest. A man who'd done his duty because he had to and never asked for the thanks he deserved. A man who owned a full plantation but treated everyone as an equal. A man who had always shown me love no matter how bad I hurt him.

In the years since I'd left, I'd thought about my family more than I'd care to admit. I wanted to see them. I wanted to embrace them. I wanted to tell them I was sorry. Though I try to forget it, I am human. Sometimes, I wished my parents had been a mite less loving. I wished my brother had been a mite less good. It'd make it easier to explain what I'd done to them. However, this time was the first I'd wanted my father here because I didn't know what to do.

As I looked at the corpses, I knew they'd wanted the same and hadn't gotten it. At first, I took the Cretoin as closer to apes than men. Watching their mothers weep, I was wrong. Some of us are bald, some of us are hairy. Some of us were black, and some of us were pale. The languages we spoke changed, the gods we prayed to in our desperate moments changed, even the way we told each other we cared changed. However, for all our differences, nine in ten parts of us were the same. That last piece didn't mean so much when you're weeping over your child. It seemed so small when you beg for mercy.

I once had a snooty academic who tried to explain his science of eugenics to me. He claimed we were too different to co-exist. He claimed the best outcome we could possibly hope for, was that the lesser be in peaceful servitude to the greater. He'd made a good argument, and I'd almost believed him, probably in part to the fact that he considered me to be one of the greater. However, I'd seen too much of the world to accept that. He'd seen too little of the people he judged. Science can be a powerful thing, a tool for the betterment of man, but listen to a Souren talk about how beautiful his new son is. Science seems to lose its edge in that moment, no matter the data.

I turned to Guther. "I'll be back." I said. "It may be years before I'm ready, but I'll be back." I leveled a finger at him. "I expect you to honor our deal."

"It'll be honored, Thomas Belson of the Donkeys." The Chief nodded back.

"Good," I nodded to Marc, "let's go."

"Lets." He picked up his pack and followed me.

When we were out of earshot, I said something to myself. "I should have shown them mercy."

Marc looked at me. "Guther should have let you." He nodded back to the camp. "Those were all his sons you killed."

That stopped me.

Marc went on. "I've spent most of my life with these people," he shook his head, "but these are a savage breed." He shrugged. "They ain't like you or me."

I nodded and kept moving. I should have taken solace in his words, but I didn't. That was the other part of what made us the same, our capacity for violence. Guther may have let me kill his sons. It didn't speak well of his culture, but a hundred thousand sons had died at Milhire. According to academics, the difference between civilized and savage was just scale.

Another snooty scholar had tried to tell me how the tribal leaders of untamed lands were far more moral than any Tyran country. He was just as wrong as the first. Some of us get certain things right. Some of us get certain things wrong. Never let evil be done because cause it's your culture, but before you condemn them completely, think to the sins of your own people. Everyone's got someone beneath them, and we didn't have a record of treating them well. However, before you raise up another people above your own, remember the good they've done. All people have their sins and triumphs. That goes for desert savages and perfumed aristocrats. Everyone's got someone beneath them, and even though we hadn't done so great in the past, maybe we were learning a bit more. I took a look at Guther. *Maybe not.*

Guther spoke to another truth of the world. I'd known he was an evil man, but when times get hard, we choose the worst of us. What did it say, that in the hardest of times, they chose me? That was a question I really didn't want the answer to. What I did know, was that if everyone in the world had parents like mine instead of Guther, there wouldn't be a war.

As we walked down the mountain, Marc started speaking again. He talked in awe of my fight. He looked to me as a savior. He sounded like a giddy child. I wished he wouldn't, and not just because I was worried about him embarrassing himself.

He knew my plan. He lived in a country conquered by Thaniel, a place I couldn't protect him. Thaniel would offer a huge reward for that information. I knew he probably wouldn't take it, but money does strange things to us. The real fear, though, was that he'd go running his mouth about who he'd taken up the mountain. Kranish agents would hear it and pick him up. They'd make him talk, and when he did the game was over.

I pulled the wire out of my pocket. What was one life compared to the millions I was set to save? What was one mountain guide, next to the fate of the world? He might have even understood it if it wasn't him. As we reached the bottom of the mountain, I knew what I had to do.

"You're going to liberate my country." Marc said still facing away from me. "You're going to free us from the tyrant." I stepped closer, wire extended over both hands. "My maw always said a hero'd come. I got older and never saw one." He turned to me as I was almost on him. "You're a hero." The look of pride on his face as I snuck behind him with a garrote was probably the height of irony.

I should have turned him around and strangled the bastard. He was strong for an old man, but I was me. I should have killed him. It was what Thaniel would have done. Something in his face stopped me.

When he talked about me being a hero, he seemed like a child in an elders body, and it was idiotic. As he looked at me, I realized he was a child in an elders body, and it was beautiful. Every boy believes that something better is right around the corner. They're usually wrong, but they have to believe that. As we grow older, we get ground down by the powerful who are supposed to protect us. As we grow older, we realize we get fleeced by those who are supposed to create wealth. Marc the Mountain Climber was no different. As far as I could tell, he'd been spit on by everyone. However Marc the Mountain Climber *was* different. He'd held onto that hope, waiting for anything to touch it to, anything to let it grow.

Maybe all men hold onto boyish hopes. Maybe all women cleave to girlish dreams. Perhaps, Marc was just to much a fool to squash them properly. Perhaps he was just too wise to let go of what made his life mean something.

Now the man who had made it worthwhile had planned on killing him. It's what the strong would have done. However, maybe I was wrong on that account too. Maybe being strong means you didn't have to make the best decision. You could make the right one. Maybe being strong was spitting at the world, and saying. "I choose a different path!"

Thaniel had the army, position, and power. I had desperate plans and a hard-bitten will. I'd thought the only way to win was to be the better fighter. Maybe I just had to be better. Thaniel picked fear and blood to build his empire on. Maybe mixed with a thin veneer of optimism, but everyone knew why they kneeled to him. Perhaps, I could build my own empire on something more.

Every great leader climbed to power on knives in the back and sacks on sleeping men. Their kingdoms had always crumbled in the end though. It was hope in something better that lead men to me. That something better wouldn't kill an old man.

"Thank you Marc." I nodded.

"It's no problem." He smiled. "Why you got a wire in your hand?" He cocked his head to one side, blessedly oblivious to what I'd been about to do.

"Oh, it's this new this new thing called flossing." I put the wire back. "Doctors recommend it three times a day."

"Eh, maybe I should do it." Marc smiled at the new science.

"Best not." I shook my head. "It hurts like a bastard."

"Oh, well then." He nodded.

"We need to have a little chat before I leave." I gave him a threatening stare.

He only laughed at it. "No need, I know what your fixin' to say."" He waved it off. "Don't tell no one your plan, am I right."

I nodded. "That's the long and short of it."

"I hate these Kransih bastards more'n you." Marc spit. "I'll not say a word."

"Good," I meant it, "that's not the only danger, though." I paused. "You'll want to tell people about today. You'll want to let your town know I'm coming." I said. "When you do, be assured that Thaniel will hear about it too." I scratched the tattoos on my arm. "He'll make you talk."

I expected him to deny it. Everyone thinks they're invulnerable until they get put on the chopping block, but to my surprise, he agreed. "I know what they do, and I'm not fool enough to expect to keep my peace, or to go announcin' my visitor to the world." He took a step towards me. "I'll let my people know, though." He smiled. "I'll let them know that things needn't always be like this. I'll let them know we've a prayer." He extended his hand. "Might be, by the time you come back we'll be able to offer more than a pass across the mountains. Thaniel ain't taken all our fight, yet."

I took his hand. "I'd prefer you just kept your head down and wait for me to return." I said. "I promise you'll all need to play a part before this thing is over."

He nodded and released my hand.

I scratched the back of my head. "You got any children."

"Two!" Marc proclaimed.

"You hoping they'll be mountain guides too?" I smiled.

He shook his head. "I keep them as far away from my profession as possible." He shrugged. "I wish me maw had done the same with me."

"Either of em smart?" I asked.

He beamed at me. "Aye, one of em's the smartest in the village." He smiled. "I spend half my money trying to get the boy decent tutors and books. I never learned to read, but I won't let it stop my boy. He's a right clever lad." Marc played with his hands. "Get's it from his mother, clearly."

I folded a small sack into his hands.

He shook his head. "I can't take no pay from you." He chuckled. "It was just my civic-" He stopped when he looked inside. "Demons

Below, sweet damn!" He saw that it was filled to the brim with gold. Finally, his face turned from wild excitement to begrudging bitterness. "I definitely can't take this."

"Good, it's not for you." I took a step back. "It's for your boy. That'll be enough to send him to university." I gestured to the sack of gold. "If he needs more, go to Lady Gerate. She'll cover the rest." I saw protest still forming on his lips, so I stopped it. "It's not mine. It's from the Anthanii treasury." I tapped the tattoos on my arm. "Vow of poverty and all." I shrugged. "If you don't take it, it'll be wasted on some road project that'll never get built."

"Well, I guess I can accept that." He smiled and put the money in his back pocket.

"Is the other son tough?" I asked.

"Never loses a fight." He nodded. "Don't go getting any ideas." Marc shook his head. "I don't want him joining the army, and even you can't beat his maw in a fight for that child's future."

"That's not what I had in mind." I tossed him another sack filled with silver. "If you think he's tough enough to make a go in the Confederacy send him there." I spit. "It's a free land. A place he can make a good life for himself, without licking a noble's boots." I shrugged. "Nothings assured, but he's got a chance."

"I can't thank you enough." He pocketed the silver. "Why you doing all this?" He asked.

I shrugged. "It's not my money, and I hate the man who gave it to me."

"Not just that." He shook his head. "Well, that too, but why you fighting in a war to free people you never met."

It took me a moment to answer. "The whole world seems to think freedom's just a chance for people to fuck everything up." I took a step forward. "I've seen what it's done, though. I know it's something worth fighting for, and even if it were just a chance for people to fuck everything up, which it sometimes is, men deserve that chance." I put a hand on his shoulder. "Sometimes, it feels like we've hoarded it all to ourselves in the Confederacy, but the world's changing." I smiled. "That change'll die if no one steps in."

I nodded to the money at his side. "The gold is because this new world needs men to help shape it." I said. "It needs the sons of mountain guides to help remember that people aren't just notes in a ledger." I took my hand off him. "The world needs to remember not to ignore the men who make it turn."

I took a step back. "The silvers because I think freedom might go out of style someday, even in my country." I shrugged. "Might be we'll need someone to remind us what oppression feels like."

Marc bowed his head. "I've not known you for a week," he said, "but I'd die for you."

I shook my head. "Dying for someone is easy." I smiled. "Living for yourself is hard, but it's the only thing worth doing." I walked off to my horse. "Remember that."

"Next time a lord laughs at me behind my back, I'll tell him to go to hell!" Marc screamed as I mounted my horse. I smiled.

I rode to my next destination. When scribes fill their books with stories about me, they'll say I was a man of contradictions. They'll say I broke armies and dueled on mountain tops. However, I hoped there'd be a chapter at the end. Maybe, a chapter that reads. "He did what was right when he could."

The Thaniel Wars

J walked with my shoulders hunched. My face was hidden by a black shawl. This wasn't the sort of place you wanted people to know you visited. This was Imor. I couldn't yet see the city, but the outskirts were beautiful. Trees blossomed with fruit even though it wasn't the season. The landscape seemed to be perfectly manicured, but who could have possibly done it?

Everything about it was wrong. It was the middle of winter, and yet as I got closer to the city, the world seemed to warm as if I'd suddenly walked into spring. It should have been pleasant, but it wasn't. The only thing I could compare it to was like taking a heated bath while a battle raged around. You felt good, but you knew something was off. You knew this pleasure had a cost.

As I walked towards it, I could feel my steps growing lighter. When I turned away for a moment my legs became lead, every foot seemed to weigh on me. I was being drawn to this city.

I'd had to piss when I'd gotten off my horse. I figured I'd do it later. As I drew closer, I felt the inhibition to hold it flake away. I'd thought the impulse had just passed until I looked down and saw I'd gone all down my leg. The funny thing was I didn't care.

I had some dried meat and hard biscuits with me. I knew they needed to last me a while, but I figured just one snack wouldn't hurt. I pulled out some food. I promised myself I would only eat half of the biscuit and then put the rest back, but it wasn't long before I was licking my fingers for crumbs. I reached down for another snack and stopped myself. I wasn't even hungry. Why did I want to eat now? I knew the answer. Food was good. Why deny yourself what is good.

Even the air I breathed felt like mulled wine. Every inhale I took seemed to take me farther from reality. It felt like thinking through a dream. It felt like swimming through syrup. I went into the Battle-Mind to escape it. That was a mistake. By the time I managed to come out of it, I'd almost forgotten my own name.

As I kept moving, I asked myself a series of questions to make sure I kept a hold on my humanity. I wanted to reassert the difference between right and wrong.

"Why don't you seduce a married woman?"

"Because it's wrong." I'd answer myself. "Because ruining a marriage for one night of pleasure is a shit trade."

However, with every step I took the answer seemed to change.

"Why don't you seduce a married woman?"

"Because the husband could find out and beat her."

"Why don't you seduce a married woman?"

"Because people could see you, and it'll cause a whole host of problems I don't want to deal with."

"Why don't you seduce a married woman?"

"I don't know why. I'm really limiting myself by only going after the single ones."

"Why don't you seduce a married woman?"

"The husband could even wind up raising one of my children. That would be hilarious."

"Why don't you seduce a married woman?"

"I could reproduce and not even have to worry about raising the bastard. After all, I'm probably a better specimen than the husband."

I could see the pattern clear as day. At first, my answers were based off my morality, right and wrong. Then they turned to what could cause pain for someone else. Then I thought about the consequences it could bring about that weren't worth it. Finally, I'd arrived at a place where consequences seemed so inconsequential. Shame was a human construct. Human constructs put a shackle over your neck. Be free! Who can say what you should and shouldn't do?

Philosophically I knew the flaw in it. Morality was universal. It didn't matter where you were, you did the right thing. Sometimes it's hard to see what that is. Sometimes it's hard to follow that path even when you know it's right. Sometimes you fail, but you always try to do what's right. Try to do the right thing, and you'll wind up happy. You're better off with a loving woman than a fistful of gold in a whore house. Your marriage will be better if you try to communicate with your woman instead of beat her. It's easier to ignore your children than read them to sleep, but at the end of your days, you'll rarely wish you took the easy way. The Three told us this in their Testament. Some people just saw it as a lie to trick people out of doing what they loved. I'd even thought that at one time, smart youngsters usually fall into that trap. As I saw more of the world, I knew those words were put there to free us not to enslave us.

Philosophically I knew this, but so close to the Capitol of Sin, it was hard to think philosophically.

"Why don't you kill a defenseless man?" I asked myself.

"Oh, no Thomas! Don't even start down that road." I listened to my own advice and posed questions less relevant to me. I didn't want the answer to that one.

"Why don't you stiff the bar owner with the bill?" That was more like it.

Finally, I cleared the trees and saw what was easily the strangest scene in my life, and I'd lived a strange life. There were people here. I tried to count them but always seemed to lose track in their twirling and galloping.

They were all naked. Men and women swaying to a beat that wasn't there, but they could all hear. Everybody seemed to be sculpted. Every face was without flaw. It wasn't just Thyrans either. I saw black Sourens, the yellowish Intes, the bearded Northerners, even a few Huego's. It seemed every people was represented in this hedonistic dance, and it was hedonistic.

I saw two men on one woman, two women on one man. In the main field, I could only see a writhing mass of bodies. There couldn't have been less than twenty in that pile. That didn't even cover the tip of what I observed. There were sex acts being performed I couldn't even describe. That wasn't saying much from my mouth. I was a recently turned seventeen-year-old, who'd devoted his entire life to soldering. I'd only ever known one woman, Lady Gerate. Most of my knowledge about human coupling was either faked, the result of overheard drunken bar talk, human instinct, and a few dirty novels that if anyone ever found, I'd deny were mine upon pain of death. However, I could have lived a hundred years of pure debauchery and still not done a quarter of what was being attempted here. *Could you even fit it in that hole?* I squinted at two people in the farther reaches. Apparently, you could. Though, I imagined it took a lot of practice. I knew Lady Gerate would never do that with me no matter how much I begged. I caught a glimpse of another group closer to the center.

Why is she squatting over him like-Oh, that's why. There weren't many things that could make me hit a woman, but if Lady Gerate did something like that to me, I'd have trouble controlling myself.

Isolated musicians strummed dumbly at their instruments. They were too far away to hear each other, and yet as I moved further into the field, they all seemed to be playing the same song. At first, it sounded beautiful, but as I listened closer with a musicians ear, I heard the truth of it. The song was shit. I'd been to a few symphonies, a couple in Thyro, a couple I begged my father to take me to. I'd always liked music. However the song I heard there had no pattern, no structure. The booming sounds and soft melodies of modern music were made great because they broke the rules. If there were none to break you were only left with meaningless humming. Still, I found myself swaying to it.

There was a table arrayed with fruits and meats of every kind. I saw the members feasting, but the food never seemed to diminish. Grease and juice flowed down their perfect bodies, but it never seemed to stick to them. It made my mouth water.

The groups that lavished in sex, music, or food were all distinctly different and yet somehow blurred. You couldn't tell where one territory ended and another began, but you knew there was a line. There was such a pleasure here. No strife of any kind made it into this field. I wanted to take part in it. There was no town to defend, no soldiers to worry over, no war I might lose. It disgusted me. There were no invaders to beat, no warriors to lead, no war I'd win.

One man rolled off his partners and walked over to meet me. His face was pure delight. "We've been waiting for you." He said, then his face twisted into agony. "Run! No, it's too late already."

I ignored the second part. "You've been waiting for me?"

He smiled. "Thomas Belson, the great warrior!" He went on. "They told us you'd come, and we can have a lot of fun with a great warrior." He looked me up and down as if my clothes weren't there.

"Who told you about me?" I asked.

"Why, it was…" He trailed off. "No, it was…" He looked around as if looking for the memory in his own mind. "Someone must have told us. I'm sure of that."

"No doubt." I nodded at the madman and went to move past him, but he stopped me.

"Where's your armor and broadsword?" He asked. "All heroes have armor and broadswords."

I narrowed my eyes at him. "We don't really go in for that stuff anymore." I patted my six-shooter. The way I fought was ahead of its time, but broadswords and armor had gone out of style more than a hundred years ago. Even the stubborn nobles had to admit that the time of knights was done.

"That's a shame." He shook his head. "I saw Sir Gawain as a boy. He looked magnificent on his black steed."

"I'm sure you did." I said it more to move past than anything, but it still didn't make sense. Sir Gawain was a knight dead two centuries ago. How long had this man been here? I looked over his shoulder to see a woman playing a lute. I almost recognized her as Caterina of Gerdald. I'd seen a portrait of her once. She looked different now, younger. Which was strange because she'd been the lady of Gerdald half a millennia ago. No, it wasn't her. She was long dead. Well, the history books said she disappeared mysteriously, but that couldn't... Could it?

The man brought my attention back to him. "Won't you stay for a moment?" He asked. "This place is wrong!" He twisted seamlessly into horror.

"I can't." I said simply, but for the life of me, I couldn't remember why.

"You can." He smiled from ear to ear.

A hand wrapped around my chest. Another reached up to stroke my face. I wasn't in the business of being snuck up on. Outside of here, I would have spun around weapons at the ready. I dumbly turned my head to see a beautiful Inte woman, and a sculpted fire-haired girl rubbing me gently. I could feel their breast against my back. I could taste the cinnamon on their breath.

"Here feel this." The Inte woman placed my hand against her naked thigh. I ripped it away.

"Let's get you out of these clothes." The redhead tried to take off my cloak, but I shrugged her away.

"What is this place?" I asked the man in front of me.

"This is The Grove. A heaven blessed by those who came before." He smiled. "This is hell, meant to torture us for our sins." He trembled.

"Oh, well, that's nifty." I said.

"Come." He took my hand and led me to a lonely tree in the field. The women followed, grabbing at me the whole time. I wished they'd leave. I wanted them to stay.

"Why have you come here?" The man asked me.

"To learn a secret." I gritted my teeth as the women reached around my body.

"Ah, I was a philosopher set on learning the truth of the world." He paused. "No, I was a poet set on writing the most beautiful verse." He scratched his chin thoughtfully. "No, I was a scientist." He started again. "Whatever the reason, my journey lead me here." The pure ecstasy of his face caught me off guard. "I want to die! Can you kill me?" It changed to torturous pain in an instant.

"Well, I have always been good at that." I reached for my knife.

"Good at what?" He'd already forgotten. "There's no good here, only perfection." His face twisted again. "Only evil!"

I took a step back but was stopped by a hulking Souren. He put a hand on my shoulder, then proceeded to rub it. "Stay." He said in a deep melodic voice. I knew men did what he wanted me to do more often than any farm boy would think. It bothered some people, but never me. Captain Seiford was one who swung that way, and he was the best man I knew. However, I'd never looked at a man like that. Still, him rubbing on my shoulders, I couldn't help but wonder if I'd been denying myself something. Maybe I should have let him do what he wanted.

"You should let Hoto take you." The Inte whispered.

"He's a masterful lover." The redhead chimed in. I doubt she knew what it meant to be someone's lover.

I swatted his hand away. "No." I gave him a nice shove in the chest. "Stay away from me." The black man didn't look hurt, just confused. He smiled and headed towards me again as if it was some game we were playing. I put a hand on my knife. "I mean it." He stepped away, though I could see it pained him.

The philosopher, poet, scientist, or whatever he was pulled me back. "There is no refusal here, only acceptance." He turned back to agony. "No one to tell you where the line is! No one to tell you when it's too far."

"I don't need someone to tell me when it's too far." I spat out. The girls went back to rubbing me.

"Here, play this." He pulled a lute out of nowhere and handed it to me.

"I don't play the lute." I said as I took it. I'd always focused my musical attention on the piano, and there wasn't much left for that after training to be a warrior. I'd always meant to learn, but deep down I knew I never would.

"Try." He smiled.

I did and found that I knew exactly where to put my hands. In fact, a master would have fawned over my technique. I played the beginning of a beautiful melody before I realized what I was doing. I smashed it against the tree, and the whole grove seemed to look at me.

"Why did you do that?" He asked. "You were playing so beautifully."

Because I won't fall for your stupid games. I wanted to say. *Because this place isn't what it seems.* "Because I haven't earned the right to play like that." I said. "I haven't spent countless hours mastering it."

"Earned? What is that?" He mumbled to himself. "Never mind, you're a strong one aren't you." He smiled at me. "Most lose themselves by now, but you'll stay. They always do." He began scratching at his chest. "Lend me your strength. Let me free myself."

"I like a strong man." The Inte woman rubbed my stomach.

"They bring a fire to it." The redhead moaned in my ear.

"You've never known a strong man." I turned on them. "If you have, you forgot it long ago."

They stepped back as if confused. The pair coped by kissing each other. "Won't you join us, Thomas Belson." They said in unison. I realized they weren't speaking Anthanii, yet I understood them perfectly. It was another subtle subversion. The borders of the outside world didn't matter. Nothing you cared about mattered, not your king, country, or creed, not your wife and children. All that mattered here was what you could grab.

"I won't."

By now a crowd had joined. "There's no pain here." Someone said.

"There's no strife."

"There's no battle." I couldn't tell who was talking in this crowd. I spit again. "That's what I live for."

The man who had first approached me stepped forward again. "Is it though?" He produced an apple from nowhere. It was the perfect fruit. I didn't know a fruit could be perfect, but it was. My hand reached out to grab it without being commanded to. I stopped myself.

"It is."

The crowd began to speak again. "You wish to relive Milhire?"

"Well, no, but-" I started, but they cut me off.

"You are proud of leaving William to die?" The face of the boy at Wuntsville flashed through my head.

"You remember fondly slaughtering innocent guards?"

"You loved watching mothers weep over corpses you made?"

I shook with rage. "It had to be done!"

The first man stepped forward. "Maybe on the outside it did." He put a hand on my shoulder. "Here you can forget."

"They're my sins!" I shouted. "I may not like them, but they're mine."

"What about your family lost and far away?" The crowd started again.

"Left in anger and pain."

"We can give them back to you."

I turned to find who'd said that with my six-shooter raised. I saw only the Belson clan staring at me with a mix of pain and hope. I reached out to them, but it was like wiping my hand through water. They disappeared.

"Stop!" I shouted through the tears. "I'll right that wrong one day!" I said mostly to myself. "When I do it'll be real!"

The man with the apple smiled down at me. "It will have been too late."

"Are you ready for what is to come, Thomas?" The crowd spoke.

"Captain Seiford?"

"The dog?"

"The Pillars?"

"What are you talking about?" I screamed in confusion.

"A monster killed who was not a monster." The voices of the crowd continued ignoring my question.

"A man broken even by your standards."

"Stepping through the final door."

"You're lying!" I swept about with my gun for something to shoot at.

"We are not." The man who first greeted me spoke softly. "I wish we were but we are not." His face contorted in pain again.

"What does it mean?" I needed to know. Their words sounded like prophecy to me.

"For us, nothing."

"For you, pain."

"It need not be, though."

The man with the apple stepped forward. "You can let it all slip away." He whispered. "The scars on your body can fade. Even the tattoos on your arm will be gone in time. The memories you hold will become distant dreams. You will become nothing as we are."

I realized what he was offering. A life free of any suffering. He was offering me perfection. I almost took it. The hard path almost broke me, but I was not born to be nothing.

If you asked me what my favorite part of Lady Gerate was, I wouldn't say her beautiful eyes, large breast, or slender waist. I'd say it was the mole just under her neck. I'd say it was that when she needed help, she looked to me. I'd say that it was the way she let me call her Abby in her arms. They were flaws, flaws that let me know her. Anywhere else they'd have been wrong, but on her it was beautiful. It made her who she was. It made her who I saw in my daydreams.

I wasn't out to save Anthanii because it was perfect. I was there because it could be better, but that betterment meant nothing if it wasn't earned. It had to be paid for with blood and pain. Thaniel was a curse, but in time maybe he could be just the sort of curse they needed.

I hadn't left my farm because it was easy. I left because it was hard. I'd left because there was something in me that wouldn't sit while others suffered. Maybe, it was part of a larger flaw, but it had called out to me, and I answered.

Perfection is nothing. A C scale is perfect. What made a thing beautiful was that it wasn't perfect. A high note played in one place sour, in another place beautiful. For a thing to mean something, it has to fulfill one of two requirements. You had to need it, and you had to pay for it. Perfection has no needs, and if something was given to you, how could you appreciate it? How could you love it?

It was easier to rape a woman than to earn her love. It was easier to burn something down than to build something new. It was easier to subjugate a people, rather than be the man who deserved their loyalty. It wasn't the right path though. Even as strong as I was, I failed often, but the effort meant something.

When you think on your favorite story, is it of a hero who has everything he wants given to him. No, that man is usually the villain. You love the heroes who got beaten down by the world and spit defiance right back. What made humanity something worth saving, wasn't that they succeeded. It was that they failed and were so stupid they tried again.

They promised to release me of my sins, but only I could do that. I'd never claimed to do all the right things, and there were few men who could match me sin for sin. Those memories might cause me pain, but I would carry them because they made me. In the end, it was my flaws that saved me from the Grove, not my perfections.

I reached out again and took the apple. I bit down hard. It didn't taste like an apple. It tasted like pleasure, ecstasy, and ease. It tasted of all knowledge. It tasted like everything pleasant in the world with nothing to drag you down. It tasted of release, but there's a difference between release and freedom. A difference so sharp it can cut you. That was the only thing missing from it… Freedom.

"Good." The man who gave it to me said. "Now, you can play in the garden with us." He beaconed me. "Come-"

He didn't finish his sentence. I spit the piece of apple at his feet and let the fruit roll. The two girls that had been trying to seduce me rushed and picked up the chewed remnants of the fruit. They wept as they worked.

"Barbarian!" The Inte screeched.

"Savage!" The redhead pointed at me.

"You serve the old masters!"

"You serve the new masters!"

I shook my head. "I serve who I choose." I stalked past them towards the ruins of Imor. I wanted nothing more to do with this place.

"Wait, Thomas!" I turned. It was the same man who had first welcomed me. "No, one has ever denied us."

"I did." I touched the six-shooter at my side. I wasn't sure how he'd react.

To my surprise, he smiled up at me. It was a pure smile. The kind the citizens of Wuntsville had given me when I saved their town. It was pride and hope. They were foreign emotions in a place like this. It was something better.

"My name is Adam." He looked at his own hands. "I came here when my wife died. I wanted to go somewhere the pain couldn't find me." A tear rolled down his eye. "I should have stayed for my children, but I was too weak."

I nodded. "You were."

"Go with the Three." Adam said, then he doubled over in pain. "Go with the Three." He repeated. Finally, the pain became too much. He went back to the soulless thing I'd seen when I first arrived.

I walked through the streets of Imor. I must have been the first to do so in two thousand years. People always kept a clear path of this place. I doubted they really knew why. They just knew anyone who sought it never came back. Now, I knew. The inhabitants of the Grove seemed content where they were, and any who wanted to see this place wouldn't get past them. I only refused the apple because I was well versed in Confederacy stubbornness. There are even those who would call me a master.

What really scared me about the things I'd seen wasn't how uncomfortable it had all seemed. It wasn't just that one weakness could mean losing Thomas Belson completely. It wasn't even the pain I'd seen on Adam's face in between gilded promises. It was what it would mean if I told anyone about it.

If I went back into the world and spoke of a place without pain or suffering, a place of orgies, food, and music, would they understand to stay away? Even if I screamed about how evil this place was, how many would still seek it out. I resolved to avoid speaking of it. If I had to, I'd spin some yarn about Demons and hellfire.

It was a blow of what made me. It was a strike to the center of my core. I've never subscribed to the view of dangerous knowledge. If a man speaks lies beat him with truths, but let him speak. Men have a right to hear whatever they want. It was all in the use of the knowledge we were given. It was up to the individual to decide. It was why I shouted defiance at the King of Anthanii. Lying wasn't my strong suit. Of course, there were some uncomfortable truths. I'd read some new physics essays that absolutely scared the shit out of me, but they were mine to read.

If I let the truth be known about this place, how many would seek out their own torment? It's a strange thing to learn your ideology doesn't quite cover the whole world. Life was complicated.

Once, as a boy, my father had taken my brother and me to the Northern Confederacy. I remembered marveling at the buildings they'd started on. When I got to Thyro I'd been impressed by castles and fortresses they'd erected, big, imposing, and solid. You could almost forget one blast of cannon could tear the whole thing down. They all paled to the majesty of Imor.

Mansions cast in solid gold, walls made of pure steel, even their ivory towers seemed to be made of actual ivory. However, they weren't right. They twisted and turned as if being tortured by the world around them. I was no engineer, but some of these buildings had no right to still be standing. Then again, who knows how ivory towers are supposed to be built. The land had been twisted by things unseen for far too long. These were dimensions not found in nature.

The pull that I'd felt as I walked to the city had let up a bit. Maybe they finally figured I was too stubborn. The tattoos on my arm burned constantly, but after a while, you get used to it. Now, the city took different methods to tempt me.

As I passed an empty building. I could hear moaning inside. The sign out front read, *we'll fulfill your deepest desires.* I kept walking. It was a rather pathetic attempt. When I passed, the building went back to darkness.

As I got further into Imor, it seemed to get smarter. I walked by a bookshop that claimed to have *all the knowledge you could possibly want.* I passed a music store with a sign that proclaimed *music lessons, one hour and you'll be the best in the world.* Finally, I strolled past what was probably a boxing ring. I could hear a phantom voice scream, "We've the best fighter the world over. Are you tough enough?"

I shrugged them all off. Then the stores got more personalized. A perfumery that specialized in the sent of my family. A shop devoted to all of Thaniel's diaries. A church that promised absolution for even the most egregious sin. I wanted to stop, but I knew if I stepped in there, I'd never come out.

It wasn't long before I realized someone was walking next to me. I turned, and it was exactly who I thought it would be, a portly man named Doctor Quarrels.

"So how do I know you're not a phantom too?" I opened up the conversation.

"I suppose you don't." He shrugged.

"How original!" I rolled my eyes. "A god telling someone to take it on faith." I stopped and started shouting. "Please, someone alert the presses!"

"Well, to be fair we are older than language itself, so technically it wasn't a cliche when we did it." Quarrels chuckled at my outburst. "You're quite a character, Mr. Belson." He shrugged. "I take it you figured out who I am?"

"You're the Three," I nodded, "or at least the Three is the New Church's conceptualization of you." I stared back at him.

"I can grow a beard if that'll make it easier." He beamed at me.

"No, that won't help. I've always preferred my deities clean shaven. Waking up in the morning to scrape the hair off your face shows you care at least a little."

"How'd you figure it out?" He cocked an eyebrow up

"It's not that hard a deduction." I huffed. "You've taken every available opportunity to reinforce some sense of divine mystery, so that makes you some type of God." I cast a glance back towards him. "Add that to the fact you only speak in variations of Testament quotes, and you must be the Three."

"I could be a figment of your imagination." The old man suggested.

"Could be," I agreed, "but you're not exactly what I'd expect the Three to be like." I looked down another corner, trying to find my way. "Therefore it's unlikely I imagined you."

Doctor Quarrels chuckled. "What did you expect?" For whatever reason, every time he asked a question, it seemed like he already knew the answer. It had seemed that way at Wuntsville too.

"Hard to say." I scratched my chin. "I don't know if I expected you to exist at all."

Doctor Quarrels shrugged. "Crises of faith are relatively common in our line of work."

"I wouldn't say *crisis*." I kept walking. "Hadn't really given it much thought is all."

"You have sworn undying loyalty to the New Church." The wry smile on his face didn't seem very divine. "One might assume that takes a level of faith higher than agnosticism."

"I wanted to fight and the New Church was fighting." I held up the six-shooter to illustrate the point. "If I'm on the right side it's just dumb luck that put me there." I kept walking but every road seemed nonsensical to me. "No point in hawking wares I've already bought."

"You are certainly a fighter." The god gave a long whistle. "The Grove really pulled it all out for you." He shook his head. "Usually people get swallowed up as soon as they start to feel the pull." His face changed to sorrow. "Poor souls…"

"Well, I'm a bit of a tough swallow." I tapped my throat. "I go down like molasses mixed with chicken bones, in case you haven't noticed."

He laughed. "Oh, we have." He gave me a bewildered look. "Taking a bite of the apple and then spitting it out." He whistled. "You're certainly an extraordinary one."

"I don't know that that's the right word for me." I kept walking.

"No, it's not." Doctor Quarrels agreed. "We made all men extraordinary, with their own skills to hone and their own weaknesses to overcome."

"Could have made my cock a little bigger." I raised an eyebrow at him.

"It's perfectly normal sized I assure you." He smiled. "After all, I have seen you naked."

I sighed. "If what they say about the Three watching is true, I'm positively terrified of what you've seen."

He shrugged. "Every man does it."

"Then why're all those monks saying it's a sin?" I asked.

Doctor Quarrels laughed again. "It's not a good thing to get wrapped in fantasy when there's real girls you could be trying to impress." He shrugged. "As far as sin goes, there's far worse trouble a young man could get himself into. Besides, it was kind of baked into the cake when you developed thumbs."

"Huh." I decided to tell brother Key's that revelation when I saw him again. "So which one are you? Of the Three I mean?"

"I suppose right now I have more of Wisdom in me." Doctor Quarrels thought for a moment. "I never go anywhere without a bit of Honor and Love to help guide as well." He shrugged. "Being only wise can be dangerous, just like being only honorable or only loving."

I waved it off. "I've read the Testament."

He laughed again. "I suppose you have." He pointed to the gun in my hand. "You can put that away."

"I find it hard to believe this place isn't dangerous." I stared at him.

"Oh, it is." Wisdom gave a solemn nod. "The most dangerous place in the world, and there's not a close second." He met my eyes and I saw the pain veiled in them. "There's nothing here that gun can kill though."

I nodded and put it away. "What happened here anyway?"

Doctor Quarrels tsk'd at me, the good natured doctor replaced the weary deity. "Come on now, George would be positively embarrassed to hear you ask that question. You know your history."

"I know this was once the center of the most powerful empire in the world." I said. "I know they used the Priests to make it that way. I know it all blew up in their faces, and no ones tried to match what they did since." I turned to him. "What exactly happened, though?"

"The Old Religion became drunk on their own power." He seemed pained as if he was remembering the day. "The Priests serve as a conduit to the Demons. One day the Demons became too strong to control." He shook his head. "They spilled forth charring the souls of the inhabitants. Men raped their mothers. Fathers murdered their sons." He looked around the city. "When it was over this was the result. One man, a blacksmith by the name Vorey, was the lone survivor. He became the first inhabitant of the Grove. It was shaped by his desires." He stared back at me. "We tried to save him many times, but to no avail."

I turned on him. "He might not have needed saving if you'd stepped in before all this." I flung my hand over the city. "Why didn't you stop it? Why aren't you stopping it now?"

He turned solemn. "We wept for those that died here." He said. "We still weep, but we cannot hurt the Demons."

"Why not?" I asked, "Are they too powerful? Am I on the wrong side of this?"

"Not too powerful," he sighed, "too weak." A question formed on my mouth, but he stopped me. "You'll understand soon."

"I doubt it." I spit venom at him.

He shrugged. "You doubted me."

"Don't think I've stopped." I turned back to walking the streets.

Doctor Quarrels laughed and followed me. "If most men walked next to a god, they'd be quivering with respect."

"So you want some more piety?" I rolled my eyes.

"No, there's a reason I choose to walk with you." He gave a knowing smile. "You're an entertaining fellow."

"Really?" I asked. "I just thought you were biding your time until you smote me."

"You should know by now, we don't smite." He tilted his head to one side.

"No, you have me do it in battle." I shook my head at the hypocrisy of it all.

"Thomas, you may be an arrogant, headstrong, lunatic," he went on, "but we both know you're not in this to smite anyone." He sighed. "Sometimes you go too far, though."

"I didn't start this war." I mumbled to myself.

"No, but the way you end it will be important." He said.

We walked in silence for a long while, before I finally got frustrated. "Where's the Imperial Palace? I'm lost."

"Imperial Palace?" He cocked an eyebrow up.

"You know, Emperor's house?" I waved my hands in despair. "Whatever you call it."

"You're speaking of Gonden's Keep." He shook his head. "It's that way," he pointed west, "but you'll find nothing inside it but old administrative reports. Interesting in their own right, but not why you're here."

"Where am I headed then?" I asked.

"The Temple." He shook his head.

"What, no foreboding name?" I scoffed.

"They tried, but all names rolled off of it." He bit his lip. "Names encapsulate a thing, and you don't have the words for the things that lie there." He pointed east. "It's this way though. Come on."

I followed. "I thought you didn't want me to come."

"I didn't, and I still don't." He sighed. "However, if you don't find what you're looking for, you'll just keep coming back."

I nodded, and we made our way over.

It occurred to me that I was standing next to an all-knowing being, and there might be some questions he could answer. Do our current principles of physics accurately depict the universe? How did the first organisms come into existence? What's the meaning of life? These would all have been worthy questions, but I chose to tackle the big issues.

"So it's right on top of the opening?" I asked.

"Yes, you'll have to feel around a bit. Every one is a little bit different, but you'll know when you hit it," Doctor Quarrels answered, "and so will she." He gave me a wink.

"That's the damnedest thing I've ever heard." I shook my head. "I've had men swear to me it exists, but I never believed it."

"It's there." He assured me.

"So why'd you hide it like that?" I asked. "Seems mean."

"Not at all!" He shook his head. "It's so a man has to spend a long time with a woman before he really understands her. If we didn't give you an incentive to stick around, you'd breed like rabbits."

"So it's to trick us into marriage?" I narrowed my eyes. "I'm not totally opposed to the breeding like rabbits principle."

"You could look at it that way." He shrugged. "I wouldn't, but you could." Doctor Quarrels turned to me. "It's like when you read a book that opens with a mystery. It's a device to keep you around long enough to fall in love with the characters, to want to know how the story ends." He sighed. "It's not a lie, but while you're learning how she works down below, you'll slowly find you want to make her laugh. You want to bring her flowers just to see her smile. You start to think maybe she's the woman you can raise a child with." He beamed brightly at it all. "You start to understand her, and suddenly her body is just a shell that holds something far more beautiful."

"Huh, so those monks were wrong about how puritanical you are." I whistled. "Brother Keys once told me if I looked at a woman, I should gouge my own eyes out."

"Well, I don't say this often, but that man is wrong." He shook his head. "If you weren't supposed to look at women, why would we make them so pretty?"

"My argument exactly!" I snapped a finger his way. "Keys said it was to test our faith."

"We don't test people's faith." Doctor Quarrels seemed absolutely pained.

"That Keys is an idiot." I laughed to myself.

"No, he's not." Quarrels shook his head. "He was clever as they come once, and his cleverness led him down the road of orthodoxy."

"Orthodoxy is the last refuge of the idiot." I shot back.

"There's value in orthodoxy just the same as there's value in originality, so long as those views are backed with reason, temperance, and humility." The god sighed. "Sometimes the answer lies in innovation. Sometimes the answer lies in tradition."

"How do you decide when to conform and when to invent then?" I asked

"You argue about it," Wisdom smiled, "both sides assuming their opponent's views are sincere and thought through." I sounded like something from the Testament, but just different enough to seem novel.

"Well argue this then," I kicked a rock out of my way. "Brother Keys is a cock."

Doctor Quarrels gave a pained sigh. "There are as many different types of people as there are stars in the sky. Every one of them needs a different path to the same goal. Some people need a man to preach fire and brimstone."

"To scare them?" I asked. "Seems out of character for you." He didn't really appear like the distant and terrifying god some monks cast him as.

"No, not to scare them." Doctor Quarrels chuckled. "I've seen in their hearts, and the people who gather around monks like father Keys aren't doing it because they're afraid."

"Why are they there, then?" I asked.

"The same reason men look to you for a savior." He put a hand on my shoulder. "They need hope."

"Hellfire and sulfur is a strange place to find it." I snorted.

"So is a sixteen-year-old Confederacy boy." Doctor Quarrels eyed me up. "People find solace in strange places. Those like Keys need to see the world in stark lines and borders, salvation and damnation with nothing in between. It's tricky to grasp the morality of the New Church so some people cling to the more easily understood ethics." He held up two hands to illustrate the point. "It helps them stick to the honest path they know. Besides, many think they've been trod on for so long, it helps them to think one day the men wearing the boots will get their punishment."

"Will they be punished?" I asked. I was thinking of a certain Anthanii monarch and his bitch of a wife.

"It's not that simple." Doctor Quarrels sighed.

"It never is." I rolled my eyes.

"We don't punish anyone. All are close to our hearts. We wouldn't cast a man to eternal torment anymore than a good father would throw out his son for breaking a vase." He paused. "However, in the end, they have to accept us of their own will. We help everyone, but it's not always enough." He turned back to me. "Every time someone errs they take a step away from us. We forgive every sin, but the trouble is they can't forgive themselves." Doctor Quarrels smiled. "However, every person, man, woman, or child, has some good in him. Sometimes it's impossible for you to see in his life, but it's there. In the end, we can bring them to us once more."

"Interesting." I scratched my chin. "Not the stuff about theology, but I can sleep with whoever I want."

Doctor Quarrels shook his head again. "That's not what I said."

"You kind of did." I egged him on.

"Thomas, *kind of* is for beings who haven't been around so many years you haven't even named the number. We don't *kind of* do anything." The god said. "Listen, sex in it of itself is a sacred thing. The trouble is when that's all women are to you." He paused. "Now, I know life gets hard sometimes, and it's not so bad a thing to find comfort in a stranger's arms for a night. There's better ways to cope with pain, but I won't deny it helps. You just have to make sure that it doesn't become only that." He stopped me. "When you discard it as just a way to relax and lay with anyone for any reason you lose something precious." He gave a soft smile. "However, when you find the right person it can be so much more. When you love someone, it can elevate the world around you." He went on. "How could someone who loves you the way we do ever deprive a man of that kind of relationship?"

"I guess that makes sense." I shrugged. "I just wanted to know where the special spot is, though."

He sighed, visibly pained. "Well, you found it. Happy?"

"Yes!" I chirped excitedly. This question, of course, came after I asked what dogs think about. Apparently, the answer was conspiring for more belly rubs and wondering why we smell weird. Of course, he'd tried to work some meaning into the explanation, but I was too disappointed to care. I always assumed dogs were conspiring to throw off their human overlords. As it turned out they rather liked their human overlords.

"So which side is right?" I asked. "You know in politics."

He cut me off right there. "I do not get involved in that sort of thing so don't ask."

"Oh," I huffed my disappointment, "What's the afterlife like?"

"It comes after the beforelife." Wisdom gave me a wink. "Come now Thomas, that's a trade secret. If I let anyone know the recipe, we might lose our monopoly on everlasting souls."

"Hmmm." I thought for a moment. "Why didn't Jaime Eldson invite me to his twelfth birthday party." It was something that had grated on me for a while.

"Because you almost burnt his house down at his eleventh birthday party."

"Damn." I kicked another rock. "I thought they believed that story about the cat." It was still a load off my mind in a way. "I thought it was because he didn't like me."

Wisdom chuckled. "Rest assured, Jaime Eldson did not like you,"

I glared at the god. "Why didn't he like me?"

"Because you almost burned down his house at the his eleventh birthday party!"

"Oh."

I was on the cusp of asking another question, but the look on his face made me hold my peace. "This is it." It was reasonably hard to read a god, not that I had to. He'd always been honest with me. I knew that's also what people said about liars who were too good to catch, but the way he talked of me seemed to go contrary to what the patron of the New Church would want. He cautioned mercy against his antagonists. He begged me to help those who helped the Old Religion.

As far as gods went, he was a decent sort. No fire and brimstone like some of the monks taught, just compassion for those who abandoned him. Only sorrow for those who strayed. I hadn't joined up to fight for the Three, and I still wasn't. The tattoos on my arm just gave me an excuse, but if I had to be a part of someone's plan, I was glad it was his. Still, I found myself wondering what he was thinking. I doubted I could even understand the things on his mind. The thoughts of the divine probably weren't meant to fit into a mortal's head, even a mortal like me.

I followed his eyes to the Temple. I'd heard stories about the majesty of the Old Religion's holy places. They were supposed to be Cathedrals that spanned as wide as a modest town and reached for the sky. They were supposed to be covered wall to wall in priceless art. The architecture was said to be so breathtakingly elegant, that people would weep upon seeing it for the first time. I'd have thought the greatest of the Priests would demand the greatest temple. I'd even looked forward to it a bit. I didn't know what I'd find. All records of the Temple had been stricken, but I hadn't expected this.

In every tangible way, it was disappointing. It was just a hole in the ground with some stone steps leading further into the earth. In an intangible way, it was more than I could have dreamed. I had gone into dark caves before and never known fear. There wasn't much a torch couldn't illuminate. In all my life I don't think I've been afraid of physical injury or failure. I'd spent many nights awake wondering on the consequences of my actions, but the thought that I might not survive the coming battle had never factored in. Sure, I had caution. I planned and trained because I knew nothing was assured. However, it didn't frighten me.

Standing before the mouth of the Temple, I was scared. I was a mouse looking up at a viper. I felt the hair on my neck stand up. I felt my hands grow sweaty. I felt a lump in my throat. For the first time, a thousand reasons not to do something came to mind. *You should probably eat and rest a day before you make that journey.* I told myself. *Why even bother? There's no assurances the secrets I'm looking for are there.* They were all lies to tell myself. For the first time, I felt the touch of a primal and instinctual fear.

It wasn't one of those tricks scientists called optical illusions that made you uncomfortable. It was just a hole. It wasn't a flourish of artistry that spoke of danger. There were just stairs. It didn't look much different than a well-made basement. It was an instinctual knowledge not to go down there. No, it was more than that. Instinct was formed by nature. This wasn't natural. It was stamped into the soul of all living things. When you see this path turn away. Everything in me said run.

I felt a hand rest on my shoulder. "You can stop now." Doctor Quarrels sounded like he was begging. "There's no shame in leaving." He wasn't staring at me. His eyes were fixed on the Temple. The prevailing thought was that the Three and the Demons Below were pure antagonists. Elemental forces in perpetual opposition. I was so sure that was the nature of it. Looking at him, I wasn't so sure.

He didn't look at it like a soldier might look at his enemy across the battle. There wasn't hatred or determination. His eyes weren't filled with fear or hunger. He didn't even hold the complicated respect I had for Thaniel. If I had to liken his face to anything, it would be a father visiting the grave of his son. No, it was more than that. It was like a parent watching his child writhe in agony, knowing there was nothing he could do. Even that description only gave one-thousandth of the emotion I saw on his face. It was sorrow and regret. It was helplessness. I hadn't thought a god could feel helpless, but from what little I knew of the Three, maybe they were the only ones who could truly feel it.

I saw something else in his eyes as well. It was guilt. I'd seen it before on him when he spoke of the path I'd need to travel. He'd even held a glimmer of it when he spoke of Thaniel. That had been guilt by omission, though. The guilt of being strong enough to act, but something stopping you. That was a powerful thing in it of itself, but it wasn't what I saw on him. It was the pain of having caused something horrible with your own two hands. I knew the feeling well. To the Three, this was their fault. I didn't know how, but I knew it was.

"You don't have to do this." Doctor Quarrel's voice was shaking. "You can turn away." He paused. "This was our mistake. You don't need to carry it."

"Is there another way to beat the Priests?" I turned to him.

"That's a complicated question." Wisdom muttered. "If by beat you mean-"

"I mean beat." This wasn't the time for semantics. "I mean when the next battle comes and Thaniel brings his Priests, is there another way to break them?"

"The Nameless Man is the only one who's managed to do that." It was as if all his attention was fixated on that hole in the ground."

"Then tell me how he did it!" I didn't want to go down there. "Who was the Nameless Man?" I asked. "What was his secret?"

Doctor Quarrels shook his head. "I won't tell you who he is. We swore that much to him." He finally pulled his eyes away from the Temple. "As for how he did it, he turned his weaknesses into strengths. He saw through to what your kind was destined for."

"The Nameless Man became more than human?"

"No." Wisdom responded. "He became more human."

"Whatever he did," I narrowed my eyes, "could I do the same?"

"You cannot." Quarrels admitted "Not the way he did at least."

I could tell that everything in the god wanted to turn away. "If you want to do what the Nameless man did, you will need to take a different path."

"This path, you mean." I nodded to the Temple. "If I don't go down there, Thaniel will win this war.".

Wisdom clinched his teeth. "You're right, Thomas, even if I wish you weren't." He gained a bit of his conviction back. "This is the only way to do what you think needs to be done." He muttered. "I've tried to caution you away, but you didn't hear it then." He sighed. "You won't hear it now."

I nodded. "Let's get this over with."

We walked down the stairway together. Nothing changed as we went, yet everything did. When you lie in your bed at night and blow out your candle. You may think you know true darkness. You don't.

"Are there dangers here?" I asked.

"Yes." He answered me honestly.

I kept walking until I heard noises. It was rats I thought at first, but then I realized rats were smarter than me. They wouldn't venture here. Nothing natural would. After a minute I realized it was mumbling and not just of one man. "What is that?" I asked.

"Pain." He answered. "Regret."

I almost yelled at him for giving me a poetic answer to a direct question. It was a peeve of mine. However, I realized it was probably the only way he could explain it so I might understand.

Finally, the stairway opened up to a large room. To my surprise, the torches were still lit. I inspected them for sorcery. They seemed normal enough to me though. "Who's lighting these?" I asked.

"Love comes down here from time to time." He said. "It's too hard for me, and Honor can't so much as look at them anymore, but Love comes every night." He stared off to the source of the mumbling. "She gives them what rest she can."

I followed his gaze again. Before I could think my pistol was in my hand aimed at the source. They were a group of six Priest. I could tell from their bloodstained uniform. They were crawling on the ground, speaking a language I'd never heard before. Still, insanity had a certain universal way of making itself known. I was about to shoot before Doctor Quarrels knocked my gun down to my side.

"No!" He shouted.

"They're Priests!" I turned to him. "Even mad as they are, they could be dangerous."

"Look again."

I did. This time I saw their faces, and it wasn't the cold beauty I'd come to recognize Demon Speakers with. In fact, it was quite the opposite. It was the most gruesome scene I'd ever laid eyes on. Each one was twisted beyond what a human could do. One was melted like wax. One had mounds growing out of his forehead. I started throwing up before I could see the rest.

"Sleep, my children." Doctor Quarrels waved a hand over them, and they stopped moving. The Priest found a modicum of peace in his words.

"Your children!" I screamed. "They've sworn to blast your church off this Earth! They've sworn to strike you down from the heavens!"

I expected some sort of empathetic response. I expected some riddle as wise at it was incomprehensible. What he said caught me off guard. "Even gods do not choose who they love."

"It'd be a mercy." I raised the gun again.

"Maybe," I saw a tear run down his eye, "but I'm not strong enough to give it to them."

I pulled him towards me. "You said there was danger here." I gestured to the sleeping Priests. "Six practitioners of the Old Religion seems pretty fucking dangerous."

"Not anymore." He finally faced me. "The danger is behind you."

The force of the blow that hit me couldn't have been less if it was fired out of a cannon. I felt two ribs break as I flew across the room. I looked up and saw a monster. People threw that word around to much. "You see that big grey animal with a trunk and tusks? That is a monster." It wasn't. It was just an elephant. The thing standing before me was a monster true.

It was shaped like a human if humans were eight feet tall and twice as wide as the biggest wrestler. It wasn't human, though. It was made of stone and magma. Fire birthed beneath every pore. Then it opened its eyes. Every holy man had an idea what the World Below would look like. They were all wrong. I knew because I saw down into the world of Demons. It almost drove me insane in that instant as it had the Priests. I was stronger, though. Actually, I was probably already insane, but arguing semantics is best done when a Monster isn't trying to kill you.

I pulled my six-shooter and emptied every round right between his eyes. They didn't just glance off. They stopped moving when they hit him. I pulled out my spare. This time I chose my targets. One where his heart would be, one where his stomach would be. Even one where his cock should have been. He had to have a weakness! I couldn't find it by the time my gun clicked empty.

"Stop!" I heard Doctor Quarrels scream. "Please, don't hurt each other..." Neither one of us seemed to be in a stopping mood.

The monster stalked towards me. He knew he had time to enjoy his work. The carelessness of it all sent my blood boiling. He expected me to crawl away on my back. He expected me to beg for mercy. I wasn't proud of it, but part of me wanted to. If he was just a stone giant, I wouldn't have had a second thought about doing just that. It was those eyes, though. I saw the evil that drove children mad. They only glimpsed a fraction of it. This was pure. There was no begging for mercy. I knew this last idiotic quest had sealed my fate. I knew I couldn't avoid death anymore, but I could choose how I died. Even if no one was there to see it, I'd leave this world in a flurry of violence.

Then, of course, there was that ever-present part of me that screamed damn the evidence. That irrational speck in my brain that would see me through. This wasn't how my story ended. I wouldn't acquiesce like his pet Priests. I jumped to my feet and realized I'd broken more than a few ribs. My leg almost gave out through its own weight. How had that happened? Probably when I landed.

Despite everything in my body telling me to lay down, I kept my footing. I pulled my tomahawk and knife. If a monster from the World Below could be surprised, he looked surprised at my defiance.

"Please!" I heard Doctor Quarrels scream. "Don't do this!"

I charged at the beast. I moved around him attacking every weak point I knew a body held. I put all my strength behind each blow, and yet every strike seemed to land like a feather. I ducked, rolled, and dodged. There had to be something, some way to take this beast down. Finally, the monster grew bored of it. I felt an iron hand wrap around my wrist.

"Fuck." I had the time to say before he flung me ten feet into another wall. This time I felt my shoulder pop out, along with a dozen other new injuries. He stood watching as I rammed the joint against the wall putting it back into place. I felt every pain to it's fullest. I wasn't in the Battle-Mind. I'd judged it too dangerous after my first attempt and almost losing myself. I tried it again but got much the same result. As I shook the fog out of my head, I knew this would have to be settled the old way.

The monster seemed to wait politely while I fixed myself. He tilted his head to one side. "You've grown stronger." He righted himself. "No matter, we will always be the greater sons."

"He's lying Thomas!" I heard Quarrels scream. "We gave you something we couldn't give them!" He shouted. "Use the Gift."

I shook his comments away. It probably wasn't the best move to ignore a god while you fought a Demon creation. I've ever been stubborn though.

I flung an extra knife at him. It had the same effect as the bullets. Then he moved. I'd judged from the look of him he weighed at least three tons of pure stone. My one hope was I was faster. I was wrong. I could spend the rest of my life training and still not be half as quick.

I barely managed to move my body out of the way before his fist punched a hole through the wall. One hit from that would kill me. His other hand grabbed me by the throat. He could have broken my neck right there, but I guessed he liked watching me squirm. He slowly pushed the air out of me, slowly closing off my throat.

I'd never been trained to fight giant stone monsters, but I did know how to fight a human who put me in a hold like that. I struck his elbow hard with one arm. I'd expected it to do nothing, but I felt it give a bit. It was stronger than any human could have been, but I did feel it give. I hit him again with both arms. This time it bought me enough time to draw a breath. I saw an almost quizzical look on his face. *How did that happen?* It seemed to ask. It wasn't worried, just mildly curious. Mildly annoyed.

I used my extra breath and drilled him in the gut as hard as I could. He backed up releasing my throat. I could see confusion on his monstrous face, maybe even a little pain. The hand I'd hit him with was clearly broken, but I ignored my wrist telling me to stop. I hit him once more in the gut, then in his big stone head. My hands were turning into powder, so I used my elbow to hit him again and felt that break as well.

Every strike cost me far more than it did him. It didn't feel like

I was punching stone, but it was definitely closer to timber than human flesh. I went to hit him again with my other arm, but he caught it slamming me back up against the wall. I felt more bones break. I struggled against him, but he was ready this time. He ripped my right sleeve down and stared at the tattoos.

The portal in his eyes full of the World Below glowed white. I didn't need a theologian to tell me that meant mad. He reared his arm back. I knew the game was done. He was about to cave my skull in. Still, I flailed out with my useless legs hitting whatever I could. I felt one of my shins splinter, but I didn't care. I bit down on the hand that grabbed me. I saw him wince with pain. I smiled on the inside. At least whatever this thing was. It'd remember Thomas Belson.

I waited for the blow that never came. I looked up in dark curiosity. Doctor Quarrels was holding it back. It didn't look like he was putting too much effort into it either, but the stone arm didn't move.

"That's enough!" The Doctor screamed, then softened up. "Spare the boy."

"I ain't a fucking boy!" I managed to choke out. However, sitting there pinned to a wall with most of my bones broken, I felt rather like a boy. The fact that they ignored me made it worse. I knew it was foolish to feel indignant with a god and monster in the same room but still…

The monster twisted his face into a savage grin. "You know we never spare anything." He lifted me then slammed me into the wall again. How many bones had I broken? Probably the same amount that were in my body.

"Just this once?" The doctor pleaded. "For the love you once bore me! For the love I still bear you…"

The beast turned his head to face the god. "The only way this boy survives is if you strike me down." He gave an earthy chuckle, and I do mean earthy, in the sense that the whole earth shook. "What? Still too weak, father?"

Father? Was this a trick?

"I'll give you something you want." Doctor Quarrels face told me this was his last card to play.

"You gave us all we needed in the Long Ago." The monster smiled.

"I can give you my life." He let the hand holding the stone arm fall. "I can give you that which you've always craved."

The monster let me go. I slid to the floor like a sack of grain. I tried desperately to stand, but too many bones were broken.

"You can't be killed." The beast turned around.

"I can if I let you." He didn't back away. The monster knew same as me, Wisdom never lied.

"You'd sacrifice yourself for this child." He gestured to me.

"I would." Doctor Quarrels nodded accepting his fate.

"I'm not a damn child." I tried to stand up, but the pain in my legs brought me tumbling down again. "Get back here! I ain't done with you yet!"

"Thomas run." Doctor Quarrels said without looking at me. "Find a peaceful place, far from the war. Bring Abbey with you. It's what she wants." A lone tear made its way down his cheek. "Forget about Thaniel, be happy."

It's what she wants? I'd rather just thought it a one-night thing. Of course, I wanted something more, but she had been hard to read, even for me. *Wait! What am I doing?* "Fuck that!" I screamed, my mind returning from a woman I'd known for a few weeks to the divine face-off in front of me. I tried to stand, but my body still wouldn't let me. I was tough but not that tough.

The monster ignored it all. "I'll admit these beasts are stronger stock." He pointed those eyes back at me briefly. "Back when the youngest dwelled in these halls, they'd have fallen to their knees as soon as look at me." He gestured to the Priests. "They didn't last long." He turned back to me. "Maybe this one's just dumb."

"Fuck you." I screamed again from my aching knees.

"He's a special one." The doctor smiled as he backed into the center of the room. "They all are." He chuckled. "It wasn't me that made them like that, though. It's what your ilk never could get. It was their trials and suffering that put the iron in their bones." His smile turned to sorrow in a moment. "I've enjoyed watching them grow."

The monster picked Doctor Quarrels up by the shirt. It seemed a lousy way to kill a god. "I hope this helps you find peace." The doctor said. "I'm sorry it had to end like this."

"I'm not." The monster reared his fist again.

Call it battlefield strength. Call it stubbornness. I managed to stand again despite piercing agony, and move towards the pair.

"Thomas, run!" He screamed it.

I looked up the stairs. I'd gotten a second wind, enough strength to make it out of this temple before the Monster could follow me. At some point, I'd be reduced to crawling, but I'd make it back to my horse. From there I could move into the Battle-Mind and last long enough to find a doctor. I'd find a way to survive, and carry on my war. I was tough like that. My body would never be the same, but I reasoned I was young enough to be able to run again eventually.

Or I could do what Wisdom had told me. I could find Lady Gerate and run far away. Maybe I could take her to the Confederacy, make amends with my family. A god thought I could find peace. I wasn't sure, but he was the Three after all.

"Run!" Doctor Quarrels screamed again. "Your god commands it."

"No!" It wasn't in my nature. I used the last of my strength to jump on the monsters back. I wrapped my arms around its throat and squeezed for all I was worth. "Die Fucker!" In the end, I guess my squeezing wasn't worth all that much. He had me in his hand before I'd had a chance to breathe. He wobbled though. I'd swear that he wobbled. It made me smile.

Well, I smiled up until the point he slammed me on my back. I felt my spine snap, and everything below my legs went numb. I'd seen enough battlefield wounds to know they'd be numb for the rest of my life. However, the rest of my life wasn't looking too long.

"Thomas, use the Gift!" Doctor Quarrels screamed. "The Nameless man did it with compassion, you'll have to use the other way."

"Fuck!" I screamed as the monster kicked me in the ribs.

"Use your suffering, your sin." He screamed. "Use your fire and passion." He paused. "Use everything that makes you Belson the Blessed."

"Fuck!" I screamed as another savage kick was landed. The beast was taking its time torturing me. Quarrels' offer had seemed mighty tempting, but this thing clearly found me irritating. A small victory while my body radiated pain.

"It's what makes you stronger than them! It's why we made you this way!" Doctor Quarrels wouldn't stop. "It's not over!"

"Of course, it is." The monster kneeled next to me, taking my neck in both of his huge stone hands.

I was running out of options, so I decided to listen to the god's advice. I believed I was greater. I reached for every pain I could remember. I hugged every sin I held in my heart. I remembered my joys as more than fleeting. I brought everything out that made me Thomas Belson.

For the first time, I saw it. The hidden path was hidden no more. It was the only path, and needed to follow it! I couldn't say exactly what I did, but I did something. Explaining it afterwards would be like explaining how you made your heart beat.

I felt something inside me crack. I felt a light go off inside of me. I felt heaven pouring from that crack, and a lot of hellfire too. Something changed in me, and I knew I could win.

I rammed my head into the monster's nose. This time it wasn't like hitting timber. It was like hitting flesh. His stone head tore back. He tried to escape me, but I held onto him with both shattered arms. Suddenly I was on top. Once you equalized everything out, the monster *was* weak. It wasn't used to true pain. It didn't know how to react.

I beat him. I let all the pain he'd given me back on the beast. I beat him until the fire went out of his eyes. I kept at it. The magma in his blood stopped running. His body started changing. I cut off my savage attack to watch. By the time the transformation was done he was a boy who couldn't have been older than twelve. He was beautiful too. Like one of those forest spirits, you hear about.

I tried to stand, but my legs were still numb. I thought what I'd done with the Gift might heal me. It didn't. Then the pain all came back at once.

"Fuck!" I screamed. "I can't walk!"

Doctor Quarrels went over to the body ignoring my agony. "I'm sorry Gothin." He slid the child's eyes closed.

"Fuck!" I screamed again.

Doctor Quarrels walked over to me and put his hand on my face. All at once, my bones started mending, sliding underneath my skin into their rightful place. It was the most pain I'd ever been in. Doing years work of recovery in a few seconds. I think I almost died, but by the time he removed his hand, I was all healed up, except for some soreness.

"Fuck!" I said one last time before I realized who I was talking to. "Sorry about all the cursing." I said.

He waved it off and went back to the corpse. Doctor Quarrels put his hand on the monster's chest. Well, apparently it was a boy named Gothin, but from the beating I'd taken, that wasn't all he was.

Flowers and vines sprung up from the stone to wrap his body. The boy started to change again, growing even smaller. In the time it took me to catch my breath, he was just a little tree sprout, barely out of the acorn. Doctor Quarrels pocketed it. This was too strange. Defeating an invincible army was easier to deal with than what I'd seen.

"You should have run." He said. "Then I wouldn't have had to bury him."

I spit. "I don't run." That was probably one of the times it was advisable, though. "Could he really have killed you?"

"I would have let him." Doctor Quarrels nodded. "It would have saved you from dying here." He touched his pocket. "It might have helped him find peace." He looked back at me. "A small payment for a great sin, but what can we do but atone?"

"Am I really that important to you?" I sat up. It added to my already growing arrogance. A god had been willing to die for me. What he said next knocked it out of me.

Despite his somber mood, he gave a sad chuckle. "Yes, you are that important." He paused. "As is the beggar at the end of his street, as is the king who sits on his throne." He gave me his caring eyes. "We love you more than you know, not all of you but each of you." He helped me to my feet. "When a man goes mad and kills innocent women on the street, we weep for the man as much as those he killed. We hope both, victim and victimizer, can find salvation in their own way."

"That's a lot of weeping." I mumbled.

"It is," Doctor Quarrels agreed, "but we smile sometimes too."

"So you'd have sacrificed yourself for anyone," I knocked the dust off my coat, "whore, pimp, drunk?"

"Yes."

"Even a lawyer?" I asked.

Doctor Quarrels rolled his eyes. "They're not as bad as you think. They do just as much defending the downtrodden as they do attacking them."

"Even a lawyer?" I repeated. The rich ones certainly did more attacking.

"Even a lawyer, Thomas." He cocked an eyebrow at me. "Though, you're probably the only one desperate enough to come down here, and certainly the only one foolish enough to try and strangle one with both broken arms."

"I thought it'd impress you." I shrugged.

"It did," Doctor Quarrels smiled, "that doesn't make it any less foolish."

"Wait," I slowly remembered the smattering of theology I'd been taught, "You're all knowing, so that means you knew exactly what I'd do." I cocked an eyebrow up. "Your self-sacrifice wasn't quite so self-sacrificing."

He paused, trying to figure out how to explain my ignorance. "We are all knowing, but it's not how you might think. It's like looking at a painting for us, less than knowing every word in a book." He shrugged. "Once you insert yourself in that painting, you lose a part of it." He paused again. "I was certain I would die, but we knew you would save me if that makes sense."

"It doesn't." I admitted.

"I expected not," Doctor Quarrels frowned, "but one doesn't have to be omniscient to know Thomas Belson has a hard time running from a fight."

"You're right on that count." I had a thousand questions, but I decided to start small. "That's a neat trick, you got with fixing my body." I said. "Any time I get a bad wound, I just pray a little, and you'll come patch me up?"

He shook his head. "Only here, and only once." The Doctor sighed. "The rules are different in this place, and the death of a First makes things malleable."

"Who enforces the rules on a god?" I asked. "I remember that bit about omnipotence from the Testament.

"We enforce the rules upon ourselves, as do you." I was about to raise an objection, but he stopped me. "I know about laws and such." He paused. "Some of them go far beyond what they should, but the basics, what makes you a good man, that is something you choose." He gestured to where the monster was a moment ago. "This creature followed no rules, and look what he became."

"What was that thing anyway?" It was the real question on my mind.

Doctor Quarrels touched the sprout in his pocket. "The Imorans used to summon them as the head of their legions, but even they didn't know what they truly were." He paused. "The Priests now summon Demons to do their will, but they don't have the power to summon one in full form." That was a scary thought. "What you see in the world, are pale shadows." He turned to the ruined Priests still sleeping. "Long ago, they learned how to summon one in the flesh. That is what you just fought."

"I fought a Demon!" It seemed too absurd even for me. "Is it dead?"

"It is." The sorrow crossed his old face. "You're the first man to do so. The Nameless Man tried, but in the end, he loved them almost as much as we did. He couldn't hurt it." He sighed. "He died that day, but at least he managed to scare them into the World Below as you call it." He paused. "Except, for Gothin. He was always so willful."

"Almost killing one Demon was enough to scare them all out of this world?" It seemed a bit extreme.

"You don't think the way they do." Doctor Quarrels said. "Every human that lives in this world has something he'd die for. It is because he knows that he will die." He cocked an eyebrow up. "Of course, some men fear it less than others and ride with donkeys into five thousand enemy soldiers, but all have something for which they would die, glory, family, even gold for some reason." His eyes turned sour. "The Demons have never known mortality. To them, even a one in infinity chance of death is too high." He touched the pocket that held his Demon acorn. "Gothen was always such a willful boy though." He turned his eyes back to me. "It's what makes you so much more powerful than they. It's why you could do what you did."

"That Gift as you called it." I looked at my fist. The feeling of it flowing through me was gone. "It'll be enough to break the Priests power?"

"Yes." He nodded. "Do what you did here, and they won't be able to hurt you or your armies."

"Can I teach it to others?" I asked.

"All can learn, but few are willing. It requires you to accept your mortality and flaws. Even humans have trouble doing that." He said it with a slight sad chuckle. "You'll have to be the judge of that."

"No warning about it being too dangerous?" I cocked my eyebrows up.

"It's called the Gift for a reason." Wisdom smiled sadly. "We gave it freely."

"You really do love us, don't you?" Of course, the Testament told me they did, but it was hard to believe in a world like ours.

"More than you could know." He answered.

"Then why make the world this way?" I threw my hands up. "Why fill it with war and violence? Don't give me the free will argument cause I've heard that." I shook my head. "Why the disease and earthquakes? Why so much pain?"

"Would you be happier in utopia?" He smiled at me.

The answer was no. I needed strife. I needed someone to struggle against. I had left paradise for horror twice in my life, once in the Grove and once from a loving family. Despite what it had cost to me I'd do the same again. "I'm not most men." I answered.

"You certainly aren't." He nodded. "As I've said, we didn't make this world for most of mankind. We didn't even make it for all of mankind. We made it for each man and woman."

"You're not answering my question." I said.

"I can't answer your question fully in a way you'd understand," Doctor Quarrel's eyes darted to my tattoos, "but I can tell you this." He paused. "You've sworn to fight the Demons, but you've never wondered where they came from."

"I never cared." That was a bit of a lie. "I always figured they were like mountains or oceans. Just there, and we don't yet know enough to understand them."

"Well, you're right. You don't yet know enough to understand them." He chuckled. "You don't even know enough yet to understand even those mountains and oceans change. You just haven't been making maps long enough to see it." Quarrels picked up some sand and let it slide through his fingers. "However, you won't explain the First with science, or at least not a science you've given a name yet. However, this new field of psychology shows promise. Perhaps with it you might one day understand the edges."

"What are you getting at?" I asked.

He nodded, realizing he'd been on a tangent. "You call them Demons we call them the First. It's because before we created this universe, before we formed a cloud of dust into a planet around a star, before we saw it seeded with life that would grow to be man, there was them." He smiled. "We gave breath to our first children. We loved them so very much. The paradise we built them is beyond anything you could ever imagine. They never grew hungry, thirsty or tired. They were never lonely or sad. All the little things you struggle against were absent in them. We wanted their lives to be free of all pain. We didn't know that free of all pain meant no freedom at all." His face twisted into sadness.

"Slowly, slower than all the time that has ever passed in this universe times a thousand, they ceased to be the loving creatures of the garden. Their gentle ways turned violent. The happiness they'd known grew to be their baseline. They wanted more of it. We tried to give it to them, new pleasures to experience, but they turned it away. They wanted a different type of joy, one we couldn't offer."

"They started small, killing the animals we had sent there with them. When they grew tired of that, they tortured them. We still remember the first beast they bludgeoned. It haunts us. These were not the animals you know today. The ones you heard, hunt, and eat. These were creatures with their own souls. They called out to us, but we deafened ourselves to their pain. We loved our children too much to believe what they had become. The games they played changed. Their hearts were not made for degrees, only absolutes. They couldn't understand anything between innocence and evil."

"Perhaps, we should have punished them. Perhaps, we should have taken their new pleasures away, but we couldn't hurt them. Even as they are now, we love them too much. In our hearts, we knew these were not the children we formed so long ago. In secret, we made a new people far away, The Second. They were a robust one, not unlike the kind you are now. They were mortal as you are. They made children and loved them. They hunted and farmed. In fact, we could have plucked one out and put them in this world, without causing much of a stir. That is if any still lived."

"The First found them, and the things they did on that day will follow us for eternity. We can never be free of them. Should never be free of them They were worse than all the crimes committed in this world, worse by an infinite degree. We watched on in horror. We tried to stop them, but that would have made us hurt our children. What do you do when two people you love equally destroy each other? There is no good answer."

"At first we thought our children didn't understand the wrongs they had committed. We thought maybe it was a miscommunication with disastrous consequences. We tried to teach them. We tried to show them our displeasure. They didn't care. They didn't love us anymore. We knew no good could exist while they were allowed to roam free. We locked them in a prison, what you call the World Below. At first, it was a gentle incarceration, not much different than the paradise they left. They turned it to hellfire and ice."

"After that, we set into course the events that would make you. You were to be a different kind of creature. You were to exist for the journey while those before lived only in the destination. You were to be what we were most proud of. We watched you grow, always creating a better world, but never perfect. It warmed us. We couldn't hurt our First, but while they lived you would never be free, so we gave you the Gift. We are so very proud of what you've become. Always falling over your feet. Always getting back up. You ask why we didn't fashion you a world free of suffering? We tried that, and it didn't work. A world free of suffering isn't free. Eternal bliss and eternal torment are indistinguishable."

The trance that story put me in faded. I could almost see their pain and their joy. Finally, it faded. "How did the Demons get set loose in this world, if you locked them away?" I stepped towards him. "How am I fighting a war you won eons ago?" I pointed an accusing finger at the god.

"You sought them out." Doctor Quarrels answered. "We cannot stop you from anything. You are free to choose." He sighed. "At first it was a village chief who figured out how to speak with the World Below. It was an accident born of his rage and impotence. We tried to warn him, and at first, he listened but then..." He trailed off.

"Then he got too angry and too impotent." I answered for him.

"Yes, and then Demons were let loose upon this world." Doctor Quarrels shook his head. "The First learned how to hunt their new prey. They left brutality aside for subtle promises. The world learned from this chief, and you were not yet ready to use the Gift, so we did what we so rarely do." He looked up at me. "We intervened. We helped found the New Church." He gave a sad little smile. "You think the Constable is less than five hundred years old? He was here before you learned how to turn copper ore into swords."

"Well, it's kept me gainfully employed." I shrugged.

"Since then the battle has raged. Each side fighting for reasons they barely understand." He paused. "We believe this to be the turning point."

"You mean me?" I asked.

"You have a part to play." Doctor Quarrels admitted. "It wouldn't do to tell you too much of your future."

"I'll win." I assured him.

"We would rather everybody win, but if you defend the innocent, that will be enough." Doctor Quarrels responded.

"Strategy aside, you've done me a favor." I said. "I can do you one too." I nodded to the Priests gently sleeping. "I can finish what you can't."

He shook his head. "Those Priest have already moved to the Next World without their tormentor to keep them alive." He paused. "We will do what we can to save them there." He gestured to the outside world. "As for the members of the Grove, we have not given up hope for them." He smiled. "Adam, that man who offered you the apple, has already found the courage to escape his torment. He too will pass to the Next World when he steps outside Imor's influence, but I think he can be saved as well."

"Aye." I nodded. I hoped it was true "Well, I guess I better get back to Anthanii. There's a war on you know?"

"We know," he smiled, "but you may want to make a stop at Gertinville on the way."

"Why's that?" Leave it to me to question the words of the all-knowing.

"You've been gone for quite a while." He said. "Thaniel has learned of your absence. You're the only man he fears."

"He's right to fear me." I shot back smugly.

Doctor Quarrels seemed to be amused by my arrogance. "The Kranish have redoubled their efforts to take Southern Anthanii. They've brought reinforcements and Priests to take the city." He paused. "Lord Corbula is holding onto the last stronghold." He waved his hand. "Also, Thaniel has led his forces over the mountains himself. That army you so tactlessly told King John to form will fight him and lose, but it won't be so disastrous as Milhire."

"That's a lot of work in a short time." I raised an eyebrow. *Thaniel had sent troops across the North in winter?* That was bold, but it sounded like it might pay off.

"It is." He shrugged. "However, if you ride now you can make it to Gertinville in time to form the defenses, then you can turn Thaniel back, buy a little time." He smiled. "It's been a long time since we've fought, but I still remember a little strategy."

"I thought you didn't want me to fight?" I asked.

"We don't," he admitted, "but you're going to do it anyway, so why not let you know what you've missed."

"Thank you." I nodded and was already running up the stairs before he could respond. I'd been too long away from the front. It was time I returned.

Present Day
Jessie's Story

Jesse waited behind a corner. It was raining, and the bread he
was eating was wet. The part of town he was in was in its own
way wealthier than the area that the aristocrats called home.
This district was for creation, not decadence, and the shops were
well used but also well kept. Still no matter how cheery the place,
even here couldn't escape the influence of the time and weather. The
bounty hunter could have been outside a palace, and it would have
still seemed gloomy. Whoever was in charge of the moon and clouds
was clearly trying to discourage the Jesse.

The street was dark and only the most devoted of craftsmen
were still out. It was fortunate that his man was one of them. He
looked at the man the letter had specified around the corner. Fenton
Cooper was the name on the note. He was looking at him now
watching and waiting. Jesse didn't know why he warranted such
special attention from Bellefellow and he wasn't sure he wanted too.
It was dark, and the man had been at work for some time in his barrel
shop. Jesse would have liked to plan it more, but the note said it was
to be carried out that night.

Truly, the man would have been dead before the rain if his
son would have ever left his side. Jesse didn't like killing what he
presumed was an innocent man. He absolutely detested the idea of
murdering him in front of his son, but the bastard wouldn't leave.
The son couldn't have been older than five and looked as innocent
a child as Jesse had ever seen, and Fenton appeared to be as normal
a man as any. The bounty hunter pulled out his knife and looked at

it with disgust. He tried to think of Mary to pass the time, but she didn't deserve to be associated with a thing like this.

The man named Fenton was coming out of his shop finally, and the child was still with him. It was the last chance Jesse would have. Boy or not, he needed to get his job done. Jesse walked around the corner towards the man.

"Keep a look out son." Jesse could hear the man say as he locked the door to his shop. Out of the corner of his eye, he could see two black-clad figures on the other side of the street waiting patiently.

Jesse reached the man just as he turned around. "Give me your money!" He screamed but didn't wait for an answer before he started stabbing.

"Please!" Most men raise their hands in defense when they're being stabbed Fenton used his last gesture to push his son away.

"Your money!" Jesse shouted as his knife went in and out of the poor cooper. He wanted to stop, but he couldn't. He kept stabbing. The first few were expertly placed in the spots that would make the man bleed out in less than a minute. The rest were to make it look like an amateur did it. He thrust again and again until something made him stop. It wasn't like whatever Bellefellow did to him, that was like it's body forgetting it's very function was to serve him. This was like his arm was rejecting the evil act it was committing.

He finally looked down to see the man's son pounding at his leg. "Get off my Paw!" He screamed tears streaming out of his eyes.

"Piss off!" Jesse screamed and backhanded the boy with the hand that still held the knife. The boy went flying and looked up still crying with a crescent-shaped outline of blood on his chin.

The man pulled Jesse close. "Please don't take my boy." He gasped blood running down his mouth.

"I want your fucking money!" He screamed again

The man wasn't convinced. "Don't let Bellefellow take my boy please."

"I-" Jesse didn't know what to say. The note just said kill Fenton and make it look like a mugging. It didn't mention a boy at all.

"Run!" He screamed at the boy and then slumped lifelessly against the door. The child was too shocked to do anything.

Jesse reached in the man's wallet and took his money. Then he looked at the door it was an impressive lock he'd have trouble breaking it. Then he looked at the glass window to the shop and shattered it with the pommel of his knife. People always spent so much money on their locks expecting robbers to be polite and go through the door. A broken window on a display wall worked just as well.

He jumped through the glass and started wreaking havoc on the meticulously well-kept store. He turned over barrels and scattered documents. Then he went to the register and took all the money in it.

As Jesse jumped back out, he saw the boy snatched up by the two black figures. He thought briefly about rescuing the child, but he told himself it wasn't his problem.

Then people started coming out of buildings to look at the damage.

"Police!" One man screamed.

"Someone get a doctor!" He heard someone yell

"Stop that man!" Some woman shouted. That was Jesse's cue to run.

He pulled up the rag that covered his face and ran down out the street. One good neighbor tried to grab him but caught an elbow in his jaw for the efforts. Before anyone could catch up, he was in an alley and running with everything in him to anywhere else. When he finally had to stop, he couldn't hear anyone chasing. He looked down at the blood on his hands and found a horse trough to wash it off. No matter how hard he scrubbed, it didn't seem like enough.

He thought about the child and the two black figures who had abducted him. He couldn't stop thinking on why Bellefellow would want some poor cooper dead. It wasn't outside the Priest's character to kill a man for making a bad barrel, but he wouldn't have sent Jesse to do it. He would have just done it. He looked at his hands which despite his washing still seemed too red. It didn't make sense. None of it did.

———◆◆◆———

Jesse knocked on the door and waited for the shuffling inside to reach him. "Who is it at this hour of the night?" He heard his father's voice say.

"It's me, paw, Jesse."

"Oh, Jesse one second please." His father said, and the bounty hunter waited for him to undo all the locks Jesse had insisted be put on the heavy door. "Jesse!" His father exclaimed as the door swung open and folded his son into a crippling hug.

"Hey there Paw." He said untangling himself from the big man's grip. His father finally released his son, and Jesse took a long look at his paw. It was one of the happiest sights he had found in this world. Renny Devote looked just like his son, same build and blocky features. Still, he was bald now, and the wrinkles in his face let Jesse know he was getting older.

"What are you doing here at this hour?" Then he looked down at the blood on his shirt. Demons below what happened to you?"

Jesse waved him off. "It's fine." He sighed. "I killed a deer earlier, and some of the blood got on me. I just haven't washed it off yet."

"It looks fresh." Renny said, not believing his son.

"It was earlier today paw."

"What's all that racket out there Renny?" Jesse heard his mother ask still sounding like she was half asleep.

"It's me, Maw." Jesse said.

"Oh, Jesse! Come in, come in." He saw his mother hobble out, and he walked up and hugged her too. His mother was to him what every mother should look like. Denise was skinny, and her white hair showed that she wasn't quite the young woman she used to be. Her eyes though were as brown and caring as ever. "Do you want something to eat? Suppers cold now but I'm sure your hungry."

"I'm fine Maw. I'm just tired."

"Well, I'm sure you are. You can tell me all about your adventures in the morning."

"AHHHHHHHHHHH!.." Jessie heard the scream pierce through the house. "AHHHHHHH!" His brother screamed as he ran into the living room.

"Bo-Bo!" Jesse rushed forward to comfort his little brother.

"AHHHHHHHHHHH!" His brother Bobby was running around the room with his hands over his eyes.

"Bo-Bo, it's me." Jesse caught his brother and moved his hands away from his face.

"Oh. Jesse, I missed you." He said and hugged his brother happily. The boy was twelve years old now. He was a beautiful boy too. He had the same dark hair and eyes of his older brother, but his were somehow more delicate. He should have had a happy life. It's what he deserved, but good people rarely got what they deserved. "Where've you been?" He asked, but he was looking around the room as if he wasn't quite sure who he was talking to.

"Oh, you know here and there." Jessie held his brothers face to look at him. "Were you having a nightmare?"

"No, I haven't had a nightmare since you started in the trading business." Bobby said proudly. "I just don't like loud noises during sleep-sleep time."

"Oh, I'll be quieter I'm sorry." Jesse apologized still kneeling and holding his brother by the shoulders, so he knew who to talk to.

"It's fine. I didn't know they were your loud noises." Bobby smiled. "I like your loud noises just not Maw's so much."

Jesse smiled back at him. "Has Jimmy Pierce been throwing rocks at you again?"

"No." Bobby said oddly sad. "After you explained to them I didn't like the rock game they stopped." He looked embarrassedly down at his feet. "I feel bad that I ruined their game. They seemed to like it a lot."

"Oh don't feel bad. If you didn't like the game, they can find someone else to play it with." Jesse said reassuringly. In truth when the bounty hunter had found out about Jimmy's "game" he'd gone over to the Pierce household and unleashed an anger not even the Puena had seen. He'd beaten Jimmy's older brother into a bloody pulp, knocked a few of the father's teeth out and screamed at little Jimmy until the boy pissed himself. The gunslinger even kicked their dog for good measure, but he didn't see a reason to tell Bobby that. "Does he give you a lime every day still?" That was one of the demands Jessie had given the boy. His brother liked limes.

"He has. It's quite nice of him." Bobby said. "Some other boys tried to play the rock game with me, and Jimmy beat them real good." That was another of his orders to Jimmy. His exact words were put said boy's head up his own ass, but Jesse wasn't a stickler for details.

"That's good well I'm gonna go to sleep now I'll see you in the morning." Jesse said standing up.

"Can I sleep with you?" Bobby asked rocking back and forth. "I don't like you being alone in the dark its scary."

"I've never said no to the company of a brave man." He extended his hand to his brother. "Come on now." They walked into his room together.

Jesse sat up in his bed. It was one of two beds in the world he liked, and his favorite person was in it, but he didn't figure he deserved it after the things he'd done. The gunslinger felt the tears sting his eyes. He wouldn't show them in front of anyone, but when they came in the night, it was impossible to stop.

He cried, not for the men he'd killed, not for the families he'd broken. He cried for what he'd become. Maybe every man would have done the same in his shoes. Maybe he was a minority, but that didn't matter to Jesse. He cried for himself. If that made him a bad person, he didn't care. He was already bad enough as it was. Who his tears were directed to didn't mean much at that point.

He could have been a good man like his father, but he wasn't. He couldn't blame anyone but himself. A man makes his own choices. He looked at Bobby next to him. What was one life compared to all the ones he'd taken. When judgment was upon him, he knew what the powers that be would say.

He sobbed loudly. Loud enough for the boy next to him to stir. Jesse felt small arms wrap around his neck, gentle but firm. "It's alright, Jess." He heard the boy whispering in his ear. "I know it's scary sometimes, but I'll always protect you."

"I know Bo-Bo." He patted the arms. He sobbed until there was nothing left. He fell back to the bed and felt Bobby put the blanket over him. Jesse knew that no matter how hard he'd try to convince himself otherwise, his brother's life meant more to him than his soul. He wouldn't have changed a damn thing if it meant Bobby wouldn't have been Bo-Bo. Jesse knew what the powers that be would say to him when judgment came. He knew, and he didn't care. Whatever those powers were, Bo-Bo's judgment meant more.

Present Day

We left for the Belson Plantation. Andrew and I rode. George, Seiford, and Ayn-Tuk took the carriage. I worked Shaggy Cow hard returning only to the rest for food, water, and at night to sleep. With the wind in your face, you could almost feel your sins struggling to keep up. I made them run hard. Shaggy couldn't have been happier in horse heaven.

Andrew had been an excellent rider when I left. Time had only enhanced his skill. I was sure I'd seen a man sit a horse better, but for the life of me, I couldn't remember when. Still, even he had to struggle to keep up. His horse was of good stock, but Shaggy was The Lightning on Four Hooves.

It wasn't just the stead that made me better than him at it. It was the skill. If you put the two of us in a horse show, Andrew wouldn't just win, he'd embarrass me. His form was perfect. Mine was sloppy at the best of times. The difference was every muscle in my body was perfectly attuned to the harshness of the saddle. I rode in a style that mixed nomad tribesmen with the knights of old. I had been thrown from dying beasts more times than I could count. There was one engagement I'd spent a full week skirmishing with a nomadic eastern tribe. Andrew had seen more of war than most, but fighting was all I'd known for fifteen years. If you do something enough in battle, you get perfect at it or die, and I had definitely done enough riding in battle.

I probably should have slowed up, but when it came down to it, for all the time I'd spent away, Andrew was my younger brother. If you can't show off to your younger brother, who can you show off to? I didn't let the demonstration of my skills end there, though.

It came when I spotted a hair running across the field four hundred yards away. I pulled my repeating rifle out.

"There's no way you can hit that." He'd laughed at it. "Not even you."

We ate rabbit that night, and Andrew changed his tune.

We talked as well in between mad gallops. We generally avoided our father as a topic of conversation. I wasn't ready to face that yet. These were happy times. I wanted to keep them that way. He understood and didn't press it.

I asked about his older son named Thomas. Andrew said he was a willful child who couldn't stay out of trouble. He also told me George counted him as his best student. The boy also used the intelligence he gained to terrible effect. All in all, my nephew was a beautiful boy and everything a father could want. He said he was working hard to be worthy of my name.

When he told me that, I nodded dumbly and made an excuse about taking a piss. I didn't take a piss. When I finally came back, I was sure he could see the tears still in my eyes. Andrew didn't mention it.

I asked him about the wars he'd fought in, something I could relate to. He was constantly humble, never failing to mention he wasn't the only hero there. Always bringing up how brave his men were. I could read between those lines though. Andrew could have fought with a cushy cavalry unit and had even been a horseman at one time. However, my brother had chosen to stand with the infantry. He'd been a captain at the time, but when things went wrong in the worst way, he'd lead as a colonel. He'd thrown back endless hordes of Puena soldiers. All in all, if it was one of my stories, it would have ranked close to the top. Some idiot would have probably put in a dragon there too.

He couldn't get enough of my heroics either, always asking about this battle and that. I told him the stories as they actually happened. I spared him some of the gruesome bits, but the facts were there. He ended up thinking more of me rather than less. My stories weren't embellished to make them more impressive. They were embellished to make them more understandable.

Finally, the topic of his wife came up. It wasn't really something you could avoid honestly. He told me about Sarah. He tried not to brag, but I saw it in his eyes. They were happy together, truly happy. The kind of marriage you hope for as a child. I gritted my teeth and nodded. "She's a good woman." It was all I could say.

He asked about the women I'd met on my journey. He was sure

there had been many. That story was a bit disappointing. Eventually, he mentioned Lady Gerate. "Is it true? Did you really carry on with *her?*"

"Aye." I nodded, mind lost to a simpler time, thinking about a life that could have been mine.

He whistled at that. "We always hear stories about her. She's one of Alexis's heroes." He was uncharacteristically oblivious to what I was thinking. "Won't shut up about her. I'm sure she'll squeal like a stuck pig when you tell her you knew the woman." He looked back at me. "How'd you ever let that one go?"

I tried to tell him. Talking about it was like a song you tried to play that falls apart because the notes can't match up. "We had our duties." I finally managed to mutter out.

He finally caught on that it wasn't something I was overly disposed towards thinking about. "Well, you sure did your duty well." He tried to change the subject. "Tell me again. How many men were at Windsbrough?"

I smiled and told him. He whistled again suitable impressed.

When it finally got dark, we headed back to the carriage to share the night with our group. George, Ayn-Tuk, and Seiford had already begun setting up off the road next to a stream that looked clear enough to drink. There weren't many bandits this far east, so there wasn't the fear of being set upon while we slept. It was a clear night, so we decided the tents weren't necessary.

After the horses were fed and the fire was started we all sat down and ate the rabbits Andrew and I had hunted earlier. Eventually, I took out a bottle of bad Ventarii whiskey and passed it around. It was empty before too long, and we were all feeling rather warm in the face by the time conversation resumed. Except for Ayn-Tuk, of course, who waved the bottle away.

"You'd think after ten years of living like this you'd have gotten a bit better at living like this." I said to Seiford as I pulled out my rifle and began cleaning. I said it more to start a conversation than to comment on his road skills. Nothing was more depressing than a silent campfire. Besides he was struggling with his bag an awful lot.

"Oh, don't be so rough on the monk." Andrew cut in.

"I'm a university student from Suffix Anthanii." The monk retorted proudly. "I apologize for having been raised in civilization, not one step away from being a Huego." From any other noble it would have been a slight, but from Seiford it was just part of our relationship. I poked at his incompetence, Seiford talked about how everyone not from a city inevitably fucked goats.

"I'm a university student from Mainstead." George chimed in with a chuckle. "I can still tell a saddle from a corset." Much to Seiford's dismay, George picked up on the relationship and more often than not chose to side with me in our constant spats at night.

"Mainstead might qualify as civilization in this backwater you call a continent, but in Thyro we have higher standards than one whore in town." The monk stared vehemently at George.

"Well, maybe one day you can visit, and it'll be two." I said not looking up from the rifle, but I could still feel the gaze move from George to me.

Seiford bristled at that. "I wouldn't want to put your mother out of business." This time I did look up. "I heard an exceptionally charming pig came to town and you went hungry that winter." He stated in a matter of fact way.

George stared wide-eyed at both of us, horrified at what he heard, then looked down at the weapon in my lap. He knew Andrew could take the joke, but the last time he'd known me, I'd had a temper. That temper had played a large part in me joining the Constabulary. "I-" George started but was cut off by roaring laughter from me and an impish smile from the monk.

"Don't pay him any mind George." I choked out when I finally got my breath back. "Seiford's still a bit sore about how things turned out. Because of me, he'll never get to fulfill his lifelong dream of being the university pillow biter." The old teacher finally calmed down and even laughed nervously. Andrew who'd also been standing a bit straighter relaxed. He knew he wasn't about to have to pull me off someone.

"Oh, I stopped dreaming about that long ago." The monk said with a chuckle back. "Being the lover of a young, slightly less handsome Constable is more than any pillow biter could possibly hope for."

I smiled and went back to cleaning my rifle. I'd finally gotten all the rust spots off, but the barrel was still a bit rough. The long voyage at sea hadn't done the rifle any good. Salt water was the constant enemy of anyone who cared about proper weapon maintenance.

"What sort of musket is that by the way?" Andrew gave it a curious look.

"It's not a musket." I held it up gesturing to lever at the bottom. "A musket shoots once, and then you have to reload it." I pulled the lever down and cocked it to demonstrate the point. "Also it uses brass casings and clear powder like a six-shooter so the barrel stay's clearer." Then I turned the rifle around so Andrew could look down it. "It's a good thing too, the grooves would catch the residue of black powder."

"Ah, you could probably shoot three hundred yards out if you had too with rifling like that." George stared down it as well.

"I've seen him hit some of those hares from four hundred." Andrew shook his head at how ridiculous it was. "They were moving too."

"It can hit even farther if the shooters good and the winds not blowing too hard." I stroked the rifle like someone would a favorite dog.

Andrew nodded. "That's a clever contraption they've been trying to make a repeating rifle ever since that man Brown invented revolvers." My brother patted his own six-shooter. "The closest anyone's got since then was those breach loading ones ten years back. They were more accurate than anything we had before, but still." He said it almost to himself. "There's a rumor John Reard has finally cracked it, clever bastard that he is, but if he has, he's not producing them." Andrew looked up at me "Where'd you get that from?"

Seiford finally came back into the conversation, talking about gun mechanics bored him, but no one could tell a story better. "Well, you see back during the siege of Wuthold, the Duke promised a great reward to any man who could best the champion of the Westenland lord." His voice rose as he went into the story. "When on the third day Thomas Belson-"

"Yes, yes I know the story." George cut in much to Seiford's dismay. "He prayed for strength for one day, for wisdom on the second, and on the third the compassion to not take one more life than was necessary." The tutor waved it away.

Andrew picked up on it, excited by the old story "Then he met their man on the field who was so big a heard of oxen followed him as their leader." My brother gave a wry smile. "They battled, and Thomas got the upper hand but spared the man because his last wish was for his people, not himself."

"Yes, that's correct." Seiford was clearly agitated that someone else had told his story. "If you want to tell it like a professor would teach an unruly student math."

"But in that story, Thomas get's three wishes." Andrew said. It was my turn to be excluded from the conversation even if it was about me.

"Aye," Seiford was desperately trying to get ahold of the tale. "He was given seven arrows that could find the heart of any man no matter where he was in the world, a cloak lighter than death but stronger than a good man's will, and a kiss from the Duke's daughter who by all accounts is considered the finest beauty in Wuthland." The monk looked off remembering the girl well.

"So where'd the rifle come from?" Andrew cocked an eyebrow up.

I chuckled at that. "What actually happened is I waited three days so clouds would cover the sky and our enemy couldn't see us come over the wall." I pointed up at the moon. "I attacked in the middle of the night with three hundred picked men. I wound up sparing their champion because he hoped out his tent with both legs through one trouser hole fell on his head and knocked himself out." I finished the story.

"He was a rather large fellow, you must admit." Seiford shrugged.

"Aye, he was huge." I whistled at the memory of him. "It's a good thing he hit that rock before he got to me, or I would have shit myself." I said through a chuckle then went back to cleaning.

"You still could have taken him though right?" Andrew poked me to get my attention. "I hear you never lost a fight."

"It's more complicated than that." I rubbed the tattoo on my arm. "I know how to move in a battle, and there's a small handful of men who can hope to give me pause when I get started." I shrugged at that. "Still, they can hold me for long enough that another man can come and stab me in the back. The battlefield is a chaotic place as you well know." I sighed. "If I had fought him in single combat, I probably would have won. I've fought men that size before." I shook my head. "People don't offer single combat much anymore and never when I'm around. The way I did it cost the least casualties on both sides."

Andrew was clearly unsatisfied with that answer and let it show.

I sighed "Yes, I could have taken him." I touched the scar on my chest Thaniel gave me. "Only one man's ever beaten me in a fair fight," I paused, "and I got him in the end."

"And the rifle?" Andrew asked. "Where'd it come from?"

I smiled patting the rifle. "A gunsmith named Hurlch in Wuthland wagered me his finest weapon against my six-shooter," I patted the weapon at my side, "that I could route their army without firing a shot." I was lost remembering that day. "It was this rifle right here. A completely innovative weapon no one had figured out how to mass produce yet and still haven't."

George nodded. "Well, that explains the seven arrows story. I can see how that jump could be made from repeating rifle to magic arrows." He stared at the weapon. "I wouldn't make it," he gave Seiford a skeptical glare, "but I can see how some storyteller might." Seiford just shrugged. "Still there's a shred of truth in every story, so where'd the cloak, and kiss originate from?"

This time it was Seiford's turn. "They actually did give us some very handsome cloaks but he," the monk pointed at me, "lost his in a game of cards, and I woke up in a ditch one night after a bit too much to drink, and it was gone." He shook his head. "I think some smelly vagrant took it, and if they did, I don't want it back anymore." He sighed and looked down at his priestly blacks. "Besides it didn't go well with the uniform." He smiled up at George. "I took that kiss from his daughter if you want to know that part as well."

"You took more than a kiss as I remember it." I said through a laugh.

"You weren't complaining while you were with her pretty handmaid." Seiford's eyes were absolutely wolfish.

"That I wasn't." I conceded, smiling at the happy memory.

"So which one of you made up that story." George stared disapprovingly at both of them. "Legends like that spring up everywhere but not that quick."

"That'd be Seif." I nodded my head to the monk. "Telling tavern girls those stories is his favorite part of the job."

"Well, way to throw me under the carriage." The monk's scathing stare only made me laugh more.

George shook his head. "At least one of you knows the truth from an ass boil." He leveled his gaze at Seiford "There's a place for long tongued liars, as I'm sure you know being a monk and all. You ought to be embarrassed."

Andrew cut in to try and de-escalate the conflict. "They lived a hard life on the road." He shrugged. "Let them have some fun where they can find it."

"It's fun when it doesn't leave the tavern." George kept on his glare. "Half the world has heard those stories."

I was about to jump in, but the monk stopped me."So they have, and I'm not ashamed to have started them." Seiford looked back unflinchingly. Well, maybe a bit of flinch, but George had one of those disappointed stares that terrified students at the other end of it. To the monk's credit, he held up far better than I had when I missed a lesson because I'd drank too much the night before.

"And why is it that you're so unashamed?" George noticed that the monk meant what he said, and some questioning seeped into his face

Seiford went on. "Well, for three reasons." He held up three fingers then put them down. "One is that the so-called "leaders" of Thyro think far too little of their men and far too much about their power and their purse." He stared at me. "If they think that the other side has a man as invincible as those in the stories I've told, it might make them think twice about marching on their neighbors. It might even save a few lives."

"Fair enough point and curious to hear out of noble blood." George said grudgingly.

Seiford nodded. "Most men are blinded by their birthrights. I chose to let mine make me see clearer." It was said shortly and too the point, a far cry away from the usual idle chit chat we shared. "Two, the Demon-Speakers have been around for as long as men have written down history. Mothers tuck in their children to stories of what the great Old Priests of Imor accomplished with their mastery of the Powers Below before it fell. Sure, the Priests now are cheap imitations of the ones that lived a thousand years ago, and even the most ambitious won't attempt a fraction of what the Imorans did, but their strength is derived from the same place, and so their majesty is tied to that of their ancestors. The Constables came into being less than five hundred years ago. Of course, they're all mean warriors worthy of respect in every sense of the word. Sometimes they fail, though, and people know those stories too. While Thomas's true accomplishments are impressive to say the least, they aren't enough to offset that superstition. However, the legend he's become can. For the first time in history, people fear a tattooed arm more than they do one with a blood-colored robe, and both me and Thomas and any other man with half a brain knows that only evil comes from trusting Demons over man."

"Aye, I know that much." George looked down at his feet, sad for a reason I knew all too well. Andrew looked away as if ashamed. It spoke volumes, and the burn on my arm seemed to hurt a little more.

"The last and most important is that the stories I tell aren't lies." The monk looked at me like a drowning man looks at a piece of wood. "Sure, they don't always tell everything that happened exactly the way it did, but sometimes there's more truth in the stories than in the history books, and the truth I tell the people in every slum and inn is worth telling."

"And what is this truth then?" Andrew asked.

"It's that everyone from king to slave deserves a hero they can believe in. Someone to right the wrongs of a too often evil world. Someone to save them when their village is about to be plundered and burned. Sure, Thomas can't always be there, and most justice won't be served in this life, but that hope makes men strong. That hope makes children believe there's honor in the world and that means maybe they can grow to be honorable as well instead of wicked. Now I know better than any man alive that Thomas Belson the man isn't perfect, he's got as many faults as anyone who's lived a hard life. However, Belson the Blessed, Constable of the New Church and defender of the weak, is a beacon of greatness. Let all men try to reach it, sure they'll fail but there's a greatness in striving to be good, and that's what they'll achieve." We all watched Seiford like a prophet sent from above. Even Ayn-Tuk looked up approvingly. This was the Monks way. When he gave his sermons, they weren't to scare or push people into submission. They were meant to inspire men to greater heights. That was why I loved him. No matter how many times I veered from the path, Seiford was always there, never to scold, but to let me know of the man I could be.

"I think I like your way." George said with respect.

"Aye," Andrew nodded, "me too."

The monk bowed his head before he continued. "People think utopia will come after we've won our final war. After we've found the leader who can shoulder our doubts and fears. We believe that once we have righted the wrongs of this world and seen the end of injustice, then we will bask in the light of our perfect society. We believe that when that day is upon us, we will feast and be merry. All we need is the man who can take us there." Seiford shook his head. "Maybe we need to believe that, but history has proven us wrong. There have been a thousand victories for goodness in the world, and all should be remembered fondly." The monk gave a slight chuckle at that. "However, I believe in the end utopia is a small thing, and we'll hardly notice when it happens. There never has nor can there ever be a utopian world. Utopia comes from the soul, from the self. It is comforting to think that an army, emperor, or god will set it into our lap. No one can blame us when we fail. No one can blame us when we don't even try." Seiford looked up to the sky as if invoking the muse. "That is a lie though. It's a comforting one, but those are the most dangerous kind. The closest we will ever come to a perfect world is one where people are free to choose the right path. The closest we'll ever come to that mythical leader is one who inspires us to choose it. Forcing men to obey the right things is not the right way."

He looked around the campfire and smiled a sad smile. "Few will try, less will follow through, at least in the beginning. One day though, men will learn and tread that path not on their own, but of their own. The perfect world we seek lies in our hearts. The utopia we crave will be ours because no army, emperor, or god can ever take that from us."

"And you think Thomas could be the man to show us that way." Andrew asked with a new kind of pride in me.

"Aye, I think he can." Seiford leveled a happy look at me, but there was an edge to it, a challenge to take up the responsibility he laid at my feet. "Let that be our tradition. Let man look upon Thomas Belson and know there lies a better way. Let him inspire, but more importantly, let him show the world what it could be." I looked down at my feet. My soul called out to be the man Seiford wanted me to be, yet there was a demon inside me that I could never fully free myself from.

After a long silence, George finally broke it by saying. "Aye, and you're right on all accounts Seiford. You're a decent sort. I'm glad Thomas has you."

"So am I." I let the monk know with my eyes how much he meant to me.

"Thank you I just…" For once Seiford was at a loss for words.

"Did the Church teach you that?" Andrew asked after a minute of thinking what to say. "To tell those stories I mean."

He shook his head. "My brother did."

"He must be a good man." George looked sympathetically.

"He was. The best I ever knew." He looked up at me and smiled. I smiled back. "Well, tied for best I suppose, there's no shame in that." He took a breath to steady himself. "His name was Bradly. The type of older brother who comes off as a god. He joined the army when Thaniel started his Demon wars. He didn't want to fight anyone, but he wouldn't let poor men die in his stead because he had a fancy last name."

"That's an honorable way." Andrew seemed like he understood that.

"That it is." He paused again. "I would have followed him, I really would have." He looked like a child ashamed he'd left off of work and made his siblings do it for him. "Only I was too young and not in the greatest health. It's probably for the best though I'm no good at soldiering."

"I've seen worse." I said thoughtfully. "I've certainly seen better too, but worse is just as common." I looked at the rest of them. "His brother was my second. A better man I haven't met."

He nodded at me. "Anyhow, I used to tell my friends about how he'd come back with Thaniel's head on his sword. I used to say he was invincible. He was the greatest hero I'd ever needed, but he wasn't invincible in the end I suppose." He made a fake yawn and wiped away a tear. We saw it but had the decency not to say anything. "Anyhow, I figured if I had a hero like that, the rest of the world should too. He was the one who started telling me about Thomas. He's the reason I'm here." He finished defiantly.

I put my hand on my friend's shoulder, and he gave me a look of gratitude. He rarely told that story. I could only think of twice before, once to me and once to a princess he'd felt something other than lust for. Neither one of us were perfect men. Seiford could be a bit pompous at times, it went with the being nobility, and he could find trouble like a rat could find cheese. He also had a habit of sleeping with the wrong women, and me… Well, I had enough sins on me stain a brown shirt black. We'd been each other's only true friends for so long we couldn't imagine how it had been before.

Seiford tried to break the mood. "Besides, you must admit that getting a woman in bed is easier if you tell her you're traveling with the man who terrified an Ice Demon into giving us an early spring, rather than you spent three months freezing your balls off waiting for the snows to break."

I laughed at that. "I remember those girls in West Ventarii. It was hard enough to get the red-haired one into my bed, even with telling her about that Eastern Campaign." I gave out a great yawn. "Well, it's best we go to sleep now. If we get up early, we can get a head start to home." I did want to make good time, but mostly I needed the night to think.

I laid into my sleeping roll, but sleep was elusive. I hadn't seen home in a decade and a half. It was almost impossible to keep my mind off what it'd be like to finally get there. Of course, deep in my heart, I imagined a sweeping welcome home party. My family would embrace me as if no time had passed, women would swoon over the returning hero, and the men there would show me the respect my reputation deserved. In short, all the things that made my heart yearn for the Belson plantation would still be there, and all the things that had made me leave would have been gone and forgotten.

However, I'd learned in fifteen years of war that those thoughts only ever brought pain. My sister had grown from being a child to a woman, all while I was two thousand and more miles away. My mother wasn't the woman she used to be from what I'd heard. How would Sarah react? She was happy it sounded like, and I didn't know how to feel about that. The only thing that had gone the way I wanted it to, was perhaps my brother. I looked up at the night sky again. The sky was the same at least. Maybe that was all I could ask for, but my father wasn't here to share it with me.

I heard the other's breath fall into the rhythmic pattern of sleep. Then I heard footsteps move toward me. I looked up, expecting to find Seiford standing there, but it was Ayn-Tuk almost as black as the night that surrounded him. "We need to talk." He whispered it as to not wake up the rest.

"Well, that's a first. Is the world finally ending?" I chuckled to myself. "It's been threatening to for a while."

He didn't respond to my goading. His stoic face wasn't meant for trading glib comments.

I sighed, shifting my gaze back to the stars. "What do we need to talk about?"

Ayn-Tuk sat down next to me. "I know how it must feel to be so close to your home."

"Aye?"

"Aye."

"You've got any advice for me?" I was still half staring at the stars.

"A warning maybe." His eyes looked down upon me like a pair of stars in the moonlight. There was regret in those stars though.

"And what's that?" When Ayn-Tuk spoke, you listened. It seems the more a man holds onto his words, the more valuable they become.

"Things change when you're gone." The black warrior said. "It's not your fault, but it still stings." He paused for a moment, speaking of a past he could only hint at. "And I've seen you scratching at the tattoos on your arm."

"I thought it might be the mosquitoes." I mused, but Ayn-Tuk wasn't the sort of man you muse to.

"This isn't a joke," the black man sighed, "but you know that I think. Go to sleep we'll deal with whatever we find same as usual."

"Same as usual." I said, and Ayn-Tuk walked back to his bedroll. I listened as he eventually found sleep, leaving me to think through all the memories of home I'd kept close to my heart. I'd buried them years ago, never really expecting to make it back, but now maybe a couple days ride away they came back to me in a flood. I thought of the times I'd hunted with my father, and how happy it'd made him. I thought of the way I'd left as well. I felt a slight burn in my arm, and I reached over to scratch it away. Ayn-Tuk was right, this wasn't the place I'd left.

I fell asleep looking at the stars they were the same at least, trying not to think about how the man my father warned me against might be the one who came home.

"You killed me!" The corpse screamed.

The dog continued it's whining.

"Stop!" I screamed.

———————◆•◆•◆———————

I woke up to a shrill scream. Battle trained muscles sprung me out of my roll and into a fighting stance. One of my six-shooters was already in my hand. *Is it an ambush? Did they slaughter the watch? Did the enemy advance in the night?* All these thoughts went racing through my head. *I need to rouse the troops. I need to organize a defense. I need to fight!*

I looked around for my imaginary army, trying to spot my imaginary enemy. I finally realized where I was. There were no enemies here, just roads and friends, but I had heard something. I remembered what happened when I attributed a noise in the night to my nerves.

It was still dark out, and I was about to go back to sleep when I heard the scream again. This time it woke Andrew, and Ayn-Tuk came out of the shadows spear hoisted.

"What is it?" My brother asked me still wiping sleep from his eyes.

I was already on Shaggy, ready to ride. "Someone screamed to the west, and it was close." I said as I put my rifle in its holster on my saddle. "I'm going to take a look."

"I'm coming with you." Andrew was already strapping on his gun belt.

I was about to tell him to stay and guard the camp, but I saw the look in his eyes. I turned to Ayn-Tuk. "Stay here and keep Seiford and George safe."

He nodded.

Andrew was on his horse, and we rode to the sound. "What do you think it is?" He asked.

"Could be someone's horse fell and broke a leg." I shrugged. "Could be a pack of wolves." I pressed Shaggy Cow and rode hard. "There's a lot of things can make someone scream like that." My face went sterner. "Could be something else though."

Andrew nodded. He'd brought his old cavalry sword. I didn't share with him my thoughts on swords.

We rode west, cautious in the night, until we found what we were looking for. It was a carriage stopped in the middle of the road. There didn't seem to be anything wrong with it. Men were moving back and forth, and three people were tied up in clever knots. I could hear them speaking a dialect I didn't understand.

"They're Huegos." Andrew said, sure of himself.

"This far east?" I asked.

"Things change brother." The lines in his face told me it was true.

It was dark, but the moon let me see things clear enough. I counted at least twelve, probably more I couldn't see. It seemed like overkill for a stagecoach with three people in it. None of the people tied up looked like warriors.

"Where's the fucking money!" I heard one of the robbers scream.

"We don't have any money!" A man's voice screamed back.

"Fucking liar!" I heard the dull thump of a kick. By the ornate look of the coach, I had to admit he was probably lying.

"What are you going to do?" Andrew asked.

I stood up. "I'm going to stop them."

Andrew put a hand on my shoulder. "We need a plan. There's a lot of them."

I've got a plan." I said. "You're staying here. It's too dangerous." In reality, I could probably use him, but he was all I had of my family and my past. I couldn't see him hurt.

"I'm not going to let my brother, who I haven't seen in fifteen years, fight twelve men alone." He stood up too. "I'm coming."

I nodded. There was nothing I could say. Even if I told him to leave, he wouldn't listen.

We walked to the coach. "Ho there." I cried out. Every face turned towards me, even Andrew's. "How bout whoever's coach this is tells them where the money's at." I kept walking closer. "Then you leave, and no one get's hurt."

"He's a liar." The man I presumed as the leader of the raid aimed a kick square in the man's chest. "We want gold, and he gave us this!" He threw a wad of paper notes on the ground.

"That is money," I proclaimed proudly, "and a lot of it. Enough to buy you some new war paint huh?" I kept walking forward. Andrew followed.

"It's a white man lie." He spat on the money. The rest of the group was looking towards the fields, wondering how many men we brought with us more than likely. "This is paper, not gold."

"No," I shook my head, "that's what we call currency." I kept moving forward. We were only fifteen paces away now. "It represents gold. You give it to a banker, and they give gold back to you. It makes things easier!" I proclaimed the wonder of civilization to them.

"Thomas, I don't think this is the right time to explain economics to them." Andrew said.

"How many white men did you bring?" The leader asked. "Ten? Twenty?" He gestured back to his group. "A brave is worth a hundred of those!"

I put up two fingers. "Just the pair of us."

I saw the leaders face turn into a savage smile.

"Why the fuck would you tell them that?" Andrew gave an exasperated look.

The leader shouted some nonsense in his Huego language. It was probably kill them. Oh, I was willing to bet it was kill them.

The Braves started walking towards us, slowly. They didn't need to hurry to kill two men. They should have moved faster. It would have made it harder.

I pulled my six-shooter, and every round dropped a Huego. Andrew was just a half second behind me. I saw him kill two and wound another. It was good shooting for anyone who wasn't me.

Then I moved. The first Huego struck over my head. I jammed my fist into his jaw and stabbed him with my knife as I came around. Andrew had his sword out and was already beating the closest man, but there were still four others.

I pulled out my own Tomahawk and caught a blow from the next warrior. I glanced it by and buried my ax in his neck. Another one was already on me. He was quick, making me take a step back. Another had a chance to join in. One struck at me, but his hand went too wide. I cut the knife out of his grip and stuck my blade in his chest. I was about to square up with the other one, but Andrew cut him down from behind.

It was too quick. A couple heartbeats and twelve men became one. Only the leader was left. He backed away slowly realizing he was alone. He held his courage to the end though. He let out a violent war cry and charged me with a weapon that looked remarkably like mine. I hit him in the gut sending him into a fit, trying to gain back the air he'd lost. I didn't let him. I ran my knee into his face.

He fell back clutching his broken nose. I pulled out a knife and was on him already. "Why are you here?" I screamed at him.

He spat blood onto my shirt. I was about to hit him again, but then something started to happen. I shouted in pain as I felt the tattoos on my arm burn like wildfire. For a second the world was still then the Huego opened his mouth, and it seemed as if all the wind was being sucked into the man. More than that, all the world was going into him. I slit his throat, and the world returned to normal. It was largely anticlimactic.

"What the fuck was that?" Andrew gasped. It was probably the first tangible thing he'd ever seen of the Old Religion. Of course, he'd seen the crops grow taller than they had any right to be. He might have averted his gaze at one of the afflicted's screams. Who knows, maybe he'd even caught a whiff of plague nature hadn't architected. He'd never seen a Demon's true nature though. The Priests were too clever for that.

That was what bothered me. Putting a Demon-Bound, as powerful as this, on a lowly Huego highwayman was sloppy. Unless it wasn't. I was the greatest enemy of the Old Religion. I had chased it to the corners of the world. I had taught a lucky few how to armor themselves from it. For all that, I was always one step behind, and I knew it. Mother Vestia called me paranoid, the ones in power called me a fear-monger, only Seiford considered that I might be right. Still, he was far from being convinced.

I'd burn the web but never catch the spider. I'd ride into town, and overthrow whatever lord had been seduced by the power of the Old Religion. I'd see the Priests hung in the streets, let them know the age of mysticism was over. However, by the time I got there, the documents were already burned. A straw man was rustled up to put a noose around, but in my heart, I knew more powerful hands were moving the pieces.

When men told stories about my victories, the things they pointed at were honor, fearlessness, and strength. They played their part, but they were far from the real reason I'd been winning for so long. I had a conviction matched only by one man before me, even that in it of itself wouldn't have been enough. My real weapon was one of the most potent analytical minds in the world. I could calculate on thin evidence. I could see my move ten steps back. I knew I was being played.

There were quiet moments I wondered if everyone around me was right. Was I so used to fighting I turned shadows into enemies? Yet, someone has to cast a shadow. Why did all my decisive victories turn more complicated? Why try to hide everything if they were acting alone? I'd learned young, contradictions are what you call it when you don't have all the facts. Maybe the rest were just too afraid to look further. It's the truths we're scared to ask about that're important. If a man trusts his wife, he doesn't mind asking why she's home so late. If he doesn't, he'd rather avoid the answer until he's raising a child that looks nothing like him.

For years I'd been calling for the powers of Thyro to launch a full investigation. Mostly I was ignored. Sometimes they chose to humor me by sending a few uniformed officers to ask questions. They never treated it like a real threat. Part of that was Constables weren't secret police. I was meant for everyone to see as a visage of righteousness. They let me know I was out of my area of expertise. Another part was that they saw me as a tool they weren't sure they needed any more. The days of pitched battles and desperate wars were at an end in Thyro, or so they thought. They thought the same thing before Thaniel clawed his way to the throne. They'd treat me with respect because I'd earned it, but they were more than happy to have me on the frontier, fighting the last remnants of feudalism.

However, before long I'd started to think maybe there were more sinister reasons for their inaction. Maybe someone high up didn't want the truth to come out. *She*. I remembered the words of a dying priest. I'd seen her hand reach where I'd never expected it to. I was doubting all of my preconceptions about who was friendly and who wasn't.

When I'd been sent across the ocean, I even saw her hand there. Of course, I never doubted Mother Vestia, but she could have been maneuvered without knowing it. She could have been forced to cut me lose. The facts could be manipulated to tell a story about how I was growing too dangerous. I was a man of consequence. When I talked, Thyro listened. Now, I was halfway across the world. Even my voice couldn't reach that far.

As I stood in front of a man corrupted by the Powers Below, old fears began to well up. They'd only send a Demon-Bound for something important. Something important like me. They had to know twelve men, not even armed with guns, wasn't enough. Five thousand with three dozen Priests hadn't been enough. It was sloppy work, and she, whoever she was, wasn't sloppy. It had to be a play. A complicated move to shape my moves. *Do I pretend I never saw it? Is that what she's expecting me to do?* Intricate plots upon plots flowed through my mind.

However, maybe some Priest just got careless and wanted to flex his muscles. Maybe he didn't even know I'd be here. Still, I'd rather check the noise behind the bush before I wrote it off as the wind. People thought the world got safer when Thaniel died. Perhaps, the war just changed shape. It was hard to stay vigilant in a time when children grow fat and soldiers can sleep on watch. I never left the war, though. I was always struggling like Thaniel was on my heels. I'd been that way since I left God's Rest.

"Excuse me, Thomas," Andrew cut through my scheming, "you still haven't answered me. What the fuck was that?"

I cut out his tongue and put it in my pouch to investigate later. "You heard about those nationalist in Pyrene?" I asked.

"You mean the ones who strap dynamite to themselves and walk into government buildings?" My brother cocked an eyebrow up. "I've heard of them. Right foolish if you ask me."

"I agree." I looked down at the body. It had aged now. The Huego had gone from approaching forty, to not a day under mummified corpse from a forgotten millennium. I could have taken him to a university, and they'd have paid a fortune to study the man if I didn't mention he was only a couple minutes dead that is.

"What do those loons have to do with any of this?" Andrew kept on.

"This man is like one of those suicide bombers." I took out my six-shooter to reload it. "Except instead of dynamite they use Demons." I shook my head. "Instead of nationalism, it's the Old Religion." I paused remembering Fowstand. "Instead of a building, they can level a city."

"Oh." My brother nodded. "Oh!" Once it really hit him. "Should we burn the body? Should we check for more?"

I shook my head. "No, he's dealt with." I tapped my knife. "Besides, it's a rare phenomena. It takes more from the Priest than they're used to giving."

"You've seen this before?" Andrew asked.

"Aye." I made it obvious I didn't want to uncover that memory.

"So the Old Religion did this?" He kept his distance from the body. "I refuse to believe they'd bite our hand like that."

"Believe, what you want. The Old Religion doesn't have a master. It has temporary patrons." I looked at the corpse again. "Very temporary." I shook my head. "However, in a way you're right. The Old Religion is universal. Every culture stumbles upon it eventually."

"What do you mean?" Andrew asked.

"The Thyran variety is the most common, and the one your Priests practice." I shrugged. "It's not the only one, though. The Souren have Witch-Women. The Inte's have Howlers. The effects are usually similar, but the rituals are different." I kicked the body lightly, sending my brother stepping a few more steps back despite his courage. "Every variation leaves its imprint which I'm trained to read." I paused. "This wasn't done by anyone trained in the Thyran style."

"Who did it then?" He asked.

"When I studied at God's Rest I saw the symbol on his tongue once." I shook my head. "It was half mentioned, and no one could point to where it came from." I looked back at my brother. "It was never in a firsthand source, never someone who was there. Only whispers half-remembered." I put my pistol away. "The one word that stuck out was 'Hervad.'" I paused. "The closest thing in our language would be 'dangerous.'"

"Well, I'll say." My brother shook his head. "A whole city, really?"

"It's not just that." I thought of how to explain it. "Hervad is a word from the Eastern dialect. It means dangerous to the very fabric of reality. Dangerous to the borders between the sky and the underworld." I shrugged. "Even that's not really doing the word justice." Finally, I realized I was just scaring him in a way that was useful to no one. "We can talk about this later." I was going to show the tongue to Seiford. He knew more than me. Maybe George should see it as well. He was a leading expert on the Huego. "You did well." I walked up to my brother and put my hand on his shoulder.

"Not as good as you." He shrugged. "Six men with six shots! That's unheard of!" He swelled with pride at me being his brother.

"I've been doing this for fifteen years." I returned the shrug. "You hit three with your quick draw, and I see you know how to use that sword of yours." I gave him the stare a proud brother should always give. "If I had to go into battle, I'd want you with me."

I meant it. Comparing someones martial virtue to me was futile, but Andrew was good. Of course, people had been telling me that since I got off the boat. However, in my mind, he was still the thirteen-year-old boy I'd left him as. I saw that he'd become a man in every sense of the word. He'd kept a cool head when we were outnumbered six to one. He fought bravely, but also with a careful training. I'd seen a number of great warriors in my day, but very few matched who my brother had become. If tonight was any indication, he'd earned his hero title.

Finally, a stirring from one of the captives reminded us we weren't alone. I was a bit embarrassed because if they hadn't squealed a bit, I might have forgotten them. I took my long repeating rifle off Shaggy and surveyed the surroundings just in case there were more to come. I also kept my ears on Andrew as he cut the bindings away. I still wasn't sure they weren't part of a ruse.

I'd counted three bodies tied up. They'd been bound, gagged, and blindfolded, so it was impossible to say what they really looked like. One seemed to be a woman, the other a man about me and Andrew's age, the last was a plump gentleman, probably the coach driver. I knew they were rich from the look of their carriage. Odds were they were Southern aristocrats.

Finally, I heard Andrew fight away the last of the ropes. "Alexander Gondua!" I heard him shout. "Good to see you again."

I moaned to myself. I remembered Alexander. As a boy, he'd noticed a piece of snot hanging from my nose. He'd taken to calling me Booger Belson. A name that had stuck with me till the day I left. I was not a fan of Alexander Gondua.

"It's good to see you as well." I heard the patting of them embracing. Of course, Alexander had always liked Andrew. Everyone liked Andrew. My brother made fast friends with senator's sons and stable hands. He could make you feel like he saw what made you special. The thing was Andrew genuinely meant it.

I heard him free the next captive. "Are you alright sir?" Andrew asked.

"Quite fine thanks to you." I heard the plump stagecoach say. "It's a shame to have failed in my duties.

"Nonsense," Andrew said. "There were twelve of them. You made the right choice."

I kept my watch on the perimeter.

"Rachel!" I heard Alexander embrace the last captive. I remembered Rachel as well. She'd been seven when I left. A skinny girl who's face was too big "I haven't seen you in ages." She'd always been a bit annoying. I'd never liked her much by virtue of being a Gondua. "How long have you been in Thyro?"

"Five years." I heard a low voice respond. It was a lovely voice I had to admit.

Finally, I turned around, convinced we weren't going to be set on again. As I looked at Rachel, any thoughts of suspicion went away from me. She'd been on the road, and most recently tied up and bound. Yet somehow she looked like she was ready for a ball. Her eyes were bright and blue as they looked up at me. Her black hair seemed to curl around her face as if even it wanted to be closer to her. She had the sort of look men carve into stone. The sort of beauty you imagine Emperors might start a war to hold for a night. She was wearing a puffy dress in what I assumed was the current style, and yet it seemed as if the style wanted to be with her not the other way around. I could see the faint outlines of her body. A mystery that needed to be explored.

I had a number of witty comments prepared, but they all left me as the air went out of my lungs. The surprise of seeing a girl like her was like being thumped with a musket. She was the sort of lady you wished was a hair less attractive so you could talk to her. The sort of lady who even thinking about feels like a sin.

I stood there, rifle hanging dumbly in my hand. It made me want to fight, to show her I could do something. It made me afraid, a strange emotion. I didn't want to talk for fear of stumbling over my words. If Seiford were here, he'd know what to say.

Alexander broke the tense silence, or maybe it was only tense to me. I hoped it was only tense to me. For all that, Rachel kept looking at me and I at her.

"We were headed to your plantation for the ball." Alexander

rubbed his hands. "We may not have gotten there, if not for you and your man." He took a few steps towards me. "I've never seen shooting like that. Whatever Andrew's paying you, I'll double it."

I finally tore my eyes away from Rachel to look at her brother. He was a handsome man by anyone's measure. His sharp green eyes looked like he considered touching me a favor. His strong chin jutting out to make sure the rest of the world was under it. His hair was meticulously groomed, and the way he looked at my ragged scalp told me he didn't approve. He wasn't quite arrogant enough to talk down to someone he'd just seen do what I did, but I could tell he wanted to. He'd seen the way I stared at his sister, he didn't like it. To him, I was just some rogue probably off the frontier.

"That's not necessary." I shook his hand. Alexander released it and tried to wipe my filth away.

"Oh, I insist." He took a wad of money from his pocket and pressed it into my hand. It was a lot, enough for a man to buy a reasonable house in the West. No doubt that's where he wanted me.

I shook my head, trying to hand it back.

"Do not refuse it." I saw then it wasn't really about the money. As it stood, I was the one in power. I'd saved him. He wanted to take the money so my saving him was just an extension of his wealth. It was a flawed way to look at the world, and I wouldn't play into it. He was the kind of Confederacy man who envied the power the lords of Thyro had. In his mind, he should have had the authority to hang a man who offended him. People should do as he wanted because his family was old, and he was constantly maneuvering to make the South more like that.

"I'm afraid I have to." I put the money back in his hand.

Rage started to well up in his eyes. He was about to let it loose, except Rachel stopped him.

"Alexander, stop being a fool!" She stepped towards me. "This is Thomas Belson." She smiled. "Belson the Blessed."

Present Day

We decided to take them with us. Actually, I insisted. I told everyone it would be unchivalrous leaving the party to be set on again. Really, I just wanted to watch Rachel. That's all I had in mind at the start. I just liked seeing her. Anyone who's ever been infatuated with a girl will understand. Anyone who's ever had to answer the question of why they went to the store across town rather than the one next to their house could probably understand as well. There was nothing sinister to it really. You didn't want to leer at her when you thought she wasn't looking. You didn't make clumsy passes at her that were doomed to failure anyway. You nodded politely to whoever it was that caught your fancy and went about your business. However, the next time you needed eggs you'd still walk to the shop across town despite the store next to you selling them just as good for just as cheap on the off chance you might get the pleasure of nodding politely to a girl you were sweet on.

Rachel decided to ride her own horse the rest of the way. George knew her too and apparently had tutored the girl. I learned from listening to their conversations, she'd been a student at LeSalle University, the most prestigious college in the Confederacy. She had a quick wit to match her education. I watched her verbally spar with every man in the convoy and come out the better. Except when she went over to Ayn-Tuk. She looked a little embarrassed coming back from that one. I wish I could have heard what the black man said. I also learned Andrew had planned a party for me without my consent.

I was thirty years old, and Thomas fucking Belson to boot. She made me feel like a child all the same, constantly looking over her way, only to avert my gaze when she returned the look.

Finally, I worked up the courage to ride up next to her. I was going to ask about the bandits of course. I was a constant professional with absolutely no ulterior motives. "Were there any others that got away?" I'd ask. "Did they come for anything specific?"

She saw through it almost immediately. "Oh, your damsel doesn't need saving anymore, Thomas." Rachel gave me a knowing smile. "I'm quite sure you got them all."

"I was just asking." I scratched my head. "It seemed strange is all." I started to turn Shaggy away realizing I was out of my depth, but she stopped me.

"That doesn't mean you should leave!" She called after me. "It's a sin to send an interesting person away." She patted the side of her horse. "Stay!" She said. "Talk to me."

Shaggy went back to her side dutifully. "Interesting?" I asked. I knew I was interesting, of course. My story was told in every place drunk men gathered. The historians at Harfow had an entire wing in their university devoted to the study of me. I was reasonably sure half the men who fought for me only did so out of a queer curiosity, but I wanted to hear her say it.

Rachel disappointed me and yet somehow impressed me at the same time. "Well, I was more or less talking about your horse." She stroked Shaggy's head. "That's an Eastern mount isn't it?"

"Oh, yes she was given to me as a colt when I fought for Khan Haldow five years ago." I smiled. "I lead the main force away so he could…" Slowly I realized bragging wouldn't help me. "Well, that's another story."

"I've heard tales about these horses," she kept petting Shaggy, "small but faster and stronger than anything in Thyro." She cocked her head to one side. "I've read her genealogy. She's mixed with the Noble Blood too."

"Where'd you find Shaggy's genealogy?" I asked.

"Where all secrets are held," she looked up at me, "the library."

"Oh." I didn't know how to respond to that.

"I heard she's smart too." She went back to the horse. "It's a shame you named her Shaggy Cow."

"Well, she's got a sense of humor." I patted my mount lightly. "Not many people know her real name."

"I'm not many people, then." She let the words shake me.

"I suppose, not." I scratched the back of my head again. I was painfully aware of my failings. My face had been left ugly after years of war. The hero reputation helped with girls sometimes, but it wasn't generally enough. Once they got past the novelty of meeting a hero, the truth started to seep in. I was ill-tempered, poorly mannered, and painfully arrogant. Women not half of her had laughed me off. Sometimes they liked me, but it had to be the right kind of woman. She was too much for me, clever, good breeding, *beautiful*. Still, it seemed like she wanted me to keep talking, so I did.

"You've grown since I left." It seemed a stupid thing to say, even to me. "The last time I was here you were barely seven."

She chuckled at that. "The last time I saw you, you were fighting a mule, because you claimed to have seen it bite a mare on the ass."

"Well, you know me always coming to the defense of helpless mares." I looked at her eyes. I'd seen so many different women. I was sure I'd seen more beautiful, but for the life of me, I couldn't remember when. I hadn't even thought Lady Gerate so pretty. She had other qualities, though. She made me happy. If I could've had Abby beside me, I would have, but Rachel was a close second in that moment.

"Always." She smelled nice, not overpoweringly so, just nice.

"Was it a big mule?" I asked. Her hair looked pitch black against her fair skin. I'd always preferred my women a bit darker, but she was doing fine work to combat my preconceptions.

"Not really," She gave me a pitying look, "and you were losing."

"I'm sure it just looked that way." I tried to regain some of my pride

"It didn't. That mule really trounced you." She looked down and then back up to give me a soft smile. It was a completely unfair tactic, but very effective as most unfair tactics tended to be. She sighed, letting the air of indifference fall from her face. "Then I went to visit Thyro for a time and heard some strange things about that boy who had lost a fight to a rather small mule."

"Oh." I was a bit surprised. "What sort of things?" *The things that make kings tremble. The things that make the weak rise up and become the strong.* I knew that answer well enough already.

"The sort of things that make a young girl swoon." Rachel rolled her eyes sarcastically. "The sort of things that make a man seem overpoweringly interesting and mysterious." This time it seemed a bit more serious. Perhaps it was just my imagination playing on me, though.

"What were you doing in Thyro?" I asked.

"Lots of things." Rachel's eyes looked positively scandalous. "Mostly studying though."

"What'd you study?" I was desperately trying to keep the conversation going.

"Medicine, mathematics, literature," she listed them off, "anything I hadn't already learned in the Confederacy, really." She turned her gaze back at me. "My area of expertise was the Thaniel Wars, though."

"Aye." For a moment my mind was torn off her, and back to a distant memory. A time of pure battle, of life and death. It seemed like ages now. It seemed like yesterday too. I remembered who I was talking to. It made me uncomfortable in a different way than her off-putting beauty. If she studied me with the same diligence she studied everything else, she might know some things. Things that weren't exactly a secret but not common knowledge either. She might know about the allies I took. She might know how powerless I'd been at the end of it all. She might know about the Pillars. "Those were dangerous times." It was all I could say.

"The times of heroes usually are," she gave a coy smile, "but they also make for some interesting tales." She eyed me up like a cat would a bird. "Tell me something interesting, Constable Belson."

That caught me off guard, but I rebounded as best I could. "There's a type of frog in Souren that can-"

"Change its sex." Rachel waved it away. "Every one's heard about that." She urged me on. "Try again."

I clinched my jaw thinking desperately. My mind wasn't working quite at smoothly as it usually did, and no man wants to waist an opportunity for conversation with a beautiful woman. "The Souren believe the moon-

"Was once the farm of the wicked god Tu'knuh before Man stole all his water." She finished for me again with a chuckle "I have read a book before, Thomas." I gazed on her face that, to me, seemed a heart shaped porcelain statue, with emeralds for eyes. I was determined to say something interesting.

"So you want to hear something that can't be found in a library?" I said it as a challenge.

"Yes," she steered her horse closer to me, "something that can't be found in a library."

I went to my emergency stories. "The Baroness of Kint-"

"Still breastfeeds her fourteen-year-old son." She rolled her eyes. "Old news."

I was growing frustrated. "Lord Halus-"

"Publishes erotic mystery novels under the pseudonym Jorge Hard." She shrugged in a way that brought my gaze to her chest for a moment too long. "I've read a few. They're not half bad."

I quickly racked my brain for any interesting tidbit that could impress Rachel. "I bet you didn't know that Earl Palazo-"

"Wears a dress each night and holds tea parties with stuffed animals." She cocked an eyebrow up.

That caught me off guard. "I was going to say he had a tattoo." I took a moment to take in her comment. "Is that true?"

"It is." Rachel smiled in a way that made me lose all control of my eyes again. "I thought that Belson the Blessed might have something more interesting than court gossip."

I finally got a grip on my thoughts. She had challenged me, and I would answer.

"So it's a secret you want my lady?" I gave a wry smile.

"Yes, a secret." She answered. "I'm sure you know one."

I nodded and put on the mask of a famed adventurer. "Fifteen years I've roamed this world. Fifteen years I'd led armies down paths others had refused to walk. I have seen many questions answered, many riddles unraveled. Beneath the desert sun and atop the highest mountains, I've heard ancient wisdoms and seen horrible paradox. Is this the sort of secret you want to hear?"

"Yes." Her eyes shouted excitement and I knew I had her.

I pressed my advantage. "I've sought out wise men and mystic sages to solve the puzzles in my heart. Surely the answer must be a dark mystery. That's how the stories went anyway, but I'd been in those stories, mysteries were just things you didn't know yet. Mysteries are more valuable lusted over than when you hold them in your hand. This was true of all currencies but doubly so for mysteries.

"The truth is that the more you know, the less it means. Those sages and wise men, did not give me enlightenment. They took what was most precious. Possibility is always more beautiful than certainty. Theres precious few things so magnificent that the imagination doesn't think could be better.

"Fifteen years I've roamed the world. Fifteen years I've led armies down paths others had refused to walk. I have seen many questions answered, but only twice was the answer more valuable than the question. You scoff at two, but I count myself lucky to have them. Search your own soul. How many do you have?

"I know many secrets worth admiring from afar, but only two worth holding in my hand. The first I have sworn to never speak of. I swore it not on the Three Above or the Demon's below. Oaths said to such things are always broken. I swore it on nothing because I could never break nothing. This answer would die with me, and the world would be better for it.

"The second I speak of often and freely because there is wisdom in the second secret, though I am not wise enough to find it.

"The second secret is the Thro'ncat.

———————◆◆◆◆◆———————

At the siege of Ostin an old mercenary had come and pledged me his service. He seemed a fighting man, so I offered him a fair pay. He refused. He needed to get to the city and would not say why. Naturally, speculation began immediately. *Was a secret lady love trapped inside? Was it a debt of vengeance that needed to be paid?*

When the battle started the mercenary fought as I'd never seen a man fight. He nearly carried the defenses singlehandedly. Seiford and I followed him through the city. *Was there a priceless gem hidden away? Perhaps secret magics slumbered in Ostin, and he hoped to awaken them!* Seiford and I saw it as our civic duty to find out.

He walked directly towards the palace, and we thought we had our answer. *Surely he is a lost prince come to claim his birthright!* He passed it up and did not look back.

Next he walked to a beautiful temple built in honor of a god who's name had long slipped from human memory. *He must be a priest looking for absolution from an ancient deity.* That would make quite the story. He paused momentarily to get his bearing and started due west.

Finally, we came upon the magnificent library of Ostin. Ostin had a reputation for the place a man went to for true learning. There are bigger collections of books in the world to be sure, and I'd seen a few of them. However, those had been carefully curated by powerful people who wanted to keep their secrets secret. Finally, Seiford and I knew. *He is a scholar in search of forbidden knowledge!* That would be quite the twist! The man looked nothing like a scholar.

It certainly showed the two of us not to let a man's appearance hide his true nature. We were quite happy with this parable, made all the more valuable because we had lived through it. Both monk and Constable counted themselves lucky to have been handed such precious wisdom.

A scholar... Fascinating!

And alas he was not. The man didn't even slow down as the library disappeared behind us.

Finally he reached a completely unremarkable merchant quarters, went down an unremarkable alley, sat down before and unremarkable wall, and pulled an unremarkable ball out of his pocket. He threw the unremarkable ball at the unremarkable wall and caught it in his unremarkable hand, over and over again. Seiford and I watched for an hour before I finally broke my peace.

"Whatcha doin?" I asked.

"Thro'ncat." He responded.

Seiford and I didn't wait till the ball left his hand again before we were tearing apart the famed Ostin library. *Thro'ncat!* Perhaps it was a mediative state one used to find true enlightenment. Perhaps it was a word of power that one must spend a lifetime pondering. I held that it was an ancient fighting style that allowed a warrior to vanquish their enemies.

In my defense it seemed plausible at the time. Though Seiford mocks me for it now, he didn't find it half so ridiculous at the time.

I'd seen him fight on the walls. I can count on one hand those that could best me in single combat. Amongst them were the most powerful ruler in living memory, a prince from one of the greatest dynasties in Thyro, a very angry blacksmith, a monster so ancient and evil that the Three Above wept for it, and worst of all, a goat named Sir Hoofington. There were more than that who could claim a victory, but those were more complicated stories. Only five could meet me sword in hand with a chance at victory. I got them all in the end, except the damn goat.

Though it galled me to admit it, this mercenary might be the one to make me use two hands when I complete the list.

We searched the library for a week. Finally, Seiford noted the mercenary had a slight Rhorii accent, but that didn't make any since. We both spoke flawless Rhorii and the word was a mystery to us. We needed an expert.

The two of us heard about a famed scholar from Rhorii visiting for research, and put the mystery that was the thro'ncat at this man's feet.

"You mean throw and catch?" He asked.

"No Thro'ncat."

"Yes, throw and catch."

I pulled his bookcase down in spite, and Seiford who was taking it even harder than me, knocked a boiling tea kettle into his lap. If the lawsuit the scholar brought against us was true, my monk had done *significant damage to four irreplaceable texts*.

We didn't even care enough to show up to the courthouse. We spent two more weeks searching the library for answers before we once again stood before the Thro'ncat wall.

"You're playing throw and catch?" Seiford asked hoping he was wrong.

"Yep. Thro'ncat." The mercenary didn't even look up.

Seiford cursed in at least six languages, and swore on things that damn near made my ears bleed.

A thought struck me. "Did you grow up here."

My monk gave me a nodding approval seeing where I was going with the question. Perhaps he was a man ground down by a hard life, looking to rekindle the joy of his childhood once more. That made sense.

"No never been to Ostin." He shrugged without looking at us. "Just heard this was a fine wall for it."

"Heard from who?" Seiford asked.

The mercenary caught the ball and paused to think for a moment. "You know, I can't remember." He threw the ball with a chuckle. "Damndest thing that."

Over the next few weeks we brought holy men of various religions, community leaders of known integrity and wisdom, even an avowed soothsayer who claimed to posses the ability to see into the spirit world.

The answer was always some variation of; "Please we have more important things to do."

The final straw was when I kidnapped the head doctor of the local hospital and bid him check the man's head for trauma. When we took him to the spot, he turned to my friend. "Brother Seiford, by your reputation you're a man of science and logic." He gestured to me. "Talk sense into this Constable."

Seiford had my six-shooter pointed at him before I realized it was gone.

"Check him." The monk said cocking hammer back to accentuate the point.

The doctor obeyed and declared that there was nothing medically wrong with the man.

Seiford shoved him against the wall and jammed the barrel of my six-shooter down his throat. "He's lying, Thomas! Beat the shit out of him." For the first and last time in our relationship, I restrained him, and not a second too soon. The monk was a hairsbreadth away from painting that alley with doctor brains.

I lost count of how long we watched after that, but it was summer when we started, and I remember snow falling. The man did sleep occasionally and took breaks from time to time for food or to relieve himself, but usually he just played Thro'ncat.

Seiford lost his nerve and broke. "I'm doing it."

"Don't! It's too dangerous." I tried to stop him, but he would not be deterred.

The monk walked in front of the mercenary and caught the ball mid air. I had a gun under my coat trained at his head in case the man was driven to homicidal rage. I was so nervous I nearly shot when Seiford grabbed the ball.

"Sir, I must protest." Seiford said in his most authoritative voice. "You are no longer allowed to play Thro'ncat here."

We'd spoken about this plan a few times, but I'd written it off as too risky. Seiford had the idea that there are some children born *touched*. Often times, these children became attached to a favorite toy. Any attempt at separating this toy was met with distress from the child, and even more distress from the thief as they tried to fight off a murderous child clawing at their eyes.

If we garnered this reaction, we could put him in that category. Perhaps he was a child who had been cured and relapsed. It seemed unlikely such a lad could have a successful career as a mercenary, but I'd seen stranger.

"That's fine." He stood up and gave a mighty stretch. "I know this game drives some people crazy."

Seiford looked at me then back to the mercenary. "Can I keep the ball?" He finally asked.

The man shrugged. "Sure. Balls aren't very expensive." He

scratched his head as if embarrassed. "Besides..." He started, then shook his head. "Never mind."

"Besides what?" Seiford demanded.

"Besides, you and your friend don't seem in the best mental health." His eyes darted between the two of us. "If the ball brings you comfort, who am I to deny you?"

Seiford tossed the ball back to him. "You know what I changed my mind."

The mercenary caught it. "Are you sure?" He asked. "Wouldn't want to put anyone out."

Seiford nodded. "I insist."

We watched him for a while longer. Finally, I tried one last time. "Say you want a drink? I'm buying."

"I'm fine." He didn't look up.

"What about opium?" I asked and didn't get an answer, so I prodded a bit more. "It's pretty fun."

"Gives me a headache."

"How about a woman." It was the final desperate card I had to play.

Amazingly, he stopped playing Thro'ncat and turned to look at me. His gaze was truly startling.

I felt my heartbeat rise. "I'll pay for one. The finest I can find."

Then he spoke the last words we'd ever hear him say. "Girls are shit at Thro'ncat."

Shortly thereafter a representative of the people came to inform us we had been tried for several crimes and had failed to appear in court. For this we were presumed guilty, but I was assured there was enough evidence to convict even if the King John himself spoke on my behalf. He was somewhat worried about that, as my early career had left me well loved in that nation

I assured the representative it was unlikely the good sovereign of Anthanii would come to my defense because that would require work, and in the five years I'd spent saving his nation, I'd never once seen him do anything even remotely resembling work.

I also informed him that whatever punishment the court of Ostin had settled on would not put them afoul of Anthanii, a matter which was clearly weighing on the poor fellow. In fact King John had his own prescription for me. I was to be hung and quartered. After that unpleasantness, my remains were to be buried in an unmarked grave, bound with salt and iron.

The representative told me this was no time for jest, so I showed him the royal edict of the Anthanii court, making the official opinion on Thomas Belson quite clear. He believed the language used unsuitable for legal documents but agreed that the seal was quite authentic.

King John's wife, ever the more creative of the two, had issued her own declaration on my person involving a honeycomb, three angry badgers, and a national holiday ever after. However, due to some clever legalese Brother Seiford had devised, this declaration only held weight in three provinces, none of which had a native badger population. We thought ourselves mighty clever for this.

The representative agreed that producing three badgers was unworkable and that while the influence of Anthanii was respected in Ostin, the actual edict was too foul to be read in court or really anywhere honest folk might hear, so we were spared that fate as well.

Instead, we had earned somewhere between sixty to eighty lashes for kidnap, assault, and other various crimes that the good and godly people of Osten should not be forced to endure. However, because I had won a certain leniency for my actions during the siege of Ostin, the whole thing would be forgotten if we left town immediately and never returned. There's been some black spots on my ledger, but the New Church went frantic trying to cover up that particular embarrassment.

The mercenaries last words were as sage as his first. Girls were shit at Thro'ncat. This is not idle sexism. We tested it scientifically with women of various ethnicities and cultures, from barmaids to duchesses. There was even a princess we studied with a bloodline that could be traced back to the God-Kings of Imor.

This caused quite a scandal, and only the swift intervention of Mother Vestia, Viverent, and secretly prince Edward, all of whom were held in high esteem, saved us from further trouble. They all assured the girl's father that, yes, we were every bit stupid enough to ask her play Thro'ncat with us. This defense worked much better than the one Seiford and I had devised in our drunken stupor. It hinged on the fact that while the nobility of Thyro's characterization of us as degenerates was not entirely unearned, we were cunning degenerates. If we had intentions of luring his daughter into an alley for unclean deeds, we would have chosen the prettier one. Instead we picked the one with manish shoulders, for science's sake of course.

If you ask me, the real scandal was that a princess of the blood would agree to accompany two men of high reputation and low repute into a dark alleyway without supervision. While I would never impugn a lady's honor, I will suggest that she was more excited than was appropriate when Seiford began digging around in his pocket and more disappointed than was becoming when he presented her with nothing more than a ball. I knew more then I'd care to admit about disappointed women too.

Despite the lengths we went to in the name of science, we came to the same conclusion as did the noble mercenary. Women are shit at Thro'ncat. We originally believed this was due to a basic lack of athleticism, but further investigation dismissed this.

We came to believe that Thro'ncat is an endeavor that involves more of the soul than the body. A far more workable hypothesis is that women are utterly and completely without souls. If more evidence is needed, watch a father of multiple girls in a tavern. Observe how many beers he can drink before he starts crying. I have never met such an afflicted individual make it past four.

However the real value of Thro'ncat goes even beyond an exploration of delicate gender relations. There's wisdom in that story even if I don't quite know what it is. The objectivity of Seiford and myself may be suspect in this case, but it should be known that the greatest mind of our age, Viverent, asked what secrets I had learned in my journeys. I told him countless worth admiring from afar, but only two worth holding in my hands.

He asked what they were.

I told him the first was a secret so powerful that it could spell humanities complete and total destruction. I had sworn upon nothing to keep it, and so nothing could break that oath. That secret would die with me. *Do not ask more.* I told him. *For knowing could be the end of all things.*

Because Viverent was an intellectual worth his salt, he peppered me with questions before I finished speaking.

Then I told him about Thro'ncat. He forgot about the first secret almost immediately.

Yes, there was wisdom in the second secret, though I am not wise enough to find it. For this reason I tell the second secret often and freely, so that another might untangle the meaning. It doesn't do so well at parties, but that hasn't stop Seiford and I from spending many a pleasant evening pondering the elegant enigma that was Thro'ncat.

Thro'ncat
Thro'ncat
Thro'ncat

"Thomas…"

"Thomas!"

I finally pulled myself away from the Thro'ncat and saw George riding next to me with a quizzical, vaguely worried look on his face.

"George!" I muttered. "Sorry about that. I must have dozed off in the saddle." I glanced up at the sun and figured I'd lost an hour.

"You were quite awake." He shook his head. "Muttering about Thro'ncat. Every once in a while you'd mention something about badgers, but mostly Thro'ncat."

"Where's Rachel?" I looked around. "I was telling her a story."

"Once you started muttering with herself she went back to ride with her brother for a bit." George looked me up and down. "What'd they do to you in Thyro?"

I waved the comment off. "I should go apologize." I pulled the reigns of Shaggy, but my old tutor stopped me.

"You should, but maybe wait a while." George scratched the back of his head awkwardly. "I think she found the whole thing a bit off-putting."

"Damn." I cursed myself. "You think so?"

"I do." The tutor answered.

I pulled a little rubber ball out of my saddle pack and let it fly at nothing in particular.

"Missed again." I muttered to myself.

The worried expression on George's face became more pronounce. "What were you aiming at?"

"The truth of all things."

"Huh…" George humored me, "You ever hit it." He asked the same question that boy at the docks had.

"No but I met a man once who couldn't miss." It was the response I always gave.

While I was upset to have wasted my chance at conversation with Rachel, I needed to talk to George and Seiford about what happened to the Huegos anyway. By the time I'd said my peace, the girl would have forgotten my indiscretion.

"Seif!" I hollered at the monk and waved him over.

"Thro'ncat?" Seiford asked.

"Thro'ncat." I nodded back. "Still, there's something else on my mind." I pulled the tongue out of my pouch and tossed it to them. "This mean anything to either of you."

"It's a tongue!" George recoiled in fear. "It means someones missing one."

I rolled my eyes. "I mean the marking on it."

"Oh." George took a closer look. "I've seen that symbol once." He paused. "Huego put it on unholy ground as a warning."

"So it's Huego?" I asked. "I had my suspicions." I cocked my head to the side. "Never knew the Huego to speak with Demons."

The tutor shrugged. "Me either. It's a huge taboo in their culture. Unlike every other people in the world, they know how dangerous it can be. If they hear even a rumor someone's been up to it, they kill everyone around and salt the field." He handed it to Seiford. "Did the former owner of this one dabble in sorcery?"

"He was Demon-Bound." I answered.

"Demon-Bound?" Seiford studied it. "You sure?"

"I've killed enough of them to know."

"That's powerful sorcery." The monk said.

"Demon-Bound?" George cut in. "I've never heard of that."

"There's a reason you haven't." Seiford said. "It's a relic of the time before the Nameless Man. The New Church hadn't seen it in centuries. They thought Thomas and I were just being paranoid but the effect became too..." The monk trailed off, looking for the proper word. "Noticeable to ignore."

George narrowed his eyes. "I think you mean more than noticeable."

"He does." I cut in. "Powerful people have Priests put a Demon inside a man. Eats away what makes him human. The effects differ from person to person." I gritted my teeth. "Soldiers who won't stop killing even after you cut their head off, warriors who can shoot fire out of their fingers, even women who can manipulate the mind of a strong-willed man with just a stare." I paused. "Priests rarely use them."

"Why's that?" George asked. "Seems like a useful thing if you lack the moral compass."

This time Seiford answered. "Man and Demon weren't meant to co-exist like that. Eventually, the creature they create goes out looking for vengeance on the one who made them."

I shook my head. "Even the Priests have some twisted sense of right and wrong, probably from the small part of them that's still human." I paused. "I've been around this world and hung every variant of Old Religion practitioner there is."

I paused. "In the end, they won't beg forgiveness for torture, rape, or genocide. Not even for the other crimes I won't speak of now because you wouldn't be the same afterward you knew." I hung my head. "They beg forgiveness for making a Demon-Bound, though, and they mean it."

George seemed shaken by that. It's a hard thing to realize how much evil there really was in the world. It's a hard thing to know some stories get so bad even poets haven't figured out the words to explain them. Still, my tutor only saw the drawing, and it was enough to stop even his inquisitive mind. Seiford and I had seen them with out own eyes. I'd like to say we didn't go mad because we were strong, but I knew that was a lie.

I was only still sane because I had him. He was only still sane because I needed him to be. Sane might even be too strong a word. It was more like we were clutching the side of a cliff, and neither of us would fall while the other was holding on.

George finally spoke again. "If it's as bad as you say, why do the Priests create them? They've got power enough. Why now after five-hundred years?"

"They were scared." I tried to leave it at that.

"Of?" My old tutor pressed on.

I turned the full weight of my gaze on him. "Me." It was barely a whisper, but it stopped him from pressing on.

"What kind of Demon-Bound was he?" Seiford asked to change the subject.

I sighed. "A Powder Keg."

"Really?" Seiford asked. "Haven't seen one of those since Fartow."

George looked confused. "Fartow? That city so destroyed by plague no one bothers to go near it?"

"When we were there it was healthy and peaceful." I said.

"Someone set a trap for us." Seiford shook his head. "Blind luck we'd gone to the outskirts of the city to inspect a farm."

I shook my head. "It wasn't lucky for them, though." It was another of my failures. Fifty-thousand lives lost in an instant. I should have realized it was too easy. That was the price for one moment of complacency. There was a reason men called me paranoid.

Seiford saw my distress and picked up where I left off. "We made up the plague story to keep people away and avoid a panic."

George seemed skeptical. "I've never known a story about plague to avoid a panic."

"Better than the truth." I said, and I wasn't lying.

I took the tongue and put it away for further investigation. Just then Andrew cantered up to us. "I see you've been chatting it up with Rachel." He whistled. "That's a formidable woman."

"Stow it." I was getting short.

"Speaking of magic," George would have been bored blind by idle talk of romance, so he steered the conversation back to something more interesting, "I know the New Church considers it a high sin, but to hear some of the stories it sounds like your kind use it too." George looked as if he'd been trying to ask that question for a while but hadn't found a tasteful way to do it.

"And?" Seiford gave the tutor a questioning look.

The tutor went on "What's the difference, or is it simply if anyone else does it it's wrong but not me." All attempts at tact were thrown out the window.

Seiford and I looked at each other cautiously. "It's hard to explain I suppose." The monk said after a moment. "For the gentry, it can be difficult to tell the difference, so we avoid the topic with them."

"Well, I'm sure you know I'm not the gentry." George was a humble man on the by and large, but he was one of the most educated scholars in the Confederacy and knew it well.

"And I'm your brother." Andrew nudged me gently. "Surely, you can reveal certain trade secrets."

"They're not secrets." Seiford shrugged. "No one's hiding anything, but it's rather uncommon knowledge."

"Well, then tell us!" George urged me on.

Seiford and I nodded at each other. I let the monk go first. "Half of those stories are more to do with the monks than the Constables." He said. "We men of the New Church pride ourselves on, science. To become a monk, you're forced to study everything from engineering to medicine to philosophy." Seiford straightened himself up a bit. "Even then, most of our order goes about preaching the Testament, teaching at University, or serving in some other capacity." He paused. "Only the brightest of us get to accompany a Constable."

George rolled his eyes. "Isn't humility a tenant of the faith?" It was a light jab.

I smiled at the monk. He returned it. "Humility is, but lying is not." I turned to my tutor. "You don't get it. Seiford is being humble." I paused. "Two hundred and four times three hundred and forty-six!" I said abruptly.

"Seventy thousand five hundred and eighty-four." He answered without a seconds hesitation.

George took a moment to do the math and got the same answer as the monk. "Let me try." He said. "Forty-fifth lord of Gesalry?"

Andrew and I looked at each other, hopeless. We were both students of history, but the obscure ruler of an obscure province was beyond our grasp.

"Lord Thyalt." Seiford answered instantly. George was about to open his mouth to gloat, but the monk stopped him. "I know you think it's Herald, but I find that the ruler during the Hissan crisis was really only lord in name. Even the official edict never proclaimed him the true sovereign."

I looked back at the tutor. "You're a smart man, George, and anyone wise should listen to your counsel. There's probably a good bit you could teach my monk." I smiled. "However, Seiford might be one of the cleverest men in this world." I shrugged. "I never did figure out why he hides it so."

"You're an ass." The monk snorted.

"Cleverest man in the world?" Andrew gave the monk another look over.

"You heard about that eight-year-old solving Ferdun's Equation?" I pointed a finger at Seiford. "It was him."

"You're kidding." George joined Andrew in gazing at the monk.

"I'll be honest with you." I went on. "A good bit of my victories would have fallen flat, without Seiford's knowledge." My friend often times didn't get the thanks he was due. "He figured a way to build trenches that only a direct blast from an eighteen-pounder could break. He jerry-rigged the cannons, so they only misfire one in a thousand times." I missed those days of living by our wits desperately. "He assisted with the logistics of all my campaigns over the past ten years." I chuckled. "The bastard even remembered a four hundred year city map of Hest that had a tunnel going under it."

"You'd have figured a way without me." Seiford scratched the back of his head.

"Aye, but there'd have been a lot more blood." I nodded. "Besides, it's not just what he did during the fighting, but what he did after." I gave my friend a respectful stare. "Seiford showed them how to rebuild what I tore down for half the price and twice the quality. He showed them how to grow their food with modern technology. After I had the Priests hung, Seiford showed the people they didn't need them." I smiled. "He even wrote out constitutions for the governments I put in place as tight as the Ironwill Pact." I shrugged. "Most legal precedents in Thyro and Souren bear the fingerprints of this lecherous monk."

Seiford was secretly pleased by all the adulation. I could tell. "You helped with that." He gestured to Andrew. "Your brother was no slouch in politics."

"So it's established that your friend has an impressive resume." Andrew said impatiently.

"Impressive?" George shook his head. "It's amazing is what it is. I was always wondering how Thyro didn't collapse in on itself after feudalism died. Now I know. It was the two of you." He gave both of us a strange look. "Why am I just hearing about it now? That's the kind of thing that belongs in every history book around the world."

Seiford seemed a bit uncomfortable. "Our doctrine used to be not to upset the powers that be, and everything would work itself out." He said. "After the Thaniel Wars Mother Vestia realized we needed a more proactive approach" The monk shrugged. "However, it might have caused a stir if the lords of Thyro realized how much of my hand was in the changing ways. We might have even lost our support, so we don't exactly keep it hidden, but you have to look hard to find it, and most don't."

I laughed to myself at how scared the nobles were when we rode into town. "Still people talked, and the rulers knew they weren't quite as indispensable as they'd been before." I said through a chuckle.

"So where did the magic come in?" Andrew had grown tired of politics.

Seiford answered. "When one of us comes to a remote village and shows them how to grow crops better or heal a man thought beyond help, some sheep buggerer always cries devilry."

"Aye, I taught a Huego how to plant good wheat, and I almost got chased out of town." George said thoughtfully.

"And we did far more than that." Seiford said. "Magic and science don't travel together, but they ride in a cart that looks awfully similar from far away. The trouble is both are too stubborn to get a damn new one." He paused. "When a tribal people see the wonders we work, superstition can blind them to the simple facts behind it."

"So no magic?" Andrew asked.

"Science is impressive in its own right." Seiford answered.

My brother clearly wasn't satisfied. "You said that was only half of it."

"Aye, I did." Seiford smiled. "The other half is the Constable."

Andrew got his excitement back quick. "That's what I want to hear."

I obliged him. "As thoroughly as the monk is trained in academics, Constables are trained in war." I cracked a wry smile. "They only take those of us who have some kind of useful background and training. Even then they only accept the boys with the mind and strength to make us more than common warriors." I paused remembering the brothers I had once. "Every Constable would have been a great warrior in his own right, God's Rest just made us better."

George nodded. "They almost didn't take you."

I didn't want to remember that day. "They almost didn't." I agreed. "The training is tough. Half of the recruits don't get their tattoos."

"They die?" Andrew shied away, slightly scared.

"In this day and age?" I cocked my head back. "Three above, no! They just get sent back home." I shook my head. "What do you think we are? A group of savages?"

"Just asking. You hear about that kind of thing sometimes." Andrew looked down as if embarrassed.

I nodded. "That comes after they set us loose." I went on. "Nine of ten Constables don't finish out their term. It's a dangerous business." There were enough of my dead brothers in Thyro, so I didn't have to illustrate the point. "However, while they're alive they fight like lions. They show us something called the Battle Mind. It lets us fight beyond injury, move even after we should have died." I scratched the tattoos on my arm. "Those battles turn into myths and myths usually have some sorcery to them."

"That's not the end of it." George said. "I read every story about you I could get my hands on. He paused looking me up and down. "There was more there than training and science, wasn't there."

Seiford paused for a moment. George was clever enough to see the truth behind the facts. "Most of the time, it's just men trying to wrap their head around what Thomas did." He glanced at me. "To a lot of people sorcery was the easiest explanation."

"But..." Andrew pressed on.

"But every once and a while, there was something more." I answered. "I won't call it sorcery, because it wasn't that." I took a deep breath. "It was something though."

"Stories like Fredua, Gertinville, the Rose Petal Throne..." George looked at me differently than he had a moment before. "They don't read like history. They read like..." The tutor trailed off.

"They read like what?" I knew what he was going to say, but it had to be him that said it.

Andrew finished for him. "They read like those tales about the Nameless Man."

"He used something called the Gift." I sighed trying to figure how to ans. "I don't really understand it, but I learned that power enough to beat the Old Religion just like he did." I paused. "The Nameless Man and I have no more in common than that."

"What makes that better than what the Priests do?" George was too far into his curiosity to come back now. "You learned it from the same place, didn't you?" He paused. "I always thought it was just some tale, made up to give your name weight."

"What are you talking about?" Andrew asked.

"You learned about this Gift in *Imor*." George had his eyes on me and with something more than a teachers rebuke. There was fear. "That's what the rumors say, anyhow."

I touched the tattoos on my arm. "There's a lot of things happened in my life." I started. "There's a lot of stories about me full of half-truths and legends." I kept on. "There's even some parts I don't like to talk about. I hold those close to me." I leveled a gaze back at my tutor. "I only have two secrets though, and that's the one I'll keep to the grave. Of all the vows I've broken, I won't break that one. What I saw in Imor dies with me." I paused. "It's too dangerous." *Too tempting.*

"You were there, though?" Andrew leveled a gaze at me. "You learned the Old Religion's secrets?"

"Aye, I was there." I swallowed deep. It was the part of the story I could tell. "I learned things about the Old Religion even their Priests don't know." I turned back to George. "But the Gift I used came from the Three."

"Came from the Three?" Andrew finally came across one of my stories he couldn't believe. "As in you had some sort of epiphany?"

"As in they walked beside me as you do now." I was growing tired of this.

My brother waited a moment, probably hoping I'd laugh and tell him it was all some kind of joke. "Never really took you for the pious type."

"If you don't believe me, then don't believe me!" The rage in my voice was barely kept in check. "You wanted the answer, so I gave it to you."

Andrew looked to Seiford for help, but when he realized none was forthcoming went on anyway. Seiford believed me. "Thomas," he called me by my name as if to remind himself I was still human, "it's just..."

"I'm not a pious man." I shot back at my brother. "I can't remember the last time I prayed, and I certainly don't live my life by the fucking Testament." I touched the six-shooter at my side. "If you have a better explanation for how I did what I did, please let me hear it."

"The Three are parables meant to lead men towards a just life." George cut it. "Maybe there's something behind the parable, but they don't-"

"Don't what?" I hissed before I finally calmed myself. "Maybe I was mad then. Maybe I'm still mad, but I know what I saw. I know what I did next." I stared at the open road ahead. I bit my lip trying to keep my voice level. "Wisdom taught me how to use the Gift, though." *And then he took it from me. I've been coasting on luck and fear ever since.* "It wasn't a parable." I said it in a way that let everyone know I was finished.

"What are you doing Constable?" I turned around and saw Rachel trot up on her horse. "Telling them that nonsense about the thro'ncat?

My face went pale. How long had she been listening to us? "Its a good story." I managed a shrug.

"So you say..." She smiled then turned towards the plains around us. "I've grown bored of standing around, though."

"We'll be home in a few hours my lady." I fumbled over my words. Lady was the wrong thing to call her. Maybe miss? Rachel seemed too informal. I saw Seiford's face go red holding in laughter.

She smiled and didn't correct me. "I know, but my attention is awfully fleeting." She patted the side of her mount. "I was wondering if you'd ride with me for a bit."

I turned to Andrew. "Don't stay on our account." He said. "I've had about as much as I can handle for one conversation." I didn't want to stay either. Beautiful women aside, I wanted to put some distance between us while they thought that story over.

I turned back to Rachel. "I would love to accompany you." *Damnit, Thomas!* I thought. Love was too much. I should have said like. No, enjoy would have been best. "What I meant to say was-"

She stopped me before I could make a further fool of myself. "Good." She cantered off to the plains, as I followed. I was even unsure of the invitation. Did she really want me to come? Of course, she'd come up and asked me with no prompt at all, but maybe she was just being polite. There's some questions so dumb they can only come from an intellectual or a lusty man. *Damn this girl!*

As I rode off, I heard George whisper. "The Three really?" He said. "You sure he's not losing his mind. I've seen some of the veterans that come home from war, and he's been at it for fifteen years."

I decided that was a problem for when a beautiful girl didn't want to ride with me, so I resolved to face it later.

I followed her expecting a pleasant trot and strained conversation. She really meant a ride, though. As soon as we were a reasonable distance away from the carriage, she bolted. I pushed Shaggy Cow into a gallop to follow her. She zigzagged around the plain at a rapid gallop, turned in circles tighter than brick and mortar, even found a few logs to jump. I could keep up. My own unique riding style was the best outside of the Step, but the girl gave me the World Below for the effort.

The real problem with me catching her was my indecision. Was she trying to shake me? Give me a subtle sign to leave her alone. She'd invited me of course, and she hadn't given me an obvious signal I'd been annoying her. Still, I'd known girls who led men on just to prove they could. People always say men are savages, but women can be just as malicious in their own way.

I knew I was just second guessing myself. Rachel didn't seem insecure enough to indulge in the worse sins on her sex, but she was riding awfully hard... Three above! I hadn't been this indecisive since the Gestin incident.

Finally, she stopped. I caught up to her. Rachel's face was perfectly composed as if she hadn't just ridden like she was trying to escape a pack of wolves. However, no one can completely hide exertion. Her breast heaved to get in the air she needed, and I saw some sweat appear on her brow. It was becoming on her though.

I reached her and scratched Shaggy Cow for the mounts efforts. The horse deserved it. I paused not knowing what to say.

Rachel pointed to an apple tree three hundred meters away. "Shoot one of them."

"What?" I asked dumbly.

She rolled her eyes. "People all over Thyro claim you're the best marksman in the world. I've heard you can shoot a flea off a dog at fifty paces." She smiled. "Hitting an apple off a tree shouldn't be so hard."

I finally felt more sure of myself. This was the kind of thing I was good at. "That story started when I shot a spider off a Rhorii prince." I smiled. "I'd never take aim at a dog. I like dogs."

"And not princes?" I saw a smile tug at the corner of her mouth.

I cocked an eye up at that. "Depends on the prince."

"I heard you and Prince Edward were quite close."

"We were." I nodded.

She nodded. "Edward still talks about you, you know?"

"That so?" It didn't shock me she'd met the Royal family. Educated citizens of the Confederacy were in style at Thyro courts.

"I thought after the way things ended..." I touched my tattoos. "He wasn't so pleased about me when I left."

"He had to act that way." She nudged her horse closer. "His father still has an unofficial bounty on your head."

I laughed. "Well, that's an improvement from what it was."

"What was it?" She eyed me up curiously.

"Any living member of my family." I turned back to her.

"King John was a piece of work." She chuckled.

"Most men are in their own way." In truth after years of hating the man, I'd come to peace with him. He was an impotent ruler in one of the harshest times in history, and everyone saw it. Every battle I'd won made him more paranoid. Even his son had fought with me. If I was in his place, would I have handled things differently? Probably, but I was Thomas Belson, and he was a soft man forced into hard times. In my story King John was a pathetic character, it's hard to hate someone like that for your entire life, and it certainly doesn't help anyone. After the war, I'd wanted nothing more than to kill him. Now, I just hoped his death might be more graceful than his life.

"Still better than his wife, though." Rachel rolled here eye's at the woman.

"There's not many things worse than his wife." I admitted. The King's consort was a different story. She was just a frigid bitch with no reason. The day she went into the ground, I'd have a feast.

"Queen Harriot ever find that statue I took." I cocked an eyebrow up.

"Yes, she did," Rachel smiled, "but she didn't want it back after where you took it." She abruptly started laughing hysterically. I'd thought everything about her was perfect, but she had a bad laugh. It sounded like a donkey braying. However, it made me like her more for some reason. I wanted to make her laugh again. "Those savages really wanted it?"

I smiled. "You'd understand if you'd seen their women."

I got another round of donkey laughter. It was even sweeter the second time.

I pressed my advantage. "Prince Edward was quite put off by that."

"I can imagine." She recovered from the laughter. "For all her faults that's still his mother."

"What does Prince Edward say about me?" I needed to know.

"In public, he says all the stylish things." She flipped her hair back. "Thomas Belson was an up jumped savage. Thomas Belson wasn't really all that necessary. His success was mostly coincidence and luck. Thomas Belson has a small prick."

"Even a broken clock is right twice a day, it seems." I smiled, desperately hoping she'd see it as a joke.

Her donkey laugh reassured me. "He was almost disinherited after you left." She brought back her composure. "The King wasn't sure where his loyalties lied. He puts on a show to keep the nobles from growing too suspicious."

"I'm sure he takes credit for the victory too." I couldn't hate the Prince, not after all we'd been through. Not after all the friends we'd lost, but there was bad blood between us. Edward wasn't like his father. He was strong and clever. He knew what right and wrong was. It made what happened so much worse. You expect a snake to bite you, but it hurt when you thought the snake a lion.

She shook her head. "He should." Rachel shrugged. "It would be the right thing to do politically. The commoners still see him as a hero for serving with you, but he can't bring himself to take the praise." She nudged her horse closer. "Even that concession has set the court tongues wagging. He mostly gives thanks to the army who fought for him."

I stared back at her. "The army could have used that loyalty at the end."

"You know that was an impossible choice." She eyed me curiously.

"Not impossible," I said, "just hard."

"Well, anyway that's what he does in public." She gave me an encouraging smile.

"What about privately?" The girl knew something.

"In private he does whatever he can to help the men who fought with you." She said. "He makes sure they get pulled off the colonies. He makes sure the families get the money they need to break into the middle class. He makes sure that the veterans get their trade licenses and gives them no interest loans from the crown." She paused. "He's even paid to send a few to university."

She went on. "Edward is trying to set things right." Rachel turned the full weight of her gaze on me. "Besides, you should hear the future he talks about. It's one of hope for the world you promised." She shook her head. "No, it's even better than that. You wanted a world where people had a say in their nation. He promises one where they are the nation." She gazed up into the sky. "One where men don't need to ask permission. One where they just do." She sighed. "It sounds a bit idealistic to me, a country closer to the Confederacy than Anthanii, but he means it."

It was hard to let go of an anger that had been brewing for so long, even if her words were sweet. "He should have stood for something, not working in secret to heal his princely guilt."

"Maybe working in secret means more." She said. "Everyone talks about doing what's right when people are watching. It's different when you do it for no one to see."

"Maybe." I still didn't want to admit she was right. What happened after the war hadn't been my first failure, and it wasn't my last. It cut deep, though. I still remembered. "Then again, maybe if you have the wisdom to say a thing in private, you should have the courage to say it in public."

Rachel lost her patience. "At least he's doing something!" She screamed into the valley. "What did you do after Thaniel fell? Overthrow backwater tyrants and kill village Priests?"

I was utterly unprepared for that vitriol. "They needed help too!"

"Yes, so you went and knocked down petty oppressors one by one, building your legend the whole way." She fired back at me. "Imagine what you could have done with Anthanii, Kran and all the nations between them behind *you*!" She stared down her nose at me. "You could have made sure your army got what was owed. You could have changed the world in one fell swoop."

It wasn't not my place!" I returned the anger. "I didn't have the authority for that!" The words rang hollow even to me. How many nights had I lain awake wondering if things could have been different, wondering if I made the right choice? Seiford thought so. Mother Vestia thought so. I wasn't sure.

"What you did have was the best army in the world." She leaned towards me. "You had the loyalty of the people. You had the power to change!"

"Like Thaniel?" I hissed back.

"That would have been up to you." She went on.

"I took oaths." I hissed back. "I'm a Constable, not an upstart."

"Well, now you're nothing." The words hit me like a musket ball. "Cut loose by the very people you served. Sent to the frontier to rot."

We sat quietly for a minute. Even the horses were too uncomfortable to neigh. I saw the regret flash through her face. "Thomas, I-"

"Is that what you really think of me?" I barely knew the girl. Her opinion should have meant nothing, but it did. And not just because I was sweet on her.

"Of course, not!" She said. "I..."

"That I'm just a relic of a different time, who's outlived his use?" I asked. "That I'm just a glorified dog on a leash, set loose on anyone who incurs my master's disapproval." It weighed on me. "That I bungle things around just enough to upset the order, but don't have the conviction to see it through." She hadn't said those things. I had. They came from me.

"Thomas..." She trailed off.

"I'm not blind." I looked to the ground. "I see the articles they print about me in the papers. I pretend I don't, but I do." I paused. "It's easy to sit back and judge events ten years past, but you weren't there. None of you were!" I gathered my breath. "Maybe if you knew the things I did to win that war, the man I almost became, you'd be thanking the Three I left!"

"Thomas, I know about what you did, the truth of it." She paused. "I'd never judge you for what happened there." She reached out and took my chin in her hand guiding it up to face her. "I've spoken to the men who fought with you, to the people you helped. Those are the ones that really matter." She did know, and she didn't judge me. "They worship you. You were the hero they needed, and even now the world is changing just because you existed."

She went on. "I don't think you're a mad dog on a leash. I don't think you're a relic of a different age who has the audacity not to die." We were close now. "I know you're the greatest hero in living memory." She paused. "I don't know what you should have done after Kran, and it's over now anyway." She moved even closer. Close enough to smell the scent of her sweat, close enough to see the lines of her lips. "I just think the world could use more Thomas Belson not less."

I didn't know what to say, so as usual, I said the worst thing. "So you spent much time in private with Prince Edward." *Well, Thomas at least you're consistent!* I thought. *Fucking idiot.*

She didn't pull away, though. She should have, but she didn't.

Rachel smiled, still holding my chin in her hand. Still just a few inches apart. "So what if I did?" She said it as a dare.

I leaned my head forward ever so softly. It wasn't a full commitment, but it was enough.

She trotted out of my reach. "As it stands, Edward was a perfect gentleman." She smiled. "I only tell you now to save his own reputation."

"Right…" I tried to cough away my embarrassment. "Right, that sounds like him." Had she seen what I was doing? Of course, she had. How many men had tried that on her? Still, it wasn't so obvious. Maybe, I could explain it away. I opened my mouth, but for once my better judgment kicked in. I decided to cut my losses. "Maybe, we should head back. They're probably wondering where we got off to."

"Let them wonder." She waved that aside. "You're not getting out of it that easy." She pointed at the apple tree again. "I asked for an apple. I expect an apple."

"The lady wants an apple." I pulled my rifle out and took aim. I could have shot an apple, it would have been impressive enough, but I needed to be forgiven for my earlier blunder. I spied what I was looking for. It was an impossible shot for most men, but I was not most men. I breathed in, then once I let the air out…

Three gunshots rang out through the valley.

"I don't think you hit one." She mocked disappointment. "Have stories about you been exaggerated." I knew she was just playing with me. I rather liked it anyway. She probably hadn't expected me to hit it. An apple is a small target.

"Just wait." I said.

Crack. The branch I'd aimed for tore off from the tree.

"Most impressive." She clapped enthusiastically.

"I don't shoot innocent apples." I smiled back at her.

She laughed. "No, you just drive them from their homes, and eat them alive while their families watch."

"That's not fair." I shot back at her. "Sometimes I roast them a bit first."

"How heroic." She rolled her eyes.

"It's all about perspective." I'd finally found my wits. I really did have a sharp tongue, honed from years of going back and forth with Seiford. Rachel had merely stolen it for a time. It was just the other parts about me that were rough.

We dismounted and walked towards our prize. I brought a sack with me to stow the apples away. We talked back and forth. The tense nature of our earlier conversation was forgotten. She was nice to talk to, always finding something else to say. I never had to force anything. She even made me laugh.

"So how far out can you hit someone with that thing." She gestured to the weapon on my shoulder. I should have put it up, but I thought it made me look manly and roguish.

"I hit a lord in Combers from twelve hundred yards out." I said. "He was pretty fat, though, so it only counts as a thousand in my book." I closed one eye as if measuring. "A regular shaped girl, though..." I paused. "Why don't you start running and we can figure it out?"

"Oh, regular shaped." She rolled her eyes. "You really know how to flatter the ladies don't you."

"I'm sorry what I meant to say was sculpted by the Three themselves." I smiled back at her. "Really, you should be more worried that I just threatened to shoot you."

"Oh, I've been shot at before." She pinched her face. "No man has ever dared to call me regular shaped, though."

"You've been shot at?" I asked.

"I didn't *just* study in Thyro." She gave me a scandalous stare. "You can't have *all* the stories."

"And why not?" I smiled back. "Monopolies are quite profitable. I'm a dragon fight away from price gouging."

Rachel chuckled. "You'll be able to charge whatever you want for tales."

I was feeling bold. "Maybe, even a kiss." As soon as it came out of my mouth, I wanted to take it back.

Rachel rolled her eyes. "Maybe, but you don't have that monopoly yet." She said. "I'd rather go to the vendor across the street who sells them for a tender touch on the shoulder."

I laughed. The girl was quick. "I have the best product, though."

Rachel rolled her eyes. "You're not the only adventurer."

"Who else have you been buying stories from then?" I asked.

"Secondhand mostly." She sighed. "Books and witnesses charge next to nothing." She turned back to me with a maniacal grin. "However, there are a few fellows who produce original tales."

"Like who?" I asked. Most of the warriors and adventurers of the world had crossed my path at some point, either fighting with me or on the other side. After Thaniel and before Souren, I'd spent much of my time tangling with mercenaries, ideologues, and other various soldiers for hire.

"Alice of Rustia for one."

"I fought with her for a time." I picked up another apple. "She helped me carry the field at Aswold." I paused. "Then she fought against me at Hornwood." I smiled. "I respected her. Not many women out there with a weapon." I remembered the stern-faced lady who still wore plate mail for some ungodly reason. "She was a good soldier, but cautious. Sometimes a bit too much. I made her pay for that in the end."

"She sang your praises too." Rachel huffed. "Said you were the only leader who beat her because you were better."

"Is she still the captain of the Long Daggers?" They'd been a good company, as far as mercenaries went.

"No, she had a child and decided to sell the company and buy a textile mill." Rachel seemed disappointed by it. "That child wasn't yours, was it."

"So what if it was." I echoed back at her. "No, it wasn't mine." I finally relented under her gaze. "Did you see the size of that woman? She'd break me in half." That got another donkey laugh from Rachel. "Honestly, the child surprised me. I thought she preferred women."

"Oh, she did." Rachel smiled wryly. "Made a few passes at me."

I stopped in my tracks. "Did you accept?"

"Like I said, you can't have all the stories." She went back to picking up apples.

"Huh." I muttered a bit disappointed. I wasn't sure if I was hoping she'd say yes or no, but I definitely wanted to know about it.

"The women's rights advocates I ran with for a time tried turning Alice into a symbol." Rachel chuckled at that.

Imagining that stern woman's response made me smile. "What'd she have to say about that?"

Ironically Captain Alice was the most stubborn conservative I'd ever come across. Thought the world worked well enough, and we'd only foul things up tinkering with it. I didn't completely agree, but I didn't completely disagree either. The fact that conservative thought might find issue with her chosen vocation and sexuality, never really occurred to her. She was one of those people who never mixed day-to-day pragmatism with high philosophy.

"She wrote an article in the paper about it." Rachel kicked a rock on the ground as she talked. "Said all those women should get back in their husband's kitchen where they rightfully belonged."

"Did she?" I asked through a laughing fit.

"She did." Rachel nodded. "I've never seen so many girls cry. Those suffragettes really idolized her." Rachel chuckled as she looked back at me. "They kicked me out of their club for laughing so hard."

"She was the only person I ever met that could be humorless and hilarious at the same time." I admitted. "Still I was proud to know her. Despite Alice's antiquated political philosophy, she turned me into something of a suffragette myself." I smiled. "I certainly wouldn't try and stop her from voting."

"That's the way the world works." Rachel nodded.

"What other heroes did you meet?" I asked.

"There was Gregory of Mes." She said after some thought.

"I shared a couple fields with him too, mostly on opposite sides unfortunately." I remembered the fellow. "Preferred fighting with him, but..." I tossed an apple up and caught it in my hand. "He had his own idea how things should work." Gregory had served as a colonel in Thaniel's military. After the war, he'd repented his ways, and vowed to the Three to seek absolution by struggling for the oppressed. He was a bit of a leftist for my taste. Saw the problems of the world and thought we could just fix them then and there. I knew better than anyone how much bloodshed that led to.

Revolutionaries were just as bad as the kings they toppled half the time, and the other half, they were far worse. However, Gregory been a decent sort despite that, not like the howling, overeducated university students he often made common cause with. "He still fighting the good fight for the working man?" I said somewhat sarcastically.

"No, they caught him outside of Rence." She shook her head. "Tore him into pieces and sent them to the corners of Thyro." Rachel paused. "As I understand it he was betrayed by his anonymous patron."

"That's a shame, he deserved better." I nodded. "He should have been smarter, though. I warned him about fighting the capitalist and bankers, while at the same time financing his crusade with money from an anonymous source."

· "He was always a bit short-sighted." She agreed. "Still, he was a decent man."

"That he was, but his revolutions generally spilt more blood than they were worth. Besides, capitalists and bankers have a profit incentive not to go about slaughtering townsmen, whatever their other failings might be." I touched the six-shooter at my side. "Some of the men Gregory took up with acted like they got a commission check for rooting out 'anti-revolutionary behavior.'" It would be funny if it wasn't so bitter. "A good many of those men they hung couldn't even read, much less shill for the bourgeoisie."

Despite all that, I took a moment to remember the idealistic liberal I'd met all those years ago. "Still, he was a good man at heart. Just wanted to make the world a better place. Sometimes he even succeeded despite himself." I paused. "I can't say if the world was better or worse for his meddling, but now that he's gone, I miss him."

I wanted to turn the conversation away from Gregory of Mes. "So who else did you meet?"

"A certain former acquaintance of yours," she smiled, "Marcius of Renton."

"Marcius of fucking Renton!" I turned towards her. Marcius of Renton was my least favorite type of soldier.

"So you did know him?" She had picked all the apples her sack could carry and stood up.

"Aye, I fucking knew him!" I was fighting a losing battle against my own anger. "You didn't believe that shit about him being a general in Thaniel's court, did you?" I turned my voice into a mocking tone. *"I fought for the last great leader of Thyro, and now I want vengeance on his killer!"*

"Well, he does call himself *of Renton*, so I expected he wasn't actually a Kranish soldier." She shrugged. "Still, everyone needs a story."

"It wasn't a story! It was a lie!" I huffed. "He was a common sell-sword with uncommon stupidity." It doubly chaffed on me because I actually *had* spent many long years in Thyro hunting down Thaniel's generals who caused a ruckus.

"He claims to have chased you off the field of battle." She moved a bit closer to me. "He says you charged him with three thousand heavy horse and he turned you away."

"Oh that's what he says, is it?" Sarcasm dripped off every word.

"It is." Rachel gave me a mocking smile.

"Well, let's forget for a moment that no one's used heavy horse in three hundred years." I huffed. "I made a feint with some light scouts then fell back. He followed with his entire army, and I blasted them to hell. He lost five thousand men." I held up seven fingers. "I lost seven, and that was mostly on account of a cannon exploding."

"He did like to embellish." She shrugged.

"Of course, he did." I flailed my arms. "He told that story loud enough for all Thyro to hear. A bunch of lords who'd been harboring Priests were about to surrender peacefully when they heard that tale." I shook my head. "They pooled their resources together and hired him and twenty-thousand mercenaries to fight." I tightened my fist. "I spent six months and took five cities before he finally surrendered." I was shaking with rage. "It wouldn't have been that bad if he knew what he was doing, but half of the towns that man was supposed to be defending starved because he couldn't manage the grain." I calmed myself. "Do you know how many men died in that war?"

"Is that why you killed him in Souren?" Rachel took a step back. "I was rather looking forward to his return. He promised me ivory, gold, even a trained lion." She regained her composure. "All the things boys do to show you they care."

"I didn't want to do that." I knew that didn't make him any less dead. "Those stories of his were causing too much trouble." I paused. "At the end of the siege in Gluswell, I made him swear he'd put down his arms."

"You knew he wouldn't." She bit her lip.

"Aye, somewhere deep down I knew, but I've executed too many men and never got the taste for it." I said. "The last straw was when he took a contract from an Anthanii trading company to put down some rebels in Souren. He put them down in the worst way." I still remembered the way he begged in the end. I thought I'd enjoy killing him. Turned out I only enjoyed the thought of it. "I couldn't let that happen again."

She sighed. "Well, it's getting to be that time." Rachel said. "We should head back."

"I'm sorry about making things so dark." I picked up my sack of apples and followed her. "There's just some memories there."

"I quite enjoyed hearing your stories." She said over her back. "I'd like to continue this conversation. We just can't keep all these apples to ourselves." She turned to me as she mounted her horse.

"I never liked Marcius anyway. Always putting his paws where they weren't welcome."

"I still don't like how it ended." I said.

"People rarely do."

We walked our horses slower than we'd come to the forest. We kept up our conversation.

"You know my brother, and his friends are worried about you coming back here." She gave a wistful sigh. "They think you might upset the political balance in this country, and side with the North."

"We still got freedom of speech don't we?" I asked.

"We do, but to people like my brother you're only free to speak the right way." She turned back to me. "Besides, I think they're worried about more than speech."

I cocked an eyebrow up. "Are they?"

"You are Thomas Belson. It wasn't orations that made you famous" She chuckled. "I told them I'd speak with you. Let them know they've nothing to worry about."

"What are you going to tell them?" I gave Shaggy one of my apples. She'd already put a reasonable dent in my supply.

"Maybe they should be worried just a bit." She held up two fingers close to each other to illustrate the point.

"Aye, maybe they should." I paused. "No offense, but your brother doesn't seem to like me much."

"Well, you were just picking apples alone with his sister." Rachel posited.

"You know how to take care of yourself." I gave Shaggy another apple at her behest. How did the horse stay so fast with all the apples she ate? They'd have slowed me down.

"That's rarely a consolation to a brother." She chuckled then grew more serious. "So if the unthinkable does happen, what side will you be on?"

"Let's hope it doesn't come to that." I tried to end the conversation.

"What if it does?" She pressed on. "Please, I'm just asking out of curiosity. I was educated in the North remember."

"I don't know." I said honestly. "I've spent my whole life fighting the Old Religion. To have it free in my homeland stings, and that's what this is really all about isn't it?" I paused. "What's more, I like McAllan. I think he means well. I like the industry and freedom they have up in the North." I took a hard swallow. "The Demons are evil, make no mistake about that, but part of this country is that we can change things without armies."

I went on "My family is from the South, though. I've always been a Southerner even halfway around the world. I don't want to fight them, especially not if my brother chooses to pick up arms." I remembered my conversation with George. "I think they've got some decent gripes too. They're not as important as they once were, and the provinces have a right to govern themselves." I patted Shaggy. "The problem is, people think one day the Old Religion will just go away. If I've learned one thing in Thyro, it's that the Old Religion doesn't just go away."

"Sounds like you haven't made a choice yet." Rachel cut in.

"Maybe, I'll follow Alice of Rustia's lead." I smiled. "Have a child, open up a textile mill," I leaned in towards Rachel, "make passes at pretty women."

She laughed that donkey laugh of hers. "I don't think that's in your nature." She paused. "Besides, even textile mills will have to choose."

I looked at her. "You got a dog in this fight."

She scratched her chin thoughtfully. "Well, I wouldn't call you a dog, but I've grown rather fond of you."

I laughed at that. "Seriously though?"

She paused. "My brother is one of the most vocal supporters of secession," she said, "but my brother is also an ass." She sighed. "Honestly, after the intrigue of Thyro politics, this spat seems rather benign."

"It'll do that to you." I mumbled then I saw a sight that made my heart catch in my throat. I stopped Shaggy Cow.

"Thomas, is something wrong?" Rachel asked.

The orderly fields as far as the eye could see. Fields I'd grown up in. Servants tending them with care. Servants I'd played with as a boy. A big yellow house in the middle of it. A house now lacking a father.

I'd wondered what it would be like for fifteen years. I thought it would be my triumphant return. I thought it would bring out all the pain I'd been hiding. The truth was both and neither. I was a different man than the boy who had left, but that boy was buried here.

"It's my home..." I said. A voice in the back of my head whispered. *Is it?*

Present Day

achel and I caught up with our band of travelers. She went to ride next to her brother. I went back to my friends. I threw George and Seiford my bag of apples mostly to keep them away from Shaggy Cow. Andrew and Ayn-Tuk were riding their horses next to the carriage.

"So you went apple picking with the lady?" Seiford chuckled as he gave Shaggy another apple at her bequest. The horse took it greedily. The damn beast was a natural beggar. I thought about taking her treat away, but I'd always been too soft to disappoint her.

"Oh, shut your mouth." I rolled my eyes. "We just talked."

"How'd it all go?" Andrew asked hopefully.

I thought about all the ups and downs. How she'd challenged me on things no one had the bones to before. "It went well, I think."

George chimed in. "I thought she might be too much for you." The tutor said. "Girl's sharp as a whip, and that was before she spent five years studying in Thyro."

"She can be a bit confrontational." I admitted.

"As opposed to you." Seiford snorted.

"I didn't say I didn't like it." I shot back. "Just saying she challenged me is all."

"Well, good." Andrew smiled. "You need to start thinking about what you're going to do now that you're retired." He waged a finger at me. "You're not so old you can't have a family."

"I went on one ride with the girl." I almost laughed. "That's hardly grounds to talk about marriage. Besides, I'm not even sure she likes me that way."

"You did save her from a group of Huegos." George posited.

"Then she offered a private ride with you, which is more than I got." Seiford feigned disappointment.

"And you're Belson the Blessed, greatest hero in the world."

Andrew reached over and tousled my hair. "Besides girls can't stay away from Belson boys."

I pushed his hand aside. "Fuck off."

"Just saying." My brother shrugged.

"No, you're not." I shot them all a look.

He grew a bit more serious. "Thomas you've been gone for fifteen years." Andrew said. "I was just hoping you'd start looking towards a future here." The real implication behind his words was clear. *Please don't leave me again.*

Ayn-Tuk surprised us all. "A wife is a good thing. It gives a man roots, makes him fight for something other than himself."

I glared at him. "Well, apparently you're married, and obviously those roots don't go too far, or you wouldn't be here with me."

The black man didn't respond like I expected him to. "Roots of love go deeper than anything of this world." I almost saw an emotion on his face. "I am always connected to my wife, no matter how far I am from home."

"Strange bastard." I mumbled to myself. "I'm not leaving any time soon." I surveyed the plowed fields of the Belson Plantation. "I got nowhere else to go."

George shook his head. "No, you could have gone anywhere, and they'd have taken you in." He said. "You came here because it's your home."

"I suppose." I gave a begrudging nod. *Is it?* I asked myself again. I didn't know the answer to that, but I couldn't deny this was one of the most beautiful sights I'd seen in fifteen years of traveling.

We passed through the first of the tobacco fields and saw the servants tilling them. They were all kinds, Thyrans who indebted themselves to pay there way across the ocean, blacks from the Souren Continent who came over after the famine took their crops, even some from the far East Inte lands, no one really knew why they immigrated to the Confederacy, but they worked hard enough to earn their keep and more.

I was caught in a trance the whole way. There were farms in Thyro, large ones. My plantation put them all to shame. The way it was run was seamless. Our techniques had been honed over the years. The need to innovate had forced us into the forefront of agriculture. It seemed we'd even added some fields to our domain.

Yet, something was off. The crops grew tall, too tall. Not a single one looked to be spotted with blight. Above everything else, the tattoos on my arm itched.

"Why are the plants so tall?" I looked at Andrew.

He clenched his jaw. "Let's not have that conversation now." My brother said. "This is a happy thing. I won't see it ruined."

I nodded and filed the information away. This wasn't something I could ignore for long.

It was about a half hour ride from the outskirts of the field to the plantation mansion. The mansion was large enough to fit a hundred families if needed. It was painted a light shade of yellow giving it an inviting feel. The exterior was beautifully built with white pillars that went down the whole four floors of the building. The summer heat was beating down on the house, so the windows were thrown wide to allow for airflow. House servants ran around doing odd jobs, some of them I recognized by name, most were alien to me. Still, I felt the call of home. I felt the embrace of it like dunking myself into a warm bath.

"Why'd you ever leave?" Seiford finally asked, awed at the sight.

"Well, you see I had great ambitions as a child of ruining some university student's dreams and turning him into a monk." Sarcasm dripped off every word. "Why do you think I left you tit?" I rubbed my tattooed arm angrily.

"Sorry, I just wasn't expecting..." He trailed off and waved extravagantly at the house.

"Well, let's go inside then." Thomas gestured. "Three be damned Seiford you've seen castles ten times as big." I said as I dismounted Shaggy Cow.

"Yes, but those were all so angry looking." Seiford hopped off surprisingly nimble then helped George down. "This was built for pleasure, not necessity."

"Built by our great grandfather." Andrew hopped off his horse. "It's the pride of our family."

A group of servants came to take the horses and coaches. They tried to take Shaggy Cow's reigns, but I waved them away. "Don't worry about this one." I turned to the horse and took off her saddle and tack. "Shaggy, go!" I pointed to the large fenced in area where the other horses were.

She neighed her disapproval.

"You know you're not allowed inside anymore." I said sternly. "Lord Fadder almost started a war after you shit in his dining hall."

She neighed again as if to say. *You threw up on everyone! I just took a little poop.*

"I know I may not have been in the right," I sighed, "but I've got two legs, and you've got four."

She neighed again as if to say. *Racist.*

"Don't go throwing around accusations like that." I put a finger out. "You know I'm a card-carrying member of the Equine Liberation movement. I can't go to war with the entire world over their bigotry."

This time her neigh said. *False friend trying to subvert our glorious revolution.*

I slumped my shoulders defeated. "There're many stallions in there you can terrorize." I gave her another apple.

Shaggy Cow seemed mollified and hopped the fence. She immediately set to abusing every horse in biting distance. "Three above, I love that pony." I said to myself.

George gave me a strange look. "She understands you."

I shrugged. "I think so. She's never given me a reason to doubt it."

"Besides being a horse you mean." George scratched his head.

"Yes, besides that." Seiford chimed in.

The servants then moved to take the rest of the horses and carriages. Andrew put a hand on the leader of the party's shoulder. A Souren man I barely recognized. "Assin," he said, "how's the wife holding up?"

"Not so good." The black man answered. "Her fever's gotten worse."

"I was afraid that might happen." My brother sighed. "I sent for Doctor Bennet while I was in the capitol. He should be here in a day or two." He said. "Don't worry he's the best I know of."

"Thank you, sir." Assin nodded with a smile. "I'm in your debt."

"I'll call it square as long as your boy keeps his marks up at school." Andrew smiled back. "How's he doing anyway?"

"Sir, he's still on the dean's list." The black man said. "He can't seem to stay out of fights, though."

"I expected that too." Andrew shrugged. "Boy's huh? My oldest is a right devil, now." He whistled. "I think his mother will straighten him out, soon."

"She will at that, sir." He smiled.

"Here give this to your workers." Andrew pressed a small wad of cash into his hands.

"I will, thank you sir." He nodded and went back to the horses.

Part of me expected that Andrew was just putting on a show to impress me, but it all seemed so normal. The servants of all type, Souren, Inte, and Tyran, looked at my brother with respect. No, not just that, it was admiration and affection.

"You treat the workers well." I said.

"The plantations doing well. The workers deserve a share of that." My brother said.

"And when the plantations not doing well?" I asked.

"I treat them well, and I work harder." Andrew smiled "It's how our father did business."

"Aye, it was." I nodded.

"It's a shame all the Southerners don't see it my way." He turned his head to Alexander Gondua, berating an Inte boy.

I walked over to help Rachel down from her saddle. "What a gentleman you Belson men are!" She chuckled.

"Don't tell anyone." I smiled back. "My reputation depends upon me being universally despised."

Alexander was still berating the help. "And if I find one scratch on this carriage, I'll have you whipped."

That became too much for Andrew. "If you lay one hand on them I'll have *you* whipped!" My brother drew himself up to his full height.

Alexander seemed startled by the outburst. "I was just-"

"You were just threatening my people!" Andrew said with a stone face. "I won't stand for it. If there's any damage to your carriage, I'll pay for it out of my own pocket, but I'm sure there will be none because my servants know what they're doing!" He paused and turned to the Inte boy who'd been the subject of the anger. "Don't worry about this, Kir-Sun. Just do what you're good at." My brother patted him on the shoulder. "Tell your mother I said hello." The boy smiled and went about his work.

Alexander looked suitably embarrassed. "I meant no disrespect." He said. "I know you're an honorable man. I just don't like the way you treat your servants."

"And I don't like the way you treat yours." Andrew stepped

forward. "Barely better than slaves. It's a good thing I don't have a say in how others run their business."

Alexander leaned in to whisper but spoke loud enough to be heard. "They'll start to think they're our equals."

"According to Then Ironwill they are." Andrew didn't back down.

Alexander was about to say something else, but his sister hopped in. "Alexander, leave it." She said.

"This is man's business." He sneered at her.

That was a step too far for me. "In my mind abusing servants is far from a man's business." I tapped the tomahawk on my side. "You ever want a taste of man's business, though, I'll be more than happy to oblige you."

Alexander was about to respond to that but thought better of it. "My apologies." He said meekly.

"Let's go inside, shall we." I walked up the steps and through the open door.

A pretty serving girl of about twenty was there to meet me. "You must be one of the surveyors." She looked over my scars and weapons. She had the green eyes of an Anthanii, but the strawberry blond hair of one of the Slaen countries her complexion was fair with freckles on her cheeks. The girl looked powerfully familiar.

"Er, no I'm..." I tried to say.

"Oh, you must be one of Andrew's army friends." She smiled. "I think it's so wonderful how he keeps in contact with you all." She sighed. "He's in the capitol on business, but he'll be back soon." The girl was polite as could be. "He's told us to offer you the guest room if any of you ever stop by."

Andrew finally stepped forward. "That won't be necessary, Ally." He said. "This is Thomas Belson." Ally that was it. The girl had been so young when I left.

Ally finally took a deeper look. From my face to the tattoos on my arm. "Master Belson!" Her face went red with embarrassment. "I'm so sorry. I didn't know."

"It's fine." I waved it off. "It's just Thomas now. I think Andrew's the captain of this ship.

"Well, hello seenii." Seiford pushed past me and used the Rhorii word for sweetheart, taking the girls hand and kissed the back slowly. Ally giggled sheepishly.

After Seiford was finished George came and folded her into a hug. "How's my best girl doing?" He said like a grandfather embracing his favorite spawn.

"I'm doing good," She caught herself "Well. Sorry, I'm still learning, you know."

"Oh it's fine, your voice is still sweet as honey." George let go and leveled a tutors stare at her "Did you study those books I left for you."

"I got through one of them, but we were so busy preparing for your return, it was hard to find the time." She looked at the party still dusty from the road.

Andrew stepped in. "Ally can you show our guests to their rooms?"

"Yes, Master Belson." She turned to Seiford, Rachel, and Alexander. "Just this way. I'm afraid we may not be able to provide the usual lodging. Lot's of guests flowing in for the celebration."

"Oh, it's quite fine." Seiford smiled at the girl.

"It's not fine, but it'll do." Alexander huffed.

Ally paused for a moment. She had a question that she couldn't hold in any longer. "Is it true you fought seven mountain wolves to save a maiden?" She asked me.

I chuckled. "There's some truth to that." I pointed to the monk. "He could probably tell you better than me."

"Just so." Seiford chirped giving me a wink. "It was a gray and stormy night…" The story trailed off as they went upstairs.

Rachel stopped for a moment. "I'll be expecting your company later." She said with a delicious smile.

"You'll have it." I nodded.

She seemed to be pacified, but her brother gave me a dangerous stare as he went to his room.

George gave a heavy sigh. "Well, I better go tend to my books." He smiled. "It's what you pay me for."

Andrew laughed. "Go on old man."

For the first time, my brother and I were alone. I didn't know what to say. Fifteen years ago my last gift to him had been tears and pain. He was a good man, and willing to forgive, but I wasn't sure he should. They'd all deserved better. Then I remembered the words of my father. *Forgiveness can only be given when it's not deserved. Otherwise, you're just accepting payment for a debt.*

"Is everything the way you remembered it?" Andrew asked.

"Aye." I muttered. The walls were filled with portraits and paintings. They commemorated all our important events. My sisters birth, my father's service, my brother's wedding. They were missing my pictures though. The furniture was still the same as when I used to play in the sitting room, but It seemed so alien now.

I'd never expected to make it back to this place. I thought I'd been alright with that. I wasn't. I felt something catch in my throat. I tried to fight it down.

"It's nice." I managed to get out.

"It's a good place." Andrew put his hands on his side. "Maybe, not the castles and palaces you've slept in, but it'll do for us."

"Aye." Those castles always seemed so lonely. They were meant to keep everyone out, not invite people in. This was better to my eyes.

"Is Mother out back?" I asked.

"She is." He smiled. "I'll go get the rest of them, and give you two a minute alone."

I walked to the back of the house. My feet showed me the way. As I saw the familiar sights, I fought the memories down. I didn't want to cry in front of them.

I stepped onto the porch and saw the back of a woman sitting on a chair. "Mama?" I asked tentatively.

She looked curiously over her shoulder at me. In the split second before she said anything a thousand questions raced through my brain. Would she even recognize me?

"Oh, Tom Tom!" She closed her book and walked over as quickly as she could and folded me into a surprisingly strong hug. "We've missed you fiercely!" We separated, and I looked at my mother for the first time in fifteen years. She was still beautiful in her old age. Her hair had lost some of the golden sheen and was slowly giving way to white. There were more wrinkles in her face, and she'd lost the easy grace she had when I'd left. The eyes were the same, though. They were my eyes. It was still my mother. "Where have you been?" She asked.

I've been to the places where titans do battle and lived to tell of it. I've been to the greatest empires in the world and watched them burn. I've been to lands distant and exotic and fought on them all.

I've been to the city gods turn away from, and I stand before you now.
"I've been around mama."

Looking at her broke my heart. Not because she was older now, not even because I'd had to leave her for a decade and a half. Because of all the times, I'd been a poor son, for all the time I'd been short with her and she'd given me nothing but love. Because she deserved a better son in me than she'd gotten. I wished I could take her to the grandest castle in Thyro and treat her as the queen she was. No, I wished I could rebuild the Imoran empire and have her as its greatest treasure. Queen Pamela had a certain ring to it. I wished I could show her all the wonders that I'd seen and none of the horrors. I knew I could never do any of that, though

I wished I'd written home at least once, to let her know I was safe. She deserved better, but that was all I could have done for her, and I hadn't even done that much. It hit me worse than any muzzle to the stomach ever could. "I've missed you fiercely as well." In her arms, I couldn't even feel the burn of my tattoos. If everyone had a mother like her, the world would have been a better place.

She grabbed my face and clucked disapprovingly. "Have you been fighting with the Helmy boys again?" She shook her head. "Your face is a mess. You should have Dante look at it."

"I will, mama." I said softly.

"Where's your father at? He's been heartbroken without you." For a moment I held a fool's hope that Andrew had just been playing some sick trick on me, and my father was waiting. I had a habit of making fools hope's pay off. Not that one, though. Dark realization struck her. "Never mind about that I'm just glad you're home." She started to dust off my clothes, then looked down at my arm. "Which one of your friends convinced you to get this? I've got an earful to give him."

"Oh, it's nothing mama." I said, self consciously rolling down my sleeve despite the heat. "Here let's sit down." I led my mother to her chair and took the seat across from her looking down at the garden.

"Everyone's always telling me how great you've become." Pamela smiled. "I just wanted my son back."

"I'm still your son." I looked up into her.

"You are," she nodded, "but there's more to you now than when you left." It seemed like she was finally starting to remember the last fifteen years. Had I done this to her?

"There is, mama." I scratched my arm.

"You've seen some horrors haven't you?" She asked.

"I have." The sins in me clawed.

"I think you've seen some good things too." She smiled.

"There was a lot of that too." I returned the smile.

"Life usually gives us both." She looked over her shoulder. "I've been blessed in that." I saw Andrew walking towards me. He was leading a boy of about seven and carrying a little bundle in his arm. Just behind him was a girl every bit as beautiful as fifteen years ago. It was Sarah.

I stood up. "Sarah," I mumbled dumbly, "It's good to see you."

"It's good to see you whole too, brother." She smiled politely. Maybe there was a bit of warmth there, an echo of a feeling long since past. Mostly, it was polite.

"Mostly whole anyway." I tapped the missing piece of my nose.

Andrew pushed the boy in front of him forward. "Say hello, won't you."

The boy took a few steps forward. "Hello, Mister Thomas." He fidgeted from one leg to the other. "My name's Thomas too, but everyone calls me Tom, so they don't get confused."

I went to a knee in front of him. "Well, it's nice to meet you, Tom." I extended a hand.

"Oh, now he's shy." Andrew rolled his eyes. "Before I left he wouldn't stop talking about you."

"I'm gettin' to it Paw!" Tom said over his shoulder. "Do you think I can shoot your gun?" He pointed to the six-shooter.

I looked up at his parents. I didn't want to step over my bounds.

"Maybe later." Andrew smiled.

"Absolutely not!" Sarah shouted horrified.

"I mean absolutely not!" Andrew amended. "What's gotten into you boy?" The anger wasn't in his voice, though. He gave me a wink.

"We'll talk about that later." I patted him on the shoulder.

"That's alright, Mister Thomas." He seemed a little disappointed.

"You know I'm your uncle, right?" I gave the boy a funny little smile. "You can call me Uncle Thomas if you want." I shifted uncomfortably. "You don't have to, of course, but I wouldn't mind it if you did."

"Yes sir, Uncle Thomas." The boy beamed at me.

Andrew stepped forward presenting his bundle. "And this is Leopold."

I stood up and scratched the baby's head. "He's beautiful." I looked down at him. To an unbiased observer, he probably looked like a weirdly shaped hairless cat, but I wasn't an unbiased observer anymore. I'd never liked babies, but watching that one sleep peacefully in my brother's arms... I liked that one.

"He gets it from his mother." Andrew smiled at Sarah.

"Oh, fathers always say that." My mother said from her chair. "Don't let him butter you up." She jutted a finger at Sarah.

"I won't," Sarah smiled, "but Andrew hasn't made a serious mistake yet, so I'll keep accepting the compliments."

"No, he's much like his father that way." My mother smiled. "They both are." I wondered if she'd say that knowing the things I'd done. Desperate and afraid, the evils I'd chosen. My father would have taken the right path.

"Would you like to hold him?" Andrew asked and pushed the baby forward.

"I would." I took him gently. As soon as he was in my arm, his eyes shot open. Leopold took one look at my scarred face and started crying. "What do I do?" I asked frantically.

"Give him here." Sarah took the boy out of my arms and rocked him back to sleep.

Andrew waved it off. "Don't worry about it, babies take time to get their courage." He smiled. "Maybe you'll get to watch this one grow up."

"I'd like that." I smiled.

Andrew turned back around. "Anyway, look who else has come to see you."

He gestured to a fat bulldog standing in the doorway. The dog licked his snout as if trying to judge my worth. It looked like the one I'd had as a boy, but that couldn't be right. Dog's didn't live that long. Only the one inside my head would stay with me forever. The one that whined in the moonlight.

"That can't be Pig." I squinted my eyes.

Andrew smiled. "No, it's Pig-Pig." He shrugged. "Pig had pups a while back. We kept that one."

"Oh." I went to a knee again and beckoned the dog to me. Pig-Pig approached slowly. He took a few sniffs and quickly retreated to licking his snout. It seemed dogs and babies could smell sin.

Tom mauled the dog quickly. Flipping him on his back to scratch his belly. I stood up.

Andrew saw the distress in my eyes. "Don't worry, coming back from war is like trying to put on an old pair of shoes." He said. "Takes a while before they feel right again."

"Aye." I nodded, but I wasn't sure if it would ever feel right again.

I saw someone spying in the doorway. "Alexis?" I called out.

"It's me." She stepped forward and gave a forced curtsy. She was almost as tall as I was now. She was pretty too, I wasn't so oblivious that I didn't notice that. She looked like Andrew, blond, green eyes, with soft, delicate features. I wanted to make her laugh, to chase her around the house like I used too. I wanted to tell her my stories so grand and impressive they couldn't have been real. "You've grown." Was all I could say.

"That'll happen in fifteen years." Alexis bit her lip. "I'm glad the road has seen you safe Constable Belson."

I shook my head. "The road tried to kill me an awful lot. I was just more stubborn." I said. "What's with this Constable Belson business?" I asked. "I'm your brother Alexis." I stepped in for a hug.

She backpedaled away from me. "No, you're some man from fifteen years ago I barely recognize now."

"Alexis!" Our mother leaned forward.

"Don't talk to him like that!" Andrew glared at her.

I waved for them to stop. "Alexis it's me, Thomas." Of all the bad things I'd done to the rest of them, I'd always loved that girl. I wanted her to grow up safe. I wanted her to love me.

"Aye, it's you, Thomas." She looked around the porch. "The rest of you may be willing to forget how he left, but I won't."

"He's family!" Andrew stated. "When one of our own comes back we welcome them."

"No!" She hissed staring at me. "You didn't have to see how Mother cried every night for five years. You didn't have to watch the guilt in Sarah and Andrew's face that you had no right to put there." She swallowed collecting herself. "You didn't have to listen while Father banged his fist against a wall. You didn't hear him calling out for you while he died."

"That's in the past, now!" Andrew hissed at her. It wasn't all in the past, though.

I tried to collect myself. "I had to go…" I muttered numbly.

"They needed me." The baby had started crying again. "I had my duty."

"You didn't have to go like that." Alexis shook her head. "You didn't have to ignore our letters."

A thousand excuses came to mind. All of them fell flat. "I'm sorry…" Was all I could say.

"Your brother is a hero!" Andrew shouted.

"He's a hero to a distant people halfway across the world." She sneered. "To his sister, he's a stranger." She stalked back through the door and was gone.

"Alexis!" Andrew screamed. "Get back down here!"

I held his shoulder, though. "Let her go." I said. "I need to take a walk."

I held my tears. Following my feet away from the distant people that called me family. I went to a tree I used to know. The tree I used to read under.

I collapsed into a ball of sobbing pain. I hadn't cried like that in a long time. Maybe not since I left. Finally, I got tired of crying. I stood up angry. Before I could think my tomahawk was in my hand. I chopped viciously at the tree.

Fuck the dog.

Fuck my family.

Fuck Mother Vestia.

Fuck everything.

The ax got stuck in the tree, so I abandoned it. I punched it, hard. I struck it absorbing all the pain. I didn't care. Blood ran down my fist mingling with the salty tears I shed.

"Thomas?" I heard someone call over my shoulder. I didn't answer. "Thomas, your brother said you might need me." It was Seiford.

"Thomas!" He shouted as he got closer. "What are you doing?"

He ran to me and pinned my arms to my side. "Stop! You're going to hurt yourself." I threw him off and kept punching the wood. The monk stood up and grabbed me again. This time I collapsed in another fit of sobbing.

"It's just like I said it'd be!" I said as he whipped off my hands. "They hate me!"

"They love you." He patted my back.

"They deserve better." I wiped the tears away again.

"They deserve to have you back."

I sat there in more silence, weeping into my friend's shoulder. It must have looked pathetic. I looked up at the tree. I'd brought it only pain after fifteen years. *That's all you're good for.* A voice said.

Over the hill, I saw a man in the distance. No one else paid him much mind if they saw him at all. He looked like a doctor who had fixed my wounds once long ago. He looked like he was crying too.

Present Day
Jesse's Story

esse Devote woke up to his mother knocking. "Someone left you a note, Jess."

"Shhh, you don't want to wake Bo-Bo, Mama." Jesse said stroking the boy's head. He was still fast asleep sucking on his thumb. "What was the man dressed like?" He said rubbing the sleep out of his eyes.

"Oh sorry, I didn't mean too." She whispered in a volume that wasn't much better, but Bobby always slept well when his brother was with him. "He was all in black. It seemed a curious dress for a trader."

"Don't think much of it." He lied to his mother. The Priest said he'd contact him soon and Jesse had been waiting a week and a half for the message. The gunslinger was curious how he'd do it, but of course, Bellefellow knew where he lived. The Priest knew everything. "They started wearing it in Thyro apparently. You know how those rich folk are, always trying to emulate the Kranish." That was true at least.

"Oh, I suppose you're right." She paused to think, "Maybe I should start wearing it. It's nice to be fashionable."

"Oh, don't do that Mama." Jesse smiled at her. "I've always seen you as the sort of person who should wear color. Genuinely happy people have no business wearing black." He stood up and buckled on his gun belt.

"Oh thank you, Jess." She smiled back at him. "Besides I'm too old to go chasing fashions."

"Don't say that." He walked to his mother and kissed her on the cheek. "If more girls had as much vigor as you, I might be married by now."

She gave her son a hug at that. "You've been so much nicer since you got back from the army." She wiped his cheek. "And since you've taken to trading." She took a step back. "At first I was distraught when I heard you weren't going to University, but I'm happy your job agrees with you so much." If she knew how true that was, she would cry her eyes out like the day when he'd left for war. He had been an awful son to her back in his youth. He always assumed his parents didn't trust him and rebelled accordingly. Of all the things he'd ever done, the bounty hunter wished he could take back the things he'd said to her when he was young.

"Thanks, Mama." Jesse told her. "Doing right by all of you makes me happy."

"Oh, I wish you'd consider that Render girl! You'd make a fabulous husband." She kissed him on the cheek. "Anyway your fathers in the kitchen. He wants to talk to you." She handed her son the note.

"Thank you, Mama." He mumbled as he looked at the letter. It was good paper, the kind rich folk used often. It read simply "Jessie Devote open at once." He did just that.

Meet at the docks at four, while it's still righteous for men to do so. Don't let your new guest distract you too long.

-Bellefellow

Jessie shook his head at the note. What guest could the damn Priest be talking about? "Fuck him." He mumbled under his breath then ripped up the letter and stuffed it into his pocket. He'd burn it later. The bounty hunter put his shirt on and finished getting dressed. It didn't take long. With a gunslinger's life, he was almost never fully naked. After he was finished, he walked out to meet his father.

"Sit and eat something boy." His father said without looking up from the paper.

"Well, I'll go fetch some water. I know you boys need to talk about something important." His mother said and walked out the house with a bucket.

"Papa I-" Jesse started when they were alone.

"One second." His father said as he finished the article he was reading. When he was done with it, he folded up the paper and stared his son in the eyes. "You're mother's not stupid you know. I wouldn't have married her if she was. She just loves you. So do I, but I was a soldier too. I know the look of a man doing violence."

"I don't think she's stupid." Jesse was taken aback.

"Well, then you're stupid for telling anyone, not a moron, those lies you do." His father said calmly. "I know you're not a trader, son."

"How?" He didn't even bother lying to the man who raised him.

"A trader doesn't come back with so many scars," he looked his son up and down, "and I've heard stories about your work."

"What kind of stories?" Jesse cursed at himself. Stories to intimidate were good if you were in the business of intimidating people. They were less good if you were trying to hide your career from a family that loved you.

"Stories about a war hero taking on a pack of savages for ear money, or subduing a band of outlaws all by himself." He stood up and gave Jesse a plate filled with eggs and sausages. "Those kind of stories."

"People exaggerate things." He said trying to backpedal away from the situation. "I ran into some trouble on the road, that's it."

His father looked at Jessie and shook his head. "People do exaggerate things." He said looking at his son. "They seldom make up stories out of thin air."

"I do what I have to." Jesse said looking at the floor.

"No, you don't." His father said still trying to look his son in the eye. "I might have lived with you being a bounty hunter, despicable as those lot are. These stories are something else." He shook his head again. "I know you were good at soldiering. A great many soldiers do that kind of work when they get out, but this thrill-seeking has to stop."

"I'm not thrill-seeking!" Jessie said, then realized he was almost shouting and lowered his voice. "I'm not thrill-seeking."

"If you're not thrill-seeking then you're desperate. Only a desperate man would go after the people you're gunning for." He paused as if trying to understand the situation. "Jim Jones, Hurton Caliper, The damned Red Scarf gang. Those are big names."

"Big names pay better." Jesse tried not to look guilty.

"Are you gambling, son?" He reached an arm across the table.

"I don't gamble." Jesse said trying to look anywhere except at his father's sad eyes.

"Then why?" Renny was pleading. "I saved my entire life for you to go to University and be someone, but Demons Below I'd rather you be a bookbinder like me than this." He took his son's hand, and Jessie looked at his father. "Why?"

"What if someone told you they could fix Bo-Bo?" The bounty hunter said with desperation. "Not just help but fix for good."

"I'd call that man a liar." His father said taking the hand away. "You think one of those damned quacks selling sugar mixed with opium is going to fix my boy." He shook his head. "You're smarter than that."

"It's not one of those people. It's someone who can help." Jessie tried to make his father understand.

"A Priest?" His father was in disbelief. "I'd take the word of a quack before I took theirs, and I'd rather you work for the Red Scarf Gang than for the Old Religion."

"The Red Scarf Gang can't fix my brother." Jessie sighed. "There's only one way to do that."

"I can't imagine they have much concern over the justice system." Renny said still in disbelief. "Why are they making you do these things?"

"At first it was just money they were asking for and too much of it to earn honestly. I saw a billfold advertising a man worth more than I could make in half a year bookbinding or soldering." Jesse unconsciously touched his gun belt. "Then when I couldn't make enough of it doing even that, they started asking for favors." His voice went to a whisper.

"What kind of favors?" His father asked, and for the first time, there was shame in his eyes.

"The kind I won't speak about now or any other day." The bounty hunter hung his head. *The kind of favors that involve killing innocent men and abducting children.* He thought. *The kind of favors that make me want to eat a bullet, so I won't have to face you or Mama knowing what I've done.*

"You can't trust those people." He said looking at his son with desperation. "It's their foul sorcery that's done this to my boy in the first place."

"That's what I used to think too." Jesse leaned towards his father. "Then after the first payment, they promised his nightmares would be gone, and they were. If they did this to him, they can undo it."

"You think you're doing this for Bobby?" He looked baffled. "I won't let one son kill himself for the other."

"I am doing this for Bo-Bo." Jesse sighed and changed his strategy. "I'll ask again, Papa, and I expect an answer this time. What would you do if someone told you they could fix your son? My brother?

"And I knew they were telling the truth?"

"Yes."

"I'd pay whatever price they asked. I'd walk into the ocean with lead in my pockets if that was it." He looked at his son like he was a Demon asking for him to serve the world on a silver platter. "But I wouldn't sell you Jess."

"Well, then you put a higher price on me than I do." Jesse looked at his father like he was a stranger. "Bo-Bo's the best of us, and you know it. He might be the best in the whole damn world for all of it I've seen. He deserves the chances I had. He'd have been worthy of them. He doesn't deserve this."

"No, he doesn't but son..." He trailed off. "The price is your soul."

"That's a price I'll pay happily."

His father looked horrified. "I know you'd sell your life son, but what about your soul? Anything that asks that can't be worth it."

"If I have to sell that in the afterlife than that's something else entirely. My soul is mine. Even a Priest can't take that from me yet." Jesse said it with a defiance that shocked even himself.

"You're wrong about that son." He paused as if his next words were too much for him to say at once. "I know at your heart you're a good man. You can try to hide it if that makes you feel better, but no one evil would care for that boy the way you do. You risked your life to protect all those men in Puena. The Prime Governor himself gave you a medal for that. The only time I've been prouder in my life was when you tried to fight all those McCullock boys for picking on that little kid from up the street, and you got your ass whipped." Renny put a hand on his boy from across the table. "You're right. They can't steal your soul, but they can make you twist it. You'll do one bad thing and another until you can't see the difference anymore. That's what makes it so evil, that you're letting them do this to you.

One day you'll come back so changed that all you can see of Bobby, is some mongoloid child you used to feel something for."

"You're wrong no one can make me stop loving that boy." Jessie said with a conviction he hadn't even felt when he was trying to save his men.

"No one but you." His father said gripping his arm harder. "People think that selling their soul is so evil and impossible. It's what makes them do it so damn often. The truth is that the world asks us that price every day, bit by bit, piece by piece. The truth is that every time we sell something to an illiterate man at an ungodly price or lay outside our marriage bed, we give it to them, and its never worth it. It's the hardest thing in the world to keep it, and that's what makes it so easy to give away. You're getting a better price than most but keep it. Please, I beg you."

"I'll do what I can." Jesse said knowing his brother was worth it.

"You were in an infantry regiment same as I was, son." His father sighed trying a different tact. "Means you marched your fair share of long miles."

"Aye and I did." Jessie admitted unsure where his father was going with it all.

"Do you remember the pain that came with it?"

Jessie remembered it. He could remember every caress and touch of the agony, almost in the same way he could remember the curves and dimples of Mary. He remembered where his pack rubbed him raw, where his rifle chafed his shoulder, even where his pistol dug into his side. He remembered that agony worse than any beating he'd ever taken because it was ever present but sharper than a bayonet. He remembered how he thought every next step would be when his legs failed to move. How the next second he'd think his soul would finally decide his back and legs couldn't take the punishment. He remembered deciding he was through and looking left and right to the men around him. He remembered seeing their stalwart faces too stubborn, too brave to give in. He remembered deciding he could move just a little farther if they could. He remembered at the end of every day when he set down his pack thinking they were the strongest men to ever live. They were George The Tall. They were Henry Holiest of Men. They were Then Ironwill. They were greater than the Three above. They were greater than the Demons below. They were gods. "Aye, I remember. There's a reason I ride a horse now."

"Why didn't you just fall out and ride in the baggage train with the other cowards?" His father tapped the table remembering his own marches.

"I don't rightly know." Jesse paused. "I thought about it every second though. I suppose it's because the rest of them didn't. I don't think I could look at myself in the mirror if I had." He looked his paw in the eye then. "I figured if even one of them could do it I could."

"You know I never realized it at the time, but I do now. Marching is like life. You're just not letting the world get the best of you at the end of the day."

"Then what are we marching too then?" Jesse asked. "Death? That's a morbid thought."

"In a sense." His father smiled. "But it's not really so morbid a thought when you think about it. We're not falling out because we're trying to meet the end of the line knowing we were strong enough to bear whatever those Above or Below could make us carry."

"If that's the metaphor I don't think I've fallen out quite yet." Jesse smiled. "They've sure made my pack heavy. though."

"Because you're the only one who can carry it son." His father reached out and grabbed his son's shoulder. "And whatever happens next, I'm proud of you for carrying it this long."

"Thank you." It was all he could say.

Just then he heard a knock on the door. "I'll get it." His father said standing up pushing the cracking and popping of his old body out of his system. He walked to the front of the house. "Who's there?"

"Mary." Jesse heard the response through the door and shot up. *Your new guest.* He remembered the note.

"That's for me." The bounty hunter ran to the door, flinging it open. He saw her standing there in the doorway. She was dressed humbly, not like a whore. She had on road clothes a stained white blouse and long purple skirt that looked like it needed a wash, and a wool cloak. However, Jesse hardly noticed what she was wearing. All he saw was that soft smile that seemed to tell him the whole world could wait a moment longer. She had the red rose he had given her stuck in her blouse. It made him happy to see her wear it and happier still to see her at all. Yet, he knew that someone thought she could hurt him or she wouldn't be here.

"Hello, Jesse." She said and rushed into his arms and laid a kiss on his mouth. Then she looked around and saw his father with a face shocked as if he'd seen a princess walk into his house and blushed red enough to be seen even through her dark complexion. "Sorry." She said softly then extended her hand to him "I'm Mary."

He shook her hand still apparently shocked. "Renny Devote." He took her dainty fingers in his rough, calloused palm.

"Oh, you must be Jesse's father I didn't know he had one." She said favoring Renny with a smile then shooting a skeptical look towards the baffled gunslinger.

"Aye, most people do." His father said giving his son the same look Mary had. "Jesse isn't really one for talking about himself."

"You're right about that Mr. Devote."

Then Bobby ran out screaming his head off. "Ahhhhhhhhhhh!" He jumped up and down in the kitchen. "Not Mama! Not Mama!"

Jesse saw Mary jump startled and rushed over to his brother taking his head in both his hands. "Bo-Bo." He said firmly. "Calm down she's a friend of mine."

"Friend eh?" He heard his father chuckle.

"Friend eh!" He heard Mary say with an edge of anger.

"A very close friend." He said ignoring both of them.

Bobby stopped his jumping and looked around the room with his typical blank stare. "Oh." He paused. Then looked at Mary. "I guess I'll be her friend too."

He gestured Mary to come over to the two of them. She did, and Jesse gently took her hand and pulled her down to her knees with him.

"This is Mary." He said gently pushing the boy's head, so his gaze met hers.

"Hello." She said softly like she was trying to give an unruly horse a treat.

"Hello, Mary." He said ignoring the hand and reaching his hand out to touch her face. "Oh, you're pretty." He touched the rose on her blouse. "I like your flower."

Her hand went down to the rose and touched Bobby's, and to Jesse's surprise, he didn't shrink away. "Me too your brother gave it to me." Then she looked at Jessie. "I see the resemblance. You're much more handsome though." She looked back at Bobby and gave his hand a little squeeze.

"He gave me a flower just like it." Bobby frowned then. "I let some boys look at it, and they stepped on it, but Jess went and talked to them, and they bought me a new one." He smiled

"Well, you're brothers a caring person." She favored Jesse with a smile.

"I try." The gunslinger managed to growl out. "Mary, would you mind if we take a walk for a minute?" He asked nodding to the door.

"Can I come?" Bobby perked up. "I want to spend more time with Mary!"

"Well, of course-" She started.

"I'm sorry Bo-Bo we have some important things to discuss." He stood up and gave his brother's hair a little ruffle. "I promise she'll come for dinner though."

"Oh." Bobby said with more than a little disappointment as he looked at Mary. "I'll see you at dinner then."

"Be safe you two." His father said as the pair walked out the door. "They never did catch the man who killed that cooper a few streets over."

"Will do Paw." He said as he hurried the girl out of the house.

"So what's this important business you need to discuss." Mary said walking down the street and putting her arm around Jesse's.

It took a while before Jessie could muster up the courage to ask her, but once they were far enough from the house he did. "Why are you here?" He asked. It sounded colder than he intended it too, far colder.

Mary recoiled as if struck. "So all that talk about you wanting me to come to Pentsville was just so you could get a better price on your favorite whore!" She seethed with anger, and everyone in the crowded street paused and looked at the couple. He even heard one man snicker. It was lucky Jessie couldn't tell who it was, or he'd have broken the man's nose.

"No!" He said grabbing Mary's shoulder which she shrugged off angrily. "I didn't mean it like that." He pulled her into an alley away from prying eyes. "I want you to be here, I really do, but things are happening here that you don't want any part in."

"So that's what being a wife is like!" She said striking Jessie in the chest and then got even angrier when he didn't budge. "I'm supposed to wait until whenever's convenient for you to see me." She was furious now. In all the time they'd been seeing each other he'd seen her happy, sad, and scared but never angry. "That seems a lot like being a whore. It just pays worse."

"I meant every word of it, Mary." He said and reached his hand up to stroke her face, but she slapped it away.

"Meant!" She hit him again. "So now that I'm here you'd rather me back in Rory's Rest, is that it?" She turned around to leave. "So turns out you were just like all those other men.

"No!" He said louder than he should have and grabbed her shoulder and pulled her to him. He kissed her then. She resisted at first, but when she felt how genuine it was, she let go of most of her anger. "You know that's not true." He said pleadingly, grabbing her hand. "If I were like the rest of them would I have left you all that money? Would I have even told you where I live?"

"No, I suppose not." She was finally mollified. "I guess I was just afraid that I'd come all this way and you'd want nothing to do with me." She looked at her feet. "Then I saw the way you acted with me in front of your family and..." She paused. "I don't know."

Jesse grabbed her face just like he did with Bobby and kissed again. "I was just surprised." He sighed. "Men get like that whenever they have to show a woman to their parents."

She looked up smiling slyly, but there was a bit of nervousness there too. "Have you taken many women home to your parents then?" She said stroking his hand gently.

"You're the first." He said returning the smile. "It's just what I've heard."

"That's a relief." She said letting out a breath, that it seemed she'd been holding for a long while. "It was a long trip from Rory's Rest, and I had a lot of time to think. I even got the notion that you might be married."

"Well, trust me you're safe on that front." He chuckled. "But I guess what I meant was, how are you here?"

"A man in black came and bought a night with me." She looked almost ashamed at the statement, and Jessie knew who was behind it immediately.

"If he hurt you he'll pay." The gunslinger took a step forward and put his arms on her shoulders. He'd comfort her now, violence would come later.

"No nothing like that." She shook her head. "He didn't even touch me. He came and gave me more money than I've ever seen in one place."

"And you took it?" Jessie took a step back and gave the girl an appraising look. He'd always thought her clever. How could she do something so stupid? "They own you now. They own us."

"I did take the money." She caught the look he gave her. "They don't own me any more than the men who pay to stay in my bed." She returned the glare in turn. "You never talk about what you've had to do to survive, and you've never asked me in turn. I think that's the reason I fell in love with you. Because you know that it doesn't define you or me." She took a breath gathering itself. "I don't want to just survive anymore. I want to live."

"That money came from the people I'm enslaved to." He turned away from Mary. "You want to talk about living rather than surviving." He sighed and turned back. "What do you think I've been doing? They've turned me from a man into an animal."

"You're not an animal." She stepped forward and put a hand on his cheek. "I could never love an animal."

"The only part of me that's still living is with my brother and you." He put his hand over hers. "Now they've gotten to both."

"I've taken their money, but I'm bound to you by a higher law." She kissed him, and he knew that he was bound to her as well.

"They'll use that." He sighed. "I hate them. I hate to see you entwined to them." It was still hard to say he loved her back.

"I'm entwined to you. Whoever they are, whatever they'll ask of us we'll face it together." Mary smiled in a way that was defiant and loving all at once.

"I'd rather that I think." He smiled back. "I just wouldn't want to see a soul like yours corrupted by this."

"That's my choice to make." She took a step back and bit her lip. "You know when I came here, I wasn't sure you were willing to be together like that."

"What changed?" He asked still smiling.

"You said we were enslaved." She looked up at him. "You didn't even think about it. You just knew you were too."

"I suppose so." He could feel his face blushing. "Let's go back to the house."

"I'd love to meet your family for longer than it takes you to shuffle me out the door." She said walking out to the street.

He didn't know how he was supposed to act with her. It seemed appropriate for them to walk arm in arm, but in all his memory he couldn't recall a time for he'd ever done it in public, besides his mother when he'd been a boy. She didn't seem to have any reservations about it. She wrapped her arm around his waist. It was as if Mary was saying she didn't belong to him like some southern belle. They were together. It was both of their choices. A thought struck him though as they were walking. "My brothers a bit..." He wasn't sure how to describe it. "Special I suppose you could say if you haven't noticed already."

"He's sweet just like his brother." She kissed him on the cheek. She didn't see that he screamed when things were too loud or that he didn't know where to look when he talked or even that he didn't know how far to stay away. She saw Bo-Bo. If he hadn't loved her before, he loved her for that.

"It's just that, well, he's a bit fragile." Jesse said carefully.

"Just like his brother." She smiled again. "You know I didn't start to feel for you because of your medals or your scars. Well, I suppose I did because that's part of what made you, but it was when I knew the sort of man you really were."

"What sort of man is that?" He asked.

"The sort of man that does what's right." She said warmly. "No more than that. The sort of man who knows what's right even if he makes mistakes."

"I've made many mistakes." Jesse said with some shame.

"And you know they were mistakes." She kissed his cheek again. "Men try to justify what they do. On the few instances that you've talked about the wrongs you've done, there was remorse there,"

"I don't think I'm done with my mistakes yet." Jesse muttered.

"No, you've a hard path ahead I imagine." She admitted. "But some false speech about how you're on the straight and narrow for good, is almost as bad as making an excuse." She sighed. "You know what's wrong, which is why I'm sure you'll always do right by me."

"I don't know that a man like me can ever do right by a girl like you." Jesse said with the same shame.

"I'm a whore, and you're a decorated war hero." She said with a laugh. "Some might say I'm dragging you down."

"Some are fools." He looked at her and smiled as they walked. "You're a good woman who was in a bad way." He faced forward so he wouldn't trip. "I believe you've only had good in your heart. There's two kinds of people in this world, those who let the evil drag them down, and those who rise above it." He stopped and found they'd finally reached the house. "Well, we're here."

"Then let's go inside." She headed towards the door and opened it before Jesse had a chance to follow her. When he made it through the door, he saw his family there. His mother was working on what was presumably dinner or a late lunch, his father was mending some old book. He was retired, but the old man felt a pang of nostalgia every once in a while, and Bo-Bo was playing a game with little wooden sticks. Jessie had tried to understand it on more than one occasion, but the rules were too complex, and his brother's explanations were wanting. When the bounty hunter cleared his throat, they all looked up except Bo-Bo who was in a deep trance with his sticks. The boy could spend weeks playing that game and had to be reminded to eat and sleep.

"Hi, maw." He said as she was the only one who hadn't met Mary. "Mary this is my mother, Denise Devote." Jessie said. "Maw this is-"

"Oh, I know who she is!" She rushed up and gave the girl a hug. "Your father's already told me about her." Then she released a surprised Mary and turned to face her. "Renny told me how beautiful you are, but I had trouble believing it. I know how my son is with girls."

"Maw!" Jesse started to object, but his mother cut him off.

"Don't act like it's not true!" She scolded her son then looked back to Mary. "After he got home from that dreadful war with all those medals, he could have taken whatever girl he wanted."

"Oh, is that so?" Mary gave Jessie a sarcastic smile.

"It was, until he spent all his time drinking and fighting." She gave her son the same look. "I was worried he'd only be able to pay for a woman." Mary looked down with a little shame that only Jessie noticed. He wished she wouldn't. It was the world that deserved the shame for forcing her to do what she'd done.

"Well, here I am." She smiled the moment gone.

"What time is it Paw?" Jessie asked remembering the note he received. His own pocket watch had been broken for some time.

"It's about a quarter after two." Renny frowned at the boy. "Do you have business?" He asked looking his son up and down.

"Aye, I have some work needs taking care of." He gave his father an angry look.

Mary saw the exchange and cut in before it could get ugly. "Well, I ought to go to Michael's inn I have a room there." She smiled at the pair.

"Nonsense!" Jessie's mother said before anyone could object. "I won't have my little Jess's woman pay for a room when she can stay with us."

"Oh that's very kind, but I wouldn't want to put anyone out." The girl said with characteristic tact.

"I haven't had another girl in the house since I moved out of my family home." Denise smiled happily. "It'll be excellent!"

"Well, if you insist…" Mary said unsure of herself, though Jesse could tell she'd like nothing more than to stay in a home for once.

"I do!" His mother smiled. "When Jessie gets back from his business he'll help pick up your things."

"I'd love to." The bounty hunter put a hand on the girls back.

Mary gave Jesse a sly smile. "I'm afraid I don't really have much in the way of luggage, but I'd be happy for the company."

"Well, I best be off." He gave his mother and father a hug like the one he'd given them after he enlisted. "I should be back before supper." Maybe they didn't know why his voice was shaking, but every time he met with the Priest, he felt like he was a little farther from the people he loved.

"I'll walk you out. I should go square my agreement with the innkeeper." Mary said seeing a bit of the distress in his voice. She grabbed his hand as they went out the door.

When they were out of earshot, Jesse turned to her. "I've got to go see the man responsible for the money you've got." He squeezed her hand

"I never wanted to cause you any trouble." Mary said slightly ashamed. "I just couldn't stay where I was."

He kissed her and saw her spirits rise a bit. "You haven't caused me anything I haven't brought on myself already." He put on his hat. "Just remember they're bad people."

Jesse walked along the street to the docks, then when he couldn't bear it anymore, he looked back and saw Mary still looking at him. He knew why Bellefellow had brought her to his house. The Priest thought he'd got some extra leverage over the bounty hunter, but the bastard was wrong. He'd given Jesse something to fight for. Jesse remembered how something had made the Priest flinch in their last meeting. Maybe it was just a cramp, maybe it wasn't, but for Mary and Bo-Bo he'd find a way to break gods.

———◆◆◆◆———

Jesse arrived early to the docks and bought a bag of honeyed almonds. Bellefellow was always late to these meetings, but the gunslinger had learned early that it pays to be at a rendezvous first. You never know when a man's gonna cross you, and it's best to see the lay of the land if he does.

He saw a ship being crafted and it wasn't for trading. It had the slick look of a war sloop, or at least what a war sloop had looked like fifty years ago. The South had relied too heavily on Northern ships for too long to suddenly start building them now. Jesse had seen a true warship in his days in the army. Now they had armor plating and steam engines. Whoever sailed on the rigs being built in Pentsville was going to die. Even the cannons they were loading on the floating casket seemed odd to his eyes. They were too big. Aye, they'd pack a hell of a punch, but they probably wouldn't get a chance to throw the second one. The game had changed. The smaller Northern ones could shoot five times before this antique could even reload.

Ironwill's Vision was written on the side. Jesse wasn't a political man, but having the country he founded tear itself apart didn't seem like anything ole Then would have wanted.

After he'd eaten half of the bag of almonds, he folded it up and put it in his pocket. Bo-Bo loved the treats, and he assumed Mary did too. They both deserved it more than him anyhow.

As he was doing it, he saw a face he knew, but couldn't quite place. The man caught sight of him gave a wave and a smile and came to sit beside him. Jessie was too baffled to provide any protest about it, so the man just sat happily.

"Mr. Devote." He said with a smile and extended his hand as if they were close friends.

"I'm sorry sir you've caught me at a disadvantage." Jesse shook his hand politely. Perhaps it was an old comrade he'd fought with, but that didn't make any sense. The man didn't look like a soldier, and the bounty hunter knew the name, face, and talents of every man who'd ever served under him.

"Sorry I realize I never introduced myself properly." The man shook his head and chuckled. "I'm Harold Jensen."

Realization dawned on him. The name meant nothing, but now up close he realized it was the waiter he'd met those weeks ago. "Oh, the waiter." Harold had dropped his pompous attitude from before and now seemed as amicable as an old drinking companion. "I'm sorry I didn't have the money to pay. It was a bit to rich for me, and I thought the other fellow would pick up the tab."

The man started laughing uncontrollably. When he finally stopped for long enough to get a word out, he clapped Jesse on the shoulder. "Don't be I got a good laugh out of it." He shook his head in disbelief. "Huego ears." He mused to himself.

"Well, I'm glad someone got a good laugh out of that night Mr. Jensen." The bounty hunter said bitterly.

The man went serious for a moment. "I know what that Priest did to you…" He gave an involuntary shudder. "Well, it didn't seem right to say the least." He paused for a second as if working up to it. "I just saw you here, and I wanted to say I'm sorry for treating you so poorly." Harold had genuine remorse in his voice.

"Think nothing of it." Jessie wanted the poor fool to leave before Bellefellow saw the waiter.

"But I should Mr. Devote." Harold said nodding his head in difference. "I know who you are. My brother served in the same regiment as you and wrote back about how you saved them all." He twiddled his thumbs while he talked. "He died in the last days of the war, but his ghost would haunt me forever if it saw how rude I was to you without giving proper apologies."

"Don't worry I know I didn't belong in that place." Jessie said with a wave of his hand. "I figured it was part of the persona aristocrats pay for. You know being rude to the rabble.

"Well, that's true I suppose." The man said scratching his head.

"I'm trying to save up enough to buy a restaurant of my own, so my boy can have something to inherit, but that doesn't make it right."

Just then Bellefellow arrived. He saw the crowds whispered panic and terrified bows before he saw the crimson robes and white acolytes. "Leave now." Jessie said under his breath.

"Sir, I just meant to apologize to you." He looked almost hurt.

Jessie looked at the man. "And I accept, but I have a meeting with the sort of folk you wouldn't want to meet again."

The man looked up and saw the Priest bearing down on them and ran before Jessie had a chance to look back. Bellefellow shooed the crowd away and saw Jessie sitting on the bench and gave a smile that might have been friendly on a different face.

"Why hello Mr. Devote." He said with a bit too much joy as he approached.

Jesse stood up and nodded his head. "Hello, your eminence." He meant it to sound deferent, but it came out like an angry dog trying to ape civilization.

The Priest sat down on the bench, and the white acolytes in perfect unison went to their knee in front of him. "Please sit. We have much to discuss." He patted the space next to him.

"Yes, your Eminence." He responded and sat.

"Is that honey'd almonds I smell?" Bellefellow rubbed his stomach. "I've always loved sweets."

Jessie took them out of his pocket. He wanted to throw them on the ground and spit on the snack rather than let this monster have them, but he remembered the helplessness of their last meeting. "Yes, your Eminence." He said meekly and handed them over. He tried to hold his tongue, but couldn't. "I bought them for my brother and…" He didn't know why he didn't want to say Mary's name in front of him, but he didn't. "Well, my brother."

"Well, I'm sure you can buy more." He popped one in his mouth and sucked on it a little. "These heathens keep working long after what is appropriate."

"I suppose you're right." Jessie nodded.

"Of course I'm right." He smiled again. "So how have you been enjoying that little present I brought over." The Priest said through a mouthful of almond.

She's not a present you damn ape. Jesse wanted to scream, but instead, he merely nodded. "She's a good woman your eminence."

"She was probably cheaper when you were paying for it." He gave one of his predatory smiles. "The only reason I waited this long was because I wasn't sure you actually wanted her full time. Then one of my men saw the way you looked back at her, and I thought you don't look back at paid company like that."

If it were any other man Jesse would have shot him dead right there and damned the consequences, instead he politely replied. "If its all the same to you, I'd rather not talk about her that way."

"Of course, of course." He nodded. "The first rule of whoring is to never call her a whore after all."

The bounty hunter tried desperately to control his anger. "I don't have any money to pay you with." He said and shook his head. They both knew what that meant. It meant favors.

Bellefellow put a hand that might have been meant to be reassuring on the man's shoulder, but all it did was make his skin crawl. "I like to think our association has moved beyond mere money." He shrugged his shoulders. "Even though you tried to kill me last we met."

"Then what do you want?" It was always like this. Jessie started off polite as a slave to his master, then his patience wore thin as he was slowly reminded that their relationship actually was that of a slave and his master.

"Oh, I just wanted to make sure you were adjusting well." The bounty hunter narrowed his eyes, and the Priest chuckled. "That is to say I have nothing more for you at this very moment."

"Then why?" He glared at the smile.

"Have you heard of your former compatriot, Andrew Belson's brother?" Bellefellow put another almond in his mouth. It was probably too much to hope that he'd choke on it, but the gunslinger hoped for it anyway.

"Thomas Belson?" He was confused.

The Priest's immaculately handsome face transformed into a vicious scowl. Jesse had never seen that reaction come from the mention of another man. "That's the one."

"Everyone in the world's heard that name." Jessie muttered thinking. "If half the stories they tell about him are true, then he's a handy man in a fight."

"More than half the stories are true." Bellefellow kept his scowl as he ate another almond. "And handy fighter is as big an understatement as I've ever heard." Maybe it was his eyes playing tricks on him, but the Priest seemed worried, almost scared.

"As I understand it he's not to keen on the Old Religion." Jesse allowed himself a smile.

"He's a heretic, clinging to a joke of a church." Bellefellow spit on the ground. "But he's dangerous, very dangerous."

"And what do you want me to do about it?" Jesse said. He could almost feel the power shifting his way

"If he were just some normal mercenary, I could have him dead on the streets by sundown." The Priest took a long breath. "However, he's a Constable."

"So you need a man to do it the old-fashioned way." Jessie nodded. "Guns, bullets, knives."

"Don't fool yourself." Bellefellow sneered. "My order was killing fools when your lot were still stabbing men with sharpened wood." He shook his head. "But every once in a while, a man needs to be beaten to death." The Priest shook his head. "Can you do it?"

The bounty hunter shook his head in thought. "You say the stories about him are true."

"They are."

Jesse shook his head in disbelief. "If I learned anything in war it's that any man can kill anyone else on a given day." He nodded looking at the docks. "I've watched a private shoot a general off his horse." He sighed. "If I had the drop on him and a good rifle… Well, I assume he's not bulletproof."

"That's good." Bellefellow nodded as if he'd just been heavily reassured, but Jesse wasn't.

"Still a man doesn't survive fifteen years of the worst fighting in a millennia, without keeping his eyes open." The bounty hunter caressed his own weapon,

"But it's possible." The Priest leered at the man.

"Aye, it's possible. It's more possible to put a bullet in McAllan's head." Jessie gave the Priest a curious look. "Still it seems unwise."

"I don't know that you're the man to say what's wise." Bellefellow said condescendingly.

"You're right, and I'm not a political man." The bounty hunter admitted. "It just seems like if the most famous Constable in the world gets shot, a lot of eyes might find themselves staring at the Old Religion." Jesse shook his head. "You can forget making it look like an accident if that's what you're thinking.

"I'm not asking you to do it now." The Priest waved his hand dismissively. "But political climates change, and one day people might find his name less than exalted, and on that day I'll need to know it can be done."

Jessie nodded then a thought occurred to him. "Do you know the first rule of being a bounty hunter?"

"Don't get shot?" The Priest gave him a leer. "I haven't the time to familiarize myself with provincial wisdom, so if you have a point get to it."

"A heavy name demands a heavy price." Jessie returned the stare. "If the day comes when I'll need to kill the man with the heaviest name in the world, I'll demand the heaviest price."

"Don't forget yourself." Bellefellow said in a voice so threatening it chilled the gunslinger's bones, but Jesse hadn't won the Iron circle for letting good opportunities pass him by.

"If I do him, I'm off your leash." The bounty hunter said threatening a smile. "I want my brother cured for good and enough money to take my family and Mary out East for a new life." He paused. "And I never want to see another blood colored cloak for as long as I live.

"Oh, so you think this is a business arrangement." The Priest said with the joy of a predator circling around its prey.

Jesse tried to object, but all of a sudden he seemed to have forgotten how to speak.

Bellefellow continued. "It's not business. You're my slave. A good master always rewards good service, but on his terms, not the slaves." He reached forward and touched the head of one of his white-clad acolytes. "You see this identity crisis all stems from one misconception. You still think you're a man." He pulled down the white hood of the child in front of him and smiled wider. It was a face Jessie knew. It was the face that used to belong to a boy begging a man not to murder his father. It might have been a beautiful face if not for a crescent-shaped scar on his chin where a man had accidentally run a knife across. "Tell me do you still think you're a man?"

Jesse couldn't speak, but it wasn't magic this time. His body rejected any words he might have used to justify his actions.

"No, I thought you wouldn't." Bellefellow pulled up the hood hiding the boys face. "If I decide you should kill Thomas Belson, and you succeed. I'll reward you as I see fit not as you do." He stood up and smiled. "And no matter how far you go the only way you'll be free of me is if you take that pistol of yours and put it in your mouth, but then you'll belong to my masters, the Demons. They don't even reward slaves." He walked away then. Jesse couldn't even tell which one of the acolytes that followed was the one who's father he'd killed.

The bounty hunter sat there until the Priest was out of sight. He ran away from the docks away from everything. He followed his feet until they took him to the inn where Mary was staying. He asked the man at the front what room she was in if the innkeeper noticed his distressed persona he was kind enough not to mention it. He ran up the stairs and opened the door without knocking. Mary was there naked on the bed waiting for him. Then she saw the look on his face and the tears in his eyes.

"What happened?" She stood up hurrying towards him.

He didn't answer. He folded her into a hug and kissed her hard.

"It's alright Jess." She pulled him towards the bed. "It'll be alright." She'd never seen her lover like this before. He wept into her shoulder as Mary held him.

He didn't know how long it was, but eventually, he composed himself enough to speak. "Do you think you could love an evil man?" He asked looking at her through the tears.

"No." She said with resolve. "That's why I love you."

"You don't know what I am." He looked to her like a man looked to a temple for salvation.

"I don't know what you've done." She replied and stroked his hair. "But I know what you are."

Jessie fell asleep in her naked arms. It was better than he deserved. Mary should have more than a slave.

The Thaniel Wars

J rode into Gertinville like I had all of the World Below chasing me. In some ways I did. I saw men wearing Anthanii red hastily preparing to retreat. If you watched the faceless prepare to tuck tail and run, you probably couldn't tell the difference between that and an advance. The difference was in the eyes. Every moving body from private to colonel had the same look. It was fear and hopelessness. It was of sacrifices made in vain and brothers lost for nothing. It was defeat.

I dismounted my horse. It was too tired to give them the message that they needed. My legs and abdomen ached from the long ride. My body screamed at me to limp from the bones I'd broken in the city of Imor, hastily healed as they were. The tattoos on my arm burned like wildfire. They told me there were too many Demons loose for one man to do anything. Even my mind told me to leave. In the end, we are all creatures of the pack. When we see those around us broken, we feel broken ourselves.

I walked tall. I marched like I was moving under arches of gold to celebrate our glorious. I moved like I imagined the heroes of old would. Victory was here because I was here. Give me one sacrifice more, and I would make it count.

I wore my uniform, black except the white Tree of the Faith on the front. My tattoos shown for the world to see. I wore my six-shooters. I let my tomahawk hang from my side. I let them see what defiance was. The world had been too long without its heroes. Every hero starts with a conviction, and mine was that if I died, it would not be unarmed. *Follow me!* My body screamed.

Men stopped working around the retched ruins of Gertinville to stare at me.

"That's Thomas Belson." I heard a private whisper.

"Belson the Blessed." A corporal with his arm in a sling said with more conviction.

"We're saved!" I heard someone scream from far away.

I didn't acknowledge that I heard them. I wanted to let them know that any condition didn't matter. Not my enemy's guns, not my ally's adulation. We would win because we would win. In the end, we're all just creatures of the pack. If they see one man say there's hope with enough conviction, people believe him.

"He's just a boy with a couple battles under his belt." I heard a salty sergeant say. "We're as dead as we were before he got here."

Sometimes when things get too desperate, the walk's not enough. You need to show them. I smiled at the sergeant's words. I always have loved proving men wrong.

I walked to the headquarter's tent where I knew Lord Corbula was. The sentries guarding it saluted me. I saluted back. I ducked my head under the flap. There were six of Corbula's staff organizing the retreat. It was an austere tent, but Corbula was an austere man.

"Gendry pack up the big guns and-" Corbula stopped mid sentence. "Constable Belson?" He gave me a queer look. "I heard you were dead in Kran."

"Not quite yet." I smiled around the room.

"Have you come to help us with the retreat?" The lord knew he had a duty to his men, and he'd do it. He wouldn't let them see how desperate he was, but I saw. I saw the weariness in his eyes. I saw that for all his discipline, the fight had gone out of him. Someone needed to put it back.

"No, I did not come to help with the retreat." I said with a sneer. "I didn't come with my ass bare to let Thaniel fuck it either if that was your follow up."

That got a laugh from the staff. It was forced and desperate, but it was a laugh. There's only one time you can change a man's conviction about the world, and that was when he laughs. Corbul's staff were probably the sternest officers in the Anthanii army, but even they knew the day was lost.

"I came to take this city back with you." I looked around the room. "I came to win."

Corbul shook his head. "It can't be done, Thomas." He stared back up at me. "We're holding onto Gertinville by the tips of our fingers. If we stay here, our entire army will be destroyed." He tapped the map. "Our only chance is to retreat, and link up with Prince Edward's men. We can throw them back there." He kept staring at the map. "We'll have his seventy-thousand and what remains of our forces."

I estimated that there were about thirty-thousand men ready to hold a rifle in line. He knew it was still hopeless. Even with ninety-thousand, we couldn't beat Kran in the open field yet. Southern Anthanii would fall and soon so would the rest of it. What's more, Gertinville was Anthanii land. It had been so for a thousand years. To lose it was to tell the world, Thaniel has a right to be here.

Corbul looked up at me with something close to desperation. "We'll also have you." It stiffened my spine, but even I knew, Belson the Blessed couldn't save the world if Gertinville fell.

"You have me now." I said simply. "What about the reinforcements?"

One of the more plain spoken colonels with a bandage across his check chimed in. "They were untrained boys," he said, "and the cannon they sent us were all but defective." He shrugged his shoulders. "Maybe three in ten of the guns worked and none all to well."

Another colonel who was clearly hiding a limp, decided to say his piece. "King John sent us a good number of cavalrymen, but in these ruins horses are useless."

I nodded at that. *Fucking idiot king!* His help had been worse than useless. It had been like giving a starving man a wax apple. He'd die from sheer disappointment.

"It still might have been enough," Lord Corbul put in, "but Thaniel's been funneling everything he has at us." He bit his lip. "His Northern army beat Prince Edward outside of Windbridge, and we're on the brink of being surrounded."

"After we've won here, I intend to ride with haste to Prince Edward and fix that as well." I looked down at the map. "From what I've heard his casualties have been minimal, and he still holds good ground." I surveyed the tent. "He's been beaten once, not routed." I said. "It was a far cry from Milhire." I didn't tell them I'd gotten the intelligence from a doctor who claimed to be the Three.

The tent gave some mumbled agreement, so apparently the information was good.

"Unless one of you can give me a good reason why Gertinville belongs to Thaniel we're taking this city back!" I smashed my fist into the table.

They all started looking at each other uncomfortably. Finally

Lord Corbula spoke. "They've brought their Priests." I saw the faces of the staff drop. I'd been on the point of convincing them, but those four words were like stones weighing on their souls. It was the one truth of the world. When agents of the Old Religion came, you ran.

"They've been trained at Threspin." The Colonel with the bandage on his cheek said. "They're not village charlatans, which would be bad enough. They're powerful," he hung his head, "and there's seven of them."

I knew what that meant. One powerful Priest could call lightning. Two could call a hurricane. Seven could suck the air out of a thousand men's lungs and laugh as they suffocated.

"So?" I said. "That's not a good enough reason."

"No one has ever beaten an army with seven Priests, Thomas." Lord Corbul started rolling up the map. "It's hopeless."

"No one until me." I stopped his hands. "I punched Bishop Harfeld." I let every man in the room see the truth in my eyes. "I watched him bleed." I moved my hands away from the map. "I'm still standing."

"It's true?" I heard one colonel whisper to another.

"Apparently." He responded.

"I will lead a group of volunteers to take the Priests position." I pointed to the Colonel with the bandaged face. "What's your name?"

"Lanside, your eminence." He nodded.

"Colonel Lanside will come with me." He'd been wounded in what seemed like close combat. A man that brave had to have some respect from the troops. I planned on using that.

"And the rest of us?" Lord Corbul asked.

"You'll marshal the men on the southern front and hit them in the flank." I looked around the whole room. "We're going to push them out of this fucking city." I sighed. "I learned something in my travels. I learned how to beat the Priests." It wasn't a particularly clever strategy, especially not when compared to what I'd done at Wuntsville. It was sound and it wouldn't work, unless I could punch through the middle.

The men didn't respond. They'd all heard my exploits, only they didn't think I could kill a Priest, much less seven. They were ready to pack it up and leave.

I didn't blame them. They weren't cowards. I'd only won a single victory that hadn't meant much, except as a propaganda point. Sure, I'd gotten some credibility after Milhire, but how much credibility could you really gain from a defeat. My name was as heavy as any in Anthanii, but it wasn't heavier than Thaniel's. At least, not yet it wasn't.

One officer with his arm in a sling said what they were all thinking. "You're risking everything on the obscure promise of a sixteen year old boy, my lord."

The entire staff listened to that. "He's a great warrior, Thendin." Lord Corbula answered him. There was no rebuke in his voice. In public. you never questioned your command, but in private, an officer who wouldn't say his piece was a liability.

"I know he's competent." Colonel Thendin sighed. "I heard about what he did at Milhire and Wuntsville." He turned his gaze to me. "Maybe if we'd had you five years ago, we'd be winning." He bit his lip. "Three above, maybe if you'd been here three month ago we'd have a chance." Thendin paused. "Maybe, if they didn't have seven Priests." He shook his head.

"Well, five years ago, I'd have been eleven, but I'd still have more bones than King John." I said with a smile.

That got a laugh out of the room, more sure than the first, but Thendin didn't seemed convinced. "I have no doubt you'll make one of the greatest warriors we'll ever see," he told me, "but we're facing *the* greatest warrior." He looked back to Lord Corbul. "I'll follow your orders whatever they are, but I caution against wagering everything on this boy's word." He turned his gaze back to me. "I believe you're good, boy, but I don't believe you're blessed."

Lord Corbul seemed to consider it.

"These men have families, my lord." Thendin scratched his arm. "I won't see them thrown away on a fool's hope."

"Maybe you're right." Lord Corbul admitted.

"Maybe he is," I echoed the sentiment, "but you all know, if we run now the war is over." I stood with pride. "We're going to have to face the Old Religion sooner or later, and I know a way to beat them here. Today!" I stared at Thendin. "You have two choices, die or follow me." I put a hand on his good shoulder. "Follow me and I'll see the sacrifices you made here mean something."

I let them know what the stakes were, victory or death. If they had any hope of winning this war, they would have continued the retreat. If they had any chance of winning the battle without me, they'd have told me to fuck off. They didn't. I may have been a fool's hope, but drowning men would cling to any straw.

Thendin took a deep breath. "I withdraw my complaint." He tore off his sling and drew his sword. "I still don't think we'll win, but we've got to try."

"Good you're coming with me." I patted his wounded shoulder.

"Aye, your eminence." To his credit he didn't complain.

I walked out the tent. A mob had gathered around it. They all cheered when I came out. "Belson the Blessed!" I heard a few scattered screams.

"I need volunteers!" I screamed.

"I told you he'd get us out of here." One private screamed.

"I'm not getting us out of anywhere!" I hollered back. "We're charging into the city they took from us, and getting it back." I saw the confusion on their faces. "We're going to mount those Priests heads on spikes and piss down their necks."

"Fuck." I heard the same private say. The mob started to disperse.

"So that's what your brothers' sacrifices are worth to you?" I challenged the crowd. "Every drop of Anthanii blood spent defending this city, and you're going to let foreigners take it from you!"

That put some iron in their backs. They knew what it had cost to hold this city for as long as they had. They were willing to grab onto any hope that would let them reclaim their land.

"Priests can't be beaten." A sergeant called out.

"They can." I said it calmly, but it carried through them all. "Many of you might have heard the rumor, but I come to confirm it." I paused. "I struck a Priest of the Old Religion, and he cried like a bitch."

That got a round of laughter.

"After that, I looked for secret magic." I said. "I went into Imor and I found a way to beat them."

The crowd gave a shocked gasp. Even the boldest of adventurers wouldn't dare those ruins.

"I read the private library of the Old Emperor!" I screamed. "There's a way to stop the Demon's below. Man has forgotten it, but now let us remember." *An old doctor told me.* "A great golden tomb told me, and it was confirmed from the reanimated corpse of the last ruler of Imor." I didn't think they needed too much truth.

"Now I call on you men of Anthanii!" I screamed. "This city has belonged to you for a thousand years. Come with me and it'll be yours for a thousand more!"

A cheer erupted.

"Let's show Thaniel what Anthanii steel taste like." I raised my six shooter.

Lord Corbul stepped out of the tent after me. "In these troubled times, where do men turn to." He caught the bait. "Look to the boy who survived Milhire with a company of men." He gave me a glance. "Look to the boy who saved Wuntsville with donkeys and scarecrows." He drew his own sword. "Look to the man who struck a Priest and lived."

The army cheered.

Lord Corbul went on addressing the crowd. "I have fought beside you." He said. "I have bled with you!" He screamed. "There are no better men in the whole of the world. With Thomas Belson, we can invade the World Below and know victory!"

I nodded at that. "Come with me men!"

They did. The wounded threw off their bandages. Clerks who had never held a weapon grabbed one then. They would fight. I had never been the sentimental type, but if I had to pick one moment that my heart remembered in my darkest times, it would be that one. It was the moment when the whole of the world pushed against a group of forsaken men, and they pushed back. As much as I'd like to take the credit, it wasn't me. They did it because they wanted to. They did it because it felt good.

<hr />

Five hundred men marched behind me. As we headed towards the sound of cannon fire, the soldiers who had been routing joined us. We became a force. We became more than we were, more than the sum of our parts.

I looked at Colonel Lanside. He was older than I'd have thought. It was hard to tell with the bloody bandage on his face. The grey in his hair spoke true, though.

Colonel Thendin was young on the other hand. He had golden blond hair, and I imagined that if he had never been forced to wear a uniform, he'd have been a happy sort. Hard times make us into things we never thought we'd be.

By the time we got to the place we'd charge from there were two thousand who stood ready to follow me. The city had been destroyed by half a year at war, but the soldiers had taken the time to fortify every inch of it. The city seemed to open up for us. Most of the buildings had been torn down by the constant barrage. Right before the hill started, there was a well dug trench, with a handful of Anthanii huddled together in terror.

I saw the enemy first. It was a line of gold cloaked Kranish infantry. They were arrayed smoothly, in perfect order. Behind them stood a battery of cannon, and behind that I saw the Priest chant. If this General Holsten wasn't suited for urban warfare, he had learned quick. It was exactly the formation I would have picked.

I felt the first cannon shot hit beside me. "In the trench!" I screamed. There were still some Anthanii holding onto a long defensive perimeter. I lead my two thousand into it under the cannon fire.

"Hold!" I screamed. It was suicide to attack with a barrage like that upon us. I'd wait till the reload.

The world around us seemed to shake. I'd stood through cannon fire before, but never like that. Sitting in that trench like trapped dogs while every big gun tried to murder us, I began to wonder if my plan was bold or just suicidally stupid.

The buildings that still stood caved quickly under the fire. The infantry was close enough to shoot as well. We took casualties on our mad dash to the trench. The defenses were well built, but still they got lucky. Even if we did charge, the Kranish held the high ground, and they were rested. Even if timed perfectly some of their cannons could still be quick enough to shred us. That wasn't even to think about the Priests that lay behind those.

I saw a few of my men try to run. They weren't cowards, they just saw how hopeless it all was. Still, any man who so much as stuck his head out the trench got it blown off. Even with the blind faith they put in me, I felt their fear rising. I needed to quell it.

"Oh you forgotten men of today!" I screamed. Even through the barrage they heard me. "Oh you abandoned by your king! Now is your hour!" I bit down. "For a thousand years in the bright future of Anthanii, men will call you their proudest ancestors!" No one else tried to run.

"Rush now into the encroaching blackness! Rush now into dark tyranny!" I went on. "Into our better world! For our children who will know nothing of war! This is our hour!" The gunfire stopped and the world seemed to take it's natural place again. "For the long night and the coming dawn! Charge now! Over the top!"

We rose as one, scrambling up the ramparts. I saw the faces of the Kranish officers. It was pure bafflement that anyone could be so stupid. We were a hundred yards from them. One of the leaders even laughed. I shot him in the head.

His replacement finally realized the danger. "Reload!" He screamed. We were seventy five yards from them. His soldiers were too curious at our foolish charge to respond quickly. Besides they had, the high ground, artillery, and the Priests. They could just sit there and watch us die.

Fifty yards. Some of the artillery was loaded hastily, and fired at us. Occasionally a cannonball would cut through our ranks, but it wasn't enough.

Twenty-five yards. I heard the booming chants of the Priest. I felt my arm burn like wildfire. For a moment all I remembered of the doctor's words was, *Nothing is assured.* Then I remembered the rest of them. *Know you are man and greater than they. Know there is a reason we formed you as we did. Know they cannot hurt you.*

I let go of the Battle Mind. I didn't know exactly what this Gift was, but it had something to do with embracing the world around me for all its faults and wrongs. I knew I couldn't achieve it by shielding myself from the world, so I let it hurt me. I let it hurt me, and I believed.

I believed until I felt something within me crack. I believed in the same way I knew I would win. I knew it the same way I knew fire burns. It felt like the light of the heavens flowed from me. I don't know if my men felt it too, but they charged on.

Ten yards. Lightning struck, but it could not touch us. Fire flared where we walked, but we did not burn. Serpents coiled around our lungs, but they could not find purchase. The Demons slipped from us. My men felt this and were emboldened. The Kranish felt the same and knew fear.

Five yards and they finally finished their reload. Their hands fumbled, though. It was too late. The Kranish were trained veterans, but they'd seen Demons roll off our back.

"It's Thomas Belson!" One screamed.

We crested their hill and for a blessed moment looked down upon them. "Fire!" I screamed. It wasn't the one rolling blast. The Anthanii shot into their enemies as they crested the hill. It was enough. The infantry broke.

I was among them. My tomahawk was in my right hand, my six

shooter in the other. I laid waste as they tried desperately to get out of my way. I caved in one skull, and shot down the highest ranking officer I could find. I had to get to the cannon before they had a chance to reload.

"Keep going!" I screamed. The infantry were already in route. They were cut down as we passed.

Twenty yards to the cannon. I saw them hastily trying to load grape shot. It would tear us apart. I ran faster than I thought I could. I emptied my six shooter hitting every officer I could find.

Ten yards. The artillerymen were looking around for orders. I drew my second six shooter and killed anyone who could have given them.

Five yards. They broke too. We chased them. In the flood of soldiers, they got the same treatment. Bayonets in the back. I hacked from left to right. They'd given up trying to fight me. The best the Kranish could do was try and escape axe. They didn't have much luck with that either.

Finally I saw the true prize. It was the seven Priest. They had stopped chanting. They knew it was futile but couldn't imagine why.

Then I saw that they hadn't come alone. They'd brought the Imperial Guard with them. It was Thnaiel's best troops. They'd been conditioned to never back away. The Guard didn't retreat. The Guard died.

There were thirty of them, all armed with the heavy poleaxes. They formed a protective line in front. The Priest hadn't thought of what happened if they needed to run. They'd never even considered the possibility in their wildest nightmares. The Guard was really just a show of Thaniel's respect.

Now two thousand Anthanii saw their greatest enemy defenseless. They didn't need to be told. They attacked.

I was the first one to hit the Guard. I went right for the middle. They stabbed at me, but I ducked underneath it, and lifted my mark up by both his legs. As I drove him into the ground I freed my tomahawk and put it right between their eyes. Just like that, a line of the best troops Thaniel could muster was broken. The pole axe was an intimidating weapon, but it was unwieldy. In this type of combat, my tomahawk held the advantage.

I cut behind ones knees and rolled. When I came up I threw two knives at Guardsmen still facing the wrong way. One stabbed at me with his weapon but I grabbed it and buried my hatchet in his neck. Then I saw the Priests. I'd put a hole in the Guards formation, and enough of my men were there to keep them busy. I turned my attention towards the Demon Speakers.

They were walking slowly backwards. Their white acolytes were moving with them.

"Now just wait a moment." A man in a bloodstained cloak held up his hand. "I am Bishop-"

I jumped on top of him and hacked at his head with my axe. His face didn't heal up like Harfeld's.

"Help!" One screamed as he tripped.

I killed them all one by one. I did it in the most brutal of ways. Afterwards, I wouldn't be able to describe it to anyone. I only spent a second with each, but they were all screaming when the life drained from their beautiful eyes. After the last was fallen, I looked up.

The Anthanii were staring at me.

"Belson the Blessed..." One said barely a whisper.

"And don't you forget it!" I pointed at him then turned to face my men. "Cut their heads off." I nodded to the white clad acolytes. "Detain those abominations, no harm is to come to them until I give the word."

They all cheered.

"This is the first step!" I screamed. "Let's take the rest of this fucking city!"

We charged together. We would rid Gertinville of anything touched by Thaniel. My men fought like cornered dogs, but a cornered dog can act like a lion.

It wasn't a plan that would carry the city. I'd done the obvious thing, break their stronghold and wheel a force around to hit them while they ran. It was obvious, but no one imagined I'd do it. My men would fight to the death because they had seen me do the impossible. The enemy would run because they knew what I was capable of.

The glow of whatever the doctor had told me to do had long faded off. I was still deep in the Battle Mind, though, so I couldn't feel the weight of my exhaustion. After we'd pushed the Kranish off their stronghold, most of them had started routing. News of my feats had made it's way through the city. I had slain a Demon. I had turned into a lion. I had eaten the heart of a dead Priest.

However, the trouble with warfare in a ruined city is that occasionally men got cornered, and when that happened, they either surrendered or fought. My reputation had grown so fearsome none wanted to be captured alive.

The fighting had raged on for hours after my initial counter attack. In that time period I had been shot at least twice, cut a dozen more, and accumulated a number of other wounds I couldn't really give a good accounting for. Finally General Holsten had realized the city was lost, and ordered a full surrender. By my count we probably had twenty-thousand prisoners, and there would be more to come.

Colonel Lanside, Thendin, and myself had finally made our way to the Kranish Generals headquarters to officially accept the surrender. They kept a safe distance away from me, though. I saw Lord Corbul and his staff approach the tent as well. They were as tired and wounded as we were, but when they saw me their eyes lit up.

"Belson the Blessed." Lord Corbul had always treated me with respect, but now I saw an awe to him. Logically he always knew I was the best. He knew that if Anthanii had a chance of winning, that chance lay in me being as good as I thought I was. However, now he had seen it. He had watched me win a battle the rest of the world had given up on. Now, he believed I was blessed, the same way he believed fire was hot.

"My Lord." I nodded to him with a smile.

"There'll be none of that." He closed the distance. "Call me Hannas." He folded me into a hug. "You can call me slave if you want. You saved my country and my men."

"Hannas will do." I managed to push him off.

He shook his head. "I never believed we had a chance." Lord Corbul looked around the staff. "I never believed we could win."

"It was your men and your training that made it possible." It wasn't just me being gracious. I was never gracious. His men had fought well. He deserved the praise.

"I don't mean the battle." He sighed. "I was committed to my duty, but I always knew Anthanii would fall."

"Well, what did you know yesterday?" I smirked.

"Yesterday I didn't know you were you." He looked me up and down. "You can save my country."

"We can save your country." I amended the statement.

Lord Corbul had never let this much emotion show. One had to stare into his face without blinking to know what lay in the General's heart. In that moment, I saw the facade crack. He let a tear run down his cheek. "You're the sort of man soldiers always pray they'll fight for one day." He stared into the ground. "The man who makes everyone around him more than they were." He turned his eyes to face me. "You're a hero like there's never been. If you died today your name would never be forgotten." Corbul clinched his jaw. "When you win this war they will erect golden temples in your name to challenge the heavens." He took a step back. "You've always had a friend in me. Now, you have a disciple."

"We follow you, your eminence." Colonel Lanside nodded.

The rest of the staff murmured their agreement, except Colonel Thendin.

He finally spoke up. "I'll never doubt you again."

"Good sentiments," I smiled, "but remember this war isn't over. We're fighting the greatest ruler who ever sat his happy ass on a throne." I put my hand on the Colonel's shoulder. "I won't win this war alone. I'll need wise council." I gave him the look all brave subordinates deserve. He'd acquitted himself honorably in the battle. "Even men who have golden statues built in their name need to be doubted from time to time." I chuckled. "It keeps us sharp." I released his arm. "If a dark day comes, I'll count on guidance like yours again."

"You'll have it." Colonel Thendin nodded.

"Good." I returned the nod. "Now, let's get this over with." I looked over at the headquarter tent. General Holsten was not an austere man. The tent was lavishly decorated in silk banners. "I'll need to meet up with Prince Edward's army as soon as possible."

"You're right." Lord Corbul nodded. "General Holsten will be a fine bargaining piece."

Just then the General walked out of the tent and threw his sword on the ground. He was a handsome man, young with dark hair and a roguish look. It was the look I generally tried to emulate. It was only somewhat reduced by the abject defeat on his face.

"Yes, he'll make an excellent captive to bring back to King John." I smiled.

Just then General Holsten pulled out an old flintlock pistol, put it in his mouth, and pulled the trigger. Brains splattered against his tent.

That knocked the smile off my face. "Or he'll make an extraordinary mess." I shrugged. "I didn't peg him for the type."

"Me neither." Lord Corbul agreed. He turned to me. "Well, that's that." He smiled at the staff. "So what should we do with the other captives."

"Have them executed." One of them put in.

"March them back to Kran naked." Another chuckled.

They went on in detail as to how to have the prisoners killed. They were honorable men, but they'd seen too many of their friends dead for empathy.

"No!" The violence of my voice surprised even me.

They all gave me a queer stare. They'd seen me fight. They'd watched me kill without thought. That I should be the one to call for mercy, seemed strange. "They're Kranish dogs." Colonel Thendin said through narrowed eyes.

"No, they're men." I sighed. "Even if they were dogs, I wouldn't see fifteen thousand of them executed in cold blood." I surveyed the staff. "The reason the fighting went on as long as it did, was because they felt they couldn't surrender to us." I bit my lip. "I will not see that duplicated." *If you were born Kranish would you have turned out so different?* I heard the question of the Three echo through me.

"So what should we do with them?" Colonel Lanside asked.

"Put them to work if you want." I gestured to the ruins. "This city needs rebuilding," I said, "but if I hear they've been mistreated, I'll know the reason why."

They all nodded. If they didn't understand the thought process, their blind faith in me wouldn't let them disobey.

"Our soldiers could be hard to control." Colonel Thendin said.

"Tell them it's my order." I said.

Thendin nodded. That needed no further explanation. They'd obey me without question.

Lord Corbul finally asked what he'd been waiting to. "How'd you do it Thomas?" He looked at me. "How'd you beat the Demons?"

"It was an ancient magic I found." It was a lie. "I'll teach it to you when our position is more stable." I couldn't explain it, is what I really meant.

He nodded.

"Now I'll need two of your fastest horses." I told the Lord. "I need to be at Prince Edward's army as soon as possible."

That took him aback. "You're wounded." He said. "Let the doctors treat you. Get some rest and food. I'm sure you haven't slept or eaten in days." He put a hand on my shoulder. "The war can wait a day."

"Could you have waited a day?" I asked.

"Probably not," Lord Corbul admitted, "but you're no good to anyone dead."

"I'll be fine." I lied. "I hadn't let any of my injuries since Wuntsville heal properly, and they were starting to catch up with me."

He took me in his arms again. "I'm sorry this burden has to fall on you." He whispered in my ear. "I'm sorry we're not strong enough."

"One day you will be." I patted his back. "For now, I have to ride." I walked away. "Tell your men I'm proud to have fought with them."

The Thaniel Wars

J rode faster than I had to Gertinville. I needed to make it to Prince Edward's camp before anything happened that I couldn't reverse. We didn't have time to train a new army. We didn't have the resources to arm that many men. Above all, if we were broken now, Anthanii's fight would leave them no matter my heroics. I had begun to forge my legend, but I knew what the rest of the world was thinking. *He's just one man.*

I'd find a way to destroy Thaniel, no matter what happened. However, saving Anthanii was never assured. I rode hard. People were looking to me, and I'd been gone too long.

As I finally made my way to the army, I discovered not all my fears had come to pass. The camp didn't have the polished, engineered look of a veteran army, but it didn't have the undisciplined, despair of peasants, thrown into the battlefield who knew they were going to die. The tents weren't in the orderly lines that only came with practice. However, the men who set them up had at least tried. The soldiers were cleaning their weapons, and they still moved with the semblance of a real army.

I knew that nine of ten of these men were fresh-faced recruits. Prince Edward couldn't have had more than a month to train them. They looked scared, but also proud. They were unsure of victory, but they weren't so certain of defeat either. My guess was that the prince had a real talent for command. I decided I was right.

The men had needed something to hold onto. I had given them the preview of a hero. I had won a battle with hardly nothing then I struck a Priest and lived. Once my victory at Gertinville hit them, they'd know for a fact, that I would save them. They also knew King John wasn't worth fighting for, but maybe Edward had convinced them there were those in the royal family who were.

I dismounted my horse and took a small burlap sack off the saddle. As I walked the usual awed stares followed me.

"It's Belson the Blessed." One soldier would say.

"He's going to help us win." Another chimed in.

"I heard he struck a Priest." I heard as a small crowd gathered around.

I stopped for a moment. These men had just been defeated, but it wasn't a route. They weren't desperate like the men at Gertinville. They didn't need a force of nature. They needed a man who would appreciate their sacrifice. None of them looked older than twenty. I knew it was the pot calling the kettle black, being sixteen as I was. However, they didn't see me as just a sixteen-year-old. I decided I needed to give them a real speech.

"I heard news of your bravery fighting against Thaniel." I looked around the crowd. "I decided I'd come see for myself." I gave them all a wry smile. "I have not been disappointed."

"We lost." I heard one of the few older looking sergeants grunt.

"No, you made a strategic retreat for better ground." I winked at one of the younger soldiers. "That's noble speak for you lost well."

The boy beamed at me. He was probably younger than I was. "We gonna lick em your emergence." He got my title wrong, but at least he tried.

"Still lost." Another of the older soldiers said.

"Aye," I turned to him, "you did." I stepped forward. "You faced Emperor Thaniel and his greatest army alone," without me was what I meant, "and they managed to drive you from the field of battle." The soldier had a long scar down his cheek. "However, you retreated in good order and with minimal casualties."

I sighed. "Most of you haven't been in the army for more than a month, and you gave Thaniel the best fight he's seen in ten years." I stepped to one of the other young men. "In another month of training, you'll be able to hold your own." I patted him on the shoulder. "The month after that, you'll be ready to march into Kran and burn the Rose Petal throne to the ground."

I turned away to address the whole of them. "You're right," I admitted, "wars aren't won with strategic retreats." I said. "However, this is the first step." I spit into the ground. "Now, Thaniel has brave men facing him, and we're going to win."

"Aye, we will, your emergence!" The same enthusiastic youngster hollered out. "We gonna lick Thaniel here, and then we'll take back Gertinville."

He was met with some scattered cheers.

"What's your name, private?" I asked the boy.

"Hooten, your emergence." He smiled his yellow teeth at me. If I had to guess, he was probably a pig farmer.

"Well, Hooten," I smiled at him, "I appreciate your enthusiasm, but Gertinville doesn't need saving anymore." I put my hand on my six-shooter. "The cities been won back, and we've managed to capture fifteen-thousand of the enemy, as well."

That got a rousing cheer.

"Bullocks." The sergeant spat into the ground. "I heard they had seven Priests in Gertinville." He waved his hand dismissively. "That city is lost and for good." He addressed the rest of the crowd. "Don't you all go listening to this pup." The soldiers shifted uncomfortably. "He's just a boy from across the ocean who wants to play hero." I let him speak. "I've seen almost a dozen of them Constables come through this country claiming they was gonna end the Old Religion." He turned his face back to me. "Thaniel killed all of em." He looked over his soldier. "We're just as dead now as we were yesterday."

I forced a chuckle. "Well, you're right about one thing," I opened the burlap sack and revealed the head of a Priest, "there were seven Priests there."

"No fucking way." I heard one man whisper in the back.

"That's impossible."

"It's Belson the Blessed." Another man in the back said as if that were explanation enough.

They all knew it was a Priest's head. No face looked quite like a Priest, even in death. The sergeant stiffened up immediately. He struck a pose of attention I was sure hadn't been that rigged since his first day in the army. I saw fear well up in his eyes. I saw the realization hit him, that I wasn't like those other dozen Constables. I was Thomas Belson, Belson the Blessed.

"I killed all of them with this here ax." I tapped my tomahawk with my other hand. I put a finger on the severed neck coating it with blood, then I put it in my mouth. "You know what that taste like?" I asked. "It tastes like victory." Actually, it tasted mildly chocolaty which was also strange. I had had vials of blood drawn from all the Priests I'd killed. I wanted to test it.

I took another finger of Priest blood and took a step forward. "Do you want a taste."

"Yes, your eminence." He said through his rigid attention. Then when I put the finger forward. "No, your eminence." He didn't actually want to taste Priest blood. I was the only one insane enough for that.

"More for me." I licked the blood off my finger. It tasted quite good. "Now, if you ever call me pup again, I'll make you do the next march naked. Do you understand me?" I said it deathly quite. The whole crowd held their breath.

"Yes, your eminence." He held his attention.

"Good." I put the head back in its sack. "Now, go teach these soldiers how to clean their weapons." I said and started to walk off. "I saw a private polishing his buttstock while his chamber was soot black."

"Aye, your eminence." He broke his attention and grabbed the nearest recruits rifle.

"Thank you, sergeant." I smiled to myself. Sergeants always deserved respect. They were the backbone of the army. I just needed to motivate this one. He'd probably seen all of his friends killed by Thaniel. He needed to know that those days were over.

I walked through the camp as the men stared at me. I didn't have time to stop and talk to all of them. I was headed to the command tent.

I passed the medics and gave the men there a salute. I had planned to come back later, but a familiar voice stopped me.

"Thomas!" It was a sweet angelic voice. It was Lady Gerate's voice. I turned and saw her wearing a blood-covered smock with her hair up high. She'd been helping with the surgeons. That was bloody work. In its own way worse than the battle. She still looked beautiful. She still looked like my Abby.

"Abby?" I said. I didn't know why she was here, but I was glad to see her. I was staring at her, wondering if I should give her a formal greeting. Should I treat her like a friend? Should I kiss her?

She solved the problem for me by wrapping me in a hug. "I heard you went into Kran all alone." She said against my chest. "I thought I'd never see you again." I felt the long-held desperation in her voice. "I heard you died."

"I'm not that easy to kill." I held her too. I didn't mention how close I actually came to dying.

"Apparently not." She released me and looked me up and down. She saw the blood that was already running through my shirt. She saw my exhaustion. She saw my chapped lips that looked like they hadn't seen water in days. How long had I been in the Battle Mind? A week? Maybe longer? Even if I couldn't quite feel it, my body gave signs to those who were watching. In God's Rest, it had been drilled into me how dangerous it was to stay in it for this long.

"Thomas," she stroked my cheek where I'd accumulated a new scar. "You need to be treated. You need rest."

I shook my head. "Soon, but now I need to see Prince Edward."

"I'll walk with you." She knew there was no point arguing. "I need to meet with him anyhow."

She led the way. "Why are you here?" I asked her.

"Some damn fool made me the head of intelligence." She gave me a wry look. "I've been with Prince Edward's army trying to set up spies ever since."

"How've you been doing?" I asked even though I knew she was skilled enough to get the job done.

"I was the one who learned Thaniel had marched an army over the mountain in the dead of winter." She shook her head. "I should have known sooner, though." I saw the regret in her eyes. "Why did you recommend me for this job? I've never done anything like this."

"You're one of the few competent, well-connected people I know." I shrugged. "I couldn't rely on anyone else to do it." I turned my head to her as we were walking. "You did well to get us this information on such short notice." I said. "Soon your network will grow, and we'll get a better warning next time."

"I hope you're right." She shuddered.

"What are you doing working in the medic tent?" I asked. "I didn't know you knew how to fix men up."

"This war has made us all do more than we thought we could." She looked up at me. "Besides, any woman worth her salt knows how to stitch up a wound." She gave me a knowing look. "Men get themselves into an awful lot of dumb trouble." I knew what she was getting at. I'd gone into Kran alone. They all thought I was dead.

"I needed to go." I said it, knowing how idiotic it would sound.

"You're needed here." She stopped and pulled me towards her. "We need you to lead us." She looked at the ground. "There's people here who care about you."

"Are you one of them?" I was happy for her saying that, despite myself.

"Maybe." She shook her head. "Yes." she finally admitted under my stare.

"I had to do it for this country." I shook my head. "We need a way to take the war to them." I looked at the soldiers running back and forth. "Otherwise, we're just delaying the inevitable. This violence doesn't end until Thaniel is off the Rose Petal Throne." I sighed. "Besides, there were things I needed to learn. I couldn't have saved Gertinville without that knowledge."

"So it's true?" She asked. "You beat the Priests?"

"Aye." I nodded.

"Well, this is the command tent." She gestured to the canvas covered in the royal sigil with guards at the flap.

I turned to go in, but she stopped me. "Before we go in, promise me I can treat your wounds tonight."

I nodded and turned, but she stopped me again. "Promise you won't leave again without telling me."

"I won't." I gave her a deep stare. "I promise, Abbey."

She gestured to the flap, and we both entered. I saluted the guards.

Inside, hovering over the map, was Prince Edward and a group of his staff. The staff looked to be interspersed equally with talented commoners, and useless nobility. Baby steps I suppose. Captain Seiford was also there, but he was wearing colonel ranks now. Apparently, the Prince had seen fit to promote him.

The newly minted Colonel Seiford was the first to notice me. "Thomas!" He gave me a back breaking hug. "I thought you were dead."

"Not until you show me your horse." I managed to choke out.

He released me. "You ass."

"I know." I smiled back.

Prince Edward looked up at me over the table. I saw in his eyes a great weight was lifted, but he had the foresight not to let his weakness show. "Constable Belson, its good to have you back."

"I'll say." I gave him a roguish smile.

The consummate professional, he looked to Abby. "Lady Gerate, what is the final casualty count?" From everything I'd seen, he'd become quite a commander. I had hoped for it, but I'd learn not to place to much hope in monarchs. Like all the kings before him, he had been schooled in war since he was a child, but sometimes lessons didn't stick, as per his father. At twenty-one years old, I knew this was his first real taste of battle, so I was delighted to see he took it seriously.

"One thousand of them will probably be able to fight again." Abby answered. "Two thousand will lose limbs." She shuddered at the final number. "About one thousand are dead or dying." She tried to force the sadness off of her. "Of course all those numbers are subject to change." She nodded. "I'll send you the final counts tomorrow, your highness."

"Three thousand lost isn't so bad." I shrugged. When they all looked at me funny, I elaborated. "Out of an army of seventy-thousand, green recruits, I mean."

Prince Edward shook his head. "I don't think their families will feel the same way." I saw the pain in his eyes. He felt like he'd let his men down.

"Aye, I suppose." I scratched my chin.

"Lady Gerate, organize a train for the wounded who aren't ready to march." Prince Edward nodded to her. "We'll march South tomorrow to link up with the survivors of Lord Corbula's army."

"Really, why do we need to go to Gertinville?" I gave everyone an inappropriate smile.

"Thomas, you've been gone for a while." Colonel Seiford hunched over. It was like those new ranks were weighing him down. "Seven Priests arrived at Gertinville along with a good many reinforcements." He shrugged. "Lord Corbula is organizing the retreat as we speak."

"Well actually-" Abbey started, but I stopped her. I wanted to hear what the Prince's plan was before I saved his hide. I knew news hadn't gotten there ahead of me. I wanted to get a measure of Edward's skill.

"Yes, Constable Belson," Prince Edward nodded. "I assume you've heard about our defeat here." He gestured to the map. "We're going to march East and make our stand with the full army, south of Harfow." He pointed to the map. "We can dig in there and have the best chance to throw them back." I saw in his face that he knew it was hopeless. Thaniel was too good. His soldiers were too well trained and led.

"What's the point?" One of the useless nobles threw his hands up in defeat. "They've got us beaten. Our soldiers were useless today." He looked around at the other noble officers who were supporting him. "Thaniel's going to crush us, and that's that." He put his nose up. "We should consider honorable surrender."

A number of the other nobles mumbled agreement. I saw the divide in the officers then. The talented new ones and the arrogant old ones, Seiford stood as the middle ground between the two.

Prince Edward looked up with deadly fury in his eyes. "This war is not lost!" He said with force so all could hear. "This war is not lost." He said it more softly as if to reassure himself. "We're going to stand at Harfow." He looked back at the noble who had spoken. "If I ever hear you disparage our brave soldiers again, I will make sure you end this war as a private!"

Prince Edward let the room feel his resolve. "If a day comes when Anthanii surrenders, no one in this room will be alive to see it, whether it's honorable or not." He made it a promise. "Am I clear?"

They all nodded their agreement. Even a noble wasn't fool enough to challenge Prince Edward.

"Clear as day, Prince," I smiled happily. "However, I went to Gertinville," I pulled the head out of the burlap sack and placed it on the table, "and my little friend here says hello."

"You rank savage!" The noble that spoke backpedaled quickly. Most of them looked a little terrified. To their credit, Abby and Prince Edward kept their composure.

I picked up the head and moved its mouth like a puppet. "Say hello to Lord Butter-for-Balls." I whispered in the head's ear. "Hello Lord Butter-for-Balls." I mimicked in a high pitched voice. I have many skills, but mummery had never been one of them.

"Thomas, you're employed as a Constable, not a jester." Prince Edward looked on impassively. "I think this is hardly the time."

"He's a damn barbarian is what he is!" Lord Butter-for-Balls said back at me.

Colonel Seiford took another look. "Hold for just one second your highness, and Lord Butter-" He stopped himself. "Lord Benton,

I mean." He leaned in towards the head. "I think that belongs to a Priest."

I moved the head forward pretending it was trying to bite Seiford's nose off. He jerked back quick.

Prince Edward chimed in. "Thomas, did you just pick the most tactless way to tell us you killed a Priest?" He tried to hide it, but I saw he was a bit in awe.

I nodded the severed head up and down to signify yes.

"Impressive as that is," Prince Edward went on, "It doesn't change our strategic position." He scratched his chin. "Though, if you can manage to do that again, it would be a great service to the king."

"Well, I have done it again." I smiled happily. "I did it seven times at Gertinville." I saw the fear mixed with respect seep into all of them. "I also smashed their army, captured fifteen-thousand of their soldiers, and General Holsten is dead as well."

"You killed General Holsten?" Colonel Seiford asked, a bit in shock.

"No, I did not." I mimed a gun in my mouth. "Some men just don't have the constitution for surrender." I paused. "You're one of them it seems."

"Oh." Prince Edward nodded his understanding. "So what you're saying is…"

I finished for him. "Gertinville is saved." I leaned into the corpses head. "Isn't that right, Priest?"

"Saved by the handsomest Constable in the land." I mimicked a high pitched mummer voice.

"That's excellent news." Prince Edward nodded. "Now we can face Thaniel without the fear of being encircled."

"If I had to guess, we won't face him at all." I said. "He'll realize he can't feed his troops, turn around and retreat." I nodded to the map. "That's what he needed Gertinville for." I put the head back down. "We can face Thaniel when this army is better trained."

"We'll still make plans for a battle," Prince Edward nodded, "but I think your right." He pulled away from the map. "This meeting is concluded. I need to think this over." He pointed at me. "Thomas stay a minute."

"Will do." I picked up the head and threw it to Lord Butter-for-Balls. "Nail this up in the center of the camp."

"I don't take orders from you." He narrowed his eyes at me.

"Do it, Benton." The Prince said firmly. "The men need to see that."

"Yes, your highness." He nodded meekly.

Colonel Seiford stopped by me on the way out. "Come by the officer tent for a drink tonight." He smiled. "I want to hear about your little adventures."

"Colonel Seiford," I pretended to be offended, "nothing about me is little." I smiled. "However, if you're going to offer to show me your horse, I would be more than willing to attend."

"You're an ass." He rolled his eyes.

"He is an ass." Abby slapped my arm. "A reckless, arrogant, egotistical ass," she slapped my arm again, "but he has an engagement for me to stitch him up tonight."

Colonel Seiford darted his eyes between her and me. "The drink can wait till tomorrow." He nodded. "Good day, Lady Gerate."

"To you too." She smiled and looked at me. "Come to my tent right after you get out." She stroked my arm. "I don't want to see you die of an infection."

"I will." I smiled at her.

Then I was alone with Prince Edward.

"You and Lady Gerate are close." The Prince nodded.

"She's a good woman." I said.

"Are you sleeping together?" He asked.

"So what if we are?" I narrowed my eyes at him. I knew how protective nobles were of their womenfolk. I also knew it was completely inappropriate for us to carry on together. I didn't care though. Prince Edward couldn't command me to stop seeing her. "Does it matter?" I asked.

"It does if you recommended her to the position of intelligence officer because you were feeling lusty." He gave me a stare.

"I'd say I lust after her because she's competent." I shrugged, realizing there was no threat.

"She is at that." The Prince nodded. "She saved our hides with that warning."

"Someone must have told Thaniel I was gone." I said. "That's the only reason he'd march his troops during winter." I considered my next words carefully. "Your father must have let slip-"

Edward stopped me. "My father is an incompetent gossip. He started a rumor that spread over half the country of your death in

Kranish controlled lands." He finished for me. "Wishful thinking, no doubt." The Prince gave a weary look. "I know what he is. You don't have to mince words in private."

"He's still your father." I said.

"He is, and I love him on that account," The Prince nodded, "but I have a million fathers to think about now." I saw it weigh on him. "I have a million more sons as well."

"I know it can't be easy." I nodded.

"You make it seem so." He stared up at me. "You rush in figure everything out, and then you win." He stared at the tattooed arm. "You're fearless." He sat down in a chair. "You always know what the best path is."

"I'm good at what I do." I shrugged and took a seat across from him.

"You're the best at what you do," he chuckled with no humor to it, "and what you do is save my country." He turned his head. "A country I was charged to protect." He sank even lower. "A country I can't protect."

"Not alone you can't." I admitted. "I'm here though, and you have good men at your side."

"And if you weren't here we would have been crushed." I saw it then. He was embarrassed. "Maybe, men don't need monarchs anymore. Maybe kings are a thing of the past."

"Honestly," I said, "I don't think they ever needed someone to rule over them, noble blood or not." I caught his eye. "Today they need a leader, though." I said. "You can be that leader."

"I'm a coward." The Prince hung his head even lower.

"The man I saw ready to make a stand for his country wasn't a coward." I stood up and looked at the table.

"Yes, I moved a little figurine on the map." He stood up as well. "You weren't at the battle, though."

"What do you mean?" I turned back to him.

"I was going to charge with the men." He shook his head. "That's what a leader does isn't it?" He pounded the table. "I was going to charge into Thaniel. I knew I was going to lose. It was Thaniel in the open field, and you weren't here!" He slumped over. "I figured I might as well make a good accounting of myself." He spat into the ground. "I thought I'd be ready, then I saw the muskets and bayonets all leveled at me." He bit his lip. "I saw the first volley, and I couldn't do it."

I gave him another look. "It's enough to give any man pause." I tried to mollify him, but in my head, I was rethinking my decision. *Are you a coward?*

"Seventy-thousand men did it." The Prince said it to himself. "You do it all on your own."

"I've had training." I touched the tattoos on my arm.

"No matter how much training I had, I still don't think I could have charged those guns." He put his hand on his side.

"There's many different types of courage." I tried to sound as sincere as possible. "There's many different kinds of leaders."

The Prince saw the hesitation in my voice. "That's not what you're really thinking."

"No, it's not." I admitted.

"You never mince words with my father, even when you should." Edward rounded the table to face me. "Why won't you tell me the truth now?"

"I'm afraid it will break you!" I said honestly.

"Tell me!" He pounded the table.

"What do you want me to tell you?" I screamed back at him. "That it's alright for you to stand behind men while they get slaughtered because of your blood!"

He took a step back, surprised at my anger. "I didn't choose this." He whispered to himself.

"You didn't eat ground oats for breakfast. You ate the finest fruits!" I took a step forward. "You didn't sleep on straw. You slept on a feather bed!" I rounded on him. "Maybe you didn't choose it, but you sure as shit didn't deny the comforts it bought!" I shook my head. "Now that you're stuck with the price you don't think you can pay it?"

"The guns..." He mumbled to himself.

"Aye, the fucking guns." I pulled out my six-shooter and aimed it at his head. I realized what I was doing and put it away. "I think you've done a good job here." I managed to calm myself. "I think you've the makings of a real leader," I took a step forward, "but one day it'll come." I turned my head. "One day, you'll need to put your chips to the center of the table." I shook my head. "One day, you'll need to save your country or your skin." I looked down at him. "On that day, I'll need you to make the right choice."

"How do you do it?" He looked to me like a man looked to the gods.

"What do you mean?"

"How do you be so brave?" He asked. "How do you kill?"

"How do you eat, drink, and fuck?" I asked back at him. "I was born for this. It's what I love." I picked up my pistol and walked to the door. "I am what I was made to be."

"You should be king." He said to himself.

"Aye, maybe I should be." I said. "It's not my choice though." I headed through the tent flap, leaving the prince to himself.

I walked to Abby's tent. I had to ask a few people for directions, but I found it eventually. I walked through the flap, and her face lit up. "Thomas!" She said excitedly. "Thomas, what's wrong?" When she got a better look at me."

"Nothing." I lied to her. "Close the flap, please."

She smiled wryly. "Wouldn't do for my honor, to have people seeing you in here, would it?" She closed the flap and rounded back giving me a passionate kiss. "We should treat your wounds first."

"Not yet." I looked at her. "I'm about to do something." I touched her face. "No matter what happens don't call for help. They can't see me like that. Promise me?"

"Thomas, what?" She took my hand.

"Just promise!" I said. "I might pass out, but don't call for help."

"I promise." She nodded.

I let the Battle Mind slip from me. The first thing to hit me was the ache of hunger. I doubled over dry heaving violently. How long had it been since I'd eaten a real meal? I'd had some dried meat and biscuits on the road, but it wasn't enough for a lazy child, much less a growing warrior who'd been exerting himself heavily for two weeks.

The second thing I felt was the exhaustion. It brought me to my knees. I felt all the strength pour out of me. At that moment a small child could have come at me with a fork, and I'd have been helpless. I collapsed to a miserable ball on the floor, wrenching and shaking. It had never been this bad.

"I'm getting help!" She said, but I caught her leg before she could leave.

"Don't!"

I almost passed out, but then the pain set in to wake me back up. My body was pure agony. I could feel broken bones in my arms and legs. I could feel where the monster struck me across a room, healed in a moment, but I hadn't felt the pain. I put my hand on the bedpost, and another wave made me break it off. I gasped out for air, but when I did, it was an agony all of its own. I had broken more than one of my ribs. It sent me back to the floor, doubling over in pain.

Then the last wave was upon me. I saw the faces of the men I'd slaughtered. The guardsmen too, even though I hadn't been in my trance when I did it. I saw the Cretoin boys I'd killed in single combat. How many men had I massacred? A hundred, two hundred, a thousand? It could have been anywhere in between. How many of those men had families who loved them? I wept on the floor in a sick, writhing, exhausted mess.

"I don't care what you say!" Abbey said. "I'm getting help."

"Don't!" I screamed back at her. "Don't." I said it softer. "It's over now." I managed to lean against the bed.

"Here, Thomas." She helped me onto the bed.

"Can I have some food and water?" I asked her.

She handed me some bread and a cup. I ate, but the pain in my jaw was too much for me to continue for long. She took it away from me.

"What was that?" She asked.

"The pain of a week felt all at the same time." I drank the water. That couldn't be ruined at least.

"Is that how you do what you do?" Abbey stroked my head.

"That's part of it." I managed to roll over. "It's something they teach us in God's Rest. Makes us fight longer."

"What's the other part?" She was clearly trying to distract me from the pain.

"Cunning, conviction, just general manliness." I tried to make it sound like a joke, but it came out as an agonized squeal.

"I see." She smiled at me. "My hero." She stroked my head.

"I don't feel like a hero." I tried to prop up my head but fell back in a frothing mess.

"A hero who doesn't suffer is no hero at all." She kissed me. "He's just an incredibly useful tool." She might have been the first person to look at me like that since I left the Confederacy. The look of someone who really cared. "You're still the man who saved my city." She stroked my chest. "You're still the man who survived Milhire. You're still the man who retook Gertinville." She took a long pause. "You're the man who gave a hopeless girl something to hang on to."

I tried to respond, but it hurt too much.

"You're the man who sees things exactly the way they are, and has the power to make them better." She went on. "You walked into a country that's a thousand years too old to change, and you changed it." Abby kissed the side of my head. "You fought the Old Religion and won. One day you'll kill it for good." She sighed. "One day you'll show us a better path."

"I'm a Constable." I managed to mutter out. "It's my duty."

She shook her head. "A hundred Constables have come through this land." She looked at me like I was a painting that was the culmination of a master artist's life. "They were good men, resourceful and honorable. They fought against the Old Religion, tried to change our ways. They tried to build a better world." She looked at me like a climber staring off the top of the tallest mountain. "A hundred Constables have come through this land, and we've never been better for it." She looked at me like she cared. I loved her for it. "A hundred thousand more could have come through this land, with exactly the same result if none of them were named Thomas Belson."

"So you finally believe in me?" I tried to smile, but my jaw hurt too much.

She laughed at that. "I guess you can't see it." She shook her head. "Everyone believes in you as soon as they see your face and hear your voice." Abbey rubbed her hand over my body. "It's not your looks, you don't really look much more than an average man." She chuckled again. "It's not your soaring rhetoric. Sometimes you talk like the worst kind of arrogant monarch, other times it's like a child with a scraped knee." She gave me those eyes of hers. "Sometimes you find a middle ground between the two, but it's not often." She shrugged her beautiful shoulders, and I watched the way her brown hair danced across her chest. "Honestly, I can't put my finger on why we have such a blind faith in you. We just do."

I let her continue.

"It's why people like the King and his court hate you." She stroked my neck. "You show them how impotent they really are." She kissed me. "At first it scares us. We're not used to heroes these days." Abby twisted her face to a hawkish grin. "Then we see you fight. We watch you save a city with scarecrows and donkeys. We watch you charge into the mouth of five thousand men. We watch you put the head of a Priest on a table." She placed her hand on my chest. "We watch you win."

I sucked in a breath. "Thank you." It was all I could say. I couldn't think of a witty response.

"I think it's time you got some sleep." She patted my chest.

"I think you're right." I nodded. She went to leave the room, but I stopped her. "I know I probably smell like death, but do you think you can sleep here?" I patted the bunk next to me. "You don't have to."

She smiled at me. "I was hoping you'd ask."

Abby slid into bed with me. I was too tired to get undressed. It seemed like she was as well. The bed was barely big enough for one person, with two it was absolutely cramped. I smelled like sweat and dirt because I hadn't bathed in a month. It was also mingled with the faint smell of piss because I had been in too much of a rush to relieve myself properly. She still had the stench of blood from wounded soldiers. She was not an easy woman to sleep next to. She constantly kicked and turned. Abby also had a bad habit of snoring. It was a wonder she didn't wake herself up.

I couldn't think of a place I'd rather be, but there was one more thing on my mind. "If I was a mite weaker, a hair less clever, if I wasn't the hero I am today, would you still care for me?"

She kissed the back of my neck. "If those cannons at Wuntsville had blown you and your donkeys to shreds, yes. I'd still feel the same way." She whispered. "The legend is made up of results, the man is an alloy of effort."

"What if I hadn't even tried?" I asked. "What if you'd come across me plowing a field or Three forbid, practicing law?"

"That's like asking if I'd like my chicken to moo." Abby chuckled. "It doesn't really make sense." She set her head down. "Get some rest, Thomas."

Being a hero was lonely business. I couldn't show an ounce of pain. I couldn't show a moment of doubt. Crowds would shout Belson the Blessed, but no one put a hand on my shoulder and called me Thomas. I wouldn't admit it, but I missed the way my father corrected my mistakes. I missed the way my mother kissed my scraped knees and called them ouchies. I missed how my brother would mess up my hair, and we'd roll around wrestling. I couldn't play fight anymore. I was liable to kill someone. I missed the way my baby sister cooed when I held her in my arm. She wouldn't be a baby when I saw her again. *If* I saw her again.

This was the life I chose. I never thought I could choose another one. I had always been too hungry. Also, I did enjoy being a hero, but I had never contemplated the cost of it. The legend I had carved out for myself was a large one, and it would only grow. People looked to me as a warrior, but there was no one to play my music for. I couldn't even attempt something I wasn't completely proficient in. If they heard one sour note, they'd start to ask what else could I fail at. Soldiers would whisper in awe at how I drank Priest blood, but I didn't have anyone to talk to about how it always tasted like sweets.

Abby saw the man beneath the hero. She saw that man and cared me for him truly. I had never been overly disposed to asking for help, but sometimes you need someone to hold you when you're hurting. Sometimes you need to admit when you're hurting.

"I love you." I whispered. I knew she couldn't hear it. She was fast asleep, and her snoring could have drowned out a cannon shot. I didn't say it for her, though. I said it for me. I said it because something in my gut made me.

I fell asleep like that, with her holding me. I drifted away to the sound of her snoring like a saw moving through thick wood.

The Thaniel Wars

J woke up at the crack of dawn. Back at home, I'd never been an early riser. I'd have slept till noon if I didn't have any pressing engagements. They broke me of that in God's Rest. I'm quite sure the only peaceful oblivion I ever got in that place was when I was knocked out. Whoever decided to put "rest" in the name must have either been an idiot or possessed an acute sense of irony.

When they finally decided to send me to fight Thaniel, I was ecstatic. Part of that had been seeing my chance to prove the man I'd be. I was finally to become a full-fledged member of the Constables, and I had my chance to win my glory. Most of my excitement was the tantalizing thought of getting eight hours of uninterrupted sleep.

When I finally got to my post, I had even less rest than when I was training. The raids and skirmishes I'd fought in required constant vigilance. I was always checking my men, standing watch, or running for the hills. When I was pulled off of that to lead a company at Milhire. I thought that was my chance to sleep. I was wrong. I was always filling out some report, doing constant inspections of my soldiers gear to make sure they were battle ready, or worst of all, arguing with the supply clerk.

"I need two hammers for a rifle." I'd make the request.

"We don't have those." He'd respond.

"I see them." I'd say as I peered through the window.

"You don't have the right request form."

"Who has the right request form?"

"My superior."

"May I speak with your superior?"

"No."

"Why?"

"You don't have the right request form."

"I will murder everyone you've ever loved."

Then he would close the window, while I kicked viciously at the ground. The supply clerk didn't care. He was basking in his surplus of useless things I needed, leaving me to stay up all night filling out forms for two rifle hammers.

It had gotten to the point where if I ever rose with the sun, I knew I had royally fucked something up. It felt like a sin to wake up after the roosters. If you want to know if a man is a good officer, look for the bags under his eyes.

So I rolled out of bed early as usual. My body tried to tell me to stop, but I didn't listen. I stepped over Abbe still snoring like she was trying to birth a small child through her nose. I took my first step off the bed. It hurt, but most of the pain had already faded. It had already started making its exit to the dull aches of a medley of other injuries.

Finally, I nuzzled Abby awake. I still needed to have my wounds dressed. She woke up and fixed me as well as she could, muttering disapproval at my recklessness the whole time. She tried to give me a sling, but I waved it off. I couldn't show that I was injured.

She had deft hands. She wasn't as good as Doctor Quarrels had been, but being beaten by a god wasn't really so bad.

"Thomas, you need to take care of yourself better." She said as I got dressed again. "Even your body needs time to recover."

"If you find some time let me know." I snorted. "I've been looking for the bloody bastard for years and haven't found it." I turned to her. "I think time is an endangered species."

She shook her head. "I'm not joking."

"I know, neither was I." I pulled on my boots. "Once I win this war, I can worry about my body." I put on my coat. "Right now, this is the way things have to be."

"The war won't be lost because you took it easy for a few days." She said as she washed up in a water basin.

"You know damn well it might." I put my weapons back in their holster.

"I do." Abby admitted. "I don't have to like what it's costing you though." She sighed.

"I know." I shook my head. "What are you doing today?" I asked, trying to take her mind off of it.

"Praying Thaniel doesn't overrun us." She folded her hands.

I walked over to her and put my hands on her shoulders. "I'll never let him hurt you." I kissed her.

"I know." She kissed me back. "I was just being glib."

"That's strange." I raised my eyebrows up. "You're usually funnier."

She slapped my arm. "You ass!" Abby rolled her eyes at me. "I have some scouts returning from the field I need to interview and some intelligence reports I need to look at." She sighed. "There's a good many nationalists in the countries Thaniel conquered who want to see us win." She shrugged. "All I had to do was give them certain assurances."

"I knew you'd take to this job." I gave her a cheery smile. "Let me know if you hear about troop movement in the Cretoin Mountains."

"Who in the Three's name would move troops over that Three forsaken place." She narrowed her eyes at me. Finally, understanding dawned on her. "You reckless idiot!" She slapped my arm again. This time she meant it. "I forbid you from doing that."

"I'm just keeping my options open." I shrugged.

"Not that one!" There was pure venom in her eyes.

"Fine." I muttered like I'd been defeated, but I still considered it our best option.

"What are you doing today?" She asked to change the subject.

"I've got to speak with Prince Edward, and then I'm going to ride out to tell Thaniel exactly why he's not going to attack us." I straightened my coat.

"Just be safe." She said.

"I will." I responded.

"You're a bad liar." She shook her head. Finally, she looked back into my eyes. "I heard you last night." She said it softly. "I love you too."

"I'm surprised you could hear anything over your snoring." I laughed.

"I don't snore!" She actually seemed hurt by the accusation. "Do I?"

"No, you don't." I lied to her again. "I was just joking. You sleep like a little angel." My ears were actually ringing from being exposed to the sound for such a long period, and I'd been shot at by heavy cannon.

"Oh," she nodded, "good."

I took a step towards her. "I did mean it though." I kissed her. "I love you."

Her face twisted into a wry smile. "So how pressing is this talk with Prince Edward?" She asked tugging on my belt.

I cocked an eyebrow up. "It's important." I tilted my head to her. "If I had a good reason to wait, I suppose I could postpone it for a bit." I had an idea what she was thinking.

"Is your body up to it?" Abby's beautiful pale face made me forgive the unintended insult almost immediately.

"Absolutely." I brought her closer. "Do you think you can be quiet?"

"I can," she shrugged, "but why would I want to."

"Protecting your reputation." I suggested.

"I'm the only woman in a camp of seventy thousand men." She rolled her eyes. "Trust me, my reputation is beyond even your power to save."

I pulled her into an embrace, and we fell to the bed in a fluster of undressing. All in all, it was the best way to start a morning I'd ever known.

The troops were all arrayed in battle formation. Prince Edward, Colonel Seiford, and I were on horses far ahead of the column. Thaniel's forces were arrayed across us. He outnumbered us by about thirty-thousand if Abby's figures were accurate. It seemed like more though. Fighting Thaniel in the open field with the numbers against us was not a particularly great position to be in.

Somewhere deep down, I knew Thaniel was better than me on the battlefield. He'd had years to hone his skill, and he had the mind of a scientist. The kind of mind that made him perfect for the ranks and columns of pitched battle. I was more of an artist. I was prone to making ridiculous gambles that somehow paid off. I knew that if I was going to beat Thaniel, it wouldn't be on a green field with armies arrayed.

Luckily, I didn't think there would be a battle. Prince Edward had sent word to the Kranish army that Thaniel and two others should come to discuss terms. I saw the three horses coming from their side of the field.

I was snacking on a pilfered piece of bread that I was sprinkling generously with Priest blood from one of the vials in my saddlebag. I hadn't had time to eat breakfast.

"Thomas, did you have to wait till right now to eat?" Colonel Seiford gave me a disapproving look.

I shrugged as I swallowed another bite. "I was hungry."

"What's that sauce you're putting on it?" Prince Edward asked.

"It's a delicacy from my home country." I lied.

"Is it good?" The Prince asked

"You wouldn't like it." I shook my head. "It's spicy." It actually tasted like a warm mug of coffee, but I knew the nobles of Anthanii didn't like spicy food. In reality, I wasn't entirely sure what drinking Priest could do to you. It wouldn't help our cause to have the Prince sprout a third arm, even if it would be neat to play with. When I thought about it a second time, maybe I should have given him some. I could have an awful lot of fun with that extra appendage.

The prince scrunched up his nose. "Never mind." He sighed. "Do you think he'll really just turn around and go home."

"I do." I said through another bite.

"How sure are you?" The Prince asked. "We're not ready for a battle."

"I'm absolutely sure." I nodded.

"How often is he wrong?" Prince Edward looked at Colonel Seiford.

"It depends." The colonel shrugged. "When it comes to women and general courtesy, almost always." He turned his stoic face towards me. "When it comes to politics and battle, never."

"Good to know." Edward put some more composure into his princely face.

"I know lots about women!" I gave Seiford an angry stare.

My comment couldn't penetrate his impassive face. "You're right." He turned to the Prince. "I've never seen someone so adept at driving them out of a room."

Prince Edward's lips curled in what could almost be described as a smile.

"And when did you become so funny?" I pointed the hand that held the bread at him.

"I've always been funny." Colonel Seiford kept his attention on the approaching horses. "You just weren't sharp enough to get the joke."

"Save this conversation for later." Prince Edward nodded his chin towards Thaniel. "They're almost here." He turned to me. "Finish your bread."

I stuffed it into my mouth and tried to swallow it before Thaniel got there. I failed.

Thaniel was dressed in his usual black uniform decorated just enough to say he was a man of consequence. He looked like the Emperor of the World on his horse. Green eyes darting around the field, like a chemist looking at his compounds. His strong chin pointed out as if he was surveying the land that would soon be his. His brown hair even looked somewhat like a crown. He was flanked by two generals in their Kranish gold. Both looked older than he was by a large margin.

"Thomas Belson." Thaniel smiled. "It's a pleasure to see you again." Strange as it was, I believed him. He gave off the impression that if we weren't on opposite sides and there weren't almost two-hundred thousand armed soldiers between us, we'd be good drinking buddies.

"Likewise." I nodded back to him once I swallowed my bread.

He turned his attention towards The Prince. "I see you've chosen the wiser option." Thaniel nodded his respect at him. Of course, the Emperor thought we were here to surrender. "This bloodshed would have been a pointless waste to a foregone conclusion." He looked over our shoulder at the army. "It's better this way. I promise I will not mistreat your subjects, and you will be given full courtesy according to your rank."

"I still think we should hang him." The general to his right said. He was clearly old. Every hair on his head had turned gray, but his light blue eyes still looked young and hungry.

"That's enough General Holsten." Thaniel turned to the man. "We are civilized people."

Holsten. I turned it over in my head. He must have been the father of the Holsten at Gertinville. The one who put a gun in his mouth. The gears in my head were already turning.

"We're not here to surrender." Prince Edward narrowed his eyes. "We're here to see you off of our land."

Thaniel looked back at his army. "How do you figure?" He cracked a smile. "You can't win," he nodded to me, "even with this little tiger."

"I'm not little!" I shot back with an indignation that could only come from insecurity.

"I think he means compared to a tiger." Colonel Seiford said.

I spit into the ground. "My father took me to see a tiger once." I said matter-of-factly. "Standing on its hind legs, it wasn't more than five feet tall." I drew myself up on my horse. "I'm almost six feet!" I lorded my victory based on facts over all present.

Seiford rolled his eyes. "You saw a stunted specimen then." He said. "The one that came to the King's Court when I was a lad reached almost eight."

"Oh, that's not so bad then!" I sat back in my saddle, somewhat mollified. "Still I can't condone any name that calls me little." I scratched my head in thought. "What about a Puma? It's still in the feline family, but we're of a height, so there's no need for a modifier." I snapped my fingers together as a thought struck me. "Or you can call me a massive alley cat!"

"Thomas…" Seiford chided me. Clearly, he was losing his patience for the game.

"What?" I shrugged. "An alley cat is a ferocious animal!" I leaned forward in my saddle. "I once saw one maul a bear over a piece of moldy pie." I nodded my respect to the creature. "Ferocious . animals indeed."

Seiford shook his head. "I really do love you provincial sort." He patted my shoulder. "Don't ever change."

Prince Edward snorted. "There is no chance of Thomas Belson ever changing."

I puffed my chest out. "Yes, Emperor Thaniel, I do hereby permit you to refer to me as a regular sized puma or more preferably as a massive alley cat." I wagged a finger at him. "Though you are to retire this 'little tiger' business."

I saw General Holsten lean in to Thaniel. "Is this really the man we're meant to be worried about?" He whispered.

Thaniel ignored him. "How about I save the confusion and call you Thomas?"

I nodded. "That would also be agreeable, as I am now and always have been a Thomas."

The Emperor let out a hearty laugh. "You're quite the conundrum to me, you know?" He eyed me down. "I can never tell what's part of the act and what's pure insanity."

Prince Edward cut in. "I'll save you the brain power." He said. "Thomas Belson is entirely mad."

I wagged my finger. "Mad like a fox!"

Edward shot me down. "No, mad like a hatter who caught

rabies and then subsequently fell into a vat of opium." He said. "In normal times I would have him thrown in the darkest dungeon so as not to infect the youth." The Prince sighed. "Sadly these are not normal times, and I've come to view his particular brand of insanity as helpful."

"You think he's mad enough to win this fight?" Thaniel eyed the Prince closely.

"We don't have to." Edward said it back as a challenge. "Those Priest you sent to Gertinville are dead. Thomas killed them." He pressed on. "The city is ours, as well as fifteen-thousand Kranish captives."

"You're a liar!" The elder Holsten shouted back. "He's lying." He turned back to Thaniel.

"It's true." I said still picking bread out of my teeth. I pulled the sword I'd taken from his son out of my saddlebag. It bore an inscription from his father, the man that stood before me. "Here I think this belongs to you." I tossed it to him, and he caught it.

"My boy..." Holsten whispered to himself. I saw Thaniel and the other general turn it over in their heads. How had I managed to kill seven Priest? How had I taken back that city? I saw the doubt in their eyes. I saw the fear.

Prince Edward ignored the weeping general to stare right back into Thaniel's eyes. "I can see you calculating the odds. You've been doing this for longer than I have, but let me tell you every eventuality that I've come up with over a sleepless night."

"Please do." Thaniel let the corner of his mouth tug upward in a smile, but there was no mirth in it. He simply didn't want to admit he'd been beat yet. "Candor is so very rare in our profession."

Prince Edward nodded. "The first is you fight us here and break us completely. This army I've raised is ground to dust." He said it like none of it really mattered in his calculations. It was a bold bluff. Edward was rare in the sense that he cared if seventy-thousand brave men who chose to follow him died. "Of course, then how would you supply this grand army of yours? You could push on to the capitol and besiege Harfow, take the head off the snake as it were."

The Prince cocked an eyebrow up. "I don't think you will, though. I think you're smart enough to realize that Anthanii is more than a capital and a palace." He said. "No, you'll probably lay siege to Gertinville again. You might have been able to take it by storm if you still had an army on the other side, but you don't." Edward leaned back. "You'll settle in for a siege that could take months, but you won't have months. Your men will start to starve after a few weeks."

"I could plunder the land." Thaniel narrowed his eyes. "I can live off stolen grain like armies have done for thousands of years."

Edward matched the glare. "Yes, armies used to do that sort of thing, but there's a reason its fallen out of practice." He said. "That was when a large force was ten thousand not a hundred thousand, and you didn't need to supply bullets for swords." The prince sighed. "Besides, it's been a bad winter. Not so bad the countryside is starving, but you will be." The Prince stared back. "If you break us today you'll find only dirt and sprouts to feed you."

Thaniel sneered down his nose. "That's all contingent upon me not taking Gertinville by storm." The Emperor said. "Maybe I can't. Gertinville is a natural fortress, but maybe I can." He gave a wry smile. "The defenders are exhausted, and too few, with a lot of prisoners to keep track of, and my army is quite good, as you've learned. There'll be a cost, but to finally end this war my men will pay it." He chuckled, and once they're out of the way, there'll be no one between me and my peace." He said peace but what he really meant was *prize*.

"You're right there will be no organized army." The Prince shrugged. "Anyone can shoot a musket, though."

"What are you talking about?" Thaniel rode in closer.

Edward matched him. "I've sent out orders that if my army is destroyed today, every storehouse is to be emptied. Not just the men but the women and the children will be given muskets too. I will arm this entire country." He narrowed his eyes. "Behind every door and every blade of grass, you'll find a bayonet to meet you." He moved his horse forward. "Maybe you take Gertinville. Maybe you even take Harfow, but our citizens will kill you off piecemeal until you limp back to your country disgraced and defeated." Edwards tone became murder. "Your rule is cemented only by victory. Once you lose so many sons and have only the promise of more war, they'll turn on you."

"You would give this country over to the mob?" Thaniel asked incredulously.

"Before I give it to you, yes. One hundred times over the answer is yes." Edward spat into the dirt. "Besides I hear everyone's got a gun in the Confederacy and they do alright."

"It's true." I finally chimed in. "I once suckled on a barrel because I thought it was my mother's own teat." I shrugged. "I turned out alright after all. My Pappy said it gave me grit." I used the Confederacy term for father to drive it home. "My maw was sore as hell over it though. She really is much prettier than a rifle barrel."

Edward went on. "Besides, an armed peasantry will be the least of your worries." He looked back at his men. "If you destroy this army, I'll die with it. Colonel Seiford will as well." He narrowed his eyes. "However, Thomas, mad as he is, will somehow survive. He's resilient like that." The Prince eyed Thaniel without looking at me. "Constable Belson, what's the farthest shot out you've ever made?"

I caught what he was really saying. "I hit a jackrabbit three hundred yards out, back on the farm." I smiled. "I've only gotten better since then too."

Edward went on. "Forgive me Emperor, but you're a mite bigger than a jackrabbit and not as agile I'm sure." He paused once again without looking at me. "How far out do you think you could hit an emperor sized jackrabbit, Thomas? Six hundred yards? Eight hundred yards?"

I shrugged. "A thousand if it's not overly windy and I have a good rifle." That might have been an overstatement of my ability but not by much

Edward went back to addressing Thaniel. "Your guard is good as far as I can tell, but to clear a thousand yards in every direction." The Prince paused. "Well, they could probably do that. The first time anyway, then the second time, then the tenth time." He smiled. "However, one day you'll want to step out for a piss. Your guard will say 'let's only send one man to check out that hill,' but one man isn't much to Belson the Blessed. You'll be whistling with your cock out, and then you won't be whistling anymore."

Edward shrugged. "Of course, there are other ways to kill a man or jackrabbit for that matter." He said. "Slip into the camp at night, put something in his food, stick a knife in his side. That sort of thing." He kept his stare on Thaniel. "What do you think, Thomas? Does killing an emperor sized jackrabbit that way sound doable."

I shook my head. "No, your highness, jackrabbits are notoriously flightily, even the Emperor sized ones." I tapped my hatchet. "However, just a regular emperor..." I trailed off. "That is very doable."

Edward smiled. "I promise this, if you take one step forward, you won't leave this country alive."

Thaniel nodded. "What's the second option?"

"About the same as the first." The Prince nodded back towards his army. "Except with the much more likely possibility that my army isn't destroyed." He stared at the Emperor. "Sure, this lot is green, and they haven't been training as long as I'd like, but they're brave lads." He pushed on. "This isn't Milhire, and as I'm sure you're learning, I'm not Lord Renton or my father."

Edward paused. "You fight us here, you'll win, but we'll retreat in good order." He said. "Everything that I've predicted will come to pass, but you'll have an army to contend with as well." The Prince smiled. "Those are long odds, even for you."

Thaniel nodded. "The third option?"

Edward gestured to the Kranish army. "Leave." He said simply. "We won't chase you. We won't harass you, just leave."

For a moment the two rulers stared at each other. Each daring the other to make a mistake. It was a battle in its own right.

Thaniel finally spoke up. "You didn't have to warn me." He said. "You could have run off with your army and let me find out the hard way Gertinville was done." He paused. "You could have had me encircled, but you chose to see me and my army off intact." The Emperor went on. "You warned me that my head was in a noose."

Three above don't tell him why! I prayed to myself. *Three above don't give him the real reason.* I knew what it was. Thaniel suspected it, but once he knew he'd have the weak spot in our armor.

The Prince didn't head my prayer. "I've seen what your armies do to a compliant population, and make no mistake you will not find mine so agreeable." He nodded. "I won't put my people through that just to see you hang yourself."

"You're right on all accounts." Thaniel smiled. "I'll leave now, but I'll be back." He said. "I know where to hurt you too. I know how far I have to twist your arm before you say uncle." He turned to his staff. "General Tiller..." He started off on some order.

It gave me time to think. Thaniel was right. He knew our weakness. He'd be back, and the next time he'd hit the Prince where it hurt. I couldn't erase that chink in the armor. Of everyone present, Thaniel and I were the only ones that saw it. I couldn't erase that chink, but maybe I could throw some paint on it.

"General-" Thaniel was about to give a command, but I cut in.

"General Holsten," I said, "don't you want to know what happened to your son?"

"My boy?" The General's eyes lit up. I could see the tears he was trying to hide running down his cheek, I could see the sorrow contorting him. "Is he..." I knew what I had to do, and I hated myself for it.

"Dead? Yes, quite." I chirped cheerily.

"Thomas, have some tact." Colonel Seiford barked at me. Clearly, he forgot who I was.

"How did he die?" General Holsten looked up at me. "Did he die well?"

I shrugged. "I don't think there is a good way to die really." I gave a fake laugh. "If you mean bravely than no." I laughed again. "Absolutely not."

"Constable Belson!" The Prince said. "That's enough."

The elder Holsten let his sorrow turn to rage. "My Emperor!" He said. "We can crush them. Don't leave!"

"I know your sorrow is great," Thaniel said, "but Edward has the right of it."

I ignored both of them. "After the defeat, which can only be described as humiliating, he met with me." I chuckled at the imagined meeting. "He went to both knees and promised he'd do anything for me to spare him. *Anything.*" I mimed a cock going into my mouth.

"Emperor, kill this monster!" Holsteen said through his tears.

"Come on Thaniel, don't you want to kill me?" I taunted further.

"General, control yourself!" Thaniel barked back

Everything in me said stop. This was too far, but I didn't. "Anyway, I told your boy I don't like that kind of thing, so I left him a pistol and let him do the work for me." I forced a chuckled again. "I had a feeling he was used to putting things in his mouth if you catch my meaning." I put two fingers in my mouth and pretended my thumb was the hammer of a flintlock.

Thaniel knew what game I was playing. "General Holsten go back to the army this instant." Even with the Emperor's perfect command voice, it didn't work. There's few things more potent than the sorrow of a father losing his son.

"Kill this savage now!" Holsten screamed.

"I'm not a savage." I mocked an offended look. "I promise I'll give you back the body when I'm done with it." I shrugged. "Well,

I may have to sew it back together first," I screwed up my face as if trying to remember the details, "and wash the drawings of cocks off his face." I shrugged again. "What can I say? Sometimes I get carried away."

Holsten's face went from fiery rage to ice cold. It was the look of a man who had lost everything. It was the look of a man who was willing to suffer whatever consequences came next.

There was a long moment of silence. Everyone looked to Holsten, face filled with cool purpose. They all knew what was going to happen, and none of them could stop it. Thaniel made a grab at the man, but he was too far away.

Holsteen pulled the flintlock pistol out of its holster. It was fumbling motion. People from Thyro weren't particularly good at the drawing of weapons. His age didn't help him much either. I shot him between the eyes, and he slumped to the ground.

In the Confederacy, the quick draw was a national past time. As a child, I'd spent countless hours, pulling a pistol-shaped piece of wood out of my belt and aiming it at the family dog. This wasn't a dog, though, and I wasn't drawing wood. It's harder to kill a man than scare a dog. It should be. Still, I was fast. To anyone watching, it probably seemed like I'd made a gun appear out of thin air.

The sound of sabers leaving their sheathes let themselves be known. Everyone had a weapon in their hand except for Edward.

"There is no need for further bloodshed!" The Prince shouted. "Put those away." He stared venom at me.

"He killed one of our men under the banner of truce." A Kranish general screamed.

"He will be punished accordingly." Edward assured them. "Emperor..." He pleaded.

"Put down your weapons." Thaniel finally said.

"We could kill them all now." Another general said. "They broke the truce."

"Holsten drew on them first. Belson was protecting himself no matter how much he deserved it." Thaniel looked from me to his sword then back again. "No sense to risk it all now anyway, when we have the same result assured in due time."

"Thomas, I will have you hung for this." Edward hissed in my ear.

"Your grace, whatever you do tomorrow please stand out of my way now." I said under my breath.

"I'm done with being ordered by you." Edward spat back.

"It's not an order, it's advice." I said softly. Then I swallowed my pride a moment more. "My Prince."

Edward nodded in a way that told me he'd have his justice, but he knew how hard it was for me to call him that. He backed off for a moment.

I looked back at Thaniel. "I lied." I said. "Holsten the Younger died valiantly. I'll see the body returned to you intact so it can be buried like the hero he was."

"Why did you do that?" Thaniel ignored the corpse to stare at my eyes, reevaluating everything he thought he knew about me.

"You know why." I answered.

Thaniel nodded his respect. I wished I could wipe it off. His respect for what I'd done felt like grime that couldn't be washed away "I misjudged you, Thomas Belson."

"I misjudged you too." I shot back at him.

"How do you mean?" The Emperor seemed genuinely curious.

"On our first meeting, I thought you to be a decent man driven too far by tragedy." I sighed. "I thought you wanted the best for your people, even if I didn't like how you'd give it to them."

That swelled Thaniel up. "Everything I do is a means to that end." He paused. "All I've ever thought about is those I rule."

"Then why didn't you ask about the fifteen-thousand prisoners?" I narrowed my eyes.

That caught everyone at the meeting off guard.

For the first time, I saw Thaniel stumble. He regained himself quickly to his credit, but it was a victory. "I assumed the cost for their safe release would be too high." He finally said.

"It would have been high." I agreed. "Still, you didn't even ask."

The Emperor didn't know what to say to that, so I helped him. "You better get going Thaniel. Once nightfall comes, the wolves will be out."

"We're the only wolves here." Thaniel said as he led his staff back to the army.

"Thomas!" The Prince screamed at me once Thaniel was safely out of range.

"What?" I turned to him. I wasn't in the mood for what he was about to tell me.

"We were under the flag of truce." There was true fury in his eyes. It almost scared me.

I nodded to the Kranish. "He drew on me."

"I would have drawn on you too." Edward shook his head. "I took you for an honorable man."

"Well, that's your mistake." I gestured towards Holsten laying on the back of a horse. "He was honorable. I won."

"You went too far!" His rage was back upon him.

"And who are you to tell me where the line is!" I screamed back at him. "Maybe, that's why you can't protect your own damn country." I spit into the ground. "You won't go far enough to save it."

"How does this help me protect my country?" Edward shook his head at the insanity of it all.

"You mean despite depriving Thaniel of one of his best generals?" I sneered. "Let me tell you how this protects your country." I pointed at our army. "Your men have been beaten ragged by Thaniel at every corner. They don't just think they're going to lose, they *know* it." I bit my lip. "Then one day they hear a story about me. They hear that I've saved a town. It doesn't mean much to them though. Then they hear I saved a city, and it means a little bit more." I paused. "Then they hear I killed seven Priest on one day, but it's still not enough. They fear Thaniel too much. Then they watch me shoot one of his head generals between the eyes, and the Emperor limps away in fear." I snarled at the man I was supposed to serve. "Now they know he's not a god. Now they know we can win."

I turned my horse back to Thaniel's army. "They saw it too." The Kranish were already turning around. "They've never seen their emperor so much as make a mistake. Sure they've heard I've been running rampant through their armies, but I've never faced Thaniel before." I paused. "Now they know they can lose."

I turned back to him. "What's more, you showed Thaniel your hand." I said. "You let him know where your line was. He would have put all his chips to the middle of the table. He would have taken this war to a place you couldn't follow, raised the stakes until you folded." I paused. "The only way to stop him from doing that was to make him think you'd call it."

"I don't want to win like this." Prince Edward said to himself.

"That's why you've been losing for more than a decade," I let him feel the venom in me, "because you won't do what it takes." I figured if I got angry enough it'd smother the guilt. It didn't. "You were too weak, now I have to be too strong. You could have picked the right path ten years ago. You didn't." I paused. "Now I have to choose the wrong one."

We rode back to the lines of our army. Prince Edward kept his distance. Perhaps, he was starting to feel his own impotence. All of his noble blood, his years spent training for this day, and the countless soldiers he could muster hadn't been enough. I had been. With a few words, I'd turned back the greatest leader who ever was. I was a foreigner. Four generations ago my family lived in the slums of a country that didn't even exist anymore. I was a pup, barely sixteen. When the world saw my face, it moved out of the way. The oldest ruling family in all of history had seen a vision of the new world. I couldn't imagine they liked it. Made them think, maybe they weren't as important as they thought.

Perhaps, the Prince kept his distance because he was afraid. No one knew my allegiances. I had sworn an oath to the tattoos on my arm and to the Three. I was here to rid the world of the Old Religion, and to show the people a better way. The first one was pretty simple, but the second one leaves for some interpretation. Still, I don't think even the most talented lawyer could argue, I had a right to take Anthanii. Yet, that's exactly what the powers that be were afraid of.

As much as I looked down on the court, I could understand why they looked down on me. They hated every one of the Free People from the Confederacy, especially those who threw it in their face as I was like to do. I lacked all the virtues they valued. Their sort of pride came from wearing ridiculously expensive clothes, inbreeding to increase their land, and bragging about their families deeds. The pride I had was frowned upon. The pride that made me challenge every one of their traditions. The pride that made me hungry. Their humility was of constant deference to the king. They saw themselves as pieces in a machine. Their duty was to make sure the state continued on as it had for a thousand years. My humility was superficial at best. Wear simple clothes, treat everyone based on their worth, not their class, but when the lightning started, scream like the thunder. I was their inverse, pride wrapped in a humble shell. It made them uncomfortable.

Constables had worked with Anthanii before against lesser leaders. We'd worked for just about every kingdom in Thyro and most outside. Some histories even suggest we played a part in the Confederacy's revolution. Until the Old Religion had cornered us in Anthanii, we were a usual sight at most courts. The nobles had an idea of what Constables should be like. They were quiet, obedient up until the point their oaths wouldn't let them serve you anymore. They were brave and competent on the battlefield, but never allow their influence be felt elsewhere. They treated the rulers to all their homages. Wherever they were from, whatever color they were, you knew what you were getting when you saw the tattooed arm. Until the day I came to fight, that is.

I was the first trained from the Confederacy, and my tutors at God's Rest made it clear they'd never take another. That was probably part of what made me different. We're a different people, scions of those too stubborn, adventurous, and stupid to remain in the old world. In the Confederacy, the Prime Governor does not kneel, and neither does the street sweeper. It's born into us, and no amount of beatings could get it out of me. The other reason I was the way I was, had to do with simple logic. Constables had been doing the same thing for five hundred years, and we were losing. I wasn't going to reverse that doing what they had done.

I was bombastic and arrogant. I didn't know my place at the table, and I didn't care to learn it. I spoke the truths no one else would say but thought in their quiet moments. My place was to lead. A fifteen-year-old runt from across the ocean, and making a fuss about how they were doing it all wrong. I'd have hated me too. They saw me as a small yapping dog, annoying but harmless.

However, my victories hadn't made them like me more. They'd gone from offhand derision to pure hatred. A hatred based in fear. I represented a new way, and I was winning. I knew what they had started to say when I wasn't listening. "If Thomas Belson decides to take our own country from us, can we stop him?" They probably couldn't. I knew if a knife found me in my sleep one night, it wouldn't be Thaniel that sent it.

Prince Edward was a child tempered by war. He had a decent heart, and as Thaniel gobbled up half world a piece of Edwards soul had been taken to. These were people supposed to be under his protection, and he wanted to save them. He wanted it enough to trust me, but I was sure he thought about a day when he didn't need our alliance.

He didn't cleave to power for the same reason the nobles did, a comfortable life on the backs of others. I could see that was far from his thoughts. In his own way, I don't even think he wanted the power. What scared him was what happened after I took the crown away. He saw the monarchies as a necessary evil, a thing to keep the people from tearing themselves apart until they were ready. He wasn't sure they were ready yet. Thyro had known usurpers before. They rarely made anyone's lives better.

In my heart, I knew they did have a reason to fear. Part of it was sheer childish anger. You'd think that someone given the name Belson the Blessed would be above it, but I wasn't. Sometimes when I came across their defaming pamphlets or heard one of their jokes I wasn't supposed to, my blood boiled. It made me think how sweet it would be to throw them to a mob of angry commoners. However, the lion's share of my thoughts of rebellion were from my upbringing. I came from free people, and it worked quite well for us. The untold truth of the world was that one day The Confederacy would be more powerful than all the nations of Thyro combined. We had unlocked the talents of every man in our borders. What people said would tear us apart, had made us stronger than anyone had hoped to imagine. There were setbacks of course, but when the cobbler made shoes because he chose to… Well, there's a reason I paid double price for boots made in the Confederacy.

However, I knew it was a fantasy. We weren't just free because our leaders were elected and not crowned. We were free because of a group conviction. White man, black man, poor man, rich man, all had a right to live the way they wanted to. Until such a day that Thyro would rather starve then kneel, the best they could hope for was an absolute monarch to guide them along. I held that Prince Edward could be that man.

I was broken from my thoughts by Colonel Seiford. "Whatever your reasons for doing what you just did," he looked back at the elder Holsten and sighed, "I can't support it."

"I'm not asking you to." I wanted to scream at him to stop talking. I wanted him to shut up and help me win the war, but it wasn't his way. After all, if he'd been the sort to meekly go along, I would have traded him in for a better model.

"Maybe, you should." The colonel said bordering on fear. "Maybe, you've been right too many times."

"Do you deny that it helped our position in this war?" I still couldn't look at him. I still couldn't face the disapproval in those stoic eyes.

"I don't," he answered meekly, "Thaniel thinks in terms of what helps him win his wars too. He'd have done what you did." I heard the waver in his voice. "That's what scares me."

"He has the better army, the larger treasury, and by far more power." I scratched the tattoos on my arm viciously. "Donkeys and scarecrows only work once. How did you think I was going to win?"

"The right way." He said it almost to himself. He said it like a prayer aimed at the Three. He was a fool to think they could change my mind. They'd tried.

Finally, I stopped to look at him. The disappointment on his face hit me harder than I thought possible. It was like a woman you didn't realize was beautiful until you took a second look. It was like being shot.

I took a moment to recover from it. "I've done worse than that in this war." I stopped my horse. "I'll do worse still before it's over." I gritted my teeth at the prospect. "The time of the knight-errant on their white steed is over if it ever existed. They failed!" I calmed myself. "This is the time for heroes. This is where the path diverges. We take the dark one." I looked at the army then back to him. "When the time comes, will you follow me?"

For the first time in our friendship, he looked flustered, as if the ground he stood on wasn't quite as sure as he thought. "I hope I'm not there for that." He finally muttered.

"What if you are?" I pressed him again.

"I hope I'm not."

I realized that was the best answer I was going to get from him. I also realized, maybe I didn't want to hear it. That's when you know you've stumbled onto a big truth. You don't want to hear it.

I couldn't hold it anymore. There was one more favor I needed of him. For saving his country and probably his life it didn't seem like such a huge thing, but it was. "Don't tell Lady Gerate about what happened here." I knew the way it'd make her look at me. "She'll hear parts of the story of course, but she doesn't need to know what I said."

"If she doesn't need to hear about it, it wouldn't matter if I told her." The Colonel started walking his horse again. "Maybe, the fact that you don't want her to know means you shouldn't have done it."

"Please." It was the closest I'd ever come to begging.

"I wasn't going to say anything to her regardless," he nodded, "and I'll ask the Prince to do the same. I don't think he will. It's not our business." He turned back to me. "You should tell her, though, on your own terms, when you're ready." He stared at the tattoos on my arm. "Not, for her but for you." Seiford moved back up to meet my eyes. "You're not the callous tool you sometimes pretend to be. I've seen the compassion in you, the desire to do what's right." He paused. "You're a man of extremes. There's other things fighting to control you, but there's righteousness in you. That's why what you did will hurt so bad." It was like he could see to the core of me. "If what you say is true, and you're yet to do even worse things, you'll need someone to confess to, someone to hold you accountable."

I couldn't say anything to that. He was right.

Seiford went on. "If you don't find someone, it'll tear you apart." He turned his horse back to the army. "Three help us when Thomas Belson breaks, but I don't know if even they can."

I stopped there for a moment as he rode on. I turned towards the Prince. "Can I speak to the troops?" I asked.

"Yes," he nodded, "they need to see you." He gave the hand signal to form up from battle order to inspection order "They're all yours."

The field band played the command, and the appropriate flags were raised. The common soldiers weren't trained to respond to those orders. To them, it was just annoying music and colored silk. "That means attention you fucks!" One sergeant screamed. It was echoed with variations across the line.

"No, you go here Daniels you daft cunt!"

"Keels I hope your mother sowed her legs back together."

"Steckly! Why the fuck is your musket between your legs."

I wouldn't want to be Steckly. I waited as the sergeants beat, cursed, and demeaned their men into line. It made me wonder how they'd survived the earlier battle. It was probably because Thaniel hadn't been in a position to pursue yet or the leadership of Prince Edward and Colonel Seiford. Most likely it was a mix.

Finally, I raised my hand for quiet. If they were going to learn how to stand at attention, it wasn't going to be right then. The army stopped at the sight of my tattooed arm. They'd heard my stories. They'd seen the severed head. They'd watched me shoot one of Thaniel's head generals, and live to tell about it.

I spoke loud so they could hear me. The ones on the edges would hear my words repeated by heralds.

"There's not going to be a battle today." They all breathed a sigh of relief. "It's a good thing too, we're not ready yet." The ones closest to me shifted uncomfortably.

I went on. "You weren't ready. A month ago you were civilians, shopkeepers, craftsmen, and students. Yet, when the war drum beat you answered. The last line between your country and an enemy who wishes to see it destroyed. You left a life of peace to be here. I ask you why?" I paused for effect. "You did it because this is your country. You did it because you won't see this world swallowed up by tyranny. There are people who will say you're just cannon fodder. There are people who will tell you your lot is to stand in line and hold a rifle. Tell them this, when they failed to save their country, you answered. When others padded their knees to make it easier to suck Thaniel's cock, you picked up a weapon and would rather die. By virtue of being on this battlefield, you've earned the title of warrior. When men speak of the ancient Anthanii knights who saved this country from savages, in the same breath let them mention the men who stood with Prince Edward today."

"For all that, courage was enough today. It won't be tomorrow. The age of knights in gleaming armor, of magic swords that deliver victory, of kings with mighty steeds, is long dead. Don't look to them to save you because they won't. This is the age of the shopkeeper, the cobbler, and the student. This is your time. I'm going to teach you a different way to fight. I'm going to teach you to be the warriors I know you can become. We're going to be ready the next time Thaniel comes, and then it'll be us coming."

That brought a collective gasp from the army.

"You didn't think I was going to wait on the border forever did you! This war ends when we throw Thaniel off his throne. I'm telling you now it can be done, and you're the men to do it. Heroes don't come from storybooks, they come from ordinary folk willing to risk everything for a cause they believe in. My father was a farmer, and so would I have been if I hadn't tattooed my arm." In reality being a plantation owner is far different from being a peasant farmer, but they probably didn't know the difference. "I stand before you now because I will not see a brave people go quietly into the night. I have made the world tremble when I walk, and soon, so will you. I wouldn't trade you for any number of noble officers because when your country called you answered. We will go where the mercenary turns away. We will stand when the slave begs for mercy. We will fight when the nobles call for terms. They've all failed this country, you won't."

"Some of you may be asking yourself why you'll suffer so much for people who've never cared about you. How is an emperor so much worse than a king? I'll tell you. We'll make them care. Thaniel claims to be the new way, but he's just a hell of a lot better at the old way. Once we show them what we can do, the world will never be the same again. The world will see that ordinary men stood against a tyrant. The world will see you're far from ordinary. This is the first step. Here and no further. Long after we've won this war, when you sit with your family in your final hours, you'll look back at your old uniform and feel the pride ring as true then as it is today. We don't just fight for this country. We don't just fight to beat Thaniel. We fight because it's the first step. For the first time, this country will belong to you because you've paid for it in blood. A new world is upon us. Will you take the first step!"

They cheered until their throats bled, soldiers with the sergeants, sergeants with the officers. I rode my horse back to the tents leaving them to scream with pride.

Colonel Seiford caught up with me. "That was a good speech." He said. "Did you believe any of it?"

"Parts of it, yes." I said. "I think the world deserves better than Thaniel or me. I think it deserves better than even Prince Edward decent as he is," I paused, "but that's likely as good as they can hope for." I sighed. "You ask me if I believed what I said? The truth is it doesn't matter." I gestured to the army. "They do."

Present Day
McAllan's Story

cAllan looked at Fennis. They were walking around one of his ponds. It was a perfectly manicured garden, and in the distance, he could see the general's servants tending the field. "I always respected you, McAllan." Fennis said looking over his plantation. It was the largest one in the South, and the name Fennis held the most weight by far. It might take three days to walk from one end to the other. "I mean that Prime Governor."

"You left your position as soon as I was elected." McAllan said throwing a stone into the pond. "Doesn't exactly scream respect, now does it."

"I left because I knew what would come." Fennis said, and the sorrow in his voice was real. "I can't do what you'd need me to do." He looked away from the pond and at him. "I was a young man when I first saw you fight in the ring."

"I was a young man too when I fought." McAllan snorted

"We were all young men once, no matter what our children would believe." He chuckled and threw a rock into the water. "Still you weren't that young when I saw you fight. They sent some stallion at you, and you took him down in the first round." Fennis sighed. "Why'd you never join the army?"

McAllan threw another stone into the pond considering the question. "I thought about it." He admitted. "My father was in during the second war with Anthanii. I went to a recruiter once, but I could never go through with it."

"Why not? You had the guts." Fennis was an old breed of Confederacy man. He believed that every man with the courage would inevitably sign on for a life of grand adventure and honor. It never even occurred to him that there were other honorable professions.

"I had a sister and a dog." McAllan said simply, and Fennis nodded understandingly. The only thing more important than duty to a man like this was family.

"Look at all this land." Fennis gestured to the plantation. "I was born with it though. I didn't believe it could truly be mine until I earned it. I believed I had to shed blood in its defense. I wasn't going to stay in for long, but it turns out I had a knack for that sort of thing, An accident really, me being good I mean, so I decided to keep at it. I couldn't leave my men to someone who wouldn't look after them like I did." He sighed. "I don't think I really took the time to enjoy my lands until I left the army." The general shook his head at it all. "I don't mean the wealth either. I enjoyed plenty of that in my youth." He looked back at the Prime Governor. "I mean the peace of it all. I mean walking from one side of a manicured field to the other, thinking about whatever it is on your mind." He sighed. "But then I think we can only really appreciate something if we've earned it."

"That's an honorable way." McAllan admitted.

"What did you inherit from your father?" Fennis asked even though he knew the answer.

"A drinking problem and a tough jaw." McAllan looked down. "That's all really. We didn't even own the house we lived in."

"You say that like your ashamed of it." Fennis put a hand on his shoulder.

"Wouldn't you be?"

"Only if you left this world with a drinking problem and a tough jaw." Fennis smiled at him. He was a handsome man even in his old age. His hair had turned stark white, and the beard he grew did a poor job of covering his scars. Still, the scars were becoming of him. He was almost as tall as McAllan and built with a broad chest. He was a born general. He gave the impression that he'd looked that way since his voice began to crack.

"There's time yet for that." McAllan smiled.

"There's time yet for me to go to Thyro, but I don't think I will." Fennis smiled back. "I respected you because you were born with nothing." He picked up another stone and skipped it across the lake. "You earned what is yours. You were an even better lawyer than you were a fighter and an even better governor than you were a lawyer."

"And as Prime Governor?" McAllan said.

"You mean well." It was all he would say.

"And do you respect Coleson?" He asked Fennis.

The man stroked his white beard in thought. "No, I don't. This country could use more men like you and less like Coleson." He put his hands in his pockets. McAllan had never seen the man without his uniform. It was strange to see him dressed in a simple shirt and work pants. He might have been a country farmer. "Coleson believes it's his birthright to be powerful, so do you I think, but it's different with you."

"How do you mean?" McAllan asked.

"He thinks it's his birthright to be powerful because of who his parents were. You think it's your birthright because of who you are and what you think you can promise this land." The general smiled. "He sees power as a privelge to be enjoyed. You see it as a responsibility to be borne." Fennis said as he frowned at a weed on the ground and plucked it up. "Damned things, but they give an old man something to do I suppose."

McAllan ignored the weed comment. He had more than enough to do as an old man. The Prime Governor picked up another rock and tried to skip it. "You agree with Coleson though?"

"I don't have to respect a man to agree with him, and I don't have to agree with a man to respect him." He chuckled. "I respect my wife, but we argue over just about everything. I have an accountant I can't stand, but I let him invest money in the railroad. It made me even richer."

"This is much bigger than either." McAllan was befuddled. "How can you remain so calm with the fate of the country at stake."

"The fate of the country is always at stake." Fennis chuckled. "I've learned that even through our triumphs and failures, the world keeps turning no matter what the borders say." He paused to pluck out another weed. "Yes, I've learned that. I wish I'd known it when I was young. It's better to approach these things with a calm hand anyhow."

"The world will stop turning for those who die in the war to come." McAllan sighed.

"Then don't try to fight us." Fennis said it like that was an option.

"You know I have to." McAllan said with a heavy heart.

"I do." The general had real sorrow in his voice. "Still those men will die for a cause they believe is right." He picked another stone and skipped it flawlessly. "Some days I wish I had done just that."

"You just didn't wish it on those days where it could have been a possibility." McAllan said astutely.

"I suppose I didn't." Fennis reflected on that. "Your aide is a black boy isn't he?"

"Yes, he is." The last thing he wanted right then was a southerners racist rant.

"Does he play the blues?" The general asked.

That took McAllan off guard. "The what?"

"The blues." He said without batting an eye. "Those Souren fellows play it. I've been trying to learn on the guitar, now that I have all this time. It sounds magnificent really, makes you cry sometimes."

"I don't think he does." McAllan said a little irritated at the banality of it all.

"Shame." He shook his head. "You know some of my countrymen think they're beneath us white folk."

"Yes, I do know that." It was one of the more frustrating parts of the Prime Governor's job.

"They call them mules like it's an insult." Fennis chuckled. "I think of them as mules sometimes too." He paused. "It's not an insult though. A mule is a tough creature, and one day they'll set the world on fire. Mark my words they will."

"And what kind of world will they inherit?" McAllan lashed against the frivolity of it all. "A broken nation, little better than slaves to those across the ocean?"

The general leveled an angry glare at his guest. "Prime Governor I invited you here, and if you can't keep a civil tongue in your head, I can resend my invitation just as well."

"I'd rather lose my civil tongue than start a civil war." He said without backing down. McAllan could feel the old boxer rage inside him.

"You think I want the blood of my people?" Fennis laughed viciously. "I want to grow old with my wife, who I've ignored too much all these years. I want my sons who all joined the army to sweat out their terms guarding a railroad against Huegos. Most of all, though, I want the South free of those who would try to govern it without any notion on what we actually do."

"We govern through a democracy General." McAllan said levelly.

"Your democracy is a bad joke, and you know it." Fennis snapped back. "It's four lambs and five wolves voting on supper."

"Then Ironwill put provisions in place for-"

"For what?" Finally, the General was showing some fire. "It was four southern provinces four north." He paused regaining his composure. "Now theres a new Northern one every year, and the middle states are little better than your lackeys." He sighed. "You don't ask anymore you just tell."

"That's not true." McAllan said even though he knew in his heart it was. "Maybe legal provisions can be made. This doesn't have to come to war!"

"Do you know my ancestor was one of the men sent to Anthanii as a delegate?" Fennis asked.

"Of course. His name is chiseled on the capital building." McAllan implored with both hands.

"Then you know what the king did to them when they presented peaceful terms." Fennis was near trembling with rage. McAllan wasn't sure if he was angry that his family had been slighted, or he bemoaned the death of a relative he never knew. However, he had the sinking suspicion that the General was one of those rare honorable sorts who was angry at the injustice of it alone. "He hung them over the river for all his subjects to see."

"Are you so far gone that you think we're capable of doing that to our own brothers?" McAllan pleaded.

"No." He said calming himself. "You'll ignore us which is worse. I would subject myself to any torture you could devise if I thought it would change things." It would have sounded like an empty boast from another man, not from Fennis though. "If you hung me, at least I'd make a statement. As it stands, I'll disappear into a stack of papers."

"You know I wouldn't do that." McAllan said with an uncharacteristic softness. In a different time, in a different place, they would have been fast friends.

"I know you wouldn't." He said placing a hand on the Prime Governors shoulder. "But your position isn't all-powerful or timeless." Fennis sighed. "Even if you win the next election, in a few years you'll be gone with less power than even me over events. Even if you choose to grant all our demands, those Northern senators will simply knock it down in the legislature. I'm not sure you'll win next term, and I am sure you won't grant all our demands." He turned back to the pond.

"You mean the Demon Worship." McAllan scowled at the man's back.

"I mean the Old Religion." Fennis turned around with military precision.

"Aye, the one that melts men's minds, the one who's Priests murder parents and abduct their children, the ones who make slaves of us all to Powers Below." *The one that took my sister from me and is taking my wife.* McAllan told himself he didn't mention it to seem objective. The truth was it was too painful to speak out loud.

"Aye, there's a cost." Fennis raised his chin. "A cavalry charge has a cost." He took a step towards the Prime Governor. "It has made us strong. I weep for those affected, but I look towards the future of my people. The price must be paid!"

"Do you think a child who can't tell a nightmare from our world, cares for your tears?" The General remained silent. "The cost is never worth it when it demands your own morality!" He lowered his voice for effect. "The price is your soul. I thought you of all people would see that."

"You think that allowing the Old Religion here makes me dishonorable?" The Generals words might have seemed defensive, but his voice made it sound like an honest question.

"No, I don't." McAllan sighed. "I think Coleson is dishonorable, I think those plantation owners who would send your people to their deaths for a few coins in their pockets are dishonorable, I've even been dishonorable from time to time." He paused again. "But not you. Never you."

"You're wrong. This will cost me my honor." The General looked down at his feet in shame. "I've been a Confederacy man all my life. This is like tearing away a part of me."

"Then let us find another way." McAllan put a hand on the old man's shoulder.

"There is no other way." He shrugged off the hand. "Don't you see the man you're dealing with. How far I'll go for my people."

"You'd die for them." The Prime Governor sounded like he was consoling a friend. "I've always known that. Every man who's ever heard your name knows that."

"Aye I would die for them, but that's easy." Fennis leveled his gaze at him. "I'm sacrificing my honor for this, my morality, the very right to look myself in the mirror and know that I am a good man." There was grief in his voice that went beyond even the one McAllan had known at the bed of his sister. "I'll burn in whatever hell there is for this sin, but I'll carry my people's sin on my back until I drown under it. That is the price I'm willing to pay. Not just my life, but my soul." A tear appeared out the corner of his eye, and he whipped it away. Both men pretended it hadn't been there. "I wish I'd been killed in battle years ago. Demons below I'd even rather die of the shits than this, but I didn't." Fennis looked on defiantly. "The price demanded of me now I will pay. Pray to whatever gods are yours, that nothing like this is ever asked of you, though I fear it will be."

McAllan realized then that he had misjudged the man. He had always thought the General was just looking for another war to satisfy his own thirst for glory or to cement his name, but the man before him meant every word he said. Fennis was the best sort of man who lived in this world. *And I will break him.* "What if your sacrifice bears no fruit."

"What if we lose, you mean." He looked up at the Prime Governor appraisingly.

"We have more men."

Fennis gave a grunt. "Just because you have more clay doesn't mean you have more bricks." He leaned down for another stone to skip across the lake. "There's a wide difference between men and soldiers."

"You've asked me not to belittle your people." McAllan said levelly. "I'd like the same respect in return." He took a step forward letting his stature and scarred face speak for him. "I know you Southerners take pride in your honor, but just because we don't boast about it doesn't mean we don't have it.

"I have no doubt you do. Honor is not a quality unique to one side of the Capitol." He picked up another stone. "There's a lot more to soldering than pure bravery though. Here we're bred to hunt and ride. The overwhelming majority of competent officers hail from here. Demons below, you don't even have a cavalry school in the North. My brethren have cut their teeth against the Puena. There's good fighters up where you're from, I'll grant you that, but the only action most of them have seen is against some Huego tribes. Most boys from the streets of New Audrey haven't even seen a proper gun fired. In Pentsville they're born with one in their hands." He pulled a long cigar out of his coat pocket and lit it puffing thoughtfully. "No there's far more to soldering than being in a few brawls."

"And there's far more to warfare than soldiers." McAllan didn't mean it as a threat, but it sounded like one. "We may not have those fine gentlemen cavalry you won't shut up about, but where do those weapons you're born with, come from?" The Prime Governor was done with tiptoe diplomacy. Courtesy be damned. If Fennis couldn't see the truth, he'd shove it down his throat.

"We have enough weapons." The General said defiantly.

"You have enough hunting rifles one step above muskets." He felt like he was back in the ring, squared up against a worthy man. "We've started producing repeating carbines by the thousands. I might be giving up valuable information, but you knew that already didn't you?"

"Aye, and it doesn't matter." Fennis said it, but he clearly didn't believe his own words. The man was a soldier, not used to lying.

"It does, even if you pretend it doesn't." He paused taking a step forward. "And that's not the end of it. If you're lucky, you can impress a few old fishing boats into your service. Have you seen that article in the newspapers a few weeks ago? We have ironclad floating fortresses!"

"It won't mean a lick of difference if you can't beat us on land." Fennis said puffing on his cigar feverishly.

"It will regardless of how well you fight!" McAllan gave a wolfish grin. "What will happen to your economy when you can't export all that cotton and tobacco I wonder? That fool Coleson's embargo has hurt you far more than its hurt the North." The Prime Governor stooped down to pick up a rock fondling it in his hand. "At least you have all those cannons we gave you to protect the territory you won from the Puena."

"Aye we have them, and we're damned good with those guns." The General said even as he felt himself walking into a trap. "A thousand good pieces to aim your way."

"Eight hundred and forty-nine by my count." McAllan nodded his head pretending to jumble the numbers he already knew by heart. "Well, that's what we gave you. I'm sure time's taken its toll on a few of them."

"They work just fine." Fennis said over his cigar.

"Aye, they do." McAllan said then with mock regret. "For last years model anyway."

"Things don't change that quick." Fennis replied darkly.

"Maybe back when we were young. Then we were lucky to get one new innovation per decade." He hunched over in his best impersonation of an old man. "Now it seems these young whipper-snappers change the world every day." He paused for a moment to get his flask out. "Rearden has discovered how to make steel twice as strong for half the cost. He's a decent man, despite what the tabloids say. He meant it to make lives easier and further our great nation. However, my engineers have learned how to make artillery out of it, that can shoot three times as far with almost no chance of misfire." He paused slyly. "I don't think I need to tell you that cannon is the future of warfare."

"You're lying." The General pointed his cigar at him.

"You know I'm not because your engineers have already tried to get their grubby little paws on it." He laughed and knocked back a drink. "Of course our engineers are worth five times over what yours are." He put the flask back. "There may be countless military schools south of the Capitol, but it's a shame science takes a back seat in all of that."

"Damn your universities. They can't teach conviction and that we have on you in spades." His words were brave, but there was a hint of fear there.

"Well, they can teach quite a lot, I assure you of that." McAllan put his hands in his pockets. "They even have this new philosophy called capitalism. Have you heard of it, back in my day we just called it earning a dollar."

"I've heard of the fiendish system!" Fennis said pinching his face in disgust. "Teaches them to only look out for their wallets. There's no honor in it!

"Well, that's a bit of an oversimplification really." The Prime Governor paused for a second looking over the ponds. "Besides it's hypocritical for you to defend the status quo, with all this as your inheritance. I'll admit it has its flaws, but it has proven a very lucrative philosophy."

"What does it matter, how you Northerners justify shameless profit mongering?" Fennis said dismissively.

"I'll tell you why it matters." McAllan turned his tone to deadly serious. "Because beyond even pure military equipment, you don't have the means to go to war. Your convictions won't matter when your boots start to fall apart, and you can't get new ones because all the factories are on the other side. You have food, but no railroads to transport it to the front before it spoils, or even a decent means of canning it for preservation." Another wolfish grin came over him. "You can't even turn the cotton you grow into uniforms."

"We'll see what our allies can do to even the odds." Fennis roared in an uncharacteristic loss of composure. It took a second before he realized what he'd just admitted to. When he did, he dropped his cigar in dismay.

"What did you just say?" McAllan said in cold fury, barely retaining his calm.

The General knew he'd made a mistake, but he wasn't the sort to retreat from any kind of challenge. "You heard me well enough."

"I'm sure I didn't." He said moving to within an inch of Fennis's white beard. He was used to towering over men, but they were of a height that their eyes were level. "Because if I did, it sounds like you just admitted to selling your country to the people your family fought to free us from."

"It's a small step from conspiracy to treason," The General said with the conviction of a man facing an enemy battle line.

McAllan gave a derisive snort then stepped away. "Legally they both end in a hanging, but morally?" He shook his head. "What have they turned you into?"

"I am what you forced me to become." Fennis said seething with anger.

"I didn't force you into anything." McAllan said not believing what he heard. "It's what Coleson and those blood colored bastards have somehow molded you into." He shook his head again. "I've heard of those Priests turning lead into gold. Now they've turned the shepherd into the wolf."

"I'll admit I was against it." Fennis said sorrow coated in fury. "But you've just convinced me with your threats."

"Those weren't threats. They were economic and industrial facts." McAllan spat into the ground. "Here's a few more. You're counting on some feckless rulers across the largest ocean in the world to help you fight your neighbor. Your brothers!" He looked away in disgust. "What did you promise them?"

"What we needed too." Fennis couldn't even hide his own guilt.

"I bet you offered the Anthanii the Yunta province, and those

Kranish the Trebia river." Of course, he knew about the talks. Samugy was second to none at spy work. It was a completely different thing to hear it from the mouth of General Fennis, hero of the Confederacy.

Fennis didn't say a word.

"I want to hear you say it." McAllan said levelly. "I want your father and his father and his father before that, to hear from beyond the grave, that their greatest descendant has betrayed that which they held so dear."

"Aye, that's what they offered them." Fennis said more to himself than McAllan.

"You can't even say we." He spat in disgust.

"I told you what I was willing to sacrifice for the good of my people." Fennis looked down.

"This won't do your people any good, mark my words." McAllan balled his fist. "I haven't threatened you yet. Here's a threat." He leveled a finger at the man. "Thomas Belson is in the Confederacy."

"It's said he won't fight."

"It's said Fennises are patriots." McAllan scoffed. "People say a lot of things."

"You think he'll fight his own people for you?" The General chuckled.

"I think he sees more clearly than you, for all your years." The Prime Governor took in the landscape. "I think he sees the whole of the Confederacy as his kin rather than just those who inherited a fancy house and some indentured blacks." He looked back to Fennis. "He knows that what our forefathers bled for was a dream we can only reach as one."

"He won't raise arms against the South."

"Do you know what the term is for a Constable?" McAllan asked then without waiting for an answer kept on. "It's twenty years. Now, why do you think the New Church would release their most famous warrior five years early?"

Fennis already saw where he was going. "You're a liar."

"Maybe they didn't release him early." McAllan smiled with no humor. "Maybe they sent him here to break you."

"So you'd conspire with a foreign church against us, and then defame me for seeking allies?" He said trying to divert the conversation.

"I didn't conspire with anyone. I just see what is." McAllan paused. "It doesn't matter though. Thomas Belson will see this country whole. He'll make sure Yunta and the Trebia stay with us." He shook his head. "Not sold to foreigners, so you can keep your abomination of a religion."

"If he does, then he has no honor." Fennis said dismissively. "I don't need a man in my army without honor."

"You know that's not true. Thomas Belson will fight for his beliefs." He said. "And he'll beat you."

"He's one man."

"No, you're one man! I'm one man!" McAllan gestured with his hand. "I'm a clever leader, and you're the general who broke the Puena." His voice went icy. "Thomas Belson has broken Thaniel. Thomas Belson has broken Empires. Thomas Belson has broken gods." He paused. "Thomas Belson will break you."

"We'll see." But his voice was unsure. "My people will do whatever is necessary to be free from you." He regained his composure.

"You saw me fight once." McAllan said calmly. "Watch me fight now. Watch what I'll do when you push me."

"I will." Fennis returned coldly.

McAllan reached down and picked up the cigar that the General had dropped. "Southern tobacco rolled in a northern factory." He opened his own coat and checked the label. "Southern cotton sewn in a Northern textile mill. When you check your shirt label tonight see if it doesn't say the same thing." He sighed picking up another rock and skipped it across the pond. "We need each other General. The Confederacy is so much greater than North and South." He turned to walk away but stopped. "One day when this is over. We'll welcome you back to us. We're brothers after all."

"I'm sorry." McAllan heard Fennis say, but it seemed almost to himself.

"Tell it to the dead." The Prime Governor said and continued walking. "They won't hear it, but it might help your soul." He headed back to his coach. While he walked, he looked around the plantation. It was beautiful. It had been beautiful for centuries, and this war would destroy it all. He walked till he saw Timothy leaning against the carriage and Samugy was there to his surprise. They appeared to be talking to a black servant who seemed almost as uncomfortable as the two bodyguards trying to look anywhere else.

"So how do blackies reproduce?" He heard Samugy ask. "Do you just plant some of your curly hair, and they rise to maturity?"

"Um sorry, sir I-" The poor Sueno was utterly baffled.

"Essentially the same as every other male in the country." Timothy cut in. "We give your mother a fish or two?" He shrugged. "Usually one."

"My mother doesn't like fish," He paused, "or blackies come to think of it." He paused seeing McAllan walking over. "Ah, fearless leader." He looked the man up and down. "You look uncharacteristically fearful."

The unlucky servant saw a chance to run and almost got away before Samugy stopped him. "Now, now. We haven't yet discovered how you make little blackie babies." The Huego looked to McAllan. "We've discovered that soldiers are formed when they place a used cartridge inside a whore." He gestured to the two bodyguards who were growing quite tired of the man's humor. "Politicians are the cleverest of barnacles who've learned to mime human traits." He stopped tapping his chin. "Blackies are still a mystery, though."

"Let the poor man leave." McAllan wasn't in the mood for verbal sparring anymore.

"Yes, sir." The man muttered and ran away as fast as his legs could carry him.

"What's got you in a pinch?" Samugy asked curtly. "No comment on how we reproduce through our ears?"

"Not today." McAllan sighed. "Get the wagon ready we're riding out."

"You said we'd be welcome here tonight, sir." Timothy cut in.

"I think we may be the last Northerners welcome here for a long time." McAllan said coldly as they filed into the wagon.

"What did he say?" Samugy asked once they were all in the wagon and putting distance between them and Fennis's plantation.

"Everything you told me he would." McAllan said looking out the window. "I couldn't believe a man like Fennis could become the wolf I saw today without hearing it for myself."

"Men become queer things when they're pushed to it." Samugy said with some melancholy like he was remembering his own past.

"That's just the thing though." McAllan said turning his view to the Huego. "I haven't pushed him. I haven't even passed the legislation I need to because I was afraid of this."

It was Timothy that spoke up surprisingly. "My uncle used to tell me a story about one of the plantation owners he worked for." McAllan expected his minister of intelligence to make some snarky remark about how that's where blackies belong, but he was listening just as intently as the Prime Governor was. "He had an overseer who used to bring a whip and threaten to beat whoever he saw slacking off. He never used it, but one day another Souren servant bashed his head in with a rock."

"What's your point?" McAllan asked though he was beginning to see it himself.

"The man did it because he felt threatened, he did it because one day the threat could turn into something else, but most of all he did it because that overseer believed he was better than him." Timothy finished.

"You think that Coleson is having his rebellion because he feels belittled?" Samugy asked.

"You think I've belittled these people?" McAllan chimed in.

"I think Coleson's a tit." Timothy nodded in agreement to what everyone else in the room already knew. "He's after power and pride." The boy paused for a moment. "But Fennis speaks for the South. With every new territory that becomes a province, they see themselves losing equality. You may be too clever to remind them of it, but you'd be a fool if you think every Northerner has your sense."

"Did some white man teach you those words." Samugy said smugly. "They sound a little too clever for a blackie."

"It's alright Huego's have a tough time hearing, all things considered." Timothy shot back.

"So what do you think we should do then?" McAllan asked the boy. Even the guards seemed a bit baffled he'd ask advise from an aide.

"Be more vigilant than the overseer." Timothy responded dryly.

McAllan nodded. "I think you're right."

Present Day

J threw Ayn-Tuk to the ground for the seventh time. He put his two fingers up in the yield sign and knocked the dirt off his glimmering black skin as he stood up.

"Again!" I gestured for him to retrieve his spear. I wanted to hit something. I wanted to be the man who toppled empires. I didn't want to be the Thomas Belson who could be reduced to a sobbing mess by a few words from his sister. I wanted to be Belson the Blessed. However, there wasn't an empire to topple. There wasn't an army to beat. There wasn't a war to fight. All I had was my Souren companion.

Ayn-Tuk paused for a moment. Even his marble chiseled body was showing signs of strain. We sparred often. Both of us were swords that needed to be kept sharp, but we this was different.

It'd been three days since my sister had sent me to the tree. I'd been avoiding my family, finding excuses not to eat with them, ending pleasant conversation before it could start, always telling my nephew I'd teach him how to shoot tomorrow. In my mind, I was already gone. I had made my decision to leave. I wasn't sure where I was headed or what I'd be doing, but I couldn't stay at the Belson Plantation. Yet, I kept finding excuses to stay another night. Shaggy needs time to rest, I wanted to see a bit more of Rachel, I'd leave after the party. They were all unimportant. Something was keeping me in my family home, but I couldn't guess what it was.

I could tell Seiford had guessed my intentions even if he wouldn't confront me about it directly. Over the course of the three days, the monk had brought me members of my family to try and coax me out of my pain. They'd tell me how much they loved me. I'd respond in turn and go back to my anger. It was a rare misstep for the monk. I knew my family loved me, which made it hurt more. No matter how many people put their hand on my shoulder, they weren't my father.

No matter how many times I was told Alexis was just angry and young, it didn't make her words any less true.

My shirt was off, scars showing across muscle. A few of the servants in the field were watching the match in between their work. By this time they were used to seeing me perform my martial stunts. I was training incessantly for a war that didn't exist. I ran, rode, and shot. When I wasn't doing that, I was reading old war tomes. I hadn't worked myself that hard since the Thaniel Wars. I told myself I needed to be ready. In truth, if I stopped for a moment, I'd turn back into the man weeping beneath his favorite tree.

"Again!" I shouted at Ayn-Tuk.

The black man shook his head and went to the bucket of water to wash himself off. He was a good fighter. He might have been the best I'd met since Thaniel, but I was Belson the Blessed. Every once in a while he'd land a lucky shot and win the match, but it wasn't often, and it wasn't today.

"Again!" I picked up my tomahawk.

Ayn-Tuk gave me a look of pure venom and went back to washing. I'd never seen him show so much emotion. It should have stopped me.

"Are you deaf, or are Souren just that stupid?" Every word was carefully measured to cause the most pain. I didn't even believe it. I just wanted to hurt someone, and if it couldn't be with my fist it'd be with my tongue. "I said again!" I screamed.

Ayn-Tuk rose from his bucket with an anger I'd never seen on him. I took a step back despite myself, falling halfway into my fighters stance. "I'm not your *fucking* slave." I'd never heard him curse before. Even in my twisted rage, I knew I'd gone too far.

I wasn't near stupid enough to continue, but I wasn't in the frame of mind to retract my words. "Fuck it." I turned away and grabbed my six-shooter, looking for a target. I found one.

An old Souren man was carrying a pale full of water on his head. I fired six shots in rapid succession. Every bullet went right where I told it to. Before the black man dropped his bucket in fear, soaking himself, there was a smiling face of holes in it.

I twirled my smoking pistol in self-satisfaction until a pain lit up the back of my head sending me sprawled on the ground. I looked up to find what hit me and saw Ayn-Tuk holding his fist in quivering rage.

"They're not toys for you to take your self-contempt out on." The words came out level, but everything in Ayn-Tuk's body screamed violence.

"Piss off!" I slammed my fist into the dirt. "You know I don't miss! It's just some fun."

"Just fun for you." The black man hissed out. "Look at him!" He pointed towards the servant I'd been terrorizing.

I looked back and saw the man hunched over his pale, waving off the people around him coming to help. He seemed smaller than he'd been a moment ago. He seemed like he was trying to hide. "It's just a fucking bucket!" I screamed back at my companion.

"It's not just a bucket." Ayn-Tuk shook his head. "You made him seem less of a man, to be terrorized by those above his station. More than that, they respect your brother because he doesn't let this kind of thing happen. Now you put him in an impossible position between his employer and you!" He said through that dark ashy voice. "You've belittled him, dishonored your family name, and given everyone a reason to hate you because you wanted to feel powerful!"

"It's just a game!" I shouted back, still on the ground.

Ayn-Tuk's rage came back. "The Anthanii who conquered my people used to play a similar game." This was the most words he'd ever spoken to me in one conversation. I could see there was more to this than shooting a bucket off someone's head. "That's all we are to you, isn't it? Just black savages to toy around with."

"You know it ain't like that, Tuk." I rubbed the growing knot on my head.

"No, it's not like that." My friend agreed. "You're not a racist. You see everyone as things to amuse you, pieces in your game regardless of skin color." He said in his ashy tenor. "Do you think that makes it better or worse?"

"Fine!" I slapped the ground again. "You're right. I shouldn't have done it."

Ayn-Tuk softened up a bit and helped me to my feet. "You need to apologize."

"Like fuck, I'll apologize!" I shook the dirt off me.

"Thomas!" There was a threat in those words, the ever so s promise of violence. I'd win, but not without doing somethin regret.

"Fine!" I turned back to the Souren servant still getting feet. "You there!" I gestured to him.

Ayn-Tuk slapped me in the back of my head. "Not as a servant, as an equal in the brotherhood of man."

"Brotherhood of lick my ass..." I said under my breath. Ayn-Tuk slapped me in the back of the head again. It was getting quite hard to control myself.

"Thomas..." He warned.

"I'm doing it!" I hissed at him then turned to the servant. "Excuse me, sir! Can I have a moment of your time?"

The Souren servant looked like he was about to make a run for it, but after seeing my shooting skills, he thought better of the idea. He headed towards us. "I'm coming, sir."

The servant hung his head humbly. He had a Souren accent which meant he'd come over himself from the continent. I knew my brother treated him well, but he was hardly the only powerful white man. Too many of the others treated anyone with black skin like a dog. Honestly, even the Souren tribal chiefs tended to act closer to master than leader, and from what this one had seen of me, he probably thought I was the former. That rubbed against me. Ayn-Tuk's words had a wisdom I was too angry to see.

"Yes, sir." The servant said meekly.

Ayn-Tuk stepped in. "He's not your employer. You don't need to call him sir."

"I called him sir, didn't I?" I shot back.

"He's acting like a man." Ayn-Tuk pointed at the servant. "You're acting like a spoiled child." He turned back to the servant. "Call him Thomas."

"Well, Mr. Thomas." The servant stood a little straighter. "It's nice to meet you."

"And you are?" I asked.

"Mathew Smith." He stuck his hand out.

I looked from his black skin and listened to his accent. "Abu at narita." It was Souren for, "No it's not."

That surprised him. "I changed my name when I came over here. Back in my own land, they called me Resta An-Sab" The servant kept using his native tongue. "Things go easier for us when we assimilate." He shrugged. "Besides, I like the Confederacy. You lot do most things right over here on the by and large, and nothing so broke it can't be fixed in time." He smiled. "It's not a shame for me to wear one of your names."

"I understand that." I nodded. "Still I'll call you An-Sab." I chuckled a bit. "In the tribes I was with, that meant lion man." I looked him up and down, getting his measure. "They only give that name to their best warriors."

He shrugged. "It's the same in our tribe." An-Sab's face was contorted by old memories. "That was a long time ago, and a different man held the spear."

"I know what you mean..." I trailed off to my own past.

Ayn-Tuk slapped me in the back of the head again. "Apologize."

I took a big sigh. "Listen An-Sab, I'm sorry about shooting your bucket." I said. "I was angry but not at you. You didn't deserve that."

"It's fine." He waved it off. "It's just a bucket anyhow."

"Well, you can take ours." I handed him our pale of water, which he took happily.

"Many thanks." An-Sab smiled.

"His shirt is wet too." Ayn-Tuk kept pushing.

"So it is." I grabbed the shirt I'd taken off earlier. "Here you can have mine."

"That's too much." He tried to wave it off.

"No, it's not." I insisted. "I'm not as tan as you are. I think it's time my body got some sun, anyway."

"Well, if you insist." He took the shirt and started to change over. "Nothing worse than working with a wet shirt."

"Yes, there is." I shuddered at my most hated memory. "Marching with wet feet."

An-Sab smiled and went to put on my gift.

I turned to Ayn-Tuk. "Is that enough, or should I suck his cock too?"

Ayn-Tuk leaned in close so the servant couldn't overhear us. "You need to learn self-control." He said in his deep voice. "I know it's hard coming home after everything you've been through, but that's no excuse."

"I always wanted you to talk." I said. "Now, I want you to shut the fuck up." I hissed at him.

He kept glaring at me.

"I'm doing the best I can." I finally said.

"Do better." Ayn-Tuk said and turned to walk away. "I have work to do. I'll see you at dinner tonight, and you *will* be there." He leveled a finger at me. "No excuses this time." He walked off to the house.

"Frigid bastard." I said under my breath. Then turned back to An-Sab.

"So how'd you come to speak my language?" An-Sab asked in Souren.

"I spent a few years fighting in your homeland." I kept using the dialect. Some people call me a show-off. They're right. "Figured I ought to learn it."

"So the story about the Golden Fort is true?" He took a step back.

My mind went back to that battle for a moment. "Parts of it." I switched back to Anthanii.

"That was a bad business." The old black man scratched his head. "Still it's nice to meet a Westerner who cares about us enough to do something."

"Honestly, most of them do care." I said. "They just don't know how to fix it."

"They could leave." An-Sab shrugged.

"I thought you liked us Westerners?" I asked.

"I like you in the West." He shrugged. "When they come to my old home they just meddle in things they don't understand."

"Well, if it were up to me, we would leave." I sighed. "Sadly, it ain't up to me."

He waved it off. "You did enough as is."

"Some people say I did too much." I scratched the tattoos on my arm.

"It's a hard balance to find." An-Sab nodded. "It might not be my place, but I was a warrior once. Things get easier after a while, adjusting to peace I mean."

"That's the trouble, though." I reached into my pocket and found a cigarette to smoke. "I'm not sure I want to." I puffed a bit. "I was a great warrior. Most say the best, and they weren't wrong." I shrugged. "I've always been shit at peace."

An-Sab nodded. "That's how all warriors think." He said. "I thought so myself until I had a son." The black man nodded. "He was a beautiful boy, and I'd rather him have an esquire at the end of his name than lion-man."

"You sent him to university?" I asked.

"I made a deal with your father before he passed." He shrugged. "Your brother seems keen to honor it."

"He's a good man." I nodded. "Better than me anyhow."

"He's a different type of good." An-Sab said. "Doesn't make your's any less."

"Thank you." I nodded. "Keep the shirt. It looks better on you."

He looked at the cloth. "I think you're right. Grey is my color." An-Sab stepped towards me. "I know I'm just a servant, but if you need someone to talk to, I live in the family quarters." He chuckled. "I want to hear about how you fought next to Rentu the Tall."

"I'll keep that in mind." I smiled back at him. "Might be I'll be around."

"Good, your brother came to me for a time after the Puena Wars." The black man shrugged. "Still does every now and again." He looked around the field. "Well, I best be getting back to work."

"Didn't mean to keep you." I nodded to him.

"It's quite alright." He picked up the bucket. "Anything for the Hero of the Plains."

"Be seeing you!" I called out to him. He waved his hand back at me.

He was a decent sort. I felt bad about shooting his bucket. Maybe he was right. Maybe peace did get easier, but then I got the feeling we were cut from different cloth.

I stowed my weapons away and looked for my shirt until I realized I didn't have it anymore. "Fucking Tuk..." I muttered under my breath and walked back towards the house.

I heard squabbling over the tilled fields. "This isn't a good idea." I heard a voice say. It sounded like Seiford. I was wondering where he'd gone off to.

"We've tried all the good ideas, haven't we!" A woman's voice chimed in. It sounded like Rachel. We hadn't spoken much since we'd gotten to the plantation. She'd made a few attempts, but even as attractive as she was, I wasn't in the mood for conversation.

"I'm not apologizing!" Another girls voice spoke up.

"I didn't ask you to apologize." Rachel said. "I asked you to talk to him." I heard her hiss. "He deserves that much."

"Fine, but I'm doing this for you, not him." The second girl said. When I heard it again, I realized it was Alexis.

I thought about slipping away before they saw me, but I realized I had to face them sooner or later. Besides, my talk with An-Sab had gone a far way towards leveling me. I took out another cigarette and puffed on it to ease my nerves.

"This is still a bad idea." Seiford said.

I pushed through the line of crops to see Seiford, Rachel, and Alexis staring at me. "What's a bad idea?" I asked.

"Well, it's too late now, isn't it." Seiford threw up his hands.

"Where'd your shirt go?" Rachel took a look at my torso covered in scars and muscle.

"Long story." I shrugged. "Should I go put another one on?"

"No, I quite like it." Rachel smiled coyly. "It looks roguish." She tore her eyes away to look at my face. "Besides, your sister needs to see it."

"I think she made her opinion of me quite clear." I glanced over towards Alexis trying to avoid my eyes. "I don't think a few scars are going to change anything."

"Don't be ridiculous." She tapped one of the pinkish lines on my chest. "You're more scar than man." She flipped her hair back letting it frame her green eyes. "Now, you've been positively boorish since that talk with your sister." She sighed. "I have absolutely no one to entertain me."

"My monk is quite funny." I gestured to Seiford.

"He's clever," Rachel admitted, "but if I wanted jokes, I'd hire a jester." She sighed. "Besides, your party is in two days."

"Two days?" I asked. I thought I had more time than that.

"Yes, two days," She repeated, "and it won't do to have the guest of honor sulking about like someone kicked his puppy, no matter how funny his monk is." She stepped aside and pushed Alexis forward. "You two need to sort out this mess out now before I have to sit through another lecture from Andrew." Rachel reached up to my mouth, took the cigarette, and stamped it into the ground. "Nasty habit. No suitor of mine will smell like smoke."

"Suitor?" I asked.

Rachel rolled her eyes. "I don't play dumb with men. They have so much more experience than I do. They always win." She put her hands on her hip. "However, if you'd prefer to just watch my ass when you think I'm not looking, that's just fine by me."

"Right." I tried not to look uncomfortable.

"Now talk!" She pushed my sister forward.

Alexis looked me up and down. She tried to hide the shock of seeing my mangled body, but I was good at reading people. "I'm not apologizing." She finally said.

"I didn't ask you too." I shrugged.

"You're the one who should be apologizing to me!"

"I have, and I will again if it helps." I said.

"You left me to go play hero!"

"I did, and I'm sorry."

That seemed to take the wind out of my sister. "Those are a lot of scars." She crossed her arms. "Do they hurt?"

"Yes, they hurt." I sighed. "Do you even care."

"No!" Alexis stamped her feet.

"Listen, girl," Rachel jumped in, "I remember the way he treated you before he left. He worshipped you like a princess." She said. "Everyone who saw you two together knew how much he loved you." She sighed. "Sure, he was an insufferable ass back then. He fought with Andrew constantly, disrespected your parents, and even ruined my favorite dress," she paused, "but he'd bring you a piece of the moon if you asked."

"I still would." I said softly.

"Fine, I care." Alexis relented a bit. "I just don't like to see an old veteran in pain, that's all!"

Finally, Seiford had enough. "That's all he is to you, is it?" He asked. "An old veteran?"

"I don't have a reason to think any more of him." Alexis sneered at me.

"Well, then let me give you a few!" The monk started. "He saved my country which was on the brink of collapse. He freed people no one's ever cared about. He stood for those who couldn't stand for themselves." Seiford paused. "He tried to do the right thing in a time when even the effort was frowned upon. He failed sometimes, but he did a damn sight better than anyone else ever had." The monk took a deep breath. "In the end, my brother decided to die for him, and I'd give the same answer if you woke me up from a drunken stupor."

"What does any of that have to do with me?" Alexis was still holding out.

"I'll tell you what it has to do with you." Seiford went on. "Every time someone asked why he sacrificed so much for people he'd never met, you know what he said?" The monk asked. "He said he wanted his sister to grow up in a better world than he had." He softened his tone. "He did it for you. I know you'd have preferred he stay here with you, but he could only do one or the other."

Alexis stopped finally. "Is that true?"

"That was part of it." After the Thaniel Wars, I'd needed some meaning to give to my life. In the end, I think it was just a smokescreen. It was a thin veneer to put over a distraught twenty-year-old with too many mistakes and too many scars. It was something to keep me going during the dark years. I had said it, though, and part of me meant it.

"You still could have written." She was a far ways from forgiving me, but the anger was out of her.

"I could have, but I didn't." I nodded.

"Why not?" Alexis said it barely a whisper.

Everyone went quiet. All my other sins had some rhyme or reason. I was a boy who'd been asked to do far too much. Then I'd been a man with too many ghosts. I could have written, though. I could have tried to give those who loved me a measure of peace. Everyone knew her forgiveness hinged upon this answer. Lie, and she'd be lost to me forever.

"I was scared." I finally said.

"Belson the Blessed was..." Alexis trailed off. "Scared?"

I nodded.

That seemed to anger her more. "That's how little you think of us?" She asked. "That we couldn't forgive some mean words said half a lifetime ago?"

"I was afraid you *would* forgive them." I looked up at her. She'd gotten so beautiful. "Since the beginning, I was called to be so much more than a scared child. I was their only hope." I rubbed the tattoos on my arm. "I had to let them think I was more than a man. I had to believe I was more than a man."

I put my weight on my good knee. "You know I limp when I'm alone." I shrugged. "It was a musket ball from six years ago somewhere outside of Hestern." I paused. "I practiced in front of a mirror for weeks to make sure no one could tell. I had to be strong, and writing home, begging for forgiveness might have broke me."

Alexis looked like she was about to open her mouth, but I kept on. "I always promised myself when the pressure let up, I'd send my first letter." I paused. "It never let up, though. The difference was it wasn't the world pushing on me. It was myself." I shook my head. "I'd made mistakes. I'd cost men their lives. So many souls weighed against me I thought a little more weight and I wouldn't be able to get up in the morning. The guilt only got worse over the years, and I wasn't strong enough to face it anymore." I looked back at her. "It's not an excuse, but it's the way things were."

"You really fought... For me?" Alexis asked.

"No." Lying wouldn't help bring my sister back to me. "I fought at first because I was hungry for glory. After that, I fought because it was habit. In the end, I couldn't tell you why I really took up arms."

"I see." Alexis nodded and took a step backward

I took a step forward. "However, after every battle is over the winner faces a choice." I said. "When a man's on his knees you can either finish it or help him up. War is only ever a means to an ends." I paused. "When the smoke cleared, and we started to count the dead, I thought of our parents, Andrew, and you." I hung my head. "I thought what would make you proud of me. I didn't always make the right choice, but I tried."

"Those are kind words, but they don't make what I said any less true." Alexis clenched her jaw. "You're still a stranger to me. The way you left hurt us, and I won't go about pretending it didn't." She paused. "I can't forgive that, not ever."

"I..." I trailed off, trying to find some excuse for my actions. There were none. "I understand." I finally said. I turned to Seiford. "Go get Ayn-Tuk, and tell him to ready the horses." I faced Alexis again. "I won't cause you any more pain."

Alexis looked away. "Maybe that's for the best."

"I think it is." I nodded.

Rachel finally stepped in. "You're just going to leave?" She looked at me. "You're just going to let him leave." She turned towards my sister.

I sighed. "Doesn't seem like there's any other path." I tried to force a smile. "I'm sorry our courtship was so brief."

"No!" Seiford screamed. "I won't accept this." He turned to me. "Show her your hands."

I glared back at the monk. "She doesn't need to see that."

"I think she does." Seiford stepped forward. "Show them to her!" The commanding tone in his voice frightened me. I showed her my fist, still bloody and bruised.

"So this is supposed to sway me?" Alexis asked. "I'm supposed to see a new bo-bo on you, feel bad kiss it, and tell you to stay." She huffed. "It's not that easy. You tried your best to tear this family apart. A bruised hand doesn't change anything."

"He did that to himself after what you said." The monk spat venom.

"Seiford stop." I didn't want the girl to have to bear that.

He went on. "Your brother beat his fist against a tree until I held him down." He said. "Then he cried like I've never seen him do before."

She wiped away what I hoped wasn't a tear. "That's not what I wanted."

"Yes, it is." Seiford stepped forward. "You wanted to hurt him because he hurt you."

"Is that so wrong?" She sneered at the monk.

"He's hurt enough for a thousand lifetimes." Seiford shook his head. "All he is to you now is a name and a legend, but he's more than that." He sighed. "For fifteen years he's been facing horrors you couldn't possibly imagine." The monk took a step forward. "Do you have any idea how many friends we've buried? How much blood he's been forced to spill."

"Of course, you don't. You weren't there!" Seiford went on. "I'm the one who has to hold him when he screams in the night, so he doesn't hurt himself. I can tell you there's more to him than just Belson the Blessed." He paused. "Fifteen years he's been fighting other peoples wars. He's had to make decisions that would drive you insane. He's had to carry burdens that would break the back of anyone else. He suffered more than you could possibly understand, you spoiled girl!" He kept on. "And at the end of it all, they cut him loose, with nowhere to go."

Seiford shook his head. "He's in pain, but the one thing that keeps him going is coming back to you, and you're willing to kick him out because fifteen years ago he said some mean things." He spat out. "It's a disgrace. He's suffered enough for that sin, and now he's coming back looking for another chance. He's not just a hero, he's a man who's paid too high a price and got little in return. He needs your help, so help him because he's your brother."

Alexis stifled a sob. "You want things to go back to the way they were?" She asked me.

"More than anything." I responded.

"I can't do that," she said, "but maybe we can try again." Alexis paused. "I want you to be my brother, but it'll take time."

I forced a smile. "I'll have to stay around for that." I said.

"You will." She nodded.

"Can I have a hug, at least?" I looked her over.

"That seems alright." She leaned in and hugged me. It was forced and awkward, but it was a start. A foothold in a mountain. That's all I ever needed. She pulled away. "I have to go see to the party." Alexis said. "Maybe after I'm done, you could play the piano for me." She paused. "Like you used to."

"I'd like that." I said.

She nodded and walked away.

"Seiford..." I said.

"I know you didn't want her to hear that," he started, "but I couldn't let her chase you away."

"Thank you." I folded him into a big hug. He seemed startled by it. "You're a good friend."

He pushed me away. "This is why people think we're lovers." He sighed. "You're a good friend too." He finally said.

"Thanks," I nodded towards Rachel, "Now if you don't mind..."

"I'm going." He nodded and headed the way Alexis had.

I looked at Rachel. "You weren't supposed to hear any of this." I said when we were alone. "I didn't want you to know that part of me." I shrugged. "If you don't want anything to do with me, I'll understand."

She tsk'd and took a few steps towards me. "You mean that bit about you being all broken, and someone needs to put you back together again?"

"Yes, that bit." I shifted uncomfortably.

"Well, let's tally it up, shall we?" She ran a finger over my torso. "You're a conquering hero returned from battle in foreign lands. You're widely hailed as a paragon of virtue in a sea of vices. You've some scars inside and out that need a woman's touch healing." She listed them off. "You're brave, well-bred, clever, and mysterious." She chuckled. "Oh, it sounds so much like one of those bad romance novels I could cry."

"It is uncanny." I agreed.

"On the other hand, you have a quite disturbing relationship with your horse," she went on, "there's stories about you and your monk that are absolutely scandalous, and you're not really much of a looker."

"That's a bit harsh, isn't it?" I asked. "I've been told I have a certain rugged charm."

"I hate to be the one to tell you, but they were lying." Rachel rolled her eyes.

"You think so?" I started walking towards the house, and she followed.

"I know so." She kept on. "Now Marcius of Renton! There was a handsome man if I've ever seen one."

"That's cruel." I smiled at her.

"The truth often is." She shrugged as if she was just stating a fact. "Marcius was an adonis, and you're about as pretty as incest."

"Please my lady," I rolled my eyes. "I don't think my ego can take this much praise."

"There's also the fact that my brother hates you." She went on.

"Does that help or hurt me?" I asked.

"Bit of both really." She scratched her chin. "After due consideration, I've decided, yes. I will allow you to continue courting me." She acted as if it was the greatest act of kindness ever bestowed upon anyone, though it was all in joking fashion.

"Well, that's very generous of you, considering how ugly I am." I laughed.

"We all must do our part to make sure Thomas Belson stays in the Confederacy." She shrugged. "You're lucky I'm such a patriot."

"They should build a statue of you in the Capitol." I agreed. "However, does this mean I can't look at your ass when I don't think you're watching."

"I'd be insulted if you didn't." She laughed.

"Thank you for helping me with my sister." I said finally.

"She's always looked up to me." Rachel said. "It shows she's a good judge of character."

"Tell me about her." I said.

"You want me to explain your own sister to you?" She asked.

"In case you haven't noticed I've been gone for a while." I sighed. "In my mind, I thought she'd be the little girl I left. I never imagined she'd hate me so much."

"She doesn't hate you." Rachel put a hand on my shoulder. "She just doesn't know where you stand, and when she's confused, she lashes out." Rachel pulled the hand away. "As to what she's like, she's clever, strong-willed, painfully arrogant, oblivious, and has a bad temper."

"So she's like I was fifteen years ago." I scratched the tattoos on my arm.

"No, she was never that ugly." Rachel smiled. "Also she doesn't have an army."

"Right." I said. We were back to the house. "Well, I better let you go now." I said. "If people see you walking back with me shirtless, there'll be talk."

"I suppose you're right." She sighed. "Fine, you don't need to beg anymore. I'll allow you to kiss my hand."

"Are you sure?" I asked. "I wouldn't want to get my ugly on your beautiful hand."

"It's a risk I'm willing to accept." She held out her hand, and I kissed it gracefully.

"Be seeing you, Rachel." I saw her off.

When I stepped inside the house, I was immediately assaulted by the young Tom and his father. "Can you teach me how to shoot now?" The boy hopped with excitement.

"What do you think Thomas?" Andrew asked over his shoulder.

"Does your mother know?" I asked him.

Andrew answered for the boy. "No, and it's going to stay that way."

I smiled at my nephew. "Go get your rifle and meet me outside."

"Thank you, Uncle Thomas!" He wrapped me up in a hug. "You're the best."

I was too shocked to respond before he darted off to collect his weapon. I stood up scratching my head. "Is this what it feels like?"

"What do you mean?" Andrew asked.

"Living a normal life?" I shrugged. "I've been afraid of it for so long, but it's not all bad."

"It has its ups and downs." My brother agreed. "I don't get much sleep these days, but no one tries to shoot me either." He took a step forward. "I take it you talked with Alexis."

"I did." I nodded.

"How'd it go?" He asked.

"Better." I shrugged. "There's still some work to do there."

"You know she loves you." Andrew said.

"I know." I responded. *I loved Thaniel, and I still watched his head roll.*

"Good, it just takes time." Andrew patted my shoulder. "Now, go teach my son how to shoot, and if he joins the army because of you, you'll hang."

I smiled. "I'll only tell your son the bad stories."

The Thaniel Wars

I was on the seventh mile and coming down the hill. What had been a steady jog was now a full sprint. Some distance runners I'd met claimed they got a second wind as they neared the final leg. They claimed the last mile was like running on air. I was not one of those men. All of me hurt. My knees screamed at every step, my lungs begged for an unlabored breath, and the cramp I'd started to feel the shadow of on mile three had transformed into a knife jamming through my kidney. In truth, I'd have preferred the knife. You can pull a blade out.

My body told me to stop. It whispered treasonous things to my brain. *Come on, no one's watching. You could walk a couple hundred paces. There's no shame in that. You did this yesterday after all.* I ignored it and pushed my legs into a speed I had thought just out of my reach. The whisper became a shout. *Three above Thomas! This isn't smart. Your wounds are still healing!* I upped the pace again. I thought it would learn to stop complaining. Bodies never seem to learn, though.

I sprinted the last mile because it was hard. I knew how strong I'd need to be to win this war. There was the type of superficial strength that let you pick up any amount of weight with ease. Then there was the deeper kind. The kind that made you say. "Fuck you, weight! You're going over my head whether you like it or not! Stop begging your friend gravity for help! I'll beat the both of you!" In the end, the later is always better. Still, a wise man would just let the weight be. It wasn't hurting anyone.

Finally, I reached my stopping point, a secluded place in the forest none of my soldiers could see me. I hit the ground immediately doing hundreds of pushups, crunches, and all the other exercises I'd learned in God's Rest but forgot the name. *You're a moron.* My body said to me.

When I was feeling suitably like gelatin, I stood up and took a drink from my canteen. I chose not to exercise with the rest of the army. I didn't want them to catch a glimpse of me red-faced and huffing.

I had a good vantage point to see the whole camp. Two and a half months of hard training had done them well. They were getting good. No, they were slowly becoming elite. I watched one company of infantry marching in the center. Another group was coming back from their own sort of exercise. The artillerymen were doing drills on their cannons. I even saw the cavalry doing a complex series of movements in the distance.

One company was gathered around their officer who was apparently giving a class on something. I recognized them. They were the Seventh. Even by the impossibly high standards Prince Edward, Colonel Seiford, and I had set, they were outstripping the rest. I knew the officer, Captain Dios, a wool merchant's son. A few months ago he'd been a top student at the university, whose specialization was advanced mathematics. When the call came, he'd volunteered, and because of his education, I'd given him some shiny bars on his collar. Now, he was one of my top officers. I made a mental note to have him commended.

It wasn't just that Captain Dios was overly strict with his men. In fact, it almost seemed like the opposite. He'd drill them hard, but I'd never heard word that he'd taken away their liberty in the neighboring towns. Three above, I'd never even seen him put a man on bread and water as was common. It was that he legitimately cared about his men. He'd grown to love them. He wanted to see as many of them go home as possible, and the only way to do that was if they were part of a crack unit.

His soldiers loved him back as well. They'd run an extra mile without him ordering it. They'd police their own, so he didn't have to. Their biggest fear was to disappoint Captain Dios. That sort of behavior had been unheard of in the Anthanii army a year ago. However, in this camp, it was commonplace. Captain Dios may have been an exceptional leader, but he was not in a league of his own. The officers I'd elevated were talented sergeants, university students, and the odd smattering of decent nobility. I'd made it a point not to promote anyone based on blood alone.

Many of my cavalrymen were nobility but not all, and the ones that were hailed mostly from lesser families. Most of the lords had avoided joining up with me like the plague. They wouldn't obey orders from a Confederacy man like myself, and they knew I'd hang them for that. Knowing both those things to be true had made them choose the prudent path of taking their services elsewhere, which was fine by me.

The ranks had also swelled since I'd taken command alongside Prince Edward. I'd opened up my army to refugees of the countries Thaniel had conquered. New recruits were clamoring to join my forces. So many I had to turn some away. Then of course, there were the mercenaries I'd hired. Not enough to make a difference when the fighting started but enough to teach my men how to do their new jobs well. I'd bought artillerymen from Rustia to show them how to properly use the cannons. Thaniel and I both knew it was the future of warfare. I'd paid Rentarii engineers to teach the soldiers how to build decent fortifications. After all being able to put up a wall in a few hours could be the difference between a slaughter and a decisive victory. I'd even brought over a number of Confederacy men to teach the army how to scout, fight in the woods, and really use a bayonet. My people were unmatched in that sort of fighting. We'd gone from seventy-thousand green boys to a hundred thousand trained fighters in two and a half months. When it came time to meet Thaniel again, we'd be ready.

I used the rest of the water to wash myself off and walked down to my own training square. I passed a few soldiers on the way going about their business and returned their salutes. Even the camp looked like it had been divinely engineered by some intelligent creator with a flair for orderly columns.

I reached my training square and saw Colonel Seiford waiting for me with a practice sword. Three other soldiers were also sitting behind him with blunted bayonets. I recognized them all. There was the oxen shouldered Sergeant Ferton with a face like a block of stone, the immaculately dressed Lieutenant Kelm who stood straight-backed and tall in his uniform, and the lean, mildly fox looking Private Rolton.

I'd ordered that the best fighters from each company report to my square in the morning for combat training. They'd go and teach their company what I taught them. It was the most efficient way, outside of their usual bayonet drills. I got a new trio every day. I had to admit they were good, and getting better. I'd learned a bit about them as well.

Sergeant Ferton was from the countryside and apparently one of six brothers. As I heard it, the smallest of the litter. That was hard to believe seeing as he stood a full head over me and twice as wide with all muscle. Growing up with six brothers anywhere is a pretty good way to hone your fighting skills, and he was good. Fought like an angry bull, that one did.

Lieutenant Kelm was a law student from university and had become a championship boxer in his third year. Apparently, in Anthanii higher education, you had to earn respect by having good blood or spilling a lot of it in the ring. He used his bayonet with the same precision I imagined earned him that respect. Every stroke was calculated to hit my weak point or give him a better chance on the next go.

The best of the group, though, was Private Rolton. He was wiry, bordering on skinny, and stood a few inches below me. No one could tell me his story for sure, but he had a tattoo of one of Harfow's most dangerous gangs. He didn't talk about it, but I knew what a killer's eyes looked like, and he had them. The slums of the Anthanii capital were a dangerous place. There wasn't a doubt in my mind he'd had to do violence before. I chose to ignore that. If the man wanted a better life for himself, then I wasn't about to deny him. The man fought like a wounded animal. Private Rolton would throw himself at you one instant, duck back the next waiting for an opening, then slither around your back without you even seeing it.

I had wanted to promote the man, but as good of a fighter as he was, he was too vicious to be a leader. He was also one of my best scouts. I supposed sneaking around the woods wasn't so different from sneaking around a city. I'd find a special place for him in the army where he could wear a few more stripes on his sleeve, but I wasn't nearly cruel enough to put a poor soul under his relentless command.

Seiford smiled at me. "You look tired." He raised his practice sword.

"Not too tired to beat you." I chuckled at him and raised my blunted tomahawk and knife.

"We'll see." He stepped forward.

The fight was on. I charged the colonel as soon as I stepped into the ring. He swung over my head, but I ducked it. *This fight is going to be over quicker than I thought.* I mused to myself as I stepped inside his guard. I was mistaken. He reversed the sword quick as lightning leaving me just enough time to catch it with my hatchet. I stroked upward with my knife, but he backpedaled quick. We stared at each other for a minute then I charged again. This time I was ready. Four blows back and forth, and I had his sword on the ground and my knife at his throat.

"Yield?" I asked him.

"Yield." He took a step back and spit into the ground.

"Now, show me your horse." I gave him an absolutely devilish smile.

"You're an ass." He muttered, picking up the practice sword and nursing his sore wrist. Seiford was an excellent swordsman, but he'd taken it up rather late in his life. He'd always planned on doing something else until he couldn't ignore the Kranish anymore. He took to it with the competence he treated every activity with, but he didn't have a killer's instincts.

"You don't want another go?" I asked.

Seiford shook his head in exhaustion. "I'm tired of you beating me every day." He nodded to the three soldiers. "Let them take a shot at you." A crowd had already begun to form up. They usually did to watch the show. They liked to see me fight. It wasn't really a crowd in the traditional sense, a group of gawkers who paid to see a fight. It was more just a bunch of soldiers who had found an excuse for their task to take them near my training ring. They did their work slow and watched me out the corner of their eyes.

I decided to oblige them and waved the trio of soldiers to come and fight me.

"Aye, your eminence." They said at once and stepped forward into the ring. They fought me as a trio. I wanted them to be prepared to work as a team, and I never really found myself one on one in battle anyway.

They spread out almost immediately trying to take me from the side. It was a good tactic. Lieutenant Kelm was in the center, Sergeant Fenton and Private Rolton on the side. Before they could surround me completely, I charged Kelm. He stabbed at me once with his bayonet. I beat it aside and kicked him in the chest, buying me a precious moment of freedom.

Fenton was already on me putting his full weight behind the thrust. I sidestepped it and used his momentum to throw him to the ground. Rolton moved in quick missing me with his bayonet, and I swung my ax at his chest. He dodged it deftly, but it gave me the space to deal with the big sergeant. The man on the ground was already using all of his strength to pull me down with him, and I had to admit he was much stronger than I.

I'd been trained in grappling though. I twisted in a quick movement pinning his one arm down and stabbing my blunted knife at his chest. All the while fending off the private's furious attacks. He knew he was dead so the oxen shouldered sergeant rolled back to the side of the ring rubbing where I'd hit him. That left two.

Kelm was back on his feet and stabbed twice at me. I dodged one and knocked away the other. It was a furious defense trying to fend off Kelm and Rolton, but soon enough, the lieutenant showed a rare weakness, extending his feet too far. I hit him once in the thigh with my blunted hatchet and then came around to wrap my knife hand across his throat.

"Yield!" He screamed, and I tossed him to the side.

Now, it was just Private Rolton and me. Usually, when I got to this point, the last man looked scared. He always knew he couldn't win a one on one fight with me. He was just worried about making a good showing of himself. Private Rolton didn't have an ounce of fear on him. He had a stare that said he was going to win. I returned it and saluted with my hatchet.

He charged. It was a vicious fight. It always was with Rolton. He ducked low then moved high. I dodged back then charged to meet him. It was a fight with no defense. We were both struggling to beat someone else, not survive on our own. He used every part of his body to hit me, and I did the same with him.

He was a crafty warrior. He'd learned it on the streets every day of his life. Until he joined up though, he'd never had any formal training. I was schooled by the best instructors in a dozen different martial arts. I brought them all against him. Eventually, he twisted my tomahawk away from me, but at the cost of his musket. We became locked in a brutal hand to hand duel. Finally, I turned him around into one of the positions I'd learned at God's Rest. They called it the arm breaker, where I took his appendage and stretched it between my legs. Enough pressure and the victim of this technique would lose the afflicted limb. He struggled against me for a while, but at last, I felt him tap my thigh in surrender.

I stood up dusting the dirt off me. The crowd had grown a bit. "That was good." I nodded to the trio. "Sergeant Fenton, you need to stop putting all your damn weight into the thrust." I was breathing a bit harder than I liked. "Anyone trained in grappling well enough will use it against you like I just did."

"Aye, your eminence." Fenton nodded back. In truth, there weren't many grapplers with enough skill to worry about getting that big monster to the ground. Still, no ones so good they can't get better.

"It was a good thought to charge me while I was distracted, though." I nodded to the big man.

That rock chin of his twisted into a smile. "Figured I should take any advantage you give me, your eminence."

"You figured right sergeant." I chuckled then turned to the lean lieutenant. "Lieutenant Fenton, your form was excellent, but we're going to battle, not a boxing square." I nodded at the elegant man. "You need to take your opportunity quicker. Waste too much time, and someone's going to stab you in the back while you're looking for the perfect strike."

"Aye, your eminence." The Lieutenant had his hands on his waist breathing hard. In truth, if I'd been a mite less skilled, he'd have skewered me at the outset.

I nodded. "You've clearly got a talent for this. I won't see it lost because you hesitated." I turned to Rolton last. "You're getting better." I cocked an eyebrow at him. "Gonna kill Thaniel all on your own?"

"If you don't get to him first, your eminence." He gave me a wild grin.

"That's the attitude." I waved for them to get back. "Now set up again."

"Why not let the soldiers rest a bit?" I heard the commanding voice from behind me. I turned to see Prince Edward standing in the square brandishing a practice sword.

"Aye, your highness." They all moved to sit down and sip water.

"You're going to take their place?" The idea of it amused me.

"I suppose I will." The Prince returned the look

"You sure, your highness?" I asked. I'd seen him practice his strokes before. He had perfect form, but I was Belson the Blessed. I didn't want to see him embarrassed in front of the soldiers. "I wouldn't want to spill royal blood."

Edward stepped into the ring. "I don't think you'll need to worry about that." He looked like one of the hero princes from a storybook, blonde hair moved like a crown on his head, green eyes filled with dignity, uniform pressed and tailored to hug his form. He struck quite an imposing figure. One that garnered a nostalgia for a lost age or maybe an age we needed to believe in that never really existed

I stepped forward raising my training weapons. I resolved to go easy on him. I'd let the fight drag on a bit so as not to see him in the dirt too early. He stepped forward with the grace of a master swordsman. I'd fought master swordsmen before, though, and it hadn't ended well for any of them. I was sure he was technically skilled, but technically only went so far in the end.

Any thought of going easy on him went out after the first strike. Well, I should say first three, but it was so quick it looked like one. I managed to deflect the first one, caught the second between my hatchet and knife, the third I barely managed to avoid, moving back furiously. Even still it was one hairsbreadth away from my nose.

I looked at him with a new respect. The quickness of it was startling, but the real fear was the force he managed to put behind him. Every blow landed like a hammer. That speed mixed with that strength was dangerous.

"Are you done holding back on me?" He kept the smile on his face.

I gritted my teeth and charged him. We went blow for blow, evenly matched. I tried to get in close enough to bring my short weapons against the Prince. He tried to keep me at a distance so his slender sword could do its damage. We wound up in a cross between, too close for his comfort, too far for mine. Every time I tried to move in, he fended me off with a savage series of blows. Every time he made to step back I closed the distance between us.

It felt like we dueled that way for an hour. There was no break in between. There was no moving back so we could each catch our breath, No pulling away to judge the best way to attack. Just the sound of steel on steel pierced the air. Instinct took over. I felt the joy of a real match. I felt the elation of challenge.

On the battlefield, I'd have beaten him. I was bred for pitched combat. The way I moved through enemies. The way I used the six-shooters at my side. The way I used every asset around me, turning cannons, corpses, and soldiers into shields. I became a wild animal. I had routed five-thousand men at Wuntsville. I had stood against two regiments at Milhire. I had turned the tide of Gertinville in a matter of hours. I had even dueled Dark Forces and lived. Now I couldn't deal with one prince. It seemed like a betrayal.

In my mind, I knew the reason, though. Those battles hadn't just been won by my skill. They'd been won by my wits, will, and unpredictability. I never did what they expected, so they could never react. I hadn't won because I was a match for five thousand men in a fair fight. I won because I made them afraid. I won because I didn't fight fair. Here in the square, it was swordsmanship that would win the day, not tricks or convictions.

I felt Prince Edward begin to get the upper hand. I knew if it went on like this he'd win. I was not about to be defeated, yet victory in this game was impossible, so I decided to change the game. He took another swing, and I moved in grabbing his hand. I flipped it over my shoulder, putting him into one of the many holds I'd been taught at God's Rest. Nobles never learned grappling. Once, I put my hands on him the Prince was mine. I was wrong about that bit.

He turned me around, and we both fell together. I slithered around him placing Edward in a hold. He twisted out of it, getting on top. We wrestled like that, the dominant position changing hands like money at a whorehouse. He knew how to fight with his hands. Finally, I managed to push him away and rolled to my knife. When I had it in my hand, I charged him, but he was too quick. His sword was on my neck, at the same time my dagger was in his belly.

"I think it's a draw." Edward finally said.

"I don't draw." I bared my teeth at him.

"You do today, Thomas." Colonel Seiford went to pull us apart. "It was well fought, though." He looked from me to the Prince. "Both of you."

"Aye, it was." Prince Edward nodded putting away his practice sword.

"You want to go again?" I needed another crack at him.

He smiled at me. "Maybe some other time." He dusted himself off. "I have work to do and so do you."

"Aye." I nodded. "Some other time."

Prince Edward gave the crowd a nod and walked off. By then the group had stopped even the pretense of work. They were standing in awe. Slowly when they realized there wouldn't be another fight, they went back to whatever task they'd been assigned.

"That concludes the lesson." I nodded to the three opponents I'd fought earlier. "Make sure to keep training your fellows. You're only as good as the man next to you."

"Aye, your eminence." They all said in unison.

"Private Rolton," I said as he walked away, "see me after dinner, will you."

"Aye, your eminence." He saluted then walked off to join his fellows.

I turned to Colonel Seiford. "Why didn't you tell me he was that good?" I asked.

He just shrugged. "I thought you could use some humility." He turned to me and smiled. "What, are you sad you can't kill everyone in camp anymore?"

"I can still kill him!" I tried not to look offended. "I bet he can't shoot like me." I patted the six-shooter on my side. Then a thought struck me. I hadn't thought he could duel like that either, or grapple. "Can he?"

Seiford just laughed and walked away to his duties. Bastard didn't even give me an answer.

Prince Edward was right. I did have work to do, a mound of the most insufferable work in the world, paperwork. When I'd just been a skirmisher, I hadn't had to worry about it. Then at Milhire, my stint of command was rather brief, though I had become briefly acquainted with this particular brand of torture and was not sad to leave it behind. Then at Wuntsville I'd just done what I wanted without asking anyone. After that my adventures in Kran, the Cretoin Mountains, Imor, and Gertinville had all been blessedly free of latrine reports.

Those were desperate times. Days when the difference between total victory and death were only a hairsbreadth away. Any day could wind up being my last. I missed them terribly. I'd have taken an army of screaming Kranish over the slow death by printed word.

Yet for all that, they were as crucial as any decisive charge could be. What happened when I forgot to record how many boots needed repair? What happened when I forgot to fill out the grain report? What happened when the shit holes filled up and no one had organized a replacement built? Disaster happened, that's what! All the hard work the army had done to prepare would be useless unless I ordered the proper amount of gunpowder and had it safely stored. I had fought across too may battlefields, killed too many men, and ripped victory out of too many defeats to be taken down by requesting the wrong type of musket hammer.

Of course, Prince Edward and Colonel Seiford had each taken a third of the workload. However, the Prince had a harem of secretaries to assist him, and Seiford's orderly nature suited him to the shuffling of papers. I, on the other hand, was not suited for this. I was made for battle, glory, and adventure. I was hopeless at this sort of thing.

Another courier rushed into the tent and set a load of papers on the desk, giving a sharp salute before he left. I buried my face in my hands and stifled a groan.

"What's the matter?" Lady Gerate was in the tent at her own little make-shift desk looking over information reports. "My brave hero brought low by a cramping hand." She usually did her afternoon work with me.

"This is miserable." I muttered half to myself. "I'm shit at this kind of thing." I looked up at Abby. "How's your work going?"

"I'm glad you asked." She smiled towards me. "I've got steady reports from every Kranish occupied country. Those partisans really do hate him. I've also got sources in the docks like you asked me." She shook her head. "I've tried to turn some members of his court, but I've had little luck there."

"Any word on troop movement?" I asked.

Abby tapped one of her papers. "Yes, it seems like he's pulling his forces back a bit. I don't think he plans to move on us anytime soon." She shook her head. "He's raising taxes though, and recruiting more men. I think he's trying to build up his army again."

"Again?" I was shocked. "He's already got the biggest army in the world."

Lady Gerate nodded. "He's also fighting far more wars than anyone in the world." She shrugged. "Besides after you mauled his forces at Gertinville, perhaps he's less sure of them."

"So the other fronts aren't going so well for him?" I asked. Anthanii was far and away from being Thaniel's only enemy. One of the countries he conquered, Sinaps, was waging a brutal guerrilla war against him, and his Southern neighbors, the Dormens, were looking for any excuse to reclaim the territory he took, launching raids and the like.

"No, Thaniel's been handling them as smoothly as he can." Abby said. "If it wasn't for all the trouble you caused him, they'd likely already be finished." She stood up cracking her hands. "There's just too many fires burning for him to launch a full campaign against Anthanii."

"He'll come eventually." I tapped the desk. "Any luck finding some of his spies."

She sighed again. "That's the trouble, there's so many of them." She walked over to me. "When I do find one he can be replaced by a dozen others." Abby shook her head. "Every time I think I've found one we can turn to our cause, he winds up dead."

"He's good at this." I looked up at Abby again. Her black hair was tied up in a bun, and she was dressed plain as one can be. She still looked beautiful though. Lady Gerate had left Wuntsville to be governed by a set of village elders. I wouldn't have asked her to do this, but she was just so good at it. In two and a half months she'd been meeting with spies, scouts, and even gangsters. Her work alone had given us a look into Kran that was invaluable. Sure, she hadn't had the years of preparation Thaniel had or the money, but one eye was better than none. "Besides that man he's got Machiev understands politics better than any of us."

Another courier ran into the room to set another stack of paperwork on my desk. "I hate this." I buried my face in my hands again.

"It's not so bad." She sat on my desk. "You can't spend every night with me when your out galavanting all over creation." She rolled her eyes. "This paperwork keeps you where you belong."

We *had* been spending every night together. Truth be told, it almost combated my nomadic nature. I'd still rather be adventuring on a horse, but her tent was a close second, and the adventuring only won when I imagined her coming with me. "It's not so bad at all." I stared up into her green eyes.

"So," she tapped the paperwork, "do you think you can take a break for a minute."

I leaned back. "That depends on what for."

She glanced over at the bed in the corner.

I smiled. "It's the middle of the day."

She shrugged. "That's never bothered you before."

"You're right it hasn't." I leaned in to kiss her, but another man walked in before I had the chance.

Lady Gerate let out a forced cough and stood up from the desk awkwardly. I looked over to see who the intruder was. I spotted Captain Dios at the flap trying hard not to look embarrassed. He was a handsome man, almost reminding me of Seiford. His uniform was pressed as always and his clean shaven chin went well with his close cropped hair.

"I can come back later if it's more convenient, your eminence." The Captain said scratching his neck.

"No, no it's fine." I gestured to a seat in front of me. "Please sit." I'd forgotten I'd sent for the man earlier.

He obliged me. "Lady Gerate," he nodded his respect to her.

"I've been watching the seventh closely." I told him. "They've become quite a unit. I'm thinking of putting them at the center when the battle starts."

"We'll follow our orders, your eminence." He nodded at that.

I found his melancholy response quite strange. Most officers would have jumped at that kind of honor. He seemed like he was already worrying about it. "Anyway," I changed the direction of the conversation. "I've noticed you're quite the officer." I tapped the reports. "With the new swell in soldiers, we need more majors and colonels. I want to give you command of the Thirteenth regiment, with increase in pay and rank to match."

Captain Dios squirmed in his chair at that. I could see the discomfort on his face like he'd been handed some nasty medicine from a doctor.

"What's the matter, Captain?" I asked.

"It's just I've only been in the army for a few months." He scratched his head again. "I'm still getting used to the company. A whole regiment would be more suited for a veteran." He shrugged. "I'd recommend Gerald or Stykes. They've been in for half a decade."

"I wasn't requesting, soldier." I turned my gaze slightly more stony.

"I wasn't disobeying either, your eminence." Dios shrugged. "I was just letting you know what I think. I have a responsibility to my men to do just that," he paused. "and to you."

"I suppose you do." I nodded.

"Permission to speak freely." Captain Dios said.

"Granted." I waved my hand.

He let up his stiff-backed ways for a moment and leaned into me. "Your eminence, I've been training the seventh for months." He said. "I can't leave them, not before the fighting starts. They trust me."

"I see." I wrote it down in my notes. "We're not hurting for officers that bad. We can fill that gap with someone more experienced." I sighed to myself. "I just figured I'd offer it to you, but if you don't think you're up to it, I'll send someone else." I leveled a stony gaze at him. "If something happens in the coming battles, though, I'll need you to take that position."

"I understand." He nodded. "Thank you, your eminence."

"I will, however, bestow upon you the Anthanii Service Cross."

I handed him my filled out report. "For your excellent leadership of the seventh."

"Once again, your eminence, permission to speak freely." Captain Dios asked.

"What is it this time?" I rolled my eyes.

"I think it's the company that deserves the award more than me." He shrugged. "They do all the work, I wouldn't want to take the credit."

"You're underselling yourself, Captain." I said.

"Maybe, but I'd rather undersell myself than my men." He shrugged. "It's what's best for the company too. If they get that award, it'll help morale for when the time comes."

"Soldier," I started, "I think you have the makings of a high ranking officer." I leaned in. "I'll be gone once this war ends, but you'll still be here." I looked at him. "You could make general one day, get your pattern of nobility." I leaned back again. "That won't happen if you keep slapping down every hand a higher up gives you."

"Your eminence, with all due respect, when this war is over, I'm going back to University." He paused. "I couldn't let Thaniel trample my lands and do nothing, but I don't want to stay in the army forever."

"Fine." I waved him up. "I'll fill out the seventh's unit commendation." I looked up at him. "You're dismissed."

"Thank you, your eminence." He snapped off a salute and walked out the tent flap.

"What a waste." I said to myself.

"I think he's a good man." Lady Gerate said to me. "Realizes there's more to life than fighting." She gave me a queer look. "You've never thought about what you'll do when this war is over?"

I shrugged. "Of course, I have." I leaned towards her. "Go on to my next station, kill more Priests, have more adventures."

She gave me a dumbfounded look. "That's all you think you'll do?"

I shrugged. "It's my duty. I've got twenty years of service." I looked at how she watched me. What was she getting at? What was she asking? I started to open my mouth, but another body came through the flap.

It was Private Rolton. "Is this a bad time?" He looked from me to Lady Gerate. Apparently, he could feel the tension.

"No, it's a perfect time." Abby stood up from her chair. "I was just leaving." The look of scorn on her struck me like a slap

"Wait! Abby!" I stood up to chase her.

"I am Lady Gerate!" She turned on me. "I have business to attend to, so you can have your meeting."

I stood there, hands at my side, wondering if I should chase after her, or let Abby have her space.

"Women, huh." Private Rolton shook his head. "What'd you do?"

"I honestly don't have the faintest clue." I muttered then realized who I was talking to. "Anyway, enough of that." Of course, the whole camp knew we were seeing each other. It was hard to keep a secret in the military.

"You wanted to see me?" Rolton asked. He stood at a lazy attention. His eyes darted around the tent as if waiting for something to come out and strike him. I knew he wasn't trying to be disrespectful. He'd probably lived his entire life on edge. It was hard for him to stand still. I wouldn't bust him on account of that, especially not in private.

"You're quite the fighter." I said. "Where'd you learn it?"

"My paw taught me." He was good at not telling the truth. I almost believed him.

"You know it's a sin to lie to a Constable right?" I said.

"Is it?" Private Rolton cocked an eye up.

"It should be." I sat down in my chair and gestured for him to do the same. "Regardless, it's not smart."

Rolton sighed. "Truth is, I never knew my paw. He ran out when I was young." He gave me a wry smile. "I didn't lie to you, though. If he'd stuck around, I might not have had to fight."

"So where'd the fighting skills come from?" I asked. "You might be the best in the army besides Prince Edward and me."

He took a deep breath. "I grew up in and out of orphanages." Private Rolton said. "I started feeding myself at six…" It seemed like he didn't want to say what came next.

"Whatever the story is, it doesn't leave this tent." I gestured for him to continue.

Rolton started again. "One night, when I was eight, I thought for sure I was gonna starve. I got picked up by a member of the Sacro Street Goats."

"Wait!" I stopped him. "The Goats?"

Roltan shrugged. "Goat's a tough animal."

I thought back to Sir Huffington, my mortal enemy. "Agreed." I waved for him to continue.

"At first, I was a pickpocket for them. Then one day they gave me a stack of money and sent me into a room with a nobleman there." Pain contorted his face. Memories buried seemed to come back behind his eyes. Finally, he realized who he was talking to. "It's not what you think... He... I... He just liked to hit kids. I got away before he laid a hand on me." I'd always been able to spot the lies. They were all over his face. I knew that nobleman had wanted more than to hit a child. I also didn't think he got away. I kept my peace, though.

Roltan went on. "After that, I wanted to be strong. I never wanted anyone to hurt me again." He paused. "I got cleverer than everyone. I got stronger, but to rise in an organization like the Goats well..." He trailed off. "You gotta do some black things." He looked up at me. "I ain't proud of it, but I did em. It weren't long before I was a head lieutenant of the Goats."

"So why'd you join the army?" I asked.

"One day a job went bad. A woman caught us in her home." He looked at his hands. "I tried to get her to shut up, but she wouldn't..." He trailed off again. "Her boy was watching from the cabinet. After that, I couldn't do it no more." He stopped. "I'd thought about joining the army before. That was back before you came, though. They treated em worse than slaves. I weren't about to go die for a country that treated me like mine did."

"Understandable." I nodded.

"I thought about going to the Confederacy, but I didn't have the money for the passage." He said. "I thought about going lots o' different places, but it'd just be the same old shit to get by." He paused. "Then I heard Prince Edward was leading this new army. I heard you was gonna be in it too." He shrugged. "Word was it might be different under your lot. People was saying you take care of your own." Roltan chuckled. "I figured if it wasn't, I'd just slip away in the night. I know how to disappear."

"And how have you found it?" I asked.

"It's what boys always imagine the army'll be like." He cracked a smile. "I don't like the marching much though."

"No one does." I chuckled. "Can you read and write?" The boy looked to be about my age maybe a year younger or older.

"I tried to teach myself a bit, but no, not really." Rolton answered.

"I can remedy that." I smiled. "How would you like to be my personal guard?"

His face dropped at that. "I didn't join up to stand outside a damn tent while more important men sleep."

I chuckled at his impudence. "Do I seem like the sort who needs someone to guard his tent?"

Roltan shrugged. "Everyone's gotta sleep."

I smiled. "I sleep light."

He looked intrigued. "What'll I do then?"

I tapped the desk. "You'll be on my special assignments. You'll be the man I know I can trust when things get heated." I leaned in. "We'll be in the heart of every battle. We'll kill whoever comes our way." I pulled a spare tomahawk and six-shooter from under the desk. "I'll teach you things. I'll show you how to use these." I leaned in further. "I'll train you to do what I did in Gertinville. I'll teach you how to kill Priests."

Rolton cocked an eyebrow up. "Thought only a Constable could do that."

"You thought wrong." I slid a paper his way. "Go to your commanding officer and give him this. You'll be signed over to me and elevated to lieutenant."

"Will do boss." He took the paper and went to the tent flap. He stopped for a moment before he got out though. "Why me?" He asked.

"When you fought me today, you knew you were going to win." I answered.

"I lost." He had a confused expression on his face.

"It's the conviction that matters for now." I put a hand on my desk. "The rest will come." Then I shooed him out the tent flap.

I spent the rest of the evening on paperwork. I considered going after Abby, but I thought better of it. She needed some time to cool off. It was just getting dark before I heard another voice outside the tent.

"Is this Belson's tent?" I recognized the voice. It was Constable Fartow, and he sounded angry.

"Yes, your eminence." I heard a soldier reply.

I sighed, knowing I wouldn't like what came next. At least, it had to be better than paperwork.

They rushed through the tent flap, and I saw two men wearing a Constables uniform, letting the tattoos show on my arm. The first was Constable Fartow, looking as solid as a brick house. His hair was greying, but it only made him look more dangerous and angry. His mean black eyes gave me the full weight of his stare.

The second man I recognized as Constable Ragner. He had a beard down to his chest and grey eyes that looked like a sea in storm. If Constable Fartow was built like a brick house, then Ragner was like a great stone wall. I could tell he was from one of the Northern Countries. Both had a reputation for being competent and reliable, but competent and reliable wasn't enough when Thaniel came to power.

Despite their furious expressions, I couldn't help but notice the six-shooters on their belt. A weapon, that when I chose it, was considered a cowardly, unreliable piece of equipment. I guessed my successes had changed their opinions.

They were followed in by a young private. I recognized the soldier. His name was Henry, a brave lad if a bit clumsy and awkward, but that was more from being one of the recent enlistees. All in all, I liked the private.

I stood up from my chair and walked to the other side of my desk, leaning on it lightly. "I thought you would have come sooner." I knew how much they both hated me. They thought I was an arrogant, selfish bastard, but the real reason was that I'd done in under a year what they and dozens of their brothers couldn't do in a decade. I'd turned the tide, if ever so slightly.

"We would have, but we were on a diplomatic mission to Rustia." Fartow glared down his nose at me.

"Securing more allied troops no doubt." I mused to myself. "Did it succeed?"

"That doesn't matter!" Fartow screamed back.

"So that's a no." I huffed. "Shame, we could have used them."

Fartow took a step towards me. "Listen here you arrogant, self-important, little shit-"

Private Henry cut in. "Excuse me, gentlemen! I cannot allow you to speak to our commander that way." I had to admit, that was brave. Challenging two Constables who vaguely resembled an elephant, wasn't the best health decision in the world.

Fartow didn't answer, but he reared his hand back as if to smack the Private.

My gun was out before he even had a chance to blink. "Touch

one of my men, and I'll shoot the offending hand off the arm." I said it cooly, but they knew I meant it.

"You wouldn't dare." Fartow answered back

"I've made a career off of doing things most men wouldn't dare." I kept my level tone.

Fartow did the smart thing and put his arm back at his side. I looked at the private. "Go have your supper, Henry. I can take care of this."

He saluted and headed out the flap. I put my gun away.

"So they're your men now, ey?" Fartow glared at me.

"Aye, they're my men." I nodded.

"You've overstepped yourself." Fartow took another step forward. "Mother Vestia may have a sweet spot for you, but even she won't ignore this."

"That's the point." I didn't flinch away from him. "The whole world can't ignore this. The whole world watched me turn away Thaniel."

"This ain't the way we do business!" Fartow spit.

"Aye, and we've been doing business your way for how long?" I asked, but I already knew the answer. "We're doing things differently now, and we're starting to win."

"Don't you dare disrespect our fallen brothers!" Fartow growled at me. "You think you know what we've sacrificed because you've won some battles."

"They were my brothers too," even though they'd treated me like an outsider since I'd got there, I still felt some kinship, "but I'm trying to make what they did mean something. I won't let them have died just to delay an inevitable defeat."

Fartow spat again. "Constable Grenwold warned us about you." He said the name of the man who trained me, although torture was probably a more apt word. "He said you were nothing but trouble. He said he'd have had you killed if Mother Vestia would've let him." He bared his teeth at me. "I waved it away. Boys always seem worse when you're training them. I thought I'd just send you out on some raids so you can learn a bit about battle. Three above, I even figured the embarrassment might teach you some humility." He glared back up at me. "Grenwold was right. I should've had you killed."

"If you had Thaniel would own all of this." I paused. "What's this really about?"

"It's about you making a mockery of our order." Fartow narrowed his eyes at me.

"It's about your whore." This time it was Ragner. He said it without breaking his gaze.

My voice went to stone fury. "Call her that again, and neither of you will leave this tent."

Ragner finally turned his head to meet my eyes. He saw I meant it, but he was a hard man. The huff he gave me could have been a cry for mercy from anyone else.

"The whole country knows about you two." Fartow brought me back to him.

"What?" I asked. "You've never taken a woman before. The road gets lonely."

Fartow spat again. "We've never taken a noble to bed." He said. "We never let the whole continent hear about it, and we didn't stay with her." He shrugged. "Makes people uncomfortable."

"That doesn't sound like my problem." I glared back at him.

"It is if you've made the wrong people uncomfortable." He took a step forward. "You were never popular with the court. They're mighty protective over their women. They've had peasants hung for that sort of thing."

"Let'em try to hang me." I rolled my eyes.

"It's made other people uncomfortable too." Fartow went on. "A Constable's supposed to do his duty and move on to his next assignment."

"I've been doing my duty." I shot back.

"Aye, you have." He continued. "You raised up an army loyal to you in all but name, the whole country's set to worshipping you, and now you're with a noblewoman. A woman who, by a complicated genealogy, has a claim to the throne."

"What are you getting at?" I narrowed my eyes.

"Some people are saying when this war is over you might not leave as easy as your supposed to." Fartow took another step. "Everyone knows you hate King John. Might be you want to see his head on a spike." He leaned in. "Might be you want to warm his throne yourself."

"Now, that is something I wouldn't dare." However, I was wondering how right he was. I'd like to say I hadn't thought of it, but I had. It was always briefly and never because the power tempted me, but I would love to see those sneering nobles kneel to me. I'd love for Anthanii to be free. It was only ever a distant fantasy, but to many people so was beating Thaniel. Distant fantasies have a way of getting closer than you'd like.

"No, you wouldn't." Fartow said. "That's because I've written Mother Vestia and told her to send you somewhere else."

Now, I took a step forward. "You do that, and Anthanii'll lose any fight I've given them. Thaniel *will* take this country." I was in inches from his face. "I've given us a chance, but we're far from the upper hand."

Fartow took a step back, hands raised above his head. "Oh don't worry, she'll ignore it," he paused, "for now. It'll make her look at you a bit closer, though." The mocking left his voice. "It'll give her doubts until the day you go too far, and I'd bet my cock you will."

"Don't be ridiculous." I sneered at him. "There's not a man, woman, or goat in Thyro who wants your cock."

Ragner gave a short laugh.

Fartow glared at him.

"What?" The big Constable in the corner said. "It was funny." He turned back to me. "Boy needs to learn his place, but he's got spirit."

I turned to Ragner. "You wrote Mother Vestia too?" I asked.

"Not yet." He shrugged. "I think you've been doing a decent job of things. Better than we have anyway. I don't want to see you wasted on some frontier in Souren while the biggest war in history is being waged here." The heavily muscled Constable straightened himself out so I could see his full size. "However, I see the same thing Fartow sees, and I'd be lying if I said it doesn't scare me." He paused. "People seem to think I'm stupid cause I'm big and don't talk much." He leveled a finger at me. "Let me tell you, no one survives as long as I have being stupid."

"I never thought you were stupid." I responded honestly. Constables always looked a bit more gristle and gut than brain and culture, but anyone who wore a tattooed arm wasn't stupid. Most of them were smart enough to be intellectuals in their own right. The New Church only took the best.

"Good." He tapped his own tattoos. "Before I became what I am, I wanted to be a professor of history."

"Really?" That caught me off guard.

"Really." Ragner said. "I was the smartest boy in my village. My paw clubbed seals well into the night to save the money I'd need for university." He shrugged. "Probably spent it on booze and whores after I left, but how can I complain. That's how I was made after all."

"You read Viverant's new book?" I asked.

He shrugged. "I have. He's a bit preachy for me, more philosopher than scholar." He wagged a finger "Now Scosher's a true historian."

"I've never read him." I shrugged.

"You ought to." The big Constable nodded his admiration for the man. "I'll send you my copy. Do you read Rhetorii?"

I shook my hand. "A little, but I get caught on the-"

"Can we please get back to the task at hand?" Fartow asked.

"Right." Ragner nodded. "Now, I've read enough history to know revolutions aren't just paranoid delusions of jumpy monarchs. They happen" The Constable threw his head back. "Three above, we're fighting one! I know most of them usurpers look a lot like you do right now." He shrugged. "Usually, those situations wind up to nothing, but every once in a while..." He trailed off. "They become more than nothing." The big Constable went on. "If you decide to do something stupid, I don't know that we could stop you."

"I'm sure you could make my life hell, though." I shot a grin at the man. Ragner had a reputation for being one of the best Constables Thyro had. He'd given Thaniel hellfire for the better part of a decade. It was probably what saved us long enough for me to get to the front.

"We will," he returned the grin, "but the people here love you, the army is loyal to you, and King John ain't so popular right now." Ragner paused. "I think you could be King of Anthanii if we're not careful."

"You have nothing to worry about." I shook my head. "I'm just doing what it takes to win this war. After it's over, I'll move on to my next assignment."

"That best be the case." Fartow hissed.

"I assume you two have your own duties to attend to." I said. "Rustia doesn't seem like it's going to pan out."

Ragner nodded. "Fartow's going to Dormia to put a bit of iron in their spine. See if we can get em to do more than raid." That had a chance to work. For all the differences we had, Fartow was a first-class warrior. If anyone could stand Dormia back up again, it was him. "I'm going to the countries Thaniel conquered to see if I can start a rebellion."

"You're a bit conspicuous for that kind of subversive work." I smiled.

"I've been doing it since before your dick could get hard." Ragner chuckled. "When everyone's looking for a scarred giant, they tend to overlook a hunched beggar in the street."

"You should try playing a moron." I said. "No one bothers a loon mumbling about fish." I thought about the guards. "Well, they usually don't."

"I'll keep it in mind." Ragner nodded. "Also, I have to ask where Brother Keys is."

"He said his legs were hurting too much to be on the front like this." I shrugged. "I let him stay at the capitol."

"That sounds like Keys. Rode with me for a year and always found an excuse to get out of work." Ragner cocked his head to the side. "I don't like you not having a monk, though. They can be useful, and they can let us know when we're outside the Church's good grace."

"Don't worry, Mother Vestia's given me leave to do what I think is necessary here as long as it's within our order's rules." I tapped a note in my pocket. Apparently, my recent exploits had impressed her. Most Constables didn't get that letter until their fifth year. "I'll keep your advice, though."

"You better." Fartow pushed his way into the conversation.

I turned back to him. "Before you threaten me again, I think you should remember how quickly this whole war almost fell apart when I left for a few months," I smiled, "and how quickly I put it back together again."

Fartow huffed and turned to leave.

"Also, tell Grenwold I do hope his nose healed alright." One day the trainer at God's Rest had gone too far. He didn't want me in his order so he'd decided to fix the situation on his own while everyone slept. I'd given him a good reason not to. The rumor had spread like wildfire amongst the Constables that a half-trained fifteen-year-old had broken the nose of the most senior man in the order. Part of that was because Grenwold wasn't well liked. Most of the active Constables had been trained by him.

Ragner laughed at that. "So it's true, you really beat the old man in a fight."

"Three above, no!" I whistled. "He almost killed me. I still got the scars from that." I smiled. "I got a lucky punch in though and broke his nose. That made him think twice the second time." Of course, to a warrior as seasoned as Grenwold, a broken nose wouldn't have meant much. What did keep the bastard away was having rumors swirl that a trainee gave it to him, and from then on he knew that I wouldn't lay down and take his beating. Even a fifteen-year-old could land a lucky punch.

Ragner laughed and followed his companion. "The boy's got fire. I'll give him that."

When they were gone, I looked back at the paperwork. I decided I'd done enough for the day. I needed to talk to Abby. I wasn't going to cut her loose like they'd told me too, but she'd seemed upset. I started the trek over to her tent.

I thought about what Fartow and Ragner had told me. Of course, I wasn't going to overthrow John like they feared, but other things were weighing on my mind. After the war was over, I'd be sent to some distant frontier to fight for another ruler. This was the biggest conflict in living memory, but after Thaniel was gone what then? I'd be sent to distant lands to fight for my life. That was how it usually went. When a tyrant wasn't knocking at the door of the New Church's closest ally, the Constable was a traveling warrior. It wasn't the fighting for my life part that bothered me. It was the distant lands bit.

When I first joined up, that was all I wanted. To have adventures all over the world. Grow my name so big they couldn't ignore it. In fact, when I was first shipped over, I'd resolved to beat Thaniel quick so I could do what real Constables do. Once I'd realized how big that job was, I decided I needed to stay for a bit. Almost two years later, I wasn't so sure.

I'd spent longer in Anthanii than most Constable's did in three jobs. The people looked to me as their savior. I had formed my own army. I had friends here. Then there was Lady Gerate... Leaving the country would hurt, but sending Abby away was like looking at an unbalanced equation. It just didn't make sense.

Piece by piece I found I cared about this land. It was far from perfect, but I'd bled to defend this country. Was this what everyone else feels like? The instinct to settle down and never leave had never occurred to me, until one day it had. Would I really be able to go away?

Fartow had said he wanted me sent to some other fight. I knew I wasn't going to do that, not before the job was done. Fartow could be an ass, but he was the senior man. His voice carried weight. I knew part of it was jealousy at my meteoric rise, but there was another bit that was true.

I knew Mother Vestia wouldn't take me away from Anthanii. Even if I was just an ordinary Constable and not our best hope. We were spread too thin. Half of our order had been called to fight the Kranish. Of the thirty that started only five still lived. The other thirty were spread all over the globe frantically trying to hold everything together in our absence, and they weren't living too long either. Thaniel had emboldened a lot of people, and the support he sent overseas was making things difficult even on the frontiers.

However, maybe I should try to use a little tact. Even as I said it, I knew how unrealistic that was.

Finally, I reached Abby's tent. I took a deep breath and walked inside.

Her green eyes lit up as she saw me. "Thomas!" She put down the pen she'd been scribbling with.

"Abby," I scratched my head. "I thought you might not want to see me."

"Well, you were wrong." She stood up and walked over to me. "I'm sorry about earlier I overreacted." She kissed me.

"I wasn't even sure what about." I kissed her back.

"Oh, it was nothing." Abby waved it away. "I just saw all the success you've been having. It made me think about when this war is over."

"I've been thinking about that too." It was the truth.

"Really?" Her eyes lit up.

"Two Constables came to see me today." I said. "They told me it was best if we ended things."

She took a step back. "What'd you tell them?"

I closed the distance between us. "I told them to go to hell." I grabbed her again.

She kissed me full of passion. We moved together slowly edging towards the bed. Abby pulled away for a moment.

"What?" I asked. "Never been shy before."

She slapped my arm. "It's not that." Abby smiled. "I got in those port reports from Kran you've been asking about, after I left."

I frowned. "What'd they say?"

"Thaniel's war fleet is docking in Fredua and Wellsport." She shrugged. "Usual thing for this time of year as I understand it." She went to kiss me again, but I stopped her.

"You're absolutely sure about that?" I asked. "It's not misinformation?"

"I've heard it from multiple sources." Abby said. "It's as reliable of information as I've ever got. Probably because no one sees the point of hiding it." She gave me a strange look. "Are you alright?"

"I need to get to the navy quick." I buckled my gun belt back on.

"Oh, no!" She stopped me. "You're not going on one of your adventures right when the army is ready to fight." *Not when I'm starting to care about you.* Her eyes said.

"Don't worry I'll be back inside a month." She didn't seem convinced. "This isn't like last time. I'm not going to be alone. Quite the opposite in fact."

"What's going on?" She asked.

"We've got a chance to even this war out." I responded. "Tell Prince Edward and Seiford that I've got some business to attend to. I'll be back soon. Keep the army training and guard the borders." I paused. "Don't tell anyone exactly where I'm going. I don't know how far up Thaniel's spies go."

"Come back safe." She gave me a kiss.

"Nothing could keep me away from you." I kissed her back and left the tent.

Present Day

Jt was the morning before my party, and the servants were in an absolute frenzy. They were being dictated to by Sarah like a general leading an army. My brother's wife who was usually so polite turned into a tyrant on the eve of a celebration.

"No, put the ribbons in color order."

"Yes, ma'am."

"That banner needs to be a bit higher."

"Yes, ma'am."

"If you put the cake there, there won't be enough room for the toast."

"Yes, ma'am."

"Oh, I'll just do it myself." Sarah went to go move the cake in frenzied anger.

I leaned into Andrew who was stealthily trying to snack on some cookies. "Does she always get like this?" Andrew seemed just as uncomfortable as I was.

"Anytime more than five people come over for dinner." He choked down a pastry.

Seiford chuckled. "She'd make a fine general."

Andrew smiled. "I've never quite hated our enemies that much."

Sarah had finished moving the cake a degree so subtle I couldn't tell the difference when she walked over to us. The purposeful steps made me try to be smaller.

I started before she could say anything. "You know I don't want you going through so much trouble." I said. "If this party is for me, I'm not really so hard to please."

"It's true." Seiford put in. "After the Gaulen Campaign, he had the victory party in the stable." The monk laughed at the memory. "We entertained ourselves by throwing darts at Count Deland's back."

Andrew gasped at the cruelty of it. He couldn't ignore a violation of the rules of war like that. "You tortured a beaten man."

"No, not at all!" Seiford waved it away. "We loved Count Deland. We helped take that country for him."

I jumped in. "Mad bastard called himself bloodless, so he painted a target on his back and had us throw darts at him to prove he didn't bleed."

Seiford shrugged. "Turns out he was just drunk."

I laughed. "Don't let that story get out, though. We never had the heart to tell poor Deland he bled like a stuck pig."

Andrew laughed at that. "I've got a few scars from that game."

Sarah leveled a glare at him. "If you ever play it again, I'll give you a few more." She softened up her expression. "That being said, this party isn't just for you strictly speaking."

"Politics?" I asked.

"Politics." Andrew answered.

Sarah nodded. "We use these gatherings to show our appreciation for trusted business companions and to cultivate new relationships."

Andrew cut in again. "There's quite a guest list coming to see you." He smiled. "General Fennis for one."

"*The* General Fennis?" I asked. I wasn't in the habit of being starstruck, but Fennis had been a childhood hero.

"*The* General Fennis arrived about an hour ago." Andrew answered. "He likes to spend some time with the servants beforehand. Rumor has it he's taken to their music." My brother sighed. "When the man heard you were in town, he was dying to meet you."

"Really?" I asked.

"Of course!" Andrew chirped. "He taught a class at Cavalry school called *Strategy and Tactics of Thomas Belson*."

"And who else has come to see my ornery friend?" Seiford asked.

"Every important man in the South, including a brace of Senators, namely Coleson." Andrew answered.

"I've heard things about that man." I tried not to let my distaste show.

"They're true." My brother nodded. "I wouldn't have him here if there was a polite way to rescind the invitation." He cheered up a bit. "The columnist Destry also wanted to come, but was involved in a debate and will be around at his earliest opportunity."

"I don't like columnists." I said. A good many in Thyro had devoted their entire existence to slandering me.

"You'll like this one, I promise." Andrew said. "I also sent an invitation to John Reard."

"You know I don't like him." Sarah rolled her eyes.

"He's too rich to ignore." He put a hand on his wife's shoulder. "Besides, he never comes to these things anyway, and I happen to respect the man."

She huffed. "A necessary evil I suppose." Finally, she took all of us in. "Brother Seiford, you look positively striking in that robe."

"Thank you." The monk bowed. He had dug out his best clerics uniform for the occasion and, as always, looked dashing.

Sarah turned her attention to Andrew. "If you keep eating you'll bust right out of those clothes."

"Sorry." He took the cookie out of his pocket and went to put it back on the tray.

She took the treat before he could. "Don't put it back you daft fool." When she saw Andrew looked a bit hurt, she softened up. "Oh you know I'd love nothing more than for you to be fat and lazy." She handed to treat back to him. "I love you, sweetheart." She kissed him.

"I love you too, even when you're mean to me." He smiled and ate some more.

Finally, Sarah leveled a gaze at me. "It was smart of you to wait and put on your good clothes later."

"Well..." I scratched my head.

"Those are his good clothes." Seiford finished for me.

I took an insulted step back. I liked my suit, even though it had gone out of style five years ago.

Sarah looked me up and down. "It's wrinkled like a prophets face, there's a hole right here," she gestured at my coat, "and is that blood?" A nun could have taken a lesson in indignation from my sister-in-law.

"I had to stop Count Deland's bleeding somehow." I shrugged.

"Do you have anything better?" She asked.

"I have a Souren Battle Robe." I smiled. "Made with real lion."

"Stay in that." Sarah huffed. "Can you at least put away the weapons?"

My hand fell to my tomahawk. "It's part of my charm." I said with indignation.

Seiford shook his head. "I've been losing that argument for ten years."

"Fine." She accepted it at last. "Just promise to be on your best behavior."

"Don't worry." I smiled. "My monk is excellent at parties."

"I know." Sarah eyed me dangerously.

"You mean me?" I asked full of feigned innocence.

Andrew shrugged. "The stories about your party etiquette, are as well known as your battles." He chuckled. "I thought they were hilarious, but…"

"I didn't," Sarah answered, "and if you ride your horse through my living room, I will have you strung up."

"But Shaggy loves parties!" I protested.

"I'll string her up too." She wasn't budging on that issue.

"Fine." I relented.

"Excellent!" She went back to ordering around the servants.

Andrew nudged my side. "What's wrong?" He asked.

I shrugged. "I just thought this would be a nice evening. It seems so stressful now."

"It is," he agreed, "but don't worry. I also invited some people you might want to see." My brother had a little glimmer in his eyes.

"Who could that possibly be?" I asked. I wasn't popular before I left the Confederacy. Of course, I had playmates, but that was so long ago I could barely remember their names. They would be nothing to me if I saw them again. I knew Andrew meant well. He always did but seeing a man I used to throw rocks with wouldn't do anyone any favors.

"Just wait and see." He patted me on the back.

I darted a curious eye at Seiford.

The monk just shrugged, with a smile that told me he knew but wasn't about to spoil the surprise.

Just then the door opened a hair as if whoever was on the other side wasn't sure he should come in yet. Eventually, the door inched open revealing the guests. It was a man who looked to be no older than me. He was well dressed but wore his clothes poorly as if he didn't feel at home in them. He had a beard that was undoubtedly grown to hide his scars.

He looked powerfully familiar, but I couldn't quite place him. Then I saw his eyes. They were the same kind of eyes I had. The ones that continually assessed whatever danger might be hiding in the room. They were the eyes of a man who had seen too much sin and had trouble dealing with it. Unlike mine, though, they had been tempered. I saw the reason why.

There was a woman with him, presumably his wife. She was pretty and more elegantly dressed than her husband. She also seemed to wear the clothes better, as if she didn't feel guilty about them. The wife held the hand of a little girl who shared both their looks. The man had both of his hands on a son's shoulder, edging him forward.

Finally, I remembered who he was. I remembered him and I, locked in battle, back to back against hordes of Kranish. I remembered the poor street urchin who had become one of the best men I'd ever known.

Andrew nodded his respect to the man. "How've you been Roltan?"

"I've been good Andrew." Roltan nodded his respect right back. Finally, he turned his eyes back to me. "Listen, Thomas..." He started. "I had to see you one last time." He put his hat in his hands. "I'll understand if you never want to talk to me again, but for all that's passed, I still love-"

Roltan was cut off by my crippling hug. His boy moving to behind his father's legs. "I've missed you." I whispered to him. "I'm sorry."

I held him for a moment too long. It was like holding onto a memory of myself, like a version of my life that could have been. Roltan had ever been made in my image, but he'd chosen the better path. Finally, I released the man.

"He's missed you too." The wife put a hand on my shoulder.

I was at a loss for what to say next, but Roltan saved me. "Thomas, this is my wife, Emma." He gestured to the pretty woman with bright blue eyes.

"You're a lucky woman." I shook her hand.

"I'm the lucky one." Roltan wrapped his hand around Emma's.

"We're both lucky." She kissed him, and then coughed after she realized they had an audience.

They were truly in love. I saw that almost instantly. The passion they felt was so strong they could never really hide it, but it was tempered with a respect that only came from years of knowing each other.

Some couples were never meant to be together. After the passion of courtship wore away, they were always just trying to fix a building with it's foundations in sand. Roltan had found the real thing, and it made my heart sore. Some old married men complain about their wives when they were in their cups. Some did far worse. As soon as I saw the way they looked at each other I knew this wasn't that sort of marriage. When Roltan drank too much, I would bet my arm he made ridiculous romantic gestures, like pick her flowers or compose poems. It was a far cry from the angry soldier I remembered, but I liked it anyway.

Roltan finally pushed his two children to the front. "This is my five-year-old Georgia," he patted the little girl with a bow in her hair, "and this is my seven-year-old Sunny." He squeezed the boy's arm. "Don't be scared. He's a friend."

"Hi." Georgia fiddled with her dress looking down.

"Hello, sir." Sunny tried to look tough.

"They're lovely." I nodded and took a knee to be on their level.

"My paw says you're the greatest man in the whole wide world." Sunny said.

"My paw says you have a nice horse." The girl kicked the ground.

I smiled. "I've been called that before," I told the boy, "but I'll never be the greatest man in a world that your father shares." I paused. "He was brave, honorable, and in the end, he was better than me."

"Thomas," Roltan started, "that's not true."

I ignored him. "He even beat me in a fight once." I smiled at the boy. "He's one of a handful to ever do that."

"Really?" Sunny stared up at his father in awe.

Roltan gave a sad smile. "That was a long time ago. I don't fight anymore."

"But you did once, didn't you Paw?" He kept on.

"Aye, once I did," He squeezed the boys shoulder, "but no one ever beats Thomas Belson twice."

I looked at the girl next. "As it happens I do have a nice horse if you want to see it."

"Yes!" The girl shrieked. "I love ponies!"

"Well, I'm sure he'll love you sweet as you are." I patted her shoulder and stood up.

"Sunny!" I heard from over my shoulder. It was Tom, my little nephew.

"Tom!" Sunny ran at the boy, and they were wrestling on the

ground as soon as they hit each other. Clearly, the two boys knew each other and were actually friends.

"Cut it out you two!" Sarah said, and they shot up brushing themselves off. She walked over to the boys. "You'll knock something down." She turned her attention to Roltan's wife. "I swear if there's a hell for wives, it's full of little boys in a pottery store."

Emma smiled. "I wouldn't doubt it."

"I love your dress!" Sarah said. "Where did you get it."

"Oh, this old thing?" Emma waved her hand to be polite. "Gloria made it for me. She's the best seamstress in the South."

Sarah gave an apologetic look to Roltan. "Would you mind if I borrowed your wife? It's been so long."

Roltan smiled. "As long as you give her back to me." He gave her a kiss. "I don't know what I'd do without her."

The two walked off, talking about things I couldn't even pretend to eavesdrop on.

The little girl faced my nephew Tom with a spark in her eye. "Hey, Tom!" She said.

"Shut up Georgia!" Sunny said. "We don't play with stupid girls!"

"Be nice to your sister!" Roltan cuffed the boy on the back of her head.

Tom looked a little embarrassed. "Hey, Georgia." He said. "You can play with us later if you want."

Andrew looked at me and mouthed, *"young love."* I stifled a chuckle.

Sunny presented a small pocket knife. "Look what my paw gave me." He handed it to Tom.

"It's neat." Tom bristled with envy. "My uncle's teaching me how to shoot!" He said proudly. "He can hit a bottle at a hundred paces."

"Oh, he can do far more than that." Roltan laughed. "You two go play outside." The boys rushed off in a scramble to get out the door. He turned to Andrew and Seiford. "Would you mind if we talked in private for a bit?"

"Absolutely not!" Andrew said, but I could see there was a tinge of jealousy there. He knew that there was bond me and Roltan shared that he couldn't emulate. I resolved to do something about that.

"Let's go have that talk." I put a hand on my old friend's shoulder, but I felt a tug on my shirt. I looked down to see Georgia staring up at me. "What is it, sweetheart?" I asked

"My paw promised I could see your horse."

I laughed. "I wouldn't want to make a liar out of your dad." I lead her outside, and gave a loud whistle, followed by "Shaggy!" Sure enough, my steed came running to me. "Be nice to her. She's little." I whispered in her ear

The horse neighed loudly.

I pushed some dried apples into the girl's hand, who fed them all to Shaggy at once. Then she started tugging on the horse's ear.

"You're sure it's safe?" Roltan had the scared look a parent seemed to constantly wear.

"It's safe." I reassured him. "Trust me."

"I trust you, Thomas." He said. "I always have." Finally, we were alone. "Listen, Thomas, I wanted to say I'm sorry..." I cut him off.

"There's nothing to be sorry about." I waved it away. "I asked you to do something you couldn't. You were right to disobey me." I sighed. "Besides, we're not in the military anymore."

Roltan gave me a strained look. "I'm not sorry about disobeying." He firmed himself up. "I thank the Three every night they gave me the strength to turn away." He said. "I wouldn't have been the same man I am today. I wouldn't be the man worthy of Emma's love or my children's respect."

I took a step back. "What are you apologizing for then?" I asked.

"I still let you do it." Roltan said, barely a whisper. "I should have argued harder. I should have made you stop."

"You really think they didn't deserve what they got?" I narrowed my eyes at the man. "Have you forgotten what they did?"

"I'll never forget what they did," he took a step forward, "but it's not up to us to pass that kind of judgment." Roltan paused. "What I do know, is what it did to you." He looked at his own hands. "I know that stain has stayed with you."

"I had to win that war." I scratched my tattooed arm.

"Aye, you did."

"It was the only way." I said.

"Maybe." Roltan sighed. "I should have stopped you, all the same." He went on. "If I couldn't have done that, I should have been with you afterwards. I should have helped you find peace."

"I was never a creature of peace." I shook my head.

"You can be." He put a hand on my shoulder. "You just need to keep trying."

"That's what my monk keeps saying." I chuckled.

"Aye, I heard you took up with Colonel Seiford's brother." Roltan smiled. "He was a good man."

"Aye, he was." I nodded, and a moment of silence came for our fallen brother. "For what it's worth Roltan, there's no bad blood between us." I paused. "I don't think there ever was." I chuckled and touched my cheek. "That was a good right hook anyway."

"I need to hear you say it." Roltan looked like a desperate man. Even more desperate than the boy I'd known all those years ago. "I need you to forgive me."

"I forgive you." I said.

"Good." It seemed as if a weight lifted off of him.

"So you made it to the Confederacy then?" I asked.

"I thought I might try my hand at the new world, seeing as how the old world treated the likes of us." Roltan shrugged. "After we parted ways I hopped on a boat and headed here."

"How'd you come to know my family?" I asked

He looked over at the children playing. "I looked up your family when I got here, I told them your stories, and we became friends." He shrugged. "I try to stop by as often as I can."

"Any of the others come to the Confederacy?" I asked, thinking back to the army.

"A lot of them did." He nodded. "After the way King John ended things most of us wanted to come to the Land of What Could Be." Roltan chuckled. "They even took to calling us the Belson Brigade."

"You stay in touch with them?" I asked.

"We used to meet every year or so." Roltan shrugged. "Life gets in the way, though. It's been a while since the last one." He smiled. "We write each other, though, have someone check on the boys who are having problems."

"That's not enough!" I slammed my fist on the rail. "I never should have let King John treat you that way." I put a hand on his shoulder. "Let them all know, if they're having trouble, if they need some help sending their boys through school, I'll find a way to pay for it." I paused. "If I have to dig ditches for the rest of my life." I stepped towards him. "I won't let my men wind up begging on the street with one arm."

To my surprise, Roltan laughed. "You don't need to worry about that." He said. "I was as angry as anyone else about how things ended, but King John did us a favor."

"What do you mean?" I crossed my arms.

"I mean this isn't Thyro, and we don't need help." He smiled. "Kelm opened up his own law firm here, Ferton has a farm out west, and me…" He touched his suit. "I went into business for myself. I'm almost as wealthy as your brother now." He gestured to inside. "Emma's from the Southrend family. They disowned her when she took up with me." He paused. "In the years since, I've had to give three separate loans to their family to keep them afloat." He kept his wide smile. "Almost everyone's doing just as well in their own way."

"That's amazing." I shook my head. There really was no other word for it.

"This is an amazing place." He turned back to his children. "I always wondered why you fought so hard to save this world." Roltan shook his head. "I'd only ever seen the evil bits." He paused. "Now, I know why. This world is worth fighting for."

"Aye, it is." I nodded.

"Now we're here to help you." Roltan patted my back. "You helped build this world. Now live in it."

"I don't need help." I said sternly.

He shook his head. "Thomas, I only spent four years fighting, and I needed help." He paused. "There's no shame in accepting it."

"Tell me about yourself." I changed the subject. "How'd you get so wealthy?"

He told me. It was the type of story that made you proud of your country. He'd come here penniless and broke, plying his soldier's trade to guard caravans. Finally, he got a loan and started shipping his own goods. He'd been the first to think of pickling items to preserve them.

Then he told me about his family. How he'd taken up with Emma on one of his deliveries. He'd still been penniless then, but she'd loved him anyway. He told me about how sharp his son was and how sweet his little girl could be. It was a good story, and he deserved it.

"I heard you never stopped fighting." Roltan finally said. "I heard you never stopped making the world better."

"How could I?" It seemed a strange thing for him to say. "It's what I was born for."

"That's what I thought once." He shrugged. "Oh, the boy's got his knife out." He turned a sympathetic look towards me. "I've got to go tan his hide. We'll talk later."

I nodded and walked back inside the house. I wasn't sure what to think of Roltan. I was happy for him, but there were more layers to it than that. On the one hand, he made me hope I could find what he had. However, the other part of me knew it was too late. He was just a totem to what I could have been. He was a path I'd only ever seen the entrance to.

I walked to the kitchen to sate my growling stomach. I passed a few servants on my way who nodded politely. I got right to the door but stopped when I heard voices. It was Emma and Sarah.

"It's good to finally meet the man I've been sharing my husband with all this time." Emma said.

"Is it?" Sarah asked.

"Well, yes of course." Emma paused. "What do you mean?"

"When Thomas left those years ago it wasn't on the best of terms." Sarah seemed strained. "We forgave him as soon as he was out the door, of course, but the scars are still there. I see it in Andrew sometimes."

"That was a long time ago." Emma said.

"Like I said, I'm not the kind of person to hold that against him." Sarah said. "I'm glad to have him back with us. I'm just not sure it's what's best for him."

"What are you saying, Sarah?"

"Think about all those stories people tell about him." She said.

"They're amazing." Emma agreed. "The way he fought hordes of tyrants. The way he helped everyone around him. He's a hero."

"He is, and no ones saying he isn't," Sarah said, "but think about the kind of man it takes to do those things. It changes someone."

"My Roltan had the same trouble."

"Maybe," Sarah said, "but I've heard the way he screams at night. I've seen the look in his eyes. He's still the warrior, and I don't know that he can put that piece of himself away."

"He'll be fine." Emma said.

"I want nothing more than for him to be fine," she said, "but he's dangerous too, and I'm not ready to trade my family for him."

I walked away before I could hear the rest. My hunger was forgotten. I didn't know where I was going until my feet lead me to the piano my parents must have kept. I sat down and started to play.

It was a mournful tune, filled with dark marches and sour notes. I'd never played it before, but my fingers seemed to know the song. I played until a figure came through the door.

I stood up for him. Almost immediately I recognized who he was. From a dozen papers that told his story from my youth, even from a few I'd read in Thyro. He was taller than me by a head and, even in his old age, covered in muscle. His beard had long since faded to white, and his hair was thinning. His face looked like what every leader ought to. What I often wished my own face looked like. Sharp cheekbones, bright eyes, wide jaw. This was General Fennis.

"General Fennis..." I was at a loss.

"No please, Mister Belson." He waved me down. "It was beautiful, keep playing." I saw he had a guitar in one hand.

I played again, the same tune filled with pain. He joined in. It took a few chords before he had the hang of it, but soon it was a duet. Two old soldiers playing. His strings bouncing off my song. It was a story of pain and regret. Of sacrifices for things we could no longer remember. Soon my hand cramped, and his fingers slipped. The song left us as quickly as it had come. Neither of us was really suited for music.

"You're better than me." Fennis said. I knew he wasn't talking about music.

"Maybe." I muttered.

"There's no maybe about it." The General said. "I couldn't have beaten Thaniel."

"My great moment, huh?" I asked.

"Everyone's got one." He said. "Mine came against the Anthanii at Grenwold's Field." Fennis chuckled. "I was just twenty-five then, with a company of cavalry."

"My father was there." I nodded without looking at him. "You charged the hole in their line and rolled them all up." I said. "You saved the day. Some say you saved the whole country."

"There were too many brave men in our army." Fennis shook his head. "Someone would have stopped them." He paused. "I saved a lot of lives, though, and I'm proud of that."

"It's something to be proud of." I nodded.

"My entire life I always wondered if that was a fluke." He huffed. "I always worried if I'd lose my touch the next time."

"You never did." I finally turned to face him.

"My life isn't over yet." He looked down at his own hands. "What about you?" He asked. "You ever wonder?"

I shook my head. "I always knew I was the best." I paused.

"Even when everyone doubted me. Even when the odds were so bad any sane person would have run for the hills." I stared back up at him. "I always knew I'd win."

"You weren't afraid?" Fennis asked.

I had to laugh at that. "I was terrified." I said. "The whole world started to believe I was the savior they'd waited generations for. Who could be that type of man?" I touched the tattoos on my arm. "It wasn't losing I was scared of, though. It was winning."

"You made some hard choices." Fennis said. "That's what heroes do."

I shook my head at that. "People have called me that for fifteen years." I said. "Some days I wonder how true that is."

Fennis nodded. "I know how that feels." He muttered. "Carpenters work wood, cobblers mend shoes, and doctors put us back together." He paused. "They're all honorable professions, but I'm a soldier. Winning battles is what I do same as them. I just wonder if it was ever as honorable a profession as there's."

I sighed. "I've killed a lot of carpenters, cobblers, and even a few doctors."

"You've let a hundred times more live their lives in peace." The general gave me a small smile. "That's what I have to tell myself." He paused. "Never wonder about if you were a hero, though. It's always a hard thing for an old man to say, but the world is a better place now than it was. You helped make it so."

I smiled back at him. "I was a hero ten years ago. When Thaniel's armies threatened the world, and I slapped them down." I gritted my teeth. "I made some mistakes. I did some things that would make characters in those old stories go pale, but I was a true hero then." I paused. "After Thaniel fell, I've just been roaming the world, clawing at the echo of the man I was."

"You did great things even then." Fennis reached over and put a hand on my shoulder. "You gave the people of Thyro their countries back, you raised the Souren up and made us all see them as men, and in the end, you made people more than they were." He put his hand back. "That's something only a hero could do."

"I'm proud of those things," I said, "but there's a part of me that wonders if I should have hung my weapons up ten years ago." I paused. "I've been fighting so long, I can't give it up now, but the world doesn't have a place for me anymore."

"The warriors curse." Fennis leaned back in his chair.

"How do you do it?" I asked. "You've got a wife and children." I paused. "Everyone keeps telling me to build a life here, but I don't know how." I scratched the tattoos on my arm. "How do I come back from the war?"

He almost laughed at that. "I'm a lucky man to have all that, but I don't deserve it."

"What do you mean?" I asked.

"I never came back from the war. Not really, anyway." Fennis looked down. "I love my wife, and she loves me, but of the forty years we've been married, I've been with her for maybe a decade." The clench in his jaw told me he regretted it. "There was always some problem on the frontier I needed to deal with, some war a politician started that needed mopping up, some fresh troops that needed to be trained." He paused. "I could have let another man take my place, and nothing would have changed really."

"That's the problem with being the best," I said, "they always need the best." I laughed. "People always say the worlds about to end if we're not on the line to stop it."

Fennis chuckled. "That's what I told my wife, and I even tell myself that from time to time." His face went stony. "The truth was I wanted to go. I needed it." He clenched the side of his chair. "That moment when the line weakens, and you send in the cavalry, when you force a march for three days and get there just before the enemy, when you wave your sword in the air trying to get the men to hold for a moment more."

He went on. "You and I aren't like Andrew and your father." He paused. "They fought because they couldn't send men to die without being there themselves, and in the end, they fought to preserve a home they could go back to." He smiled. "We don't return home from battle, we return home to battle." Fennis looked me in the eye. "The cost is something you don't count until you need a home that isn't there."

Fennis kept talking, and I wasn't about to stop him. "My wife had an affair a while ago. It was some aristocrat she found comfort with." He shook his head. "She broke down when she told me. I should have raged and punched through a wall, I should have found the bastard and beat him bloody, I should have..." His voice trailed off. "I should have promised to be a better husband." He looked at me. "You know what I did."

"You went back to the front and made the world feel your pain."
I knew it was what I'd do.

"For three years I didn't see her again." He said. "When I got
home, I found out she'd been punishing herself. Fasting, kneeling on
rice and the like. She shouldn't have. It was my fault." He paused.
"Now I'm retired, and I'm trying to make up for all my sins, but
my wife is almost a stranger to me. My boys are in the army giving
everyone hellfire because they think it's the only way I'll love them.
I try to tell my children I just want him to be happy, but they don't
believe me. Why should they?" Fennis paused. "The worst is my
daughters. They try to make me dinner, but they don't even know
what flavors I like."

Fennis paused for a moment. "I waited too long to try to make
things right." He looked at me. "They retired you early though.
Maybe you can find some peace. I hope you do."

"I don't know if I want that." We were silent for a moment, but
there was still a weight between us. I should have let it lie, but I've
never been that sort. "How permanent do you think your retirement
will be?"

Fennis perked up at that. "About as permanent as yours, I
suppose." He knew what I was asking. We were both professionals.
I wanted to know if I'd have to break him one day. "McAllan talked
to you too, I suppose."

I nodded.

"He wants your help beating the South, I'm guessing." Fennis
eyed the six-shooter at my side.

"No, he wanted my help avoiding the need." I smiled. "He
seemed a decent sort for a politician."

Fennis nodded. "He's the most honest man in the Capitol." It
seemed like he regretted it. "He's competent, hard-working, and he
cares about this country."

"Is he right?" I asked. "Is there a chance the Confederacy
doesn't go to war with itself?"

Fennis's face fell. "Years ago, maybe there was." He said. "Even
today, if it were just me and McAllan, we could probably work it out,"
he paused, "but it's not just the two of us, and it's not years ago."
He eyed me up again. "The gears are already in motion, and I don't
think anyone can stop them."

"Why not?" I leaned into him. "I see two leaders who want the
best for their people."

Fennis sighed. "You're a great warrior," he said, "but you're too naive about the politics of this land."

I stood up. "Naive is it?" I asked. "I've fought in a dozen civil wars. I've watched countless nations tear themselves apart. I've seen the dead pile up." I paused. "I've watched people try to put their country back together again, and it never fits the way it used too." I stared at him. "What grievance could possibly be worth that price?"

Fennis stood up to tower over me. "We're not equal anymore. Our politics are dominated by an ever-expanding nation. Our farms are locked in servitude to Northern businessmen." He went on. "For the South to be free, we must stand alone."

"We both know this goes beyond provincial rights." I took a step towards him.

He understood what I was saying. "The Old Religion and the provincial rights are linked."

"Then someone should break the link." I glared up at him.

"What do you know of the way this land should work?" Fennis shook his head.

"Nothing, but I remember how Kran worked." I shot back.

"Thaniel was an evil tyrant." Fennis bit his lip.

I sat down. "Thaniel may have been a tyrant, but he wasn't evil." I stared up at the general. "He was just pushed, and it was the Old Religion who did most of the pushing." I paused. "I'm telling you right now. If you think you or anyone else in this world is better than him, you're wrong." I touched the tattoos on my arm. "If you think you can walk the path that he did and come out better, you won't."

Fennis sat down across from me. "It's all we can do."

"You could lay down your arms." I said softly. "You could find a better way."

The corner of his chin curled at that. "A moment ago you were telling me how much you missed the wars." He said. "You'll finally be the hero of the Confederacy, just like you are the rest of the world."

I shook my head. "I don't want it to be like this." I whispered. "Not against my home."

Fennis reached over to me. "Then fight with us." He said. "Coleson's never been a real leader, and I'm too old to last much longer." His eyes met mine. "The powers that be think you're the man to helm our new nation."

"I can't." I said it with a firmness I didn't quite feel.

"Why not?"

"Because I can't!" I screamed, then lowered my voice. "It's not my place."

"You know I taught a course on you at the academy." Fennis sighed. "At the end of every lesson, someone would ask, 'Why'd he leave all that power to men who couldn't hold it? Why'd he walk away'?" The general paused. "I never had a good answer for that, and I suspect you don't either."

"Because they needed a hero, not a tyrant." I said. *"Because I wouldn't have been any different."*

"I think they needed a ruler." Fennis bowed his head.

"I don't want to talk about that anymore." I turned back to the piano. "Will you play another song with me."

He obliged, and we made our music together.

Present Day

"**C**astrate him!" I heard the voice scream. "Take his fingers and toes!" It went on. "Make him a cripple and parade him through the streets!"

"Fuck you!" I screamed back. I struggled against the leather restraints that held me down. For all my strength, for all my cleverness, for all my will, I was helpless. I couldn't move.

I looked up at the men smiling like wolves, brandishing their tools for causing pain. They weren't soldiers. A soldier could never have done those things to me. A soldier might go too far if his blood's up. They could commit horrible crimes to be sure, but the glee of causing pain to a once proud man would have turned their stomachs.

These monsters were pockmarked and twisted things. They would never respect bravery or honor. To them, such words were a forgotten language long past its use. I felt fear rise up in me. A fear I'd never known before.

"I'll kill you all!" I screamed, but the words were meaningless. I was beaten in the truest sense. This was the end of my glorious tale.

"Impudent till the end, Thomas." The voice said with an unnatural joy, like the sickly smell of rotting meat, with a tinge of sweetness. "I'll make a deal with you *Belson the Blessed*." It said my title, making it sound as pathetic as it was in that room. "If you prostrate yourself before me now, I'll let you out of here to crawl back to the hole you came from."

"Fuck you!" I screamed again.

The voice laugh. "So be it."

The torturers started their work, bringing the scalpel to my ribs.

"Wait!" I screamed. "My King! I am sorry for all insults given in the past." I wept as the words came out. I wept my fight away. Everything I'd cleaved to given up to escape the table for a moment more. "You are wise and generous. This victory is yours. I am but a humble worm before you."

"Not enough." The voice continued.

"My countrymen should have stayed loyal to you." I said through the tears. "I will run back to them and proclaim your glory. I will ever be your loyal dog."

"I will not share a dog." The voice said. "You yet have other masters."

"I renounce the Confederacy and the New Church!" I screamed. "I renounce the Three for you!"

"They were never your true masters." The voice continued.

I turned my head and saw a small mangy dog wailing. It wanted to help, but there was nothing it could do. "I renounce myself. I am nothing compared to you." I finally let out. "Please don't hurt me!" I screamed.

The voice let out a vicious laugh. "You are nothing," it said, "but I lied."

The pockmarked tortures cut into my ribs.

"Stop!" A shout screamed with the authority of all the time that had passed and all that was yet to pass. The leather straps that had held me down were gone. I sprung up snarling like a wild animal. I was ready to kill. However, my tormentors were gone and so was the voice.

"Where are they!" I screamed. "Let me kill them!"

"Stop…" This time it was softer. It wasn't a command, it was a request for my own good, almost pleading.

I turned to it. Where the torturers had been there now stood three people. One I was well acquainted with. It was Wisdom. He still had the shades of all knowledge with him, but it was grounded by the form that comforted me, Doctor Quarrels.

To his right stood a creature I hadn't seen in some time. To call him a thing of martial valor would be incorrect, yet inside him, I saw every sort of military archetype, from the dutiful private to the proud general. However, there was also the weary old man who plowed his field despite his failing body. There was the father who came home to play with his child after a long days work. I saw the young boy who stayed home despite his hunger for glory because his home needed him. The reaction to me was visceral. I wanted to proclaim I would follow him to the ends of the earth. I would fight any battle he told me too. I would die for him. My rage kept the snarl on my face, though. Still, I wasn't so blind I couldn't tell he was Honor.

To Wisdom's left stood a woman of all shades. The pretty little girl you said you would marry as a boy. There was the woman in her prime who you wanted to make laugh. There was the mother who always tucked her children in. There was the grey-haired, wrinkled thing who despite her years was still beautiful. I wanted nothing more than to spend my days on a porch with her. I wanted to touch her. I wanted to show her all the great things I was. I wanted her to see me as a hero. I was too stubborn to do it though. She was Love.

The full Three had never appeared to me before at the same time. Even that wasn't enough to stem my anger.

"Is this what you want!" I screamed at them. "You want me to relive…" I paused not sure how to explain it. "This!" I was quivering with rage. "You want me to humiliate myself like that!" I screamed.

Honor shook his head. "We never wanted this." He said. "It should never have happened."

"Then why do you send me these dreams?" I punched the table.

Wisdom stepped forward. "We don't send you these dreams." He whispered. "They come from you."

Love folded her arms. "It would have gotten worse if we hadn't stopped it." She said. "Much worse." The sorrow in her voice hit me hard. "I couldn't watch you suffer like that anymore."

"Don't pity me!" I screamed. "I have trampled armies. I have broken empires." I shook my head. "I dueled a Demon and won." I sat down on the table. "I'm not afraid of him!" I screamed again. "I'm not afraid of my fucking family!" I looked at my own hands. "I'm not afraid…" I broke down and wept into my hands.

A hand reached out to my shoulder. I expected it to be Love or maybe Wisdom. I looked up to find Honor staring down at me. "It's alright son." He patted me again. "It's alright."

"This was the moment, wasn't it?" Honor asked.

"Aye, this was the moment." I nodded. "The moment they tossed me aside because I wasn't useful to them. Because I was dangerous!" I screamed. "I should have marched out from that hole and killed every one of them." I said. "I should have put his head on a spike and taken what was mine."

"You didn't though." Love took a step forward. "Why?"

I looked up at her. I expected a screaming rebuke from Wisdom. I could have handled that. Instead, I was left with the implication that once upon a time I knew the right way and had lost it. It burned me.

"I wanted to. I really did." I looked up into her eyes. "I was so close to reaching up and taking it." I shook my head trying to clear the memory of it all. "There was a time maybe I should have, and it would've been right." I paused. "But the things I did in the end... They changed me. I wouldn't have been better than any of them, just harder to kill."

"Besides," I let a snort of laughter escape my mouth. "I swore an oath." I let slip a sad little smirk. "Swore it on your name as a matter of fact."

Wisdom returned the smile. "Aye, you did and the same oath we gave the Nameless man." He took a step forward. "Why do you think we gave the words to him all those years ago?"

I laughed at that. "You wouldn't be very divine if men didn't have to swear all manner of restricting oaths to you." I shrugged. "It'd be like a cook feeding me when I'm hungry rather than when he decides the stew is burnt enough, not in your nature."

Love let out a quick laugh. "You're right, he is quite funny."

Honor was less amused. "Also quite impudent."

Wisdom just smiled. "The best humor is always a bit impudent." He steeled his face. "No Thomas, we did not set those oaths down just to put a thorn in your side." He paused. "I'll admit, many scholars take a liberal view on our words."

Honor nodded. "We never actually said burn those who worship the Demons."

Love chimed in. "There's a monk out in Swendel who claims all redheads are touched by the World-Below." She chuckled. "Says they're unfit for marriage. Can't imagine where he got that idea."

"His mother was probably a redhead with some loose morals. Usually, how that sort of thing goes." I smiled. "Seiford once got drunk and told a village in Souren the second week of every winter is to be celebrated with tits and wine." It felt rather like ratting out your friend to his boss, but they probably already knew.

Wisdom laughed. "Yes, and the custom is slowly spreading across the continent." He shrugged. "Mother Vestia would have intervened by now, but it's brought a rather large crop of tourist to the region." He said. "Good for the economy and all that."

"See!" I said. "People say lots of stupid shit when they think they have the backing of their gods." I shook my head. "Why should I be bound by a set of oaths said half a millennia ago?"

"Repeat to me that oath." Wisdom said lightly. It wasn't an order. It came across as a concerned mother telling her son to bring an extra jacket for the cold.

I nodded and said the words burned into my soul. "I do not say these words to any king or government. I do not pledge these things before any crowd or brothers in arms. I swear only by myself and the Three Above." I rattled off the preamble.

Wisdom seemed pleased and motioned me to continue.

I nodded. "I swear to fight the Old Religion wherever they might be. I swear to take the authority of any ruler who sullies it with the Demon-Speakers. I swear to fight till my dying day the tyranny of the World Below." It was the first part of the oath. Most Constable's remembered that part before the rest.

"I swear these things, but there is much between this day and my death. There is much between oppression and freedom." I paused. "So I swear these oaths more to guide me in the space between. I swear to set the example for men to follow. I swear to stand between the innocent and those that would subjugate them. I swear to do what is right because it is right. Let me not fail in my duties. The world deserves more than what has been."

"Remember that."

"Remember that."

"Remember that."

And I was falling.

I woke up in a cold sweat. My eyes adjusted to the world around me. *Where are the assassins? What battle have I forgotten? Where am I?* Finally, I realized I was in my own bed. I had drifted off waiting for the festivities to start, and the noise I heard was of a home, not gunfire.

I stood up and went to the wash bowl. I lit one of my cigarettes to kill the nerves. Next to my bed, there was a fine blue suit, tailored to me in the current fashion, but it wasn't my fashion.

I smoked on the cigarette a bit longer. On my dresser was a series of letters I'd received. They were addressed to Seiford and me and already opened. I wasn't quite ready for the party yet, so I read them while I smoked. I'd hoped they would ease my nerves. I was wrong.

There were a few from Mother Vestia wishing the two of us well. They were sweet, polite, and kind. I put them to the side. There were more though, from a series of aliases we'd used. I recognized them immediately. They were from Viverent. They spoke of troubled times in Thyro. Every newspaper on the continent had started a vicious campaign against me. They called me an arrogant imperialist who was a dog on the leash to higher powers. They slandered anyone who defended me as an apologist for my crimes. What was worse, the only debate amongst the newspapers and intellectuals was if I was the worse criminal in history, or I served the worst criminal in history. They'd done it before, but this time it was different. It was coordinated, by some power unseen.

I hadn't made enough allies amongst the ruling class that they put up any defense against me, not that I'd have asked them to. From the way Viverent told it, the people I'd helped still swore by me, but they were getting older. If they were peasants, the newspapers called them ignorant. If they were higher up, they called them traitors. It hadn't worked much with the population who remembered the horrors I'd saved them from, but those who were too young to know the fear of fifteen years ago, they were already calling for my statues to be pulled down. What was worse, they were calling for the Old Religion to return.

The last thing Viverent wrote put the chill in my bones.

Ask yourself why they're doing this. Ask yourself
why they waited till you were gone.

I did, and I couldn't find any answer that warmed me. They were apparently headed by some scholar known as Malix. He called for every system in place to be torn down. He spoke of some new utopia. I smoked another one.

The next letters were from Prince Edward. He spoke of the same thing. Apparently, his efforts to set his people on a better road were being thwarted at every turn. Edward was competent enough to deal with those problems but still… The fear was that they weren't from any of his father's holdovers. This came from a different threat, and he couldn't pin it down. Then there was the usual drivel I hadn't responded to in ten years. *I'm sorry about everything. Please forgive me.* I threw them to the side as well.

Apparently, the troubles in the Confederacy hadn't gone unnoticed in Thyro. There was a sizable element that wanted a war in my home, and they weren't going to put their support behind McAllan.

I read as I smoked until a sound made itself clear. I could hear the thump of many boots striking against the wood floor.

I was probably late for the party, and so they'd sent a group to come retrieve me. It wasn't an uncommon occurrence for me. Then I realized I didn't hear the sounds of revelry from below. Had they deemed it appropriate to wait for me? That was a possibility. I was the guest of honor. They'd probably hold off on the toasts and cake till I arrived, but to remain completely silent until I graced them with my presence was a politeness I'd never observed. Not even in the cities I'd saved from destruction.

My mind fell into the cold calculations. Something was wrong, and even I didn't have the evidence necessary to make the deduction.

My fear was confirmed when I opened the door to see Andrew, George, and Seiford waiting outside. All of them had a distraught look in their eyes.

"I assume you didn't come to tell me the cake was vanilla instead of chocolate." The smirk on me was probably inappropriate.

"No brother," Andrew stepped inside, "the cake was chocolate as you requested."

"Then the guests must be partial to vanilla." I sat down on the bed. "Judging by the mournful silence below."

George might have chuckled if he had any blood in his face. "It takes people for a mournful silence." The tutor said. "You'll find no guest down below, just the regular type of quiet."

"Must have decided they couldn't go a full night smelling me then." I shrugged. "It's quite alright. I'm not unused to that complaint."

Seiford finally cut to the point. "Word came while you were asleep." The monk gave a cautious glance to the rest. "The National Assembly has passed a law. It forbids the training of new Priests."

"I suppose I'll have to go back to hunting deer then." I leaned back in my bed.

"I educated you well enough to know what this means." George gave me an appraising stare. "You know this isn't the time for jokes."

I stood up letting the scars on my chest show. "I know what this means." I glared at him. "It means more politicking and clever speeches careful not to go too far. Until then, it means a politician finally did the right thing."

George shook his head. "This on top of the South's embargo, it means people might start clamoring for more than votes in the Assembly." The tutor didn't back down from me. I respected that. "It means some of these speeches might stop being careful."

Andrew folded his arms. "Everyone worth their salt is headed to Madisonville for the debate." He threw me my old riding jacket. "It's not about a measured legal response. It's about war, and I want you to be there."

I nodded. "I'll go with you."

George and Andrew gave Seiford a nod and left him in my room.

"I received a letter this morning." The monk handed it to me. "It's from McAllan."

Dear Thomas Belson

> *The vote was made by the more radical elements in my party. I had hoped to put off any action this drastic until such a time that it might be better received. I had a plan, but you know how the Three generally choose to treat plans. In the meantime, you must put off this madness. I myself have a choice to make, on whether to veto or allow this bill. Either decision makes me weaker and our enemies stronger. You should know this before you play your role. This was not a political mistake. It was orchestrated by powers that I cannot put my finger on. You are a clever man, and you will see the hand as you draw nearer. Be careful.*

It wasn't signed McAllan, but I'd have had to be a fool not to know. I held the note up to Seiford. "You read this?"

The monk nodded.

"You read those as well?" I kept my eyes on him.

Seiford didn't answer right away. "I think we need to face the possibility that you were not being wholly paranoid before we left."

"And Mother Vestia sent me away." I snorted and stared back at the ground.

"Don't do that." Seiford stepped closer to me. "Don't start making enemies of friends. There's not a better woman in the world than that one."

"All, I'm saying is she sent me away." I shrugged. "Maybe it wasn't malice, but someone pushed her into doing it." I paused. "Forces were at work to make me seem like a liability."

Seiford shook his head at that. "Aye, that force was you."

"What are you saying?" I stood up.

The Monk stepped towards me. "You know what I'm saying." I did, and that made it all the harder. "Now, let's go stop a war." He stepped out of the room.

"Why don't we ask the opium dealer to solve addiction while we're at it!" I called after him. Still, I might have had a point. Doctors made the best poisoners. I knew that from personal experience, so the inverse could have been true

I walked downstairs and saw Sarah taking down all her careful decorations. I decided to approach her. "I'm sorry, your party got ruined." I scratched the back of my head uncomfortably. "You must be awfully sore."

She sighed and turned around to face me. "I am sore." Sarah had a strange way about her, almost like concern. "I'm sore that politics might send my husband back into war. I'm sore that my children may never see the country I love whole." She put a hand on my shoulder. "I'm sore the brother I haven't seen for fifteen years might be torn apart because of our failings."

"Concerned about me?" I asked. "I always get the impression you don't like me much."

Sarah cocked her head to one side. "Where'd you get that idea?"

"I heard you talking to Rolton's wife." I shrugged. "Don't worry, I didn't take it personally."

She stared at the ground. "Aye, I'm worried what having Belson the Blessed in my home might mean." Sarah started. "I do love you though Thomas. You've suffered enough, and I want my kin to find peace here." She nodded to the door. "We can speak about this later. You're needed elsewhere."

I nodded and put on my hat. "I'd like that." I said as I walked to the door.

"And don't think you've gotten out of this party!" Sarah hollered after me. "You're still the guest of honor, whether you like it or not!"

I smiled as I walked towards Shaggy.

"Thomas!" I heard a girl scream as she chased for me. "Thomas!"

I turned back to see my younger sister hurrying to catch me before I left. "Alexis?" I ran towards her. "Alexis! What's wrong?"

"I heard the news." She managed to say out of breath. "I just came to say..." She trailed off.

"Yes?" I urged her on.

"Don't go to war Thomas!" She grabbed my coat and pulled me close. "I love you, Thomas. I don't want to lose you again."

"I-" I paused not knowing what to say, so I folded her into a hug. "I love you too, Lex-Lex." It was the name I used to call her before I left. I wondered if she'd even remember it.

"Don't go to war." She repeated in my chest.

I released her to look in the girl's eyes. "I'm going to Madisonville to stop a war not to fight one."

"What if you can't?" She asked. "What if the war starts whether you want one to or not?"

"I'm Belson the Blessed." I smiled at her. "I always do what I set my mind to."

"Stop with that." She slapped my chest.

"Aye." I nodded. "I've got a duty one way or another." I put my hand on her shoulder. "I can't control the future, and I can't let history pass me by." The girl tried to move away, but I held her. "I can say that this isn't like it was fifteen years ago. I'm never leaving you alone again. I'll always be Belson the Blessed, but I'll never stop being your brother again."

"I suppose that's as good as I'm going to get." Alexis said. "I love you, brother."

"And I love you too." I had a duty, though. I mounted Shaggy Cow and rode off to meet my party. I wouldn't admit it to anyone, but I found myself having to wipe tears out of my eyes I couldn't entirely blame on the wind. Whatever things were, they weren't the same.

The Thaniel Wars

J was on the Captain's bridge of the Anthanii Flagship, *The Jorg*. It was so named for an Anthnaii king who ruled almost a thousand years ago, before it was even a real country. King Jorg was not a renowned monarch for his diplomatic acumen, charismatic leadership, or legal reforms. Most historians agreed the man wasn't even literate. He was not celebrated as a champion of the people, with a pension for charity and giving. Jorg had done an excellent job silencing his critics, but if I had to guess, he was probably one of the most hated rulers in his own time. Today he was considered the lesser of two evils and just barely. He wasn't even a great war hero in the traditional sense. There was no single decisive victory bearing his name, no famous charge for the bards to sing of.

King Jorg had clawed his way to the throne during the invasion of the then savage Northmen. He had rounded up all the squabbling nobles, too divided to mount a real defense, and put them all to the sword. He had elbowed his way into history by being the hardest bastard the world had ever seen. He'd mounted countless raids, waged savage guerrilla wars, and overseen campaigns characterized by fire and blood. He'd taken any woman he'd found even mildly attractive, regardless of if her husband was watching or not, regardless if she'd screamed for him to stop or not. He'd had any girl growing a Northman's baby in her beheaded. He'd slaughtered any Anthanii man who had given assistance to the invaders, and assistance under Jorg was rather loosely defined.

I knew that if I'd been born in the same time he'd been running around, I'd have killed him. However, by the time he died in battle, the Northmen had gone back to their isles. By all accounts, they'd been a truly savage place at the time, but nothing was more savage than Jorg. I chose to avoid studying military leaders like him. That wasn't the man I wanted to be, but you couldn't deny, without him there would be no Anthanii.

As I looked upon the set of admirals arrayed before me, it was all too obvious why they'd chosen to name their flagship *The Jorg*, despite the fact King John had been furious over the decision. It was because these men only cared about one thing. Were you hard?

I'd heard stories about these officers in the court. They were perhaps the only people considered lower than I was. Half of them were nobility. However, they more resembled the nobility of a thousand years ago. Back when it wasn't just the blood and royal tradition that made a ruler. They had been anointed lords because they were the only bastards that could protect the village. It was the dirty secret of all the noble families. Before they'd been cultured nobles, before they'd been knights riding in full plate, before they'd been seated in great castles, they were warriors blessed in blood who probably couldn't even spell "divine right." The court would rather the secret of their ancestors be forgotten. The ancestors probably would have slaughtered their descendants and laughed while they did it. They'd have liked the navy, though.

In the corner of the room, there were the colonels, Blip and Slip, of his Majesties Royal Marine Corps. Both of them had elegant names and titles but call them anything other than Blip and Slip, and they'd open your stomach. The pair had abandoned an officer's sword, and instead wore heavy sea axes on their sides. In addition to this, Blip always held a loaded blunderbuss which he'd somehow managed to mount three knives on, and Slip had no less than eight flintlock pistols strapped to his body. Despite their fiery hair and beard, they more closely resembled wolves than human beings. They even had their own strange telepathic link that let them speak a peculiar bastardization of Anthanii.

It went something like…

"Oy!"

"I reckon!"

"Weeblow Fucker!"

"Oy!"

I had been assured each spoke five languages, but they for some reason insisted on whatever it was they communicated in.

At my side stood Constable Waterson. As the Constabulary had been forced to extend its reach. The order had taken to training new men equipped to deal with the pirates and raiders. We called them Water-Saints. They were taught like the rest of us, but they received an extra year to learn how to fight with ships, being schooled in land strategy and naval. I'd thought about trying to go with them, but I didn't much like sailors.

Constable Waterson was a lean, hardened man only a few years older than me. From what I'd heard, he'd been recruited from some captain's son. He walked with that permanent bow-legged dance that was more at home on the seas than land, where the rest of us had evolved. He was a renowned warrior, and more civilized than those he served next to. The man had earned my respect.

There were a number of other sailors and marines present. It was entirely different than the ethnically uniform army. Filling up the numbers, were black Souren men, brownish Tulthers with their heads wrapped in turbans, even a few of the yellow Inte's. Anyone from the colonies could join the navy, and despite an edict from the court, they could rise as far as their talents let them. They had ceased to be Souren, Tulther, Inte, or even Kranish. They were warriors, and the bonds they felt for each other had long since displaced nationality or race. All it took to join the navy was balls and a general disdain for civilization.

Blip and Slip were the prototypical members of the fleet. One could look at them and tell they were closer to animals than men. However, each captain and officer gave off the same kind of air, if not as distinct. They wanted to fight.

At the head of the meeting was Lord Nelard. He was a folk hero in his own right. Children went to sleep listening to the stories of how he'd taken the fight to every climb and reach he could sail a ship and even a few no one else could. The man had royal blood on his mother's side, giving him preferential service to the crown, but he'd thrown it away to join the navy. Nelard had been offered a ship-of-the-line but had refused it, preferring instead to start his career as a lowly ensign and work his way up. He had done that shockingly fast. Some of his detractors suggested it was nepotism, but that was impossible because he'd served under a pseudonym. Also like any man with talent, he was not in favor with the court. Still, he was now commander of the fleet.

The man was a handsome fellow, blue eyes, strong chin, hair going grey in all the right places. Even his scars seemed to add to his mystique. He wore his uniform pressed and cleaned. Every man in the room regarded him with a certain deference. He still held his court training. One could tell he was a man with his foot in two worlds. One was that of a noble who stood for king and country.

The other was given only to the sea. He was the perfect go-between for the barbaric navy and the desires of the court. Besides Corbul and the handful of Constables, he'd been the only thing standing between Thaniel and disaster. He'd been giving the Emperor hell since Thaniel was only a mercenary.

I had brought the newly minted lieutenant Rolton with me. He wouldn't even wear the bars of his rank yet. The whole time he'd been whispering in my ears. "The first rule of the slums is never get involved with anyone in the fleet." I had to agree. The slums had a certain wisdom.

For all the advantages Kran had, their fleet was relatively new. Anthnaii had been a naval power for a thousand years. More importantly, they went mostly untouched by the foolish edicts the court imposed on the army. They were the most autonomous force that swore allegiance to the king. However, I was willing to bet they didn't actually have allegiance to the king. Who knew what sailors actually wanted. They were a strange breed. I made a point, that when I retired, I'd become the anthropologist that definitively proved sailors weren't actually humans. They just looked like us by pure accident. There was no relation to the rest of mankind. They just evolved in caves and waited until people got smart enough to build ships. At first, I thought maybe they were actually from fish, but that was an insult to fish. Our finned and gilled neighbors in the sea were much smarter. A fish would see a hook with a worm on it and bite. A sailor would see the same hook, climb to the top, and ask where the rest of the worms were. If you told them they were in the cooking fire, they'd no doubt jump in and ask why it was so hot. Strange bastards.

They'd fight for the king though, simply because they didn't care enough to say no. Unless the king tried to take away their grog. That would indeed be a war without end. I'd thought of withholding the foul liquor and starting a rumor that Thaniel was hoarding it all for himself. However, even I didn't hate the Kranish that much. When I died, I did not want to stand trial before the Three and have to explain why I did that. There was no excuse for war crimes so great. I could probably make them see that my mass murder had a purpose, but they'd never forgive me for setting thousands of sailors to tearing Kran apart looking for grog. That was an unpleasantness I wouldn't deliver upon the Priests of the Old Religion or even the Demons Below.

If there was a hell where men were punished for their crimes, I'd take an endless torture chamber over a room with a sailor thirsty for grog any day of the week. I'd have had them all castrated to purge the world of their ilk if only I didn't need to sail places. I wasn't even sure it would do any good. Sailors did enjoy whores even more than the rest of us, but I was reasonably sure their primary means of reproduction was to spit on the deck and water it with grog. Eventually, a full grown sailor would spring forth, asking how far away the next port was and constantly complaining about being a sailor but never doing anything about it. If they hated working on a ship as much as they claimed, they'd find a reputable job like selling opium on the street, killing people for money, or becoming lawyers and bankers. Well, maybe not that last bit. Even a sailor has some dignity. I just can't figure out where they hide it. All I knew, is that if I saw a sailor and a dog starving in the street, I'd give my last coin to the dog. It might actually know what to do with money. A ship dweller would just try and squeeze grog out the metal. I felt bad for the barnacles that had to dwell so close to them. They didn't deserve that.

Still, for all their many failings as human beings, Anthanii sailors were quite good at sailing. I had spent a week on an Anthanii warship. I hated the sea, but between my constant heaving over the side, I had been impressed by the competence of it all. They worked like clockwork. I had a plan, and as much as it pained me, I'd need the navy. I had tried burying a set of bones at a crossroads and making a deal with whatever sprung up. I occasionally heard evil spirits came up to make arrangements for your soul. None came. Probably because I smelled like sailor. It would have been preferable to dealing with anyone who worked on a ship.

That was not to speak of the Marines that made their home on the ships. If sailors are a different species than humans, we'd need another term besides living to describe how ship born infantry generally exist. Marines were always the hardest soldiers in a military. They never knew what theatre they'd fight in next, so they trained for all of them. Above all everyone knew the hardships being a marine came with. They endured the meager rations of sailors and the harrowing battle of regular infantry. There was only one reason they joined that outfit. It was because they wanted to fight. The Anthanii Marines were no different.

I needed warriors that wanted to fight. Men who left their

peaceful lives behind because they saw a cause worth shedding blood for or thought they wanted some adventure, were useful. I had no doubt that the Three would judge them better than the Marines, or me come to think of it, but every military needs the sort who relishes the sight of blood not cringes from it. After all, you'd rather have those men wearing a uniform, far away from your city, than causing mischief in the seedy parts of town. Especially when that mischief usually resulted in that town being burned to the ground.

Marines had a reputation for that sort of thing, and I always believed it wasn't the uniform that made them that way. Of course, if you put a bunch of madmen together on a ship, they usually didn't become more sane. However, at their core, they were cracked, and it seemed like hellfire came from that crack.

I once came across a couple crying in the street. In a rare moment of charity, I asked them what was wrong. They told me their son had joined the marines. I walked away. There was nothing I could have said to consul them. You could try and make an argument, that maybe if the child had a better upbringing, he could have become contributing members to society. That argument was wrong by whatever measure of logic you used.

Marines were born that way, Three help them. I had met a young man from the slums of Harfow who enlisted as a private and bragged about stabbing three men in a bar because someone had called him a soldier. I had met a well-educated university graduate whose father was a wealthy cloth merchant and had purchased a commission as captain in the Marines. He also bragged about stabbing three men in a bar because someone had called him a soldier. I had spoken with a general in the Marines who was the first born son to one of the most respected noble families in Thyro. Guess what he bragged about. If your answer was stabbing three people in a bar because someone called him a soldier, you're wrong. It was five, and one of them had been a prince. Usually, I think stories like that are lies, but I believed it.

There were three rules one needed to follow if you wanted to live a long life. Don't tell a king what to do, don't punch a Priest in the nose, and don't call a Marine a soldier. I had broken two of those rules, but for all my boldness, I would not break the last. Though, I doubt that Marines need an excuse to stab someone in a bar any more than a normal man needs an excuse to lay with a beautiful woman. It just came naturally. Why do dogs lick their balls? Why do

Marines stab people in bars? Same question really and in the end, same answer, because they enjoy it.

For all that though, they were good at what they did. They fought till their heads were blown away, marched until their feet fell off, and I had never seen a deeper, or more strange, camaraderie in a group of warriors. I met one Marine who spent an hour telling me about how the white race was greater than all the rest, and how a smart ruler should go about enslaving anyone even remotely tan. He did all of this while his best friend listened. It is important to note that his best friend was a Souren immigrant named Accun-bae and was so black I could only find him at night by looking for a floating smile of white teeth. When I inquired about this contradiction, I received no more answer than "Whatcha talking bout? He a Marine."

As far as I could tell, their only fault as a fighting force, was that there weren't enough of them. The Three, in their infinite wisdom, had made very few men insane enough to join the naval infantry. If I went to an asylum where men lived their lives in padded rooms so they wouldn't harm themselves and asked, "Who wants to be burned alive?" Most of them would think it sounded like good fun. If I walked into the same room and asked the same people, "Who wants to join the Marines?" I'd hear pure silence. Even the crickets would be too afraid to chirp. Believe me, I wouldn't have been the first to try it.

If I was going to beat Thaniel, I'd need every advantage I could get. As much as I hated to admit it, the fleet would give me that advantage. The Anthanii navy was second to none. If I threw an old book in the water with a bottle of grog on top, a sailor would follow, drink the grog, and sail the old book on a search to the ends of the Earth for more grog. Marines don't even need the encouragement. I heard stories that a group of them had burned down the largest trading post in the East because they got bored. It was unsubstantiated, but there was a city on the map that was missing, and I was reasonably sure if I looked through their footlockers, I'd find pieces of it.

At the moment beating Thaniel's Kran was impossible. It was like a bear in a cave. You had to jam a stick in and coax the damn beast out. Still dangerous, but doable. Using sailors and Marines was like pushing a stick in the cave covered with dynamite, parasitic diseases, and bad poetry. The animal would fly out of its hiding place, but by the Three it'd be angry. Angry enough to make a mistake, but also angry enough to take your head off.

I started the meeting. "Have you been practicing the raids and dock assaults?"

Lord Nelard nodded. "Aye, we have," he said, "but for the life of me I can't imagine why?"

"How good have you gotten at it?" I asked.

"Pretty good." Nelard answered.

"That's what I've been hoping for." I turned to face the rest of the council. "Gentlemen-"

"Who he calling gentle?" Blip cut in.

"Oy, show his moms how gentle I is." Slip caught on.

I thought the grumbling might be relegated to those two animals, but it wasn't. The rest of the council chimed in.

"Pup must've got us mixed up with them whores at court."

"See how gentle we is when he on the plank."

"Oy, I'll smack them tattoos right off his arm."

"Gentle me ass."

"Ain't no one ever go gentle on your ass, Halby!"

The whole crew erupted in laughter. I suddenly got the feeling I was an outsider on this ship. I'd always fit right in with the army, and I'd never cared what the court thought of me. This was the first time I'd ever been looked down upon by men I needed and held something more than contempt for. This was the first time I'd ever been looked down upon because I didn't know what I needed to.

"Don't call them gentleman." Constable Waterson whispered in my ear. "They don't like it."

"Aye, I've gathered that much." I hissed at the man. "What do I call them?"

"They'll only accept Seafarers from a Land Lover." Waterson repeated. "Try that."

"Alright, Seafarers then." I conceded. I was sure Land Lover was an insult, but I did love the land quite a bit. "The order to practice those maneuvers came directly from me." I tried again.

"Oy, you the reason we ain't gotten an honest fight in almost a year?" The glare I got from Blip couldn't have held more hatred if I killed his puppy. However, the reason he'd have been angry over that would have probably been because I killed his puppy before he could.

"You stole our damn war!" Slip jumped in with the same vitriol.

"Oy, I've been shaking like a drunk with no grog!" Blip raised his hand to show he was, in fact, shaking for a fight.

"Admiral, that the reason you've been keepin' us cooped up?" Slip tapped his sea ax.

"You been listening to this Weebalow!"

"Lil Joby more like."

I didn't know how to respond to any of that, but Waterson saved me. "Oy, this man's got a reputation in my order." He said. "He ain't Weebalow nor Joby." The lean Constable gave me a look filled with respect. "This brother here is a Gorby through and through."

That got a muttering of respect from everyone around. I still had no idea what was being said. I had never bothered to get fluent in sailor.

"I seen many a Gorby on land turn into a Weebalow on the deck." Blip shot back. That also got a mumble of agreement.

"That's enough!" Lord Nelard finally brought order to the room. "This is the man who saved Wuntsville. This is the man who reclaimed Gertinville." The admiral surveyed the room. "This is the man who turned back Thaniel with not but wits and balls." He turned his face back to me. "I say that makes him a Gorby wherever his feet stand."

"Oy, so it's true then?" Blip scratched his chin with one of the many knives on his blunderbuss.

"Me maw lived in Gertanville." Slip said.

"Got a cousin in Wuntsville." Blip said proudly. "You ever meet a boy named William?"

The thought of the boy getting run through flashed in my eyes. "I knew him." I nodded. "Fought bravely, but it'd probably have been better for him if I never came to town." I scratched the tattoos on my arm. "He fought with me though. I'm asking you to do the same."

"Might be I will." Blip nodded.

"Me too." Slip smiled. "Still a fucking Joby."

"You think we could take em, Admiral." Blip said tapping his blunderbuss and eyeing me up in a way I didn't like.

Lord Nelard smiled. "That's a question I won't answer," he said, "but if you try, I'll see you both strung up."

"Ain't no rope strong enough to beat us." Slip tapped his pistols.

"Oy, I beat the piss out any rope!" Blip declared proudly.

"Still, we like you, Admiral." Slip shrugged.

"Don't want to ruin your day." Blip agreed.

Lord Nelard chuckled and turned back to me. "They may be thick as a cannonball, but they're the two best Marines I've ever served with." He nodded for me to continue. "I would like to hear why you've relegated us to training when there's a war to fight, though."

I looked down at the map in the middle of the room. "Thaniel's conquered every country between Kran and Anthanii." I said. "For the time being it's the best we can do to fend off his attacks." I shook my head. "That'll only work for a while, but sooner or later we'll make a mistake. With Thaniel fighting against us, I'm willing to bet sooner." I looked up at the meeting. "What's more, I've met the Emperor. This war won't end until one side's beaten. Harfow or the Rose Petal throne will burn by the end of this."

Lord Nelard nodded. He was a military man and clearly understood the dire straights in which we found ourselves. "I assume you've got a plan to make sure it's not Harfow."

I nodded. "I do. I can't reveal all of it on account of Thaniel's spies, but it's there." I said. "I've begun training a real army. They're almost ready. Thaniel's got his hands full with some revolutions we've started, but he's got the largest army in the world. They're too well trained and lead to show a real weakness." I sighed. "As it stands, I'll have to do things the old-fashioned way. Take all the land between Anthanii and Kran and launch a full invasion."

"I don't like the sound of that." Lord Nelard said. He saw the predicament.

"Oy, it sounds like a whole lot of war to me." Slip smiled. "I'm right jealous of the bastard."

"Shut up, Slip!" Nelard screamed, then gestured to me. "Continue."

"I don't like the sound of it either." I said. "War like that'll cost too much. Even if everything goes right, we won't have the strength to invade." I gave a wry smile. "Luckily, that's not what I'm planning." I turned back to the map. "We need to open up a new front on the Kranish. However, the only enemies he hasn't beaten into submission are his borders to the West and North."

"The sea you mean." Lord Nelard smiled.

"Can't beat the sea." I shrugged.

"Oy, I beat the piss outa the sea!" Blip said.

"Shut up Blip!" The Lord called out again.

"You're right, the sea." I agreed.

"We've been trying to open up that front for a while now." Nelard said. "Thaniel's fleet is too big for us to face on open waters, and still have the strength to be effective against their shores if we win at all." Blip and Slip looked as if they were about to say something, but Nelard dealt with it before they could. "Can it, you two!"

"Sorry Admiral." They both said to varying degrees of sincerity.

The lord went on. "I've seen what you've seen." He said. "We've been fighting desperately for an advantage."

"How's it going?" I asked.

"It's had its ups and downs." This time it was Constable Waterson. "Things aren't as bad as they are on land, but not as good as the Anthanii navy is used to. We've been sending frigates and sloops at them. Trying to whittle em down." He nodded at the officers. "The Kranish have never been great sailors. We destroyed some frigates, and even captured a couple ships-of-the-line." He nodded. "However they've been learning quick, and they can produce new ships faster than we can. We lost four frigates this year alone, and a few man-o-wars beaten too badly to go on."

"It could be worse." I shrugged.

"Could be better." Constable Waterson said.

"Man-o-wars are expensive." Nelard nodded.

"Well, I've got a plan to make this easier." I went on. "I've received word that Thaniel's fleet is holed up at Fredua and Wellsport." I said. "It's the moment we've been waiting for."

Lord Nelard shook his head. "You think we ain't thought of that?" The man said. "Every ensign knows it's better to catch a fleet at anchor." He gestured to the map. "Thaniel is powerful clever. He only chooses ports we can't move into." He tapped Fredua. "The waters here are too shallow." He moved to Wellsport. "Here they got a natural barrier. Only a few ships can sail through at a time. Plus they're Priests at Fredua." He seemed a bit scared. "I've seen what their fire can do to a ship."

I smiled. "That was before Thaniel started excavating those ports." I pulled out my own findings and set them on the table. "I measured the depth of every port suitable to house a war fleet. I looked at their guns." I tapped my drawings. "The guns at Wellsport can't be leveled at anything past this point." I showed him. "Fredua is clear for deep boughed ships if you follow these paths."

Lord Nelard took the drawings and spent a moment examining them. "How'd you get these?"

"I went undercover and did my research." I answered.

"That took balls." He cocked an eyebrow up. "It still could be a trap. Thaniel's a wily one."

"It could be," I agreed, "but I don't think so. Still, there's a risk to this plan."

"There always is," Lord Nelard agreed, "but I'd be willing to take it if it weren't for those Priests."

I took a step back. "You heard about Gertinville?"

He nodded. "Aye, I did, but that was just propaganda." He eyed me up curiously. "It was just propaganda wasn't it?"

"It wasn't." I smiled.

The admiral scratched his head. "I've heard of Constables hunting Priest before." He snorted. "I even think I got one a few years back with a full broadside while he was sleeping." He looked back up at me. "No one beats a Priest in a fair fight, though, and that's what's needed here."

"Oy, I fight any Priest." Blip mumbled under his breath.

"Oy, I beat the piss out a Priest." Slip whispered back.

I'd have disregarded that as idle boasting from most men, but out of Slip and Blips mouth it sounded like they believed it. Part of that might have been the fact that they didn't actually know what a Priest was. I honestly thought they just heard people say the names of things that sounded remotely threatening and promised to beat the piss out of it. However, The extraordinary thing was that I believed it. I'd charged five thousand men at Wuntsville, and these two scared me more.

Lord Nelson ignored the two of them. "You're telling me you defeated five Priests in single combat."

"Seven, actually." I held up seven fingers to illustrate the point. I didn't know why. Sailors and Marines couldn't count anything except bottles of grog and scalps. "It was a battle, not single combat, but if I had to, I could do that as well."

"Then you've got our backing." He slammed his fist on the table. "Let's just see the order from the king."

I scratched the back of my head. "That's the thing…" I mumbled. "It would have taken too long for him to deliberate on a matter like this, and King John hates me too much to give me command of his navy." I shook my head. "Even if it wasn't, there's spies in the court who would hear about it. Then it becomes a slaughter."

"That is quite a thing." Lord Nelard agreed.

"It is." I said. "This isn't an order. I don't even think I have the authority to give one." I shrugged. "This is an opportunity. If it goes well, King John can take credit for the expedition." I said.

"If it doesn't?" Lord Nelard eyed me up.

"We'll all be hanged as traitors." I gestured to Blip and Slip. "Maybe they'll be put against the wall."

"Oy, I fight any wall." Blip said.

"Oy, beat the piss out a wall." Slip chimed in.

"I'm sure you would." I nodded at them.

Lord Nelard nodded. "I'm tired of wasting my boys lives like this." He said. "I want a way to take the war to them." He turned to the council. "Go back to your ships. We sail in the morning." The admiral gave me a wry smile. "Besides, if it does go bad, it's not like any of us will survive to be called traitors.

"Oy, we going to war?" Blip chirped.

"Gorby given us the war back!" Slip put in.

"Aye." I smiled. "We're going to war."

Present Day

Seiford, George, Andrew, Ayn-Tuk, and I were all headed to make our cases against the war at Madisonville. It usually took three days to make it to the meeting place, so I saved my extra set of clothes for the morning we were set to arrive after I bathed in a creek.

The meeting was for six bells past, and Madisonville was about two hours away by the time my brother chose to bring up what was on his mind.

"I know your views, Thomas." Andrew said dropping back to ride next to me "These people don't though. You'll need to temper them if you want people to listen."

That made me cock an eyebrow. "Do you really want people to listen to me?"

"We don't see eye to eye on a lot of these things." Andrew admitted. "I don't think you see how much good the Old Religion has done for us."

"I do, which makes it all the more dangerous." I gave my brother an angry look. "But this isn't all about the Old Religion to you, is it?"

"No, it's not." Andrew sighed. "This is about stopping a needless war based on nothing more than arrogance." He looked at me desperation in his eyes. "People like me. I'm not too much a fool to see that. People fear you, and you're not too much a fool to see that either. Between the two of us, well, maybe we can stop this."

"You're afraid of having me here." I didn't want to meet his eyes. Probably because I suspected he was right in his caution.

"I wasn't sure you were ready for this." Andrew shook his head. "I'm still not." My brother reached over and pulled my head to face him. "I wanted people to see you for you, not just your legend."

"My legend is all that matters tonight."

"It's not." Andrew said returning the glare. "Your legend is impressive, but a legend can be manipulated to serve either side. A man, a good man, stands straight and does what's right."

I cocked an eyebrow up at my brother, he always surprised me. "Maybe the legend should belong to you." He'd have handled it better.

"I didn't earn it. You did." Andrew gave a small salute which I returned.

Next Seiford pulled up to me. "Thomas this isn't like Tyro." The monk said. "If we're going to stop a war, we need to understand that."

"You've been here a little more than a month." I laughed. "You're gonna tell me how my home is supposed to work?"

"Fine then." Seiford mocked offense. "I guess I won't give you advice that could potentially keep this country whole." He shrugged. "I'll just go think Anthanii thoughts."

"Stop Seif!" I pulled him back. "You know I want your advice wherever we are." I smiled. "Just can't admit it that's all." I took a second to compose myself. "What were you saying?"

"In Thyro, we threaten, flatter, and tell half-truths to get our way." Seiford said. "Three know, I've done enough of that." He paused. "I don't know that it'll work here, though."

"I-" I was about to say something snarky, but then I realized he was right. It wasn't ground I was used to. "What should we do then?"

The monk snorted. "I haven't the faintest." He shrugged. "This is new territory for me too."

"I know." Ayn-Tuk rode up beside us on his black destrier.

"Do tell then." I gestured Ayn-Tuk to continue.

"The countries of Anthanii were forged thousands of years ago in shadows and superstition." The black man started. "Power there is based on tradition and fear. A place that needed to grow the way it did, but a place corrupted by the necessary evils that gave birth to it."

Ayn-Tuk went on. "This place is different. A land forged by a truth that would not abide by the old ways. A people made powerful by what they could be not what they are." Seiford and I were both staring at the man in a different manner. "In a country like this only honesty will change the rudder to a better path."

The black man turned to us. "You want to steer history towards peace, speak honestly." He said. "Even more than that, you must be the man who wants peace. You must become the man who wants to lead your people through."

Everything about him shocked me. "I hadn't realized you held the Confederacy in such high regard." I shrugged. "Considering the way we sometimes treat your people."

"This is the greatest country to ever exist." Ayn-Tuk spoke it and made me believe. "Yes, a place with faults, but the men and women here will lead us all to greatness, whether we go kicking and screaming or not." He paused. "As for the way you treat my people, it does speak poorly upon you, but it gets better. That's as much as I could ask. Honesty wins here."

"Anyway," I nodded. "It appears we're here."

We were in the town of Madisonville. It was small and meant to support the needs of the plantations surrounding it, but tonight it was bustling with activity. When I was a boy, Madisonville had seemed the hub to all culture and adventure. Now, I was utterly unimpressed. After all, I'd seen cities that were old when Imor fell. Three above I'd taken those cities by storm. There were a few taverns and inns in addition to a number of other buildings that undoubtedly held various stores and trading post that a small plantation village couldn't justify. In the center was the town hall. It was likely the only reason Madisonville existed. It looked to be well built and maintained, but it wasn't any bigger than a plantation house. It was brown and white without any flair or color. I heard Seiford sigh when he saw it. Our party got more than a few looks as they rode to the town hall, some were dirty, some were admiration, some were just plain curiosity at the strange dress. Most seemed to land on Ayn-Tuk and his polished spear eventually.

We all dismounted and tied our horses to the post outside the building. "Be good I don't want people to get the wrong idea about us." I told Shaggy Cow who I knew could easily untie the knot. After that, we filed into the town hall with the rest of them.

The building was stuffy with all the bodies in it already. If the outside was unimpressive than the inside didn't do much to improve the opinion. The walls were unadorned save for an oil painting of Then Ironwill that hung at the front. It showed him austere and intimidating, riding his stallion into what was presumably a battle for independence. At one time the founder of the Confederacy might've seemed like a god in his own right. I still respected the man's vision, but I'd killed men who had lead ten times the soldiers. Things had changed since I was a boy. The world had gotten bigger.

We moved through the crowded room. A man gave Ayn-Tuk and

his spear a laughing gaze until I stepped in between and showed the six-shooter at my side. They kept their thoughts on the shirtless black man to themselves after that.

Our party found a good seat near the middle, and I watched the crowd, evaluating the audience. It was a mix of all sort of people, some were wealthy plantation owners, others were craftsmen and traders of all types wearing their work clothes with pride in their careers. Most were the small time farm owners clearly trying to scratch out a living one expects to find everywhere. The room bustled as people conversed with their neighbor about which side they were on.

A man stood up and went to the podium, and a hush fell around the room. He was dressed in second-hand homespun but had clearly made an effort to look presentable. I saw he was missing his left arm. He wasn't hiding it with a pinned up jacket as most choose to but instead had cut the sleeve off and wore it with pride. He was plump but old enough for it to seem becoming. Despite his unimpressive figure, his stride spoke of a man to be respected, and men did, in fact, look to him in deference. Even a few wealthy aristocrats nodded their heads in respect.

"That's Jordan Jeffery." George whispered to Seiford, Ayn-Tuk, and I. "He's a good man and respected despite the poverty he was born into. The man worked like a ox behind his plow, and while he'll never be as rich as your family, he's made a good living." There was respect in the old tutor's voice. "He's educated despite his station, which is admirable, but he's on the belligerent side." He paused. "It's hard to say he has no case either."

"My name is Jordan Jeffery." He bellowed in a voice an Anthanii orator would have envied. "Many of you know me." He looked around the room. "I've fought twice for this nation I hold so dearly. When the Huego's raided our people me and so many others stood up to stop them." A cheer rose up in the crowd. "Then again when men were called to fight the Puena menace, I set down my plow once more and took up the rifle in defense of those who would not lay down silently to any man not elected by us!"

"Here here!" A man in the crowd said raising a fist

"For the people!" Another man chimed in.

"I lost my arm at San Sebastian." He raised the nub into the air. "I don't hide it because I say that if the Capitol can ask me to fight for our freedom, then they can bear to look at the receipt." He shook his head in sadness. "I don't ask pity or special treatment for it. A thousand men lost so much more than I that day."

"My boy died there!" One man called out.

Jordan looked at the man with sympathy. "I knew your boy Mr. Thorsin." He looked up at the crowd. "And I knew the man he became because of that war!" He found a man in the crowd. "I knew your brother!" He said to him, then looked at another man who couldn't have been older than twenty. "I knew your father!" He looked at the whole room. "I was there when they all died. If it comforts you to call your kin, boy, then I won't stop you, but in my heart and my most private thoughts, I call them men! They have earned that, and you should all know it! If I had my way, they would stand in bronze in front of every place men look at in awe, each and every one of them! I saw the Capitol once. It was as great as every one of you has heard."

Jordan took a moment to control the sorrow welling up inside of him "However, when I look upon its arches and pillars, it is not the beauty of the building that makes me weep. It is not even in memory of the great Then Ironwill. It is with thoughts of those who have died to make it sacred. It is with thoughts of your son rising up against a dozen Puena soldiers that I shed my tears." Jordan bowed his head at the man. "It is in remembrance of your brother walking steadfast into the barrel of a cannon." Jordan went to the other man. "Those tears hold the memory of your father baring his chest to a musket ball not intended for him so that another might live." He knelt down at the foot of the boy he had spoken to earlier. "And so that his son might grow to manhood with the pride that his father fell protecting a freedom our people bought one hundred years ago. It is for them and not myself that I speak for tonight. They paid the price, all men who fought paid a price. And what did they receive in turn? Where were the Capitols armies who are pledged to protect all citizens of the Confederacy, not just the North?"

"Tyranny!" One man shouted

"Injustice!" Screamed another.

"Nowhere!" A farmer in the front belted out

"Yes! They were nowhere!" Jordan bellowed. "And to add to that McAllan and his looters have claimed our practices and traditions barbarous! They've passed laws that they had no right to even consider!" His voice finally went down. "I've always been a Confederacy man through and through, but these slights cannot be borne. To protect the intent of Then Ironwill we must move against his words. We gave him that most noble of names because his will was of iron. Iron does not bend to the touch of bureaucrats and snakes! Iron breaks!" He received a cheer and some nods of heads. "We are iron formed in our founder's image! We have tried to reason with those who would see our liberties broken. When the hand of reason and diplomacy is scorned, that hand must become a fist and reach towards the sword!"

A cheer rose greater than any of the ones before.

"Down with McAllan!"

"Give us independence!"

"We will show those Northerners what we are made of!" He lowered his voice. "I have a son who has pledged to fight their tyranny. I have a wife who will cry to see him go, and hate me for not stopping him." His voice rose again like the thump of a battle drum. "And yet I am proud of him for standing up for what he knows in his heart to be righteous! I will see him become the man I've always believed he was capable of being! This is the only thing that remains to us after McAllan, and his pack have abused our people. The only thing that remains to us is to stand up and as a unified people and raise arms at those who would see us in chains!" He walked off the stage and found his seat looking upon the crowd with grim purpose challenging anyone to disagree with him. Conversation resumed around the room, all talking about what they had heard.

"That was a good speech." Seiford said in my ear. "Worst still, he meant every word."

"I bet he spent weeks on it. We should have written one down." I whispered back to the monk. I didn't know how to top that.

"Well, I guess that's my cue." Andrew said and stood up and walked to the middle of the room and another hush fell over. They all knew Andrew and respected him. My brother was probably the most decorated hero of them all. He held up a hand that silenced any lingering conversations. "My name is Andrew Belson." He said and looked around the room. "I was a lieutenant in the Huego conflict and a captain in the Puena wars." He reached into his pocket and pulled out a medal made of iron with a face in the middle. "For my actions in the latter, I received the Ironwill circle. Our highest honor." He put the medal back into his pocket. "I also knew your kin who have fallen. Everything Mr. Jeffery said was true. They died gallantly. Mr. Jeffery himself is far too humble to admit it, but he deserves this medal as much as me. The man is a hero." Andrew looked at the ground and sighed as if he were about to perform a painful labor, then looked back to the crowd. "But for every man who fell valiantly in the field of battle, there were two who died of infection, dysentery, or by snake bite. These men did not go quietly and bravely. They died screaming in pain, pissing and shitting themselves. I will not name them now because I have sworn not to." Andrew didn't shout like Jordan did. His was a quiet whisper that somehow made itself heard over the entire crowd. "My family has paid a high price for this nation, and I'd ask you to hear my piece now on that account."

A murmuring agreement spread out through the crowd.

"The Belsons are a noble people!"

"Andrew is an honorable man!"

"I am as my father raised me to be, and my father cautioned me on his deathbed against senseless violence." He sighed. "I won't say there isn't reason for unrest. There is, but we need to ask ourselves if it's worth it."

"Of course it is!" One man screamed

"They can't treat us this way!" Another chimed in

"You're right they shouldn't, but who really wants this war." He looked out at the crowd, his voice rising. "Coleson and his like started that embargo, and who has suffered from it?" He gestured to the people. "The same ones who suffered from the wars. Good people only trying to get what's right in this world. If war comes, do you think those dandies who have done so much to herald it will fight?"

"They're craven!"

"Can't be trusted!"

I was starting to think it was the same two men screaming swayed back and forth or simply wanting to be included.

Andrew demanded my attention again before I could do more investigating. "Aye, my family is an aristocrat one. However, my father taught me that our station was a responsibility, not a privilege, and I stand more with you than with them. It's a shame they don't all view it that way, but if war comes, it'll be us and ours who'll die in it. The aristocrats won't see the horrors, only the profits."

Andrew sighed again. "I have the nightmares you know. Everyone who's fought knows of what I speak. There are nights I wake up covered in sweat, and I see my wife cowering in the corner for fear of me. She's too good a woman to leave though. I'm sorry that she must bear that. I wish she didn't have to, but she does it well." He shook his head in anger. "My wife, my children, my trusted servants, these are the real casualties of the last war." His voice rose again. "Who will be the casualties of the next one?" He paused to collect himself. "They want to see the Old Religion burned away from this land. I don't like the Priests. I doubt there's a man here who does. They've made us prosperous though, and for that reason, the good outweighs the bad."

Andrew let the words sit for a moment before continuing. "We can show the politicians this. Whenever one man chooses to pass judgment on something he does not understand it is wrong. So let us show them. Let us make them understand." My brother looked around the room imploring everyone to listen to him. "It's worth trying because of the alternative. We go to our weapons because we think that as the only thing we can do. I'm here to tell you it's not. If we decide to go to war, I'll fight at your side, but this war won't be like the last ones. It'll be bloodier. Even if everything goes our way and it won't, of that you can be sure. Hundreds of thousands will die and not just on our side. Northerners who have never done wrong by us will be sent to die on our bayonets, and Southern men will die right there with them. I can't be sure what the outcome will be, but whatever it is those of you who come home will wonder why we ever went to war at the start."

Andrew began to hone in on his point, and everyone leaned in to listen closer. "If there's even a chance at another way, we need to take it." He looked up at everyone with conviction. "If you men go to war, I'll be there with you. I am proud to have fought at your side and would do so again if need be. I'd ask you though, to think what you'll be spilling your blood for." He gestured towards Jordan. "Is it for freedom and justice for the fallen, or will it be because Coleson and his pets tricked us into it. I'd like you to consider that before we draw our blades because baring steal is so much easier than putting it away. We have nothing left to prove to anyone north or south, except that we have the wisdom to consider peace."

Andrew walked back to his seat. There wasn't the clamor that accompanied Jordan Jeffery or any other call for righteous battle. It was the silence of men quietly contemplating what they were about to do.

Another man stood up he was young and obviously a plantation owner or at least the son of one. He walked into the center of the room with the cold indifference and pride that only comes from being born handsome and rich. He stood silent for some time. "My name is Nathaniel Hammond of the Hammond Plantation. One of the oldest in this fine land." He stopped looking around the room waiting for the recognition he believed he deserved because his family had gotten there first. My father had always believed that one should live his life knowing that a man's worth came from the first name not the last. The first existed to honor the last, not the other way around. Clearly, this young man thought differently. "I have heard Andrew Belson talk about the character of our fine leader Coleson." He said leveling a glare towards the party. "Coleson is a patriot and a hero. Your failure to see this calls into question your reason and devotion to the South. Your father would cringe to hear you say such filth."

Andrew stood up angrily at that. "I bled my devotion from Little Timber to Sentua boy!" He said the last word as a curse. "And my father taught me how to reason child, perhaps yours should have done the same."

The youngster smirked at having elicited such a reaction from my characteristically stoic brother. "Yes, you did bleed your devotion there. I wonder if you bled it all away. War makes some men heroes, others it renders more cowardly than ever."

"You'll bleed more than your devotion if you call me a coward again." Andrew was shaking with fury, and I saw his hand move towards the revolver at his side. I considered stopping him, then saw Nathaniel's smirk and decided against it.

"Hold! Both of you damnit!" Said the man sitting at the front of the room, which typically housed the mayor of whatever town hosted the debate. He was old but well dressed. His hair was greying, and he had the look of someone who had achieved complete contentment out of life.

"Who's that?" I whispered to George.

"That's Mayor Hawke.". George whispered back. "He's a decent sort but a bit stuffy."

"I haven't threatened anything." Nathaniel said calmly.

"Except for decency!" Andrew screamed back.

"You're right, you haven't," The mayor said trying to placate everyone, "but you've put Mr. Belson in a position where he had to threaten you."

"It's not my fault he can't handle the truth." Hammond was still wearing that stupid smirk.

"I'll eat a bullet if what you say is true, boy!" Andrew screamed back.

"Perhaps you should, it'd be one less craven in the Confederacy." He looked around the room. "After all it was a Northerner who gave you that little medal."

"Boy, I swear-" Andrew started.

"Hold your tongue Nathaniel!" This time it was Jordan who spoke up. "Me and *Captain* Belson may not agree on this subject." He put a special emphasis on the captain. "But he's a good man, and I'll have words with anyone who calls him otherwise!" He calmed down a bit and straightened his coat. "I watched him lead a charge on an enemy that would make you piss yourself if you saw a portrait of them. Trust when I say that if it comes to a duel, it won't end well for you."

"I don't take orders from farmers no better than serfs." Hammond spat out the words. The idea that a man so below his own position should insult him was enough to knock the smirk off his face. It was replaced instead with a look of contempt

"Boy, I'll cut your balls off!" Jordan drew his weapon, and the look of terror on the boy's face made me chuckle, but the draw was a bit to slow for my taste. I assumed the man was left handed. "I lost my good fucking arm for the right to speak at this council! What did you do?" He screamed. I shrugged at that. I was right which hand he liked to draw with. "You sat in your diapers and harassed poor serving girls, is what you've done!"

"Put your damn weapon away!" The mayor screamed, but Jordan kept his gun leveled at Nathaniel. "You all had your chance to speak let the boy have his." Nathaniel might have raged against being called a boy if it hadn't had the desired effect of getting the one-armed man to holster his weapon.

"Thank you, mayor." The boy said resuming his smirk.

"Don't thank me, child. I have half a mind to let either of them blow your head off right now." The mayor was clearly as angry as Jordan and my brother, but his position prevented him from letting it loose. "I served right there with them. I know their worth," he leveled a finger at Nathaniel, "and I'm pretty sure I know yours as well." Mayor Hawke took a moment to collect himself. "I just wouldn't want to see a good man hung over a spoiled prick." He paused looking around the room. "As mayor, I have to tell you, everyone here has the right to speak freely. You can read a damned cookbook on the stage if you want, but as a man, I tell you not to defame two war heroes in the presence of the men they saved."

"Noted." Nathaniel said coldly, but without the smirk. Andrew and Jordan sat down at that, but neither was quite happy. "I'm simply cautioning the people here against accepting political advice just because a man has shown aptitude in war."

"A fair point." Mayor Hawke admitted back to his impartial self. "Sacrifice should be important though."

"And who measures sacrifice?" Nathaniel asked the crowd. "My family came here and helped build this nation with sweat and blood." I guessed the indebted servants did most of the sweating and bleeding, but I held my peace. "That prosperity is under attack. The Northerners want to see us brought low." He looked around the room, the boy was a good orator, I had to admit. "We have our way of doing things, and it works. The Capitol has tried to pass worker reforms despite that it is our right to discipline those who's passage we paid for. After all these men are not slaves, despite how Northern smut has portrayed them, they can leave our plantations and find work elsewhere if they so choose." *So long as their debt is paid, and you don't have your thugs lynch them.* I thought. "They don't because they are happy with us." Happy was probably a stretch. I had an idea of how Nathaniel treated his people. "The idea of slavery in the Confederacy is laughable. They've suggested peaceful solutions with the Huego and Puena!" He shouted. "They are savages! There can be no peaceful solutions with savages!"

"The lad's got a point." One man admitted.

"I can see where he comes from." Another piped.

"And most importantly they've threatened our most sacred of customs. Our worship of the Old Religion!" Nathaniel went on

"Aye!"

"It's our right!"

"The way our government works is through majority rule." Nathaniel continued. "The simple fact is that now the North has the majority. They reproduce and head west as fast as our crops can grow to feed them." He paused for effect. "They can vote for whatever they see fit, and we cannot stop them by peaceful means."

"Here, here."

"War is our only option."

The crowd was turning in his favor. I could see too many men nodding in agreement. "You are right our only option is violence. Any man who cannot see this is either a fool or craven."

The boy looked as if he were wrapping up, so I decided it was my turn. "Are you calling me a coward?" I said as I stood up.

"What?" The boy said with disdain and then looked at who had spoken. He saw the black clothes marked by the Tree of Faith, the scars that littered my face, and then most importantly to the tattoos on my right arm. People had heard I was home, but seeing the greatest hero in living memory was different than hearing about it.

"I don't want a war. So according to you that makes me a fool or craven." I walked to the staircase between the rows of chairs. "I speak seven languages, and once beat Viverent in a game of trabus." I walked down the steps slowly. "I'd say that disqualifies me from being a fool, so that leaves craven."

"You're..." The boy started in disbelief.

"I'm Thomas Belson." I said still walking down the stairs, taking my time. Constables do not hurry. "I turned the Rose Petal thrown to ash. I held the city of Dunsbrook with one hundred and fifty men. I rode into the Principality of Fieldsbrough with not but my horse and wits and overthrew their king. I broke Thaniel over my knee, and I stand before you today." I finally reached the floor and headed towards Nathaniel. "They've written songs about me in every language that exist. To say my name is considered a prayer in some cultures, a curse in others. Kings have run from their castles when they hear a rumor that I'm coming for them." I stood toe to toe with the boy. Our faces were a hands width away. "So I'm asking you now. Do you think I'm a coward?"

"I-Well I-" The boy was stuttering as if he had suddenly been confronted by his worst fear.

"Spit it out, boy!" I bellowed.

"You haven't been in this country for fifteen years." He said regaining some of his demeanor, but he kept glancing down at the tattoos on my arm, no doubt wondering what magic they held at bay.

"Stop looking down there. If I choose to kill you, it won't be with my fucking tattoos." I said levelly but loud enough for the whole room to hear. "You were saying something about me not having been round these parts in a while."

"I-I-"

"You what?" I shouted again. "Spit it out, or I'll kill you out of sheer boredom." The mayor stood, but after an angry glare from me he thought better of it and sat back down.

"What do you know of the South? What right do you have to speak here?" The boy said but without his former condescension. "I come from a lineage longer than-"

"Longer than what?" I spit out. "I've ended lines that were old when Imor was a shepherd outpost." I looked around the room and found the crowd looking at me horrified. "If we can't accept an opinion because a man's a war hero, then we shouldn't accept one because your family has managed to pop out a brat with a cock every generation." I gave the boy a wry smile. "Or at least what passes for a cock since I've been gone." My look turned from biting sarcasm to biting rage. "Sit down boy or your line may not last much longer." Ayn-Tuk had cautioned me against threats, but I was still Belson the Blessed.

He hurried to his seat quickly without the strut he'd used to leave it.

"He has a point Mr. Belson. What right do you have to advise a land you haven't been to in fifteen years?" Jordan Jeffery spoke up. From his voice, I could tell the man had respect for me, but Jordan was proud and would not be cowed the same way the boy had been. "I respect your family, and I know your stories, but this is a place for the present."

"It is a fair point, Mr. Jeffery." I said circling the stage. "I haven't been here long, but I remember what it was when I left. I remember my honorable father's hopes for this country. I don't believe this is it." I looked around the room trying to be the Constable I was. "As for why my opinion should merit anything, this is a council on war, a subject I am well versed in."

Jordan Jeffery nodded his head. "Then we would appreciate what you have to say."

"Thank you, sir." I nodded in respect to the man. "You all want to go to war with the North for your independence."

"That's right!"

"Freedom from McAllan!"

"And how do you think you'll win it?" I said levelly. That caught everyone off guard.

One man stood up. "With Southern bravery!"

Another followed him. "We've got Fennis!"

"They have industry and numbers." I said cooly, and both men sat down. "How many cannons can Southern bravery produce? Will Southern bravery raise a fleet of warships for you to break the blockade they'll set?" I paused letting it sink in. "I don't think it will."

"Fennis will find a way. He's never been beaten." One man in the back said, but I could hear the doubt in his voice.

"Thaniel had never been beaten, until someone did." I looked around the room. "And he had more cannons and men than you do now." I paused. "I know what you're all thinking. That the Old Religion will help you." I pointed to my brother. "When I first returned from Thyro, I spoke with Andrew about the Priests. He told me that they were only used for growing good crops and other pursuits, that can only be called beneficial to your people." I paused and shook my head. "If it comes to war you'll plan on releasing those Demons they talk to all over the Confederacy. That's a door that doesn't close once it's opened. You'll use them for more and more evil things, and those Priests will twist your morality to abide by their every depraved will."

"The Old Religion is our right." One man shouted. "It exists to serve us!"

"Is that what you think? It might be your right to worship the Old Religion, but it isn't your will. I can promise you that. The New Church teaches us that a man must trust in the Three Virtues given to us by the Three Gods. Honor, Wisdom, and Love." I counted them all off on my fingers. "Trust in the will the Three gave us and let the Three Virtues guide that will. The Demons have their own will, and it is not guided by you no matter how much you'd like to think otherwise."

"So you'd have us give up our long-held customs for your paranoia?" Jordan spoke up.

"It's not paranoia. I've seen it. I know," I looked Jordan in the eyes then turned to the crowd, "but no, I won't ask that because I know it seems unreasonable. This is a council on whether or not you should go to war, and the first question you must ask is can you win it." I sighed to myself. "You can't without the help from Demons. You know what those Priests do in the privacy of their temples. You know how they become what they are. You've all heard the rumors. Even if you won't admit to yourself they're true. I'm here to tell you they are. If you unleash them against your fellow man, then when you return home from war this won't be the place you remember even if you win…" I trailed off. "Especially if you win." I massaged my burning tattoos absentmindedly. "They'll twist it and corrupt it worse than you can ever imagine."

"We wouldn't let it!" A man shouted across the room.

"It'll happen whether you let it or not!" I addressed the speaker directly then turned to the rest of the crowd. "In Kran, a Priest came to their king and grew a throne of roses so beautiful the ruler couldn't help but agree to let them practice in his country. They grew crops bigger than they'd ever been before, prevented plague from spreading in their land, even stopped natural disasters from landing on decent men." I paused. "Before long one of his successors started wondering if he could use the power to protect his people and it worked, at first." I paused again.

"Fifty years later, a leader named Thaniel came to power. He was a good man from humble beginnings, who just wanted to make the world better for those he loved. The Demons corrupted him, and when we finally triumphed, more than a million men had died, I burned that throne because it was created through evil means. That is where you'll be leading your people if you continue on your path. That is the legacy you'll leave for your children, ash and death." I let them see the fear I held. "Besides your working under the impression that the Old Religion will bring you victory. The Church will send Constables here, and I've taught them quite a bit about killing Priests."

Ayn-Tuk had told me not to lie, but that was about as close as I came. It was true more Priests were killed these days than before, but that was mostly because I slew all the dragons in my crusade. The other men with the tattoo arm were mostly squashing lizards, and I wasn't sure I could do what I had.

"You're saying we can't win this war." The mayor asked

"Maybe you can." I answered solemnly. "General Fennis is as good as they come." I sighed. "But you'll be fighting for all the wrong reasons, for a place that doesn't exist anymore." I put a hand on my six-shooter. "If there's one thing I know, it's that victory isn't always worth what you pay for it."

A hush fell over the crowd, and I was foolish enough to think it was my words that had caused it. Then I felt my arm burn white hot. I looked up and saw why everyone in the room was too scared to speak. Standing there in his blood colored robe, surrounded by his little children in white was a Priest. There was something different about this one then the clerics I'd met in Thyro. I could sense his power. I was sure I'd met worse, but I couldn't remember when. This Priest was dangerous.

"It was a fine speech, Mr. Belson." His handsome mouth moved, but the voice seemed to come from everywhere and nowhere. It was smooth and sonorous as any singer I'd ever heard. It felt like the sea breaking against old stone slowly eroding it to nothing. "It's a shame none of it is true."

"Every word of it is true." I snarled back at him.

"Every word is in it of itself is true by nature." The Priest sauntered to the center, and the children in white followed closely as if moved by forces beyond into perfect unison. I knew that they in fact where. "Words like is, was, or war are completely neutral, but when you string them together and spoken by a man such as yourself, then they become falsehoods. Words meanings and verity are affected by the men who use them." The Priest reached the center and looked around the room. "Such can be said of the Old Religion."

I strode towards the Priest, and the two white-clad boys stepped together to block my path. I unceremoniously pushed them aside to the collective gasp of the crowd. No one dared touch anything associated with the Old Religion. "So your powers are neutral then?" I was standing a foot away from the cleric's face. "Then why don't you tell these people how you came by these children?"

"Why they're volunteers." He said not shrinking away from the challenge. "The Old Religion takes in many orphans and outcasts." He looked me up and down "Not unlike the New Church."

"Orphans made by you." I growled.

"It's quite humorous you would speak of the welfare of children after what you did to them in Kran." He paused letting the words wash over the crowd. "Or would you name me a liar for that."

"I would say you have the truth of it," I said not looking around to the collective gasp, "and on that day I learned what high ideals could do to a man. On that day I learned the costs of war."

"So what your saying is that you and all your immense power can be used either for good or evil?" The Priest walked around me, and the white-clad children followed in unison except for the one closet to me who pointedly stayed an arms distance away. He addressed the crowd next. "Truly the same can be said of any great power that it has the capacity for good and evil." The Priest paused at that. "To those of you who may not know my name, I am Bishop Bellefellow." Everyone in the room was uncomfortable at the mention of it. They knew his reputation and unlike the title Belson the Blessed that had seemed far away, his had been formed in front of their very eyes.

Bellefellow went on. "I will be the first to admit that my people have not always been just and good. Great horrors have been wrought through the use of our powers. However did the first steel furnace not explode, injuring its workers? Did the first locomotive not slip from its tracks? Did we not learn from these mistakes?" He paused again letting his words sink in fully. "Have they not catapulted us to success? Can we not then apply that my humble order? Even though it is called the Old Religion, we are not so stuck in our ways we cannot learn." His words had the feeling of a fine orchestra that was drawing to a close. "We have learned, despite what the Northerners would have you think, and the only way we can continue to learn is to escape their tyranny!" There it was the final crashing cords and the applause of the audience. They were being swayed, and Bellefellow knew it. "What do you have to say to that Mr. Belson?" He said turning a smile my way. It was so mocking I almost shot him dead right there. I realized though that most of my anger stemmed from the fact that I didn't have any argument other than the Old Religion was wrong, and these men hadn't seen enough to be convinced of that yet.

I stood there, thinking furiously. I hadn't felt that helpless since I left God's Rest.

"Why do you keep saying north and south like they're different countries and not just different directions?" I recognized that voice. It was Seiford.

Everyone looked back to see the black-clad monk. Even Bellefellow seemed a bit shocked before he composed himself. "And by what right do you speak at this council?" He said the voice turning from sonorous to roaring anger.

Seiford to his credit didn't back down or even flinch. "By the right that I have ears to hear a contradiction and a mouth to ask about them." He said and got a small chuckle from the crowd.

"You're not from our glorious South!" Bellefellow spat out in disgust. "You're not even a citizen of the Confederacy!"

"Well, this decision affects the world, of which I do happen to be a citizen." Not even George who had been in the South for longer than some at the meeting had been alive spoke at these things. Seiford had always had the queerest sort of courage. He would scream like a baby taken from the tit when confronted with cannon fire, but he could stand in a room of strangers against popular opinion and state his case like a general staring into a battle line. "And geographically speaking I am in the South, so I have a stake in this argument I think."

"Why should we worry over the words of some lecherous monk from a religion most take as a metaphor anyway." Bellefellow shouted with a force that made every man in the audience cringe.

"Maybe you shouldn't." Seiford nodded in agreement. "Still if you won't worry about it, then what's the point of not letting me speak?" He looked to the mayor. "Legally speaking me and my partner are the same person. New Church laws and all. If he can speak," the monk pointed at me, "Then so can I."

"Well, I don't see how your words can hold any weight." The mayor said reluctantly to a hesitant agreement from the crowd and a sly smile from Bellefellow.

"I wouldn't want to stand on obscure laws alone." Despite the pressure against him, he slid to the stairway. "Still, I don't see a reason why my words can hurt you, and in contrast to a full civil war, the time for me to talk is a relatively insignificant thing."

Seiford started walking down the stairs to the podium. "Most people consider me a clever man. It seems to me this is the time for clever men to speak. Disregard my words if you want, but the only reason to not let me say them at all is that you're scared of what they'll mean." He looked around at the crowd. "Surely if you're brave enough to go to war, you won't be frightened by a lecherous monk of a religion most take as a metaphor anyway."

"Fine, then say your piece." The mayor grunted and this time received a few grumbled assents. The crowd may have seen Seiford as a foreigner, but he'd dared to speak against a full Priest of the Old Religion. Only I had shown that much bravery. They'd listen to him, even if it was only out of morbid curiosity.

"If you take the words of this filth over your own countrymen, then you don't deserve a country of your own." Bellefellow said with a rage I had rarely seen before. However, I noted something else. This Priest was afraid of the monk.

Seiford somehow managed to ignore it though. "Once again I ask why this strange distinction between north and south?" He let the words ring for a moment before they were answered.

"They don't understand our ways!" Someone shouted.

"They're yeller bastards!" Screamed another.

"My name is Seiford." He said to the crowd. "I've been with Thomas for over ten years now." He paused. "But before I took my vows, I was a noble from Anthanii."

"You're a damn leech is what you are!" Bellefellow said out of turn, but no one else dared silence a Priest of the Old Religion except for me, but I was too curious by Seiford to notice.

"Might be," the monk nodded, "but once, a century ago, we were countrymen." That brought a rumble from the crowd. "Then one day my people started saying things like, 'Those damn Westerners, they're not even from our side of the ocean.'" He paused. "And my forefathers mistreated you. Your rebellion then was just, but avoidable." The monk was greeted with a rumbling agreement. "Even in my homeland, there are divisions like that. I'm from Manrieth, a city in Anthanii I'm sure you've heard of it."

"Aye, who hasn't?" One man in the front chuckled. It was one of the biggest city in Thyro, and a good portion of the cotton and tobacco from the Confederacy went there.

"Well, whatever you've heard about it is all true." Seiford chuckled. "Especially about the women." That made the whole crowd laugh. "I swear there was one barmaid who could suck-"

"We're not here to talk about barmaids Brother Seiford." The mayor said stopping the inappropriate story.

"I want to hear about it!" A man in the front said in a half-joking manner.

"Aye, what could she suck?" Another screamed.

"Well, that's a story for another day." Seiford smiled longingly. "But if you want to hear what she could suck through a hose buy me a beer afterwards, and I'll tell you." He said giving the men who shouted a little wink. "Anyway, what you may not have heard is what folk on both sides of the river scream at each other. Those east of the Edwin call those west poshes and those west call the men on the other side degenerates." He shrugged his shoulders. "Well, that's not all they call each other, but I'd like to keep this civil." That brought another wave of laughter. "All my life I heard how one side of the river was better than the other." He looked around the room. "I heard it all the way up until Thaniel started his war."

Just like that, the monk's tone went from joking to deadly serious. "Then my brother from the west side went to fight together with those from the east. Then I read his letters about how brave his men were, whatever part of the river they called home." He surveyed the crowd they were all listening to him now. If there was one thing every man in the world understood, it was bravery. "And when my brother finally fell, it was one of those men we'd called degenerates who came to tell me about it. It was one of those 'scum' who held my mother while she cried. It was one of them who comforted a 'posh' boy who had just lost his hero."

I saw Seiford stifle a sob. "They fought together and died together on the same battlefield because they were countrymen. No one cared what part of the country they called home because they all called that country home." He let the weight of the words sink in. "It didn't matter then east or west. Maybe you can't see it now, but neither does north or south."

I tried not to let it show, but a tear rolled off me as well. If anyone saw it, they had the decency not to say anything. I still missed Seiford's brother dearly. He should have come out alive, and I should have died in that war.

"Anthanii is hardly the Confederacy." Bellefellow said to the crowd. "He knows nothing about our people!"

Seiford looked at him with something close to sympathy. "I do know something about your people." He pointed to me. "I had the privilege to ride beside one of your own for ten years. I know the greatness Confederacy men are capable of, which makes it all the worse that you should fight among yourselves." The crowd rumbled again in agreement this time more forcefully. "I know something else too." He held up a hand to the crowd. "I know whenever Thomas came across a man from your proud country he greeted them as a brother and was returned in kind." He lowered his voice then for effect. "Wherever in the Confederacy, they called home it didn't matter." He looked longingly at the crowd. "You can't see it now, but travel far from here and meet any man from the land of Then Ironwill. See if you don't call him brother too. I know if I were to see one of my countrymen that's what he would be to me, degenerate or posh."

"He's got a point!" I heard a man cry.

"How many of you have friends up north, or cousins, or even siblings?" He said more firmly. "That's who you'll be fighting."

"And should we let them strip us of our rights just because we like them more than a foreigner?" Bellefellow said. Despite his crimson robes and imposing voice, he'd been largely forgotten. "Our way of life is at stake."

"No," Seiford said firmly to the crowd as if that was just the question he'd been waiting for, "but neither should you quarrel with your brother while a thief ransacks your house." He was gaining momentum now. "And make no mistake that is what will happen. The powers of Thyro are the only ones who gain from this disunity." He beat his own chest. "They will exploit you unless you can stand together."

"Well, you and your pet Constable exploited Kran's Old Religion quite well." Bellefellow said sharply.

This time Seiford turned to face the Priest. "As they exploited the citizens of Kran right back." Then he turned back to the crowd. "This Old Religion is not your way of life despite what he would have you think." He gestured to the crowd. "Your forefathers came here to forge a better world with not but their own resourcefulness. While the rest of us hid behind our traditions, afraid of savages and untamed wilderness, the bravest stepped forward to form a new land. You didn't need the Priests then. You forged a new tomorrow. Whether you know it or not that is the very core of the New Church. The most sacred thing in this world is the sweat of a man's brow." Seiford cast a hand towards Bellefellow. "He has drawn comparisons of steel furnaces and railroad track. Those are the only things you should pay homage to. Those came from you, from your suffering and blood. Likewise, though the evilest thing in this world is taking that which you have not rightfully earned."

"Don't listen to his blasphemy!" Bellefellow shouted, but it was too late. They were listening.

"The only blasphemy is that you would allow the Demons below to infect your most holy of temples!" Seiford's voice rose to meet Bellefellow's shout, and somehow it did. "Your fields which you have planted. Your shops where you have created your masterpieces. This is where you pray! A gift from the Old Religion always holds a price, even if you choose not to acknowledge it! You are the greatest of men who made greatness where before there was nothing!"

"Aye!" Came a shout which was followed by more.

Seiford smiled at that "I won't preach my faith to those who do not want it. It's not our way to force a man to our way of thinking. To me the Three are more than a metaphor, but if that's all they are to you than so be it." He raised up a fist. "You're greatness, I would see you protect, and I will preach that greatness to you now! What would you sell that for? Not having to rotate your crops? The future is yours, not some red Priest's. To the passerby who sees this town in his quest for worthy things..." He paused letting the silence fill the room. "Here stands the worthiest of men!"

The crowd erupted in shouts some were angry and dispelling, but most were in hearty agreement.

"If we're so great alone than why should we be one country?" The mayor asked, but it was a question born of curiosity rather than rhetoric.

"No man is great alone, no city is great alone, and no country is great alone." This time Seiford received a questioning rumble. However, he had earned their respect with his words, so they were willing to let him finish. "Even Thomas Belson had his army. Your mistake is that you believe that the utopia you have sought will come after this war and be protected by giants. The utopia you wish for is here in your fields and your workshops. Your freedom is protected by the blacksmith's song and the farmer's sweat. Men like Coleson and even the great general Fennis would have you believe that they protect your freedom, but it is not something any state can promise you. It is something you must forge of your own. Men protect freedom not giants. What will you do with that freedom? Kill your own brothers?" Seiford paused. "The great pianist relies on those who craft the wood of his instruments, just as you rely on the North to provide your tools. They rely on your food and grown products as well. It does not make either of your achievements less, to say that you lean on other great men."

"So why is it a sin to rely on my Priests?" Bellefellow asked sharply, but he knew he had lost.

"Because your Demons are not men are they." Seiford didn't even turn to face him. "They will seek to take your suffering from you, but a man who cannot choose what it is he will suffer is not a man. He's a slave. Rely on your self. It is all you need. Trust me in this. No, to trust me on this would be akin to relying on their foul demons. Trust yourself in this. You know it in your heart to be true. And if you would refuse to hear me because I am foreign, then how much of a fool are you to trust those not even men?"

Seiford walked back to his seat with every eye in the room

watching him. I walked after him and whispered, "Wasn't that the same speech from Vuntland?"

"Eh, it was similar." Seiford whispered back.

"Except you were sober and weren't fucking half the rooms daughters." I said with a chuckle.

"Not yet I'm not." Seiford said.

"Now we vote on whether to go to war with McAllan." Said the mayor. "All in favor." A few scattered ayes, but even they were unsure. "All opposed." The room as a whole shouted nay even Jordan Jeffery raised his hand. "It's settled then Madisonville casts its vote against the war."

On the way to the meeting, the vote of one small town to abstain seemed an insignificant thing, but George had informed me that although Madisonville didn't have the population of Pentsville, it was seen as a certain cultural heart of the South. The larger cities were seen as more of a bastardization of Northern and Southern ways. Madisonville was always the first to cast its vote in matters such as this, and the rest of the South tended to follow.

"You'll regret this! All of you!" Bellefellow shouted angrily and turned around to storm out the room followed by his acolytes. Then turned and leveled a finger at Seiford. "But you will know the true meaning of this word I swear to you that." His anger was palpable in the room, and all flinched at it, looking down at their feet hoping to avoid his rage, even I caressed the pistol at my side in anticipation. All except Seiford that was.

"I already know the true meaning of the word." Seiford smiled back. "Only those who have had a case of Anthanii crabs really do." Everyone in the room looked at the monk in awe of his bravery. Bellefellow looked like he was about to call a demon to strike my friend down right there, but I smiled and gave a slow nod. If he hurt Seiford, I would hurt him. The Priest narrowed his eyes but said nothing and continued his furious walk out.

"That was foolish." I whispered.

"So was bedding the bitch that gave me those crabs." Seiford chuckled. "You don't have a monopoly on courage."

"I'm proud of you." I put a hand on my friend.

Seiford didn't respond to that, but I saw him smile. Then when he was sure Bellefellow was out of earshot spoke up again. "I told you nothing from a Demon can be as great as from Man. I'd rather let his

demons tear me apart than spend another night with that wench."
The whole crowd erupted in laughter, even the mayor cracked a
smile.

"Didn't you do it again?" I said with another chuckle.

"I was shaved the second time." Seiford said then stood up to
visibly scratch his crotch and looked around the room. "Besides I
didn't say it wasn't worth it!"

When the mayor had finally wiped the tears from his cheek, he
resumed his stoic appearance. "Motion to close."

"Seconded." Someone said, and the crowd funneled out of the
theatre shaped room.

When we got outside, everyone shook Seiford's hand promising
future drinks. He was always polite and charming saying to meet
him in the tavern later. They even gave Ayn-Tuk a measure of respect
because he rode with us.

The whole assembly walked to the inn and Andrew told the
Souren boy at the front that they needed to stable their horses. The
boy knew who Andrew was, but then he got a look at Ayn-Tuk.

"You're..." He paused staring at my shirtless friend. "Yes, sir!"
Then he headed out to do the work, but not before my brother
pressed a generous tip into his hands.

After that, we walked inside and were greeted by a loud cheer
from the men who'd got their first. Someone gestured to a table saved
for us with four beers already purchased on the crowd's behalf. We
sat down, and all the spectators gave us our privacy for a time, as
was the custom with important people.

I noticed that they'd left a drink for Ayn-Tuk conspicuously
absent. "Thank you all for not buying me a drink. I've been told I like
my beer a bit too much." I handed the mug to the black man. Then
I ordered one for myself. I knew he didn't drink, but he'd at least sip
on it to enhance my gesture.

"You were good in there." Andrew said to Seiford.

"Aye, now we know why all those women bed you." George said
raising his cup to the monk. "It's for your silver tongue."

"Well, it's for my tongue." Seiford said taking a drink. "However,
it has much more draws than the words that come out of it, I assure
you of that."

The group laughed at that. "I don't doubt it," Andrew said with
a smile. "but I'd rather not hear about the other qualities."

"Are you sure?" Seiford said over his drink. "Your wife might give me your home to thank me for my lessons."

"Maybe another time." My brother said with a chuckle then grew serious. "The question is do you believe what you said in there?"

"Seiford looked up at the man. "Do you know I might be the only man who actually understands the truth of this country." He smiled. "I always tell the truth. I just dress it up a bit first."

Andrew was unconvinced. "So those stories about my brother wrestling an Ice Troll to the ground in exchange for an early spring is true?"

"It didn't really happen if that's what you mean." Seiford said levelly. "He did, however, give a freezing man his last piece of firewood and found a warm refuge for us all. He did ride into a backwater village on his own unarmed and got the supplies we needed to survive." He looked over at me. "Without him, we would've died that winter, and that's a fact."

"But he didn't wrestle an ice troll." Andrew said skeptically.

"No, but the only way to make the world understand that he put his own body in danger to save his men is through that story. I could tell the world the facts and one day we will, but they'd never understand the truth of it." Seiford paused for another drink. "I believed every word of that speech same as I believe every word of those stories I tell about your brother."

"These men are smarter than you give them credit for." Andrew said. "They may not be from Anthanii, but they don't need to be told a tale every time you need to get a point across."

I saw the real issue then. Andrew was worried that Seiford thought less of his people.

Thankfully Seiford saw the same. "As an individual, people all over the world are cleverer than anyone gives them credit for. It's when they get together and start screaming angrily, they do something foolish like start a civil war." He paused. "Education, morals, breeding, always goes out the window when they think they're on the wrong side of popular opinion. To sway the individual, you need to sway the crowd with colorful stories. I didn't lie here, and I didn't even use my stories. I believe your people are destined for a greatness that not even you can possibly imagine. As a servant of the New Church, it is my most sacred duty to protect that. Me with my words, your brother with his guns."

Ayn-Tuk patted him on the back.

Andrew looked at my monk and chuckled. "I don't understand your Church. There are a thousand variations of the Old Religion. The Sourens have their tribal Dead Speaker, the Mong have their Sky talkers, even the Inte have some strange emperor worship, that no one understands." He took another sip of his beer. "Yours is the only one I know of that has gods that encourage no worship at all." He paused again. "I tried to find out more when my brother joined your ranks, but the only monks in the South got run out or keeled over pretty quick. What facts I have are mostly from what George says about it and some obscure books I've found written by people damning them as blasphemers. All I really know for sure is the story of that Nameless fellow and not much of it."

"The Old Priests are pretty successful in curbing the New Church here." George unhappily sipped his beer.

"They usually are in other places too." I said and spit at the ground.

Seiford considered this for a minute and figured out where to start. "Well, for one it's not Three gods. It's One God with Three Aspects." He listed them off on his fingers. "Honor, Wisdom, and Love. Those are the Three Gifts given to all people, black and white, men and women, even a successful seducer of women and a pillow biter." He gave me a scowl. "Which I am not despite your vicious rumors."

"I'll be sure to include that in our history." I said cocking an eyebrow.

Seiford continued on. "They all manifest in different ways though but are none the less equal. For instance, a man who loves other men, pillow biter as your brother so rudely calls me, can love another man as much as you love your wife. Even a man who never takes the time to get married, but prefers his work can be said to love that on the same level as either. A woman who is burned alive because she holds the 'heretical' belief that she deserves the rights of those blessed with impressive genitals between his legs or unimpressive," he gestured to me, "has the same honor as a warrior in the field. A man who some might consider dull, but lives a good life because he knows what is right, is as wise as a great philosopher."

A crowd had started to form around the group. They wanted to hear his lesson, and the monk obliged them. "However, it is only through using these three aspects together, that we act piously. A wise man can use his cunning to manipulate people against each other. An honorable man can find himself on the wrong side of things and never think twice about it. A loving man can seduce another's wife for the sake of his own twisted desires. It is only by the using of all three that we tread our path to righteousness, and those gifts become what they were meant to be, a blessing not a curse."

"That makes sense I suppose, though the powerful ones might take offense to that." Andrew said finishing his beer and signaling for another one.

"They often do." Seiford admitted. "That's why we employ Constables, but that's skipping a few years. Let's start at the beginning."

"You're the storyteller." Andrew gestured for him to continue.

"Most people don't know this, but the monks who worship the Three Aspects of God are as old as those blood colored fools. However the Imoran Empire took offense, many of their early wars were fought against those who believed as I did. Followers in that day were often fed to lions and killed for sport." Seiford looked down at his drink somberly. "Our early works were burned so we have no written record of how they started or who the first prophets are. After the desolation of Imor, some sects formed, but there was no real unity, and many warlords sought to reconquer that magic and did the same to us as their imperial counterparts." Seiford looked around and saw the crowd was interested.

"Finish the story." One man who was close said. "It's been a while since I've listened to one I haven't heard."

Seiford shrugged and kept on telling it. "About five hundred years ago, one of the more powerful kings marched on a village and ordered their obedience both politically and religiously. The leader of the town refused, and the king set his Priests to wreak havoc on the people and his soldiers to kill what was left. The leader organized a defense, but the Demons sent fires and plague to ravage the town. Besides that, the king's host was quite vast. Defeat and massacre were almost inevitable." Seiford paused not sure how to continue. "The leader saw the death and torment around him. Something inside him broke and what came out turned the tide of battle. We still don't understand it, but he did something. The New Church's best guess is that he reached within himself and found a fourth Gift wrapped inside the other three. The Demons were sent away, and the defenders of the town were filled with enough fire to beat the king back. Other feats similar have been recorded, but nothing like that. After, many who followed the Three came to him, and they organized the New Church under his writings which have become known as the Testament."

"So he used magic?" One man said skeptically.

"How is that different than what the Priests do?" Another chimed in.

It was Andrew who asked the most pointed question though. "How can you be sure he didn't call on Demons as well. Men will do contradictory things when they're threatened."

"That they do." Seiford said with a nod. "However Demons have great power, but they cannot lend a man strength as the story tells us he did, only take that away. It wasn't magic though. Magic comes from Demons. It was within his self, using the Three Gifts. It was a force of his will. My Church teaches that what comes from the individual is good. To trust in the Demons Below is akin to trusting a charismatic leader rather than your own morality. The leader of that town knew this and demanded his name never be recorded, and that all men know him as an individual following his own will. To this day we don't even know in which country it took place, but evidence points to western Kran. He met with others who knew this truth at the Summit of Nancia which we now call God's Rest. They went about spreading the word that what lies inside men is more powerful than any magic the Demons can work. It's just harder to use, but the only true way to greatness is through hardship. Still, the rulers who pledged their allegiance to the Old Religion fought them viciously, but for the first time in history the New Church was united, and the Priests divided so what the Imorans did, couldn't be repeated. Then they discovered the Constable."

"That's where my part comes in." I raised my cup to the crowd.

"That it does." Seiford raised his in answer. "The position has evolved since then, but their goal is the same. They fight for the freedom of man from mysticism."

"So if what comes from the individual is always good, then when a man beats his wife or murders it's because of the Demons." Andrew asked curiously.

Seiford answered the question deftly. "No, it's not, a man's action is his own responsibility and no one else's. If a king orders a soldier to kill an innocent its as much the soldier's fault as the king's, even if he would be killed for not doing it. It's its own type of slavery to blame your wrongdoings on another. The Church teaches us that we can never judge a man, no matter how great or evil, because men are infinitely complex and impossible to understand, and we can only judge what we truly understand. An action is different. All actions must be objectively viewed as good or evil, whatever the circumstances and punished or rewarded accordingly. However, a deed is not one-third right or four-fifths wrong. Righteousness is an absolute. It would be easy to attribute any wrongdoing to some force beyond our power, but it wouldn't be right. Sometimes a man follows another's evil action because he trusts their judgment over his own. Sometimes men delude themselves into thinking they're working for the greater good. Sometimes men can't even find what they know is good. Men er for a thousand reasons and no one is free from it, but the only true way to better yourself is to know that your actions are your own. The Three love us more than we know and gave us each the ability to know what is right and wrong so that we will never have to trust our judgment to others."

"So if the Three love us so much why didn't they make a world with easy women and enough beer for everyone to have a drink?" One man asked and received a chuckle.

Seiford laughed at that. "It would be nice. However, that is assuming that our suffering and the strength we use to overcome it are the means to an end. They are the end itself. If you pay for a woman or take her against her will, would you feel the same as if you had earned her love?" Seiford stopped and looked around to the grumbling agreement in the air. "In a world with no struggle, there is no triumph. How could a god who loves us rob a man of that."

"Aye." I heard some of the crowd mumble their agreement.

"Now who wants to hear about what that girl could suck through a hose." Seiford moved to the bar leaving me with George, Andrew, and Ayn-Tuk.

"That's a clever little monk isn't he." Andrew said over his drink.

"Too clever by half." I chuckled to myself. "But he means well, and I'm afraid I've become affectionate over the years."

George smiled. "I hope not too affectionate. I don't know how things are in Thyro, but here…" He let the sentence peter off with a laugh.

I smiled back. "Don't worry. I have no desire to catch what he's got."

I noticed the man Jordan Jeffery with his missing arm approach the table, but he wasn't looking at me. He was staring at Ayn-Tuk. I put a hand on my six-shooter, but the man didn't seem to have malice in him.

"Excuse me mister…" Jeffery started.

"Tuk." I answered.

"Mister Tuk." He started. "I ain't never met a man like you."

Ayn-Tuk nodded graciously. "I don't believe I've ever met a man like you either." Jeffery cocked an eyebrow up in confusion. "All men are of a different type mister Jeffery."

"I see." The one-armed man went on. "Well, regardless most people here ain't used to folk like you." He pulled his hat off. "Sometimes that can make us treat people worse than they deserve." He kept on. "But you seem like decent folk, and you keep good company. That means something to a man like me."

Ayn-Tuk stood and extended his arm. "You gave your arm for a cause, and you speak to what you believe in." The black man embraced Jeffery. "That means something to people like me."

Mister Jeffery nodded his thanks. "That's kind of you."

"Does it ever feel like that arms still grabbing for something." Ayn-Tuk nodded to the stump.

"Every bloody day I'm alive." Jeffery nodded.

"My people have a way of dealing with it that I could show you." The two walked off in unison, and after seeing a man they looked up to embrace the outsider, they all afforded Ayn-Tuk a new respect.

I turned back to Andrew and George. "The rest of the South was waiting for what we decided here today. They'll have their own debates and arguments, but where Madisonville goes, the rest seem to follow." I smiled self-assuredly. "Seems we stopped a war today." I took a long draught from my beer. "I rather like Thomas Belson, Forger of Peace."

George gave a mournful shake of his head. "They might have said the same after the first Iron Council presented terms to the Anthanii king." He leaned in a bit closer. "They might have said the same when Thaniel agreed not to go west of the Routland."

Andrew gave me a wistful look. "Thomas, I know how you see the world. You're a warrior through and through. I don't imagine there's been time in your life for much else." He took a deep breath. "You're thinking like this is a battle. Route the enemy off the field and claim your victory."

I cocked an eyebrow up. "As I recall, you're a military man as well." I leaned in closer. "A pretty good one too, and I reckon you wouldn't be if you didn't think like I did as well."

"Aye, and I am." My brother paused. "I know enough to be afraid of any war between this country, and I know how to fight in one as well."

Andrew took a moment before he went on. "Thing is, I've also been a farmer, a husband, a father. I can think in different terms." He said. "Peace isn't like a battle, a few hours of hell and what you want is in your hands. Peace is like tending your fields. It's a day in and day out struggle." He looked to George. "Yesterday's work might make tomorrow's a bit easier, but rest on your laurels long enough and you'll starve once winter comes."

"Try considering it like this." George cut in. "Let's say you need an army."

I shrugged. "I have found myself in need of an army quite a few times."

The tutor nodded. "Well, you need to train that army, so you spend three months drilling boys into soldiers." George nodded. "Once they're good enough, do you let them lounge about all day?"

"I see your point." I said. "You've still got to march them, exercise them, keep their discipline up." I sighed. "You got to flog the boy who fell asleep on watch even if he's a good lad. You've got to make them dig trenches, so it's second nature when they need to." It hit me that maybe I'd just started the work I might not be able to finish. "The only thing standing between a crack unit of warriors and a group of veterans drinking to how things were is a leader who keeps the fat off them."

Andrew nodded at my understanding. "When the Council voted to prohibit the training of Priests they took a bandage off and saw the festering of the wound." My brother said sagely. "We dealt with part of it, but we can't just put back on the linens. We need to face this."

Andrew took a draught of his beer before continuing. "The vote was one thing, but what happens when the Council sends men down to enforce those laws?" He said. "We'll be back in this place arguing the same thing." My brother shook his head. "The only difference is it'll be harder to stay their hand with Northern soldiers imposing laws the South didn't vote for. People here might start to think democracy is just the fifty-one percent telling the forty-nine how to live their lives." He paused. "Those fifty-one percent don't know much about our ways either. They'll begin to wonder how that's much different than the king we threw off." Andrew looked me in the eyes. "That wasn't what Then Ironwill had in mind when he wrote his pact, and honestly, if things keep going the way they are, people like Nathaniel might have a point."

George cut in there. "Worse still, what happens if they don't?"

I cocked an eyebrow up at the tutor.

The old man explained himself. "If they don't impose the edicts passed by a lawful legislative body. It weakens the law. This isn't like any of the nations in Thyro, bound together for eternity by blood and soil." He paused. "The Confederacy is a great experiment, there's so many different peoples here we can't even count them all."

Andrew chimed in. "It's a noble thing that a man with Anthanii blood is free same as a Rhondo. It makes us stronger than our forefathers ever dreamed. It's one of the reasons we've gone from a backwards outpost to a major player on the world stage in less than a century." My brother beamed with pride in his country. Our country, I supposed. "A thousand different peoples bringing with them the skills and virtues of their own land. Even the Souren is equal to the Thyran in name, though I'll be the first to admit we've got some work to do on that front."

George picked up where he left off. "Then Ironwill was wise with what he put in his pact. He was wise to keep us one country instead of a rabble of provinces." The tutor paused. "He founded a country that swore allegiance to a set of ideas. We are united in that no man needs to be afraid of another, no bureaucrat can tell us what to do with our body or property, and no king can regulate how we pray to our gods or even if we choose not to. In short, we are united by liberty not bound in loyalty to Ironwill's bloodline."

"This is all manner of patriotic speech," I waved my hand dismissively, "but what does it have to do with not enforcing a law prohibiting those bastard Priests from not reproducing?" However, I was starting to grasp what my tutor was fearful of.

Andrew responded. "What makes us strong also shows a spot of weakness. If a country is whole because they swear fealty to a king, then that country can stay whole even when its laws are oppressive and unenforceable." My brother paused. "When the set of ideas we pledge our allegiance to are not followed, then we're just a thousand different people with not much in common but that our forefathers swore by the same old document."

George finished it off. "One of our most sacred traditions is the legislature. If their laws no longer have any bearing upon us, then this country might start to think of itself as whole in name only." The tutor shrugged. "How long before people here believe they should drop the name? How many thousands would be willing to die over that bit of semantics?"

"I see your point." I waved for another beer. "Still that Then Ironwill document is near perfect. Seiford and I used it as a model when we designed the governments we helped create." I leaned back in my chair. "No one single man or body for that matter has the authority to tear this country apart. The Prime Governor, the Principle House, the House of Provinces, even the judiciary all sort each other out."

Andrew nodded at that. "Aye, it's a good way we've got going. It's hard to pass things into law." He sighed. "However, that was before everyone's mind was forced to turn to one problem first and the rest second. Once a representative might be for higher taxes, but against certain provincial privileges. Same goes for judges, senators, and Prime Governors too. Men had to reason with each other on the basis of ideas and compromise often as not." My brother paused. "Now everyone's forced to pick a side on one issue and stay on it."

"The Old Religion." I muttered.

"Aye, the Old Religion." Andrew nodded.

"We've always had parties, swinging this way and that." George said through his beer. "But people were Confederacy men before they were anti-taxation or pro-tariff. Now both sides reckon to be a decent Confederacy man, you've got to line up on their side of the fence all the way down."

Andrew knocked on the table. "There's two sides pulling at this country, those for and against the Old Religion." My brother looked solemn over his beer. "Sooner or later one of them will win in the courthouse, and I'm afraid the other won't abide by that." He paused. "Might be they'll try their luck on the battlefield."

George nodded. "It also seems to me both sides have stopped trying to find a mutually beneficial solution."

"What's that supposed to mean?" I asked.

George steeled himself for the answer. "They're both working within their power to hurt the other one. The South starts a war with the Puena without anyone's but their own's consent. The North helps settle a peace deal that the South doesn't think goes far enough. The South puts an embargo on grown goods to the North. The North puts a back-breaking tariff on all business going to Thyro, aiming at Southern cotton and tobacco." The old tutor couldn't have looked more serious if he was telling me I had a month to live. "Neither party is thinking about what's best for the country, just what hurts the men on the wrong side of the Capitol."

I realized that maybe George had it right to look so serious. A nation that hated their countrymen that much wasn't headed anywhere good. I would be the one to know. I'd stood between pogroms before and usually to mixed results.

"You sure its as bad as you say?" I asked. "I've talked to McAllan. Seems to me they're decent people on both sides with their eyes on better things."

"Aye, there are people on both sides who see what this is doing to the country our fathers died for." George went on. "You got folk like McAllan. He hates the Old Religion as much as anyone, but he loves this country first and won't see it torn apart." The tutor nodded. "There're people like your brother here who think the Old Religion has its benefits, but they're too much of patriots to secede over that issue."

Andrew tried to ignore the praise. "There're also men like Jordan Jeffery. He's as decent a man as I've ever known." My brother paused. "He sees that Ironwill's promise is actually better served with two countries instead of one." He shrugged. "Decent men driven onto a hard path."

I took a mournful drink. "I've never claimed to be decent, but I know the feeling."

"You are decent, Thomas, just in your own way." Andrew smiled up at me, then went back to explaining the way things were. "The trouble is that decent men are being listened to less and less." My brother looked towards George. "Wise old war heroes who fought for the Confederacy are being drowned out by the sort of warmongers in the army that can't stand a decent peace. Statesmen trying to guide this country to a better future are being outnumbered by politicians with their own agendas. Businessmen who want to build things up the right way have to fall in line with profiteers thinking on how many uniforms they can sell." Andrew paused. "More and more decency seems like a type of currency you use in the debate hall, and decency doesn't last long that way."

George chimed in. "They've stopped trying to figure a way to peace, now they're just looking for the advantage once the time comes." The tutor waved for another beer. "McAllan was a respected politician and the leader of the Northern party. He wanted an amicable way to deal with the Old Religion, but he wouldn't have put that legislation to the vote. He's lost control of his own party, and now he either looks like a turncoat or a partisan."

Andrew tapped his table anxiously. "What's more, the Southern Party holds a majority in the House of Provinces. They could have stopped that legislation from ever going through." My brother went on. "The Southerners chose to walk out in 'indignation' rather than vote against them. They acted like it was the moral thing to do, but I think both sides were wagering the time was right for arms."

I drained my beer ordered another one and finished that before I said any more. "So this peace work isn't even halfway over?"

"Not even halfway started." George said.

I nodded as the barmaid brought me a new cup. "There's one thing I think you two might be missing." I said.

"What's that?" Andrew cocked an eyebrow up.

"You talk about the Old Religion like it's a neutral thing." I paused. "It's not. I've fought it. I've seen friends struck down by it."

"It's brought us prosperity." Andrew leaned in closer to me.

"It brought Kran prosperity too." I leaned in to meet him. "You think men go mad following blood and tyranny. They don't." I breathed out deeply. "They go mad looking for gold and treasure, but it always winds up bloody in the end."

"It's the only thing that lets us compete in this market." Andrew said levelly. "With it, we're the capital of cotton, tobacco, and a dozen other cash crops. Without it, we're just backwoods hill and swamp people who can't keep costs down."

"It's a damn crutch is what it is!" I hissed at my brother. "You've been riding in a wagon so long you've forgotten how your legs work."

"Then throw us out and if we can't walk so be it?" Andrew hissed back. "You're strong, Thomas. The strongest man I've ever known, but you've never had to worry about the weak the way I have. You don't have to consider the people in the wagon who can't do what you can."

We stared at each other in silence for a moment. It was the first real argument we'd been in since my return. Partly, it was reassuring. You don't argue with someone you plan on spending a week or two with. You try and make it as blissful a time as you can. You only argue with someone you need to live with.

However, the other part was painful. We weren't having it out over some difference in politics. We were both changed men, and the world both of us saw was different. I could see his point. In his mind he was a shepherd, wanting the best for his flock. He respected the way others chose to live there lives, even if he didn't agree with it. He'd been forced to live next to his fellow man and had to find ways of doing that. He even saw that by allowing a necessary evil, he'd be saving his kinsmen some suffering. There was merit to that I couldn't deny.

I was a different creature. Yes, I could see through another man's eyes. I could see what he valued, what he thought was safe. I could take it from him. I could break him. I'd gotten my bloody way whenever I wanted it because people needed me, or they feared me. However, where Andrew had seen the good of humanity and tried to make it better, I'd seen the worst of it, and I usually had to make things worse still before anything halfway decent could come of it. I'd faced true horror, and at times become a horror myself.

Andrew saw that he was just living next to people he didn't wholly agree with, but to get along, he'd have to compromise. I saw the line between good and evil. You didn't compromise with evil. You fought it to the bloody end. I knew one inch given and they'd take everything you owned piece by piece.

It was a strange thing, my brother and I set so starkly against each other. We'd each waded into the others pool, but we would always be defined by our own waters. Could we ever really exist together? One brother ruled by hope the other by fear. Maybe the answer was no, but it wasn't an answer I liked.

On the other hand, he loved me, and I was starting to suspect I loved him as well. Perhaps, it wasn't in the uncomplicated way we had before, but in another sense, it meant more. Perhaps that was enough. Maybe we even needed each other, to make up for what both of us lacked. On our own, we were powerful men. Together, we might do the impossible. But love wasn't always enough. I'd loved people before, and it rarely had a decent ending.

George broke the tension. "Take the issue of the Old Religion out of it." He said. "Who decides what's good or evil? Who decides what another man can do?"

"The Three." I said without hesitation.

"And you serve the Three?" It was a beautiful singsong voice that said it. I turned and saw Rachel standing there. How had I missed her? She was beautiful in that red dress of hers, black hair dancing along her neck framing those emerald eyes. She was as perfect as I was flawed.

"Rachel?" I asked dumbly. "What are you-"

"Who decides what's right and wrong George?" She slid into the seat across from me. "That's an interesting question, with a very uninteresting answer." She smiled at me. "It's the strongest of course."

George nodded at her. "Who decides who the strongest is?"

Rachel snorted her ugly laugh that made me want her more. "That's the thing about being the strongest, it isn't something you debate." She stared right into me. "You just know."

"Thaniel was strong." I posited to her.

"Aye, he was at that," Rachel leaned closer to me, "but he wasn't the strongest now was he."

I didn't know what to say to that, so in a rare moment of clarity, I kept my peace.

"A true leader can choose the right path where others would fail." Rachel said. "He knows when to go to build his might to keep the peace. He can cut away those who would tear society back down to stone weapons and campfires." She paused letting her words ring through me. "Legislatures are all well and good for when the ship's in fine waters, but when the storm comes, a man has to step forward and take the rudder." Rachel leaned ever closer. "War, famine, chaos, a strong leader can make the hard choice of what to sacrifice."

I had regained some of my wits, so I responded in turn. "Have you ever seen war, famine, or chaos?" I asked, not expecting her to answer. "If you had-"

She cut me off. "I have seen those things and more besides." Rachel surprised me. "I know what it is to be under the yoke of weak men protected by nothing but tradition."

"Sometimes it's the strong man's place to step aside and let others find their own footing." I shot back at her.

"Maybe," she admitted, "but ground tilled by the weak is slippery. They need a hero to steady them." Rachel stared at me like George and Andrew weren't even there. "You've seen Anthanii and Thyro besides. You know the troubles that face that place." She paused. "How many could you alleviate if you didn't have to worry about tradition and the right way of doing things?"

"All of them." I whispered.

The girl pressed her advantage. "You remember the evils King John did after you won his war. How many would you have let stand if propriety hadn't sent you off."

"None of them." I whispered again as if for only myself to hear.

She smiled a deadly smile. "You're right, Thaniel was strong." She said. "He was strong, and many people put their hopes in him, but he wasn't the strongest." She kept at it. "The strongest broke him, and then went to play hero in feudal castles and primitive deserts."

"I don't think I want to talk about this anymore." I said.

"Of course not." She turned to Andrew and George for the first time since sitting down. "Would you mind giving us some privacy? I do so love speaking with Thomas."

In the past, they'd have leapt at the chance of setting me up with a girl like Rachel, but they were just as shaken at what she said as I was. They stood up slowly. Before they were gone, Andrew put his hand on my shoulder. "She's wrong you know." He said. "You're as good a man as I know for what you did," my brother paused for a moment, "and for the things you didn't do."

I nodded at him. "You to brother."

Finally, it was just Rachel and me. She was beautiful, that couldn't be denied. She was smart too. I was just as taken with her as I had been before. There was an edge to it, though. I wasn't chatting it up with some village girl I'd like to take a tumble with. She was an equal. She was someone I respected. The last woman like that had been ten years ago, but even Lady Gerate was different.

Abby, as I still called her in my quiet moments, cared about me deeper than I'd ever known at the time. She'd been the hand that stilled me. She wanted me to be the man she saw. In the end, she'd wanted a better life for me than a warrior, and I'd been too much a fool to take it.

Rachel and I were like mongoose and cobra. Talking with her was a duel as true as on the battlefield, and she saw into me. She saw the thing that I'd been fighting with since I was old enough to remember my own thoughts. My desire for greatness and the fear at what I could become. Ever since I'd become powerful enough to take the world in my hands, a voice inside of me had whispered, "do it." It was a dangerous voice.

Every friend I'd ever had, warned against that road. Seiford, Mother Vestia, even the Three themselves knew the evil inside of me. I could conquer! It wasn't just my vices that urged me on. How often had I looked at the world around me and found it corrupt? Probably since the day I left God's Rest. I often wondered how much better the world would be if it were me sitting that throne. I could right the wrongs of this world and for good.

I'd stayed my hand though, and for what? For a tired ideal of freedom? For an oath, I really only took half seriously? No, that wasn't it. I hadn't done it because the people I loved told me I shouldn't. I hadn't done it because the world deserved a better way. I hadn't done it because I'd seen the man who had, and I took his head for it.

Then I left. I left and the world filled with murky conspiracies. People trying to tear it all down. The smoldering embers I'd held in Thyro had become a raging fire. I started to wonder more and more if I was wrong. Should I have taken the scepter? Should I have ruled? I couldn't. It wasn't my place.

Yet, how many battles had I fought trying to protect people no one else cared about? Would I have even had to fight them at all if I had an army, a treasury, and empire? My whole life I'd been waging a war with myself, and here was this girl telling me I could put down my arms. It was dangerous, but I've always loved dangerous places.

"I don't want to talk about politics with you." I finally said.

Rachel smiled. "Because I'm a girl?" *No, not because you're a girl!* I screamed in my head. *Because you're tempting me down a road I thought closed! Because you're making too much damn sense! Because if I admit your right, then everything I've fought for is meaningless. All the sacrifices, all the dead friends could have been avoided! Because you aren't talking about politics, you're talking about everything that's ever made me, me! Because you shake me to my very core!*

"Aye, because you're a girl," I smiled back, "a pretty one at that. I wouldn't want to waste such an opportunity on politics." I took another drink and ordered her one as well. "Besides, I'm still courting you aren't I?"

"You are." She admitted wistfully. "I've found your attention somewhat divided, though."

"Well, you have all of it tonight." I eyed her up. "What are you doing here anyhow?"

She scoffed. "My elder brother was busy and was forced to send Alexander in his stead." Rachel sipped the wine I bought her. "He doesn't trust Alexander to move without my guidance."

"You have an elder brother?" I asked.

"Lesslie Gondua." She said matter-of-factly. "He's a colonel with the army these days."

"Ah." I drank some of my beer and felt it go to my head. "Are you sure Alexander takes your advice?" I remembered how he treated her when she spoke out of turn.

She scoffed at that. "Alexander is a misogynistic ass who never tires of telling me what a woman's place is." Rachel shrugged her shoulder. "He'll take my advice though, or I'll tell Lesslie about it."

I smiled. "And what side were you on?"

Rachel laughed at that. "Dear Constable, I thought you didn't want to discuss politics."

I shrugged. "Curiosity."

"I'm on the wait and see side, as it stands." She chuckled. "I'm also on the make sure my younger brother doesn't make an ass out of himself side."

"That's a losing battle." I toasted her. "Any man who thinks a woman's place is silent agreement is bound to make an ass of himself sooner or later."

She stared into me with those dark green eyes. "What do you think a woman's place is?" I asked.

"Not silent agreement." I ordered another beer.

We talked for some time after that. We talked until all, but the most dedicated drinkers had gone to bed. At first, the conversation was of places we'd been, and things we'd seen. Then she started asking me about art, and we talked about music, paintings, and books I fancied. I'd ever been a complicated man, and it shocked her a bit to hear how cultured I was. I liked to think it was a pleasant shock though.

"Well, it's getting late I suppose." She finally said.

"Are you staying here?" I asked.

"No, I have a room at Frederick's Inn." She held up a little key. "Would you mind walking me there?"

"I'd love to." And she took my arm and started strolling down towards her inn, passing up the drunks bent over in their seats.

"You know, you're different then I expected you to be." Rachel looked up at me as we walked.

"What'd you expect of me?" I stared down into her eyes. I'd seen so many different women. I was sure I'd seen prettier, but for the life of me, I couldn't remember when.

"Well, I remembered the boy set on fighting the whole world, set on proving he was the smartest, or the bravest, or the meanest." She smelled nice, not overpoweringly so, just nice. "Then I heard your stories, and it sounded like he succeeded. I expected a man like a raging fire." She paused. "Then I heard about you fighting for those who couldn't stand for themselves, and I thought here's a man like one of those bad knight's tales." She paused. "Then I met you."

"And what did you find?" I asked.

"A man too interesting and mysterious for any story to capture." She said it, and it sounded like a song.

"I did do some rather interesting and mysterious things." I tried to keep my voice level. Why was it so much harder saying clever things now than when she was farther away?

"I'll say." She set her hand on my six-shooter. "Is this what you killed Thaniel with?"

"No." She was looking down at the pistol, and I was looking down at her. "Thaniel deserved better than to be shot in the back like a common criminal." Three above she was pretty. "I let him die like a soldier.

"Oh." She said it like she wasn't really waiting on an answer. "I used to imagine that you'd come back to Kran and find me." She looked up at me then, and her eyes seemed to hit my gut worse than any musket thump to my belly ever had. "I used to imagine that you'd take me with you on your adventures."

"They weren't always so great you know." I said to her. I didn't know why I felt guilty for not coming for her. It was completely irrational I didn't even know she was there or who she was, really.

"I'm sure they weren't." She said holding my gaze. "But they were interesting and mysterious, and that was enough." I thought she looked a bit sad. "You never came though."

"I was rather busy at the time." I said trying to explain my absence despite myself. "Besides I wasn't very popular in Kran after the war ended." I looked down at the pistol remembering Thaniel's proud face.

"That's fine." She said looking up at me. "I didn't really want to be in Kran. All the adventuring to be had there ended with Thaniel."

"Where did you want to go?" I asked, thinking in my mind I'd take her there.

"Anywhere you went really." She sighed and looked back at the sword. "Anywhere we could go to see the real side of the world."

"You might not like the real side of the world if you saw it." I said and stood straight. "A lot of the things there can break a man."

She looked up at me, and the effect was much the same as the first time. The same as every time. We were at the inn she was staying at, but she didn't seem to want to leave, so I didn't mention it. "It didn't break you."

We were face to face then, inches away from each other. "You haven't known me nearly long enough to assume that."

"No, I haven't." She looked embarrassed. "But I've heard the stories, for fifteen years."

"Stories aren't always true." It was my turn to look embarrassed "Still if I'd have known you were waiting for me, I might have come."

"It's quite alright." She had an impish little smile on her. "Some other adventurers came to entertain me." Rachel whirled around. "I had more than a few rogues to keep thingS interesting." She listed all the things she'd done on her fingers as she spun around. "I gambled, drank, got into a few bar fights, learned to properly spit." She danced in the night air, and I wanted to follow her. "I've even seen a battle waged."

"That sounds like quite a bit of fun." I chuckled at how quickly she became a little girl again.

"It was a lot of fun actually." She nodded her head as the red dress swirled around her. "But it wasn't what I was looking for."

"What were you looking for?" I asked but tried not to sound too concerned.

"You." And she whirled into my arms. "But none of those adventures had you in them." She leaned her face to within an inch of mine. "Most of them are dead now, and I put a flower on their grave." She paused. "What kind of flower will they give you?"

I realized I was breathing too loud and stopped myself. Then I remembered the old Confederacy tradition.

"I'm not sure there's one for men like me." I finally shrugged.

"There aren't any men like you." Our lips were inches away. "There's only one Thomas Belson, and he's standing in front of me."

I kissed her deep and long. I kissed her like a sailor come up for air. I kissed her like all the pain I'd been carrying would wilt away if I just held her long enough. I don't know how long she had me, but I was hers.

Finally, she pulled away. "My dear Constable!" Rachel put her hand on my chest. "There's some fire in you yet."

"I suppose it's getting late." I looked up at the moon and found it was well past midnight. "Best to get to bed I suppose." I left to go, but she held me.

"Where were you planning on sleeping?" She smiled an absolutely devilish smile. "I didn't see you buy a room, and I'm afraid they're all booked up for the night."

"I brought a sleeping roll." I put on my best roguish hero face. "It does a man good to be out in the open air. Truth be told, I rather miss it."

"So you'll sleep on the hard ground?" Rachel pulled me close again.

"I was planning on bunking next to Shaggy Cow, she'll be looking for me." I gathered my coat about me.

"Well, if you think your horse can spend a night alone," she kissed me again, "my bed is awfully large."

"What about your brother?" I pulled her in closer.

"He's got his own room."

"He could hear us." I pulled her closer still.

"I'll be quiet." Rachel whispered in my ear.

"That's what you say..." I rolled my eyes.

"Oh, the conquering hero!" She swooned. "So what if he hears us! I have Thomas Belson as my protector."

"What about propriety?" I knew the answer to that one already.

"Fuck propriety!" And we were off.

Present Day

e made our way up the stairs. Our bodies never entirely our own. When I finally pushed through her door, I wasn't looking much at the room. She got undressed quicker than I'd have thought possible, and of all the castles and wonders I'd seen, her body would forever be seared in my mind. I wanted her as much as I'd wanted anything else, and I took her.

After it was all done, and after it was all done again because a girl like Rachel seemed to warrant more than once, we were laying together. Rachel had her head in my shoulders and was tracing the scars that crossed my body. "What's this one from?" She'd ask, and I'd respond a bullet from somewhere far away. I honestly got them confused most times, but I told the stories like Seiford would. Rachel liked that, and I didn't see a reason to disappoint the girl. Finally, she got to a scar just above my nether regions. "What happened here?"

"That one is actually from an arrow."

"People still use bows and arrows?" There was more than a bit of skepticism in her.

"Steppe Nomads do." I responded, looking at the girl. "They lace the ends with poison too. That wound laid me up for a week." I cringed at the memory of it. "I might have died if it weren't for Seiford's clever hands."

"Give Seiford my thanks then." Rachel said through a laugh. "They have many Steppe Nomads in Thyro do they?"

"No, they don't." I admitted.

"Ah." She kept tracing the scar. "After the Thaniel Wars, your story gets all kinds of muddled together."

"I suppose it does." I nodded. "I spent most of those fifteen years in Thyro, but I went to Souren for a bit and some of the Eastern continent." My hand was moving through her beautiful hair. "After the Thaniel Wars, they were too afraid to let me stay in all those huge nation states, so they sent me to the more remote parts of the world."

"I've got the gist, but where?" She asked.

"When I crushed Kran, I broke most of the hold the Old Religion had over Thyro," I said, "but there were lords and counts who still wanted to try their luck." I sighed. "Mostly out in the east where feudalism is still the law of the land, a bit in Rentarii too, the fractions country it is." I paused. "I spent most of my time helping this peasant revolt or that lord who was sympathetic to our cause. Seiford and I changed half the map around."

"Then where?" Her hands drifting further south where I was thankful I had no scars.

I remembered Sterling, the city still burned. "Then a mistake got made, so the powers that be decided I was too dangerous to have in Thyro at all." I kept stroking her hair. "They sent me to Souren and the far East after that."

"What was the Steppe like?" She looked up at me. "I've never met anyone from there."

"Thank the Three you haven't." I chuckled. "It was pretty much like you'd think it'd be." I smiled down at her. "The horses were excellent though. That's where I found Shaggy Cow."

"Star-crossed lovers that you are." She snorted. "It was dreadful then."

"Not all of it." I admitted. "A man can be a man out there." I smiled wistfully for those days. "Riding, hunting, and dancing, it was how we were always meant to live in some ways."

"So you liked it?" Rachel rolled her eyes.

"Not really." I grimaced. "The food was bad, the women were hairy, and those bastards are far too accurate with their bows for my taste."

"That doesn't sound fun." She made a face at me, and her hand touched something that definitely wasn't a scar.

"It's not," I said, "but I missed it when I was gone." It was the story of my life. Rushing through something, hurrying to the end, then wishing I could go back once it was over.

"So do they hurt?" She asked.

"Arrows?" I exclaimed. "Yes, they hurt quite a bit."

"No, I mean all of this." She gestured at the scars.

"Did you ever break a bone when you were a child?" I asked her.

Rachel thought for a minute. "I broke my arm when I was fourteen riding my horse." She sighed. "Nothing like this though."

"Well, does it ever hurt still?"

"Sometimes when it's cold or wet." She shrugged.

"That's the same principle." I chuckled. "Except it's all the time. Not just when it's cold or wet."

"But they're everywhere." She exclaimed.

"I know." I sighed. "Believe me I know."

"Poor Constable." She gave me a kiss and settled back into my shoulder. We were silent for a while after that, so long I almost fell asleep. "Would you do it again?" I could tell by the way she said it, that it was what she really wanted to ask, not my scars. I could also tell she wasn't talking about her or anything venial I could avoid or explain away with an impressive story.

"I usually try to avoid telling women things like this," I sighed, "but I suppose I ought to be honest about it."

She chuckled at that. "So I'm to believe I'm so different than all those girls in Thyro of which I'm sure there are many." She kept moving her hand under the blanket. "Really Thomas I'm not so naive to think you see me as special after a few weeks of courtship."

I turned to her. "All girls are special," I said then kissed her, "but it's not really that. You're not like those girls in the sense that we won't see each other after this." I paused. "I plan to be here for a while, and I intend to see you more, so I won't lie."

"I usually don't believe men when they promise not to lie to me." She kissed me back "But, oddly enough, I do now, so tell me the truth."

"What did you hear of the Thaniel wars?" I looked away from her and back at the ceiling. It was easier that way.

"I heard everything. Everyone talked about you, even without knowing where I was from." She had stopped moving her hand around me and had settled on a place over my heart. It was for the best. This wasn't pillow talk. "Those adventurers all had stories about you, the nobles told their own tales, and the peasants had their own version." She shrugged. "It's hard to know which ones to believe.

"Did you ever meet Viverent?" I asked.

"Yes, I did." Rachel said proudly. "Interesting fellow, that one."

"What did Viverent tell you?" I kept my eyes on the ceiling.

"Nothing at first but after a few drinks... Well, I can be persuasive."

"I'm sure you can." I laughed. "All those stories are true in their own sense, but Viverent usually tells what actually happened."

"He came off that way." She said with a sigh. "He told me the good and the bad. Usually, you only hear one or the other."

"There was good." I paused. "But there was bad as well." The girl deserved the truth. "Mostly it's just moments between so muddy you can't tell."

"It was war." Rachel said for the first time since we'd gotten to bed not sounding like she was talking to a childhood hero.

"Men use that excuse all the time, and usually, people who haven't been to war just accept it because to them it's just a story they can't understand." I paused again. "But it's not just a story it's real, and the mistakes we make affect real people." The words were hard to say. "The day I left here my father told me not to hide behind that excuse. He told me to remember I wasn't some story figure. He told me that why we did something doesn't matter to The Three, only that we did it." I wanted to believe those words, and part of me did. The truth though was that I hadn't always followed them.

"Leopold Belson was a good man." She said in my shoulder. "Even though he worshipped The Three down here, people still respected him, even if they didn't like him."

"He was a good man. The best I've ever known." I sighed. "But I didn't really understand it back then." I stopped trying to keep the memories away. "I didn't understand it until I marched into Kran, and set fire to that damn Rose Petal Throne." I couldn't stop the memories. "I didn't understand it until I did what I thought was necessary."

"The pillars… They were true? Not just propaganda?" She couldn't bring herself to say, so I said it for her.

"Aye, they were true." I couldn't really say it either, but I had to. "The men, the women, the children, all of it." I couldn't do anything but look up at the ceiling. "In my eyes, they were all corrupted by the Old Religion and beyond saving, but the way they screamed and begged in the end… Well, in the end, they didn't call for Demons to save them. They called for me to do it, and I just kept up the nailing." I wished there were stars instead of a blank ceiling. Stars helped on nights like those. "I rationalized it by saying that once a man's corrupted by Demons he'll never be freed of them, and I'd have to come back and fight the war again." Damn, I needed those stars now or at least a drink. "But they weren't men. They were women and children."

"You were probably right if that helps." The words didn't match the voice though. "I've heard about what the Old Religion did in Kran." She was trying to rationalize it, just like I had.

"I was probably right." I saw the face of one boy as he put him to the pillar. "I probably made the world a better place with those nails and pillars." I saw my fathers face too, which was even more painful. "But I made myself a worse person. I'll pay for those nails and pillars one way or the other, in this life or the next."

"How many worse things did Thaniel do in his time?" I could tell she was trying to make me feel better, but I'd been carrying those sins around for too long.

"Countless." I responded it was the first easy question she had asked me since the scars. "Don't try and convince me I wasn't a monster because in that moment I was." I tried to shake the figure of my father but I couldn't. "You can convince yourself if you want, but every argument you can use, I have a thousand times against myself. It even works sometimes," I stroked her hair. "In the end though I did what I did, and no clever rhetoric or philosophy can change that."

"If you had tried to explain it away, then you'd be as bad as Thaniel." She whispered into my shoulder. "Demons Below even I did. The fact that you didn't means you're not a monster."

"You're wrong. It's not because you're stupid or naive. It's because you're smart. You realize you can't imagine why I did it, so you're not going to demonize me for it." I didn't just feel lust for the girl, but respect. "You're wrong still. The fact that I did it makes me a monster. Thaniel thought he was doing the right thing right up until the point I ended it. Every evil man who ever lived thought he was doing right in his own way. The thing, the only thing, that can keep me from becoming one permanently is that I realize it, but that doesn't change what I did." I looked at her with the affection she deserved. "You're right I'm not a monster now because of that fact. I made a vow that day to never let the ends outweigh the means. I've broken that vow since. It's a hard one to keep in my line of work. Sometimes I can only see a thing that needs doing. Some days it's only Seiford that lets me know the difference between right and wrong. That monk usually keeps me on the straight and narrow. I've done my best to keep my vow. I think I'm not the same man who put those people to the pillars a decade ago, but I have been a monster, and you should know that if you choose to share your bed with me again. Those things will stay with me."

"Initially, I was thinking I'd like to spend a few more nights in your arms." She said. "You are quite the veteran you know." She gave me a look that said she wasn't talking about scars

"I aim to please." I mocked humility. "Mostly myself, but if the girl is too, just as well."

She gave me a playful slap on the arm. "Don't ruin it." She was smiling though, then she grew more serious. "But after this little talk, I think I'd like to be around for more than a few nights. At first, I thought you were just a novelty hero. The sort a girl can have for a night or two, but any longer is just living in a fantasy world. I figured I'd be cured after this, and I was right I'm done with the novelty hero."

"Most girls feel that way about me." I said wistfully.

"You're not some distant story though." Her face softened more. "You're just a man with his faults and triumphs, both greater than most men, but they're both still there. Your name holds more weight than anyone I've ever read about. The world needs a man like you, and you need a woman like me." She was an angel for saying that, even if she didn't mean it. Especially if she didn't mean it. "Still, in the end, you have your vices and your virtues. A girl can admire a man's virtues, but she can only truly love his vices, I think." She sat up and stroked my face. "That takes time though, and certainly more than one night."

"Good." I sat up. I was slowly realizing I'd been wrong. She wasn't just some clever girl who'd heard too many stories and read too many bad poems. She was... Well, I wasn't quite sure what she was, but I was willing to take the time to learn. "You're the sort of woman that a man likes to see more often, not less." I sat up and kissed her, my hands moving ever south.

"Not so fast!" She pulled away. "You've told me more than I expected to hear, but you still haven't answered my question."

"Would I do it all again?" I mused to myself. "I left a boy, not all to well-liked mind you, with a decent horse and the family pistol on my hip." I chuckled. "I lost the pistol in a card game, and the horse got shot." I looked her in the eye. This was the sort of thing I was proud to answer. "I returned with the most famous steed known to man, a legend as big as anyone's ever had, and four six-shooters."

"I only saw two?" She said curiously.

"It pays not to let them all show." I smiled wryly. "I'm the greatest hero wherever I go. That's not boasting I haven't boasted in a long time. I say it now because you warrant the truth. I did what no other man could have done, That's a fact. I made the world a better place where everyone else failed. The only ones who don't stop in awe when I say my name are the Inte, and who knows what they think." I paused. "Still to say I did it all for the betterment of man wouldn't be entirely a lie, but it also isn't the truth." I kissed her again. "And I'd be remiss to leave out that heroism comes with many benefits. Certainly, no girl like you would look my way if I'd stayed home. I got everything I was looking for and more. Fame, glory, and I proved to everyone who ever doubted me I was worth something and more. Most didn't think I'd survive the first year. Now they wonder if they'll survive meeting me."

"So you would do it again." She said sarcastically

"Not exactly." I smiled at her. "I left the wrong way and for all the wrong reasons, and because of that it was never really my decision to leave. I was tricked into it, by myself I'll grant you, but tricked all the same."

"So you wouldn't do it again." She sighed wistfully. "It's a wonder you won any battles at all with your indecisiveness."

"Once again not exactly. I left because I was angry at my brother for some reason that made no damn sense. I left because I thought it was the only way to make my father proud of me. I left because there was no chance of happiness here at fifteen." I stroked her face and decided it was a good face to stroke. "I don't know that I found happiness out there, at least not the way my brother has it, but I found something in my travels. Besides, I was good at war, and despite myself, I love it. I know that's an evil thing to say, but it's true."

I looked at Rachel again. By the Three, she was pretty. "It was what I was meant to do. I know that for a fact. I even came to believe in the reasons I was fighting for, but I was a child when I left. The man before you sees things differently." I turned my voice solemn. "At fifteen my only hope was to leave and a slim hope at that, I really only saw a glorious death when the Church came. I never expected to live through it, and I never thought of the beauty I'd see because of it."

I remembered the child I'd been. "There was a lot of horror across the ocean, and it changed me. However, there was some good too. It was like the minor chord that gives perspective to the major, the beauty." I looked at the tattoos on my arm. I hadn't liked them at the time, but they'd grown on me. "If I were fifteen years old again, I

would have done it without question, but if I could turn back time…
Well, I'd go back earlier."

I kept on. "I'd have known my brother didn't owe me what I thought he did. I'd have known my father was proud of me even without the glory. Most of all, I'd have known a man can have happiness wherever he is." I smiled again at her but softer this time. "I'd have realized there was horror and beauty everywhere, maybe not as dramatic, but drama is for plays." I kissed her for no better reason than because why not.

"I might have still gone, but I'd know what I was leaving behind. To a child, one mistake means the story's going to have a sad ending but it doesn't. The end is just where the storyteller decides is fitting. No one's story is just happy or sad, and if it is, I pity the person because it's just one note being played over and over again. I would have liked to know that."

"I don't know why I was so great. Sometimes I think its more curse than blessing. It makes everyone think you're the man to beat." I shook my head. "Like I said, I love war, but the men my challengers bring didn't have a choice in the matter. Every time someone marches an army at me, I feel something in myself rejoice. Then I look at the men I've killed, and something inside me asks how long until they just stop trying." I saw all the ghosts of my past.

"The dead would be better served if they did stop. That's the dangerous part of being great, and it's made more dangerous by the beast inside of me. I can't bemoan that now, though. I forged my reputation. It's no one's duty to carry but mine."

I stilled myself. "Still I may have handled greatness easier if I had realized these things. Then again maybe my hunger made me great. That hunger that's been with me all my life has served my cause well, but me less so. I've got a demon inside of me, and the whole world knows it. That demon's done a lot of good and evil. Is it worth it? Who can say?" I paused thoughtfully. "I don't have an answer for 'would I do it again?' All I can say is that I did what I did and nothing can change that. All I can really give you is that I know all these things now, and I hope I'm a better man for it. Is that good enough?"

"It is." She smiled and kissed me passionately. "You're wrong though."

"About what?" I thought I'd made quite a good case,

"You didn't have to be a hero for me to look at you." She stroked my shoulder. "I liked you ever since you fought that mule."

He laughed at that. "Even though I lost?" Thomas asked.

"Only because you lost." She gave a fake frown. "If you would have won it would have seemed like you were beating on a poor animal, not the heroism it was." She fixed on a scar below my right eye, the one the mule had given me. "I think this is my favorite of all your battle wounds. It's a shame you tried so hard to disguise it."

"It was other people who tried to disguise it." I said with a smile. "I would have just as soon left it lonely."

"Ha." she chuckled then moved on top of me. "There's just one question left to ask."

"Ask away." Thomas said looking at her. She was beautiful in her nakedness.

"When war comes to the Confederacy, which side will you stand with." She smiled at me seductively, but there was an edge to it.

"*If* war comes to this land, that'll be a hard decision for me." I frowned at her.

"It takes a hard man to make a hard decision." She said moving her hips on top of me.

"No hard decisions are for wise men." I leveled my voice. "I fight for those who can't defend themselves, but it's not my place to tell them what to do after the war's over. My church serves men, not some abstract creed."

She smiled at me like what I said was cute. "Sometimes people need a great man to push them in the right direction."

"No, they need great men to show them." I looked up at her. "They need great men to prove they can be good. They need to be inspired.

"And what happens when that fails?" She kissed my neck.

"We try again."

"That's a decent way," she stared down at me, "but if war comes, you may not be able to keep it."

"You want to know if I'll lead the Northern forces down to crush the rebels." I sat up on my elbows. "Or if I'll stand with my people to shake off their tyrants." I paused. "I thought we weren't talking about politics."

"A girl can't help but be curious." She purred at me.

"Aye, I suppose not." I sat back down in the bed. "I'd rather help them shake hands as friends, but if war comes, it ain't in me to stay away."

"I guess whatever side you pick will be the winner." Rachel eyed me up and down.

"Maybe, but I'm thinking this'll be a harder fight than either side is ready for." I looked at my pistols on the dresser. "You should know Rachel, I'm not the same man that beat Thaniel."

"What do you mean?" She sat back on my waist.

"I'm as clever as I ever was, maybe even a good deal more." I flexed the muscles on my arm. "I can't run quite as far as when I was a lad or move quite as quick, but I'm still one of the best fighters in the world." I paused. "Only a handful of men have ever beaten me once, and I got them all in the end." I thought on my years marching at the head of an army. "I haven't forgotten how to run a campaign or orchestrate a battle. As far as I know, I'm the best at it, and time has only honed my craft."

"So you're better than you ever were?" She gave me a queer look.

"I couldn't beat Thaniel again if that's what you're asking." I muttered out. "In the end, it wasn't my wits, or my weapon skill, or my strategy that won." I paused. "It was the things I sacrificed that I couldn't sacrifice again, the risks I took that I couldn't stomach now, even a bit of luck I wouldn't count on having twice in a lifetime." I shook my head. "This war is going to be harder than either side is counting on, and I wouldn't expect whoever's fighting to put their chips on me winning a few battles to end it quick."

She smiled down at me, hips firmly clasped around my waist. "I don't feel like talking anymore." I didn't either.

<hr />

I woke up to boots on a wood floor. My hand instinctively reached for the pistol at my dresser before I realized where I was. I let the weapon lie there. I figured I had to make a better attempt at being a civilian. Arming myself every time I heard people walking around an inn was something a Constable did in the field, not something a man did when he was trying to build a home.

Still, there was something strange about it. I counted at least three pairs of boots, but they were quiet. They were so quiet most wouldn't have noticed them. Maybe they were making their way home after a night of drinking, but they weren't walking like drunks.

What time is it? I wondered. There couldn't have been more than an hour or two before dawn. That was late, even for a drunkard. Still, I didn't grab my pistol. That's not the sort of thing a civilian does. I hadn't even put on my clothes.

It was suspicious, but I'd woken up to thousands of suspicious noises in my day, less than one in a hundred were any reason to disturb my sleep. Still, that one in a hundred could be my last if I wasn't wise to it. I wasn't going to arm myself, but it went against everything I knew to stay in bed.

I stood up and went to the door.

"Thomas, what are you doing?" Rachel wiped the sleep from her eyes. "Come back to bed."

I smiled at her. "Just a minute."

I heard the boots make their way up to our floor. They were muttering something I couldn't make out. It probably had some rational explanation, but I wanted to be sure. Finally, the muttering died down.

"It was nothing." I turned back to Rachel. "Just the wind."

I was wondering whether she'd be up for another go before the sun rose, then the door caved in.

I took the head of the first man that came through and slammed it against the doorframe. I heard his skull crack and knew he wouldn't be standing again.

The next man came at me with a tomahawk. I caught his arm in mine and pushed until I felt the bone snap and kicked him with his partner into the hall. I tossed him aside for later.

The last man attacked me with a long knife. I put it in his throat and watched as he bubbled his lifeblood away.

It was all over in less than a few seconds. They couldn't have known who they were attacking or they'd have brought more men. Maybe they had known and thought I'd lost my edge. Maybe they forgot that Belson the Blessed once made Thyro tremble. Why they made their mistake didn't matter anymore. They were dead men.

The assassin with the broken arm was moaning on the floor. He could wait for later. They were all Huego's. That explained the silence of their footfall. The killers weren't wearing their standard tribal dress and had instead opted for passable looking suits. However, the complexion of their faces and the braids in their hair spoke the truth.

I saw a note on the ground and read it. I read it once and then read it again to make sure I wasn't seeing things.

A head poked out of his room.

"Get the fuck back!" I roared at him, and he hurried to the safety of his bed. There weren't many men alive who'd disobey an order like that.

I felt the rage well up in me. It was always there, always smoldering deep in my belly. What I read on the note ignited it again. It was the fire I'd felt before Wuntsville. It was the heat I'd had at Sterling when their First Citizen thought he could mock *me!*

Sometimes men pushed themselves into a white-hot anger in the midst of battle. They'd shrug off fatal wounds and crush men's skulls in their hands. I'd always had a piece of that, but I'd never considered myself a berserker. My greatness was the ever moving mind between my ears. No matter how slim the odds were, there was a way to win, and I'd find it. Part of that was training, cunning, and skill, but without the last ingredient I'd just be a tattooed man with a talent for killing.

The last bit was drive, conviction. It was a drive born when the world doubted me as a pup. It was the conviction reignited when they wondered if the wolf's teeth had all fallen out. It was when the world forgot how dangerous I was, and I had to remind them. I was Belson the Blessed once more.

I grabbed the man with a broken arm by the throat and slammed him against the wall. It wasn't the best technique. I could have gotten out of it certainly, but I wanted to show my raw power. If age and injury had taken some of my speed, it had left me stronger than ever. I stood their naked, muscle coiling beneath tattoos and scars. My hand was over his throat, my scarred face spitting in his eye.

"Who sent you?" I screamed and felt him cower before me. "Who gave you this fucking note?" This time it was a dead whisper.

Then I felt my tattoos burn white hot. I looked down at them, then back up into his eyes. The arm hanging limp and useless, twisted back into place as muscle and bone realigned themselves.

I was struck hard in the chest. I'd never been hit by a cannonball, but if I had, in the faint moment between life and death, it would have felt like that. He was stronger than any human had a right to be. He was Demon-Bound

I landed hard against a wall. I had barely shaken the brightness from my vision when I felt some power aiming my way. I didn't know what it was, but I flung myself onto the opposite wall so I wouldn't find out. An icy blast ripped by me caving the wall in. If my body had been there, it would have caved that in too. I felt the power come again and barely had time to jump to the floor before the same blast hit that wall as well.

I back peddled naked on the floor, looking for anything to help distract this monster. Even with all my cleverness, he would have hit me. Then a shot rang through, hitting the beast in his shoulder. I saw Rachel with my pistol still smoking in her hands.

That shot wouldn't kill the monster, but it gave me time to do it. I sprung up and drove him into the ground. The Demon inside of the man made him stronger and quicker, but I had the skill. I wasn't taking any chances this time. I pinned one arm between my legs and twisted it till the bone snapped. I did the same with his other arm.

Finally, I put my hand over his throat. "You think I've lost it do you!" I screamed. "You think I'm not the man from Thyro! I'll break you ten times over and with more to spare! I'll find who sent you and kill everyone *she's* ever touched!" I ripped his throat out and watched the Demon in him try to escape. "I'll show you why you feared me! I'll show you who I am, and I won't have to do it again!"

I stood up covered in blood and sweat. Rachel had possessed the good sense to cover herself with a blanket.

"Thomas, what's going on?"

Now that the noise was over, men started to peak out of their rooms.

One such man was Alexander Gondua. He looked from me standing naked to his sister covering herself with a blanket. Even for a man as thick as him, the truth was obvious.

Alexander took a step towards her. "Why you little-"

The glare I sent his way stopped him. "Finish that statement, and I'll feed you your own teeth." I growled at him. In a rare moment of good sense, he shut his mouth. "Get dressed." I told him coldly. "We're leaving as soon as the horses are loaded."

Alexander slunk back into his room.

Next, I addressed the crowd of people looking out of their rooms. "If I hear a word uttered against the good lady Gondua's reputation, I'll know the reason why." I made sure they could all hear me. "You saw what I did to these three. Imagine what I'll do to you."

They all nodded their heads and went back about their business.

"What's going on?" Rachel repeated again.

I took the weapon out of her hands and uncocked it. "You wanted to see the man, who brought Kran to its knees? You want to see the man who took Thaniel's head?" I whispered at her. "He's here." I pointed at her clothes in the room. "Get dressed, we'll be leaving soon."

I picked up the note and read it for the last time.

Room 4. Kill the girl. If she gets her hooks in Thomas, he'll become the man we always feared he would.

-Her

I knew who sent that note. I'd been betrayed before, but never quite like this. The world had seen fit to test me again. It wouldn't like what came next.

The Thaniel Wars

I was over the edge of the ship puking up what I ate for breakfast. The sky was so dark with clouds I never really knew what time of day it was.

"We'll hit the port within the hour!" Lord Nelard screamed. "Man your stations! Prepare for action." He was the acting captain of *The Jorg*. There was a bit of a learning curve. The naval chain of command had very little to do with its cousin in the army. It had it's reason though. When the battle started, there wouldn't be messengers to take the officer's orders. It would be done by flag and signal and generally not well as I understood it. The other captains had gone over the plans fastidiously, but in the end, every Captain would be an Admiral on his ship. A naval engagement always turned into a brawl sooner or later. Another reason to hate ships by my estimation.

I tried to lower myself into the Battle-Mind, but another dry heave brought me out of it. "Fuck the navy." I said to myself.

I must have been overheard by Blip and Slip because they both came to pat me on the back. "Oy you just got to beat the piss out the sea." Blip said.

"Oy beat the piss out it." Slip chimed in.

I responded with another dry heave.

Blip looked mildly disappointed. "Oy, we all weren't meant to be warriors."

Slip slapped my back. "Someone's got to be the poet and the artist."

"I'll show you who the fucking-" I tried to spit venom at the pair, but I was caught in my own sick.

"Oy and then there's the working man." Blip went on.

"The foundation of society." Slip continued.

"See war isn't for everyone." Blip did his best to smile politely. "There's honorable work all over."

In an effort of pure will, I dropped myself into the Battle-Mind and felt the sea sickness go away. I still had a vague feeling that ground wasn't supposed to move like this, but it was manageable. "I'm fucking fighting." I snatched the musket they'd brought for me.

"Oy that's the spirit." Blip smiled.

"Oy beat the piss out of workers and artist." Slip finished.

"You want a rock." Blip handed me a small smooth stone

"What the fuck do I need a rock for?" I asked.

"Swallow one before every fight, we do." Slip held up his own rock. "This is my lucky one."

Blip pointed at the rock in my hand. "I passed that one at Serlon." He said proudly.

I shoved the stone back into his hand. "Are your men ready?" I was done talking about stomach stones. "This won't be an assault against savages with spears. It's determined resistance we're facing."

Blip turned around to his thirty marines. "Oy are you ready boys!"

He was greeted by savage battle screams and muskets thumping on the deck of the ship.

"Oy they're ready." Slip smiled.

"Zeal and bravery are a good thing," I pulled them both close, "but if they don't know the plan, we're facing disaster."

In a rare moment of clarity from Blip, he nodded back. "These are the picked men that'll take the fortress and blow the cannons."

Slip followed suit. "I'll secure our retreat at the docks, with the following units."

Blip put his hand on my shoulder. "We've briefed every marine, and quizzed them besides."

Slip finished for his companion. "They know the plan, your eminence."

"Good." I walked off. The brief moment of professionalism quickly left the two as they started screaming about who they were going to beat the piss out of. I wondered briefly how much of their insanity was an act. I doubted either really knew where the man ended, and the persona began. It was strange to think I was, in a way, like them.

The plan was as simple as I could make it. The Kranish ships would likely be completely surprised, but there was a fortress on the Eastern Dock that was too high for any of our cannons to fire back at. Lord Nelard would take his Ships-of-the-Line in a circle, blowing up anything that could muster determined resistance. The frigates would come by to mop up the rest. However, that still left the problem of the fortress. I would dismount with the marines, spike the cannons and break the sights.

Meanwhile, Slip would secure our way out. We would have cover from the swiveling guns, but besides that, we were on our own. If all went according to plan, it would be a quick fight, but it was all dependent upon the information I had gathered. For some reason, I couldn't shake the feeling something would go wrong.

"Constable Belson!" I heard Lord Nelard scream from the helm. I rushed up to meet him.

"Admiral." I nodded politely. He had earned a certain measure of respect.

He took me by the shoulder and moved to a modicum of privacy. "This is a risky maneuver we've planned."

I shrugged. "In case you haven't noticed we're losing the war." I said. "I'll have to take more risks than this one before it's over."

"I know we're losing this war," Lord Nelard shook his head, "but I don't like the idea of dying for your glory." He put a hand on my shoulder. "I know you don't like the king, and I don't know why you give a shit about us, but promise me your glory isn't why we're here."

I chuckled. "I feel like this is a conversation we should have had before we left port."

He cracked a smile. "Men are generally more honest right before the fighting starts." He shrugged. "I can still turn around, after all."

I considered my next words carefully. "I broke the Kranish at Wuntsville for glory, and I fought my way out of Milhire because I refused to die there." I paused. "There was a time it was only about glory, but it's passed me by." I went on. "That's still part of why I'm here, but it's far from the only reason." I smiled at him. "When we make it out of here, we'll have a long talk on the why. For now, I can see the shoreline."

"That's good enough for me." Nelard nodded. "How old are you anyhow?" He asked.

"Sixteen." I answered too quickly. "No, I made seventeen just the other week." I paused. "What does that have to do with anything?"

"I've read about Wuntsville, Gertenville, and the rest." Great victories all of them, but you've never tasted disaster. A man like you can get too confident in himself."

"If I can break, it hasn't happened yet." I smiled.

"Be sure it doesn't happen today either." The admiral let out a heavy sigh. "I know I shouldn't, but I love these men." He said. "I want to take as many home as I can."

I nodded and went back to the marines.

"Here." Blip pushed another stone into my hand.

"I told you, I don't want a stomach stone." I tried to hand it back.

Slip was there shaking his head. "It's a grenade." He handed me a small lighter. "Big boom."

"Right." I pushed it into my pocket with every intention of dropping it in the sea. Grenades were notoriously dangerous. Worked about as often as I didn't, and when grenades broke the man throwing them often did as well.

Finally, I addressed the Marines. "This is the day we turn the tables on Thaniel!" I screamed. "In a hundred years, they'll be writing poems about today."

"Fuck the poems!" A marine with a scar down his jaw screamed. "We want blood!"

"Oy, Tarry!" Blip screamed what I assumed was the man's name.

"What've we told you about bad mouthing the poets?" Slip chimed in.

"Only Dernay and Gerdin." Tarry scratched his head embarrassed.

"That's right!" Blip patted the boy on the back. "Only Dernay and Gerdin. Good Lad!"

Slip shrugged his shoulders at me. "We ain't savages like them army boys." He shook his head. "I hear most of them bloody fuckers ain't even read Godfrey."

"You're probably right about that." Godfrey was hailed by literary figures one of the seminal writers of the past two hundred years. He dealt with the relationship between the divine and man, reason and the immortal soul, even the individual and society. He had done this through a two thousand page tome written in blank verse. My tutor George had ingrained in me an innate respect for the man, but even as well-educated as I was, I'd never been able to make it through one of his full works. It stood to reason that most of the army had not read Godfrey either. These marines were all sorts of strange.

"Let's give em hellfire anyway!" I screamed and got a rousing cheer back.

"We're here!" Lord Nelard screamed. "Fire!" Then as one, the left side of *the Jorg* exploded with cannon fire. My ears were ringing as I watched the nearest Kranish ship turn into splinters and fire. I turned to see the docks, filled with people all running for safety. I saw our pier coming up too. Hopefully, the civilians would have the sense to leave us alone.

"Jump!" I screamed, and all thirty of the marines followed me as I hit the wood. Before I could give any orders, the men had already formed a protective square. A group of Kranish dockworkers were eying us up, caught between patriotism and good sense. For a brief second, it seemed like they would charge.

"That's Thomas Belson!" Someone screamed.

"Run!"

Just like that, the crowd dispersed. I lead my men through the twisting streets to the fortress. We met a few guards, but they were too small in number to oppose us, and they knew it. We were followed by the sixty marines who got off the next two ships, and Slip stayed back to organize the defenses.

A few muskets hissed at us, but Blip's men shot back with deadly accuracy. They checked corners, reloaded on the move, and never left their position. These men were professionals, and I saw how the Marines had earned their reputation. I was so used to desperate acts of heroism, it was nice to walk in the middle and aim my gun at buildings. It was also rather dull.

It wasn't long before we were at the sprawling cannon emplacement. It was a long zig-zag path up to the top. An assault straight through there would be suicide. They'd blow us to bits with a good canister shot. Luckily, I'd also planned for that.

"Blip, move up the front." I slapped him on the back. "Don't go through the final leg until you've heard me give the order."

"Right, you are." Blip turned to his ninety men. "Up and at em boys." He went up the stone ramp.

The fortress was well built for a siege. There were almost no weaknesses to it, but Fredua had grown to fast around the emplacement. A tall apartment had been erected using it as the back. I shouldered my musket and started the climb up its face. I'd always been a spry boy, and the exercise regiment I put myself through only made it easier. The trouble was I was deathly afraid of heights. I tried not to look down as I got closer to the top.

"It's one of the invaders!" I heard a man scream from inside the building.

"Grab em!" Another voice said.

I felt strong hands wrap around my boot. "Fuck off!" I screamed and kicked the attacker in the face. He let go but was still hurling abuses. I pulled my six-shooter and shot a round through the window. It didn't hit him, but I imagined the citizen figured he'd done all his patriotic duty demanded of him. The climb was rough, but I finally topped the building. From there I flung myself onto the wall and scrambled up the side.

Just as I'd feared, there was a small cannon facing the entrance. If the defenders had any sense, they'd have it loaded with grapeshot, but round would be almost as bad. A line of Kranish soldiers was forming up around the cannon preparing to throw the Marines back. I waited till I heard the marching of my ally's boots.

"Why are they here?" I heard a voice whisper in fear.

"Shut up Tarn!" A sergeant yelled.

"What if Thomas Belson's with them?" Another boy sounded off.

"Then we'll throw him back too!" But I could hear the wavering in his voice. He was afraid.

Just then I heard my men getting close enough.

"Steady!" The sergeant screamed.

I leapt from my position on the wall and landed smashing the head of the sergeant into the ground. "Charge!" I screamed to the marines who were following me. I whirled around, six-shooter in one hand, tomahawk in the other ready to do violence. What I found surprised me,

No weapons were leveled at me. Every soldier on that fort was staring with their mouth open. I paused for a moment. If I struck out now, they'd start fighting, but maybe there was a way to end it quicker than I'd originally thought. I held my fighting pose for a moment. One private finally threw down his musket as the ninety marines filed in. "Fuck this!" He screamed. "I ain't fighting Thomas Belson." The rest followed.

Blip's men went about kicking the weapons to the side and rounding them up without orders. They'd done this before. Blip approached me. "Oy, Belson why you always stealing me fight?" He said as he clapped me on the shoulder. There was a mix between a joke and real indignation there.

"There'll be more than enough to come." I looked around at the prisoners. Them putting down their muskets and going into a corner wasn't enough. As soon we left they'd be up and firing those guns. The game would be over. I hated myself for what I was about to say, but I steeled myself to the reality of it. "We can't leave these men behind us. We need to deal with the prisoners." I took a deep breath. "We need to..." I trailed off.

"Oy, we know how to deal with prisoners." Blip gave me a challenging look. I didn't understand that, but I was glad he didn't make me say it. "Oy, boys you heard the Constable! Get that there rope and tie em all to one another. Two double knots for the hands, one for the legs. Frisk 'em first for knives and such. Break the sights off every gun you see, spike the cannons, and if you've got to piss, do it now." He smiled. "If they got any gold watches on 'em, they should've swallowed 'em like we do." He paused. "If they got any pictures of sweethearts or pretty mothers, leave it to 'em. We don't want a repeat of the Tarry incident. No women's image deserves to be blackened so."

"I told you I was just itching, Colonel!" The boy I knew as Tarry screamed back.

"Oy, I know I wasted a week's pay to get an itching like that in Inte." Blip belted out. That brought a laugh from the crew who were already diligently going about their business. "Hop to it lads! If the sailors can do it quick, we can do it in half the time." The colonel looked back at me with a strange emotion. It looked vaguely like disgust on his wolfish face. He'd known what I'd been about to ask.

He went to assist his men in the detaining of prisoners, but I caught his shoulder and pulled him back towards me. "If we leave them tied up, they could get free and turn their guns back on us." I looked at him imploringly. "This could take time. Time we don't have."

"They won't get out of my boy's knots, and they'll be finished in a moment." He cut me off.

"What if someone comes along and free's them?" I asked. "All I'm saying is that-"

Blip didn't let me finish. "I know what you're saying, and there's not a chance in hell I'm giving that order!" He whispered it to me so none could hear, but I felt the anger behind it. "If you want it done, you'll have to do it yourself and kill me and my men first." For a moment the mask of insanity slipped. For all the mad colonel's persona unsettled me, the real man behind it scared me more.

I took a step forward. "You're willing to put this whole battle and maybe even the war at risk because you wanted to save thirty enemy soldiers?"

"Aye, there's a hundred reasons we should kill 'em but one good reason we shouldn't." Blip whispered. "Because we're warriors meant to save the innocent not slaughter 'em. Because yes thirty innocent lives is worth a kingdom for any decent sort of man." He paused. "Because the only thing that separates us from Thaniel are moments like this."

I shook my head. "We might regret this."

Blip looked me in the eyes. "Even if every worse thing you've predicted comes to happen, and we all die, I won't regret this." He sighed. "I might be crazy, but you're mad Thomas Belson."

"Fine, tie them up!" I shook my head and waited the painful minutes until the work was done. I wasn't angry at Blip. I was angry that the hero of Wuntsville who was supposed to be the paragon of virtue, needed a man so mad he should be put in a padded room to tell me right from wrong. Blip had been the better man than me at Fredua. I knew I'd never forget that, and maybe I never should.

When the prisoners were suitably detained. Blip gave the order to move out. Before he did that, though, he put a finger in his mouth and jammed it deep into one of the Kranish soldier's ears. *So that is the sad state of my moral conscience.* I thought.

We made our way through the maze-like streets of Fredua. It was a windy path, but I had studied it well. There had been no sightings of enemy forces, but that didn't mean they weren't there. "Where's the fucking Kranish at?" Blip screamed, searching frantically. I could barely hear it over the cannon fire from the ships.

"They're likely still forming up!" I screamed back. "All of Thaniel's veterans are at the front. These are his green troops and old men. They weren't prepared for this!" I took another look around. "If we hurry maybe we can beat them to our ships!"

"Better fucking not!" Blip screamed back.

I ignored him and kept running. We crested the next block and turned to find Blip's wish had come true. An entire company of men was standing idle.

I calculated all the odds in a moment. "We need to break them before they realize there's only ninety of us!" I screamed. "Charge on me!"

We were about thirty yards away before they saw us. I could see their eyes go wide in fear, but they didn't break. Then Blip let loose with his blunderbuss. It was the most violent sound I'd ever heard or ever wanted to hear. The world exploded with sulfur and pellets. My ears were still ringing when the smoke cleared, and I saw a full dozen of the Kranish lying dead. Another score were twisting around in agony. I couldn't help but wonder, what the fuck did Blip put in that thing.

"Charge!" I screamed. The Marines whooped and hollered behind me. I fired off three shots at anyone who looked important. We barreled into them with a force that surprised even me. I slammed my elbow into a Yellow-cloak who tried to run me through, fired at a man who looked to be leveling his rifle and twisted my tomahawk to land with a satisfying thump on their captain's head.

I danced and moved, becoming the wild animal I tended toward in combat. What surprised me is that the Marines weren't fairing much worse. Blip's sword was out and cutting down anything that stood in his way, the rest were clubbing the ill-equipped Kranish soldiers, even the lad Tarry who liked to "itch" himself was facing off against three enemies with his bayonet raised and looked to be winning.

Finally, the enemy broke and ran. I looked around our casualties and saw two men dead and Tarry ripping a bayonet out of his leg. We'd inflicted almost a hundred casualties on the enemy. It was good odds.

"Fuck!" Screamed Blip. "Gather up Willy and Hert. I have some bad letters to send." Two marines lifted the corpses onto their back.

"Blip, that'll slow us down." I said to him. "We need to save who we can."

Blip gave me a look of pure venom. "Then we'll move slower!" He screamed. "No one gives a shit about us, so we have to care double for our own."

I nodded. I'd heard this was how Marines did business, but I never believed it.

Blip looked at Tarry who was surrounded four six corpses. "I got four of 'em, Colonel!" He screamed.

"Aye, I knew you were a fighter son. That's why I picked you." Blip pointed at his leg. "Can you walk on that?"

"I think so." Tarry tried to stand but collapsed under his own weight. He grimaced in pain then looked up with an iron face. "I'll stay and slow 'em down." He said. "Just give me a few extra muskets."

I put away my tomahawk and reloaded my revolver. "Like hell, you're staying." I scooped him up and threw him over my shoulder. Blip would be my moral touchstone no more.

Blip nodded something that almost seemed like respect. "Let's move!" I screamed out.

We ran down the streets with the Kranish dogging our every step. It wasn't like the first all-out attack, but we were playing a constant game of firing and loading on the move. If we got bogged down, we were all dead. Some of our men got hit, but nothing that could keep them from running. We pushed on until we finally saw Slip holding the dock.

They were fighting from cover and making their shots count. The Kranish were trying to do the same, but they had never practiced anything like that. Slip would hold. However, we still had about a hundred yards and two companies of enemy soldiers till we were in the clear. We couldn't fight our way through the enemy again, but luckily we might not have to. A slim edge of the dock was clear for us to make a run for our comrades, but we'd be running through the open with no cover.

I thought furiously for any other way, but there was none. "Fuck it!" I finally said. "We have to run and hope the Kranish are shitty shots." The men nodded.

Even with all my training, Tarry was heavy. I was starting to slow down. I took a moment to catch my breath. "Go!" I screamed. We ran like madmen to the cover of Slip's safety. The Kranish were too surprised to turn their weapons on us until we were halfway there, but halfway was too long with enemies firing at me. Every step I took, I was convinced would be my last. Every crack of the musket, I was sure had a ball destined for me. I kept running, though.

The two men who were carrying the bodies and I were towards the back of the group. We were almost at the end when one of the men in front of me fell. The rest of the marines didn't see him. "Fuck!" He screamed doubling over with a shot to his side.

"Fuck!" I echoed. I couldn't leave him there. I holstered my six-shooter and grabbed him up by the scruff of his collar. He leaned on me while I helped him run. Well, between Tarry on my back and him on my side, it was closer to a walk than a run, and probably closer to a crawl than a walk. There was no way they could miss us now, no way I'd be able to evade the bullets, but there was also no way I could leave either of them.

"That's Thomas Belson!" I heard one of the Kranish scream.

"Shoot him!"

The musket balls skimmed across the ground. I was close, a foot away if that. I thought for a second, *maybe I could make it!* Then one found a home in my leg. I couldn't really feel it through the Battle-Mind, but the force sent me tumbling all the same. I fell over and tried to drag the two men to safety with me. I knew I wouldn't get there, but I had to make the effort anyway. Then a group of marines grabbed the three of us and pulled us back to the barricade.

Slip was there. "That leg alright?" He asked me.

I put my hand to my thigh, and it came away bloody. "It' alright." I lied.

Slip nodded. "You did your job?"

"Aye." I nodded. "It's done."

"Good the ships are coming to pick us up now." He gestured to the battle on the water. More than a dozen Kranish warships were on fire, sailors jumping from them, and the unprepared and undermanned crews hadn't managed to put a single one of Nelard's out of action. It was a complete success. Everything I'd hoped for. "We'll be safe for now."

Blip came up behind me. "Oy, you're a bit more utilitarian than I like my decision making, but your good when it counts." He clapped me on the back. "Tarry owes you an 'itching.'"

"Is this really the time to talk about that?" I asked.

"There's always time to talk about philosophy." Slip nodded. "You ever read Viverent?"

"Yes, I've read Viverent!" I glared at him. "Now, shoot!"

Then my arm grew white hot. It felt like it'd burn its way down to the bone. Slip, Blip, and every other Marine was gasping for air. I looked over the barricade and saw what I already knew I'd find. It was a Priest in his magnificent red robes. The ground was beating, the wind was howling. He was too far away for me to make out his face, but I knew it would be handsome and evil. The Kranish had stopped shooting and had all fallen to their knees. I pushed myself into the Gift and grabbed one of the suffocating Marine's rifles. I saw the lightning in his mouth and the fire in his hand.

"Cheeky fucker!" I screamed. The bullet hit him right between the eyes, and everything returned to normal.

"Oy!" Blip screamed.

"Weebalow fucker!" Slip responded.

"The ship's here!" I screamed as the frigate came by the shore. "Get on! Wounded first!"

The Kranish soldiers, seeing the dead Priest and the ship's guns, decided to run. I finally had a moment to breathe. I ripped a piece of cloth off my shirt and wrapped it around my leg. I stood up to test its strength. I was walking with a limp, but it wouldn't slow me down too much. I allowed myself a small moment of triumph. The plan had worked. Every ship not flying an Anthanii flag was on fire, and the Marines were loading up the frigate.

I let out an enormous sigh, then I took another look. The ships weren't moving out of the harbor. I heard cannon fire, and it wasn't one of ours. It was coming from the fort. The prisoners must have gotten free. The cannonball went wide and hit nothing. Without the sights, it would take them a while to get on target, but they would eventually.

Why were they still in the harbor? Then my eyes moved to the reason. There was a chain at the mouth. An enormous metal monstrosity, hidden under the water that would have stopped anything from getting out. It was an old trick. I'd read about it used, but not in a hundred years. It wasn't really viable now that ships had the firepower to blow the tower into the water, but that would take time. It was time I didn't have. I should have seen it, but I didn't.

I took a deep breath. "We're going to have to push through to those towers." I nodded to the colonels. "Think your boys can make it that far?" The tower on our side of the river more than two miles away. The marines were tired, and badly outnumbered, but if we could hit them before the rest of the army could mobilize on the dock, it was possible.

"Oy our boys can make it." Slip gave me his wild grin.

"Good." I muttered.

When I heard a lull in the firing, I jumped up to a high spot and then dived back to cover right as the musket balls hit. Any optimism I had was gone. The army was there in force and surrounded us entirely. The Yellow-cloaks had grown thick. The guns of the ship were keeping the soldiers around us from charging, but there was no chance we'd be pushing through. Our only escape was on the ships, and there was no escape for the ships. The colonels saw what I saw.

"We're fucked." I whispered to myself. It was a rare moment of despair. A crack in the armor I never showed in public and above all, not in battle. "We're fucked."

Blip and Slip were the only ones around. They were war dogs, as much made of iron as they were of flesh. Even they let the persona slip off for a moment. I saw acceptance, a queer peace, and a bit of fear I'd never call them on.

"Let's give em hell this one last time then." Blip put an arm around his comrade.

"Oy we'll beat the piss out of them." Slip smiled back, but there was a bit of mourning in that smile. Even a madman as touched as Slip probably had a girl he was sweet on who never knew, or maybe a parent he loved but could never find the right words for. All works that would be left undone on these docks.

"No." I said to myself, remembering who I was. "No!" This time it was louder. I looked around one more time, desperately hoping for something I hadn't seen before. I didn't find it. There were only buildings tightly packed together, and soldiers filling the street. There wasn't going to be some divine force of nature to save the day. There wasn't some revelation that would hit me in the nick of time. I'd have to make a chink in the armor and then pound it till the enemy dropped.

"Order your men to fire double time!" I screamed at Blip and Slip. "Give me enough cover to climb up that wall." I pointed to the closest building with enough boxes packed at the side to allow me a quick way up. "From there I'll make it to the towers. Keep loading your marines on the boat."

Blip and Slip stared at me like I was insane. When two men like that look at you as if you're insane, you know you've just had a bad idea, but I was all out of the good ones. What I wouldn't give for some donkeys and scarecrows.

"You've been shot in the leg." Blip hissed at me.

"So I'll limp there." I shot back as I made sure my six shooters were all loaded.

"The streets are crawling with soldiers." Slip put in.

"So I'll limp quick." I turned to him. "This is our only chance, and I have to take it."

"Aye." Blip nodded.

"Aye." Slip did the same

"Right as the shooting dies down." I waited for my chance. "Now!" They gave the order, and the marines started shooting everything they had. It still wasn't enough to take all the fire, but it increased my odds from zero to slightly more than zero. I ran with a six-shooter in one hand and the other cupped over my precious genitals. In hindsight, I should have covered my face. For all my pride, I had never made the claim that my manhood was bigger than my head.

I shot twice and saw two men fall clutching their chest. I saw the boxes loaded up next to the building I had planned to go over. I holstered my pistol and jumped on top of one then another. Finally, I started climbing the brick wall finding handholds. I was on the ledge when I felt a dull thump just below my shoulder. I lost my grip for a moment and then reclaimed it. The Battle Mind let me move through the injury.

I vaulted myself onto the top and started running. I was hoping being on top of the building would provide some cover from the soldiers below, but it was too slanted. I could see right down the muskets below.

Still, it was an incredibly stupid stunt, and like all incredibly stupid stunts, it takes people a while to realize someone's stupid enough to do it.

"That's Thomas Belson!" I heard a soldier scream. I was getting rather tired of hearing that. "Oh fuck! He's gonna break us! He's going to use his magic like he did at Wuntsville!"

That was another advantage of doing something that approached the realm of being ungodly stupid. People thought there was no way someone would do something so dumb. *It must be part of some master scheme.* They'd think. They'd start to question everything they knew. In that moment, you might be able to get away with it.

"Fucking shoot him!" I heard someone with authority scream.

The bullets started whizzing past me. That was the trouble with doing something ungodly stupid. Eventually, you're just running across rooftops in a hostile city. It took them a while though, and their aim wasn't particularly good. I jumped through to the next building.

I was running as fast as my legs could carry me. All those years spent training served me well, but even I was at my natural end. Even through the Battle Mind, my wounded leg was starting to slip.

Whatever hit my shoulder had restricted me. Even my lungs were about to pop out of my chest, but I was still keeping one step ahead of the soldiers. They couldn't know where I'd arrive from next, so if the brief moments of me running across rooftops in between covered houses wasn't safe by any stretch of the imagination, it was possible.

I was close. I could see the towers maybe less than a hundred yards away. The bullets started to whizz over my head again, so I jumped through to what looked like a housing complex. It was walled in. I thought I had a brief moment of peace.

Then my head lit up with a blinding light. I was thrown to one side of the wall holding my face in my hands.

"He's in here." I heard a monstrous voice scream. When my vision settled back, I looked up at him.

He was as big a man as I'd ever layer eyes on. His shirt was off, so I could see the rippling muscles that ran over him. If he was an inch under seven feet, I'd be a dwarf. In the monster's right hand was a heavy looking hammer. *Must be a blacksmith.* I thought dumbly. Only a blacksmith had muscles like that.

I went for my gun. Even through the wound in my shoulder, I was quick but not nearly quick enough. The blacksmith swatted the weapon out of my hand with that hammer, and the six-shooter went flying.

"You're Thomas Belson, ey?" The blacksmith clearly didn't care for an answer because he subsequently kicked the wind out of me. "Aye, you're Thomas Belson alright. Only bastard mad enough to be running around here."

I heard soldiers marching. They were closing me in. I had to get this dumb brute away and quick. I struck him in the side, but it was like hitting iron. Did me more damage than it did him. The blacksmith swung that hammer of his at my head, and I barely had the time to move. If this was a fight, he'd win, at least with me in the sorry state I was.

I was in as good of shape as any man. I was strong and fast, and I could fight. However, this fellow was a monster born. I had trained for the trying endurance of battle. I wanted to be quick and nimble. My muscles were taught enough that my blows could break wood, but this man was different. Perhaps, the blacksmith couldn't do the things I'd done, but I sure as hell couldn't do what he did either. In an open field, I'd have had a prayer. In a closed off passage, wounded and disarmed, I was doomed.

"I never cared much about this war, you know?" He stalked closer to me. I unleashed a flurry of blows, but one punch in the gut left me reeling again. "My maw was Anthanii. My paw was Kranish, so I figure whoever wins, the family honor was safe."

"I don't think your paw was Kranish." I managed to gasp out. "I just don't think he noticed the bear sneaking into your house while he was at work." If you have to go out, better to go out on a laugh.

"Ha." He hit me again. I don't think it was because of the joke. He seemed to like it. "Anyhow, I never cared much for this war." He stepped forward. "I never cared until you came to my city and started blowing everything up."

He picked me up and put me against a wall. "There's people here. Innocent people with jobs and families who had no part in this fight." He sneered at me. "How many do you think are dying right now?" He asked.

"Too many to count." I spit back.

"No, they'll be counted." He said. "Not by the government surveys or historians, but they'll be counted alright." He raised that hammer of his. "They'll be counted by their wives, children, and parents. The people that loved them." He said. "I can end it all today. It'll be the holiest work I've ever done."

He reeled back to land the last blow. That was my moment. I leaned forward and bit him hard in his face. "Fucker!" He screamed. Then I hit him over the head with a piece of brick. The blacksmith was out cold. Well, I thought he was out cold.

I ran to the next opening. I still had my work to do. Then I saw the time I had spent fighting the monster had let soldiers cordon off my exit. "Fuck." I paused.

"I'll kill you!" The blacksmith started to rise.

I took my chances and jumped to the next building. The soldiers fired, and I felt two dull thumps in my chest while I flew through the air. I hit the rooftop sputtering. Even through the Battle Mind, I could feel it. It was bad. As bad as I'd ever been hurt, and that's saying something. I kept moving anyway.

I wasn't nimble or clever anymore. I was just limping. Forcing myself to move faster so they couldn't catch me. My mind started to go a bit dark, and I willed myself back into consciousness.

I jumped through the chain-tower window and saw a group of yellow-clad soldiers looking horrified. I drew my tomahawk and went about my business.

It wasn't the skillful dancing I usually did or the vicious animal I could sometimes push myself into. I didn't even remember most of it. All I could say for certain was that everyone in that room besides me died.

I kicked the lever down, and the chain went back into the sea. Finally, I stopped and gasped for air. Then I looked out a window and saw a battalion coming my way. It wasn't enough for me to lower the chain. They'd raise it back up after they stormed the place and killed me. I reached into my pocket and pulled the last gift from Blip and Slip.

It was a grenade. I didn't know what would happen when it went off. Maybe the explosion would kill me. Maybe it would take the whole tower down. Maybe some weird mechanical phenomena would occur, and the chain would rise again. I wasn't an engineer. I didn't know. All I knew was that at that moment I was fucked and couldn't possibly get more fucked. If I lit the grenade, maybe I would be less fucked, so I did.

I set the little ball of death right under the raising mechanism and jumped out the window overlooking the sea. There was a frigate under me, maybe a story or two down. The ships had finally started moving out. I jumped and hit the deck hard. Then all I saw was blackness.

I woke up to Blip and Slip putting an awful smelling stone under my nose. "You did it, Thomas." Blip whispered.

"Aye, you did." Slip put in.

I tried to get to my feet, but it was still too hard. I was laid out on the deck. "How long was I out?"

"Not but a minute." Blip said.

"But we was worried about you." Slip nodded. "So I let you smell me stomach stone."

I pushed it out of my face and made myself stand up.

"Three above." Blip muttered as he finally got a look at my injuries.

"We need a doctor!" Slip screamed. I didn't understand the fuss. They'd seen soldiers hurt before. I'd live.

I pushed them aside and went to the back of the ship to see for myself. A man with linens came at me, but I shrugged him off.

The Anthanii warships were leaving. The Kranish harbor was on fire. I'd done it.

"I'm a fucking god..." I whispered to myself. "I'm a fucking god!" I screamed. "Fuck you Thaniel! I'm going to tear your whole fucking empire apart! Piece by fucking piece!"

"The wounds are making him mad!" Someone called out for help, but I didn't care. I barely even heard him.

I started to scream again. "I fucking-" Then the fire went up. The tattoos on my arm burned as hot as I'd ever felt them. All the ships still in the harbor were ablaze in colors that boggled the mind. I abandoned my Battle Mind and tried to go into the Gift. For a moment the blaze died down. Then my body started to convulse in pain. I'd never felt anything like it before. The flames went on, and I saw little specks on the ship begging for mercy. I'd seen a demon though. The first had no mercy left in them.

"Turn back!" I screamed. "Turn back! I can save them." But my body seized with a crippling agony.

"He's mad!" Someone screamed.

"Grab him!"

"Turn back!" I kept screaming, but no one listened. Finally, my brain began to shut down, but the last thing I saw was the ships going up and brave men dying.

The Thaniel Wars

To say I was conscious at any point would be as bold a statement as calling my actions at Fredua a success. Every once in a while I could remember opening my eyes, but the few glimpses I had were feverish and racked with pain.

Once in a fit of panic, I reached out to grab the doctors arm. "The fires!" I begged of him. "Were the fires real?" When I looked to see the rest of the body, it was attached to the Demon I fought at Imor. I tried to kill him then, but strong arms wrestled me back and shoved putrid medicine down my throat. I slept well for a time after that.

I'd always fancied myself a tough bastard. Three above, I'd taken a sword through my chest and still killed my man. Laying in my own piss and convulsing in spurts did much to humble me. No one would ever call me on it. No one would ever say a word to me about it, but I called out to my parents. "Mama!" I'd scream. "Papa!" I'd holler. "It hurts so bad! Can't I come sleep in your room tonight?"

In rare lucid moments, for the first time, I thought I'd made a mistake. Not at Fredua with all the sailors who had died. I wasn't even fully aware of that yet. My mind wasn't ready to face that failure. I thought I had chosen wrong when I'd made my way to God's Rest. I thought I should have stayed at my plantation and grown to manhood under smiling parents.

I was so bright. I could have been a surveyor, a doctor, maybe even a powerful senator one day. Most of all, I could have stayed at my plantation. Helping servants pick cotton and tobacco didn't seem so bad when half of your body is cut open and filled with infection.

I was a shade over seventeen. I was supposed to be drinking and making mischief with my friends. I was supposed to be chasing girls and failing horribly until I finally got it right. Instead, I had taken the fate of a continent in my hands. I had decided to fight the greatest empire in two thousand years, headed by the greatest emperor anyone had a record of. I shouldn't have been there.

How many millions of young boys had loving parents and a warm home? Why was I the only one who couldn't stay put for a good thing? Why did *I* need to leave?

I knew the answer. I wanted glory and greatness. I wanted it as much as a drowning man wants air. No, I wanted it more. The thing was, I found it to a measure. They were already singing songs about me, and there was more of both left to take. Much more of both. Glory and greatness in spades.

Lying there, body racked with pain, I thought glory and greatness made empty meals. In that moment, I'd have traded it all to be curled in my family bed. Mother tending me. Father sitting by my side, smiling about all the things we'd do once I was better.

It'd have been one thing if I'd never had that. But I had. Seiford, Roltan, Prince Edward, even Thaniel all had a reason to be fighting. There was some sense of duty they couldn't shirk. There was some desperation that made them think this is the only way out. There was something in their past that had broken them so thoroughly, this was the only way left. I had none of that. I was just a spoiled boy, too blind to see.

When I got to God's Rest, we were all trying to be strong. We didn't want anyone to know there might be a human under our uniform. Eventually though, if you spend enough time with people, you start to learn their stories. There's were all much the same. I heard about a lot of drunk fathers who beat their son so often he decided to become so powerful no one could ever hurt him again. I heard about towns that had been burned down, and a lone survivor who'd sworn he'd never let it happen again. I heard about family members who withered and died under the yoke of the Old Religion. Only thing a man can do after that is seek out a higher purpose.

I heard a lot of stories, and then they asked for mine. I told them it was too hard to talk about. It wasn't quite a lie. It was hard to talk about, but they'd all assumed my story was worse than all theirs put together. It was in a way. Their stories made sense. They had a reason to be the way they were. A boy that wanted to rebel against parents whose greatest sin was that they loved him, well… That wasn't much of a tale to speak about. I always figured the poets would give me some good reason after my deeds were done. I thought I'd never need one, until I did.

"Mama!" I screamed. "Papa!" I hollered. "It hurts something fierce! Can't I come and sleep in your room tonight?" I grabbed the arm next to my bed.

Whoever was by me answered. "Their bed is too messy right now." The body that hand was attached to was Slip's.

Standing next to him was his brother Blip. "They're coming to your room, right now." Blip patted my shoulder softly.

Slip grabbed my hand. "They sent us to tell you not to worry."

"Oh good." I said. If it seemed strange that two Anthanii marines would be sent to herald my parents, I was too feverish to notice. "I'm not scared." I mumbled. "Just don't want them to be worried about me is all."

"They're not worried about you." Slip squeezed my hand tighter. "They know how tough their boy is."

"They just love their son too much to let him suffer alone." Blip smiled at me. "Good parents that they are."

"That's alright." I smiled back. "They can come sleep next to me if they really want." A thought struck me. "Just don't tell Andrew about it. He won't believe I let them sleep here because they're worried." I said. "He'll think I'm yeller."

"Andrew will never know." One of them said.

Another convulsion of pain ran through my body. I started seizing, and the two marines put callused hands on me. "Hold him, so he don't hurt himself!" Blip screamed.

"Oy!" His brother grabbed me tight. "I hate seeing him like this!" I saw a tear drop from his eye, but I wasn't in a state to know what it meant. "Maybe we should just let him die. Seems like the kind thing to do."

"He didn't give up on us at the docks!" Blip screamed at his brother. "We ain't giving up on him here."

Finally, my body calmed down, but there was a fear in me. "Don't let them take me across the ocean!" I grabbed the closest thing to me. "I don't want to leave!" I squirmed around. "It'll be so cold, and I'll be so alone."

"No one's taking you anywhere." Blip did his best to calm me.

"Good." I said matter-of-factly. "I'm not scared, though. Nothing scares me."

"We know." Slip smiled down at me.

"I just couldn't take Pig with me, and I love Pig." I thought of the fat bulldog licking his prodigious chops. "Pig gets sad when I leave for the day. He'll be devastated if I have to go for all that time."

"Pig does love you too much." Blip patted my hand.

"I love Pig." I said mostly for myself. "Couldn't leave him." I looked around myself. "Where is Pig anyhow?"

"He's coming with your parents." One of them said.

Another wave of pain racked me, and the two Marines were forced to restrain my body again.

"Mama!" I screamed. "Papa!" I hollered.

"Blip..." Slip let the words trail off. "Maybe it's time."

"No!" He screamed. "He'll get better!"

I was unconscious for a while after that.

I opened my eyes again to see a kindly old doctor standing next to me. His face was a jolly one, but his eyes were sad. It looked like he'd been weeping. It was Doctor Quarrels. I was more lucid than I had been with Blip and Slip. I knew I was rocking on a ship. I couldn't say how I got there, but I knew I was on a ship. I remembered who Doctor Quarrels was.

"Dear-Dear." He shook his head. "You have too many scars for a boy so young."

The first time he'd told me thus, I'd met him with bluster and pride. All that had bled out of me though. "Am I dying?" I asked.

"Your story does not end here." He stared at me with those eyes of his. The eyes that could have belonged to a helpless father at his child's deathbed. "Maybe it would be a good thing if it did though. Before it does, you'll have more scars."

"Did you heal me again?" I asked. "Like you did in Imor."

"I told you, my son," he stroked my arm, and I felt the love of a thousand mothers and fathers, "that was only once and in a time where the rules were different."

"Why are you here then?" I managed the strength to turn my head.

"To tell you I'm sorry." Quarrels meant it. He always told the truth. A god couldn't lie, but he meant it in a way I'd never heard before.

"Sorry?" I tried to laugh, but it hurt too much. "Sorry for what? Everything that's happened is no one's damn fault but mine."

"No one came and kidnapped you into this war, you mean." Quarrels smiled at me. It was the smile of a star slowly twinkling its last. "You chose this, and I'm sorry you had to." He put his hand on my breast. "I'm sorry we made a world where there had to be fire." He paused, and in that pause, I saw the eternity he lived weigh on him. Even a god sometimes felt his burden. Maybe he always did. "I'm sorry you have to do what we couldn't."

"You mean whip Thaniel?" I scoffed. "If you'd done that I might've become an atheist. Rascal gods trying to steal my glory."

Quarrels gave a sad little laugh, humoring me. "Wouldn't want to do that."

"Jokes aside." I rested my hand on his. "I'm not exactly sure why you can't step in for this. I reckon I'm not supposed to. I don't even think I have the words to start asking the questions." I sighed. "If time's water, I'm a raindrop next to the ocean."

Quarrels patted my hand. "More than that, the ocean ends eventually."

I chuckled. "I don't even know enough to know what I don't know." I stared up into the god's eyes. "What I mean to say is that even if I don't know exactly why, what I saw in Imor let me know that theology isn't so simple. I think I saw the shape of it though. The beginning of the path you're on." I paused. "If I don't know the exact reason why, I know there's a reason, and it seems like a good one." I'd always assumed my lot had been the hardest. Looking at Doctor Quarrels, made me see the absolute folly of that. "There's no need to be sorry for me having to win this war."

"I'm sorry for what has passed." He said simply. "I'm sorry for what will come to be." Something inside me knew that Quarrels wasn't talking about Thaniel. At least he wasn't just talking about Thaniel. There was something bigger. What could be bigger than the Emperor of Kran? I had no idea.

"It's alright." I patted his hand, trying to ignore what I was just beginning to understand. For some reason I needed him to be speaking about the war. I couldn't face the future he saw for me.

"I'll win this war, and it'll easy sailing from then on." In the past, I'd wanted to go explore the edges of the world. Now, I was less sure of that. "I'll go back to my home steeped in glory and fame." I smiled at the thought. "I know I left some bad blood, but they'll forgive me. It'll be just like before." I gave a mighty yawn. "Father, Andrew, and I will be hunting. Mother will kiss us when we get back, and my sister..." I trailed off. "She'll be older by then, but I'm confident she grew up well."

Quarrels didn't answer. I knew what his silence meant, but I carried on as if saying it would make it so.

"I'll bring Lady Gerate home with me." My voice was growing more nervous. "Of course, then she'll just be Abby, but my family will love her all the same. One day I'd like to make her Abby Belson!"

Still no answer.

"Maybe, you can even visit me there." I stared into the eyes of a god. "It'd be a nice change of pace from you always seeing me like this."

"I want that." Wisdom said softly. "I want that more than anything."

"So it'll happen!" It was more of a statement than a question.

"You know I can't lie, Thomas." A single tear dropped from his eye. A tear that might have given life to a barren Earth. A tear that grew into bacteria that grew into apes that grew into me. "Don't make me tell the truth..."

"Will it happen?" I demanded from him.

"Don't ask me that." Wisdom was pleading with me.

"Will it..." A faint whisper.

"You will be changed, Thomas." Wisdom said softly. "You already are, but you will be changed farther." He put a hand on my shoulder. "Your family will change. Your home will change." He stroked my face, and I felt all of the heavens brush against me. "Even you can't stop the grains in an hourglass."

"I could break the damn thing!" I screamed at him. "I can do anything..."

"Aye, you could and you can." He whispered. "But then you'd have to watch the sands slip away. We did that once. It's better to just watch them at the bottom." He put his hand over my head. "Remembering." I felt something wash over me. "Sleep now, my child."

And I slept.

Present Day

We rode into the Belson Plantation as fast as I could remember riding anywhere. Everyone with me was winded to some degree. I hadn't let them sleep any more than a couple of hours at a time. I needed to make sure my family was safe.

Andrew handled it well. He was originally trained as a cavalryman before he'd been pulled into an infantry unit. Seiford was used to my galloping like the World Below was on my heels, even if he wasn't built for it. Rachel had surprised me. I knew she was excellent in a saddle, but this sort of cross-country ride had a way of wearing at people. George was far too old to find any part of it enjoyable, and Alexander Gondua was a dandy through and through.

Ayn-Tuk could have kept pace, but I'd left him behind to ask questions. I trusted him to be able to deal with any danger that still lurked. I trusted him to get those questions answered. I needed to know how far this conspiracy went.

I jumped off Shaggy Cow as soon as I got to the plantation, and Seiford followed my lead. Andrew went about to make sure the family was accounted for. I didn't know who else she'd try to hurt.

"Thomas, we need to talk." The monk put a hand on my shoulder. I'd filled them all in to some degree of what had transpired. I hadn't let anyone but Seiford and Tuk know about how deep I suspected this went.

"About what?" I said without turning to him. "You saw the note. You know there's only one person with the reach to do that." I kept walking. "You know there's only one person who could have given that order." I stopped for a moment. "It was Mother Vestia."

"We don't know that." The monk said.

I turned to face him. "You're the smartest person I know, Seif." I took a step towards him. "Right now, you're looking through a haze of emotion." I took a deep breath to steady myself. "Approach it like you would a math proof, unbiased. What's the answer?"

"Same as yours." The monk said. "But that woman loves you as much as anyone in this world." He stepped towards me. "She wouldn't use us like this."

"People do strange things to those we love." I turned away. "Sometimes, they're the only ones we can really hurt."

Seiford shook his head. "What are you going to do, Thomas?" He kept saying my name like it would make me more human.

"I don't know." Now it was my turn to shake my head. "I've been thinking about Sterling lately." I gave a heavy thought. "The Pillars too, the Golden Fort, and all the rest."

"That's not something I want you thinking too much about." Seiford scowled.

"Why didn't we stay?" I asked. "Some of the people we leave in power are decent enough, but others seem just as bad as the tyrants we tear down."

Seiford took a second to think. "We had business elsewhere." We both knew that answer wasn't good enough.

I shook my head. "I mean what if the New Church started ruling places. Think about how much easier that would be." I shrugged my shoulders. "We wouldn't have to borrow other armies or operate on lent authority. We could really change the world," I paused, "and keep it changed."

The monk looked at me curiously. "It's not our way."

"What if it could be?" I took a step back.

"It shouldn't." Seiford said firmly. "We serve to inspire men to greatness, not force our version of it upon them. Every man has his own path in this world. We only serve to let them choose it. We don't rule over people because it's not our right."

"Who has a right to rule?" I asked dismissively. "Monarchs who inherited their position, bureaucrats who stole them?" It was all too much for me. "Forget about it. Just a thought I've been having." I turned to go back into the house, but Seiford grabbed my shoulder and stopped me.

"You're right maybe they don't," the monk admitted, "but that's why we can't take their place." There was a steadfastness about him that shocked me. "That's why we can't become them."

"Then how does it change?" I growled back. "If we don't replace the men we unseat, it's just the same old breed who takes the throne."

"You're right again. They probably will." Seiford took his hand off me. "But we inspire people. We teach them a better way, a way of wisdom, honor, and compassion. One day that'll be enough. One day people will look to men like you and break their shackles." The monk's words didn't mean as much to me as they once had. "You can do things no one else can." He put a finger in my chest. "The whole world couldn't stop Thomas Belson if it wanted to. We can be the epitome of the systems that have enslaved men since we started writing down history, or we can be something better." He sighed. "We can be the men that proved them wrong."

"What if that takes too long?" I shook my head. "What if there isn't a better way?"

"Then we keep trying." Seiford clenched his jaw.

"Why?" I was dismayed at how he wasn't. "It hasn't worked in the five hundred years we've been trying it! What makes you think it'll work now?"

Seiford looked like he'd been struck. "Hope." He said simply. "Faith." The monk looked into my eyes. "I don't care if it doesn't work. I'll die telling your stories and teaching the Three Gifts because I don't want to live in a world that needs to be forced into civility." He stopped and leveled a proud look at me. "But I don't think I'm wrong. People don't just look to you as a savior, they look to you as an example, and it's working bit by bit."

"Maybe they should find a better one of both." I spit into the ground.

"Maybe they should, but for now you're all they have." He shook his head. "What's gotten into you, Thomas?"

"Since I became powerful enough to change this world, people have been telling me I shouldn't!" I screamed.

"You did change the world!" Seiford matched me. "You're still changing it, whether you see it or not!"

"Aye, for a few years." I shrugged. "Then what? Then as soon as I leave, the same old people try to undo everything I gave up so much for." I put a hand on his shoulder. "What your brother died for." It was a low trick.

"And what did my brother tell you?" Seiford narrowed his eyes.

"Let's go find my family." I turned to leave, but Seiford held me.

"No, not until you answer my question." He pulled me closer. "What did my brother tell you?"

I shook my head. "He told me that being strong meant I could do what no one else could." It came out barely a whisper. "He said I could walk the path no one else can, but I had to do it the right way."

"Then do it." Seiford said. "The right way."

"Let's go find my family." I turned into the house.

I was caught by George. "We accounted for everyone except your sister." He said. "She's probably in the library, though."

"Let's be sure." I led the way to her.

"Wait! There's a visitor you should see." George held on to me.

"I'll deal with that after I see my sister." I shook off his hand.

I pushed into the door and saw Alexis reading some dusty old tome. When I was a boy, it felt like all the knowledge of the world was held in that room. Since then, I'd seen libraries bigger than cities.

Alexis closed the book and stood to greet us. "It looks like you three rode through the World Below?" She cocked an eyebrow. "What happened."

I ignored the comment. She didn't need to know the danger I suspected could be on her. "What's the topic today?" I was just happy to see her safe.

"Anthanii colonialism in Souren." George responded with a forced smile. "By the look of that tome?"

"I understand you spent a good bit of time in Souren." Alexis posited curiously.

"Well, as a matter of fact, we did spend some time with the blacks, little one. That's where we met Tuk." Seiford sat down in the seat across from her. Our previous altercation seemed to have slipped from his mind at the prospect of a good tall tale. "I could tell you some stories about those people."

"You'd better not tell the wrong stories." I gave him a warning stare.

"You fought with them?" Alexis asked, trying to hide the admiration. "I heard they eat the hearts of their enemies." She said excitedly. "I heard when a man comes of age he has to wrestle a lion." She leaned in close as if telling a secret. "I hear their greatest warriors can split a tree with one blow."

Seiford and I smiled at each other. I gestured for him to go, so the monk started. "They don't usually eat each other's hearts. Sometimes men go a bit wild in battle, but it's not often." He rolled his eyes. "The two of us have seen white men act just as brutal on a Thyran battlefield. Things like that don't seem to be isolated to one race, as far as I can tell."

"Didn't Tukna eat a heart?" I cut in.

"It was a goat heart." Seiford said reassuring the girl. "And he was very drunk." He gestured to me. "You want to explain lion wrestling?"

"Of course I do." I kept the smile. Seeing my sister in good spirits raised mine enough to forget my argument with Seiford too. We were friends, and nothing could keep us apart for too long. "When a warrior gets good enough at fighting they give him the title An-Sab. It means lion man, sometimes it's translated as lion fighter."

"Didn't you wrestle a lion?" Seiford cut in.

"It was a baby one." I shrugged at my sister. "And I was very drunk."

"So the part about breaking tree trunks with a single punch?" Alexis asked.

"They punch trees to make their fist stronger, and sometimes they break." I said. "It's still impressive, but the trees that grow over there aren't very big."

"Are they usually drunk when they do this?" Alexis rolled her eyes.

"Almost always." Seiford said through a grin. "We'll make an anthropologist of you yet."

"So what did you two do over there?" The girl asked wide-eyed.

"Lots of drinking." I answered.

"Lots of whoring." Seiford shrugged.

I picked up a pen and threw it at my friend. "Remember your audience." Seiford kept that big grin on his face.

"You know what the girl means." George answered through a laugh. "Why were you there, besides drinking and whoring?"

"Some of the tribes started using Demon Worship to try and master the rest. After we weren't needed in Thyro, they sent us there." Seiford said.

"Essentially, we did the same thing we'd been doing for the past ten years, but the battles were usually smaller." I shrugged my shoulders.

"I got to ride an elephant in one of them." Seiford said excitedly then turned mournful. "I still miss Surus."

"Your elephant died?" Alexis was shocked. "How did they kill an elephant?"

"It didn't die." I cut in. "The ship captain wouldn't let him take an elephant with us."

"You got to keep Shaggy." He barked.

"Shaggy fits on a boat." I shot back, the same argument we'd been having for years.

"Did you fight with the Anthanii at the Golden Fort then?" The girl asked trying to turn the conversation back to the stories.

Seiford and I looked at each other, this time not knowing what to say. "We were there." I said eventually. That wasn't something I wanted her asking too many questions about.

"How did you escape the massacre?" She asked

"Well…" Seiford began but didn't know how to finish.

"Our orders were to not interfere." I said for him.

Alexis didn't seem disappointed exactly. She just couldn't believe that we'd done nothing, but the truth was worse. "So you just watched while they slaughtered those soldiers?"

"Well, not exactly." Seiford muttered nervously. It wasn't one of the stories that he wanted told, but to many people knew for it to be a secret. If either of us lied, my sister would find out, and our renewed relationship was already tenuous.

"We didn't stand by." I said it colder than I meant to

"What do you mean?" The girl's eyes darted between the two of us. Understanding finally dawned on her. "You didn't fight with those savages did you?"

"The Souren might not have a written language or founded cities, but they weren't the savages in that place." I said grimly.

"They were trying to bring technology and civilization to a backwards people." Alexis said in disgust.

"Up north it's different." Seiford put in. "The relationship is more mutually beneficial. The New Church let Anthanii know what would happen if they abused those people." He paused for a moment. "The Golden Fort was farther south. We can't keep eyes on it all. Things get darker down there." The monk shook his head. "At the end it was too dark to be redeemed."

"So you killed them all!" She looked horrified.

"We spent a month trying to negotiate fair treatment," I was lost in my memories, "but my name didn't carry quite so much weight down there."

"You killed your own people?" She tilted her head as if she couldn't quite grasp it.

"I won't call anyone who steals, rapes, and murders like they did, my people." I shot back with more venom than I meant to. "I wanted it to be peaceful, but they wouldn't let it be."

"It wasn't supposed to be a massacre. We were just going to push them off their foothold." Seiford tried to salvage the situation. "Your brother screamed for it to stop, but the Souren warriors had been abused too long for mercy." The monk shivered remembering that day. "We almost had a peaceful surrender with the survivors, but some Anthanii private wanted to be a hero and got a hold of his musket."

"That's supposed to make it better?" Alexis eyed the two of us in disgust. "You didn't mean to?"

George reached out a hand to calm my sister. "Alexis, you don't know how easy it is for something like that to go bad. You've never seen a battlefield."

"I don't need to see a battle to know that's not how heroes act!" The girl stood up.

I was done asking forgiveness for doing what other men couldn't. "It is when it's necessary." I snarled back at her. "See if they treat the Souren like that again." I took a step forward. Everyone in the room was quiet. Perhaps they were seeing what my sister saw, what Thaniel saw. "Now, the whole world knows what happens when you kill a people's men, rape their women, and enslave their children."

"And what happens to them?" She shot back.

"Thomas Belson happens to them." I said levelly.

"You're a monster." She said it barely a whisper and stormed out.

"Alexis-" I called out for her, but she didn't turn around. "You don't understand!"

George frowned at me. Not in the way a friend might, but in the way a disappointed teacher would. "I'll talk to her." He patted me on the shoulder and went to follow.

I grabbed the tutor's arm. "You know I'm not a monster." I said.

George looked into my eyes. "I know I wasn't there. I've heard what the Anthanii did, and I can't say I'd fault anyone for trying to stop it." He reached up with his other hand and removed mine. "I also know a girl deserves to think better of her brother than that."

"What's the difference between killing white men for black men and killing white men for other white men." I shot back at my tutor.

"Maybe there isn't a difference. We just see it clearer." That hit me in the gut. I couldn't respond. "In the meantime, you have a guest. She's on the porch."

Seiford came over to me after we were alone. "We tried to make things better." Was all he could say.

"Maybe we should have tried harder." I stared at my friend. "Maybe we should stop inspiring people to be decent and start making them."

We walked out to the porch. It was a sunny day, so my mother would be out there too. Rachel caught me as I stalked outside.

"What is going on?" She pulled me close to her. "Why am I here?"

"Someone tried to have you killed to get to me." I kept walking. "I didn't want to leave you alone."

"That's all very chivalrous of you," she said, "but who?"

When I stepped out back, the guest stopped me dead. I didn't answer Rachel.

It was Mother Vestia speaking pleasantly with my mother. She looked just the same as when I'd said goodbye to her. Same gray hair tied up. Same regal look despite the sackcloth she wore. Was that how deep she thought she had me? She thought she could have Rachel killed and come around for dinner.

There was a boy standing next to her, couldn't have been older than twenty. He was a Constable by the tattoos on his arm. He wore two six shooters on his side next to a curved blade. It was the type the Easterners used, and judging by his olive skin and prodigious beard, he was an Easterner himself. He was tall and lean, covered in muscle. I sized him up as soon as I saw the lad.

"So then he marched up to the instructor and said, 'you don't know shit about shooting.'" My mother laughed with Vestia. "Oh, you know your son."

"I do, and that sounds just like him." Pamela responded.

Then they looked over and saw me. I thought I would rage at her. I thought I might shoot her on the spot, but seeing her again made me feel like I was fifteen years old.

"He really didn't know shit about shooting." I said softly.

"Oh, Tom-Tom." My mother stood up to hug me. "I heard you were back." She finally let go. "Mother Vestia's been telling me all manner of stories about you."

Vestia came over to me next. "Seiford and Thomas!" She exclaimed. "My favorite pair of miscreants." She hugged us both, but when we didn't embrace her back, she took a step away puzzled. "And who might this be?" She turned to Rachel. "You're so lovely."

"I'm Rachel Gondua." She shook her hand. "I've read so much about you."

"Well, to keep a man like Thomas in check, I'll probably be reading about you soon too." Mother Vestia smiled. She smiled like she hadn't just tried to have her killed. She smiled like she didn't know.

"My name is Constable Ahmed." The young man with the sword at his belt extended his tattooed hand. I ignored it.

"Oh, be nice to him Thomas. He's such a nice boy." My mother exclaimed as she went back to her seat. "He made me this tea." She raised the glass up.

I took it from her. "I'm sure Mother Vestia would like some of this too." I handed it to her.

"I drink his tea quite a bit." Vestia cocked an eyebrow at me. "It helps with my joint pain."

"Then you'd like some now." I gestured to it. "Ease those joints."

"I wanted your mother to have some." She narrowed her eyes. There wasn't fear or hostility there, just bewilderment. It was like she didn't know the game we were playing.

"I insist." I kept her eyes.

"Tom-Tom, this isn't how we treat our guests." My mother was just as confused.

"I insist." I kept on.

"Thomas Robert Belson, you knock that off this instant!" Pamela was quite sore with me over the rudeness, but I couldn't care in that instant.

"It's quite alright." Mother Vestia nodded to my mother and took a sip. It wasn't poisoned. "I'm glad your son is so paranoid. It's kept him safe." She handed me back the cup.

I emptied the contents. It could have been some dangerous herb she'd accustomed herself to in an attempt to soothe my nerves. I'd seen that trick before. It probably wasn't, but I didn't want to give her the satisfaction of letting my mother drink my replacements tea."

"I could make more if that wasn't to your liking." Ahmed took a step forward.

"Don't trouble yourself." I waved him off. "Why are you here?"

"To see you of course." She smiled at me like there wasn't a thought in her mind besides my well being. "I wanted to make sure you're adjusting."

"I find getting away from Thyro has given me perspective." I put an edge on my voice even she couldn't miss.

"Anyway..." Mother Vestia sat back down. "I also wanted to introduce you to Constable Ahmed. He's the best of the new crop. Some people are even comparing him to you." It made my blood boil.

"No one compared me to a hero when I left God's Rest." I looked the boy up and down. "They laughed and scoffed and hoped I'd die."

"You should know I don't compare myself to you." The boy took a step forward. "I've read about everything you've done. I just try and emulate it."

"And emulate it you have." Mother Vestia beamed with pride at her new charge. "You should have seen him at Herow. I thought I was hearing a story about you." She sat back. "Still, there's only one Belson the Blessed."

"Don't you forget that." I whispered cold anger at her.

"I won't." It was like she was trying to read a book in a language she didn't understand. "Is there something wrong Thomas."

"I think it's best we speak alone." Seiford cut it.

"If that's what you want." Mother Vestia stood up.

Vestia, Ahmed, Seiford, and I walked to the garden out back, leaving Rachel and my mother behind. "What's this all about, Thomas?" She asked. "Why are you acting so strange?"

"We could still be in earshot." I said. "Let's head up to that tree."

"No, I want to do it here." She stopped and wouldn't be moved. Maybe she finally saw the danger she was in.

"Fine let's do it here." I hadn't wanted an audience, but it didn't matter to me much anymore. "The worlds gone to hell in a handbasket while I've been away." I stared her down. "Since you sent me away."

"I think that might be a bridge too far." Mother Vestia shrugged. "Sure, there's some unrest, but there's always unrest. There's no wars, poverty has gone down, and the nations of Thyro are signing agreements so that nothing like the Thaniel Wars can happen again." She sighed. "You're right though, there is unrest. That can be healthy, though."

"Not this kind." I pulled out a cigarette and started to smoke. "I hear every newspaperman in Thyro decries my deeds. I hear they teach a class in universities called the Crimes of Thomas Belson."

I smoked some more. "I hear they've whipped the younger crowds into quite a frenzy."

"Enemies are the price of success." She waved it off. "You changed the landscape of the whole world. You ruffled some feathers when you did that."

"Aye, I suppose so." I smoked some more. "This seems organized though. At least that's what Viverent and Prince Edward seem to think." I tapped my head. "Those are powerfully clever men."

"You're a powerfully clever man." Mother Vestia rolled her eyes. "It doesn't stop you from being powerfully paranoid either."

"A lot of clever men point to the same thing." I shrugged. "Might be enough of us see it, there could be something there." I took a step towards her, a step filled with violence. Constable Ahmed saw it and took a step forward too, hand falling on his sword. "Remember what that Priest told me at Sterling?"

"Is that what this is about?" She laughed it off. "The last words of some Priest." She shook her head. "They were just meant to scare you. To turn you towards a darker path."

"They did scare me." I said. "Doesn't mean they weren't true."

"It doesn't mean they are." Mother Vestia tried to put a hand on my shoulder, but I stepped away. "He would have said anything to get out of a hangman's noose."

"You know I had a conversation with Thaniel right before I ended him." I tilted my head. "Might be the most honest conversation I ever had." I shrugged. "I never knew a man to lie with a rope around his neck. If anything that's the only time he's honest."

"And what did Thaniel say to you?" She asked.

"He warned me." I said. "About what, I won't say. Whatever he was at the end, he deserved one sacred conversation."

"You want me to say there's no conspiracy around you?" The way she looked at me cut deep. "Of course there is." She laughed. "There's thousands. I found one group that wanted you to go into Inte so they could set up a tea trading business. That doesn't mean we should go and try to root them all out." She paused. "You're a powerful man, Thomas Belson. There's a good many who'd like to use you, so don't let them."

"This one seems to control the papers, the universities, and maybe in time the mob." I flicked some ash. "That's something we should maybe deal with. Don't you think?"

"Are some reporters paid to write pieces on you? Of course, they are." She was baffled by my naivety. "Are some professors trying to slander your name? I'd reckon so." She took another step forward. "Is it part of some grand old plot? No!"

"I know what reporters and professors are like." I shrugged. "Might be it is just some folks trying to get back at me or seem smart by taking an extreme position." I smoked my cigarette. "Might be that's all it is, but what about this fellow Malix?" I asked.

Mother Vestia stopped dead. "You mean that radical preaching that the only reason we want to eradicate the Old Religion is to keep the oppressed, oppressed." She shook her head. "Is that the man you're talking about?"

"Aye, that's the one." I stared back at her.

"He is dangerous, and we should treat him as such." Mother Vestia nodded her head.

"Then why haven't you dealt with him yet?" I asked.

"I've written a thousand papers denouncing him." She rolled her eyes. "I have the monks preaching against him till their throats bleed."

"No!" I shouted, and the violence of it shocked me. "Why haven't you *dealt with him*?"

"We're not cloaked thugs!" She screamed at me. "We don't assassinate people!"

"No, you have me do it in a battle." I hissed back at her. "What's the difference?"

"The difference is we fight people who send daggers in the night." She plucked the cigarette out of my mouth and stomped it. "We don't become then."

"Aye, the old take the high road speech." I shook my head. "How's that working for you?"

"It's worked fine!" She spat back at me. "You've almost wiped the Old Religion off the map."

"Almost being the keyword." I hissed back. "How much headway have you made since I left?"

That caught her off guard. "I admit your absence has been a hindrance." She swallowed. "But we've been working to finish them off." She pointed to Constable Ahmed. "Just last month Ahmed tracked down a cult it Roston."

"Ahmed." I turned to him. "Did any of those Demon Talkers even have a blood-colored cloak?"

He shook his head. "They'd just managed to make a crop grow when I got to them."

"Aye, you're really doing the Three's work." I turned back to Mother Vestia.

"Those huge temples are almost all gone." She rolled her eyes. "You burned them."

"In a few years, I'd have had them all." I lit another cigarette. "But you sent me away before I could finish what I started."

"So that's what this is about." She strode towards me. "You're right. You'd have seen that plague ended." She faced me then. "You'd have ground it all into the dirt with fire and blood, but I stopped you because I knew what it'd done to you." She paused. "You talk about all those who decry your name. Well, on the path you were headed, they wouldn't have had to lie." This was something Mother Vestia never wanted to say out loud, but I'd made her. "Those last few years, Thomas…" She took a deep breath. "You got bad."

"I did what was necessary." We were inches away from each other.

"That's what you never understood, Thomas." She sighed. "The only thing separating you from your enemies is what you're headed towards."

"That's what people have been telling me for so long." I shook my head. "After I beat Thaniel, I could've overthrown that bastard, King John!" I screamed. "I could've had the most powerful empire anyone ever saw!" My voice dropped to barely a whisper. "I could have set the world right, but I believed all the lies you told me."

"Who decides what's right?" She asked.

"The strongest." I didn't need to think about it.

"The one with the fastest draw, you mean." She hissed back at me.

"If need be." I paused. "But none of that makes a difference now. I did stop." I turned towards Ahmed. "You tried to replace me, right before I could end it all." I sucked in some more smoke. "The more I think about it, the more I think this isn't run of the mill incompetence. I never did find out what woman that Priest was talking about."

"You think I betrayed you." Mother Vestia couldn't believe what I was saying.

"I've got the knife in my back to prove it." Seiford handed me the note. "You know that girl I met? She's been saying things I've been thinking for a long time." I said. "Always telling me about how I should've gone farther. I think I'm starting to believe her." I handed her the note.

"You think I wrote this?" Mother Vestia turned to Seiford. "Do you believe this too?"

"I think there's evidence to support our friend's claim." The monk said. "The things he's seeing, I see them too." He shook his head. "I think you're far too competent to let matters get like this. Maybe it's more than incompetence."

"I didn't even know the girl's name till today." She threw the note in the mud.

"I figured you'd say that." I stepped towards her. "I want to hear you admit to it!" I screamed. "I want to hear you say that you wanted her dead." My hand was on the tomahawk. "People always speak the truth when their head is in a noose." I tapped the weapon on my side. "Consider this the rope."

Fear finally found it's way into her face. "Thomas, I…"

"Say it!" I screamed.

"Thomas this has gone too far." Seiford stepped in. "Whatever's going on you're not going to hurt this woman." He put a hand on my shoulder. "She was like a mother to us."

My elbow hit him hard in the nose. He hit the ground. "I love you Seiford, but this is a game of absolutes." I turned to my friend. "Either she's guilty and deserves to be punished, or she's innocent. I think it's the former." I stepped over him. "Don't interfere."

I pulled out my ax and stalked towards her, but Ahmed met me. "Please, don't do this." He said. "You're my hero…"

"Step aside boy." I hissed at him. "I got no quarrel with you."

"This isn't the Thomas Belson I read about." The Constable drew his sword.

"No, this is the one that actually existed." I stared him down. "No one would have remembered me if I'd walked the peaceful road. Glory is paved with corpses."

"You were supposed to be a savior." He fell into his stance.

"Then I'll try and be yours." I said. "Step aside."

"Do it!" Mother Vestia screamed. "Run away! He'll kill you."

"I will." I spit the cigarette out.

"I reckon you probably will." Ahmed smiled. "It's not the ends though. It's the way we get there."

He leapt at me, sword grasped in both hands. I met him with

my ax. The boy was fast, and he knew his business. Metal clanged against metal. He was quicker than me. Three above, he was probably quicker than when I was fifteen years ago. He didn't have what I had, though.

I felt the battle-joy come on me. This was how I was meant to be. This was how Belson the Blessed had been born. I'd searched half the world for a worthy opponent when Thaniel fell. Ahmed wasn't Thaniel, but he was as close as I'd come in a long time.

Our steel met again and again. It felt like an hour. It was probably under a minute. Finally, he exposed himself. A strike that didn't go back quite fast enough. I twisted the blade from his hand and struck him in the face hard.

Ahmed went reeling, but to his credit, he was back up in a flash. Eyeing me up. Figuring how he was gonna beat me.

"This fight is over." I hissed at him. "Stand aside."

"Run!" Mother Vestia screamed.

I saw his eyes drop to the six-shooter at his waist. "Don't." I knew what he was thinking.

His hand darted to his belt quicker than I'd have taken him for, but I was always the fastest draw. My gun went off first, and the boy dropped.

"No!" Mother Vestia screamed.

The boy moaned in pain. I didn't want him dead. I wanted him out of my way. A bullet to the shoulder would do that.

"What have you become?" Mother Vestia looked on in horror. It was like she'd finally finished the puzzle, but the picture on it was too horrible to face.

"I'm what you made me." I pushed the muzzle into her head. "Do you know what hurts the worst?" I asked but didn't wait for an answer. "That all these years, I thought you loved me like a son." A tear ran down my cheek. "I was just your fucking dog."

"I've always loved you like a son. I still love you like a son!" She grabbed the barrel of my pistol. "Pull that trigger, and I'll go to the Three begging them to forgive you." She pushed the muzzle into her forehead. "If my death would've brought you even an ounce of peace, I would have taken a swim with lead in my pockets." She held her grip. "Kill me if you have to, but don't go down this road." She was crying now too. "There's no turning back once you do."

"Do it, Thomas!" Rachel screamed. She must have come for the show "She's holding you back. Do it and be the man you were always supposed to become." She had a look of sick pleasure on her face.

My eyes darted from Rachel to Mother Vestia. One weeping before me, one urging me on. Could I really do it? Could I kill an old woman in cold blood? A woman I'd loved once. I uncocked the pistol. Turns out, I couldn't.

"Leave this place and never come back." I holstered my weapon. "If I see you again, I will kill you."

"I'll always be at your side." She whispered up to me. That hit me in the gut.

"Leave!" I screamed at her.

She gathered up Ahmed and hurried off. She looked back once. Her eyes didn't look like the kind that saw me as a dog. They didn't look like the eyes of someone who would send an assassin to my bed. They looked like the eyes of someone who cared. They looked like they were in pain.

"You should have killed her." Rachel stepped up to me.

"I'm done doing what everyone says I should do." I touched the tattoos on my arm. "I'm doing as I see fit now."

I kissed her deep then. "Send a letter to McAllan." I said when I stopped. "Tell him I'll fight." Belson the Blessed was back.

Present Day

We rode into the Belson Plantation as fast as I could remember riding anywhere. Everyone with me was winded to some degree. I hadn't let them sleep any more than a couple of hours at a time. I needed to make sure my family was safe.

Andrew handled it well. He was originally trained as a cavalryman before he'd been pulled into an infantry unit. Seiford was used to my galloping like the World Below was on my heels, even if he wasn't built for it. Rachel had surprised me. I knew she was excellent in a saddle, but this sort of cross-country ride had a way of wearing at people. George was far too old to find any part of it enjoyable, and Alexander Gondua was a dandy through and through.

Ayn-Tuk could have kept pace, but after he saw the Demon-Bound's corpse, he said something about needing answers. He rode off into the night, giving none of us the faintest clue what questions he was asking. I didn't need an answer anymore. I already had one.

I jumped off Shaggy Cow as soon as I got to the plantation, and Seiford followed my lead. Andrew went about to make sure the family was accounted for. I didn't know who else she'd try to hurt.

"Thomas, we need to talk." The monk put a hand on my shoulder. I'd filled them all in to some degree of what had transpired. I hadn't let anyone but Seiford and Tuk know about how deep I suspected this went.

"About what?" I said without turning to him. "You saw the note. You know there's only one person with the reach to do that." I kept walking. "You know there's only one person who could have given that order." I stopped for a moment. "It was Mother Vestia."

"We don't know that." The monk said.

I turned to face him. "You're the smartest person I know, Seif." I took a step towards him. "Right now, you're looking through a haze of emotion." I took a deep breath to steady myself. "Approach it like you would a math proof, unbiased. What's the answer?"

"Same as yours." The monk said. "But that woman loves you as much as anyone in this world." He stepped towards me. "She wouldn't use us like this."

"People do strange things to those we love." I turned away. "Sometimes, they're the only ones we can really hurt."

Seiford shook his head. "What are you going to do, Thomas?" He kept saying my name like it would make me more human.

"I don't know." Now it was my turn to shake my head. "I've been thinking about Sterling lately." I gave a heavy thought. "The Pillars too, the Golden Fort, and all the rest."

"That's not something I want you thinking too much about." Seiford scowled.

"Why didn't we stay?" I asked. "Some of the people we leave in power are decent enough, but others seem just as bad as the tyrants we tear down."

Seiford took a second to think. "We had business elsewhere." We both knew that answer wasn't good enough.

I shook my head. "I mean what if the New Church started ruling places. Think about how much easier that would be." I shrugged my shoulders. "We wouldn't have to borrow other armies or operate on lent authority. We could really change the world," I paused, "and keep it changed."

The monk looked at me curiously. "It's not our way."

"What if it could be?" I took a step back.

"It shouldn't." Seiford said firmly. "We serve to inspire men to greatness, not force our version of it upon them. Every man has his own path in this world. We only serve to let them choose it. We don't rule over people because it's not our right."

"Who has a right to rule?" I asked dismissively. "Monarchs who inherited their position, bureaucrats who stole them?" It was all too much for me. "Forget about it. Just a thought I've been having." I turned to go back into the house, but Seiford grabbed my shoulder and stopped me.

"You're right maybe they don't," the monk admitted, "but that's why we can't take their place." There was a steadfastness about him that shocked me. "That's why we can't become them."

"Then how does it change?" I growled back. "If we don't replace the men we unseat, it's just the same old breed who takes the throne."

"You're right again. They probably will." Seiford took his hand off me. "But we inspire people. We teach them a better way, a way of wisdom, honor, and compassion. One day that'll be enough. One day people will look to men like you and break their shackles." The monk's words didn't mean as much to me as they once had. "You can do things no one else can." He put a finger in my chest. "The whole world couldn't stop Thomas Belson if it wanted to. We can be the epitome of the systems that have enslaved men since we started writing down history, or we can be something better." He sighed. "We can be the men that proved them wrong."

"What if that takes too long?" I shook my head. "What if there isn't a better way?"

"Then we keep trying." Seiford clenched his jaw.

"Why?" I was dismayed at how he wasn't. "It hasn't worked in the five hundred years we've been trying it! What makes you think it'll work now?"

Seiford looked like he'd been struck. "Hope." He said simply. "Faith." The monk looked into my eyes. "I don't care if it doesn't work. I'll die telling your stories and teaching the Three Gifts because I don't want to live in a world that needs to be forced into civility." He stopped and leveled a proud look at me. "But I don't think I'm wrong. People don't just look to you as a savior, they look to you as an example, and it's working bit by bit."

"Maybe they should find a better one of both." I spit into the ground.

"Maybe they should, but for now you're all they have." He shook his head. "What's gotten into you, Thomas?"

"Since I became powerful enough to change this world, people have been telling me I shouldn't!" I screamed.

"You did change the world!" Seiford matched me. "You're still changing it, whether you see it or not!"

"Aye, for a few years." I shrugged. "Then what? Then as soon as I leave, the same old people try to undo everything I gave up so much for." I put a hand on his shoulder. "What your brother died for." It was a low trick.

"And what did my brother tell you?" Seiford narrowed his eyes.

"Let's go find my family." I turned to leave, but Seiford held me.

"No, not until you answer my question." He pulled me closer. "What did my brother tell you?"

I shook my head. "He told me that being strong meant I could do what no one else could." It came out barely a whisper. "He said I could walk the path no one else can, but I had to do it the right way."

"Then do it." Seiford said. "The right way."

"Let's go find my family." I turned into the house.

I was caught by George. "We accounted for everyone except your sister." He said. "She's probably in the library, though."

"Let's be sure." I led the way to her.

"Wait! There's a visitor you should see." George held on to me.

"I'll deal with that after I see my sister." I shook off his hand.

I pushed into the door and saw Alexis reading some dusty old tome. When I was a boy, it felt like all the knowledge of the world was held in that room. Since then, I'd seen libraries bigger than cities.

Alexis closed the book and stood to greet us. "It looks like you three rode through the World Below?" She cocked an eyebrow. "What happened."

I ignored the comment. She didn't need to know the danger I suspected could be on her. "What's the topic today?" I was just happy to see her safe.

"Anthanii colonialism in Souren." George responded with a forced smile. "By the look of that tome?"

"I understand you spent a good bit of time in Souren." Alexis posited curiously.

"Well, as a matter of fact, we did spend some time with the blacks, little one. That's where we met Tuk." Seiford sat down in the seat across from her. Our previous altercation seemed to have slipped from his mind at the prospect of a good tall tale. "I could tell you some stories about those people."

"You'd better not tell the wrong stories." I gave him a warning stare.

"You fought with them?" Alexis asked, trying to hide the admiration. "I heard they eat the hearts of their enemies." She said excitedly. "I heard when a man comes of age he has to wrestle a lion." She leaned in close as if telling a secret. "I hear their greatest warriors can split a tree with one blow."

Seiford and I smiled at each other. I gestured for him to go, so the monk started. "They don't usually eat each other's hearts. Sometimes men go a bit wild in battle, but it's not often." He rolled his eyes. "The two of us have seen white men act just as brutal on a Thyran battlefield. Things like that don't seem to be isolated to one race, as far as I can tell."

"Didn't Tukna eat a heart?" I cut in.

"It was a goat heart." Seiford said reassuring the girl. "And he was very drunk." He gestured to me. "You want to explain lion wrestling?"

"Of course I do." I kept the smile. Seeing my sister in good spirits raised mine enough to forget my argument with Seiford too. We were friends, and nothing could keep us apart for too long. "When a warrior gets good enough at fighting they give him the title An-Sab. It means lion man, sometimes it's translated as lion fighter."

"Didn't you wrestle a lion?" Seiford cut in.

"It was a baby one." I shrugged at my sister. "And I was very drunk."

"So the part about breaking tree trunks with a single punch?" Alexis asked.

"They punch trees to make their fist stronger, and sometimes they break." I said. "It's still impressive, but the trees that grow over there aren't very big."

"Are they usually drunk when they do this?" Alexis rolled her eyes.

"Almost always." Seiford said through a grin. "We'll make an anthropologist of you yet."

"So what did you two do over there?" The girl asked wide-eyed.

"Lots of drinking." I answered.

"Lots of whoring." Seiford shrugged.

I picked up a pen and threw it at my friend. "Remember your audience." Seiford kept that big grin on his face.

"You know what the girl means." George answered through a laugh. "Why were you there, besides drinking and whoring?"

"Some of the tribes started using Demon Worship to try and master the rest. After we weren't needed in Thyro, they sent us there." Seiford said.

"Essentially, we did the same thing we'd been doing for the past ten years, but the battles were usually smaller." I shrugged my shoulders.

"I got to ride an elephant in one of them." Seiford said excitedly then turned mournful. "I still miss Surus."

"Your elephant died?" Alexis was shocked. "How did they kill an elephant?"

"It didn't die." I cut in. "The ship captain wouldn't let him take an elephant with us."

"You got to keep Shaggy." He barked.

"Shaggy fits on a boat." I shot back, the same argument we'd been having for years.

"Did you fight with the Anthanii at the Golden Fort then?" The girl asked trying to turn the conversation back to the stories.

Seiford and I looked at each other, this time not knowing what to say. "We were there." I said eventually. That wasn't something I wanted her asking too many questions about.

"How did you escape the massacre?" She asked

"Well..." Seiford began but didn't know how to finish.

"Our orders were to not interfere." I said for him.

Alexis didn't seem disappointed exactly. She just couldn't believe that we'd done nothing, but the truth was worse. "So you just watched while they slaughtered those soldiers?"

"Well, not exactly." Seiford muttered nervously. It wasn't one of the stories that he wanted told, but to many people knew for it to be a secret. If either of us lied, my sister would find out, and our renewed relationship was already tenuous.

"We didn't stand by." I said it colder than I meant to

"What do you mean?" The girl's eyes darted between the two of us. Understanding finally dawned on her. "You didn't fight with those savages did you?"

"The Souren might not have a written language or founded cities, but they weren't the savages in that place." I said grimly.

"They were trying to bring technology and civilization to a backwards people." Alexis said in disgust.

"Up north it's different." Seiford put in. "The relationship is more mutually beneficial. The New Church let Anthanii know what would happen if they abused those people." He paused for a moment. "The Golden Fort was farther south. We can't keep eyes on it all. Things get darker down there." The monk shook his head. "At the end it was too dark to be redeemed."

"So you killed them all!" She looked horrified.

"We spent a month trying to negotiate fair treatment," I was lost in my memories, "but my name didn't carry quite so much weight down there."

"You killed your own people?" She tilted her head as if she couldn't quite grasp it.

"I won't call anyone who steals, rapes, and murders like they did, my people." I shot back with more venom than I meant to. "I wanted it to be peaceful, but they wouldn't let it be."

"It wasn't supposed to be a massacre. We were just going to push them off their foothold." Seiford tried to salvage the situation. "Your brother screamed for it to stop, but the Souren warriors had been abused too long for mercy." The monk shivered remembering that day. "We almost had a peaceful surrender with the survivors, but some Anthanii private wanted to be a hero and got a hold of his musket."

"That's supposed to make it better?" Alexis eyed the two of us in disgust. "You didn't mean to?"

George reached out a hand to calm my sister. "Alexis, you don't know how easy it is for something like that to go bad. You've never seen a battlefield."

"I don't need to see a battle to know that's not how heroes act!" The girl stood up.

I was done asking forgiveness for doing what other men couldn't. "It is when it's necessary." I snarled back at her. "See if they treat the Souren like that again." I took a step forward. Everyone in the room was quiet. Perhaps they were seeing what my sister saw, what Thaniel saw. "Now, the whole world knows what happens when you kill a people's men, rape their women, and enslave their children."

"And what happens to them?" She shot back.

"Thomas Belson happens to them." I said levelly.

"You're a monster." She said it barely a whisper and stormed out.

"Alexis-" I called out for her, but she didn't turn around. "You don't understand!"

George frowned at me. Not in the way a friend might, but in the way a disappointed teacher would. "I'll talk to her." He patted me on the shoulder and went to follow.

I grabbed the tutor's arm. "You know I'm not a monster." I said.

George looked into my eyes. "I know I wasn't there. I've heard what the Anthanii did, and I can't say I'd fault anyone for trying to stop it." He reached up with his other hand and removed mine. "I also know a girl deserves to think better of her brother than that."

"What's the difference between killing white men for black men and killing white men for other white men." I shot back at my tutor.

"Maybe there isn't a difference. We just see it clearer." That hit me in the gut. I couldn't respond. "In the meantime, you have a guest. She's on the porch."

Seiford came over to me after we were alone. "We tried to make things better." Was all he could say.

"Maybe we should have tried harder." I stared at my friend. "Maybe we should stop inspiring people to be decent and start making them."

We walked out to the porch. It was a sunny day, so my mother would be out there too. Rachel caught me as I stalked outside.

"What is going on?" She pulled me close to her. "Why am I here?"

"Someone tried to have you killed to get to me." I kept walking. "I didn't want to leave you alone."

"That's all very chivalrous of you," she said, "but who?"

When I stepped out back, the guest stopped me dead. I didn't answer Rachel.

It was Mother Vestia speaking pleasantly with my mother. She looked just the same as when I'd said goodbye to her. Same gray hair tied up. Same regal look despite the sackcloth she wore. Was that how deep she thought she had me? She thought she could have Rachel killed and come around for dinner.

There was a boy standing next to her, couldn't have been older than twenty. He was a Constable by the tattoos on his arm. He wore two six shooters on his side next to a curved blade. It was the type the Easterners used, and judging by his olive skin and prodigious beard, he was an Easterner himself. He was tall and lean, covered in muscle. I sized him up as soon as I saw the lad.

"So then he marched up to the instructor and said, 'you don't know shit about shooting.'" My mother laughed with Vestia. "Oh, you know your son."

"I do, and that sounds just like him." Pamela responded.

Then they looked over and saw me. I thought I would rage at her. I thought I might shoot her on the spot, but seeing her again made me feel like I was fifteen years old.

"He really didn't know shit about shooting." I said softly.

"Oh, Tom-Tom." My mother stood up to hug me. "I heard you were back." She finally let go. "Mother Vestia's been telling me all manner of stories about you."

Vestia came over to me next. "Seiford and Thomas!" She exclaimed. "My favorite pair of miscreants." She hugged us both, but when we didn't embrace her back, she took a step away puzzled. "And who might this be?" She turned to Rachel. "You're so lovely."

"I'm Rachel Gondua." She shook her hand. "I've read so much about you."

"Well, to keep a man like Thomas in check, I'll probably be reading about you soon too." Mother Vestia smiled. She smiled like she hadn't just tried to have her killed. She smiled like she didn't know.

"My name is Constable Ahmed." The young man with the sword at his belt extended his tattooed hand. I ignored it.

"Oh, be nice to him Thomas. He's such a nice boy." My mother exclaimed as she went back to her seat. "He made me this tea." She raised the glass up.

I took it from her. "I'm sure Mother Vestia would like some of this too." I handed it to her.

"I drink his tea quite a bit." Vestia cocked an eyebrow at me. "It helps with my joint pain."

"Then you'd like some now." I gestured to it. "Ease those joints."

"I wanted your mother to have some." She narrowed her eyes. There wasn't fear or hostility there, just bewilderment. It was like she didn't know the game we were playing.

"I insist." I kept her eyes.

"Tom-Tom, this isn't how we treat our guests." My mother was just as confused.

"I insist." I kept on.

"Thomas Robert Belson, you knock that off this instant!" Pamela was quite sore with me over the rudeness, but I couldn't care in that instant.

"It's quite alright." Mother Vestia nodded to my mother and took a sip. It wasn't poisoned. "I'm glad your son is so paranoid. It's kept him safe." She handed me back the cup.

I emptied the contents. It could have been some dangerous herb she'd accustomed herself to in an attempt to soothe my nerves. I'd seen that trick before. It probably wasn't, but I didn't want to give her the satisfaction of letting my mother drink my replacements tea."

"I could make more if that wasn't to your liking." Ahmed took a step forward.

"Don't trouble yourself." I waved him off. "Why are you here?"

"To see you of course." She smiled at me like there wasn't a thought in her mind besides my well being. "I wanted to make sure you're adjusting."

"I find getting away from Thyro has given me perspective." I put an edge on my voice even she couldn't miss.

"Anyway..." Mother Vestia sat back down. "I also wanted to introduce you to Constable Ahmed. He's the best of the new crop. Some people are even comparing him to you." It made my blood boil.

"No one compared me to a hero when I left God's Rest." I looked the boy up and down. "They laughed and scoffed and hoped I'd die."

"You should know I don't compare myself to you." The boy took a step forward. "I've read about everything you've done. I just try and emulate it."

"And emulate it you have." Mother Vestia beamed with pride at her new charge. "You should have seen him at Herow. I thought I was hearing a story about you." She sat back. "Still, there's only one Belson the Blessed."

"Don't you forget that." I whispered cold anger at her.

"I won't." It was like she was trying to read a book in a language she didn't understand. "Is there something wrong Thomas."

"I think it's best we speak alone." Seiford cut it.

"If that's what you want." Mother Vestia stood up.

Vestia, Ahmed, Seiford, and I walked to the garden out back, leaving Rachel and my mother behind. "What's this all about, Thomas?" She asked. "Why are you acting so strange?"

"We could still be in earshot." I said. "Let's head up to that tree."

"No, I want to do it here." She stopped and wouldn't be moved. Maybe she finally saw the danger she was in.

"Fine let's do it here." I hadn't wanted an audience, but it didn't matter to me much anymore. "The worlds gone to hell in a handbasket while I've been away." I stared her down. "Since you sent me away."

"I think that might be a bridge too far." Mother Vestia shrugged. "Sure, there's some unrest, but there's always unrest. There's no wars, poverty has gone down, and the nations of Thyro are signing agreements so that nothing like the Thaniel Wars can happen again." She sighed. "You're right though, there is unrest. That can be healthy, though."

"Not this kind." I pulled out a cigarette and started to smoke. "I hear every newspaperman in Thyro decries my deeds. I hear they teach a class in universities called the Crimes of Thomas Belson."

I smoked some more. "I hear they've whipped the younger crowds into quite a frenzy."

"Enemies are the price of success." She waved it off. "You changed the landscape of the whole world. You ruffled some feathers when you did that."

"Aye, I suppose so." I smoked some more. "This seems organized though. At least that's what Viverent and Prince Edward seem to think." I tapped my head. "Those are powerfully clever men."

"You're a powerfully clever man." Mother Vestia rolled her eyes. "It doesn't stop you from being powerfully paranoid either."

"A lot of clever men point to the same thing." I shrugged. "Might be enough of us see it, there could be something there." I took a step towards her, a step filled with violence. Constable Ahmed saw it and took a step forward too, hand falling on his sword. "Remember what that Priest told me at Sterling?"

"Is that what this is about?" She laughed it off. "The last words of some Priest." She shook her head. "They were just meant to scare you. To turn you towards a darker path."

"They did scare me." I said. "Doesn't mean they weren't true."

"It doesn't mean they are." Mother Vestia tried to put a hand on my shoulder, but I stepped away. "He would have said anything to get out of a hangman's noose."

"You know I had a conversation with Thaniel right before I ended him." I tilted my head. "Might be the most honest conversation I ever had." I shrugged. "I never knew a man to lie with a rope around his neck. If anything that's the only time he's honest."

"And what did Thaniel say to you?" She asked.

"He warned me." I said. "About what, I won't say. Whatever he was at the end, he deserved one sacred conversation."

"You want me to say there's no conspiracy around you?" The way she looked at me cut deep. "Of course there is." She laughed. "There's thousands. I found one group that wanted you to go into Inte so they could set up a tea trading business. That doesn't mean we should go and try to root them all out." She paused. "You're a powerful man, Thomas Belson. There's a good many who'd like to use you, so don't let them."

"This one seems to control the papers, the universities, and maybe in time the mob." I flicked some ash. "That's something we should maybe deal with. Don't you think?"

"Are some reporters paid to write pieces on you? Of course, they are." She was baffled by my naivety. "Are some professors trying to slander your name? I'd reckon so." She took another step forward. "Is it part of some grand old plot? No!"

"I know what reporters and professors are like." I shrugged. "Might be it is just some folks trying to get back at me or seem smart by taking an extreme position." I smoked my cigarette. "Might be that's all it is, but what about this fellow Malix?" I asked.

Mother Vestia stopped dead. "You mean that radical preaching that the only reason we want to eradicate the Old Religion is to keep the oppressed, oppressed." She shook her head. "Is that the man you're talking about?"

"Aye, that's the one." I stared back at her.

"He is dangerous, and we should treat him as such." Mother Vestia nodded her head.

"Then why haven't you dealt with him yet?" I asked.

"I've written a thousand papers denouncing him." She rolled her eyes. "I have the monks preaching against him till their throats bleed."

"No!" I shouted, and the violence of it shocked me. "Why haven't you *dealt with him*?"

"We're not cloaked thugs!" She screamed at me. "We don't assassinate people!"

"No, you have me do it in a battle." I hissed back at her. "What's the difference?"

"The difference is we fight people who send daggers in the night." She plucked the cigarette out of my mouth and stomped it. "We don't become then."

"Aye, the old take the high road speech." I shook my head. "How's that working for you?"

"It's worked fine!" She spat back at me. "You've almost wiped the Old Religion off the map."

"Almost being the keyword." I hissed back. "How much headway have you made since I left?"

That caught her off guard. "I admit your absence has been a hindrance." She swallowed. "But we've been working to finish them off." She pointed to Constable Ahmed. "Just last month Ahmed tracked down a cult it Roston."

"Ahmed." I turned to him. "Did any of those Demon Talkers even have a blood-colored cloak?"

He shook his head. "They'd just managed to make a crop grow when I got to them."

"Aye, you're really doing the Three's work." I turned back to Mother Vestia.

"Those huge temples are almost all gone." She rolled her eyes. "You burned them."

"In a few years, I'd have had them all." I lit another cigarette. "But you sent me away before I could finish what I started."

"So that's what this is about." She strode towards me. "You're right. You'd have seen that plague ended." She faced me then. "You'd have ground it all into the dirt with fire and blood, but I stopped you because I knew what it'd done to you." She paused. "You talk about all those who decry your name. Well, on the path you were headed, they wouldn't have had to lie." This was something Mother Vestia never wanted to say out loud, but I'd made her. "Those last few years, Thomas..." She took a deep breath. "You got bad."

"I did what was necessary." We were inches away from each other.

"That's what you never understood, Thomas." She sighed. "The only thing separating you from your enemies is what you're headed towards."

"That's what people have been telling me for so long." I shook my head. "After I beat Thaniel, I could've overthrown that bastard, King John!" I screamed. "I could've had the most powerful empire anyone ever saw!" My voice dropped to barely a whisper. "I could have set the world right, but I believed all the lies you told me."

"Who decides what's right?" She asked.

"The strongest." I didn't need to think about it.

"The one with the fastest draw, you mean." She hissed back at me.

"If need be." I paused. "But none of that makes a difference now. I did stop." I turned towards Ahmed. "You tried to replace me, right before I could end it all." I sucked in some more smoke. "The more I think about it, the more I think this isn't run of the mill incompetence. I never did find out what woman that Priest was talking about."

"You think I betrayed you." Mother Vestia couldn't believe what I was saying.

"I've got the knife in my back to prove it." Seiford handed me the note. "You know that girl I met? She's been saying things I've been thinking for a long time." I said. "Always telling me about how I should've gone farther. I think I'm starting to believe her." I handed her the note.

"You think I wrote this?" Mother Vestia turned to Seiford. "Do you believe this too?"

"I think there's evidence to support our friend's claim." The monk said. "The things he's seeing, I see them too." He shook his head. "I think you're far too competent to let matters get like this. Maybe it's more than incompetence."

"I didn't even know the girl's name till today." She threw the note in the mud.

"I figured you'd say that." I stepped towards her. "I want to hear you admit to it!" I screamed. "I want to hear you say that you wanted her dead." My hand was on the tomahawk. "People always speak the truth when their head is in a noose." I tapped the weapon on my side. "Consider this the rope."

Fear finally found it's way into her face. "Thomas, I..."

"Say it!" I screamed.

"Thomas this has gone too far." Seiford stepped in. "Whatever's going on you're not going to hurt this woman." He put a hand on my shoulder. "She was like a mother to us."

My elbow hit him hard in the nose. He hit the ground. "I love you Seiford, but this is a game of absolutes." I turned to my friend. "Either she's guilty and deserves to be punished, or she's innocent. I think it's the former." I stepped over him. "Don't interfere."

I pulled out my ax and stalked towards her, but Ahmed met me. "Please, don't do this." He said. "You're my hero..."

"Step aside boy." I hissed at him. "I got no quarrel with you."

"This isn't the Thomas Belson I read about." The Constable drew his sword.

"No, this is the one that actually existed." I stared him down. "No one would have remembered me if I'd walked the peaceful road. Glory is paved with corpses."

"You were supposed to be a savior." He fell into his stance.

"Then I'll try and be yours." I said. "Step aside."

"Do it!" Mother Vestia screamed. "Run away! He'll kill you."

"I will." I spit the cigarette out.

"I reckon you probably will." Ahmed smiled. "It's not the ends though. It's the way we get there."

He leapt at me, sword grasped in both hands. I met him with

my ax. The boy was fast, and he knew his business. Metal clanged against metal. He was quicker than me. Three above, he was probably quicker than when I was fifteen years ago. He didn't have what I had, though.

I felt the battle-joy come on me. This was how I was meant to be. This was how Belson the Blessed had been born. I'd searched half the world for a worthy opponent when Thaniel fell. Ahmed wasn't Thaniel, but he was as close as I'd come in a long time.

Our steel met again and again. It felt like an hour. It was probably under a minute. Finally, he exposed himself. A strike that didn't go back quite fast enough. I twisted the blade from his hand and struck him in the face hard.

Ahmed went reeling, but to his credit, he was back up in a flash. Eyeing me up. Figuring how he was gonna beat me.

"This fight is over." I hissed at him. "Stand aside."

"Run!" Mother Vestia screamed.

I saw his eyes drop to the six-shooter at his waist. "Don't." I knew what he was thinking.

His hand darted to his belt quicker than I'd have taken him for, but I was always the fastest draw. My gun went off first, and the boy dropped.

"No!" Mother Vestia screamed.

The boy moaned in pain. I didn't want him dead. I wanted him out of my way. A bullet to the shoulder would do that.

"What have you become?" Mother Vestia looked on in horror. It was like she'd finally finished the puzzle, but the picture on it was too horrible to face.

"I'm what you made me." I pushed the muzzle into her head. "Do you know what hurts the worst?" I asked but didn't wait for an answer. "That all these years, I thought you loved me like a son." A tear ran down my cheek. "I was just your fucking dog."

"I've always loved you like a son. I still love you like a son!" She grabbed the barrel of my pistol. "Pull that trigger, and I'll go to the Three begging them to forgive you." She pushed the muzzle into her forehead. "If my death would've brought you even an ounce of peace, I would have taken a swim with lead in my pockets." She held her grip. "Kill me if you have to, but don't go down this road." She was crying now too. "There's no turning back once you do."

"Do it, Thomas!" Rachel screamed. She must have come for the show "She's holding you back. Do it and be the man you were always supposed to become." She had a look of sick pleasure on her face.

My eyes darted from Rachel to Mother Vestia. One weeping before me, one urging me on. Could I really do it? Could I kill an old woman in cold blood? A woman I'd loved once. I uncocked the pistol. Turns out, I couldn't.

"Leave this place and never come back." I holstered my weapon. "If I see you again, I will kill you."

"I'll always be at your side." She whispered up to me. That hit me in the gut.

"Leave!" I screamed at her.

She gathered up Ahmed and hurried off. She looked back once. Her eyes didn't look like the kind that saw me as a dog. They didn't look like the eyes of someone who would send an assassin to my bed. They looked like the eyes of someone who cared. They looked like they were in pain.

"You should have killed her." Rachel stepped up to me.

"I'm done doing what everyone says I should do." I touched the tattoos on my arm. "I'm doing as I see fit now."

I kissed her deep then. "Send a letter to McAllan." I said when I stopped. "Tell him I'll fight."

Present Day
Jesse's Story

Jesse Devote was happy. It'd been a long time since he'd last felt it. Mary was sharing his bed, Bo-Bo was getting better, and his parents seemed to think their son was finally on the straight and narrow. Jesse was happy until he got a message that read,

Meet at the docks at once

-Bellefellow

Jesse told his family he was going on a walk and would be back in a bit. When he was free of the house, he sprinted to that part of town. It was an unusual message. Most had a time attached to it that Bellefellow would promptly ignore and arrive an hour late anyway. This time when he got to their usual spot, he saw that the Priest was waiting for him already, and he looked impatient. His white clad acolytes projected the emotion as well even still as stone. They weren't exactly inconspicuous, but only a fool eve drops on a Priest of the Old Religion.

"What do you want?" Jesse asked.

"No your Eminence, or how are you?" The Priest was trying to spar, but his heart wasn't in it today.

"I figured you're in a hurry." The gunslinger said. "Seemed best to just get on with it." He said as he sat down next to the monster.

"A coach is coming up the Highland Road in a week's time."

"He's dead then." Jesse knew better than to ask any more questions.

Bellefellow nodded in understanding. "This time you need to know who's in the coach."

"Then tell me." The bounty hunter knew something was off.

"It's the Prime Governor." The Priest said waiting for a response.

"Funny I didn't hear he was in town." Jesse said as if it meant nothing because it did. "He's still dead." The gunslinger liked McAllan for all he knew of him. Thought he was a good man, but he'd die all the same.

"He's traveling with only two guards." Bellefellow said looking around to make sure they weren't overheard. It was long after sunset though, so most people were gone. "He doesn't want us to know he's here, but our sources are good."

"I can see why he didn't." Jessie said sharply.

"Kill him and do it bad." The Priest leaned in. "Make him suffer."

"A Prime Governor commands a heavy price." The bounty hunter said trying to fish for more leverage. He remembered how their last conversation on the subject had gone, but he needed something.

"You're brother will be cured. Your family and your woman will receive a hundred thousand dollars each, and they'll be granted a nice plot in the west." Bellefellow paused. "They will never hear from me again."

Jesse was shocked. "Really?" Was all he could say.

"Really." The Priest nodded.

"That seems a bit generous for one head. Even if it is attached to the Prime Governor." The bounty hunter said skeptically.

"That's because it is." Bellefellow was serious as the grave. "After you've done it you'll ride back here and brag about what you've done. Then you'll be hanged."

Jesse looked at the Priest, seeing his plan in full. "You want me to start your war?" He shook his head and looked at his feet. "You want me to fire the first shot in a conflict that will kill hundreds of thousands." He looked at Bellefellow's beautiful face. "You want my name to live in infamy forever. The lone fanatic who killed the Prime Governor, so when the North wants revenge you can claim ignorance." Jesse shook his head. "No one will really believe you, but its enough armor to keep whatever secret alliances are in place."

Bellefellow gave a nod that almost spoke of respect. "Clever for a hired gun."

"It's what my paw keeps telling me." Jesse said as he stared into the sky.

The Demon-monger gave a sigh. "I want McAllan dead, and I want you hanged for it." The Priest looked at the bounty hunter coldly. "What happens after is of no concern to you." He leaned in closer. "And what happens to your name is of no concern to me."

"It's a heavy thing to do all the same." Jesse said looking at the six-shooter that hung from his belt. "To condemn myself to that." He said it more to himself than anyone else.

"As if you weren't condemned before?" The Priest cocked an eyebrow up.

Jesse gave a sad little nod. "I know there's no paradise waiting for me after the things I've done." The gunslinger paused. "Still, I imagined one day I might become a good man. Maybe not for long. Maybe for just an hour." He stared at his hands thinking of an old man he'd met. "Meet my death with something more than regret, like that barber did."

The Demon-monger cocked an eyebrow up. "Barber?"

Jesse waved it off. "Don't matter now." He paused. "Even if I couldn't get that. I thought people might be able to see where things went wrong. That if things had been different, I'd be a better man. Might be a lie but I like to think so." The gunslinger shook his head. "If I do what your asking, I won't even get that small sympathy. I won't deserve it."

Bellefellow sighed. "I'm usually not in the business of making my slaves feel better." He looked at the port in disgust over what he was about to do. "But I suppose if you're going to send a man to his death, you can't be too cruel." The Priest was almost acting humane. It was terrifying. "What do you think makes a man a hero or a villain?"

"Doing the right things." Jesse looked at the port, thinking about the place he called home. It might be the last time he could look at it. He'd never been a sentimental man, but now... "Being a hero's doing the right things because you're the only one who can."

Bellefellow snorted dismissively. "Right, wrong, good, evil, they're just matters of perspective." He looked at Jessie. "You can't help one person without taking something from another. If you take things from other people on a grand enough scale, they call you a hero." The Priest looked at his own crimson robes. "That's the secret at the heart of the Old Religion, and no one wants to ask about it." He looked then at his own acolytes. "Nothing comes free in this world. If you give something to someone, then another must suffer." He looked back at Jessie. "You think I'm evil don't you?"

"Yes." He said simply. He should have been more polite, but he was a dead man already.

"I know I'm not a good man, but you have no right to judge me. You think the battles you've seen were hard? You think crying over the bedside of your brother hurts you?" Bellefellow shook his head. "That's all a fairy tale compared to how I Ascended."

Jesse couldn't help himself he was curious. "What do you mean?"

"I wasn't always Bellefellow, that's the name of a powerful Imoran Priest, and I wasn't always so handsome." He chuckled to himself. "Most days it's like remembering through a dream if I can even remember at all. Some days it's easier though." He gave Jesse a look like he almost respected the man. "My name was Jude, and I was the miserable, ugly son of a poor farmer." He sighed. "No matter how hard I try, I can't remember the name of the people you'd call my parents. Sometimes, I remember things about them. I remember how beautiful my mother was, and how mean my father got when he was drinking." He shuddered. "I remember looking into a mirror and being disgusted with myself. I had a deformity on my head, and my limbs were misshapen. I had so much trouble breathing, the doctor thought I'd suffocate in the night." The Priest looked up into the sky. "If my mother hadn't been so kind, I'd have likely been left in the woods to die."

"That doesn't excuse what you've done to my family." Jesse said looking at the man in a new light. "That doesn't excuse what you've done to me." *But does it?* The bounty hunter thought about the barber he'd shot in cold blood. He thought of all the people he'd killed that didn't deserve to die. What had he become when he was pushed to it? "Just because you looked like a monster doesn't mean you had to become one." Jesse expected the Priest to suck the air out of his lungs again, but he didn't. He just looked at the bounty hunter thoughtfully, like a parent might a child.

"If you treat someone like a monster for long enough, what do you expect they become?" Bellefellow looked almost sad. "Even still when the black-clad men came and took me, I never thought to become a monster, just powerful enough to change the things I thought needed to be changed."

"That's what all monsters say." Jesse wasn't sure though.

"You see even a child needs to be properly motivated if he's to be successful." The Priest looked again at the children who followed him. "They offered me women and subtle drugs, as they offer all acolytes. I took them of course. It's hard for a boy to resist such things." Bellefellow turned his gaze on the bounty hunter. "However, to truly Ascend, more was required than just pleasures of the flesh." He looked away at that. "I won't go into what I had to do, but as I've said all the things you've suffered in your life pale in comparison to it." When he was done mourning he looked back at Jesse. "They let me remember how my family had gone hungry because the crops wouldn't grow, they let me remember the sounds of a Huego raiding party, they let me remember all the evil there was in this world. Then they offered me the power to change it." He grabbed the bounty hunter's shoulder like they were old friends. "I wanted that more than you even want Mary."

"Please don't talk about her." Jesse said, but the Priest went on anyway.

"I wanted so that no child would grow up hungry and scared." He kept his hand where it was. "I wanted so that everyone who had ever been called a monster would know that the power they craved was at their fingertips." He took his hand back and looked at it. "That desire drove me. My face changed, my name changed, and I was ready to become their hero." He shook his head. "I was more powerful than any had been before me, and the crops grew, and the outcasts saw." He paused. "I deal with Demons so much it can be hard to distinguish between human morality. Sometimes, I forget I'm dealing with men not ants."

Bellefellow paused collecting his thoughts. "But all the things I've done, I've done for the greater good." The Priest sneered. "Then, after all I've given up to help them, people question my methods. After all I've offered them, they ask about the costs." He looked at a few random people walking along the docks. "After what I've gone through for them, they look at me like the monster my father saw so long ago."

"You could have proved them wrong." Jesse mumbled, but was he talking to the Priest or to himself.

"Imagine yourself in my position, you can kill anyone who crosses your path easy as thinking about it." He bunched his fist. "A man treats me like a monster, without even trying to understand my story, and I think, and the man dies." He opened his hands then. "Imagine if everyone you ever casually imagined hurting, died. I think the corpses in your path would number far more than mine."

"You asked for the power." Jesse growled. "Don't bemoan the responsibility that comes with it."

Bellefellow chuckled at that. "Exactly my point. Such power can't be in the hands of those not perfectly trained in its use. That's what the New Church wants." He sighed. "Even though I mock the Three, I know they exist, perhaps even more than their own followers." He looked at Jesse. "The gifts they gave to men were real. Their mistake is they gave them to all men, and they are misnamed. They made us clever, not wise, and men used it to build war machines and factories that destroy our land. They made us delusional not honorable, and that delusion has made us kill the fellow across the river because of an insult irrelevant before they were born." The Priest paused and stared deep into Jesse's eyes. "They filled us with the lust, not love, that causes us too look at our neighbor's field and wish it was ours."

Bellefellow looked back at the port. "Things were better when the Imorans ruled, and the power of the Old Religion was unfettered. We brought stability!" He lowered his voice. "We brought peace." He said barely a whisper. "And then those damn Three lovers thought to count the price of what we did." He looked at the golden chain that was draped across his neck. "Man cannot handle the blessings of the Three."

He looked up to the sky as if cursing it. "I don't remember what I was all the time. The name Jude is meaningless to me. I am only Bellefellow. Somedays, I don't think I'm even human, but that's the price I chose to pay. I give my soul to make this world a little better. I give my soul, and they count a few scared children as too high a price!" He slammed a fist into the bench. "Men should worship Jude." He whispered it softly. He wasn't using his voice tricks. This was more powerful. This was true emotion. "He did what he had to, and so will I."

"Why are you telling me this?" As far as Jesse knew it was probably a sin to share such intimacy with a man, not of his order.

"Because you'll be dead soon." Bellefellow said calmly. "But more than that, it's because I like you. I understand you better than you understand yourself. I understand what you're willing to sacrifice for the things close to you." He sighed a bit. "Somehow you help me remember the way I used to be."

"I'll profane my name for you." Jesse said cringing at the very idea. "But I want two hundred thousand for my family and Mary." He paused looking at his gun. "And I want that plot next to a river. It'll make the crops grow better, and Bobby loves the water."

"They'll have it." The Priest nodded. "And I promise that I will never let a man in the South profane the man who started our just revolution."

"I don't know that I want to be beatified for killing McAllan." Jesse shook his head.

"You think he's a good man?" Bellefellow nodded to himself.

"I didn't vote for him." The bounty hunter said. "But he's grown on me, and I don't think he deserves to die."

"He is a good man." The Priest said to Jesse's surprise. "But he needs to die. Idealist only ever muddy clear waters."

"He'll die then." Jesse said to himself. "And my family will live in prosperity."

"That they will." Bellefellow stood up, and his acolytes followed in unison. "I'm sorry it had to be you." He turned to leave, but before he did, he turned back to the bounty hunter. "I'm sorry for the way I treated you. It was the only way to make sure you were ready for this." Before Jesse could say anything, he walked off to wherever Priest go to think on their sins.

Jesse went back to his house. The sun was rising, and people were waking up to go about their day. He tried to tell himself the Priest was just lying about it all. That the apology was only meant to ensure he did as he was beckoned, but he knew it was true. Something inside Bellefellow was a man, and Jesse above all others knew what a man could become when he was pushed. He'd always hated the Priest. To know that his story may not have been all that different from his own... It was a hard thing to hear.

The bounty hunter opened the door quietly his family was still asleep. He walked through the cozy room to where he and Mary slept. He saw Bo-Bo snoring beside her. She was so beautiful. Everyone always thought that angels were pale things bathed in light. He knew the truth. They had brown skin, dark hair, and eyes that could make a man want to be better. Angels comforted a scared boy trying to sleep even though they barely even knew him. Angels deserved better than Jesse Devote.

He shook her awake gently. "Jess?" She looked up at him rubbing her beautiful eyes.

"It's me." He smiled at her.

She looked at Bo-Bo and smiled back at her lover. "He got scared while you were gone, so I let him sleep with me." She looked at him affectionately. "He's a beautiful child."

He kissed her because he needed to touch the goodness in the world. "I have to do something." He stroked her face. "When I do, a man's going to come to you with money and a deed to good land. Take it and go west, I'll meet you there soon enough." It was hard to lie to her, even if it was best.

"Jesse, what are you going to do?" There was worry in her voice.

"What I have to." He said putting his forehead to hers.

"You don't have to do anything but stay here and be happy with me." Mary's voice was so convincing he almost agreed to it.

He shook his head and looked at her. "That comes later." He leaned back. "After I do this you'll have money and land." He paused to look at her face. "You can forget about everything bad that's happened to you."

She shook her head. "I don't care about the money or the land." She reached out and put a hand on his cheek. "I care about you." She looked at him like an angel would. "We'll scrape by. I'll sell my body again if I have too. All that matters is that I'll have you."

"I won't let you live any kind of life like that!" He touched the hand at his cheek. "I'll be there with you soon I promise." He lied.

She moved her hand to the gun at his side. "No man who lives by this can ever promise anything about tomorrow."

Jesse smiled at her. "I know. You've told me that before."

"I've never told you my story." She said desperately trying to convince him to stay. "I know you've wondered how a Peuna women came to be a whore in the South."

"I know your story." He kissed her again. "I know all the parts that matter. The rest doesn't concern me."

"I fell in love with you for that, but if you think I care about money and land, then you need to hear the rest of it." She looked at him in a way that made him want to be better. "You need to hear about how my mother died in childbirth, about how hard my father beat me during the day, and…" She paused stifling a tear. "About what he did to me at night."

"Stop." He said looking away. It was as hard for him to hear as it was for her to say.

She went on ignoring him. "You need to hear about how I was

picked up by a band of cattle rustlers when I was thirteen, about how they passed me around and dropped me off in town naked."

"Please! I don't want to hear this..." He was pleading now.

"You need to hear about what I had to do to survive, about the horrible men I let between my legs." She reached out and touched his face. "You need to hear about how the only good thing that ever happened to me was a mean bounty hunter, paying for a night, and how I counted myself the luckiest girl in the world for it." She kissed him again. "You need to hear about how I'd do it all again just to have you safe and at my side."

"You deserve better." Was all Jesse could say.

"I don't care what I deserve." She looked at him like he was the only man in the world. "I want you."

"I have to go." He looked at Mary like all men should look at her.

"Where are you going?" Bo-Bo said wiping the sleep from his eyes.

"I've got to do something, but after that everything will be perfect for all of us." He rubbed his brothers head. "The nightmares will go away. You'll be just like the other boys."

"I don't want to be like the other boys." He looked at his brother, then around the room as if he'd forgotten its shape. "I want to be like you."

Jesse tried to stop from crying, but a tear made its way down his face. "Be better than me." He told his brother. "You'll need to protect mom and dad while I'm gone." He said touching Bo-Bo's shoulder. "And Mary too, especially Mary."

"I will." Bobby said proudly. "She got scared without you so I promised I'd protect her from the nightmares."

"Don't go." Mary said pleading with him.

"Don't make this harder than it has to be." Jesse kissed her like it was the last time he'd see her. "I'm leaving now, and you can't stop me."

She nodded fighting back tears of her own. "I know, but I figured I should try."

He picked up his rifle and headed to the door. He was almost out the house when a voice stopped him. "Where are you going with that rifle, son?"

It was his father. "You don't want me to tell you." He paused. "About a week from now a man will come to you with money and land rights. Take Bobby and Mary and go as far West as the train will take you. Then keep going." He said turning to look at the man.

"Don't do this." He said softly.

"I have to." He said looking around the house. "Promise me you'll treat Mary like your own daughter." He looked at his father. "Promise me you'll find her a good husband." He said it softly, so she wouldn't hear it in the other room.

"It sounds like you're not planning on coming back." Renny took a step towards his son.

"Things happen." Jesse said more to himself than anything.

"Not if you don't let them." His father took another step forward.

"Yes, they do." Jessie sneered. "I didn't let them drive Bobby to the point of insanity, but they did it anyway."

Renny didn't have an answer for that. "You owe it to your mother to tell her goodbye." He nodded to her room. "If you can't do that, maybe you shouldn't go."

"I owe it to my mother to let her believe her son was a good man." He shook his head. "Just let me leave."

"I can't stop you son." Renny sighed. "Whenever you're about to do whatever it is you think you need to, remember that your mother thinks you a good man."

Jesse bit his lip to keep from crying. "Tell her…" He couldn't think of anything. "Tell her a comfortable lie." He looked at his father. "And promise me about Mary."

"I'd have treated her like a daughter no matter what you did." He reached out to his son and gave him a hug. "Please don't do this."

The bounty hunter pushed him away and put on his hat that sat at the door. "I have too." He said and walked out. If anyone noticed the tears streaming down his face as he rode his horse out of town, they were kind enough not to mention it.

Present Day
McAllan's Story

McAllan had moved through every part of the South and talked to any man who could possibly avert a war. Coleson had already turned them all to his side. The only one who'd had any success was Samugy. He'd set some agents to deter the commoners fighting, but the Prime Governor knew it wouldn't stop much, even the Huego himself had called it a drop in a bucket that would likely be thrown out anyway. He'd gotten a letter from Belson though. If it was going to be a fight, that was a man to have on his side.

"Once enough men start enlisting even those who think it's a bad idea will sign on for fear of being called a coward." Samugy mentioned on the way to meet Belson. "The trouble is most of those men will make the best soldiers."

McAllan knew that the type of anti-war sentiment Samugy had spread would only be useful if the fight dragged on for years, by that time it might be too late because the North would be thinking the same thing.

"So it's war then." Timothy said under his breath. He'd noticed McAllan's mood getting worse and worse with every meeting.

"Aye, it's war." Samugy muttered with as foul a disposition as the man he worked for.

"Aye." McAllan muttered.

"How do you think it'll start?" Timothy asked.

McAllan had moved his clever mind from how to stop it, to how best to start it. "We'll try and make them throw the first punch. It's the best way to keep the middle and western provinces from choosing the wrong side."

"The trick is taking the first punch." Samugy muttered. "We

need to appear like we weren't preparing for it, but if we're not prepared enough…" He let his words drop off.

"Then we'll lose, and their Anthanii and Kranish allies will be emboldened."

"It'd be better if they symbolically attacked us." Samugy said. "Like declaring war or bombing a recruiting station."

"Or killing the Prime Governor while he's in the South." McAllan said morosely. "We'd have a reason to fight, and I'm afraid the country wouldn't lose much.

"Fennis won't let that happen. He's too honorable a man." Samugy said to the two bodyguards stroking their weapons. "Besides I would have heard something by now."

"And Coleson?" Timothy asked pointedly

Samugy gave the aide an appraising look. "What about him?"

"Don't tell me you haven't thought about what that snake might do?" Timothy looked incredulous.

"Of course I have. I want to know what you think." The Huego sat back and waving his hand for the boy to continue.

Timothy looked around the room as if he expected a trap. To McAllan, it seemed the boy was thinking he shouldn't have spoken at all, but he finally did. "I don't think Fennis would kill a fly if he didn't consider it honorable." The aide looked at the Prime Governor who nodded encouragingly. "But even though Coleson plans to use the man's honor and reputation as the face of his rebellion, he still considers himself its leader. I don't think it would be out of character for him to order our assassination without telling the general, and then blaming it on some extremist faction to stay on good terms with Fennis." Timothy paused again. "Especially after the way you embarrassed his embargo."

McAllan and Samugy looked at each other approvingly before the Huego spoke up. "No, it wouldn't. That's a clever thought for a mule brain."

"That's a clever thought in your's, mine, or any other man's brain." McAllan beamed with pride at his young prodigy.

"It is." Samugy nodded in begrudging respect. "However I've thought about it. Yes, it's possible, but I have eyes and ears in Coleson's office. Men who follow a man like that are often easy to turn."

"You have traitors in Coleson's office, and you didn't think to tell us?" Timothy looked baffled.

"No, I didn't think to tell you." Samugy chided the boy. "My work is very secretive in case you haven't noticed. I don't disclose everything to the Prime Governor's paper bitch."

Timothy looked down at his feet a bit embarrassed. "I'm sorry. I was being presumptuous." McAllan stayed quiet. The boy was intelligent and honorable, and he was preparing the aide for great things, perhaps even to hold office himself. However, despite the trust McAllan put in him, he was for now just an aide. It wasn't as though McAllan didn't want the boy to know all the secrets of governing he could, but the lesson that he had to earn those secrets was more important.

"Now that you've mentioned it, they're not traitors exactly." Samugy admitted. "One senator has a whore he tells to much too, an ambitious chief of staff wants a higher position and is informing to an agent of who he believes is a political rival, and there's a head tax overseer who loves to talk politics with his barber." The Huego let the news seep in. "It's almost impossible to completely turn a powerful man to the other side, but I own the whore, the agent, and the barber, but even the whore, the agent, and the barber don't know I own them. They just have friends that I own too, and some of those friends don't even know it."

"I understand." Timothy said nodding his head.

"Tell me exactly what you understand." Samugy said like a teacher testing a student.

"People never like to think of themselves as traitors so you can't treat them like one." The aide responded. "You have to give them an excuse that lets them keep believing the story they tell themselves about how they're good people."

"Very good." Samugy nodded.

"There's one question I have though." Timothy looked around the room. "It seems that these stories would be third sometimes fourth hand before they reach a trained intelligence officer. How can you trust their reports are accurate, or worse that they're not purposely feeding misinformation."

"Very clever." McAllan said happily. "I'm curious as well. The boy brings up a good point."

"Well, because of redundancy." Samugy nodded as if it were the simplest thing in the world. "Preferably, I have five separate reports from different sources, if one piece of intelligence isn't corroborated than it's likely untrue and the result of idle boasting or speculation.

If time doesn't permit me to place enough agents in a space, then I still won't take the information seriously unless I have at least two."

The Huego leaned back happy that people were taking such an interest in his work. "If I receive a report unconfirmed that contains news so important it will shape the landscape of the political arena, it's almost always purposeful misinformation." Samugy sighed. "It rarely happens though, only four times in my entire tenure with McAllan." The Hugeo had been working hand in glove with the Prime Governor for ten years, even before he'd been elected to the office. "Well, rarely happens without my influencing it."

"What do you mean without you influencing it?" Timothy looked on the spymaster curiously. He was a bright boy, but Samugy was a master of masters in his field.

"If I know they're sending me misinformation, that's almost more important than receiving true information." The Huego explained proudly.

"How do you mean?" Timothy retorted.

This time McAllan answered. He was tired of taking a back seat to the conversation. "Because then you know what the enemy wants you to think. You know what he wants." McAllan saw Samugy chuckle out of the corner of his eye. The Huego respected the Prime Governor, and this was why, because he was wise enough to spar with the spy as an equal

"Wouldn't it just be better to know the enemy's plan instead?" The aide was out of his depth. He was smart but lacked the fundamental understanding of how the world worked. That only came with time learning the wicked ways of the world.

McAllan looked at Samugy, who gestured for him to answer, so the Prime Governor did. "If a man tells you he's rich and he is, what do you learn?"

"That he's rich." The boy looked confused

"And if a man tells you, he sleeps with many women, and he does, what do you learn?" McAllan continued.

"That he might have the cock rot." Timothy said which got a laugh out of everyone in the cart, even the typically stoic bodyguards.

Once the Prime Governor wiped the laughter from his face, he continued. "And what if he tells you that he's a great powerful man and he is?"

"You learn he's a great, powerful man."

"Now what if you learn he lied about all that?" McAllan said honing in on the point.

Timothy's face lit up. He finally understood it all. "You learn he cares about those things." He looked at the two like they were wise prophets sent from the Three Above. "You learn how to move him."

"Exactly." McAllan smiled at his protege. "Politics at its heart is just knowing with what currency to buy off your opponent, and most men don't even know themselves what currency they'll accept."

Corporal Sally with the scar on his jaw finally couldn't control himself. "So what do they want then?"

McAllan thought for a second. "Fennis wants what's best for his people, but he refuses to see his people as larger than the South. Coleson wants a shot at executive power and knows he'll never be elected by a country that includes the north and west, the rambunctious youths who will join the fight want honor and glory, and the rest of the people want tall crops and healthy babies. The trouble with the last is that Coleson's convinced them they can have both without sweat and toil."

"It's things like this that make me not trust the government." Corporal Sally said half to himself, earning a disapproving look from the sergeant next to him.

"Keep that impulse." McAllan said with a chuckle. "In peaceful times I'd have men like Samugy hung for being too dangerous."

"You'd never succeed." Samugy smiled.

"Probably not, but it's the principle of the thing." McAllan shook his head. "I'd rather my people not give a cow's shit about their government, than worrying about them starting a war." McAllan's mood had been slightly improved by the talk. He enjoyed stimulating conversation about politics, at least in the abstract when it wouldn't cause a war that could kill half the countries young men.

"So we head north to prepare?" Timothy asked

"Not quite yet." McAllan said with a wince. "We've talked to every man in the South who might help us stop a war, but there's one man yet who could help us end it."

"Belson again?" Sergeant Harmon asked gripping his sawed off.

"Aye Belson." Samugy muttered.

"You think you can convince him to join us?" Timothy asked halfway to himself.

"I don't think I could convince him the sun would rise in the east and set in the west if he was otherwise disposed." McAllan said.

"Still I'll hear his answer for myself. If we're to have the greatest warrior in living memory fight for or against us, I'd like to know about it. Wouldn't you?"

"So what do you think Belson wants?" Corporal Sally asked gripping his pistol hard.

"I haven't the faintest clue." McAllan said truthfully. "Maybe he's the sort that wants even more fame and glory than he already has. In which case he'll join the South because he believes them to be the weaker side. Maybe he's the sort that's tired of war and wants to find a woman and raise a family. In which case he'll go west. Maybe he's the moral sort who believes that the Demons need to be banished from this world and Then Ironwill's legacy is worth fighting for. In which case he'll join us."

McAllan put his hand in his head and looked up. "Maybe he's the pugnacious sort, maybe he's the greedy sort, or maybe he's the heroic sort, but I don't believe he's any of those. I believe that in all the years the world has turned, there's never been a man we can compare him to. I don't think there's any kind of flower to put on his grave, and the Three didn't create one because even they don't believe he can die." The Prime Governor shook his head dismissively. "Who knows what the greatest man to walk this earth wants."

I woke up in a cold sweat gasping for air. It was morning, and the sun was flitting through the blinds in my window. I sat up and saw Rachel staring at me. I was happy she was in my bed, but I didn't want her to see me like this. The dreams had gotten worse since Mother Vestia. I couldn't fall sleep without waking up shouting

"You were screaming." She said propping her head on her elbow.

"I had a dream." I said and quickly put on my pants.

"It sounded like a nightmare." Rachel said with a bit of concern.

"Nightmare is a relative term." I said as I put on my boots. "To a pillow biter waking up to a beautiful woman in his bed might be a nightmare." I paused for a moment to kiss her.

"And to a great warrior dreaming about taking a city might be pleasant." She said standing up to reveal her nakedness.

"Aye." I stopped dressing altogether looking at her. "Although waking up to a beautiful woman isn't so bad." I kissed her hard, and we went back to the bed struggling against the clothes I had already put on. She had given up being quiet for the sake of decency. Rachel wanted me, and I wanted her. If the world found the act indecent, it wouldn't say it to my face. The world was too scared of me.

I thrust and growled, and she clawed at my back moaning. I'd known many women before, and I suspected she'd known a few men, but this was different. I had searched the world looking for a worthy match after Thaniel but hadn't found one. I'd never thought to look at women that way before. Every time we coupled it had the feel of a battle, both trying to take pleasure from the other. Still, it wasn't as if I was trying to conquer her. It was as if we were testing each other. We wanted to know if the other was as strong as we thought we were. If she had been a man, I would have boxed her, but this was how we came to know each other. It was as furious as any fight had ever been.

After Lady Gerate, I had only thought of women as momentary distractions or a pleasant way to spend an evening. The women who didn't find my scars so hideous were nice, and I treated them well. They wanted to spend a night with a hero from the stories. After it was all over, and I left the next day, they didn't mind. Some of them were princesses some were whores, some were kind, and some were harsh. It never really mattered to me as long as they were pretty enough, and when I was drinking even that rule got a little hazy.

I never cared about any of it because I never cared about them. They wouldn't remember the night as it actually happened. They'd tell the story to themselves as a glorious warrior who came and loved them for a night and couldn't stay because he was needed elsewhere. They didn't see it for what it was, a broken man needing comfort for a moment. They didn't realize I left in the morning because no one battle, country, or empire could sate my hunger, much less one woman.

Rachel was a different breed altogether though, but so was I. I'd never had sex like that, and I was sure she hadn't either. We were equals. She was fierce as I was, she was as talented as I was, and I was slowly discovering she was as hungry as I was. We'd taken different paths in life. I was a warrior, and she was, well... I wasn't quite sure what she was, but whatever the answer, she was damn good at it.

I knew she'd lain with more men than society would consider appropriate, but I had always found those rules a bit unfair anyway. Some men said they wouldn't touch sullied women as if them having loved others made their nights less special. It didn't mean that to me. I didn't feel cuckolded. I felt as if she'd sampled men from the world and found them wanting. She hadn't let lovers steal her virtue. Rachel had mastered them. She had tried to master me and failed. It was probably why she stayed in my bed.

The sex hadn't always been like this. At first, she just thought me a flavor she might like to taste, and I'd thought the same of her. There had been some respect there. Both of us knew the other had merit, but we never suspected that merit would be equal to their own. Over time the pleasant coupling had turned into a furious ravaging. Every night we spent together we learned the measure of our lover.

I thrust into her one last time and heard her moan while she dug her nails deep into my back. It hurt like a bayonet, and I loved it. I rolled over exhausted as if I'd ran ten miles. I was sure the girl was trying to kill me.

"Ha." She chuckled through her own labored breathing. "You are a rare sort of man Thomas."

"The same goes for you." I said panting for air. I was thirsty.

"So you're going to fight then?" She kissed the back of my neck

"Suppose so." I let her kiss me. "I've had my fill of war, but it hasn't had its fill of me."

She gave me a knowing look. "No, you haven't. You just say that sort of thing because it's expected of you." She paused leaning back in a seductive pose. "It's true most men fight because it's their duty, and once that's done they hang up their weapons and hope they never have to pick them up again." She stared into me deep. "You fight for the same reason a master artist paints, because you're the best at it."

I searched for some words to deny it, but I couldn't find them. The girl was too smart for that.

"You miss the fighting don't you." It wasn't a question. "I think there was a time when you imagined putting your weapons down, but fifteen years of adventure and glory changes the men it doesn't kill first."

"I hate seeing good men die." I said simply. "I hate killing peasants who's greatest crime was being born on the wrong side of the river." I looked at my own tattooed arm. "I hate the smell, sound, and sight of a battlefield after the bloody work is done."

"But…" She urged me on.

"I love the way I feel when I chase an enemy three times my number from a battlefield." I caressed the curve of her. "I love holding the line with brave men." I looked at her eyes. "I love the way women look at heroes." I sighed. "I know it's not good of me to feel that way. A hero should do what he does because it's right."

"You don't believe you were fighting on the right side." She gave me a curious look.

"I don't know anymore." I looked up trying to find the answer. "I always figured the side Mother Vestia was on was the right one." I paused. "I'm not so sure these days."

"You did good works, I've heard." She ran her finger down my spine.

"I'm glad I left a peaceful world in my wake, I'm glad I broke the tyranny of the Old Religion." I paused. "But I didn't fight for those reasons in the end. I fought because I loved it." I stood up suddenly. "I've dueled fifty men in my life with gun and blade and won them all." I did a quick draw with the pistol on my dresser and holstered it remembering the days. "I shattered armies with more soldiers than there are in the entire Confederacy. I broke the greatest warrior who's lived since the Imorans." I paused looking back at her. "I fought for the weaker side in every war and not always because they were just. I did it because joining the winner presented no contest. I sighed looking down at my own weapon. "When Mother Vestia let me go, it felt like a drunk ripped from his bottle, like a lover ripped from his beloved." I shook my head in shame. "She may have been a liar, but she didn't lie about everything. It got bad towards the end."

"I thought you left because there was no one else to fight?" She stood up and draped her arms over my shoulder.

"Oh, there's always someone to fight." I turned away from her, too consumed in my own thoughts. "In my last year, I developed a reputation." I turned toward her seeing the look in her eyes. "They don't tell stories about it, because no one wants to hurt my name, but if you listen in the right taverns around the places I've been, you'll hear them whispered."

"What will they say?" She moved forward. She was a bit afraid, but also curious. It was like I was a half-tamed lion who could snap at any moment, but too wondrous to stay away.

"That maybe I wasn't blessed I was cursed." I gave a soft sigh. "Hard to argue with that come to think of it."

"That's the way of blessings and curses." She whispered.

I reached out and touched her cheek. "They said I was

dangerous, no matter what side the men were on." He pulled her closer. "Some said I was a mad dog who'd outlived his use."

She leaned in despite herself. "Were you?" She said it so softly I could barely hear it.

"Yes."

I thought Rachel would retreat as if struck. Instead, she smiled. "On our first night together you told me those women and children you killed in Kran were your greatest regret." She drew closer. "No man's ever successfully lied to me before."

"I meant it." I touched her again because I couldn't stop. "I was young when I did that. I thought there was such a thing as the greater good and necessary evil. I thought I just wanted the war to end and to live out my term in peace. I know now I was wrong on both accounts." I bunched up my fist. "After the war, I was happy when they sent me to fight elsewhere." I kissed her neck. "It wasn't until years later I realized the truth. I was the necessary evil."

"And if war comes again." She asked softly.

"That's like asking a drunk if he'll stay sober." I shook my head. "I hope I'm strong enough to resist it, but I don't know." I sighed. "Do you think I'm an evil man?"

She kept that smile on her. "I don't know." She stroked my face. "I think maybe you've been pushed too far." She whispered. "I also think there's been a hand on your reigns."

"I've never taken a woman against her will." I whispered to myself "I've never given orders for a city I took to be razed, even though it happened from time to time." I could still feel the heat of all my sin. "I've never even killed a man just to watch him die." I still couldn't shake those nightmares. "There's a thin line between my enemies and me, thinner every day, but I've never crossed it." I reached out and touched her chin till she looked me in the eyes. "I try to help those I knock to their knees if I can." She seemed to revel in it all. "War is a tricky business though. No one really comes out clean." I paused for a moment, collecting myself. "Sometimes to win, you've got to take the bad road."

"I don't think you're evil." She said simply. "But there's evil in you, and you know how to use it."

"I do."

She sighed clasping my hand to her cheek. "Would you ever hurt me?" Rachel looked deep into my eyes.

"Never."

She kissed me then. When she pulled away, she looked around and said. "I do believe I should head back to my own room now." She stood up to leave, and I watched her go.

A few minutes after Rachel was out. I heard a knock on the door. "Thomas, McAllan's here." It was Seiford

I hurried up and got dressed, then walked out to meet him. He was still sporting a bruised face since I hit him. We hadn't spoken much about it, but I saw a shadow of doubt in his eye. I'd seen it in his brother before he died. "I don't like what that girl's doing to you." He said.

"Well, I do." The edge on my voice let him know I wasn't about to talk with him about it. "McAllan's here?" I asked.

"Carriage just rolled in." The monk nodded. "What are you going to do?"

"Same thing I always do." I said. "This time though, I won't let anyone stop me from doing it all the way."

<hr/>

McAllan waited for the two to make their way to the front of the house. They seemed different somehow. The monk had a bruise on his face, but besides that... There was something there that hadn't been before. A tension maybe.

"You wanted to speak?" McAllan said to Belson as he walked outside.

"I do." The Constable lit up a cigarette.

"Then let's retire inside." The Prime Governor gestured to the house.

"Better not, my mother doesn't like smoking in the house." Belson took a look at the cigarette. "Or smoking in general, but she can't smell it outside."

"Besides by the look of those carriages in your stable, you have some notable guest in your house." McAllan gestured to the stables which were now housing ornate coaches. "I don't think you want those guest knowing I'm here."

"My last homecoming party was ruined by politics." He laughed. "My sister-in-law decided it would be a good idea to have another." Belson shrugged. "Most of the guests are dandies and fools, though. I don't much care what they see me doing." The Constable said defiantly.

"But you care who they might tell don't you." Samugy said over the Prime Governor's shoulder. "And it's an easy precaution." McAllan looked over at the Huego then at the Constable they were appraising each other like they had the first time, but now they both had a smile on their face.

"What they don't know won't hurt them, I figure." Belson said to the spymaster. "Besides, I wouldn't want politics to ruin this ball as well."

"That's a poor thing to say to a man who's spent the better part of his life trying to learn things." Samugy said right back to him. "However, I do understand the detrimental effects of intrigue on a nice dinner."

"Well, maybe it's best to leave these fools in the dark then?" The Constable gestured to an obscure shed that seemed secluded enough.

"Very well." McAllan said. "Lead the way." The party walked toward the shed flanked by Corporal Sally and Sergeant Harmon. Belson opened the door, and they funneled inside. It was dim, lit by the cracks in the wall where the sunlight streamed through. The tools on the walls were clearly worn and rusted.

The Prime Governor had spent much of his childhood working in sheds like the one they were in, trying to earn enough money to put food on the table and buy his sister's medicine. He hated sheds like the one he was in. They reeked of impotence. It was half the reason he'd taken up boxing. The money being the other half.

"So judging by the look on your face the talks aren't going well." Belson said as he sat down on a bale of hay puffing on his cigarette.

"They aren't." McAllan leaning against a workbench opposite.

"I assume the propaganda campaign hasn't worked to your liking either." The Constable gave a coy smile.

"It's worked alright." The Prime Governor shrugged. "I just didn't realize how far gone most men were."

"Well, not to make your day worse, but I had a woman on that very same bench you're leaning on earlier." Belson kept up that damn annoying grin.

"So that's the life of a retired Constable?" McAllan said moving from the bench to a stacked bale of hay high enough to accommodate him. "I assume this is clean then."

"Nothing in here is clean." Belson gestured to the dirty walls. "But I haven't fornicated on it if that's what you mean."

"Good enough for me." The Prime Governor made himself

comfortable then gestured for his party to do the same. Samugy, of course, had already done so, but he wasn't lounging like he usually was. Behind his eyes, calculations were forming. McAllan would have paid good money to know what it was.

"A man having as bad a day as you, deserves a cigarette." Belson offered him a cigarette, which he took and lit. Then he offered one to his bodyguards, Timothy, then Samugy. They all shook there heads politely to decline.

"My wife doesn't like me smoking, and she's almost better with spies than I am." The Huego said, but McAllan could still see the gears turning in his head, which was rare. Most problems usually only took him a few seconds to work through, and the ones that didn't he held as beyond the scope of human reason.

"Well, better not then." The Constable pocketed the smokes. "So you couldn't stop a war from happening and neither could I." He paused to puff on his cigarette. "Now you want to know if I'll fight with you for the glory of a united Confederacy?" He said with a queer smile on his face.

"I know you've said you won't fight but-" McAllan started, but was cut off by a hand from the Constable.

"Save your breath and my ears." Belson said smugly and leaned even farther back in his hay bale. "I'll fight for you." He said as if he had worked out the whole course of the war and was already bored.

"Really?" McAllan asked incredulously. There was no way it could be this easy.

"Suppose I wasn't as retired as I thought." I paused wistfully. "You just can't quit what you're good at, I suppose." He gestured around as if pointing to the whole country. "I've had my eyes on things here and found things wanting." He sighed again in a bored manner. "I had considered defending my people from a persecuting and distant government, but from what I've seen the country fits together as a whole well enough. You don't seem like the persecuting, distant type, anyway."

McAllan didn't think he was lying, but something about the whole situation irked him. "Well, good I've drawn up a plan. You're to lead-" Once again the Constable held up a hand to cut him off.

"I'm sure you've worked your plan well enough. You don't seem the sort to go into anything unprepared. I imagine that's why you were as good a boxer as are a politician." Belson said it like he was humoring a child.

"However..." McAllan said leading the man on.

"However..." The Constable said catching the lead. "I know how to run a war better than any man alive, and I've put a great deal of thought into how to beat Fennis since I've gotten here. I think I can end it quicker than you thought possible."

"And how's that?" McAllan was getting tired of being schooled by a man half his age like a pompous professor would teach a slow child. He felt the familiar rage he'd use in the boxing ring boil up inside of him, but there was perhaps one man in the world he was too afraid to unleash it on, and that man was Thomas Belson.

"I'll raise my army just north of the Capitol. That army should have three regiments, four batteries of mobile cannon, and two batteries of heavy." He scratched his head as if he were forgetting something. "Oh yes and as many units of cavalry as can be spared without weakening the other theaters of war, with an appropriate baggage train for an army that size." Belson sighed "Some commanders prefer foraging, but that's a relic of a time before men required ammunition. Besides, what happens if someone on the other side gets clever and decides to torch the land. I'll tell you what happens. We starve in the winter!"

"And assuming I trusted a man I've had two conversations with enough to give him three regiments, what would you do with them?" McAllan said gritting his teeth

"I'd spend two months training them, while you start the blockade you no doubt have planned already. After that, I'll march just south enough to harass and embarrass them, but not so far I can be surrounded. Coleson will feel his purse tighten. Political and economic pressure will make him urge Fennis to start a battle before he's ready. I'll win. I've already planned it, but I won't get into that now. Today's a day for strategy, not tactics. After that, half the army will march into Pentsville and force a truce, while the other half moves north to fend off the Anthanii that will inevitably come to invade Yunta."

Belson looked up at the shocked face on McAllan. "Yes, I've guessed they might come for Yunta, but your look confirms it. The Kran will take Trebia for the winter, but that's marshy land and full of disease. Once it starts to warm, we'll push them out easily and be home to watch our gardens bloom in spring. The Old Religion will undoubtedly cause problems, but there are ways of dealing with that." Belson looked around the room smugly. "Any objections?"

"You forgot the victory parades and women throwing themselves at us." The monk said to the Constable.

"I did." He shrugged his shoulders. "I also forgot. I want my army to be made up entirely of white regulars and veterans, not any draftee who is unfortunate enough to walk by your recruiting station." Belson said with a matter of fact attitude. "I understand you've been experimenting with mixed units, but that can wait until the war is over." The Constable took a puff of his shortening cigarette. "Do what you will with the rest of your army. They'll mostly be involved in skirmishes anyway, but the men under my command will be uniform.

"I had intended you to lead a fully integrated group of volunteers." McAllan said rankled by the man's racism. He had thought the Constable to be more enlightened. "The future of this country is united, not driven apart, by arbitrary distinctions of skin color." He tried desperately to control his fury. "Shedding blood on the battlefield together will make men of all colors and creeds look upon themselves as citizens of one great nation, not a group of different people struggling for dominance over each other."

Belson looked as if it was something he'd like to change, but didn't have the time. "With all due respect, we can worry about this country's future after we've secured its present." He looked at Timothy who was showing visible signs of anger. "I'm not a racist I promise. I fought with just about every people in the world, and they all soldier well enough if they're properly motivated."

"Whites just soldier the best." Timothy shot back with venom.

"Generally yes, but that's more due to better weapons, and a modern military doctrine." Belson looked on apologetically. "I just don't need immigrants, blacks, Intes, and Huego's quarreling with experienced soldiers. That kind of thing could set my plan back by months."

"I understand." Timothy shook his head in disgust. "We'll fix spitting on the blackie mule's at a more convenient time."

"Well, that makes it sound bad, but essentially yes." He paused for a second. "If it makes you feel better I'd just as soon raise an army of all blacks. There just aren't enough seasoned soldiers or trained officers to outfit three regiments." He sighed. "In my experience diversity in an army breeds dissent."

Timothy was about to make another comment, but McAllan raised a hand to stop him. It wouldn't make things better. The

Constable was too set in his ways. What was worse McAllan agreed with the boy and another comment like that might gall the Prime Governor to lose his temper, and like it or not they needed Belson. "Other than the all-white army, it seems like a sound strategy." McAllan said begrudgingly.

"It's not just sound it's bulletproof." The Constable smiled self-satisfied. "Three above its cannon proof." He shrugged his shoulders. "It's the quickest way to win this war. Well unless you pick the smart way, but governments usually don't pick the smart way, so here we are."

"The smart way?' McAllan squinted his eyes.

"You declare martial law. Send in Confederacy soldiers before Fennis has a chance to raise his army." Belson threw his smoke away and lit another one. "You reinforce them with draftees as soon as possible and govern the South like what it really is, a group of rebellious provinces." He smiled again. "Then you round up Coleson, all his cronies, and anyone you can get your hands on wearing a red cloak and hang them from the highest tree in town." He mimed a noose on his neck. "See the smart way!" He chuckled. "And I tell you what! You can use any color soldier you like for that."

"No! Absolutely not!" McAllan surprised himself with the violence of the statement.

"Why?" Belson looked genuinely confused. "It's the way with the least bloodshed." He rolled his eyes. "I know there'll be backlash, but it's well within your power to declare martial law I assure you."

"In times of emergency!" McAllan shook his head in dismay.

"And you don't think civil war qualifies?" The Constable rose an eyebrow.

"Maybe he has a point." Samugy whispered in his ear. McAllan was more than aware of the Huego's opinion on the subject. It was the one unnamed entity that stood over all of the Prime Governors councils of war. It had been mentioned by a few of his cabinet, but McAllan had refused immediately, and he had never heard it proposed so casually.

"This is not some flood or riot that would make me enforce a curfew. This is the single most important moment for our country since we revolted one hundred years ago." McAllan paused to collect himself. "I will not punish men for crimes they have not yet committed. That isn't what Then Ironwill intended when he wrote the law."

"Who cares what he intended." The Constable muttered dismissively. "The law is on the books, so why not use it. If old Ironwill had meant the law to be so strict, then he should have left it less open for interpretation."

"He didn't because he never imagined anyone would have the gall to twist his words." The Prime Governor was seething.

"Sometimes things need to be done for the greater good." Belson said it calmly enough, but the monk behind him looked at the man curiously. It was clear Seiford did not share his friend's opinion on the greater good.

"If I do as you're suggesting, you're right. The South won't have time to raise an army, and they'll be under my thumb." The Prime Governor shook his head "I don't want them under my thumb. I want them to come into the fold. I'm not a husband beating his wife, so she stays. I'm a leader of one people who don't see themselves as one. There's more at stake than just beating them. If I do what you want, I'm proving that they're right." McAllan raised his voice. "The wounds on this country will never heal, and if the festering is to stop now, then it must be addressed, not covered in rags hoping it will go away, or else the whole animal will die, and die painfully."

"Sometimes a limb must be severed for the patient to survive." Belson shrugged again.

"Not while my people live on that limb." He shook his head. "And once I have done this thing, it can never be undone. Martial law can be repealed, but the precedent will stand for any politician clever enough to get elected. The great faith of the men who founded our country will be thrown out the window, and we will be left as nothing more than hypocritical reminders of the land of what is." He paused looking around the room for help but found none so went into the breach on his own. "I will not set us down the road of tyranny because I wanted the easy path."

"It's not just the easy path, it's the path with the least blood." Belson implored him. "A few hundred men, guilty as a hand in the pie, will die rather than thousands of soldiers trying to do right. I don't understand why not."

"And you'll never understand why, boy!" McAllan said in hushed rage that left everyone in the room in awe. No one talked to Belson the Blessed that way. The man who broke Thaniel, the man who broke empires, the man who broke gods.

"For the sake of the Confederacy, I'll give you one more warning than I'd give anyone else." The Constable said in a matching tone. "Be careful who you call boy." Thomas took a deep breath to calm himself. "It's what I would do if I were ruling in your place."

That was the final straw. McAllan was too far gone to practice caution. Even if it cost the nation, he would not let fear determine the fate of his people. "I do not rule boy." He said the last word as a curse. "I lead."

The Prime Governor stood, throwing the butt of his cigarette on the ground and stamping it out. "I lead the greatest nation this world has ever known. We are the land of what could be, not what is. I am not some lord of Thyro who believes that his country exists to please him. You talk about the greater good? So do the Priests, so do the rulers of Thyro who enslaved half a continent, so did Thaniel. There is no greater good, there's only good."

Belson stood up. He was much shorter than McAllan, but he had the bearing of a warrior. If the Prime Governor were in his usual state, he would have had the sense to feel scared, but he was feeling righteous. "You'll sacrifice your country for principle."

McAllan finally realized what irked him about the meeting. It was the nonchalant attitude Belson had about waging war against his own people. It was the way he put morality away for his political calculation. It was the way he put winning before why he was fighting. He was like Fennis, except far more dangerous. He had no cause to ground him, but the abstract thought of victory, whatever that meant, and everyone around him was too afraid to tell him when to stop. The monk might have served as the angel on his shoulder, but what he needed, what the world needed was for a righteous man to stand in his way, not whisper in his ear. "Tell me, when you battled Thaniel, when you started your mission of pressing every nation you came across into submission, did you even believe in the Three?"

That took him aback. "I came to believe when I saw enough."

McAllan shook his head. "I'm not asking if you came to believe." He leveled a finger at the most dangerous man who ever was. "I'm asking whether or not, when you started your crusade, you even believed in the gods you were fighting for."

"I thought they were a fine metaphor of what man could achieve on his own right." Thomas muttered angrily.

"Did you believe!"

"No!" Belson lashed out. "I thought power was power and it didn't matter where it came from!" The Constable screamed furiously.

"I thought Thaniel had a point! I thought that up jumped peasant leagues above any other ruler I've met!" Belson finally realized what he'd said and lowered his voice. "I've learned since then."

"Then why did you fight Kran?" McAllan asked sharply. "If you didn't believe in your own cause than why fight the most powerful ruler in Thyro."

"I beat him to stop the war." The Constable knew he hadn't answered the question.

"You could have ended the war by surrendering Every war can be ended by just surrendering. There has to be a reason not to." McAllan took a step forward. "If the New Church was a lie, then what's the difference between Thaniel and King John?" He paused. "I'll ask again. Why did you fight the most powerful ruler in Thyro if you didn't believe he was morally wrong?"

"Because he was the most powerful ruler in Thyro!" Belson screamed back at the man. "Because he was there, and I wanted to tear that Rose Petal Throne apart!" He was furious now, but the Prime Governor thought he was more angry at himself than anyone. "Things changed."

"Not as much as you thought maybe." McAllan said it in a deathly calm. "You wanted to tear the Rose Petal Throne apart. Now that's exactly what you want to do with Fennis." The Prime Governor went on. "You don't want what's best for the people. You want to be able to look on a map and say you beat the entire world in a fist fight."

"What does it matter why I fought? I did it, and people were better off for it!" The Constable spit on the ground. "There's been millions of good men on this planet, but there's only one Thomas Belson. Only one man who could shatter the world that was. I killed tyrants, freed millions from bondage, and saved more people than there are living in this whole damn country, while you sat on your ass and begged some aristocrats not to be too nasty!"

"And what's the use of shattering the world that was, without building a new one." McAllan looked away. "There's more to a war than winning it. You have to prove you deserve to. Otherwise, what's the point?" The Prime Governor looked at Timothy. "I'm going to fight this war, Thomas, not because I'm backed into a corner. I'm going to send young men to die by their thousands because I believe that this country represents an opportunity to be better men than we were. We don't go to war because we're desperate. We go to war because there's hope."

"When the country tears itself apart you'll get desperate enough to beg for my methods." Belson shot back.

McAllan shook his head. "When this country tears itself apart, I won't force it back together. I'll inspire it to embrace each other." He sighed knowing the futility of it all. "More likely I'll die trying, but that doesn't matter." He whispered to himself. "I won't do what you did to Thyro. I won't sacrifice what makes me a man because I hate the Demons.

"What do you know about Thyro or the Demons." Belson spat out.

"Pray to the Three you never learn what I know of the Demons!" McAllan screamed with more venom than he thought he had in him. "I was at my sister's side when they tormented her into insanity. I listened when a black-clad man came to me and said the Priest would help her if I helped them. I watched her get better when I killed a man with my bare hands and stole his son. I saw something change in myself afterwards." McAllan shook his head.

"I watched her mind eat itself until all she could do was scream about nightmares." He paused for a moment wiping his eyes. "I felt the tears sting my eyes when I put the pillow over her head until she stopped." He looked at the man who was supposed to rid his country of their plague. "Now I sit at my wife's side and wonder when I'll have to do the same to her." He looked around the room. Samugy knew of course, and Timothy had suspected, but the rest of them were as shocked as he was that he'd finally said it out loud. "The Demons have taken everything from me except my morality, and I will never let them have that. I hate them more than you ever will, which is why I won't stoop to their level!"

Belson finally mustered up the courage to answer that. "So you want me to fight for your conscience?" It was obviously meant to come out as sarcasm, but it sounded more like a plea for help.

"You won't fight for me at all!" McAllan screamed at the man. "Thaniel's mistake was he turned to powers he didn't understand to do his bloody work. I don't understand you, and I will not give the wolf permission to hunt my flock."

The Constable was furious. "Then I'll fight for the South, and I'll take your damn flock from you."

"Then kill me now." McAllan smiled as his two bodyguards drew their weapons, but he put a hand up for them to stop. "You won't though because you don't care what happens to these people. You just want a war to win."

"I'll defeat you."

"Maybe you will." McAllan said as he turned to leave beckoning his men to do the same. "But that's all you've ever cared about, defeating men not freeing them." He looked back at the Constable. "Maybe we will lose, but I'll lead a lawful army of blacks, whites, Intes, Huegos and whoever else believes in something, to stop you. If we lose, then we'll lose the right way, and if we die, we will meet the Three as good men." He said walking out of the shed.

———◆◆◆———

I watched them go. The Huego lingered for a moment. "The woman you took on that bench, what was her name?"

I looked at him angrily. "I don't see how it's any of your concern."

"Was it Rachel Gondua?"

"Maybe it was." I narrowed his eyes.

"Maybe means yes where women are concerned." The Huego smiled infuriatingly, then followed his master.

I stood there, fist balled in anger till Seiford broke the trance by standing up behind me. "Is he right?" He asked the monk.

"He doesn't know what you did for those people." Seiford put a hand on my shoulder. "He doesn't know how you helped up the people you knocked down."

"Damn the results!" I screamed not looking at the monk. "I want to know the reasons! Is he right? Did I beat men just to prove I could?" Seiford knew me better than any man alive. If he said it was nonsense from an angry politician, then it was. I needed my friend to say McAllan was wrong.

"Yes, I believe he's right."

"Why didn't you say so then?" I turned around to face the monk. "You're my friend, not my lackey!"

Seiford took a step back. "I was never sure until he named it. Now, I know he spoke the truth."

"Damn you and all your stories!" I put a malicious finger in his face. "You were sent to be my conscience. To make sure I was a good man, not herald me down an evil path."

Anyone else would have pissed themselves, but Seiford stood firm. "I think you are a good man." He said simply. "I saw a morality and honor in you when the rest of the world saw a war machine." The monk stepped forward. "There was a darkness in you too though, a hunger. I've only ever seen it show through in battle, but even in peace, there's a shadow of it. I wasn't sent to be your conscience, though. If you need another man to be that, then you're already lost." He took another step forward. "I'm here because I'm your friend. I told those stories about you because I believed that what you represented was true enough, but there's another reason. I did it because in the Thomas Belson of those stories I saw what you could be one day."

"And what's that?" I spat.

"The kind of man that McAllan is." He paused. "The kind of man that doesn't just win, but does it because he cares about something."

"Fuck you and fuck him!" I seethed

"I lied to you when I said you were one of a kind." Seiford went on undaunted. "There's been a million men like you. You were just the best." He put a hand on my shoulder. "But let go of the darkness, let go of the hunger, and then you will be the greatest to have ever lived."

"What about the people I helped?" I screamed. "What about the people who I freed after the battle was done."

"Noble acts all of them." Seiford looked me in the eye. "But you did them because after you knocked an army down, your morality demanded you help them." The monk gestured out the door. "The sort of man that McAllan is defeats an army because he wants to help those people. He doesn't do it as an afterthought."

I put my hand on the six-shooter. "You sound like Mother Vestia." It was a threat, the first one I'd ever leveled at Seiford.

"Fuck Mother Vestia, fuck this war, and fuck Thaniel." He didn't back away. "Be the man you can be because it's right." He whispered.

I was a heartbeat away from accepting the monks words. I almost gave up the hunger inside of me, but my pride won out. "Take a horse and leave this place. You're not my friend anymore if you ever were. Take all the money we have and write that damn history if you want." I couldn't look him in the eye. "Just leave."

"You know I won't." Seiford said softly. "You know that the money, women, and fame meant nothing to me."

"Then what was the prize?" I screamed at the man.

"Knowing you." The monk said. "Standing next to a man I believe will break the shackles of this world."

"Leave, or the next time I see you, I'll kill you."

"You're a powerful man." Seiford smiled at me. "But you'll never be powerful enough to keep me away from your side."

I pulled out my six-shooter. "I'll kill you if you don't."

"No, my friend, I don't believe you will." Seiford took a step closer.

"Bang!" The bullet landed between the monk's feet. "Leave." I said it almost pleadingly.

He didn't even flinch at the shot. "Once you've realized what you've done, I'll stand beside you again." Seiford walked out the door McAllan had left through, but turned around before he disappeared entirely. "I'll be there when you need me most." Then he was gone.

I need you now! I wanted to scream, but I didn't. I was alone for the first time in ten years. I'd thought I'd known loneliness, but without Seiford there, it was like the plug being taken from the bottom of a ship, and the most powerful man in the world sat on a bale of hay and wept like a child.

I remembered the dream of me standing over my closest friend. His corpse in my hands. I didn't know what path I was on, but it wasn't the right one.

McAllan and his men got into the carriage and didn't talk much until they were away from the plantation. Oddly enough it was Timothy who broke the silence.

"I'm sorry about your sister." He paused. "And your wife." The aide didn't know what else to say. "I suspected about her, but I didn't want to ask."

"You don't need to be sorry. The people that need to be sorry will feel it soon enough." McAllan shook his head in anger. "Though without Thomas Belson I don't know how." He looked at his bodyguards. "What will you say when you tell the story to your men about how your Prime Governor had a chance to win the war but didn't take it?" He paused letting his self-loathing flow. "Corporal Sally, will you laugh about it? Sergeant Harmon, will you scream in anger."

"I'll tell the story of how our leader refused to compromise." The corporal said with a smile. "I'll tell the story about how our leader stared down the most dangerous man in the world because he had a dream about what this country could be." He patted his own gun. "I'll tell them I'm willing to die protecting that dream."

McAllan nodded then looked at Sergeant Harmon. "I'm not much of a talker sir, but if they ask, I'll tell em to fuck off."

That got a chuckle out of everyone. Especially Samugy, who held the smile for too long. "And what were you thinking during that talk. I saw you calculating something."

Samugy looked at him happily. "You've saved us. Thomas Belson will fight on our side."

McAllan cocked an eyebrow up. "And how do you figure."

"Before he'd have led our armies for a time." Samugy chuckled. "He'd have defected. I'm sure of that."

"And you're not now?" The Prime Governor looked up curiously. "After he's said something exactly to that effect."

"Now he'll fight for you on whatever terms you offer." The Huego laughed like he was sharing an inside joke.

"I don't follow."

"It's because he's sleeping with a woman who'll push him." Samugy couldn't hold the laughter back now. "And if there's one thing I know, it's that when someone pushes Belson the Blessed, he pushes back."

And the carriage echoed with laughter for many miles.

The Thaniel Wars

I woke up in a dank cell with water dripping on me.

"You think he'll wake up?" I heard a voice say as my eyes adjusted to the darkness.

"That's Thomas Belson in there." Another voice answered. "I was at Gertinville, and I had a friend at Wuntsville."

"The question stands. You think he'll wake up?"

"I've never known a man to stand back up with that many wounds, but if anyone can, it's him."

I put my hands out to steady myself, but I found they were manacled together. Must have been done to prevent my hurting myself. I tried to get my legs up under me, but they were chained to the wall. That probably wasn't for my own benefit. The cell probably wasn't prescribed by a doctor either.

The rattling of my chains alerted the guards. "Oy, he's awake!" I heard one of them scream. "Go tell the captain!" I heard the pitter-patter of boots on stone.

"What's going on?" I asked. "Where am I?"

"My names Corporal Haldt, your eminence." I could see the man well enough. He had on the red uniform of a soldier. His face was rather bland and a little beaten as happens to most who spend long enough in the army.

"It's a pleasure." I nodded.

"As for where you are, these are the dungeons of Harfow." He shrugged as if he'd just brought mutton when I asked for beef. "Weren't my idea."

"Well, it's awfully kind of the powers that be to protect me so with stone walls and my own guard," I looked him up and down, "but I'm feeling much more like myself." I held up my manacled hand. "If I could just have my coat and hat back, I'll be on my way." I was completely naked except for some sackcloth pants.

"I'd like nothing more than to let you loose, so as you could continue your fight with Thaniel." The guard tapped his musket nervously. "Trouble is, I like my head where it's at."

"Ah." I nodded as if I'd been expecting that, part of me had. The other part was still hoping this was some sort of sick joke. "So, I guess I'm not in here for my own protection." I was arrested, but for what?

That made the guard laugh. "I don't think there's much a bloke like me could do to protect Belson the Blessed." He nodded to me. "Even in the state you arrived."

"So I've been arrested for being too devilishly handsome." I snapped my fingers. "I knew it was a crime being this good-looking, but I thought they'd wait till after the war to try me."

"You're a funny one." The guard laughed again. "It's good to keep your spirits up at a time like this." He chuckled at something. "Back when I was in Rustia, it was terrible cold. Winter like you'd never seen." Haldt slapped the bars. "We had this fellow with us, Private Derbas. You'd have liked him." The corporal rolled his eyes at the memory. "Drew a cock on the back of the Colonel's coat, must've marched a hundred miles following that cock."

I laughed at that too. It was a funny story. "Sounds like quite the man, this Private Derbas. I'd love to have a beer with him."

"He's dead now, your eminence." Haldt's smile dropped a bit.

"Well, I suppose I don't want the beer that bad." I drew a little cock in the dust, in memory of the man. "Say, I'm a bit hungry. You got any food for me?"

"The soup cart don't come till noon," the guard glanced over each shoulder as if to make sure no one was watching, "but you don't want none of that anyhow. You deserve something better."

"I'd settle for soup." I shrugged my shoulders. I had an idea that dungeon soup was probably a step below army stew, which wasn't that far up the ladder either.

"I won't have it!" Haldt said adamantly. "Thomas Belson won't slurp up the same slop as murderers and rapist." He put his foot down. "Least not while he's a guest in my cell."

"You're a decent sort of man." I nodded at him.

"I try to be." The man made sure no one was around and unlocked the gate. "I weren't always. Was a right bastard not too long ago, I was. The kind to steal a coin out a blind man's cup."

"What changed?" I asked.

"Me daughter started asking for stories about you when I was home." He stepped through the gate. "Wanted to hear about how Thomas Belson punished the wicked and protected the innocent." He scratched his chin. "Really, got me to thinking. Why weren't she asking for stories about me? I been places. I done things."

"Anyhow, the answer came to me." He leaned his rifle against the wall. "I had been places, and I had done things, but I if I was punishing the wicked or protecting the innocent, it were only a matter of geography that put the wicked in front and the innocent behind." He sighed. "Besides, I'd be a fool to think all the people I was protecting were innocent, and all the men I was punishing were wicked." He used the key on his belt to open the gate.

"I decided my little girl deserved better of me." He gave a mighty huff. "I decided the next time Thomas Belson came up, well maybe I could say I did right by him."

"You should know all those stories about me aren't exactly true." I smiled up at him.

"Oh, I know that. I was at Gertinville. Weren't no dragons or maidens, but you were there." He pulled out a sack of cloth. "I don't give a polished turd if it's all true, enough of it was."

"That means something I suppose." I gave a manacled salute.

"Reckon it does. Here." He opened up the sack. "Me wife packed you something." It was fresh bread and a good slice of roasted lamb. It made my mouth water.

"Thank you, Corporal Haldt." I said as he placed it right in front of me.

"It's the least I could do." He waved it off and pulled out something else. It was chocolate wrapped in wax paper. "Here, me and the boys all chipped in for it."

"Chocolate's expensive." I cocked an eyebrow up. "Must've cost you all a week's pay."

"It's nothing. The boys would have bought you a wedding band if they thought you'd say yes." The guard said. "You've saved most of our hides in some manner or another."

Haldt reached down to hand me the chocolate. I waited for my moment. Then right as his hand touched mine, I spun him around. Chained wrists over his neck.

"Are the keys to my manacles on that belt?" I nodded down to his belt.

"Yes." He nodded.

"Reckon I could break your neck right now, grab those and escape." I whispered in his ear.

"Reckon you could." Haldt managed out.

"But then again." I smiled. "You brought me chocolate." I relaxed my grip on him and helped him up. Then picked up the lunch and started eating.

"That was a poor joke, your eminence." He was smiling though.

"Just wanted you to know I could." I winked at him. "Wouldn't want people to think I'd lost my edge."

"I reckon there ain't a round surface on you." He walked back out the gate and shut it. "Truth be told if you asked me nicely and were truly repentant of your sins, I'd let you out and suffer the consequences."

"Say, what are my sins anyhow?" I asked. "Why'm I in here?" I said through a mouthful of bread.

"You really don't know?" He asked.

"Not a clue." I shrugged. "I don't remember much, state that I was in."

"Treason." Haldt said it like it pained him.

"Treason?" I made the word chewing on my lamb prize. "How'd I catch that charge."

"The king alleges that you lied to the navy in order to catch them in a trap." Haldt shook his head. "Says you lost them ships at Fredua on purpose."

"Fredua..." Then it all came back to me. The battle, the fighting, the blacksmith... The fires. It was like remembering through a drunken haze.

"The fires they're..." I started. "They weren't just my mind playing tricks on me."

"They were real." He said.

"How many men died?" I asked.

"I don't have the exact number, but..." He paused. "It was a lot."

"Admiral Nellard?" I asked hopefully.

"He was one of em."

"Constable Waterson?" Maybe he got out.

"Aye, him too."

I pushed the food away. I wasn't hungry anymore.

"It isn't true, right. You didn't send those men there to die?" Corporal Haldt looked over his musket. "Did you?"

"Aye, I did." That made the man take a step back. "I sent them to die. Just like I would've sent you to die if my charge at Gertinville hadn't worked. Just like I would have sent all of Wuntsville to die if I'd failed there too."

"You didn't do it for Thaniel though?" The Corporal couldn't understand my answer.

` "In a way I did." I wiped the food off my mouth. "I was so obsessed with the man, I pushed things till they finally went wrong."

What went wrong?" Haldt asked. "I realize that might be privileged information, but I ain't telling."

"No, it's quite alright." I waved my hand. "There was a chain at the entrance. Who the fuck uses a chain in this century?"

"Thaniel?" Haldt posited.

"Suppose so." I muttered. "Anyhow, I managed to take it down, but not before the Priests got there." I rubbed the tattoos on my arm. "I had a plan to deal with them too, but..." I trailed off, remembering the horrible convulsions that had run through me. "Well, you've been in the army. You know how it goes with plans."

"I do at that." The guard nodded.

I looked back up at the guard. "If you're asking me if I sent those men to their death..." I stared up at the lone window in my suite. "It was my plan. If I hadn't given the order, those men would still be alive."

"For a time at least." Haldt said. "Until Thaniel wins this war eventually." He paused. "I don't need to tell you, we weren't doing too well before you got here." He caressed the musket in his hands. "Still aren't."

"You'll be doing a lot worse if I hang for this." I sighed. "Have I gotten any visitors?"

"Quite a few." Haldt said. "There's one in particular, though."

"Who?" I asked.

"A Lady Gerate comes to the guardhouse every morning threatening to skin you alive." He whistled. "You're a lucky man Thomas Belson."

I held up the manacles. "How do you figure?"

"Wish my wife had enough passion to threaten me like that?" The guard seemed happy to finally give some good news. "It shows the relationship is still alive and well."

Haldt and I chatted for some time before I heard footsteps coming. It was a lot of them. "You've got a visitor." He said.

"Who's that?" I asked

"Queen Harriot." He widened his eyes.

"Must've finally missed her bust." I chuckled to myself.

"What's that?" The guard cocked an eyebrow up.

"Sorry, that is privileged information." It still gave me a laugh, though. "Does she look angry?"

"No, as a matter of fact, she doesn't." Haldt said. "Almost pleased." He smiled. "Lucky you."

I steeled myself for whatever was coming my way. "That's worse." She hated me, and only the thought of my impending execution could give that woman a smile. "She's been waiting for me to make a mistake like this for some time."

"Oh." He muttered. "My condolences then."

He went to attention and saluted as she drew closer.

Finally, I saw her. Blond hair laying across her emerald dress and jewels. Face puckered up as if she was above all creation. Green eyes with nothing but scorn in them. I had to admit she was a pretty lady, all things considered.

"Open the gate." She said without looking at Haldt. He obliged. He was a good man, but he couldn't protect me now. She was flanked by six of the royal guard. They wore their red underneath polished armor plate. All of them would have been nobles, and their uniform showed it. They'd likely never see a battle. I could tell under all that tough armor, they were soft. There was one man in the back who stepped forward. It was Colonel Seiford looking much more grim than usual.

"Leave." She told Haldt. The queen didn't want any witnesses for what she was about to do. What the royal guard lacked in combat skills, they more than made up for in discretion, and Seiford was a colonel, trusted to keep his mouth shut. However, Haldt was a corporal and corporals were notorious talkers.

Haldt didn't leave.

"Did you not hear me?" She finally deigned to glare at the man.

"I did your grace it's just that…" He didn't want to leave me in the hands of this witch. He wanted to protect me if he could. He wanted to bear witness if he couldn't. He thought I deserved better than to die tortured to death by Queen Harriot. "He could be dangerous."

"I am at that." I discreetly nodded for him to go. Whatever he thought he owed me, it was paid by his kindness. "The queen should be fine though, as long as she stays away from my mouth."

Haldt turned to leave, but the Queen saw that he followed my order, not hers. "Grab him." She wouldn't let her rule be undercut by me.

Two of the royal guard took the man, and one produced a knife at his throat. They knew how that order usually ended.

"Your grace!" Haldt screamed. Seiford looked like he was about to intervene, but I stopped him with a gesture from my hand. That would only make things worse.

"I don't much like the idea of having a man in my army who takes orders from foreigners rather than his queen." She took a step towards the poor soldier.

"Your grace! Please, I was just-" The corporal pleaded.

I stood up or tried to at least. I managed a strange half-sitting position. "Whatever you want to punish me for, this man had no part in it."

"I'd just as soon kill him because you like him." She smiled sadistically, looking at a flesh and blood man who had pledged his service to her like he was a fly she was about to tear the wings off of.

"Well, I don't like him that much." I shrugged. "He's a decent fellow, though. I was just trying to save you some trouble down the road."

She sent a glare of pure hate my way. "You! Save me trouble?"

"Of, course! I've pledged my assistance to your country, after all." The manacles around my hands somewhat undercut my point. "It's easy to cover up one dead prisoner. Prisoners die all the time." I went on. "But Private Derbas here is well liked. If he shows up dead too, well that's too many coincidences." I paused, desperately thinking of what to say. "No one will call you on it, but eyes will turn your way. We live in times of revolution, don't we? Slaughtering a well-liked private won't make the army more inclined to protect you."

"I will not let you threaten me!" She hissed, and her hand was about to give the order.

"It's not a threat!" I screamed despite myself. "You can only hurt one of us with impunity, and who means more to you?"

I saw the gears turn behind those queenly eyes. Harriot was a frigid bitch, but she wasn't stupid. "Run along then." She let the man scurry off. No doubt, that wasn't the end of it in her mind. She already had plans to send an assassin to his door, but they'd be looking for a poor cock drawer who died in Rustia years ago as opposed to the man who showed me some kindness in a dungeon.

She probably wouldn't remember long enough to send a second attempt.

"Queen Harriot," I said from my half-sitting position, "now that we have some privacy, I can express my-"

Two of the royal household stood me up, and two more punched me in the gut hard. I hit the ground gasping for air.

"My queen!" Seiford stepped in. "This man is recovering from injury." He spared a glance down my way. "If you keep doing this, he may not survive."

The Queen snapped her fingers and the royal guard set to kicking me. I fumbled for some way to stand. When I couldn't do that, I tried in a pathetic attempt to grab the feet and protect the important bits. I'd been beat before. I knew how to handle it. I'd felt worse, but that was in battle. It was a different sort of pain. I refused to admit it to this bitch of a queen, but as far as ordering beatings went, she was pretty good.

I tried to slip into the Battle-Mind to numb the pain, but it wouldn't come. Between all the injuries suffered, and the rap of their boots against me. I couldn't manage it. I'd have to get through this the old fashion way. Grit my teeth.

Even through it all, I could see the game. I knew the rules. Every human interaction had them, and a savage beating was no different even if the stakes were higher. Harriot wanted me to plead, to beg. If I did, she won. That could mean the end of the beating, but it could also mean it wouldn't stop. If I held out for long enough, then my silence made me the winner, and no one wanted to play a game they were losing. Still, everything in me wanted to scream, stop. I wouldn't give it to her.

"My Queen!" Seiford finally screamed.

"Yes." She said it softly, but it still managed to carry over the thumps of boots.

"He's had enough…" The colonel spared a glance my way. It was only for a heartbeat, but it was one filled with as much emotion as I'd seen on him. It wasn't pity, not exactly. It was the look you gave to someone who didn't deserve it. Did I deserve to die? Maybe. Did I deserve to be punished for my arrogance? Undoubtedly. Did I deserve to be beaten to death in a musty cell? No!

"I'll say when he's had enough." And the boots continued to land.

She waited a good minute before she called it off, with a flick of her hand. I understood that. She couldn't let it seem like Seiford had made her stop.

I knew why Seiford was here too. It was common knowledge that he was my closest ally in Thyro. If the queen could make even him consent to my destruction, she'd have back whatever imagined power I'd stolen from her. Those were the only terms Harriot could think in. Power.

I managed to scurry back to my sitting position, spitting blood and bile. "How many?" I asked. "How many did we lose."

"Sixteen ships of the line and four frigates." Harriot didn't seem upset by that. There was a smile on her face. To her mind, it was a worthy price to pay for my destruction. "Not to mention a lord admiral and the honor of the crown."

"Three thousand and thirty-six." Seiford muttered out. The disgust in him was bubbling over. I didn't think it was directed at me.

"They were good men." I gulped down a breath and tasted the iron of blood. "I know I used to make jokes about sailors and marines, but..." I paused. "They were good men to the end of it."

"They were." Seiford agreed.

Queen Harriot had her men pull me up. "I told my husband not to trust you." She hissed in my face. "I told my son not to trust you." She scoffed. "Those small victories you won with your Confederacy tricks, convinced them you might be worth the headache, but I knew you to be a feckless dog."

"A dog's a loyal animal." I shrugged.

"Loyal to who I wonder?" Queen Harriot produced a slim knife from her bodice. "Certainly not loyal to us."

"To the Three and the New Church." I hissed back.

"Maybe to Thaniel as well." She smiled. "I heard about that private meeting you had with him." She paused. "We still don't know exactly what you did in Kran over the winter.

"You don't actually believe that do you?" I narrowed my eyes. "Everything I've done has been to win this war." I eyed up the guards around her, hoping someone would see sense. "He'd already be sitting on your throne if it weren't for me!"

She reeled back with that knife of hers. She wasn't going to stop. She didn't just hate me because I bucked propriety. She didn't just hate me because I was a Confederacy man. She didn't even hate me for my arrogance. She hated me because, in this world where peasants became emperors and foreigners protected the crown, I'd shown what her power was really based on. It was smoke from a fire that had gone out long ago.

She would have killed me then, but the blow didn't land. Seiford was holding her arm.

"You would touch a queen." She turned to face him. "That's a hanging offense, Colonel."

The colonel stayed firm. If nothing else, he was steady. "I know."

"You'd die for this man?" She didn't seem angry, only perplexed.

"I'd die for this country." He took a step back. "I'd die so that Thaniel doesn't undo centuries of hoping for something better." He looked me in the eyes. "I'd die for justice, and whatever this man deserves, he doesn't deserve this."

For a moment I'd thought I'd been wrong. Maybe this queen had just devised some trial to test my resolve. Maybe Seiford's words had softened her aching heart. "Grab him too." She finally said. I wasn't often wrong in these matters.

All six of them attacked the Colonel. He was a good fighter, and maybe if he'd been armed, he could have won. Still, he managed to send two to the dirt before someone clubbed him from behind.

"Stop!" A voice rang out. A kingly voice, the kind of voice you follow. It was Edward, standing there with his sword drawn.

"You?" Harriot asked.

"She's going to kill Thomas!" Seiford screamed but was cut off by a blow to the jaw.

"Leave this place, Mother." The prince took a step forward. "I won't allow this."

"I told you to stay in your room, my son." Now there was venom in her, but even a frigid bitch like her, probably wouldn't hurt her own son. "Take him away." She nodded to her guards. Probably was the keyword.

They took a step toward the prince, and the first man to touch him had his arm broken before he could even scream. "The only way to kill these men is to kill me." He was the leader everyone hoped to serve in that instant.

"They're traitors!" The queen said.

"Even you don't believe that!" Edward took a step forward, and the guards stepped out of his way. No doubt looking at the man gasping on the floor who had tried to stop him the first time. "You're just afraid that this man might be more of a king than your husband." He hissed at her. "Than your son, even."

"Ah, so you've heard the whispers over the past year too." She smiled wickedly. "You know what the peasants say when they're in their cups." She matched her son.

"Aye, I've heard them." Prince Edward sheathed his sword. "I haven't just been listening for the past year, though." He gave a glance to me. "I've been listening all my life."

"Then let's make them silent!" Queen Harriot handed him the knife.

The Prince took it. "I was listening when Thaniel first started this war. I was listening when they whispered that we couldn't protect them." He turned that blade over, looking at it like it wasn't just steel. "I was listening before even then. I was listening when they said that all they did was serve us, and we didn't return the favor. I was listening when they begged us for permission that wasn't ours to give."

"Ingrates!" The queen hissed. "And this man is the leader of them." She pointed at me.

"Ingrates..." The Prince was still staring at the knife. He was staring at the knife like it was the sharp edge between right and wrong. "I've been listening for a long time." He tossed the knife to the ground. The message was oddly clear to me. Blades aren't the border between right and wrong, good men are.

"You were never fit to be a king!" She slapped him, hard.

The Prince put his hand to his face. "Maybe..." He paused. "But I don't think anyone else is either." He stepped past his mother to face me. "I've read our histories. I know kings are made by knives in the dark." He kneeled down, so our eyes met. "But people are bettered by decent folk who stand in the light."

"He'll still hang for this!" The queen screamed. "You've done nothing here."

"Maybe he will." Edward shrugged without looking at her. "It'll be in the light, though. Where everyone can see."

"There'll be a price for this." The Queen knew she was beat.

"Then I'll bear it!" The Prince rounded back on her. "Leave Mother..." This time it was barely a whisper.

Without another word Queen Harriot stormed out of the room, followed by the household guards in their pretty armor. They let Seiford be.

"You promise you won't try and escape?" Edward asked.

"I do."

He laughed at that. "Why should I take your word?"

Corporal Haldt stepped from around the corner. "He won't, your highness." It appears he hadn't run as far as he should have. "Constable Belson's already had the chance." He scratched his head. "I'm a better soldier than I am a prison guard."

"Haldt, you daft bastard!" I smiled at him. "Thought you would've run back to your family by now." He'd obviously been hiding nearby.

"You didn't run back to yours." The guard smiled back.

I couldn't hold back the laughter. "Aye, and take life advice from me." I raised my manacled hands. "See how far that gets you?"

"Ivory towers or a musty cell," Haldt smiled, "a good man's a good man, doesn't matter where you put him. I think that's the only path we should follow."

"I think you're right." Prince Edward reached his hands out for the keys.

The guard handed them over. "Your Highness, I don't mean to overstep my bounds..."

Prince Edward put a hand on his shoulder. "You signed on to die for my kingdom." He smiled. "Whatever we have to be in the public eye, you can speak to me true in private."

The guard smiled and shook his head. "I didn't sign on to die for your kingdom." He said. "I was the seventh son of a poor fletcher. I signed on for a good meal and steady pay." Haldt's eyes glanced at me and then the prince. "Whatever I signed on for, I'm here now because it's something worth dying for." He paused. "Your mother was wrong. You'll make a fine king."

"Well, first we have to make sure there's a kingdom." The Prince undid all my bindings and lifted me to my feet. "I trust you can still fight, Thomas."

"Aye, I can fight." I rubbed the blood into my wrists.

I stared at them all for a moment. Edward, Seiford, and Haldt. A prince, a noble, and a commoner I barely knew. They were all willing to die for me. It wasn't just because I'd won some battles in hard times. That had made them notice me, but it wasn't why they'd stood up to a queen. It was because I'd been the man they wished they could be. I'd stood for a people not my own. I'd fought for something they couldn't see. I'd made them more than they were. That's the man they thought I was anyhow. They deserved to know the truth.

"I know what you all think of me." I tried to make my voice firm, but it came out a whisper. "I've killed men with knives in the dark, though." I met the Prince's eyes. "I've done things that'd make you weep." I took a deep breath. "They make me weep even." I went on. "I've slain men who've begged for mercy. I've made deals with shadows." I paused. "I mocked a grieving father's dead son and killed him when he had the audacity to object." I shook my head. "I'm not the man you all see when you look at me. I'm a killer same as all the other evildoers in this world. I'm just better at it," I looked into Edward's eyes, "and maybe I had the good fortune to be on the right side."

I went on. "I didn't do it for your country. I didn't do it for high ideals." I looked down at my hands. "I did it for me. I did it because I wanted to be the hardest bastard that ever walked this earth." I wondered how much blood would have been saved if those hands had been cut off at birth. "I wanted glory, greatness, and a name so heavy only I could lift it." I spit into the ground at the memory. "If Thaniel could've given me that, I think I would've taken it. The uniforms my allies wore never really meant much to me." I paused one last time. "I didn't do it because I was wise, honorable, or caring. I did it because I was foolish, angry, and scared."

I took them all in. "If there's a noose at the end of this, maybe it's more than I deserve." I looked down on my shackles. "Those men at Fredua, they died on account of my arrogance. It could've happened at any battle, just bad luck it happened with men that weren't mine to lead." I paused. "I wanted victory, and I didn't care much who got hurt in-between."

Seiford finally spoke up. "I knew all of that before Wuntsville." He said. "Still followed you then."

"Why's that?" I asked him.

"Because I knew that was who you were." He took a step towards me. "I hoped that wasn't all you'd be, though."

"Fools hope." I snorted.

"Aye, but so were donkeys and scarecrows." Seiford gave a snort of faint laughter. "Thomas Belson's got a way of making fools hopes pay off." The colonel took a step back. "Hard times make hard men do hard things, and these are the hardest times of all." He paused. "Sometimes they make us more than we were though." He smiled one of the few smiles I'd seen on him as long as I'd stood next to Seiford. "The world needs Belson the Blessed, not just as he is, but as he could be." That smile almost made me believe it. "You asked how many men were lost, not ships. Might be you're on the way there."

"Never did show me your horse." I snorted at him.

"And I never will." He kept that smile. "Might be I'll show you my brother though and have been proud to do it."

"What's your brother like?" I asked.

"I think he'll grow into a fine man." Seiford said.

"I think he will." I agreed.

Prince Edward stepped forward. "You've made mistakes, Thomas." He said. "You'll have to pay for those mistakes." He put a hand on my shoulder. "You've done good works too though. You won't have to pay alone."

"Thank you." So that was how it was going to be. I made them a little more than they were, and they made me a little more than I was. People always thought of decency, kindness, and charity as some sort of zero-sum game. If one man's got it, someone else has to suffer. That wasn't the way it worked at all. It was like a snowball rolling down the side of a mountain. No one notices it at first, then one day it grows big enough to shake the world to its foundation.

"Well, we've got an army to get back to." Prince Edward turned around to leave.

"How're they coming?" I asked.

Seiford answered me. "They're going to change this world." He paused. "That I believe." He turned to follow his prince, and they were gone.

"Some friends you've got." Haldt said as he returned to his post.

I chuckled a bit at that. "I never really saw them as friends." It was true. "In my mind, they were allies. Men I trusted to do a job. Men I thought might help me win this war. I didn't come to Thyro to make friends."

"Oh!" The guard said it like I was all sorts of fool. "Some friends you've got."

"Aye." I smiled through the bar. "Some friends indeed."

The Thaniel Wars

It was a few days before the royal guards came for me. I could hear the commotion in the streets already. Apparently, the whole city wanted to see me walk to the gallows. I was still weak from my injuries. I'd tried to do my exercises, but I always wound up aching on the ground.

"Today's the day?" I asked Haldt.

"Aye, today's the day." He undid the gate and let it swing open.

"They're gonna walk me from the dungeons to the Palace?" I asked.

"Seems that way." The corporal said.

"That's a lot of people between here and there." I whistled to myself. "How do they usually treat these men?"

"Poorly." Haldt admitted. "You're well liked in the city, but when crowds start at something..." He trailed off. "You know how they can get."

I laughed. "Back where I'm from, twenty men is considered a crowd."

He shrugged. "Same principle. Don't take it personally, though."

The royal guards walked towards me with their polished breastplates and clean uniforms. "Why isn't this prisoner in irons?" The leader said, a man with a pristine face, that I could tell was a little pudgy beneath the uniform.

"They broke." Haldt shrugged. "This one's been behaving himself though."

"Then you find another!" The lead royal screamed at the man.

"You know all the irons I tried to throw on him broke too." The Corporal shook his head. "Damndest thing. I've never been a religious man, but I've heard about the Three's miracles." It was a lie of course, and the guard knew it.

"We've brought our own." He shackled my hands and feet. "Seems divine intervention doesn't happen to my irons."

"No." Haldt agreed. "The Three want nothing to do with your shackles."

"The Queen will hear of this." The lead guard threatened.

"Oh, go easy on poor Private Derbas would you." I implored the royals. "He's not very bright you know." I turned around and gave the man a wink.

"March." He pushed me up through the stairs and went out the dungeon. We arrived at a plot of mud. All I had were my sackcloth pants. No shoes or shirt.

"I'm confused." I turned towards the royals. "Where are the masses calling for my blood?"

"They're waiting for you to get dressed." He pushed me into the mud.

I finally floundered my way to my feet. "That's polite of them." I spit out the mud. There was a trough filled with water, still enough for me to see my reflection. I looked pathetic. My catatonic state had left me malnourished. Haldt had snuck me some food, but it hadn't made up for a month of being force-fed soup. The muscles I had worked so hard to develop looked withered and beat. The scars seemed less intimidating, sadder. Even the tattoos on my arm looked faded.

"You thirsty?" The guard asked.

"A bit parched." I admitted.

The lead guard snapped, and his lackeys pushed my head into the trough while I struggled against it. They finally pulled me out after what seemed like an eternity. "Still thirsty?"

"Think I've had my fill." I shook the water off

The guard shook his head. "You've ruined your outfit." He said. "Best to get you another." They threw me in the mud again.

They walked me out front, and I saw the crowd, lined up twenty deep. However, they weren't shouting and jeering. It looked more like they were mourning something.

"We'll take it from here." I heard a voice say from behind.

I turned around to see Private Roltan with his same old fox like gaze, only he was wearing his lieutenant bars proudly now, like he felt worthy of them. He was flanked by eleven men I recognized. Sergeant Fenton was there with all his bulk, Lieutenant Kelm too. They were all wearing their army uniforms.

"We've been ordered to take this man to the palace by the King himself." The guard took an arrogant step forward.

"He'll get there." Roltan matched him for swagger, but the lieutenant's was earned. Somehow that showed. "He'll be accompanied by men who know his worth though."

The guard saw now that the shield of royal authority, wouldn't do much against men who knew how to fight. "The King will hear about this." He said.

"I'm quite sure he will." Roltan sneered down at him. "I'm still here though aren't I?"

The men fell in behind me. "Prince Edward told you to be here?" I asked over my shoulder.

"Didn't have to." Roltan said to my back. "I wasn't with you at Fredua. I won't make that mistake again." He jerked his head back to the soldiers behind him. "They felt the same way." He shrugged. "Not for nothing but the whole army shared the sentiment as well."

"It's probably a good thing they didn't all come." I chuckled. "Marching an army on the capital wouldn't help me with this being accused of treason business." I looked back up at the street thug who'd become noble in all but name. "Still, I'm glad you're here."

Roltan nodded. "Like I said I should have stood with you at Fredua."

"I needed you with the rest of the fleet." I knew Roltan was steady as they came.

"All the same, I wish I would've been there." The lean killer answered.

"How'd your raid go?" I asked.

"Flawless."

I sighed. "Guess we better get this over with then."

"Suppose so."

I marched forward through my shackles.

The first of the crowd I saw were some boys with rotten tomatoes in their hands. I didn't begrudge them that. It was just their custom. I'd have probably done the same at their age. Still, as I walked by, they dropped the fruit on the ground.

"That ain't the way we treat heroes." I heard an old man tell them.

The young boys did what young boys so rarely do. They listened to their elder. They wanted to believe in some thing worth living to manhood for. Maybe the children figured they found it marching defeated through their street and decided it wouldn't be improved with the addition of rotten fruit.

When I walked by, men took off their hats. A couple women threw flowers in my wake. No one screamed at me. No one said a word.

There were other gangs of boys with rotten fruit, but they kept them at their sides. People think young boys are evil little demons. There's some truth to that assessment, but mostly they were just wild. They picked up the behavior of the adults around them and took it to the extremes only young men can really get to. Not evil, just trying to find their place in the world. However, maybe they were secretly looking for a better way.

The walk was long, and my legs were weak. My feet blistered, and my shackles chafed. I fell before long. Roltan went to grab my arm, but a little girl with pigtails ran from the crowd before he could drag me up.

"It's alright." She whispered in my ear. "It's not much farther."

"Thank you." I put my hand on her shoulder.

She took out a white cloth and wiped my face. Then she cleaned the tattoos on my arm. "A Constable's marks should always show." The girl helped me to my feet.

"So they shall." I said.

I walked for what seemed like an eternity. I didn't fall again, though. These people deserved a hero.

I walked on until the silence was broken up by a man's voice piercing through the crowd. As I got closer, I realized he was one of those corner preachers dressed in sackcloth. Every city had them to some degree. I generally didn't like what they had to say, so I tended to ignore them. This particular preacher looked like they all did. He was old, shaved, and standing on top of a wooden soapbox.

"We were hopeless!" He preached. "We were beset by a beast none could slay. We were dead men all of us." The crowd around him seemed receptive. "We prayed to the Three for deliverance. We prayed to anyone who would listen and thought our invocations fell on deaf ears." He pointed to me. "But they were listening. They sent us a hero, like the knights of old."

He stepped off the wooden box, and the crowd parted before him. "We thought all was lost until the Three sent us their champion." He met me, and my procession stopped. "They sent us a warrior who could free us from Thaniel's yoke." He looked me in the eyes. "They sent us a man greater than the Old Religion and their Demons Below."

I realized the whole crowd was staring at me, waiting for my response. "I don't know about being the Three's champion." I shook my head. "I don't know about answering your prayers either." I paused. "I fight, and some say I do it well." That got a chuckle out of them.

"If you want a man who's greater than the Old Religion, it's you." I surveyed the crowd. "Each of you is greater than that plague, you just haven't realized it yet." I took a deep breath. "As for freeing you, I can't do that either. Search for freedom within yourself." I stared back into the preacher's gray eyes. "I fight though, and some say I do it well."

He took my shoulder. "Then keep fighting just a little longer."

I nodded and kept walking until I felt a presence beside me. It was Doctor Quarrels. "You're the only one who can see me so try not to talk too loud." He said. "I wouldn't want people to think you've gone mad."

I chuckled. "Who knows? Might be I am mad." I whispered out one side. "I am talking to an imaginary friend only I can see."

"Seeing is a strange thing." Quarrels chuckled. "Maybe they don't observe a doctor here in this street, but I think the world knows the Three walk beside you all the same."

"Thought the Three didn't choose sides in war." I said through the corner of my mouth.

"We absolutely do!" He cried out. "We choose everyone's side, and hope they're better off for it."

"In my country playing both sides is a hanging offense." I paused. "Same in every other country, come to think of it."

"It's a good thing we're not in the business of selling arms or secrets." Quarrels smiled.

"Then what are you in the business of selling?" I asked more to be cheeky than anything else.

"You don't really have the words for it." The doctor shrugged. "Let's call it salvation." He paused. "Let's call it something better."

"Doesn't get much better than this." I raised my shackles.

Quarrels gave a hearty laugh. "I know you're saying that because you think it makes you sound clever," he paused, "but you've stumbled onto something truly wise."

I cocked an eyebrow up. "Not sure I follow."

"No, you're not ready to follow us where we're taking you yet," he looked me up and down, "but one day you will."

"I hope so." We walked in silence for a while. "So is John gonna hang me?" I finally asked.

"It's like I said." Wisdom huffed. "Omniscience is like a painting-"

"I know, I know." I waved him off. "Is John going to hang me though."

"If you call him John, he probably will." Quarrel's admitted. "Show a mite of humility, and it'll go far." He paused. "You already knew this, though."

"I do." It chaffed at me even still. "Humility has never been my strong suit."

"No, it hasn't." The god admitted. "What is life without change, though?"

"Well, if I don't change, there may not be much life left." I kept walking, my feet had started to bleed.

I had moved past the peasants, in their glum silence to the nobles in their arrogant silence. I'd always found it strange how silence can mean different things, and we know exactly what it implies without having it pointed out.

All the lords and ladies didn't even lower themselves to spit at me. It was as if they thought noble spit might improve me. In all the years the world had turned, I doubted anyone had been so offended at having not been spit at. They looked pretty. I wasn't too angry to give them that.

I looked into each of their faces. *I saved you all!* I shouted inside my own head.

Finally, I saw King John staring down his nose at me. This was what he'd been waiting on. The only question left was if he had the strength to carry it through. He was wearing a dark green doublet, cloaked by Anthanii crimson. In his eyes was pure delight.

Slightly to his left was Queen Harriot. She looked as beautiful as ever, dressed in her emerald dress and emerald eyes. She gave off the impression that if you took her to an appraiser, she'd be regarded as one enormous jewel.

To the King's right was Edward. He wore his military uniform and a scowl that could cut through diamond. He gave me a nod, that was imperceptible to anyone watching but me.

Rolton marched me up the steps until I stood directly under the gaze of the king.

"You stand accused of treason." A herald shouted so that the royal voice wouldn't have to go sore on my account. "You stand accused of consorting with Thaniel to destroy our fleet."

"I'm guilty as a hand in the pie." I shrugged my shoulders. "It was my plan that saw those men there that day." I hung my head. "It was my arrogance that killed them as much as the fires."

"So you plead guilty to treason?" The herald's voice rolled over us all like silk and honey.

I bared my chest to show the wounds I'd received. "I've been hit enough times to kill a dozen men." I screamed back. "The only thing that keeps me on my feet is beating Thaniel. Any man who says otherwise is lying or ignorant."

I cringed at the wording of it. "Not that I would accuse your highness of either these sins." That got a murmur from the crowd. They'd never heard me talk like a beaten dog. "We Confederacy folk are prone to hyperbole."

"So you are." The king hissed through a smile.

"I am guilty though." I hung my head in shame. "There were lives lost on that raid, that can never be got back. Admiral Nelard was a hero, and he deserved better than he received." Again another rumbling, this time of agreement. They hadn't much liked the man while he was alive, but death plays strange tricks on our memory. "Those sailors and marines were just as good too. They deserved better as well."

"They didn't get it though." The King stepped forward. "All they got was death by your hand."

"Like I said." I shrugged. "I'm a guilty man." I let a pause break the silence. "I was arrogant and cruel. I've done things to make the Three turn away. I placed my own hunches above the wisdom of the sovereign." I went down to one knee, to a group gasp. "If I had consulted *my* king beforehand, the carnage could have been avoided."

John should have seemed pleased at my humility before him. I saw a frown twitch on his face for half a heartbeat. If he killed me now, there would be riots. The army would refuse to fight. Even the nobles would mutter about it. One thing was assured, Thaniel would conquer them all.

"Father this man is innocent of treason." The Prince finally spoke up. "Why train an army he wanted to betray? Why save us when-"

King John cut him off with a slap to the face to more muttering.

"He doesn't save us." The man hissed. "Divine right placed me on this throne."

"All the same," Edward should have stayed silent, but he didn't, "it didn't put you there to punish men for faithful service."

"I should be punished, though." I said it to spare the prince. "I will prostrate myself before you now." I went onto my belly. It looked clumsy with all the chains. "Whatever, you so judge appropriate will be done to me."

King John walked off his pedestal, slowly. He made his way to me in quiet strides. Finally, he stood right before me. "Kiss the royal shoe." He smiled down at me. "It is an honor to do so, after all."

I wanted to grab him at that moment and break his neck. I wanted to tear him apart, and even in my weakened state, I knew that I could.

Then I thought about the faces of the men I'd led. I thought of the captain who just wanted to do right by his country. I thought of the soldiers, who chose to help me. I thought of the men I'd killed. I thought of the men who'd died under my command and the boy at Wuntsville who I could have saved but didn't. I thought of those who put their trust in me. It was a responsibility I'd sought out. I couldn't turn my back on it when things got hard.

I kissed his royal shoe, and he kicked me in the mouth. It was subtle. None saw it but the two of us. It didn't even really hurt, but the blood dribbling down my mouth was a message I read clearly.

"Don't ever forget this." King John whispered to me.

"I won't." He took it as some base complement, rather than the threat it was meant as. It always struck me as strange how two men can hear the same thing and take it differently.

"Thomas Belson is not to be hung today." The herald shrieked.

I'd cheated death a hundred times, but it had never felt like this before. I was needed elsewhere, and that painting Quarrels talked about still had me in it.

Present Day

I dressed for the party in sullen silence, not that there was anyone to hear me anymore. Every gala or ball I'd ever been too, I'd had Seiford clucking disapproval over my shoulder. I'd always thought I'd just ignored him. It turns out I hadn't. While I hadn't listened to the wardrobe advice, formal functions still had a way of unnerving me, and Seiford had chosen the most annoying way possible to let his friend know he was there for me.

Now he was gone. I had told the monk I'd sent him away because he hadn't been honest with me. That seemed flimsy even to myself. The truth was, I finally saw what Seiford wanted me to be. What he believed I could be, and I wasn't sure if I could muster that. Now that I knew, I couldn't bear it, and to look at my friend was to know.

"And why the fuck didn't he try to tell me earlier?" I seethed to myself. The monk may have thought that after I'd won enough victories, I'd be content. Somewhere deep down maybe even I'd thought that. The truth was that every army I'd shattered, every country I'd conquered, and every Priest I'd hung, had just cemented who I was. It had just made me more hungry. Now the wall I'd built around my identity was impenetrable, well almost impenetrable. The Prime Governor of the Confederacy had only been able to give me a momentary pause. My own brother had tried to make me accept my humanity and failed, but an Anthanii noble and reluctant monk who I should have felt no kinship towards had somehow wormed through my defenses and started a civil war against myself.

He was more than that, though. Seiford had been my only true friend for ten years. The monk was lecherous, foul-mouthed, and vain, but he was moral. He was a good man. How many times had he stayed my hand? The old bastard I'd had before Seiford was chaste, devout, and orthodox. He spent ten hours a day reading the Testament and the rest lecturing anyone within earshot. When I had marched into Kran and rounded up every man woman and child, he'd whispered in my ear. "Kill them all." He'd said. "And make them suffer."

I'd listened.

My father had taught me all the sins I committed were my own and no one else's. It would have been easy to blame Father Keys. To dump my sins on the old bastard and then rage against him. It would have been easy, but it wouldn't have been right. After the New Church had discovered what I'd done in the name of the greater good they knew even at twenty years I was dangerous, dangerous and useful. They pulled Father Keys on the excuse that he was too old and replaced him with Seiford. Someone told me he died of a heart attack shortly after. I wondered if he heard the same voices that screamed for mercy in my head. I suspected that if he did, he read the Testament until they went away.

I hadn't liked my new monk at first. He was too lecherous, too foul-mouthed, too vain, and what's worse, he was noble, pretty, and charismatic enough for it to seem becoming. How could a man like Seiford succeed where Keys had failed? How could Seiford know the difference between right and wrong?

It was more than that, though. I told myself I didn't want him because of all his failings. Truth was I didn't want him because of my own. In him, I saw the brother that was dead because of me. I saw a man that no one could replace, and it felt dirty just to try. There was no one like Colonel Seiford, so it was best if I just let things lie.

We'd gone out drinking enough to like each other, but I was secretly looking for a replacement. Then a month later I conquered a city with a fourteen-year-old duke. The duke was an ally to the Old Religion, and no one else could be installed until he was dead. I had put a gun to his head. I knew how to kill a man quick.

"No." Seiford stepped between the two of us. "There has to be another way."

"There isn't." I knew what had to be done, even if it was unpleasant. "This is for the greater good."

"What do you think he said when he let the Demon's loose in his land?" Seiford took another step forward. "The same thing you're saying now with your gun pointed at a child's head."

"What's one life compared to the thousands that live in this city?" I was prepared to shoot the monk to get to that boy.

"Nothing." Seiford had said pushing the weapon down. "But

8itssϊ

I'm not trying to save his life. I'm trying to save your soul, and that means more to me than all of Thyro."

We'd spent two weeks drawing up a new document to govern the province. It was a constitutional monarchy. The duke would rule only by the consent of his people, and in the years since, the city had never let a Priest of the Old Religion within its walls. By all accounts the Duke had grown into a fine young man as well.

My father had always told me that the sins I committed were my own and no one else's. He also told me that an angel on my shoulder never hurt. Now the angel was gone, and I was alone.

There were more than enough reasons for me to be happy. I'd announce I'd side with the South, and receive praise and adulation from my people. I would march side by side with my brother. I wouldn't have to choose between duty and family, and most importantly I would come home to Rachel. Maybe we could be married and have children. That's what men were supposed to want after all.

I wanted desperately to want that. Still, no matter how hard I tried I couldn't get the Prime Governor's words out of my head, and they would have meant nothing if Seiford hadn't said they did.

I didn't wear my uniform. After all, I wasn't fighting for the New Church anymore. I did want to appear as a warrior though, so I wore what I did in battle. I was dressed in worn cotton pants, a dark green shirt, with a thick leather vest, and on top of it all my trusty brown duster. I went to roll my right sleeve up but thought better of it. Things wouldn't be helped by reminding people of my old allegiances. I also buckled on my pistols, one handle facing forward, the other back, for a twist draw if need be. The pouches along my weapon belt were each filled with a round except the place my hunting knife went. I had another pistol in a holster next to my vest, half concealed, plus a two-shot hidden in a pouch I'd sewn on the inside of my sleeve. I always kept my tomahawk at my side. Once I'd adjusted myself thoroughly in the mirror, I put on my hat which had been black at one time but was now faded gray. I had bought it to keep the elements off but kept it because Seiford hated the unfashionable thing. I didn't know why I wore it then except that I wanted to.

When I was finally ready, I stepped out of my room and went downstairs to the party. People were gathered, and the affair was already in full swing. Everyone looked up at me with respect, but they couldn't hide their initial look of disbelief at what I was wearing. It suited me just fine. There were many men in the room who looked to have seen hard military service. A few even wore gilded uniforms that they could never, in good conscience, take on a battlefield. The difference was they weren't just soldiers, they were plantation owners, aristocrats, and family men. They had a life away from conflict. I had only war. The other reason they had some disappointment in their eyes, was that they'd heard the stories about me. They expected Belson the Blessed to be seven feet tall and handsome as a prince. The scarred man of average height who favored one leg more than the other left a lot to be desired. In this crowd of well-built men in expensive suits and beautiful women in elegant dresses, I was the least impressive among them.

I smiled as genuinely as I could and muttered some greetings. I looked around the crowd. The usual serenity of the yellow sitting room seemed hostile now. Everyone was looking at me, even the servants carrying the food had stopped to get a glance at the conquering hero. There must have been a hundred people crammed into the room.

Thankfully, I didn't have to stand there long. Andrew and Sarah hurried to my side. "The man of the hour has finally arrived!" My brother said to the crowd then turned to me. "The most famous warrior in the whole world and he's a Belson." He paused with pride. "Belson the Blessed." He looked over the crowd. "I'll give another speech for him later when we've all had a bit more to drink." Everyone laughed at that. Andrew had a gift for making people laugh. "Until then I'll reintroduce him to all you fine people he hasn't seen in fifteen years."

Now it was Sarah's turn to play the gracious host. "Until then eat whatever you like. It'll go bad if you don't."

Andrew leaned close to me after the guest had gone back to mingling. "I know you're uncomfortable, but it's custom to have these things." He patted me on the back. "Anyway, people are dying to meet you." He said as he shuffled through the crowd.

"This is miss…" Andrew would say to me, and I promptly forgot they ever existed.

"Oh, I heard you wrestled a mile long snake." She'd ask.

"Only the one in my trousers." I would always make some rude remark, usually involving my trousers, before my brother shuffled me along to avoid embarrassment.

"I heard you have a magical sword."

"I do in my trousers."

"I heard you boxed Gregory the Strong and won."

"I did, but to his defense, he was very drunk." I couldn't work my trousers into every conversation.

"I heard you rode a dragon."

"Only the one in my trousers." I did my best though.

It went on for a while before Andrew and Sarah pulled me aside. My brother was clearly recovering from a laughing fit. My sister-in-law clearly disapproved, but Andrew interjected for her. "If you don't stop mentioning your trousers people are going to start believing that smut they write about you and your monk." He looked around. "Where is Seiford anyway? He's always raving about how he loves a good party."

"He left." Was all I could say.

"Pity." Andrew frowned. "I'm sure he'll be back soon. He never likes to be far from your side."

"I wouldn't count on it." I looked away.

"Regardless," Sarah cut in disapproving, "you have a duty to uphold your family name."

Before I could make a snarky comment my brother cut in. "He's done enough in Thyro to uphold our family name for ten generations. To our father, actions are what mattered, not words." He said disapprovingly to his wife, then TO me. "Still the words are a formality, so if you feel a comment about your trousers come up, just smile and nod."

"I will." I smiled and nodded at the obvious trouser joke in the comment.

"I appreciate you not saying, 'I always feel my trousers come up.'" He looked around and found who he was searching for. I looked down caught in my own melancholy. I hardly heard my brother say. "This is Senator Coleson. We invited him thinking he'd be too busy to come, but when he heard Belson the Blessed was here he couldn't stay away." I, however, did perk up a bit when I heard my brother say. "And you already know Rachel Gondua,"

I looked up at the senator. He was taller than me, about the same size as Andrew. He was handsome too, for a man who was clearly closer to forty than thirty. Still, there was something about him that was unpleasant. Maybe it was the slicked back hair. Maybe it was the green eyes that viewed me with mild distaste. Maybe it was the air of superiority that I would have bet my life, was unearned. I hated the man immediately. The fact that he was standing far too close to Rachel didn't help either.

Rachel looked stunning as always. Her dark hair was hanging loosely curling around her breast. Her fair skin looked not just fashionable, but beautiful. The red dress she was wearing wasn't in the puffy style, it was laying along the natural curves of her body. She looked as good as I'd ever seen her, but the way she standing next to Coleson was more than polite.

"Thomas Belson, it's nice to meet you." I extended his hand in greeting

"Oh, no introduction necessary." Coleson said the words politely but didn't even try to hide his superior attitude. He shook hands with me and made sure to show the full strength of his grip. I showed him mine in turn. The senator took his arm away trying to hide the pain.

"I'm sure Rachel has spoken enough on my behalf anyway." I said with a loaded smile then took her hand in mine and kissed it gently.

"Oh, she has spoken glowingly of your conversationalist skills and military record, which of course needs no explanation." Coleson gave her a look that made my fist clinch.

"Oh, she has?" I gave the girl a sideways look.

"I have." She smiled then mouthed. "He doesn't know about us."

"And praise from her is always a sign of an extraordinary man." The Senator smiled at the girl. "She is, after all, a formidable woman."

"I learn something new about her every day." I said. Then in Renarii, a language I was sure no one spoke. "Assu van tera hull." I said it like a compliment, but it translated too. "You're sleeping with this asshole."

"Gegar tas huntu." She followed my lead saying it in the same manner, but it meant. "Let's talk about this later."

"I'm afraid I don't speak Kranish." The senator frowned as if learning any other language than aristocrat Anthanii was beneath him. He was so up his own ass he didn't know there wasn't actually a Kranish language.

"We were just exchanging pleasantries." Rachel put a hand on his shoulder seductively.

I nodded. "Neither Rachel or I are used to this stagnation of languages. It can get very boring." I said politely.

"Oh, I understand." He nodded in a way that showed he didn't and put a hand on the small of Rachel's back, which made me grind my teeth furiously.

Andrew who had remained largely silent saw my anger and stepped forward. "Where is your wife this evening senator? Sarah does love Angela's company." He turned and gave me a wink.

They both immediately ripped their hands back to their sides. "She's fine." He said indignantly. "Angela doesn't like to leave the house much."

"Pity." Andrew said politely, but couldn't wipe the smile off his face.

"Yes pity." Coleson gave him a look of extreme displeasure, then turned to me. "I was very much hoping to talk with you." He smiled like a wolf does when he sees a lonely sheep. "My associate Fennis did as well, but he said he was busy practicing some nonsense called the blues with his Souren servants." The senator rolled his eyes as if there was too much wrong with the statement to begin explaining. "I keep telling him not to fraternize with those savages."

"Oh, I like the blues." Andrew said but was largely ignored.

"I've fought with Souren men before, and more than a few women besides." I said defiantly.

"I'm sure it was beyond easy after cutting your teeth on real Thyro men, especially with Anthanii regulars at your side." Coleson smiled at his race's on superiority.

"Not in the least." I smiled at taking the man down a peg. "There may be some confusion I didn't fight against them I helped them overthrow various rivals who practiced witch magic."

"Well, I suppose you had to choose the most civilized tribe." The senator said dismissively. "Witch magic sounds dreadful."

"They were actually quite a bit more civilized to my eye than their Anthanii oppressors." I said matching the senator's tone. "But you're right witch magic is dreadful. It's essentially the Old Religion, with a more honest name."

That comment earned a second of awkward silence and an angry glare from Coleson, but he tried to salvage the conversation. "I've always felt those Anthanii were simply trying to impose civilization on a backwards society."

"They certainly imposed a lot of things on those poor people." I paused dramatically. "They imposed their taxes, their whips, and their weapons on them." I smiled. "However, their favorite things to impose on them were themselves on their women. Sometimes they even made the husband and children watch the imposition." I scratched my head as if in thought. "Now that I think about it, civilization was about the only thing they didn't impose." The awkwardness around the conversation was palpable.

"You can't believe those savages should be left to their own devices." Coleson was the only one around who lacked the self-awareness to stay silent.

"Oh, I do believe it." I said levelly. "Have you ever heard about the Massacre of the Golden Fort?"

"If you mean the Final Stand of the Golden Fort, then yes, I have." The senator was desperately trying to control his temper

"Well, it was very final I'll give you that." I chuckled at his dismay. "Officially the New Church told me not to interfere, but unofficially…" I let the words hang for a second. "I interfered. You're right though they can be quite savage, or at least as savage as any other breed of man."

"Well, we can't always choose the right side." Coleson said offering an olive branch.

I shit on the olive branch. "You're right we can't." I was thinking about how I was about to offer this man my service. "But that time I did."

"Well, what happened years ago across the ocean is of little concern." He said clearly losing his patience. "It's what happens now that matters to us."

"You want me to fight for you." It wasn't a question.

Everyone was taken aback. Andrew put a hand on my shoulder. "Now, isn't the time to air your political allegiances."

"Why not? I'm facing a politician." I said without looking at my brother. I spat politician as a curse.

Andrew was about to speak again, but the senator held up his hand to silence him like a man would quiet a dog. That infuriated me more than anything. That my brother, a good and honorable man, could be silenced by a worm like Coleson, and worse, that my brother would obey. "I know your stance on the Old Religion, but it is our custom. However, that is not the only issue in play here." The senator said like he was explaining something to a willful child. "It's about us being forced to accept laws not our own, without being entitled to the protection that comes with it." He did his best to sound principled, but it came off like a bad actor trying to play a part he was horribly miscast in. "I know McAllan has spoken to you, and that damnable monk probably whispers some unfound nonsense in your ear, but we are your people."

I looked at the man. "McAllan views you all as his people, not just those north of the Capitol."

Coleson looked around in disgust. "What can I say? The man is an idealist."

"You're right he his." I didn't know why, but it didn't sound like such a bad thing. It always had before, but it didn't then. "You can stop your drivel. I've already made the decision to fight on your side." I hated to hear myself say the words, and I didn't know why.

"I'm glad to hear it." The Senator did, in fact, look happy as a cat looking over a dead bird, then his face turned stony. "But you should take care to remember who you're talking to."

"I'm talking to a senator of a government who doesn't even think that government should exist." I said levelly. "And you should take care to remember who you're talking too." I took a step forward. "The Thomas Belson who broke Thaniel. The Thomas Belson that forced an entire continent and more to bend to his will. You should also remember that you need me far more than I need you. I'll fight your damn war, but don't expect me to lick your boot."

Coleson smiled at that. "Yes, I am a senator today, but when the war starts, I will be much more." If there was any doubt in my mind about why this worm wanted a war, it was gone. Senator Coleson wanted this war so he could become Prime Governor Coleson, maybe even more than that.

The bastard sighed. "I suppose it doesn't matter much anyway which boot a mad dog licks, as long as it's turned on the right people." He looked at Rachel and kissed her cheek. "I'm afraid I have to go and mingle, but I'll be seeing you later." He turned to Andrew and me. "The war council will begin in an hour at the library, it would behoove you both to be in attendance." Then he left, and I could almost see a trail of slime following the worm.

"Thomas we need to talk about this." Andrew said in my ear.

"We'll talk at the war council." I shrugged my brother away.

"We need to talk about this." He repeated.

"What's there to talk about?" I said with more anger than I thought I had in me. "I'm fighting on your damn side aren't I?"

"We need to talk about why." He said putting a hand on my shoulder.

I glanced at Rachel then back at Andrew. "We will. Just give me a minute."

"Fine." My brother said, but he still wasn't happy. He gestured for Sarah, and they both left.

"You're sleeping with that asshole." I said in Renarii. I could tell people were still listening over our shoulders. Especially after the two most powerful men in the room had just gone at it.

"He's the most powerful man in the South. It behooved me to have his ear." She followed my lead and switched back to the language as well. "Why? Are you jealous?" Rachel said like we were still playing a game.

"I think I have a right to jealousy." I said trying to control my voice. "Besides it seems like you have a lot more than his ear." It wasn't a game for me. I felt something for the girl.

"You're right I do have a lot more than his ear. I have his favor, his obedience, and his resources." She said finally catching how angry I actually was. "Besides I'm not sleeping with him. I slept with him. Twice. Before I ever even met you. It's just better for my interest if he thinks I might sleep with him again."

"And how do I know you aren't doing the same thing to me?" I asked angrily.

"Men like Coleson are disposable." Rachel said rolling her eyes. "Despite his self-importance, he holds position now because his resources are vast and his name rings loud here, not because of any sort of competence." She stroked my cheek. "Men like you and women like me are different. We're powerful because we forced the world to yield for us. After this war ends, I plan to rip his position away from under him like a rug." She gave me a sly smile. "The time of great men bowing to weak ones is about to be over. A new day comes. Our day, and together no one can stop us." She could tell I wasn't convinced. "Also I like you quite a bit. Don't worry tonight I'll stumble into your room tonight, not his.

"And what if I don't just want tonight?" I finally admitted.

"You mean you…" She trailed off not able to say the word.

"Yes." I said belligerently. "I want you to be with me."

She looked around to make sure no one in the crowd was watching. When she felt we were safely secluded, she kissed me quickly, but passionately. The spectators had grown bored of them talking in a foreign language, so no one else saw, Then she leaned in close and whispered. "If you mean that then I'll show you something special tonight." Then she pulled away. "And we can talk about tomorrow afterwards." She smiled. "I have to go mingle, but I'll see you tonight." Rachel gave me a longing look as she disappeared into the crowd leaving me standing there.

There were fifty women there who would gladly go to bed with the Terror of Thyro. Why did that one matter? I looked out the window and saw a figure sitting in a chair. I knew who it was and needed to talk to her, so I left the party for the back porch.

My mother was on the porch, reading a book, and sipping on her tea. "Mama?" I said cautiously. I hadn't talked to my mother as much as I should have. I approached her every day, but sometimes she was having a fit. I didn't like seeing her that way. I needed my mother now. I needed the woman who tucked me into my bed as a child. If she wasn't there, it would break my heart. "Mama." I said again.

"Tom-Tom?" She turned to look at me. "Why aren't you enjoying your party?"

I felt relief flood over my body. She was lucid. "I was. I just wanted to come talk to you." I looked at the book in her lap. "Why aren't you there?"

"I used to love parties." She said as I walked closer. "I thought it was a great chance to meet a good husband. It wasn't." She smiled. "Then one day your father came by my house in his uniform to tell me some cousin I'd never met died in battle against the Anthanii." She sighed wistfully. "After that, I liked parties less. Your father never went to them. When we got married, I couldn't stand them." She stared up at me in a way that let me remember I was her son. "Now, I figure parties are for people trying to make their lives a little more interesting and fun. They aren't for those of us who have already lived a life without a single regret in this world." She smiled again.

I nodded to my mother. "What are you reading?"

She flipped it over to reveal the cover. *The Exploits of Thomas Belson by Viverent* it read. "Your friend, Seiford, gave it to me." She chuckled to herself. "He's a good boy. I just wish he'd watch his mouth more."

"He's a good friend." I smiled and took a knee next to my mother.

"Well, I'm glad you had him then." She put a hand on my

shoulder. "I'm at the part where you fought that ox man after praying for three days."

I didn't have the heart to tell her the real story. "That's a good part, mama." I looked at her. Still beautiful, even without her blond hair, even with some of the wrinkles. I wished I'd gotten her hair, but I was happy I'd got her eyes.

"It is." Pamela smiled at me. "What did you want to talk about?"

"Are you proud of me?" I asked desperately.

"Oh, Tom-Tom." She stroked my hair. "You're my son I'd have been proud if you stayed here and farmed the rest of your life." The softness in her gaze let me know it was true. "I'd have been proud if you'd have been the town drunk, even though I knew you wouldn't be." She touched my face. "I'm your mother. I'd have been proud of you no matter what."

I wiped a tear away. "Are you proud of what I've done?"

"Up until your friend gave me this book, I wasn't quite sure what you'd done." She looked down at the tome. "I knew you won a lot of wars, but that doesn't make a mother happy. I didn't know how you did it or why. That's what a mother cares about." She put her hand over mine. "This book tells me you helped the poor, saved innocents, and built a better world than the one you found. It tells me you did it because it was the right thing to do." She stroked my hand, and it felt like the tender piece of flesh I'd had fifteen years ago, not the scarred, calloused piece of meat my body had become. "That does make a mother very happy."

"Some of the stuff in that book is a bit exaggerated." I tried to hide the shame.

"I'm sure it is. Dragons aren't real, and your father told me only fools use a sword." She took my head in her hands and lifted it to face her. "What matters is that the man who wrote this saw you that way, and he doesn't seem like a fool to me." She paused for a second. "Your monk friend sees you this way too. That woman who came and visited you saw you this way, even if she didn't leave happy. Your brother sees you this way. Even your sister sees you this way though she doesn't say it, and most importantly your father saw you this way."

"Did he really mama?" I asked. I needed to hear it.

"There was never a doubt in his mind you weren't exactly the man this book says you were." She frowned at me. "Now you have to be that man. Not just for your family, but for everyone in the world who looks to you as the legend you are, and I expect there are many. The world needs this man." She tapped the book. "It needs this man because he proves that once upon a time there was a hero who did the right things, the right way, for the right reasons, and if a man like that existed then maybe they can do the right things, the right way, for the right reasons too." She paused. "As much credit as I'd like to take for raising your brother to be the way he is, I think you're the reason he's so good."

"What do you mean?" I looked up at my mother.

"I mean that every day since you left, he was emulating you." There were tears in her eyes now too. "Every time he was offered a choice, he wondered what his older brother would do." She saw the look of despair in my eyes. "It's a hard thing, to have the eyes of the world look up to you, but the Three chose you. Maybe it's because I'm your mother, but I think they chose wisely."

"What if I can't win?" I implored her. "What if I can't win the right way, for the right reasons."

"Then maybe losing means more." She stroked my head. "Might be it's easy to win and keep your morals. I think it's harder to have the world beating down on your head and not give in." She kissed my forehead. "People will remember the man that held fast then." She shook her head. "I wish this load never fell on your shoulders. I wish it wasn't my son." Pamela looked at my face like she was seeing it for the first time. She looked past the scars and into what made me who I was. "So much like your father, but even he never had this asked of him." She gave me a look that let me know she believed every word she'd said. "I think too many people spend too much time arguing over what it means to be a good man." She opened up her book again. "Waste no more time on that foolishness. Go be one."

"I love you, Mama." I said kissing her forehead then turned around and walked back to the party because I couldn't bear it anymore. She deserved to sit on a throne and have the whole of the world worship her, but she was happy in that rocking chair reading her book. I was going to be the man in that book.

I knew what I had to do. I was a Constable. I would always be a Constable, sworn to the protection of the weak. Sworn to defend them until a day when they chose to be something more. It was not my place to force them to be righteous. It was my place to inspire them.

My mother was right. It wasn't all that hard to be a decent man. You just had to do decent things for decent reasons.

I walked through the party. People greeted me, and I nodded back. Before long I was where I needed to be, in the study for a war council.

"Jeremiah your battalion will be posted here." I heard Coleson lecturing. I looked around the room crammed with all its books. Space had been cleared on which a large map was placed with miniatures that were supposed to represent various armies. Ten men were looking at the map. I saw Andrew in the corner shaking his head in disgust. I recognized Leslie Gondua, Rachel's quiet brother, sitting in the corner, stoically listening. The rest I vaguely knew from fifteen years ago, but couldn't recall any of their names. Some looked like they'd seen a battle before. Some looked like they hadn't even graduated from the cavalry college yet. Some looked dead serious. Some looked dead bored. All of them looked surprised to see Thomas Belson barge into the room.

Coleson looked up and smiled. "Ah the mad dog himself." He gestured to the room around him. "I'd introduce you to the rest of the war party, but I don't think you care." He pointed to a miniature far north of the rest. "You'll lead this regiment, raising whatever hell you can. Burn villages, rape women, I don't care. Make them hurt like the mad dog you are."

"Thomas we need to talk." Andrew said taking a step towards me. "This isn't the man I thought you were. You're not a mad dog!"

"Be quite Andrew!" A man in the corner who Thomas thought was named Jackson said sharply. He had the bearing of a soldier who'd seen combat. "He's Belson the Blessed, the man that broke Thaniel. With him, we'll be invincible."

"Before he was ever Belson the Blessed, he was Thomas Belson, my elder brother." Andrew looked at the man sharply, then back at me. "He's my brother, and I love him." He closed the distance and put a hand on my shoulder. "I loved him when he read me to sleep because I was scared of the dark as much as I did when I heard he was the greatest hero in the world." He looked me in the eye pleadingly. "He was always the greatest hero in the world to me."

"That's very touching." Coleson smiled in a way that said it wasn't. "I don't care what you call a mad dog as long as he obeys when I tug on the leash."

Andrew shot a disgusted look at the senator. "I'll be a dead man before I stay silent when the worm insults the lion."

Coleson narrowed his eyes. "You'll take care to speak more respectfully to me." He looked at me now. "And you'll stop encouraging him to disobey orders before I have you tried for treason."

"I don't care what you'll be tomorrow." Andrew looked back unflinchingly. "But for now a senator doesn't have that power."

I cut in before it had a chance to go farther. "You're right Andrew." I folded my brother into a hug. "I'm not a mad dog." I pulled away. "I'll spend the rest of my life asking what you would do. I should have started years ago." I released my brother. "I'm going to be the man you think I am."

"Can we get back to the war planning." Coleson rolled his eyes.

"Why, sure we can." I adjusted my gun belt nonchalantly. "So I'm to set the North on fire from The Capitol to the Trebia river." He walked closer to the map. "You want me to twist their arm till they scream mercy."

"Well, that is the essence of war isn't it?" The senator said sarcastically.

"The essence of war is to do something you think is right, and another thinks is wrong." I circled the table where the map lay, studying it intently. "I never used to wage wars of attrition because they didn't work." I glanced around at the crowd. "I've always found that when you try to push a people into the dirt, it has the opposite effect. They rise up unified and stronger than ever." I chuckled a bit. "People are so strange. You'll spend a year with them speaking their language and eating their food until you think you understand them. Then one day they do something so insane you couldn't have anticipated it if you spent a century studying them." I shook my head in dismay. "When the chips are down, and their backs are against a wall, they surprise you. They act like people." I smiled fondly as if all the goodness of my great species was incapsulated in that one sentence.

"Is there a point in all this." Coleson said as if he was losing his patience.

"Craftsmen work around the clock without pay, to give their people a fighting chance. A starving family will share its last loaf of bread with their neighbor. Beardless youths and crippled old men beg to join the army, just to have the chance to protect their city, and above all, no one runs, not even when their kings and nobles abandon them. No one runs, not the rich, not the poor, not the women, not the children, not the healthy not the sick." I chuckled again as if remembering an old joke. "I remember one man missing a leg, half an arm, and not a day under seventy, came to me with his rifle." I couldn't stop laughing at the memory. "Do you know what he said when I tried to turn him away?"

"I don't care, but I figure you'll tell us anyway." The senator said trying to move things along.

"He told me, 'you might have stopped Thaniel, but you won't stop me.'" I frowned. "He died in that battle, but I've never seen a king fight more bravely." I looked around at the crowd. "That's why I never fought battles of attrition because I've never come across a wall harder to break than human spirit."

"So you have a strategic objection to our plan." Coleson rolled his eyes. "You could have just said so."

"No, I said I used to never fight battles of attrition because they don't work." I sighed. "A tall man with a black aide changed my outlook."

"So you will follow the strategy?" The senator looked confused in the worst kind of way.

"No, I used to never fight wars of attrition because they don't work." I smiled to myself. "I don't do it now because it's wrong. The world deserves better than a man who shoves peoples faces into the mud."

Coleson pinched his face angrily. "Fine. You're really just there for redundancy. The Old Religion will make their lives hard enough." He pointed at the map. "Your regiment can go-"

I cut him off. I was done listening to the worm. "You know all those stories they tell about me say I inspired those people." I looked back at the map. "I even told that to myself. It made me sleep better after a hard battle." I shook my head dismissively. "The truth is they inspired me. I figured if a starving peasant could keep going a little farther, then maybe I could too." I looked up at Andrew who was staring at me, proud of his brother as his brother was of him. "All those educated thinkers who write that a government is the only thing keeping people from eating each other, have never been in a city under siege after every politician has fled." I looked up to the heavens. I believed in the Three but never prayed to them for help. I prayed then, not for strength or wisdom. I prayed to thank them for the goodness of man. "The world doesn't need a government to force them into mutual submission. It needs an idea to reach for together." I looked up at my brother again. "It needs a hero to inspire them."

"What are you saying?" Coleson looked at me narrowing his eyes.

"I offered to fight for McAllan before I agreed to fight for you." I sighed. "I offered to lead his armies, but on my terms." I regretted the conversation I'd had with the Prime Governor. "My terms were logical and made sense, they weren't right though." I turned to Coleson. "He refused my help because he'd rather lose the right way than win my way."

"Are you saying you agree with the idealist?" The senator was fuming now.

"He is a rare idealist. He'd rather court disaster than abandon his principles." I sighed. "The world is terribly full of pragmatist though." I looked around the room. "You plan on letting Demons loose in the North. You plan on selling lands, not your own, to Anthanii and Kran. You don't care what happens to them."

Coleson looked indignant. "And should I?"

"You shouldn't. There's no logical reason for it." I laughed. "There's no logical reason for McAllan to care about a few rebellious provinces." I went on. "But he does. He cares about every man who lives in this Confederacy." I looked around the room meeting all of their eyes. "He cares about the people in this room, even as you plan to destroy him."

"Idealist care about many stupid things." The senator said dismissively.

"You're right they do." I looked at my brother. "They're even stupid enough to care about their older brother's soul when the fate of a country lies in the balance." I looked back at the map. I saw it as McAllan did. I saw it as one country. One nation. I saw it for what it could be, not what it had been. "Like I said the world is terribly full of pragmatists, but I don't think it's better off for it. Maybe what it needs now is an idealist."

"You can't mean..." Coleson said not believing what he was hearing.

"You want to divide and conquer." I shrugged. "It's a sound strategy. It's been done for as long as there have been armies to fight." I looked back at the map. "McAllan wants to unite and lead. That hasn't been tried half as much." I let out a great sigh. It seemed like all the sin I'd been holding in me left at once. "Maybe it should be." I paused looking at my brother. He was the only man in the room that mattered. "That's why, following this party, I'm going to ride straight to the Prime Governor fall to my knees and beg him to let me serve in his army in whatever fashion he sees fit. If he makes me a store clerk, I'll do it prouder than when I led a hundred thousand men. If he makes me a private than I'll die as a man should. I'll die for an ideal."

"You're a traitor!" The senator said in disgust.

"To you maybe." I stood tall, taller than I ever had before. "But to the people who see me as a hero, to my gods, and most importantly to my soul, I finally stand true."

"He's a traitor!" Coleson repeated to the room. "Shoot him!" He gestured to the room.

"He's my brother." Andrew said with venom before anyone had a chance to move. "You'll not be shooting him in my house."

"Then you're a traitor too!" He screamed. "Shoot them both." No one moved.

I backed up towards the door adjusting my hat. "Is this the man you're going to fight for?" I said to the crowd. "Is this who you'll throw your lot with?"

"I won't shoot Andrew." Leslie Gondua said. The stoic man suddenly talking had the same effect as a statue coming to life. "He's a good man."

"Then shoot his brother." Coleson spat out.

Gondua pulled out his pistol. "He seems a good man too." He looked down at the weapon. "But I don't owe him my life."

"You'll have to shoot me to get to him." Andrew stepped in front of me. I put a hand on his shoulder and moved him aside.

"You've done enough." I told Andrew. "I'll not stand behind good men any longer." I looked at Leslie. "Do what you have to." I nodded to him.

Leslie nodded back in respect. He raised his gun to shoot, and faster than the eye could see I drew and shot the pistol out of his hand. The entire room looked in awe as the gun flew across the room and landed on the floor broken. It was a hard shot, impossible for all but a handful of men in the world. There was even a chance I would miss and be shot dead. I aimed for the gun anyway.

I didn't do it because I thought Rachel would be angry at me for killing her brother. I didn't do it to propagate my legend. I did it because I was trying to be a good man. Good men didn't shoot guest in their own house, and the best found a way to save everyone, even if it was hard. Especially, if it was hard. I turned the gun to point right at Coleson's slimy head. "Before I met McAllan I'd have shot you dead because it's the easy way. Three above, I'd have shot you for offending my pride." I looked at my brother who smiled. "I'm trying to be a better man though." I holstered the pistol. "Whatever filth you might say about my leader remember this, I'd have shot you dead if McAllan hadn't staid my hand." I looked at the map. "Don't worry about me seeing your plan. It's shit anyway. If Fennis has half a brain, he'll tear it up."

I turned around and walked out the door. I smiled to myself. I was pretty sure Coleson pissed his trousers. When I reached the crowd, they all stared at me. "Don't worry! It wasn't a gunshot. we were just opening champaign." It was a flimsy lie, but it was a good enough excuse to continue partying. I looked around the room and found Rachel staring at me. I walked up to her. "Can we go upstairs now?" I asked.

"Someone can't wait." She smiled seductively and drained the drink in her hand. "Lucky for you, neither can I." She headed up the stairs, and I followed. When we were safely alone in the hall, she turned around to kiss me. "I'm glad you decided to fight for Coleson, even if he is a tit." She leaned closer running a finger down my face. "I have such great plans for us here."

"That's what I want to talk to you about." I looked into her eyes. "I'm fighting for McAllan." I grabbed the back of her neck in what I hoped passed for romantic. "He's a good man, with a righteous vision of what this nation could achieve." I looked her up and down memorizing the curves of her body, and the beauty of her face. "That vision won't be if Coleson wins."

She looked up at me in despair. "I need you here, at my side."

"And I need you with me." I looked into her beautiful hazel eyes. "I love you." I hadn't said that to a woman in ten years. I meant it both times. I was hoping this time would wind up better though. "When this war is over, I'll come find you. We'll live in the new world together, but first I have to win that new world."

"Why do you always look for a master to fight for?" Rachel said as if she were a great enlightener. "You're the sort of man who needs an equal to stand with. You need me." She stroked my chest as if she was trying to reach my heart, thinking she could change it. "You're the only man in this world who can equal me. We were meant to stand together." She leaned in to kiss me. "I love you too."

My heart broke at that. "McAllan represents something greater than anything I've seen in fifteen years roaming this world." I kissed her back. "But he needs me to win, and I need him to restrain me."

"You don't need to be restrained." Rachel looked at me pleadingly. "You need to be released." She touched the pistol on my belt. "This weapon has served lesser men for too long. The world belongs to you. It is your birthright." She touched my cheek. "We are the greatest beings on this planet, let us take it." She was whispering now. "Let the rest of the world bow down to us like they should."

I took her hand. "And who decides what man is greater than another." I shook my head. "Who decides when we've gone too far."

"People like me and you can never go too far." She searched my face looking into my soul. "You were right when you pillared those people in Kran. You should have gone farther. Your only mistake in Thyro was that when you had them on their knees, you left them to follow lesser men or worse. You left them to their own devices." She was saying what I'd wanted to hear since as long as I could remember. "You and I could rule this world." Rachel was so close I could smell her breath. It smelled like desire and worth. It smelled like what I'd fought fifteen years searching for. It smelled like the thing that could slake the hunger that had been growing inside me since birth. I wanted nothing more than her at my side, but I couldn't accept it and be the man in my mother's book.

"It wasn't my right to subjugate them." I said wishing it was.

"It was your right." She laughed. "It was your right because you were the strongest."

I shook my head in dismay. "The strongest have been forcing the weak to submit for too long." I was pleading with her now. "It's time for the strong to lend their strength to the weak. To teach them how to stand on their feet."

"What about Mother Vestia?" Rachel hissed. "Aren't you tired of being used?"

"Whatever Mother Vestia did, doesn't matter." I paused. "I want something better."

"I can give you that." She whispered in my ear, and I believed her.

"I think you could." I let out a sad smile. "It wouldn't be the right way, though."

"Thomas…" It was the ashy voice of Ayn-Tuk back from asking the questions I wanted answers to.

"Can it wait?" I didn't want to look at him.

"I'm afraid not." The black man said, and I turned to him. There was something in his voice that I'd never heard before. Something akin to fear. "That girl," he nodded to Rachel, "is *Her*."

"*Her*?" I asked. It sounded ridiculous. "The same *Her* playing all of Thyro for fools, pulling the strings in conflicts unseen?"

"Not just Thyro apparently." Ayn-Tuk stepped forward. "There are people who want to make you into a weapon." He hissed. "People who you to lead their armies. They thought Thaniel was the one, but he wasn't." She stared up at me. "This woman leads them. She want to turn you against the things you served."

"That's ridiculous." I gestured to Rachel. "She's a clever woman, but she's closer to twenty than thirty."

"How old were you when you tore Thaniel off his throne?" Ayn-Tuk shot back.

"That was different…" *But was it.* I turned to Rachel. "Tell him it's ridiculous."

Rachel smiled. "It's ridiculous." No matter how good the liar, when you make an accusation that lands completely true, it shows. Rachel didn't even try to hide it though. Almost like she wanted me to know.

"How do you know this?" I asked Ayn-Tuk, not looking away from Rachel.

"I know it." The black man responded. "That's all I can say."

I believed him. Something in me knew Ayn-Tuk was right. "She tried to have herself killed?"

"She wanted to turn you against the people who restrained you." Ayn-Tuk's eyes darted to the girl. "A clever play, and a risky one." He paused. "I heard about Mother Vestia. The clever play worked."

Things fell into place. The Huego's, the note, the Priest's last warning, all carefully planned to turn me from the people that had always staid my hand. They didn't want it staid though. When I looked at it through the lens of emotion, the pieced didn't fit, but when I looked at it like a math equation, unbiased, I saw the answer. "Almost worked, anyway."

I turned to Rachel. "You knew Marcius of Renton." I said coldly.

"I did." She responded in turn. All talk of love and a future together dropped from her face.

"While he was dying, he said he came to Souren because a beautiful woman promised him her hand if he could kill me."

She returned the gaze. "What are you saying?" Her hand moved to her back.

I caught the move. "I'm saying that I was supposed to be somewhere else the day I killed him." I whispered. "I heard Marcius was talking about how he defeated me to anyone who was listening. It angered me, so I killed him." I paused for a moment looking at the girl I thought I loved. "I missed a summit, and the decision was ruled in a way that I would have spoken against." I chuckled to myself. "I always thought it was a coincidence, but maybe someone knew my pride demanded I fight him. Maybe someone didn't want me to speak at that council."

"Maybe someone didn't." She said still moving her hand behind her back.

"Then I hear another beautiful woman was following my trail, adjusting the countries I left in small ways." I smiled, but the smile never reached my eyes. "I had more important things to do, and the ways she changed them seemed small enough. I ignored those stories." I looked down at my six-shooter. "Maybe I should have paid more attention."

"Maybe you should have." She looked at me differently, with the same desire, but tempered with something dangerous.

"Then in Sterling, a Priest threatened me with his dying words about some woman playing us all like puppets." I put an edge on my voice. "I got sent out of Thyro after that. I got paranoid and started doing some things maybe I shouldn't have. Finally, they drummed me out of the Constabulary." I hissed. "That would have been that, but there was a war brewing in my country. A war certain people had a vested interest in. Then as soon as I leave, the papers start printing lies, and some upstart starts sewing dissent." I shrugged. "Could all be a coincidence. I wouldn't bet on it, though."

"You'd probably lose that money if you did." She glared up at me. "Then again, we play for bigger stakes than coin."

I looked back at her. She was just as beautiful now, but twice as alluring for some reason. "Maybe they were the same beautiful woman." I watched her. "Maybe she had her hand in Sterling too. Maybe she decided she wanted me on her side." I knew what was coming. "Maybe she fucked me to make sure that happened."

She moved her knife quick as a rabbit in the snow. If I were another man, it would have hit the mark. If I wasn't expecting it, the knife would have been in my throat. The move was practiced, she was trained, but so was I, and I was stronger. I caught the knife, pushed her against the wall, and jammed it into her shoulder. I knew my business. It wouldn't knick an artery or cause any lasting damage tomorrow, but it would hurt like hell today. Still, she didn't scream, like most would. She hissed at me. You learn a lot about a person when you shove a knife in their shoulder. She was strong. "Belson the Blessed, ey?" She spat out the words.

"I told you I loved you..." I whispered in dismay.

"And you meant it." She chuckled at my pain. "You still mean it, or you'd have killed me." She was right.

"The Huegos... The note... It was all you." I whispered back at her.

"No use lying now." She nodded.

"You used me like you used Coleson." I put pressure on the wound until she winced.

"No." Rachel said defiantly. "Coleson was a tool. You were the prize." She smiled at me. "I meant what I said. I love you too. I want you at my side." She looked at me imploringly. "This civil war isn't the end, it's the beginning of my reign." She frowned at me. "It could be our reign."

"Then I said no, and you tried to kill me."

"I wasn't going to kill you. I was going to wound you." She looked up at me in desire.

"Why?" I asked. When she didn't answer I put my thumb on the wound and pressed till she squirmed.

"If you're so attached to having a master there's only one solution." She smiled like a snake about to strike. "Take away the master." She gave a devilish smile. "Of course there were different reasons when I gave the order, but two birds one stone right?"

"What do you mean?" I searched her face in desperation. She stayed quiet. I was scared in a way I hadn't been since my first battle. I hit her hard in the side and felt the bones crunch.

"Umph." Rachel grunted as she gasped for breath.

"Don't make me do it again." I hissed in cold anger.

"I want you to remember this moment." She spat out. "For all that talk of being a better man. I want you to remember the moment you hit the woman you love, for that greater good you claim not to serve."

I took a step back looking at my hands horrified. "I didn't mean..."

"But you did it." She slumped to the floor clutching her side. "You did what you had to do. I don't blame you, but you blame yourself." Rachel looked at me standing there. "Give in to the thing inside you. Pull this knife out my shoulder, fuck me like there's no tomorrow, and let the pieces fall." She whispered seductively. "Let my agents kill McAllan. Let me free you."

I knew she was talking about killing the Prime Governor, but her saying it out loud made it real. "I won't let that be my legacy." I fixed my hat and turned to walk away.

"You won't get there in time." She called out to me. "He's a two-day ride from here, and he'll be killed tomorrow if not today." She said through a laughing fit. "You'll be late, and he'll die." She changed her tone to affectionate. "Then you'll come back to me."

I looked at the women I loved. "You've seen Shaggy Cow." I wanted to stay with her, but I couldn't. "You think she can't make it?"

"Yes." Rachel said, but she wasn't quite as sure as she usually was.

I smiled at her. "Never underestimate Shaggy Cow." I turned and ran down the stairs with Ayn-Tuk in tow.

"Tuk, head up to the Capitol. Shaggy is the only horse that can make it in time." I said. "I'll meet up with you when I'm done."

The black man nodded as we hurried down the stairs.

I headed to the door before someone stopped me. "Where are you going?" I turned to see Alexis looking at me. "You have to stay for the speech." We hadn't spoken much since the history lesson, but George had gone a long way in making her not hate me.

I looked at my sister. "I can't. I have to do something." I looked over her shoulder and saw Alexander Gondua gave me a curious look. How much did he know? Probably nothing considering the estimation his sister held him in. Leslie Gondua needed to be watched though.

"I haven't been the best older brother. I know that." I had to leave, but I couldn't leave her like I had the last time. "I wish I'd been there to watch you grow up."

She wasn't expecting this, but she nodded her head. "I know why you weren't. I don't blame you." She sighed. "You were busy being a hero."

I looked at her. She looked just like our mother. She had the same beautiful eyes. "I should have been your hero."

"You were." She said trying not to cry. "I'm so proud of you. I just didn't realize it."

"I'm going to be the man you think I am. You were right. That's not how heroes act." I stroked her face. "Until I come back, I want you to promise me something."

"What's that?" She looked up at her brother.

"Live well." I told her. "You deserve the world, don't settle for less." I gave her a hug. "Everything I do, I do for you."

"I will." She wiped her face. "I love you."

"I love you too." Then without another word, I opened the doors and left.

"Shaggy!" I screamed and heard a neigh in reply as the horse jumped over her fence and galloped to her master.

"What are we doing?" I heard someone say behind me. It was Seiford. I turned around and gave the monk a back breaking hug. He pushed me away finally. "I'm not actually a boy lover you know." He said dusting himself off. Seiford looked uncharacteristically dirty, like he'd been hiding out in a stable, which knowing the man he probably had.

"It's good to see you." I smiled.

"I told you, I'd be here when you need me." The monk smiled back. "You always need me, so I never left." He saw the distraught look in my eyes. "What are we doing?"

"Someones going to kill McAllan." I went to the stable and grabbed my saddle. "I'm going to stop them."

Seiford followed him. "So we're on the right side again." He considered the statement. "Good for us I suppose." He scratched his head. "Is Rachel the one trying to kill him."

I stopped and looked at the man curiously. "How'd you know?"

The monk smiled. "No girl that pretty would sleep with you unless she's up to something."

I chuckled as I buckled on the saddle. "Go back into the house and get everything I need to fight a war." I tightened the girth. "My uniform, my compass, anything you think I'll need." I snapped my fingers remembering. "And my rifle. Go get my rifle!" I went back to fixing the horse. "I don't have time to pack. Go get it all, take a horse, and ride north to the capitol with Ayn-Tuk."

"Hold on one second." The monk said as he hurried behind the stable and reappeared brandishing his rifle, shined to a mirror's perfection and a small sack. He ran back to me and thrust them into my hands.

"Why'd you take my rifle?" I said confused. "You always hated guns."

"I know, but you taught me how to make bullets, and they don't sell this kind of ammunition here." The monk shrugged. "I figured we'd need it." He gestured to the sack. "I'd have made more, but I didn't have enough money for extra powder or casing."

I mounted my horse and stowed the rifle, looking in the sack before securing it. It was full of shiny rounds. "It's perfect Seif."

"Remember that the next time you call me a boy lover!" He called after me and hurried off to collect our belongings.

I put the heels to Shaggy, and she galloped at a speed faster than any mount could match. If there was one thing someone should never do, it was underestimating Shaggy Cow.

Present Day
Stories Collide

Jesse waited by an oak tree. He'd been there for a week watching the road. The Priest had sent eight of his black-clad servants to make sure he didn't have a change of heart. The bounty hunter wished they weren't there. He wanted to be alone. However, when he tried to turn them away, they refused to leave. "We have orders." Was all they'd say. They didn't talk much, but Jesse had caught one of them torturing a squirrel. He had pushed the man aside and put the poor animal out of its misery. After that, he'd started taking his meals alone.

He just wanted it all to be over. He sat by the oak while one of the servants watched him intently. It was almost dusk on the last day when he finally saw what he was looking for. It was made to look simple, but it was well built, and from the way it sagged against the axel, probably armored. "Is that the carriage?" The servant asked.

Jesse didn't answer he just put the rifle to his shoulder and fired at the driver. The distance was about two hundred yards. It would have been a hard target for most, but the bullet found its home.

McAllan heard the gunshot, but before he had a chance to do anything he felt the carriage tip and horses neigh in pain. Someone was trying to kill him, and they'd probably succeed.

Jesse walked calmly to the cart with the servants trailing him suspiciously. Without the driver to guide them the horses had run straight into a tree, making the whole damn thing flip. The driver was writhing around in pain from the shot in his shoulder. The bounty hunter needed witnesses for this, and he had no interest in killing more innocents than he had to.

Jesse shot the horses to end their screaming. Their legs were broken. There was no reason to prolong the suffering. Someone should probably have done it to Jessie after that war. End his suffering. He stepped on top of the carriage dropping his rifle and grabbing the pistol, it was better equipped for this sort of work.

The door, which was now facing up, opened and a man with a curious scar on his jaw came out with a sawed-off shotgun. He looked big, strong, and experienced but the crash made him slow. Jesse kicked the man in the face then pulled the weapon out of his hands. The scarred man fell back into the carriage. The bounty hunter turned the weapon into the open cart door. "Come out with your hands up, or I'll fill this damn thing full of lead.

"Alright, just don't hurt anyone." He heard come from inside the cart. It was a deep voice full of authority. Jesse took a step off the wagon and trained the weapon on the opening. The first man to come out was as tall as any the bounty hunter had ever seen. His face looked like an old anvil from the number of times it'd been hit. He sported a sizeable dark beard to hide the scars, but it didn't help much. It was McAllan. He almost fired then, but something stopped him. The next man to come out had a face built like a brick, he was holding a pistol in his hand.

"Drop it, or I shoot the Prime Governor right here and now." He said, and the man looked at McAllan who nodded for him to obey. The bodyguard threw the weapon to the side. There was something familiar about him, but Jesse didn't have time for remembrance. He was followed by a slimy looking Huego, a young black boy, and the man he'd unceremoniously kicked in the face, only now he was holding his bloody nose not a shotgun. "Get off the cart." Jesse gestured for them all to step down in front of him. They did.

"Let's just kill them all now." He heard one of the black-clad men say with venom.

"And who's going to tell the North this story?" Jesse shot back. "Shut up! Only one of them has to die."

"Over my dead body." The man with the brick face stepped in front of McAllan.

"Be careful what you say." Jesse spit out. "I might make you mean it."

"Fuck you." The scared man with the bloody nose moved next to, brick face.

"Stop this nonsense!" McAllan said to the two bodyguards and stepped past them. "No one's going to die for me today." He looked at the bounty hunter. "Do what you have to, but leave them alone."

Jessie dropped the shotgun and pulled his pistol. "I don't want to hurt them."

"Then don't." McAllan responded. His hands were up, but even still the Prime Governor didn't have surrender on him.

"I know you." Brick Face said.

"Shut your fucking mouth!" The bounty hunter hissed.

"You're Jesse Devote." He finally recognized the man. It was Corporal Sally. "You saved my unit in Puena."

"Shut up." He said pointing the pistol at the corporal.

"Don't do this." Sally echoed his father's words.

"You don't understand." Jesse pointed the weapon back at the Prime Governor.

"But I might." McAllan took a step forward, and Jesse cocked the gun to stop him. "Who did they promise to help?"

"Shut up!" He said anger running through him, almost enough anger to pull the trigger but not quite.

"For me, it was my sister." The Prime Governor implored him.

"It's my brother." He said almost to himself.

"I beat a man to death because they told me to." McAllan looked at the servants all of them with weapons leveled. "I've spent the rest of my life trying to wipe that filth off me."

"I'm too dirty already." Jesse went to pull the trigger, but couldn't.

"That's what they want you to think." The Prime Governor was clearly trying to shield the men who followed him. Was this really the type of man he could kill? "They want you to imagine you've gone so far you can never go back."

"Maybe I can't." Jesse said. He just wanted it to be over, but something about the man stopped him.

"Maybe you can." McAllan took a step forward. "They've made you so filthy you think the only way to the end is deeper into the river.

I remember the man who won the Iron circle. He was honorable and brave in a way that few are. The kind of man you were doesn't just go away, no matter how much muck they try and smear him with." He took another step forward he was too close now. "You don't see a choice, but it's there. Be a good man."

"I need to help my brother." The gun in his hand was shaking, Jesse's gun never shook.

"Let's just kill the fuckers now." One of the servants said over his back.

"No, it needs to be him." Another hissed.

"And what would he think if they saw you drawing down on unarmed men for Bellefellow." McAllan said ignoring the servants. "What would your parents think?" He took another step forward. "What would your woman think?" He was in arm's length now. "You're right. You need to help them all." He paused. "You need to be a man they can look up too." The Prime Governor gently put a hand on the gun and pushed it down.

"If I don't do it then they'll kill us all." Jessie looked at the man's eyes. They were compassionate, despite the scars.

"Then we'll all die good men." McAllan put a hand on his shoulder.

"Fuck this." The leader of the servants said and cocked back his rifle.

Just then Jessie heard hoofbeats of a horse running fast. Then six shots so close together it almost sounded like one. He turned and saw six of the men drop clutching their chest. Without thinking the bounty hunter turned and shot the other two.

<hr />

I saw the scene in my heightened Battle Mind. I thought I was going to have to kill the other two black-clad men and the queer one standing in front of McAllan, but for some reason, the bastard turned and did the other two on his own. I dismounted and moved towards him drawing my other pistol. The man might have had a change of heart, but not two seconds before he had a gun trained on McAllan. He was big, not much taller than me but about twice as wide and all muscle. The scars on his face spoke of battle wounds, and the quickness he shot with said he was handy in those fights. I didn't care. I aimed my gun at the man, waiting for him to defend himself, but the big man just let the weapon in his hand fall away.

Something about the killer made me want to put my pistol away too, but I'd been shot in the back by surrendered enemies before. I put my elbow against the big man's throat and drove him into a tree. "Are there any more of them?" I hissed out.

"Urgh." The big man grunted. I was about to hit him when I realized how much pressure I was putting on his throat. "No." He said when I finally let the man take enough air to talk.

"Constable Belson, I think you can release him now." McAllan said over my shoulder.

"I've seen men pretend to surrender then pull a spare out of their boot." I said, then thought for a moment. "Three above, I've done it myself! It's a damn effective tactic!"

"If he wasn't going to shoot us with eight armed men, then why would he shoot us now?" McAllan said sharply.

"It's something about my face." I said. "People always try to shoot at it. I really am working on being more personable."

"Maybe start by not pointing guns at people." The Huego interjected.

"You're right." I holstered the weapon and let the big man go. "I figure this man's earned the benefit of the doubt."

"Thank you." The big man said rubbing his throat. I ignored him and walked to McAllan.

"You were right." I said to the Prime Governor. I went to one knee in front of the man. "You were right about all of it." I pulled out my pistol and gave it to the leader handle faced up. I'd only done it once before, and I hadn't meant it then. I meant it now. "I was a mad dog, and you were justified to keep me in my cage. I don't want to be a mad dog anymore. I want to be better. I'll fight for you on whatever terms you give me. If we win, we'll do it the right way, and if we lose, I figure we'll do that the right way too."

"Stand up you bloody fool. I'm not royalty." McAllan said helping me to my feet. His words were harsh but there was pride on his face. "And take your pistol back. You'll need it again soon."

"Sorry, it seemed traditional." I fixed my belt, it really wasn't meant for kneeling. "I meant what I said, though."

"If I say you'll serve as an armory clerk?" McAllan gave me an appraising look.

"You'd never lack for weapons."

"If I say you'll serve as a private?"

"I'll die for you as prouder than when I led army."

McAllan finally looked satisfied. "No, you'd die for this country proudly." He looked at the two bodyguards and smiled. "I won't have good men dying on my behalf."

"You think me a good man?" I hadn't known how much I needed to here it.

"Getting better maybe." The Prime Governor gave a wry smile.

"So be it." I said in a way I hadn't in a long time, maybe ever. I said it humbly.

"You'll lead a regiment of volunteers of every race this nation has to offer." The Prime Governor put a hand on my shoulder. "You'll pick up the pieces of this country and help me forge them into one."

"I'd like that." I said with a smile. It was a good moment, between a good man and one who was trying to be better. However, the moment was ruined by the assassin I'd let live.

"Fuck!" I heard the big man scream, then punch the oak tree hard enough to break his hand.

"What's wrong with him?" I said pointing at the assassin.

McAllan turned me around to face him. "Why don't you ask?"

I nodded and straightened my coat. "Excuse me Mr..." I paused realizing I didn't know the assassin's name.

"It's Devote." McAllan interjected.

"Really that's Jesse Devote?" I whispered incredulously. My brother had told me stories about the brave men he'd served with, but Andrew had been clear that Jesse was the hardest of them all. "Sorry about your throat, Mr. Devote."

"It's fine." He said nursing his hand. "Fuck!" He screamed again and hit the same tree.

"Stop that!" I said stepping in between the assassin and the tree so he couldn't do it again. "That tree's done nothing to you."

"Sorry." Jesse said rubbing his hand.

"What's got you in such a fuss?" I asked, trying to be polite.

"A Priest sent me here to kill the Prime Governor." Jesse said looking like he was about to take another swing at the tree, then thinking better of it. "After that, I was to turn myself over to the authorities in Pentsville to be hanged."

"Why would you do something like that?" I asked even though I knew the answer. I'd seen that story play out before.

"He said he'd give my family and my woman two hundred thousand dollars each and a good plot of land." The big man paused. "He said he'd cure my brother."

I laughed in his face. "And you believed him?" I said still chuckling. "Were you hit in the head with a cannonball?" I meant it as a joke, but judging by the scars on Jesse's face, it was definitely possible.

"Yes, I believed him!" Now it looked as if Jesse was about to take a swing at me. He'd find my body less forgiving than the tree. Trees were known for their patience, being trees and all. "What choice did I have?"

"You should have taken everything not nailed down and ran as far west as west goes." I gestured to the flipped cart.

"Well, I didn't." Jessie said through an angry snarl. "And now I've failed." The big man looked down at his hands.

"And you think that now the powers that be will take their frustration out on your family." I scratched my chin expecting to find stubble but forgot I shaved for the party.

"Would you put it past them?" Jessie said sarcastically.

"No, but if it makes you feel better, they were probably going to kill them anyway." I shrugged. "The Priests can't really undo what happened to your brother, just make it seem like they're trying."

"Why the fuck would that make me feel better?" Jesse had a face of pure fury.

"Well, I said if." I took my empty pistol out of its holster and started reloading it. "That's the oldest play in their little Priesty book. They coerce a man to do their dirty political killing, then when he's done it. They wipe out anyone who might say the man was pushed into doing it."

"So they're already dead?" Jesse looked like he was about to turn one of his own weapons against himself.

"Hmm?" I said over my pistol. "Sorry I was getting ready." Then I looked at the man. "No, they wouldn't yet. They still need confirmation that the job's been done. That's the good news." I loaded the last bullet and smiled. "Want to hear the better news?"

"What's the better news?" The man was clearly growing tired of my shenanigans. It was understandable if I was being honest.

"Well, in the olden days I'd have thought logically and gone back with McAllan to start raising that army he's promised me." I holstered the weapon.

"One regiment." McAllan interjected.

"We can argue about that later." I rolled my eyes. "I'd have left you to deal with this situation on your own. It's the smart move, and shooting up the biggest city in the South will no doubt give Coleson good reason to go to war." I gave the Prime Governor a look of respect. "That was until a certain leader told me heroes ought to act heroic."

I looked back at Jessie. "What's more heroic than walking into Pentsville, the Priests stronghold, saving your family, not to mention a damsel in distress, then fighting our way out tooth and nail?" I paused with a grin. "Nothing I'll tell you!"

"So you'll help me?" Jesse was finally starting to like me. It takes a while sometimes.

"I will and lucky for you." I smiled. "On your own, it's certain death."

"And you think one man makes it possible." Jesse said skeptically. Apparently, he didn't believe the stories about me.

"Nothing is certain death when I'm involved." I looked at the men I'd shot in my rescue. "Well, except for these poor fellows." I scratched my head. "And death is certainly still a heavy possibility when I'm involved, but I'll help you."

Jesse smiled for the first time in the exchange. "I served with your brother."

"He told me about you." I nodded. "Said you were the meanest bastard he ever met. I hope you haven't gone soft in your old age."

"Not a bit." Jesse snarled. "He's a good man though. Your brother I mean."

"He's the best man, far better than me." I smiled.

"Aye probably." The big man's smile grew wider. "But you're the better shot. I think I'd rather the better shot for this one."

"I'll come with you." The bodyguard with the brick face said.

"Absolutely not, you'll take these men's horses and make haste to the Capitol." I gestured to the dead men. "Someone needs to protect McAllan. He can't guilt everyone into fighting for him."

"I can do that." The corporal nodded.

"Good." I looked back to Jesse. "I have a question before we leave."

"If you ask how pretty my woman is, I'll shoot you." The big man said with some menace.

"I have another question then." I paused. "Was that Priest who coerced you Bellefellow?"

Jesse nodded his head. "Is that a problem."

I adjusted my hat. "Not at all. We have a score to settle." My smile grew even wilder. "He threatened my idiot."

Present Day Stories Collide

Jesse spent all night trailing Belson. When they'd started the journey, he'd looked at the horse, aptly named Shaggy Cow, and thought the damn thing would die if the Constable rode it all night. The bounty hunter was riding a good horse taken off a very rich bounty, and even then the hairy pony could have run circles around him and kept pace.

What was even more impressive was Thomas himself. He hadn't believed the stories. He still didn't believe the ones about magic swords and dragons, but he was starting to see that maybe there was some truth to them. Sometimes aristocrat whelps got lucky and had a talent for bragging. There were even some plantation owners who earned their reputations on the battlefield like Andrew and Leslie, but the tales they told about the Constable were different. They were too outlandish to believe. That was before Jesse met the man himself.

Jesse watched Belson empty a six-shooter without a moment of silence between each shot, and every bullet found a man's heart. The bounty hunter had never seen someone use a gun like that, but being a good shot didn't make a soldier, even though it helped. Then he'd felt the Constable push him against a tree. The bastard was stronger than he had a right to be, but there was more to it. The way the man's knee had driven Jessie off balance and his elbow had pressed against his shoulder in a way that his whole arm wouldn't work. Every part of the bastard's body had a purpose, and the bounty hunter had rarely felt so helpless in his life.

Jesse thought in a fair fight he'd still win, but only by the skin of his teeth, and only fools fought fair. However, actual battle was only a fraction of war. What counted more was what you did in between. Twenty-mile marches, staying awake and vigilant for days at a time, doing shit work when you were bone tired, that's where you found a man's mettle. Thomas had that mettle. He couldn't have slept in at least two days, and it didn't show. The Constable scanned the tree line constantly, doubled back for safer paths, and rode like a demon with hellfire on its tale. Aye, the bastard was a good fighter, and that was important, but more than that, he was careful, methodical, and quick all at the same time. The man was more than a hero. Thomas Belson the Constable was a professional soldier. Jesse had followed heroes, and he'd followed professionals. He'd even followed men who were a little bit of both and a lot of fools in between. He'd never fought for a man like the one he was following though.

They reached Pentsville in the dead of night. Judging by the position of the moon they had about four hours of darkness left. They dismounted at a carriage rental store right outside of town. "We'll need one of these to put your family in." Thomas said going to the stable and examining the lock on the gate frowning.

"I'll get this one." Jesse said walking to the stout wooden gate drawing his elbow back and hitting the wooden plank with his forearm. He felt it give a bit, but the damn thing was well built. He pulled back to hit it again, but Thomas stopped him.

"Wait." The Constable said grabbing him. "We don't want to wake anyone up." He moved to in front of the gate and set his fist an inch away from the beam. The fool must have been cracked from Thyro if he thought he could break a piece of wood like that with no wind-up. Thomas took a deep breath and struck the board, and the whole thing came apart with a sickening crunch.

"I loosened it." Jesse said defensively, but secretly he was wondering if he could beat the man in a fight, fair or not.

"I'm sure you did." Thomas whispered with a smile. He pushed open the gate gingerly. They set to work preparing a stout wooden carriage with two big looking horses.

As they worked Jesse's curiosity won out. "How long has it been since you've drank, eaten, or slept." He asked quietly.

Belson stopped what he was doing and thought for a second. "Two days, no three, since I slept last." He shrugged his shoulders. "I ate a little on the ride. I always keep some jerky stashed somewhere. You want some?" He reached into his pocket and pulled out a piece of dried meat.

"Sure." Jesse accepted it and went to eating. He'd forgotten how hungry he was.

"As for water, I finished my skin a while back." He drank deep from a horse trough. "Thank you for reminding me. I get a little forgetful when I feel a fight coming on." Then he filled up his water skin as well.

"How are you still moving then?" Jesse asked louder than he meant to as he buckled the horses in. "What I mean is, I'm a tough bastard, but after three days of no sleep and hard rations even I start to wear down."

Thomas waved his hand dismissively. "This is nothing. At the siege of Rant, the bastards attacked for ten days straight, and I had to organize the defenses day and night." He rolled his eyes. "That's why I'm so glad modern cannons have made sieges obsolete."

"How?" Jesse asked making sure the straps were tight.

"I spent a long time training in God's Rest." The Constable shuddered at the memory. "It's as bad a place as you've heard and twice as cold. They taught me a great many things, but the most important thing they taught me was the Battle Mind."

"And that is?" The bounty hunter asked as they lead the carriage out.

"A secret." Said Thomas. "But we'll both probably be dead soon anyway, so I'll tell you." He stopped for a second collecting his thoughts. "It's a state where you can ignore the pangs that usually plague men." He took some coins out of his pocket and laid them on the counter. It looked like enough to fix the gate and buy two carriages besides. "You can go weeks without sleep and eat and drink sparingly without feeling it. You can ignore wounds that would usually leave you screaming in pain. Your body becomes more efficient, and your mind gets sharper. Time even seems to move slower."

"Can you teach it to me?" Jesse immediately saw why a tattooed arm was so feared throughout the world.

"I can try." Thomas shrugged his shoulder. "But it took me months to master enough to use, and that was considered fast." His eyes went dark. "Besides, there's a cost to it."

"What kind of cost?" Jessie was curious.

"If you've ever had a nasty hangover, it's like that, but all over your body and much worse." Thomas stopped. The carriage was safely out of the stable. "Besides ignoring thirst, hunger, exhaustion, and injury doesn't mean they don't exist. Most Constables die because they come out of it, and their body can't handle the shock. That's why they say Constables don't die in battle, because in the middle of a battle only a bullet to the head or heart can stop them, but I'll tell you a great many drop dead when it's over."

"Still, it seems a useful thing to know." Jesse said stepping on top of the carriage.

"It is." Thomas walked to Shaggy Cow, and the bounty hunter heard him talk to the horse. "Go into those woods and wait for me to run out screaming." He said and grabbed the strange looking rifle off his saddle.

The horse neighed in a way that somehow seemed angry.

"Oh come now, pulling a carriage is beneath you." He said and offered the pony a treat out of his pocket. Jesse hoped it wasn't the jerky, which tasted a lot like horse.

The beast seemed satisfied and trotted to the tree line. Thomas climbed up next to Jesse like nothing strange had occurred. He couldn't ignore it though. "You talk to your horse?"

"Yes." The Constable said as if it was a completely normal thing.

"And it understands you?" Jessie asked as he urged the carriage on.

"Shaggy understands more languages than I do, and I understand a lot." Thomas beamed with pride at his stead. "Three above, I love that little mare more than life itself."

"You need a woman." The bounty hunter snorted.

"Shaggy's never tricked me into fighting against my principles." Thomas's mood darkened. "And she's never tried to stab me." He said it in a way that made Jesse stop talking about women.

They rode through Pentsville searching the streets for anything strange. Jesse eyed up the tall stone cathedral that reached far into the sky. He usually tried to ignore it. The grey stone contrasted unpleasantly with the wood and thatch buildings that lined the city streets, but it seemed prudent to keep an eye on the place where hundreds of enemies could swarm from.

When they were about a block away, he stopped the carriage. "Best go on foot from here." Jesse said stepping down. They crept to his house and saw exactly what the bounty hunter was afraid of. Four men in black watched the house intently, two at the door and two in an alley about fifty feet up the street. The stark black made them easy targets the uniforms were meant to intimidate, but they were too dark. All it took was dim light to see their silhouette. The brown jackets Thomas and Jesse wore were much better. "We need to take them quietly, I don't want to bring the entire cathedral down on us." Jesse said.

"You're right. It's knives then." He nodded. "You take the two in the alley, I'll get the pair at the door.

The bounty hunter nodded and quietly snuck across the buildings to move behind the men. He'd moved past Huegos unseen before, and these men weren't Huegos. Thomas took a different tact. His stride went from proud and purposeful to sloppy drunk in a heartbeat.

"Hey, you two!" He screamed at the guards on the door. Jesse was about to run over and knock the man out cold, but the damage was done. They had seen the Constable.

"Fuck off." One of the guards snarled. All Jesse could do was keep moving towards the men in the alley praying to whoever was listening that the Constable wasn't completely insane.

Thomas tripped, tumbled, and swerved his way to the guards. "I'm new in town." He said through a burp. "Where's the bestestest whores at?" He tumbled back a bit. "Sorry I mean the cleanest, I don't want another case of the Kranish drip." Jesse kept frantically moving along the side of the houses. Luckily they all had careful eyes on the odd Constable.

"If you're new in town you don't know we're not the sort of men you talk too." The guard at the door said furiously. "So fuck off."

"Do you mind if I piss here then." Thomas went to unbuckle his pants. Jesse sent up a silent prayer.

"If I see your cock you die." The guard pushed him to the ground.

Thomas stood up blinking his eyes. "Wait! Is yous whores?"

"He's going to wake the family." The other guard whispered.

"I'm warning you now." The first man in black put a menacing finger in Thomas's face. "Usually you'd be dead already, but we're here on business. So fuck off." He moved his jacket revealing a six-shooter of his own.

"No, I'm warning you morer." Thomas drunkenly poked the guard in the face. "Stop hiding the whores."

"Fuck it you're dead." The man went to pull his six-shooter.

Jessie was finally in position he moved quick putting his knife in the first man's throat. Then before the second one could react, he grabbed the man's head and slammed it against the wall until all that was left was a bloody red pudding. Thomas took the cue and elbowed one in the throat hard, pulled his knife and stuck it in the man chest, both died without a sound.

Jesse heard a rifle cock back. He looked around for the sound. While he did Thomas rolled. The rifle went off and struck where he'd been not half a second earlier. He came up with his pistol and fired once, and the bounty hunter saw a body fall from the top of a building across from his house.

"What the fuck was that?" Jesse hissed menacingly.

"Would you have preferred I wait for him to shoot again?" Thomas hissed back.

"I mean about that drunken, lunatic act." Jesse shoved the man in the shoulder.

"It wasn't an act." He said defensively. "I am a drunken lunatic." He waved his hands. "Besides, the first rule of stealth is, never appear like you're trying to be stealthy."

The bounty hunter shook his head. "We need to get my family before more come."

"By all means." He gestured to the door.

Jesse hurried in the door. His family was already awake. His father was already dressed in his trousers and boots with a shirt hurriedly put on and an old dusty six-shooter in his hand. Mary and his mother were still wearing a nightgown, looking terrified. Thomas's drunken ravings and the sound of the gunshot had probably jarred them awake. Bobby ran out of his room screaming "AHHHHHHHHHHHHHHHHHHHHHHHH."

Jesse grabbed his brother and folded him in a crushing hug. "Shhh, Bo-Bo." He whispered. "The bad noises are gone."

"Bo-Bo?" Thomas mocked over his shoulder. "Didn't take you for the cute nickname type."

"Shut up." Jesse hissed.

Bobby took his brother's face in his small hands. "It wasn't the noises, I had nightmares you were going to do something bad." He wiped tears from his eyes. "You were gonna do something bad, and it was my fault."

Jesse smiled at his brother. "I was, but I couldn't do that to you." He squeezed his brother again then stood up, and Mary hugged him almost as distraught as Bobby.

"What's going on?" She asked frantically when she finally let him go. "I heard some drunken lunatic raving about whores, and then there were gunshots."

"I can explain later." He held her face in his hands. "Now, we need to leave, quickly."

"And who's this?" His mother gestured towards the Constable.

"Why I'm the drunken lunatic screaming about whores." The Constable said with a flourish of his hat.

"That's Thomas Belson." Jesse said pointing a thumb over his shoulder.

"Wait, the same Thomas Belson…" His mother stared in awe, as did the rest of his family, much to the bounty hunter's distaste.

"Yes that Thomas Belson!" Jesse was trying desperately to hurry it all along.

"Demon's Below, son!" His father exclaimed. "What have you gotten yourself into?"

Now, it was Thomas's turn to speak. "Well, that's just the trouble." He started. "We seem to have run afoul of some Demons, so we should probably have this conversation later."

The pair hurried the family out of the house and towards the carriage. "Are you gonna let me ride your dragon?" Bobby asked Thomas as they walked.

"I'm afraid I had to trade the dragon for a horse." Thomas said whimsically. "Do you know what the costs of keeping a dragon are? They're outrageous." He shook his head. "That's not even to speak of the taxes on such a thing. Damn bureaucrats! Telling a free man what kind of fire breathing lizard he can ride. That's not the country my father fought for, I'll tell you."

"Oh." The boy said, disappointed.

"You can ride my horse though. It's a magnificent animal." The Constable said scanning the buildings for threats.

"What's his name?" Bobby asked perking up a little.

"*Her* name is Shaggy Cow." Thomas said emphasizing, the her. "She gets upset if you call her a boy."

"Shaggy Cow." The boy said trying it out. "That's a wonderful name!" He exclaimed.

Thomas stopped with a smile. "You know, so do I. No one else seems to appreciate it." He gave the boy a pat on the head. "It's nice to finally meet someone who shares me and Shaggy's comic sensibilities."

"Would you move." Jesse said sharply. He was growing impatient. "We can talk about how the only two people who think you're funny are a twelve-year-old and a horse later."

"Ass." He heard Thomas whisper under his breath.

They reached the carriage, and Jesse hurried them in. When Bobby finally sat down, he stopped and looked the boy in the eyes. "Listen there's going to be some bad noises outside. I need you to just cover your ears and stay quiet." He rubbed his brothers head. "Don't worry! Constable Belson is going to protect us."

"I like it better when you protect us." Bobby said then leaned in close. "Besides he doesn't even have a dragon." The boy whispered.

"Ass." Jesse heard Thomas whisper again.

"Good." He gave his brother a kiss on the head.

He turned and saw his father standing next to him. "Son, what is going on?"

Jesse looked at his father. He knew he wouldn't get in the carriage without an explanation. "A Priest told me to kill a good man and offered me everything I've ever wanted."

Renny looked somber. "And?"

"It wasn't his to give." Jesse said putting a hand on his shoulder.

His father folded him into a hug. "You're a good man Jess."

"Trying every day, paw." He said then pulled away. "But the people I've offended are coming after us. You need to get into the carriage."

"I'm not letting you fight this alone." He held up the pistol he was carrying.

"I'm afraid it's probably for the best Mr. Devote." Thomas put in. "You've been off the battlefield for a while."

Renny scoffed at that. "I may not have run around Thyro or Puena, but I was a seasoned veteran before either of you were born." He jumped onto the driver seat with more spryness than his son would have thought possible from the man.

Thomas shrugged and joined him. "Here you go, sir." He produced a pistol from somewhere. "You'll need more than one."

Jesse didn't like the idea of his father trading bullets, but he didn't have the time to argue him down. He jumped up with him and whipped the reigns hard. They flew down the street fast. They were about half a mile to the end of the city, then Jesse heard the first shots.

<hr/>

This was what I lived for. Violence. I hated the fact that I loved it. To me, violence was like a beautiful woman with a heart of ice. I knew I should stay away, but the bitch kept luring me back. There was something inside me that craved it. When I heard a battle was on the horizon, I'd be in the middle of it, even if I didn't particularly care who won. I was trying to be a better man, but that was in the calm. I may have been done fighting for the wrong reasons, but I wasn't done with fighting, and the beast inside was hungry.

Many soldiers I'd talked to spoke of battle like weathering a vicious storm. Those men weren't me. I was the storm. I was vengeance, rage, and justice released upon those the Three found wanting. I was fire, blood, and death incarnate, sent to fill the earth with men. I was the gods' mistake, and now that they had realized their folly, it was too late. I was too powerful to be killed.

People were right to be disappointed when they met me in peace. That man was a shell to be filled with hellfire and gunpowder when men needed to be struck down. The real Thomas Belson could be seen at Sterling, at Willow's bridge, at Kran. Three above, how I missed Kran. Two titans had battled for five years, scarring half a continent. It was a fight not seen since the Three cast the Demons into the World Below. After Thaniel was beaten, I had wandered the world looking for another man to match my first adversary and found them all lacking. I'd fought in the largest battles remembered by man. I had jumped onto the back of a twenty-foot crocodile. I had boxed Gregor the Big, strongest man to be found in the world. I had won them all.

Women, drink, wealth. They were all pale distractions from my true love. Now that I saw her again, I wondered how anything less than her could satisfy him.

There were two sides in the world, the New Church and the Old Religion. One wore robes stained in blood. One released Demons from worlds beyond and spoke with the voice of evils older than time itself. The other side had Thomas Belson. Men who survived both in their full glory, had nightmares of tattooed arms and prayed to the Three.

I was deep inside my Battle Mind. Black-clad men came through alleyways with their rifles trying to stop our escape. They might as well have been blowing against a hurricane. All weapons not in my hands were pale imitations. I killed them all. I may have been the god of Death, but I was not a cruel one. They died quickly.

I saw the way Jesse shot. He was calm, collected, and precise. A good warrior. Despite the high speed of the carriage he even managed to kill some of the men he aimed at. I had seen better, but few and far between. Still, he was mortal made of flesh and blood, not forged in fire and steel like I was.

A thousand things were coursing through my mind. I counted the bullets I shot from my repeating rifle. I saw the men who crept up the alleys. I knew the speed I traveled at. All of these things and more converged to serve one purpose. How many men would die?

The servants sent against me were poor shots. They were thugs and sadist, not pure warriors. They aimed at us sitting atop the carriage, but it was moving too fast, and their bullets went wide. If they were thinking clearly, they'd have aimed for the large horses. They were the easier targets, but unless men were perfectly trained in chaos, their minds seldom reasoned well.

However, there was something else in play besides the high speed of their targets and the stress on them. They were afraid. They knew the man they faced. They saw the wild grin on my face and the crazed look in my eyes. They saw how each man caught in my crosshairs was marked for death. They took their shots before they were ready with shaking hands and sweaty palms. They feared the Demon in front of them more than the ones at their back.

I only knew of fear second hand. I'd seen it in the eyes of my victims, but it was a strange phenomena to me. Some called it self preservation, but there was no real self to preserve outside of battle.

We were almost to the edge of the city, and there hadn't been a single challenge to meet us. Then I saw it fifty feet away. Sixteen men with rifles trained, blocking the way. One hundred thousand men had not been enough to stop me. Sixteen was insulting. I would make them pay for it in blood.

For a moment, I forgot why I was there. Somehow I remembered I had to keep the family safe. They hadn't had the time to block the road, which was fortunate, but if sixteen men fired some would get lucky, hitting the horses, and the escape would be ruined. Some would likely even hit Jessie and his father. I didn't want to escape. I wanted more blood, but that would come later when the real battle raged.

I took the situation in all at once. They weren't a line of soldiers. They were thugs, not used to battle. Their weapons shook. They could barely hear the order to ready their rifles through the fear. They were at thirty feet. These men lacked discipline. They saw my tattooed arm and scarred face, and for the first time in their lives knew true fear. They were at twenty feet. I needed to do something unexpected. I needed to break them. Renny pulled hard on the reigns. The horse's hooves skidded as they tried desperately to stop. My two companions held on for dear life, but I leapt. Belson the Blessed flew towards them.

Someone screamed fire, but no one listened. They watched as their worst fears came flying towards them. The carriage was forgotten. I heard a few scattered rifles go off and felt a dull thump in my shoulder. I didn't care. I still held the gun in my right hand. I saw my first target as I came down. I slammed the buttstock into the man's head. I felt it crunch like a melon between the street and my rifle. I dropped the weapon and rolled to take the weight of the fall. I came up with my pistol. There were men all around me. I saw rifles being leveled from my right and grabbed one man as a shield against them. Then I let the full storm loose.

I charged. When you're outnumbered in a fight there could be no retreat or defense, only attack. I put my pistol in one's mouth and squeezed the trigger. Whatever was inside a man's head went into the rest's faces. They were blinded by it, and I was on them. I spun, ducked, and dogged my way past as men tried to touch. It would have been easier to catch smoke in their hand. I emptied my weapon, each bullet finding its mark. I dropped it and pulled another, then emptied that one too. I picked up unfired rifles and used them, all the while moving like wind in a storm. I drew my knife and tomahawk to do my bloody work with. It was all a mix of the precise martial arts drilled into me at God's Rest and the furious anger of a wild animal I'd learned on the battlefield. How were there still men to kill? I was sure I'd killed sixteen.

I saw the carriage was moving out the corner of my eye. Jesse had joined the fray. He was a good fighter. Now the black-clad men had two enemies, but only one Belson the Blessed. I felt the necks crack beneath my iron arms. I felt ribs shatter, puncturing lungs leaving the victim coughing blood, waiting for death. I felt skulls fracture as I slammed them against whatever surface I could find. I felt shoulders dislocate, bones snap, and eyes pop as I moved through my enemies like a tide through stone. Men with bullets in their muskets tried to shoot me, but I was too quick. Most didn't even have time to pull the trigger before I put my clever hands on them.

I exploited weak spots they never knew they had. I hit nerve bundles that left half their bodies useless. I taught them what their bodies were. They were clay to be molded into corpses. Then all at once, there were none left. They ran. They knew their masters would have them flayed alive when they learned two men had broken them. They didn't care. All they wanted was to be free of Thomas Belson. From now till the day they died, they would pray to the Three in their hearts. They would have nightmares about tattooed arms.

I looked over at Jesse and smiled. The big man stared wide-eyed at the carnage. If he didn't believe the stories before, he would now. Even the ones about dragons and magic swords. I heard Renny step off the cart and survey the scene.

"Three above." He said making a sign to ward off evil. I looked around myself. There must have been fifty corpses, all killed in the most brutal of ways. More moaned out and crawled on battered bodies, the ones I hadn't had time to end properly. They begged for mercy, and I would give it to them. There was no point in killing beaten men. I was not a child burning ants. I was a lion looking desperately for a challenge. I saw none there.

"We'd better leave." Jesse said cautiously. Him and his father were looking at me like I might do the same thing to him. They didn't understand. They thought I was out of control. I wasn't. I was the master of all creation on that street in Pentsville. I wasn't a mindless creature. I was an artist, and this was my painting. It would not be made better with the addition of Jesse or his father.

"We better." I smiled grimly then the tattoos on my arms started to burn like wildfire. I turned around to see a regal looking Priest dressed in blood-colored flowing robes chanting in a booming voice. He had the same face all of them had. That face so beautiful it had to be evil. *Bellefellow.* I recognized the power. All Priests looked the same, but in fifteen years I'd only felt Demons so strong once. I knew it instinctively almost before the winds started to pick up and the familiar popping and cracking of a man touching something that gods couldn't handle.

I had to move quick before the Demons were set loose. Usually, all they could muster was a couple of distant lightning claps, but this was different. I saw a loaded rifle next to me and aimed it quickly. I pulled the trigger and heard the click, but nothing happened. The powder must have fallen out. *Poor luck.* Was the last thing I thought before the wind hit me in the gut like a train. I was flying again.

Jesse had joined Thomas to fight their way out. He killed a few with his pistol before it ran dry. He'd used too much ammo on the carriage. He'd wrestled a few muskets away from men, stabbed some people, and even bashed one man's skull in with the butt of his six-shooter. Jesse was more than a competent fighter. As far as the bounty hunter knew, he was the best in the South. That was before Belson the Blessed returned from Thyro.

The man killed the same way most breathed. He looked around at some fifty odd bodies twisted and deformed by his hands. More cried out for mercy. The bounty hunter didn't know if that meant they wanted him to spare them or finish it, but regardless the sight filled his mouth with bile.

Now, Jesse believed all the stories, even the ones about dragons and magic swords. He was grateful to the man. They wouldn't have made it out if it weren't for his little flying stunt, but there was something else besides gratitude. It was fear. The way he murdered men with that manic look on his face. The way the black-clad servants were helpless to stop him. The way they watched and could do nothing as he tore them apart. He never quite grasped why people in Thyro talked about Thomas the way they did. "No one could kill like that." He'd say to the traveling soldier who'd had the misfortune of sharing a battlefield with the man.

They'd just shake their head and order another shot of whiskey to wash down the memory. "You don't understand." Was all they could say.

Jesse understood now looking at the man. He'd thought he was afraid of the Old Religion. There was no Demon below who could do what Belson the Blessed could.

"Three above." He heard his father say.

"We'd better leave." He said to the Constable cautiously.

The bastard smiled at him. How the fuck could he smile. "We better."

Then he heard crackling and popping, like lightning without the strength to strike yet. He felt the wind pick up. Then he felt his lungs forget how to breath. He went for a rifle next to him, but his hands forgot how to grab. He looked over and saw Thomas fly like he was hit by a cannonball.

"Jesse Devote." He heard the voice say. It was Bellefellow. He looked up and saw the Priest angrier than he'd ever been. Wind was blowing his crimson cloak. "Don't you know it's a sin to work after five." The words were filled with rage and seemed to come from everywhere at once.

His father raised his pistol to shoot, but a gust of wind slammed him against the carriage. "I was going to have them killed quickly if you'd have done like I told you." The Priest was coming closer wreathed in wind and fire. "I wasn't lying. I did like you." Lightning struck twenty feet away, and a gust of wind tore a wooden pillar free. "You should have killed McAllan. Now they'll suffer."

Jesse felt his legs forget how to stand and he fell. All he could do was watch his father. He watched as the man who raised him turn his head left slowly, then when it should have stopped it kept moving. "AHHHHHHHHH." His father screamed in an agony the bounty hunter hadn't heard in years of battlefields and gunfights.

He looked back at the Priest. "Please Jude, don't do this." He managed to croak out. He stopped in his tracks like he was struck. The wind and lightning abated, and his father stopped screaming.

Bellefellow looked at Jesse curiously. "Why would you call me that?" His face twisted. He looked like he was trying to think through a dream.

"It's your name." Jesse said as he felt the air rush into his lungs. "It's the one your mother gave you. You said she was beautiful."

"I did?" He eyed the bounty hunter curiously.

Bobby ran out of the carriage screaming and hugged his brother. Jesse finally remembered how to put his arm around someone to show you'd protect them. His mother rushed out the carriage too and went to his father. "Renny, are you ok."

"I'm fine dear." He said patting her cheek weakly.

Then Mary rushed out and tried to pull Bobby away, but he wouldn't move. "Come on Jesse we have to run." She looked over the carnage and started dry heaving.

In the bounty hunter's mind they were all probably dead, but maybe there was a chance. "You used to want to be powerful so you could help people." He whispered to the Priest. "You said you were angry because no one knew your story."

"I'm Bellefellow." He said confused. "I've always been Bellefellow." He whispered to himself.

"No, once you were Jude." Jesse said with as much compassion as he could muster. "I know your story."

"We have to run." Mary said frantically. She didn't understand there was no running.

Jesse ignored her. "You don't need to do this."

The bounty hunter heard a shot fired it sounded like one of the little pistols prostitutes got to defend themselves. "Jesse you can't reason with this monster!" He heard Thomas scream. Then the wind and lightning returned, and Thomas was blasted into a wall.

"Monster!" Bellefellow was back, and Jude was gone. "And what's the difference between me killing with Demons and him with his fists?" He gestured at the bodies strewn along the ground. "Do you know how many he's sent to the grave on his own?" The rage seemed to reverberate against the world. "Do you know how many more have died because of his 'heroism'?" The Priest laughed maniacally. "Even if I told you, you wouldn't believe me." He walked closer. "But I'll tell you this, even if I lived a thousand more years, my number would never be anywhere near his." Lightning struck again, and another pillar flew free, but this time they were closer. "So I'll ask you one more time, what's the difference between him and me?" He waved his hands at the destruction. "Were these men not as helpless to him as you are to me?"

Jessie hugged his brother tight. Even if they were going to die, he wouldn't let Bo-Bo die alone.

"I'll tell you the difference." He said walking closer. "I use my power to achieve peace and stability. Concrete goals for a concrete world." He gestured to the wooden planks where Thomas had landed. "He uses his for some abstract idea of freedom." He shook his head dismissively. "Or at least that's the excuse he uses to trick young men into killing more young men." He was close now. "I will forge an obedient world. He talks about freedom." He paused with an evil smile on his face. "Freedom to do what? I will free the world from hunger and war because I am a caring god, unlike those absent Three." He sneered down at them all. "We both fight for a greater good, but only I see an end to the road." He spat into the ground. "And you chose him!"

"AHHHHHHHHHH!" His father screamed as his neck was twisted past what was humanly possible and then there was nothing.

"Renny!" He heard his mother cry out.

Bo-Bo sobbed into his shoulder.

"The only way to the end of the road is through obedience, and disobedience must be punished harshly." He whispered it, but it was as if the whole world whispered it too. "Maybe I'll make your brother claw his own heart out. Maybe I'll make your mother and your whore kill each other, but one things for sure." He leaned over them all. "I'm going to make you watch."

Something inside Jesse snapped then. He wanted to protect them so much it became a real thing. It was real enough to push back at the Demons controlling his body. He pushed hard, and the Priest winced. That was all he needed, proof that he could hurt him. He pushed harder, and Bellefellow took a backwards step. He thought about teaching his brother how to read, about his mother kissing him to bed at night, he thought about the nights he spent with Mary. He pushed hard and felt the pressure abate. It wasn't hard enough, and the rage of the Old Religion came crashing down on him. He felt the air being driven from his lungs, and then he saw Thomas Belson walk up and shoot the Priest in his distracted face.

<hr />

It was a common misconception that Constables were immune to the Demons. This probably stemmed from reports of Constables being untouched in a plague caused by Priests, or the fact that Demons couldn't worm their way into our bodies like they could with most people.

The truth, of course, was more complicated. While a Demon couldn't directly touch a Constable. A Demon could move wind with the force of a cannon ball, and that cannonball wind could most definitely touch a Constable.

This, of course, was harder to do, giving said Constable a chance to fire a musket, but if that musket didn't have any powder in it, then he might be fucked.

I knew my body was in disrepair. I couldn't feel the pain through the Battle Mind, but I did the careful evaluation of the injuries I'd learned at God's Rest. My left leg didn't move quite right, probably something was torn. When I breathed my right side was pressured, that spoke to an impaled lung. Worst of all was my right ear. The rest of it would probably heal with time. I'd feel the shadow of the pain for the rest of my life, but I'd be able to run and breath again. My right ear heard nothing expect a painful ringing that might never get better. The wind could have ruptured my eardrum irreparably. I closed the ringing off like closing a door, leaving only my left ear to send its vital warnings. My weapons were dry my knife was broken, and all I had was the prostitute pistol in my sleeve. It was only accurate up to ten feet, and even then it missed often.

That was true for the first shot. I never missed, but sometimes weapons malfunctioned. The Priest hit me again, I didn't even bother with the self-check the second time. *Why doesn't the Priest finish me yet?* I wondered to myself. I was clearly the greatest threat. For some reason, though, Bellefellow was intent on Jesse. I only heard every third word, but it was too strange a conversation to comprehend anyway. I couldn't even see the family in my coffin of broken wood. Still, I'd never seen a Priest act like this one, but then again I'd never left one alive long enough to observe it.

When the Priest hit me again, I'd given up hope of trying to save the family. My only chance was to play dead long enough to take the last shot. I wouldn't do that. I wouldn't let Jesse pay so heavy a price for being a good man, but to rush Bellefellow now wouldn't help anything. I felt the Demons take a life and knew I had to move. I stood, and my left leg gave out immediately. I tried again, but it still wouldn't work. Most men wouldn't try a third, but no one defeated Belson the Blessed, not even my own body. I stood up and held my leg together to make it work. I expected to be blasted back again, but then I felt it.

I felt it in the same way I could feel the line of an army. Jesse was fighting back, he was losing, but he was fighting back. It was a skill that had been gone from me since Thaniel fell, but I recognized it still. It was the Gift. This was a long enough distraction. I couldn't run, but I walked quickly. I was almost there, ten feet away, I felt the surprise of the attack wear off, and now Bellefellow was on the offensive. I was five feet away, still not close enough. I felt the battle end, and now I was right next to the Priest. I shot the bastard in the head and watched him fall. Then I let go of my leg. This fight was done.

Jesse watched Thomas fall to the ground. A few minutes ago he'd been the greatest warrior the Three had ever created, and the Demons had ever feared. Now he couldn't stand on his own.

He ran to the Constable. "Are you alright?" He said picking Thomas up.

"Your brother was right." The cheeky bastard chuckled. "I should have brought my dragon."

"You're still not funny." Jesse said then found he was smiling anyway. When they were out of the city, he needed to talk to Thomas, but that could wait. "We need to leave now."

"We could stay as long as we want." The Constable said leaning on him heavily. "We've killed the most powerful Priest in the South. They won't touch us." Thomas looked at Jesse's father seeing it for the first time. "I'm sorry."

"Get in the fucking carriage." He couldn't let himself think about that.

"That won't be necessary." He stopped for a moment. "Shaggy!" He screamed. The horse came running, and he somehow managed to hobble on. "Let's go then."

His mother was still weeping over the corpse of her husband. "Get in the carriage." He said firmer than he meant to. He looked at the body. "I'll take care of him."

She nodded unable to speak through the tear and took Bobby with her. He wasn't crying yet. Jesse would have to explain it all later. He grabbed Mary's arm.

"What?" She said it through her own tears. She didn't mean it as mean, but she was scared.

"Do you have that rose I gave you?" Jessie asked trying desperately to control his own emotions.

She reached into her breast. "Don't give it to your father." She said through the tears. "He was a good man, but he was lucky till the end I think."

He kissed her on the forehead. "He'll have a different flower."

She nodded and gave him the rose, and then walked into the carriage, shutting the door behind her.

He walked up and placed the red rose on Bellefellow's chest. Then stifling a tear walked to the front stepping up to the reigns.

"Bellefellow doesn't deserve a flower." Thomas said spitting towards the Priest.

"Your right Bellefellow doesn't." He wiped his eyes. "But Jude does I think." The words just confused the Constable. "Can you take my father with you." He paused not able to say the words. "My family shouldn't have to ride with him.

Thomas nodded, and Jesse took the body and slung him over the little pony. It didn't seem to be bothered by the weight. The bounty hunter wished he could say the same about himself. Renny looked just like the dozens he'd thrown over his own horse for a bounty. He looked like the old barber. He whipped the reins and the carriage set into motion. When Thomas was safely out of sight, scouting the woods, Jesse wept.

He wept for his father, but also for his own sins. He wept for the men whose heads he'd so arbitrarily put a price on. He wept for his family. He even wept for a little boy named Jude. They all deserved better than a flower.

Present Day Stories Collide

esse drove the horses all night at a decent speed. They weren't followed. Thomas was probably right. They were too scared. When they were safely away, Jesse stopped the cart and buried his father next to a large oak tree. He had cried his last tear on the road. He didn't need to do it in front of his family.

Thomas walked off as soon as they stopped to do whatever it was Constables do. Jesse wasn't angry about it, the man couldn't possibly dig a grave in his state. Belson came back shortly, though, with a white Silesia, a real one at that, before disappearing back into the woods. Silesia's rarely grew in the wild. They needed to be cultivated, it was part of what made them sacred. Jesse had planned on just finding any old white flower, but that was better.

His mother said the burial words. When it was time for the bounty hunter to speak all he said before placing the flower was. "He was born a good man, he lived as a good man, and he died as a good man." Long orations were for the wicked. The sort who's lives had been full of so many twists and turns it was hard to figure where it all went wrong. They deserved to have their story told. They deserved to be remembered a little better than they were. For the decent, simplicity would do. As he said it, Jesse wondered how long his own story would be.

I gave the big man the Silesia and hobbled off into the woods. I found a spot where I could be alone and went to work. I took off my shirt and ripped it into bandages. First, I staunched the bleeding in my arm and then splinted my leg. I realized my shoulder was dislocated and ran into a tree until it went back in place. There was nothing I could do about my lung or ear. Only time would tell with those. I ate some of the jerky in my pocket and sipped from my replenished skin. I even found a plant I could chew to help with the pain. Then I set my back against a tree and sat down slowly. I let the food digest until I realized I was putting it off.

I lowered myself from the Battle Mind, and there was a split second before the pain came back. I wondered if it would finally be too much for me. I wondered if my body would succumb like the rest of the Constables. Then it hit me hard.

I was a tough man. For all my faults, no one claimed I wasn't tough. I had pain tolerance like a bolt of steel, but even still, when it came, I threw up everything. If I wasn't so underfed and dehydrated, it would have been more. I felt my lung burn, it wasn't popped, but it wasn't comfortable either. My ear rung like a bell, and my shoulder felt like an anvil being punished for being a lousy anvil. The worst was my leg though, sharp and coursing. Then I ate more of the pain plant and prepared myself for the worst part.

I saw the terrified faces of the men I killed, if they could be called men, most were barely old enough to shave. I saw their helplessness and pleadings. I even felt the joyous way with which I broke them. I threw up again. It was all too much for me.

I'd promised myself and everyone that mattered that I'd be a good man. Could a good man do what I did in Pentsville? I knew those black-clad servants stories. They weren't good men exactly, but neither were they evil. They were helpless boys found on the street, offered money and a better life. One of those boys probably wanted to open a store, another probably wanted enough money to court a girl he was sweet on, and most probably just wanted to fill their bellies. They'd never do any of those things now. However, the most sickening part of it was that while some part of me mourned the boys, another part was proud, happy even, of the carnage I'd caused. I tried to blame it on the Battle Mind, but there was a dark voice in my head that still called what I did on that street, art. *What is art without suffering?* It said. I lit a cigarette to help silence it, but it would never be silent. It was a chain I could never be free from.

I heard rustling in the trees and Jesse presented himself.

"You ought to learn to be more stealthy." I said through a puff of smoke.

"Next time I walk through the woods, I'll be sure to act drunk and scream about whores." The big man slid down a tree opposite me.

"I don't think you'll find many whores here." I said with a laugh. "Pretend you ate some bad mushrooms." I remembered the time Seiford and I had run around the woods looking for the hallucinogens. Viverent had not lied about their potency. Then my mood turned solemn. "How's your family?" I asked. "All things considered?"

Jesse locked his jaw. "They're doing alright." He sighed. "All things considered."

"And you?" I asked,

"I have my own way of dealing with it." The big man pulled a flask out of his jacket pocket and drank deep. "You want some?"

I nodded and caught the flask taking a big gulp of the burning whiskey. "Thank you." I said and drank more offering the man a cigarette.

Jesse shook his head. "I have my own vice for that." He pulled a bag of chewing tobacco out of his pocket. "Mary doesn't like me doing it, but I can't bring myself to quit."

"She seems a good woman." I nodded. "And pretty besides."

"She is." The big man nodded back. "She's scared of you."

That hit me hard. "She should be." I said, taking another drink of the whiskey before throwing it back. "I'm sorry for that, but she should be."

"Don't be sorry." He said drinking again through the chewing tobacco. Try as I might, I never understood the skill. "I'm scared of you too." He paused. "You got a woman?" Jesse asked

"I got an enemy." I said it darkly. Jesse caught the hint. I saw the look on his face. He had a question but he wasn't sure he wanted to know the answer. "What are you afraid to ask me?"

"Some people say if a Demon kills you they drag you down to the World Below with them." The big man nodded, and I saw why he was scared. "Is it true?" He asked.

I took a long draw on my smoke. "The New Church is divided on that." I said flicking the ash. "Some say that dying by a Demon places you too far from salvation. Others say if you die fighting the Powers Below, your place next to the Three is assured."

"And what do you believe?"

"I don't know about all the theology. Doubtless, my monk could give you a suitable explanation, but he's running an errand." I took another long smoke. "I've met the Three, though."

"Aye?" Jesse asked.

"Aye." It was a hard thing to believe. "I know them as well as any man alive."

"Before last night I'd have been hauling you off to an asylum for that kind of talk," the bounty hunter let out a big huff, "but I believe it today."

"I've got that way about me." I shrugged.

The big man met my eyes as if it were the last thing he wanted to do. "So what did your friends say about my father's soul?"

I traced a figure on the ground with my finger. "Well, they're your friends too." I paused. "They're also friend to McAllan, Coleson, that Priest you killed, and even the bitch that cut me, believe it or not," I gave a sad sort of chuckle, "and I won't fault you for not because I'm not sure I believe it either."

"I don't need friends." Jesse said it shortly. "I need an answer. Is my Father with the Three above or the Demon's Below?" He shook his head at the futility of it all. "Not that their answer will change things one way or another."

"They don't really answer things, at least not the way you want them to." I gritted my teeth. "Their words are wrapped in riddles." I paused. "Try not to fault them for it. They have to hint at whatever wisdom they hold because we don't have the words, breadth, or whatever else is needed to understand them."

Jesse shook his head. "So you don't know."

"I know them, even if they don't tell me much." I looked into the big man's eyes. "I know they won't let a man like your father go to the World Below." I said and meant it. "I don't really think they let anyone go to the World Below but especially not your father from the little I knew of the man." I paused. "They've got a plan for each of us..." I trailed off, remembering what Doctor Quarrels had told me in Imor. "Or a fool's hope at least, and I don't think eternal torment is a part of it."

"Thank you." That seemed to mollify Jesse. The big man spat out some brown. "What happened to you in Pentsville?"

I gestured for the flask again and drained it. I knew what he was really asking. *How could you kill that way?* "I'm a different man in battle."

"The way you were so calm and calculating." Jesse looked

confused. "The way you shot so carefully and quickly." He sighed. "I don't think I watched you miss with a single round."

"Except the one that mattered." I said with some self-loathing.

Jesse ignored that. "Then when you fought, it was like watching a wild animal," He shook his head. "Except, every move was so precise. I've seen a lot of good soldiers in my time but nothing like that." He paused. "How?"

I shrugged. "There's already a dozen books written trying to answer that very question." I'd been trying to answer it all my life. "The best I can tell you is I was born touched by something." I took another drag on my cigarette. "I want it more than anything, and I wish I didn't."

He looked down at me. "It's like you didn't even see them as people."

"That comes later." I finished my smoke and lit another.

"Maybe it shouldn't." Jesse said looking up at the sky.

"Aye, maybe it shouldn't." I agreed then gestured back to him. "Have you ever heard of Constable Fowler?"

"No." Jessie looked confused.

"He never killed a man when he could avoid it." I said thinking about the warrior. "He always tried to find a peaceful way. If it came to combat, he'd only ever wound men. He said all were the Three's creation." I took another smoke. "Probably why you haven't heard of him. Didn't last long. I did."

"I see." He nodded, but I could tell he didn't, and I didn't want to explain it to him.

"What did you do to the Priest?" I finally asked even though I already knew.

"I was going to ask you that very question." Jesse shrugged.

I sighed. "My best guess is that you unlocked the Gift. It comes from man, but it's sporadic." I took another drag. "I used to have it, but only those who stand in the light can unlock the power." I remembered the man I'd been so long ago. I'd still been rough around the edges. Still did some things a decent man shouldn't. Still had dreams the righteous weren't troubled by. I hadn't been the beaten creature I became, though. I hadn't had to look at the Pillars yet. "I haven't stood in the Three's light for some time." I finally answered.

"I hear stories about you doing things like that." Jesse twiddled his thumbs. "Gertinville, Haslow," the big man paused, "the Pillars."

He took a step forward. "I hear you deadened their powers somehow. Made you able to kill them."

"Aye, I'm reasonably sure you did what I did." I paused. "It's lost to me now though. After Thaniel, well…" I shook my head. "Things weren't the same." I took another drag on my shortening smoke. "I never really understood what I was doing. It has to do with embracing the truth of yourself, bravely facing the suffering of existence or something like that." I sighed. "I haven't been able to do that for some time."

"You've still killed Priests aplenty." Jesse raised an eye.

I laughed at that. "I've killed more Priests than you have men." I hardened my face. "I've really been coasting on their incompetence and fear since the Pillars. All the powerful ones died in the Thaniel War anyway anyhow." I remembered the things Bellefellow had done. Things I hadn't seen since Kran. He was more than a village charlatan. He may have been stronger than the ones I killed ten years ago. "I thought they did at least."

"How are you still alive, if you can't break their powers." Jesse asked the next logical question.

I let my hand rock on the six shooters. "I'm still quick and mean as anyone, but if they knew I couldn't do what I did in Kran, I'd already be dead, so keep that bit secret."

Jesse smiled. "Why are you telling me now?"

"From what I've seen you're a decent sort." I inhaled more smoke. "Besides there's things you should know now."

That took the wind out the big man. "The first time you saw me, I was about to kill the Prime Governor." He sighed. "If you'd seen the things I've done, you wouldn't say that."

"That's what I mean." I took another smoke. "It's easy to live a good life and keep doing it. Harder for a bad man to try to be better. Besides, maybe I just need to believe someone like you can stand in the light. Puts me a little closer, I figure."

"Makes sense." Jesse nodded. "Still think I'm a far cry from any kind of decent, though."

"But you're trying to be better." I threw a small stick at nothing in particular. "That means something to a man like me."

Jesse seemed to meditate on that for a moment. "So can you teach me how to use it?" He asked with hope in his voice. "This Gift thing, I mean."

"Probably not." I admitted. "But maybe." I'd let Seiford explain it later. "Why'd you call Bellefellow, Jude?"

"It was his name." Jesse said grimly. "Somewhere deep inside him, it was his name."

"No!" I was angrier than I thought. "There's nothing deep inside those bastards."

"I think you're wrong." The bounty hunter said softly.

"There can't be!" I was still angry.

"And why not?" Jesse cut back sharply.

Because then I've killed thousands that could have been saved. Because then I wasn't putting down mad dogs but real men. Because then death wasn't a mercy, but the end of their story with no redemption. "Because there isn't." I settled on.

That ended the talk, but I knew we'd rehash it soon.

We sat in silence for a while before Jesse broke it. "I guess the war's on."

I lit another cigarette. I should really have tried to cut back. "Guess it is."

"You're going to need a sergeant." Jesse said spitting another brown glob.

"Aye, I will." I paused. "But not one looking for vengeance." I took another smoke. "Men like that have a habit of going too far. I ought to know. I've been that man."

"I'm not looking for revenge." Jesse said to the ground, barely a whisper.

"Then what are you looking for?" I asked.

"Atonement." Jessie looked up. "Maybe even a little redemption" His gaze turned steely.

"Atonement is in short supply." I nodded. "And redemption is rare as diamonds." I smoked on my cigarette. "But if there's a man who can give it to us, it's McAllan."

"I think you're right." The bounty hunter nodded.

"So you'll fight for me?" I asked, most men who saw me fight these days didn't want another taste.

"I'll fight with you." Jesse corrected me. "And if the day should come, I'll restrain you."

"And if you can't?" I was genuinely curious.

The big man opened his jacket revealing a six-shooter. "Well, then there's an answer to that too."

I nodded. "I suppose there is." I smiled. "Can you make a

private's life hell?" I smothered my cigarette. "That's the only way the dumb bastards learn."

Jesse smiled back. "What'd your brother say?"

I laughed at that. "He said you could make a general's life hell."

The big man laughed back. "Generals need to learn too."

Seventeen
Years Ago
A Different Boy

My entire family was gathered in the living room. I sat in an armchair on the other side of the room from them all. I pointedly tried to ignore my brother. Andrew knew how angry I was at him, but even at thirteen, he had the grace to bear it silently. At fourteen, I didn't. Sarah was next to him on the couch squeezing his hand until her own turned white. Alexis was too young to see this. She was playing in her room. My mother Pamela, who always looked so young and kind, was distraught. She tried to hide it, but the way she gripped to her husband's coat was telling. Leopold put a comforting arm over her. His once brown hair was streaked with gray, now. His strong angular chin twisted into a sorrow. Yet, despite his age, he sat up proudly. George was there too watching from the corner. After all, we were as close to family as he had.

The men who came recruiting were a Constable and a monk. Constable Hanku was about thirty years old and Souren. He was coiled in lean muscle, and the tattoos on his arm showed in contrast to his dark skin. He was a handsome man. He had scars, but they seemed becoming on his face. Besides that, he had the confident bearing that seemed to attract women. More than anything Hanku had a face like a hard man about to do a hard thing.

Brother Aquina was Anthanii and couldn't have been a day under fifty. He seemed like every kind old man who had ever lived. His gray hair and uniform were completely unkempt. In contrast to the black Constable, he gave my family a mournful smile. Perhaps like a doctor trying to tell his patient it wasn't so bad when it clearly was.

"What are the chances he survives?" Leopold asked holding his wife.

"He'll be well trained and armed." Hanku said with a nod.

"What are the chances!" My father demanded.

"They're not great." Brother Aquina said sadly. "Some make it for the twenty years, but most don't." He sighed like he was carrying the weight of the world on his shoulders. "Those are in peaceful times. Things are far from peaceful these days. Thaniel's only growing more powerful, and Thyro as a whole is moving towards chaos in his wake."

"Which is why we need every Constable we can train." Hanku cut in. "Someone has to be there to stop the bloodshed."

"Does he have a choice?" Leopold said as he comforted his wife.

"We do not have the authority to abduct children." Hanku answered crossing his arms.

"Even if we did, we wouldn't." Brother Aquina gave a sympathetic look. "Morality aside, a man won't do what we need him to if he's conscripted."

"Your family will receive a generous stipend." Hanku looked at him with a hard face. "You can live like kings."

"Damn your money!" Leopold screamed. "Don't bother sending it." He looked to his son. "It's not my place to choose for you. Make your own decision, Andrew."

I went white with anger at that. I wanted my brother out of the picture, but not like this. I wouldn't take Sarah while my brother fought all across the world winning glory. I had the small sense to stay silent, though.

"I do have a duty to protect the weak." Andrew said looking to Sarah. "I have a duty to my family as well." He smiled at Sarah then back to Hanku. "As it stands I believe your Church to be a metaphor." He looked down mournfully. "I won't shed blood for a metaphor."

"It is not. I can assure you that." Hanku said with his stern face.

"No, you can't." Andrew shot back then kissed Sarah on the cheek. "I'm needed here. Someone else can run around Thyro collecting glory and fame. If war comes to my people, I'll fight but not before."

Brother Aquina nodded. "I understand. There are others who may be more willing." He paused. "I can't say you're making the wrong decision."

The pair turned to walk away, and the room breathed a

collective sigh of relief. Everyone except for me. I looked around and saw nothing to keep me there. There was no happiness to be had in the Confederacy. I didn't want happiness, anyway. I wanted men to fear me.

I stood up. "What does it take for a man to become a Constable?" I asked, and the pair turned back surprised.

"Thomas," my father was as close to begging as I'd ever seen, "please, for once in your life stay silent!"

"Shut up!" I hissed back. In normal times my father would already have me bent over his knee. Now, he was too shocked to respond. "I asked you a question." I turned back to the warrior and monk. "What does it take to become a Constable?"

Brother Aquina looked me up and down. "Honor, wisdom, and a loving heart."

"Fuck that." I hissed at him. "I don't want to know what some bastard scrawled on your charter half a millennia ago." I took a step forward. "I want to know what it takes."

Brother Aquina opened his mouth to answer, but Constable Hanku stepped forward. "We take boys with a military background. We want educated lads who already know there way around a weapon." He answered my challenge. "In times like these, they also need cunning, bravery, and a hard edge."

"I've been riding, shooting, and fighting since I could walk." I gave a smug smile. "I've got all those qualities, same as my brother."

"Yes, you do." Brother Aquina answered.

"Is there anything else?" I asked. There was more to being a Constable than that. I knew it even then.

"There are other less tangible qualities to having a tattooed arm." Hanku looked me up and down. "Something we don't understand that's needed to fight the Old Religion, but we have ways of finding whatever it is."

"Do I have that as well?" Even though it was a question, I already knew the answer with the surety of a fourteen-year-old boy.

"You do." Hanku nodded. "Stronger than we've seen in some time. We never used to observe this phenomenon in the Confederacy, but our order has reason to believe we'll find a savior here?"

"A savior from Thaniel?" I asked, already imagining the Emperor's blood on my blade.

"Maybe, that." Brother Aquina shrugged. "Maybe more."

"Than why not ask me?" I hissed.

"It's not customary to take the firstborn." The monk said, but it was a lie.

"These are dangerous times." I smiled back. "Customs are meant to be broken."

"I don't think you'll make it." Hanku gave the real answer. "You might be clever, brave, and hard as bad iron, but you've got arrogance, anger, and recklessness in spades." He nodded to my brother. "He can be trained." He turned back to me. "I don't think you can be." The Constable paused. "If you take whatever's eating you to the battlefield, there will be a cost."

"I'll pay it then." I said it like a challenge. "Take me!"

"Thomas, don't do this!" Leopold couldn't hold his peace any longer.

"Tom-Tom!" My mother had started crying again. She could barely get the words out.

Andrew of all people walked up to me. Even though he was younger, he was still the taller of us. "Thomas I know we're not on the best of terms now, but this…" He gestured to the pair and put a hand on my shoulder. "There's better ways to spend your life than fighting other people's wars."

I gave my brother a sneer. "There was until you took them from me." It sounded petty even to myself. The look of hurt on his face didn't make me feel any better, but fourteen-year-olds are slow to admit their mistakes I shrugged Andrew's hand off.

"Damnit! Don't throw away your life to spite your brother!" Leopold rushed to me as well. "You could be a good man here."

I ignored them. "You don't think I'll make it, try me." I hissed at the Constable. "I'm not interested in being a good man. I want to be great." I paused. "Take me!" I repeated to the pair.

"Listen to your family, son." Brother Aquina looked at me with pity in his eyes. It was the look that made my blood boil. "Don't do this to hurt them. You may never forgive yourself."

"Take me, and I'll break Thaniel and anyone else you set me against." I took a step forward. "I'll be the greatest warrior who ever wore those tattoos." I took a step forward. "Take me!"

"There's a darkness in you son." Brother Aquina almost seemed scared of me then. "I don't know that I'm willing to set you loose on anyone."

"The world has grown darker in recent years." Hanku said with a nod. "Might be we need some of our own." The black Constable looked at me with something approaching respect. I resolved to earn the full thing. "I still don't think you'll make it."

"I don't care." I shot back, and I didn't. I'd read about the Constables since before I could remember. I'd never thought to stand amongst them, but I always knew I wanted to fight. If it was for the glory of the Confederacy or the New Church, I didn't care. If Thaniel had come before these two, I would have likely been wearing Kranish gold already.

Hanku nodded at that. "Good." He gestured towards his family. "It's customary to let you stay with your family for three days to say goodbyes."

"That won't be necessary."

"I didn't think it would be." Hanku smiled for the first time.

"Thomas, don't leave like this!" Leopold pulled me back. "Don't leave in anger." He folded me, his son, into a hug. "I love you more than anything else in the world."

My mother rushed to me as well. "Tom-Tom, why can't you just stay here and be happy?"

I pushed them away, and even then, I knew they deserved better, but there's a sureness in being fourteen. Nothing was going to dissuade me from my path. "You think I can be happy here?" I hissed. "Just small men on a small farm in a small country." I scoffed. "I've got ambition. I won't be happy until the whole world knows my name."

"Do you think a mother cares about that Tom-Tom." She cupped my face in her hands.

"Stop calling me that! I'm a man!" I shot back, and my mother recoiled as if she'd been struck. I should have stopped then, but I didn't. "I don't care what you want! I care about a world that doesn't quake when I walk!"

"She just wants you to be happy." Leopold said in disgust. Perhaps, he finally saw the man I'd become and cursed himself for it.

"And I want glory." I sneered.

"Don't let that cloud you." He said looking at me like I was a completely different person. "Be a good man." Even if I'd hurt him, he still wanted me to know I was his son.

"I'll be a great one." I said with a proudness only a child could have.

"And which one do you think is more important?" Leopold asked, but it wasn't a question. Even at fourteen, I knew the answer.

Even as a boy, I knew my path would lead to nothing but pain, but a boy like me can't stop himself from making a mistake once he seizes on it.

They'd been nothing but good to me. I had no right to act the way I was in that moment. A hero needs a chip on his shoulder though, and I wanted to be the greatest hero of them all. It let me find offense where none existed. If I became as powerful as I knew I could be, how dangerous could that become? I didn't care.

"Thomas-" Andrew started.

"I've got nothing to say to you!" I shot back. Andrew couldn't comprehend how cruel his brother had become.

"Take this." Leopold drew the pistol out of his holster and thrust it into my hands. "If you learn how to use it well enough, you might live to make amends for this."

I just smiled. "I'll be back, don't you worry." Then I looked to Hanku. "Let's go."

That was how I left them. In anger. Brother Aquina was right. I would never forgive myself. Even at fourteen, I knew that. That was how history changed. One boy wanted to make the world bleed.

———◆•◆•◆———

They stopped at a dozen more plantations looking for recruits. Brother Aquina and Constable Hanku found nothing but shaking heads and closed doors. Only one boy heard our case, and he'd possessed the wisdom to say no.

The people who came to get me thought they'd find a savior in the New World. The warrior and monk had been searching for someone taller, stronger, better tempered. They loaded up the ship to God's Rest with only me. Hanku muttered something about hoping it was enough.

It sounded like some strange prophecy to me. I didn't care about prophecies. I didn't care about being a bad son, either. I just wanted someone to hurt.

The Chaniel Wars

J walked toward the command tent still stinking of running and training. Men saluted me at every step, and I returned it. Lieutenant Roltan followed me smelling much the same.

"You probably ought to slow down." The bodyguard lit up a cigarette. He was talking about the exercises We'd done.

"You a doctor now?" I asked him.

"I ain't a chemist, but I don't have to be one to know it's a bad idea to mix gunpowder and fire." He smoked deep. "Those wounds you took should have killed you. Don't finish their work for them."

"You're a good bodyguard," I waved a finger at him, "but you're a shitty mother. Best stick to being a bodyguard."

Rolton chuckled. "Well, if you want my professional opinion on the guarding of bodies, it's a bad idea to run five miles a month after you woke up from a coma."

"Cheeky fucker." I shook my head. "How're the reading lessons coming?"

"They're coming." Rolton shrugged. "Captain Dios!" He saw the officer headed towards us and greeted him.

"Lieutenant Rolton." The man who'd turned down my promotion and award nodded. "Your Eminence."

"What brings you my way?" I asked Dios. The tall, well-built officer rarely had to come to me with problems. Come to think of it, I couldn't remember a time I'd had to solve something for the man.

"That's the thing sir." He scratched his head. "I'm not really sure."

"Please explain." I waved my hand.

"Well, this morning fifty men came into my camp." Captain Dios said. "They're all wearing Anthanii uniforms and claim to be a part of my company, but I know every soldier under my command by name and talent. I've never met them before."

"You think they might be spies trying to infiltrate our camp?" Roltan asked.

"I always assumed spies would be more inconspicuous." Dios crossed his arms. "Every one of them is wearing a horrible fake mustache. Instead of trying to eat at the mess, they just shovel grass and dirt in their mouth. They're under the impression that's the army's preferred meal."

"They're probably not spies." I shook my head. "Have you tried to send them away?"

"At least a dozen times." Captain Dios gave an exasperated sigh. "They look like fighting men, so I told them to go to the volunteer office." He shook his head. "They usually just eat more grass."

"It's probably worth our attention." I agreed.

We headed towards where the seventh was camped. I was met with the typical chorus of "good mornings" and salutes. The seventh's camp seemed divided between the members of the company and the fifty men wearing bad mustaches looking for a choice piece of grass.

Two of the impostors were conspicuously armed. One was wielding a blunderbuss with bayonets somehow mounted to it. The other wore six flintlock pistols on his harness. Both had a wild wolfish look despite their fire colored hair, and they also gave off the impression of being completely insane.

"Blip and Slip!" I walked over to the pair, each wearing ridiculous mustaches.

"Oy!" Blip screamed. "We ain't no Blip and Slip."

"It's a common mistake, being that we both sport devilishly good looks." Slip nodded.

"However, them's good seafaring folk. We's just dumb land lovers." Blip smiled.

"We can't even read!" Slip proclaimed proudly. "Would you like some of this here grass." He handed me a handful of weeds he'd plucked from the ground. "It is especially choice today."

"Afraid lunch was only an hour ago." I shook my head. "What are you doing here?"

"Oy, it seems our deception is up!" Blip shook his head.

"Oy, I beat the piss outta any deception." Slip gritted his teeth viciously.

"You's a clever man to see through our ruse." Blip clapped me on the shoulder.

"It's been said before." I rolled my eyes.

"Now that there ain't much fighting left to do on ships, we figured to take up with your lot." Blip looked on me pleadingly.

"Oy, we even take to your army customs, such as eating grass and being illiterate." Slip munched on a handful to illustrate the point.

"Who are these men?" Captain Dios asked over my shoulder.

"They're Royal Marines." I hissed back.

Dios's eyes went wide. "Seventh!" He started giving the orders. "Grab your weapons and form perimeter!" There was an innate fear in the army of their sea-born cousins.

I waved them down. "You'll do no such thing!" I screamed. "These men are on our side."

"They're loons!" The officer was still concerned for his men.

"Oy we ain't loons, you weebalow!" Slip shouted.

"There will be no fighting between my own men!" I reiterated the point, then turned to Slip and Blip. "I'll take you on!" Every soldier who heard me seemed unsettled at it. "But no more eating grass!" I ripped the weeds from their hands. "And all soldiers of mine will be clean shaven." I ripped the fake mustaches off their faces.

"Oy, many thanks!" Blip smiled and walked his men off.

"Rolton, go make sure they don't kill anyone." I nodded to the bodyguard.

"I'll try." He took his rifle and walked on after the marines.

"Are you sure you want them fighting with us?" Dios asked again. "They're mad."

"They are." I agreed. "But they don't care about uniforms. They just want something to hit." I paused. "If we don't let them fight with us, they might join the other side." I turned to the captain. "You want that?"

"Please keep them far away from my men." Dios was begging.

"Just keep the grass mowed down." I walked back off to the command tent.

———◆◆◆———

When I arrived, Colonel Seiford, Prince Edward, and Lady Gerate were already there. I gave Abby a nod. She'd already given me the World Below for my stunt at the docks. Then she'd made it up to me, and that had been worth it all.

I noticed two boxes sitting next to the map. "What's in those?" I asked.

Prince Edward ignored it. "You getting your strength back?" He shot an eyebrow up.

"I'm healing up, I suppose." I said it with a shrug, but the motion hurt my shoulder. "Bit by bit." I turned to Colonel Seiford. "Injuries like those don't heal all at once." I paused. "I'm ready to fight though, and soon, I'll be even more ready to fight." In truth, my body would never really be the same after the punishment it had endured on the docks. We were never the same men who set out on our quests, after all.

"Ready to go on some damn fool mission without telling anyone." Lady Gerate raised an eyebrow. No one raised an eyebrow like she did.

"I went out because there were things I needed to learn." I washed myself in a bowl of water. "I know what I need to now."

I could see she wasn't really understanding what I said, so I made it easier. "Little Tommy's not going anywhere." I splashed the water at her. "At least not for some time."

"You've broken that promise before." She put one hand on her hip. It made me want her.

"There'll be more promises broken before this war is over." War made liars out of us all. The worst one was, "I'll be home one day."

I went on "From here on, who wins will be decided in the old way." I pointed on the map. "It'll be our army against Thaniel's. We'll fight desperate battles for ridges, hills, and valleys no one cared about five years ago, and no one will care about once it's over."

Colonel Seiford stepped forward. "The men are ready for it." He nodded. "I've never seen a force quite like them."

"Hopefully, Thaniel won't be." Prince Edward's hand fell to his sword. "You've got more of those tricks, don't you?"

"We've played too many of them." I shook my head. "If any of my bluffs had been called this past year, we'd be worse off then before." I stared up at both of them. "Donkeys and scarecrows only work once." I straightened myself up. "This has been a hard war, and it'll only get harder."

Prince Edward allowed himself a rare smile. "Maybe, but your donkeys and scarecrows have done a bit to even the odds." He tapped the Kranish coast on the map. "We still have most of a fleet, but they don't. He'll need to deploy troops there to defend the coast."

Lady Gerate finally spoke up. "The Rhorii nationals are also giving Thaniel one hell of a fight." She touched my shoulder just the way I liked. "They won't win, but he'll need to waste troops there as well."

"So what's next?" Colonel Seiford asked what they were all thinking. "We'll fight him hard for our own land, but you want to end this war not prolong it."

"That's right I do want to end this war." I let my hand rock on the six-shooters. "For now we'll defend our border. We'll win some, and we'll lose some." I loved the way the grip felt in my hand. "Those allies who've been dragging their feet will see this isn't as hopeless as they thought it was."

Prince Edward nodded. "More will come and stand with us." He agreed. "Rustia is thinking of throwing their lot in, Gillen too."

I let my joy tug at the corner of my lips. "They'll come, and even that won't be enough." I paused. "Thaniel's too powerful." I knocked on the map. "He'll think we've played all the cards we can, and then I'll use one of my clever tricks."

"And what might that trick be?" Colonel Seiford asked.

"It'll be tricksy." I assured him.

"So you don't have a plan." He rolled his eyes.

"I've got the edges of a plan." My eyes fell to the Cretoin mountains. "I've got a plan by the legs, and I'm not letting go."

"So you don't have a plan." Colonel Seiford crossed his arms.

"Fuck you." I hissed back.

"It'll have to be enough for now." Prince Edward rolled up the map.

"What's in those boxes?" I pointed again to the wooden crates.

Colonel Seiford shrugged. "They arrived right before you did."

"Well, let's open them up." I took out my tomahawk and started to pry it open. It was a well-made box, but wood against ax is an unfair match at the best of times. Finally, I looked inside. I drew back immediately, heaving up whatever breakfast I'd managed to put down.

"Three above." Lady Gerate put her hand over her mouth. I was the only one who was sick. It was probably the surprise of it all.

I finally stood up and grabbed the head by the hair. "It's Fartow." It was the other Constable. The one who had warned me off a path. "Ragner is probably in that one too." They were both steady men. I hadn't liked either of them much, but they deserved better than this.

"Is it a threat?" Lady Gerate asked.

"Men like Thaniel don't play in threats." I put my hat on. "Neither do I." I walked out the tent flap. "Get the soldiers ready. We're marching before midday." This was going to be a hard war.

Present Day

J marched through the camp where my regiment was stationed, followed closely by Seiford. They all looked at me in awe and stood at attention as I walked by. I waved them down and even gave a few smiles and encouraging words, not that they needed much encouragement. My monk was the one who really knew what to say, anyhow.

The camp was sloppily erected with no rhyme or reason, their uniforms were utterly wrong, and though every other soldier was cleaning his new breech-loading rifle, courtesy of John Reard, they were doing it all wrong, just wiping a dirty rage on it over and over again. Most of them had never soldiered before, which was a scary thought. Yet, there was something else running through the camp.

It was the same feeling that accompanied all armies when they learned Belson the Blessed was at their head. It was the blind faith, the undo trust, that if I was leading them, they would taste victory. Still, there was something else behind that faith. It formed an alloy of the sort I'd never felt before. There was more there than the knowledge that I would win. Somewhere deep in the hearts of all these soldiers lied an unshakable hope, a pride even. *We would do it for the right reasons and the right way.* That's what I thought anyway. Maybe I was wrong, but a voice in me said I wasn't.

I thought an army built around more than one race would crumble from disunity. The effect was precisely the opposite. They were bound together by something other than where their ancestors came from. *Perhaps to them, it was just that the "infallible" Thomas Belson had ordered it, and he was always right.* I thought. After all, no one would argue with the man who broke Thaniel. I rolled my eyes at that. *No one but McAllan.*

Still, that kind of bigotry didn't die because a powerful man ordered it. It wasn't just me that ended it. They didn't see the race of the man who stood next to them. They saw what they could be.

They were going to fight for their country, and any man committed to doing the same deserved some respect, regardless of how easy he tanned. They had finally left the land of what is behind. The land of what could be would begin today. It had been staved off for too long. The new world would not wait any longer to draw breath. This army would protect that breath fragile though it was. The flickering fire of a hope that would not die while a single of these men yet lived. They were committed to that. They were bound together by something other than who they were. They were united by what they all could be.

Maybe somewhere down in their hearts they knew it was wrong to judge a man based on his color or creed. Maybe they just needed a reason to stop. War was as good a reason to unite as any, but they weren't drawn together by fear. They'd been offered a chance to be better men, and they'd taken it. I shook my head at the ridiculousness of it all. I remembered the speech I'd given Coleson. *When the chips are down, and their backs are against the wall, they surprise you.* I'd said. *They act like people.*

I couldn't keep the smile off my face. I'd fought my entire life just to prove I was the best. Now a bunch of store clerks, farmers, and even the odd lawyer, perhaps repenting for the sins of his profession, had shown me I wasn't. They'd decided to stand for something when the greatest hero in the world had written it off as impractical. I shook my head again. *Men always surprise you given half a chance.*

I looked back at Seiford as he shook the hand of a soldier. This was what he'd been working towards. The stories he told had finally born fruit in the hearts of men. This was the first step towards the righteous path. A small step along a great journey. The road ahead wasn't an easy one. There was nothing harder than this. Yet, even though it was small, it was an affirmation of everything Seiford believed. There was nothing harder than this... Nothing more worthy, either.

I felt it too. It was almost enough to beat the hunger inside of me. Maybe it would one day. Maybe after this, I could lay down my weapons. I could start a family of my own, but I knew my heart still called for Rachel. I wanted to accept what she'd offered, but a man's got a duty. No man's was greater than Belson the Blessed. Besides, what she'd offered would have destroyed me in the end. Even I could see that, though I wanted to see something different.

This army was untrained and green as the grass beneath my

boots. I had led untrained armies before, but it had been a long time since I'd led one with hope in its heart instead of desperation. Even then, with Thaniel knocking on the gates, it wasn't like this. These men would do.

Seiford and I walked into the command tent. We were the first ones there. Well, except for an old doctor who had tended my wounds fifteen years ago. He smiled at me, and it felt like taking a warm bath.

"Hello, Thomas." He nodded. "Hello, Seiford."

"I'm sorry, do I know you?" The monk gave a queer smile. He knew this man was more than he seemed, but when you meet a god, sometimes it takes a moment to process. Doctor Quarrels didn't even have a big white beard.

"More by reputation than personally." Quarrels chuckled. "I think you're familiar with my work."

"Thomas…" Seiford turned, looking for me to explain.

I put a hand on my friend's shoulder. "You remember that fellow Wisdom, you always go on about?" I patted his shoulder. "I've been meaning to introduce the two of you but never found the time."

Doctor Quarrels took a step towards the monk with his hand extended. "I think Seiford's done far more introducing me to you than the other way around." He nodded his respect. "For that I'm grateful."

"So this man is…" He glanced between the doctor and me ignoring the hand. Finally, he resolved himself. "I'm an admirer." Seiford didn't know whether to prostrate himself or not, so he dumbly took the hand. "Listen, I'm sorry about the lechery, drinking, and swearing! Times are stressful."

Quarrels waved it off. "If anyone knows how frustrating following this one around is, it's me." He took a step forward. "Anyhow, I'm far more concerned with men's virtues than their vices." He put his hand on the monk's shoulder. "You've been as good as anyone in that regard."

"So why are you here?" I asked.

"Thomas!" Seiford hissed at me. "Could you for once in your life, use a little courtesy?" He turned back towards the doctor. "You know how he is." He jutted a thumb at me.

"Aye, I do." Quarrel's nodded.

"I must admit a bit of curiosity to your…" Seiford trailed off, not really sure how to address the maker of the universe. "Highness?

Apologies, there isn't really a chapter for this in the edict books. What do I call you?"

"Well, I am I am." The god smiled. "You can just call me Doctor Quarrels, though."

"Doctor then." Seiford gave a weird little bow. "Despite my friend's impudence, I must admit I am curious as to why you're here as well."

"Just a thank you." Wisdom took a step back. "It seems our mutual friend is finally on the right path. It's in no small part to you."

"I do what I can." Seiford shrugged.

"No, you do what you must." He winked. "There's worse still ahead, but I'm proud of you both."

"I'm proud of you too." Seiford started than realized how far his foot was in his mouth. "I mean... I'm just..."

Someone opened the flap to the tent, and as we turned to face it, the god was gone. It was like he'd never been there.

It was Rolton, my old comrade from the Thaniel Wars. He looked so different from the street thug I'd known so long ago... From the man who tried to stay my hand in my darkest hour.

He looked like the man my parents had wanted me to become. The man who'd been a killer in an Anthanii slum and had become what kings were supposed to be.

"Who were you talking to?" Rolton asked.

"Just praying." I gave Seiford a wink. "Never hurts." I paused. "What are you doing here?" I asked.

"I've come to fight with you." Rolton nodded his head.

I shook my head at the old soldier. "Absolutely not."

"I wasn't asking your permission." Rolton smiled a bit. "I was just stating a fact."

"You've got a family now." I leaned against a table. "You've built a life. I can't let you throw it all away because you owe me some imagined debt."

Rolton shrugged. "I have made a life here." He answered. "I've got a woman I love and children who'll grow up strong." He took a step forward. "I've got a business that doesn't require as much attention as it used to." The old soldier looked me in my eyes. "I've got many regrets and a chance to set the biggest one right." He shrugged. "That's more than most men get, isn't it?"

"If it'll change your mind," I paused, "you were right when you left. I went too far."

"That's what makes it worse." Rolton shook his head. "I should've done more."

"We'll talk about this later." I waved him off. There was too much on my mind.

"Afraid it can't wait." Rolton's lips curled up in a smile. "Got Kelm, Harris, and all the other lads waiting down at the camp." He paused letting the wolfish grin I remembered grow. "Should I tell them to head to the armory, or should I just finance them to buy their own equipment? I'm rich enough for that, you know?"

I pulled out a slip of paper and scribbled the orders down. "Give this to the clerks." I handed it to him. "I'll talk you out of this tomorrow."

"Wouldn't bet on it." Rolton put on his hat and backed up to the tent flap. "It's good to be back, your eminence."

"It's good to have you back." I nodded, and he was out the tent. Despite me trying to refuse him, I wanted my old bodyguard with me. For practical reasons, he knew how I fought. Roltan and the veterans would be instrumental in training the recruits. For less practical reasons, I needed him all the more.

"I'm trying to give it out more freely these days." I smiled as she left. "Where's Ayn-Tuk?" I asked Seiford.

"Praying." The monk answered curtly.

"Really?" I asked. "What to?"

Seiford shrugged his shoulders. "I'm not sure, but he was on his knees by the river." He chuckled "That's how you pray isn't it?"

"We should have asked Doctor Quarrels while he was here." I turned back to the map and lit up a smoke. "He'd probably give some response about how praying is anything we do to better ourselves, and it wouldn't make any bloody sense to you or me."

"Almost forgot." Seiford pulled out a sealed envelope and handed it to me. "Mother Vestia sent this to you."

I took it from his hands and tried to open it. I found that I couldn't. "I treated her wrong." I said finally.

"You did." Seiford agreed.

"Reckon I'm not ready to face that yet." I put it in my coat pocket.

"You'll have to eventually." The monk shrugged.

"I will." I nodded. "Just not yet." I turned back to the map. "Let's plan a war."

Jesse gave Mary another hug. The rest of his family had stayed up north. He wanted them safe, and McAllan had assured the gunslinger he knew a place. However, the woman who had been a whore refused to leave until she'd said her goodbyes.

He still mourned his father, but in a strange way, Renny was more alive than he'd been in years. Somewhere the man was watching his son, and for the first time in a while, Jesse thought he was proud. He finally wore a uniform again. He had a cause to fight for. Thomas and McAllan talked a lot about building a better world. To him, none of that mattered. All he cared about was being the man his father wanted him to be.

"I won't promise anything about tomorrow." Jesse looked his woman in the eyes. "I know a man who lives by this." He grabbed the pistol at his side. "Can never really promise anything about tomorrow." He put a hand on her face. "But I love you."

She put her hand over his. "I wish you'd come up north with us." She smiled at him. "Thomas said Bo-Bo wouldn't get any worse up there. We could live a happy life." He saw a tear move down her face. "You could be a carpenter like you said and put those guns away for good."

Jesse wiped the tear away. "To tell you the truth I was never much good with wood." He smiled back at her.

"Then I'd be the poor wife of a bad carpenter, and that would be enough." She moved closer and kissed him. It was inappropriate for him to show affection in uniform, but he didn't care. "But you're not the same man you were when you came into the Western Rose all that time ago." She took his hand and played with it as if remembering all the nuances. "Back then there was always something dragging at you. Like you wanted to be a good man and didn't know how."

He felt her hands too, remembering how the softness felt against his calluses. "There was something dragging at you too."

"I know. It was my past." She smiled sadly. "That's why I liked you at first. It was because you didn't care about what I'd done, only who I was." She was still looking at his hands. "I started loving you because of the way you could see people like that." She looked so beautiful wearing her yellow dress. She looked beautiful in a whore's rags too though. "All I wanted was for you was to see yourself that way."

Mary stared at him proudly. "You finally do, and I'd never be so evil as to ask that you leave it behind." She straightened his uniform for him. "I told you once, a man who lives by the gun can never truly promise anything about tomorrow. I think I was right." She stared at him with those beautiful brown eyes. "But I don't think you live by the gun anymore. I think you live by a code now. I think you see something that needs doing and you'll do it. A man that lives by a code can always make promises, even if it's just that he'll die a good man."

Jesse folded her into another hug. "I'll come back to you when this is over."

"If you don't I'll know why." She said taking a step back. "You're needed here. That man Thomas Belson, well..." She paused not knowing what to say. "There's a greatness to him everyone in the world knows that." She took a step forward again. "There's a darkness to him too, though. I saw it when he helped us escape. I think he needs a man like you next to him." She shook her head. "I wish he didn't, but that's the way things are."

She reached up and stroked his battered face. "He needs the kind of man who can look into the eyes of a Priest about to murder his whole family and see something good in him." She wiped away one of his own tears. "He needs the kind of man who can lay a red rose on that Priest's grave even after he killed his father."

"I'll miss you." It was all Jesse could say.

"I'll miss you too." She said and left with a kiss.

After she was gone, Jesse walked off like he had to take a piss. It wouldn't do for the men to see him cry.

◆•◆•◆

McAllan shook Timothy's hand. "Are you sure you want to do this." It was strange to see him in a blue infantry uniform. The boy cut a handsome figure even if he only wore a private's rank.

The black boy laughed. "Three above of course I don't want to do this," his face grew sterner, "but I need to."

The Prime Governor smiled at the boy. "I'll need a new aide."

"Maybe you'll finally pick a white one." Samugy chuckled behind him.

Timothy ignored him. "You talked about building a better world, about the promise this country has." The boy nodded to himself. "I think I believe in the things you said." He clenched his jaw. "I don't figure I've got a right to do any less than this."

"You're a good lad." McAllan took a step back. "I never had any sons. I figure you're the closest I'll come."

"I-" Timothy didn't quite know what to say to that. "I'm proud you think of me like that."

"I've always had high hopes for you." McAllan said patting him on his shoulder

"I know that." The boy beamed back at him.

"Of course you did. You're a sharp lad." The Prime Governor looked at him. He'd grown so much in the three years they'd been together. "But I don't think you know how high." He sucked in a breath of air. "I think one day you might hold my office."

"But I'm black." Timothy scratched his head.

"I never said it'd be easy." McAllan smiled. "Nothing worth doing is."

"I won't disappoint you." The boy smiled back then hung his head a bit as if he didn't know how to say what was next.

"Even if Constable Belson drums you out the army today," McAllan took a deep pause, "you're the thing I'm most proud of."

A silent moment stretched between them. Not quite tense, but young men had trouble being sentimental. They tended to learn that in their later years.

"I always suspected about your wife." Timothy said finally meeting his eyes. "I never knew about your sister though. I'm sorry about that."

McAllan nodded. "We can't always fix what's wrong with the world, and maybe it's wrong to try and avenge it. All we can do is be better men." He touched the part of his uniform where the private patch was. "I think you'll be the better man one day if you aren't already."

"Thank you sir."

McAllan was about to leave for the council until Samugy took a step forward and shook the boy's hand. "Keep your head down." The Huego said with a frown. "War isn't like the stories they tell. There's too much chaos and shit for it to be that glorious." He released the boy. "Just listen to your sergeants and train hard. Above all, keep your head down when the shooting starts. Even a blackie mule like you might come out of this alive."

A curious look played across the boy's face. "You were in the army?" He asked.

"Not this army." Samugy looked around the camp. "But I've seen a few battles in my lifetime."

"Oh." McAllan could watch the moment Timothy began to see the Huego in a new light. "I never thought..."

"And try not too." Samugy said smugly. "Blackies aren't very good at it. Private blackies are even worse."

The spymaster dropped the callous act for one blessed moment. "Take care, Timothy. You're a good lad. The world needs more men like you not less." McAllan had never heard him address the boy by his actual name. "Whatever it is McAllan sees in you..." Samugy paused for a moment. This time it was tense. Sentimentality was the only trick he hadn't learned in his long mysterious life. "Well, I see it too."

"Thank you." Timothy shook the Huego's hand again and then turned to walk back to his company.

McAllan and Samugy watched as he was greeted by his comrades. They teased him for talking with the Prime Governor, but it was good-natured. They saw each other as soldiers, not by any race or former rank. It was what he had wanted, but he never expected it to happen so quickly.

"It's like watching my little nephew go off to his first day of Huego school." Samugy said spoiling the mood. "Wept like a little girl I did when he killed his first buffalo and learned how to give things ridiculous Huego names."

McAllan sighed, and they turned to walk towards the command tent. "Why'd you never tell me you were a warrior."

Samugy shrugged. "It was a long time ago." He said simply. "I'm not overly proud of the things I did." He turned to McAllan and smiled. "Besides you never asked."

"Cheeky fucker." The Prime Governor said with a laugh. "I wouldn't even know where to start asking."

"That's how a master liar operates." The Huego gave a slippery smile. "Keep things so close to the chest you only ever have to tell the truth."

"Penny for your thoughts?" Seiford asked as I looked over the plans.

"You wouldn't want them." I chuckled. "They're awfully bleak today."

Ayn-Tuk who had finally come in from doing whatever he had been doing, cut in. "Keep those thought's bleak, and they might stop a bleak reality." He put a hand on my shoulder. "Keep your heart light, though. Nothing's ever really so bad as it seems."

"Sage advice." I nodded to the black man. Finally, I got up my courage. "Ayn-Tuk, I feel I've a right to know. Why have you followed me all these years?"

"You do have a right to know." He nodded back. "But I can't tell you the full truth yet." The black man paused. "Only this, you needed help, and I was sent to guide you."

"You talk too little for someone sent to guide me." I huffed.

"The Northmen have a saying." Ayn-Tuk nodded. "It is the stagnant ore you notice, not the busy ones."

"Sounds a lot like a Northman was trying to get out of rowing." I mused to myself. "You never told me how you came to sail with them?" I asked.

"Not much sailing." Ayn-Tuk gave a rare smile. "Mostly rowing."

"One day I'll figure out who you are." I shook my head.

"One day you will." He agreed. "But on the day that you need to, and it's not today."

"Ah Thomas!" McAllan walked in with a smile. "I was hoping we'd find our hero here already."

"Well, if your tired of hoping you can settle for me." I said with a smile then turned to Jesse as he walked through the flap. "Sergeant Major, Devote." I nodded.

"Your Eminence." He answered. McAllan hadn't liked giving Jesse that title, and not just because he'd tried to kill the Prime Governor. I had made him the highest ranking enlisted in the regiment. He was second only to me. McAllan understood a good war record, but Jesse had only been a sergeant when he left the army. Still, oddly enough I trusted the big man, but there was more to it than that. I'd seen what he did to the Priest. Not many people could do that. The other side of the argument was that I needed as many people to reign me in as I could find. After colonel Seiford died was when I made my worst mistakes. I was trying to be better, but I still had a mean streak in me.

McAllan looked at the map and went on with the meeting "We have a division west to deal with Huego and Southern units up the river, and another two regiments north to give the Anthanii pause. I've put good generals in charge of them all." He pointed them all out. "The other regiments are farther north. They'll reinforce you as soon as they can, but make no mistake, the war hinges on you. The border provinces haven't declared yet, but they will soon."

"For us?" I asked.

"We thought so." Samugy cut in. "But Rachel's done her work well. The Anthanii are dragging their feet. Apparently the crown prince Edward has come out publicly against the war." He paused. "However, I have word that the Kranish might be closer than we thought." The Huego looked as if he hadn't slept in a week. "We may be more alone in this fight than we anticipated."

"We're outnumbered then?" Jesse narrowed his eyes.

"Right now, yes." Samugy answered.

"What about in a few months?" I caught the bait.

"We'll be outnumbered far more." The Huego said dryly.

"Desperate fights are my forte." I forced a smile.

"Might be they are, but being surprised isn't mine." Samugy looked back at the map. "Your girl is effective."

"That she is." I replied with a bite. "Do we have any advantages?" I took off my hat and wiped my brow.

This time it was McAllan's turn to answer. "We have better weapons and more a steady supply line. We can move our units quickly with railroads. Not to mention, we have our impressive navy."

"Well, that's good." I said trying to be the optimist.

Samugy grimaced. "Not as good as we thought though. Rachel's managed to secure contracts with Puena factories. They can't make things as quickly as we can or as well, but it's a damn sight better than what I thought they'd be able to do." He scratched his head. "I'd give my first born child to learn what she promised them. The Puena hate Coleson more than we do."

"She's that good?" Seiford asked with a cocked eyebrow.

"Ha." Samugy gave a dry laugh. "Is she that good he asks." He looked around the room to make sure we understood the gravity of it all. "This bitch has turned every advantage we thought we had against us." He looked back at the map. "This'll be a tough war to win. Make no mistake we're fighting Rachel Gondua, not Coleson. If that doesn't scare you, then you're a damn fool."

"Is she better than you?" I was thinking about how to win this war, but I would need good intelligence.

"Yes." The Huego didn't have to think about it, and that was frightening. "I've already had a few of my agents found face down in the river. It'd be impossible for her to completely blind me, but she's doing a damn fine job of obscuring my gaze. Many of the reports I get are conflicting or don't make much sense."

"Is that all?" I asked.

"No." Samugy reached into his pocket and drew out a blood-covered note. He opened it on the table, but it just seemed like random numbers and letters to me. "It's my code, but the agent who sent this died before I got my hands on it. It's like she wanted me to know this."

"What does it say?" McAllan chimed in.

"The Southern leadership is involved with the First." Samugy read it then looked around the room. It didn't have the effect he thought it would, except for me of course. "It has something to do with the Old Religion, but I don't know what."

"So?" Jesse asked. "Everyone knows they've got the Old Religion on their side, and Thomas just killed their most powerful Priest."

Samugy was about to respond, but Seiford answered first. "It didn't say the Old Religion. It said the First."

"What's the difference?" This time it was McAllan.

"The First refers to a sect of the Old Religion that's been inactive since the fall of Imor." There was more to it than that, but they wouldn't understand my explanation. The First was something you needed to see.

"So she can use the powers of the Imoran Empire?" Jesse seemed suitably terrified.

"Maybe." I scowled.

"She could be lying." McAllan proposed to the council.

I shook my head. "I don't think we should risk underestimating Rachel Gondua again." I felt my heart ache as I said her name.

"Regardless, she's the most dangerous woman in the world." The Huego appraised me up and down. "Maybe the most dangerous person in the world too." He shook his head. When you said that in a room with Thomas Belson in it, you meant something. "You should have killed her when you had the chance."

"Maybe I should have." I gritted my teeth. I'd told them about our last exchange, or at least about the parts they needed to know.

"This isn't looking good for us." Seiford said mostly to himself then perked up. "Good thing 'this isn't looking good for us' is Thomas's specialty."

"And that advantage might prove more important than all the rest." McAllan looked at me. "We have Belson the Blessed."

"I'll fight like as hard as I ever have." I stared back at the Prime Governor. "Still it's one regiment, seven thousand men."

"You beat Thaniel with one regiment." Jessie put in.

"No, I delivered the death blow with one regiment." I rapped my knuckles against the table. There were almost one hundred thousand men in that army." I shook my head. "Even then it still took five years and close to a million corpses. I'd rather not see what happened there happen here." I looked at the map. "Even if I win every battle there's a chance this doesn't end like we want it to."

"I know that, but there's more to it than the battlefield." McAllan straightened his coat. "Your reputation has power."

"I'd rather more cannons." I mused

McAllan ignored that. "People know your name, and they fear it." He said with an appraising look. "They're afraid to fight you."

"That didn't stop 'em in Thyro." I shot back.

"It's more than just that though." The Prime Governor walked up to the map. "They respect you. They love you." He smiled again. "The men who'll enlist in this war have grown up listening to your stories, and the parents who will send them off, told those stories. Their entire lives they've heard how you defend the weak and right the wrongs of this world. Now you fight for the Confederacy." He paused letting it sink in. "All of it, not just North or South." McAllan looked around the room. "They're not just afraid to fight you, they don't want to. The South has already started drafting men because every boy knows that any side you're against is the wrong one."

McAllan took out a cigar and started to smoke it. "Meanwhile, we haven't needed a draft. Our recruiting stations are overrun with requests to serve under you. We're still trying to outfit all of them. They've dreamed their entire lives of standing by you on the field of battle. Now nothing will stop them. You've got a regiment now, but it will grow in time." He chuckled through his cigar. "Young men even sneak across the border to join your cause."

"Really?" I asked.

"We've already caught a few thousand." McAllan gave the room an optimistic look. "And that's just the ones we've caught. We're not very good at catching them."

"What do you do when you catch them?" Seiford looked worried.

"We direct them to the nearest recruiting station." McAllan smiled. "I told you. This war isn't about the North. It's about The Confederacy.

"That's all well and good," I responded, "but the rest are still at our throats."

"Not exactly." Samugy cut in. "Rachel convinced the provincial governments to fight for her, but she didn't convince the people." He gestured to the middle provinces on the map. "The popular opinion is with us. They've already started rioting over it." He pointed at Seiford. "That little speech you gave at the assembly is already being printed and the powers that be are trying to stop it." He went back to the map. "Even in the South, there's a large group of people who want to put down their arms and find a better way." He looked up at me. "The whole country believes in you. I've always been a cynical man, but maybe this could win the war for us."

"Well, I'll just have to figure a way to keep us going until it does." I nodded at McAllan. "You'd better go give a speech to the men while you're here." I'd heard of the Prime Governor's oratory skill.

"I just so happen to have a speech planned." McAllan said smiling over his cigar.

"Sergeant Major Devote go form up the men. I'll be out shortly." I said without looking up from the map. The men needed to learn to take orders from him.

They left the tent. Samugy went to follow, but I stopped the spymaster. I waited until the form up command was called and looked at the Huego.

"You knew what Rachel was?" I asked.

"I suspected." Samugy nodded grimly. "I didn't know how powerful the girl had become, but I knew she was something."

"How?" I looked at Seiford then back at the Huego. Was I the only one who couldn't figure it out?

"She had a silence about her that's uncommon in my line of work. She slept with Coleson, and no one could tell me much about her." The Huego looked like he'd been beaten.

"What did you hear about her time in Thyro?" That was what I really wanted to know.

"Only whispers."

"What kind of whispers?" I pressed him.

"The same kind that follows you. She's not known by many, but those that do talk about Rachel Gondua the same way peasants talk about Belson the Blessed." Samugy clenched his jaw. "She rubbed elbows with powerful people. She manipulated things to go her way, but no one could tell me exactly what her way was." He sucked in a breath. "Some say she's even gone to the ruins of Imor." He looked at me. "Just like you.'

"That's one of the stories I don't like people telling." I narrowed my eyes. It was mentioned from time to time. I even used it to give my name a bit more weight, but I had never spoke the truth of what I saw in those ruins.

"So it's true then?" Samugy looked like he was trying to understand it all.

"It's true." I nodded

"What'd you find there?" The Huego asked, but it didn't seem like he really wanted to know the answer. He wanted me to tell him the broken city was just your regular sort of broken city. He wanted me to tell him the myths were just wive's tales to keep children on the straight and narrow.

I disappointed him "One of my secrets." I snarled at the memory. "Things that shouldn't be found, not even by me."

"You think she found them too?" Samugy looked at my tattoos.

"Time was, I didn't think anyone else could have come out of that place." I pulled out a smoke and lit it. "Times change."

"Aye, they do." Samugy said cautiously. "I'd better go see McAllan unless there's anything else you need to know."

Does she love me? Did she ever love me? "Nothing you could tell me." I said it barely a whisper and when Seiford and I were alone, I hunched my shoulders over the map. "She's good Seiford."

"So are you." My friend smiled that dumb smile he had. "No man's ever gotten rich betting against Thomas Belson."

"I don't know that people should be betting a country on me these days." I gestured to the map. "I'm not the man I was."

"No one ever is." He put a hand on my shoulder. "I think you're better for it, though."

I sighed. "Despite everything Samugy said about the populace, she's winning right now."

"So was Thaniel at one point." Seiford kept up that damn optimism.

"And you remember what I had to do to end that." I shook my head. "I can't do it again."

"We'll find a way." Seiford patted my shoulder.

'What if it's the wrong way?" I shook my head. "What if I can't win and be the man you all seem to think I am?"

"We'll find another path." I wished I had his faith.

"What if there isn't one?" I stared at Seiford, wanting what he said to be true.

"We'll make one." The monk patted my shoulder. "Or we'll die trying."

I nodded. "For once in my life, I'm fighting to win, not just beat someone else." I sighed. "I believe in this country."

"It's a good thing to believe in." Seiford said it softly

"You never asked what Rachel offered me." I turned back to my friend.

"It doesn't matter." Seiford smiled. "Besides, I don't want to hear about how she agreed to wear a mask of me in bed."

That made me chuckle. "She said we'd be king and queen over all the earth." I grew grim. "She offered it to me, and I believed her." I showed my friend what I was. I showed him the broken thing I'd become. "I wanted to accept it more than I've wanted anything else."

"Why didn't you?" Seiford asked.

"Who knows?" I laughed to myself. "Maybe I'm so used to fighting, I fought her too." It could have been true. "Maybe I'm finally starting to believe those stories you tell about me." That was probably closer.

"Who do you think I tell them for?" The monk kept his dumb smile.

"Well, I guess I better go give the men a speech, don't I." I said straightening my coat.

"Have you given any thought to what you're going to name them." Seiford chuckled. "Every army deserves a name."

"I was thinking the Theben Regiment." I smiled at my friend.

"The redemption regiment." Seiford knew that Rhorii word well.

"Why not? We all need it from time to time." I said and walked out of the tent.

"-For the Confederacy!" I heard McAllan end his own speech. It must have been a good one. The soldiers seemed filled with fire.

I walked over to the podium. My leg still hurt, but it wouldn't do to limp in front of the army. I climbed on top and saw the eager faces looking at me. A rumbling went through the crowd.

"I heard he killed fifty Priest in Pentsville."

"I heard he dueled a giant."

"Where's his dragon?" I was used to being greeted like that.

I held up a hand to stop the talking. When they were silent, I began. "For as long as I can remember my father called this the land of what could be." I looked back at Seiford who smiled encouragingly. "That seems to mean different things to different people though. Some saw it as a land where a man can choose his own way to live his life. Some saw it as a land where they could find new ways to oppress people. Some people thought it meant a land where all men were equal, but still, some thought they were more equal than others."

Def

That got a chuckle out of them. "My father told me it was a place where we could build a new world." I continued. "I don't think I really understood what that meant until I saw the old one. This will be the land worth shedding our blood for! This will be the land where men can ascend to any height! Without scraping to the Demon's Below!" I let the words ring out. "We forge that land today!" I ended with a scream, and the men returned it.

"Three hundred years ago, the first Anthanii settlers arrived here. They faced untamed wilderness and unlivable conditions. They faced a world that wanted them gone, and they stayed. They wrote home of the horrors they faced. Starvation, disease, and death waited around every corner. They told their kin about the fresh hell they had made home, and more came. Not just Anthanii, not even just Thyro's, people from every corner of the world sailed across this ocean, two thousand miles from civilization. They did these things because they knew what this land could become. They would build their better world and damn anything that tried to stop them!" That brought another cheer.

I went on. "One hundred years ago our Anthanii masters saw the flame we lit even across the ocean. They feared what that flame might become. They feared it because their people saw it too. They tried to stamp it out, and our forefathers screamed back in one voice, we will see this fire engulf the entire world!" They cried out again.

"At times we have fallen. At times we have failed. We bickered amongst each other. We pushed our brother's face into the mud while the wolf waits at our door. Yet we picked ourselves up. The flame grew! It is still growing!." I paused for a moment. "It will not die while I breathe."

"Some may ask why we'll fight and die to bring our wayward brothers back into the fold. If they wish to bask in the old ways than let them. We will bring them back because they are kin. The Old Religion promised them something that was not theirs to give. They promised them a utopia. The Old Priest built them a grand castle with its foundation in sand. The cost of that goes beyond tortured children and crimson masters. The Priests take their very souls. That utopia they have promised will never exist. The Demons cannot give it to us. Men must build it. Men must die to protect it."

I sucked in another breath. "Some of you may look to me as the hero who can save this nation. That is not me. Giants do not defend the rights of man, men do that. I will lead you though. I will show the world that watches us now, that while the emperors, kings, and politicians, who claim to protect us hid, the brave men of the Confederacy stood fast." They cheered again.

"I anoint all you now men of the Theben Regiment. From now till the end of days, our scions will look upon us and know what it means to be free. It means, free to live by an ideal. It means, free to die for it." I looked around the men. They were untrained, but they would do. "For ten thousand years our decedents shall ask what would the brave men of the Theban Regiment do? We will show them the path. We build our new world today. We spread our fire over all creation. The whole world watches what we do next. Should we disappoint them?"

"No!" They screamed back at me

"Good." I pointed at the mountain behind them, and they looked. "That hill looks like it needs to be climbed. It's three miles up and three miles down." I smiled at them. "Forges only work when it's hot you know." I jumped off the podium and started off running despite the pain in my knee. The men followed in turn. All hurried to be at my side. The land of what could be would not die for lack of effort.

It was late in the night, and despite the training I'd led my men through, sleep would not find me. I meant what I said to the army. They would become something better than they were. They would fulfill the promise Ironwill had made a century before, but there was much work to be done. I even thought of Rachel and the burning she'd left me with. However, it was not these things that kept me from the sweet oblivion.

The Priest I killed, Bellefellow... He was more powerful than even Thaniel's great Demon Speakers. It was blind luck I killed him and perhaps a bit of his arrogance. Then Samugy had found a note that mentioned Dark Forces. I remembered what Rachel had promised me. We would be king and queen of the world eternal. She had believed it. One man had made that claim before. He had believed it too.

The Huego were perhaps the only people in the world who didn't speak to the World Below. In the three hundred years Thyrans had been observing them, no one found a hint of it. Now I had encountered two Demon-Bound. It was powerful magic. At least some of the Huego tribes were turning back to a distant past. No one knew what that past might be. No one except for me.

The Old Religion was evil. I knew that to be true, but there was worse still in the world. I told people the Pillars had been to prevent another war, to finish Kran and for good. That had been a half-truth.

In the end, in Thaniel's desperation or arrogance, he'd turned to powers he thought he could control. I knew he couldn't. The magic his Priests worked in chambers below the Rose Petal Throne was more dangerous than his armies ever were. They would have destroyed us all. Not just one city or country or continent, all of us. I nailed children up to wooden pillars to make sure that didn't happen.

I thought I'd ended it that day. As it turns out I hadn't. Now, in a distant land, ten years later, someone sought to do what Thaniel couldn't. That was the end game, and I felt it in my bones.

What would I have to do to end it again? Could I end it again? Neither were questions I liked the answer to. I didn't sleep well that night. I knew I wouldn't for some time.

Epilogue

Red Bear walked to the council. He wanted to weep at what his world had come to, but he needed to be strong today. He was the youngest chieftain to be represented. He remembered why that was, and he remembered why this title had been given to him. He was a good man and had won his name for his unyielding bravery, yet he was scared.

He walked into the large tent. It had been sewn together from a hundred pelts of bison. The tent was sacred and only used at the most important of gatherings. Red Bear was the last to arrive. The chieftains were sitting around the fire in the center. It burned blue to show that the Three Great Spirits watched them. Would they like what they saw? Red Bear thought not.

Swift Deer was there, so was Silent Eagle, and Plain Horse. There were a hundred representatives from a hundred different tribes all set to one task taking back their land.

Above them all sat Stone Lion. He'd fought the white men longer than most had been alive. He'd even won a few of those battles, which was getting rarer. A black mark had hung over him since his brother, Slippery Snake, had gone to work for the Confederacy. He raised his hand for the meeting to begin.

"Since the first white men came, our people have been pushed to the edges of a land that is ours by every right that matters to men." Stone Lion shook his head angrily. "They take our ears for sport, they poison our crops, and they have the gall to call us savages." He scowled at the memory. "It is time to push back. Back into the sea where they belong."

"And how should we do that?" Biting Mule asked. He had a reputation for being a pragmatic man. "We've fought them since they came on their wooden horses from the Easter Lands. We are losing. They have better weapons." He looked around at the council. "Not just their guns and steel but the most secretive and dangerous weapon. They have discipline." He shook his head. "In the battles I've seen, white discipline is worth ten fold what Huego bravery is."

"You think their warriors better than ours?" One man Red Bear recognized as Sleeping Rabbit asked.

"I think warrior to warrior we are the stronger. That is not the question that keeps me awake at night." Biting Mule paused. "Battles are not fought warrior to warrior. They are fought army to army, and there they are the stronger."

"You're a coward." One man Red Bear did not know, spat the ground.

"I think you know in your heart I am not." Biting Mule responded levelly. His way was always calm and slow to anger, but men knew what his anger could become. "I have bloodied my tomahawk in many battles." He returned to the council. "They can sweep entire battlefields with their cannons that shoot fire and death, they can make their soldiers hold the line against great numbers of Huego Howlers, and most frightening of all to a clever man, they can feed and water their men over great distances with this sorcery they call logistics. I have tried to emulate them, and in many cases, I have succeeded." It was true. With the implementation of this Confederacy discipline Biting Mules tribe had gone from small and unimportant to one of the greatest in the land. They even rivaled Stone Lion's. "Still mine is just one tribe in a sea of men fighting with the old ways. Our people fight as individuals striving for glory, not soldiers fighting for victory."

"So if we can't fight the white men what shall we do?" A younger chieftain called Walking Tree asked. His name came from his size. He was large even by the white man's standards.

"We must find ways of making them fear us on the battlefield first, but this is not the end of it." Biting Mule raised a hand to illustrate the point. "That is the short term victory. The long term one is to adopt some of their ways. We need to learn how to forge weapons from fire and metal as they do. We need to organize our armies so that we can establish discipline. Most importantly we need to start teaching the younglings their magics of trapping stories on paper. They call this reading and writing. I myself have learned, and it has done my tribe great benefit. With this magic all other things become possible."

"You want us to become them!" A man Red Bear couldn't see screamed.

"I want us to acknowledge that our world has grown, and we must grow with it." Biting Mule said with his typical calm. "War is but one part of a wider game. We must learn to trade and prosper with them. We must make them need us. This capitalism, as they call it, could benefit us greatly. We must think of things not as disadvantages, but opportunities to grow greater as a people. As the old proverb says, when the rabbit runs, search for the deer. We scour our land looking for the rabbit while the deer nuzzles our shoulder." He looked around in empathy. "We must change the weapons we fight with both on the battlefield and, as these strange easterners say, the market." He took out his own tomahawk and looked at it, then threw it into the blue fire and pulled a piece of twisted metal. Red Bear recognized it. It was a six shooter. He had one of his own but dared not bring it inside the holy tent. "We cling to our old ways as if they are planks of wood keeping us from drowning. Maybe it is time to build wooden horses of our own." Biting Mule sat down and waited for a response. Red Bear had to admit he agreed with much of what the older Huego said.

Another man stood up. This time it was Silent Eagle. "Do we use muscles to wrestle the big man? Do we use speed to outrun the fast man?" Silent Eagle looked around to see that he was understood. "Then why would we try to beat the white man at his own game." He gestured to his clothes. Even in the blue light of the tent they seemed to blend with everything. "Our strength is tied to our lands. We can hide two paces away and be invisible. We can cause havoc and be gone before they have time to wield their great cannons that sweep battlefields with fire and death." He gestured to Biting Mule. "Perhaps on a set battlefield there is little hope for victory, but where the bison fails the snake may succeed." The man stroked his tomahawk gently. "We turn their formations against them. Pride in the past has made us foolish. We have formed lines against them. We have shouted 'Here we are! Do your worst!' and they have!"

"We are not so weak as to let them take our pelts and women with no challenge." Red Bear heard a man he knew as Coming Storm.

"Yes, but do we need to announce so loudly where that challenge should be?" Silent Eagle proclaimed for the council. "When they march on our people we must needle them from every direction, and when they reach our camps they will be gone like the shifting wind." Silent Eagle was a clever man. "Turn our weakness to strength and their strength to weakness. While defeating them entirely is impossible we can make them pay so dearly they will know it is not worth it." He paused to let the point sink in. "When we lose a match, the correct decision is not to continue fighting to show our courage, but to change the nature of the game and win that one."

A rumbling agreement ran through the tent.

"I agree with much of what Biting Mule has said. War is but the beginning. After they have gone back to their cities, we should trade our pelts with them." Silent Eagle continued on his momentum. "However, our solution is not to bend to their culture, but to show them the strength of our own." He took out his necklace laced with thirty white ears. Red Bear knew that was just the beginning of the men he had killed. "They take our ears now because we taught them that savagery. They know nothing about us but what they have seen on the battlefield." He paused knowing the point he was going to make would not sit well. "And what they have seen is barbarism in victory and shame in defeat. We must learn to trap stories on paper not to read theirs, but to show them our own." He threw the necklace of ears into the blue fire and they crackled next to the tomahawk. "We must teach them of the Three Great Spirits that guide our lives and freed us from the Ancient Prisons. We must show them the way of the great plain within. There is good and evil to every people. Where they have seen only evil let us show them good. First on the battlefield and then through our own stories." He looked around the tent again. "Perhaps, the white man is not so alien to ourselves, and it is time to show the white man that we are not so alien either." Silent Eagle sat down and waited for another to speak.

Both had made excellent points, but both were reflections of their own tribes. Bitting Mule's people lived closer to the Confederacy than any other, and had learned the ways of the white man. He had seen their skills and had come to adapt them. Silent Eagle's people claimed the southern desert as their home. He was many days ride removed, and the ones who came to him were often men seeking adventure. He had come to respect their ways and they had come to respect his. Both men had found much success in their strategies, more success than most of the other chiefs. Still, they were wise men in a desert of vicious anger. Many at the council even called them traitors, though not within hearing distance. Their plans were good, but they would not drive the white man into the sea as most at the council wanted done. However, that goal was impossible. Also the rage felt at the council was not entirely unjust. The Easterners had killed thousands and displaced many more. The way of the Three Spirits was waining, and soon all Huego's would speak Anthanii, at least the ones that weren't dead.

Red Bear had not spoken yet. He was respected but young, and his words would be written off as such. Still he had to speak now for his wives and his children, for the whole of his tribe, and for the ways of his people. He stood up.

"I am young in flesh, but old in spirit." Red Bear said calmly. "Biting Mule and Silent Eagle have raised good points, yet I would like to expand upon them." He looked around the room. "I have killed many white men myself, and like many here, I speak their language as well." He looked to his own tomahawk. "When they lie dying the things they say are not so different from when we join the land. They cry out for water, maybe hard spirits if the wound is bad enough. Above all they cry out for one more touch of their mother." He paused. "I do not think at their core, the Easterners are so different from ourselves. I have even found myself weeping in the night for those I have killed."

"Another traitor." A man said angrily. Red Bear silenced him with a look and continued.

"You overlook the way they govern themselves." He went on. "They do not rule by chieftains proven in battle, but by politicians elected through a majority vote. I must admit I found it strange at first, but now I have come to see the wisdom in this. We must show their citizens what is done to us and they will pressure their government to leave us be. They know only of our raids and battles and nothing else. They count only the dead as we do."

"And our dead are numbering more every day!" This time it was Wild Mustang who spoke. He was a good man but impetuous.

"Aye." Red Bear agreed. "But those who have gone back to the land don't care about revenge. Our thoughts must turn to the living. This man McAllan has helped us."

"And what happens when another takes his place?" Jumping Frog asked. It was a good question.

"We must petition their people to elect another man such as him." He looked at the blue fire. "War has failed us. Now we must reach out with the open hand. When they first arrived it was just white men, but now black and yellow have joined them. Why do we not ask to join and share the land as one?"

"And have you seen how they treat these new men." Wild Mustang spoke out angrily again.

"Aye, many were mistreated at first, but as people saw them as men, things have begun to change. Maybe we should look to them as examples." Red Bear said.

"We will not put our people at the mercy of theirs." Jumping Frog said angrily.

"If you still want war than consider this." Red Bear looked around room. "We could not beat their armies as they were, but I have word another man is here. We will be fighting him"

"These are rumors." Howling Wolf muttered.

"These are true." Red Bear addressed them grimly. "Their greatest warrior is returning from across the wide water. This man has broken every enemy in the circle of the world. Are you vain enough to think you can stop him?"

"We can kill anyone." Walking Tree spit into the ground. "I boxed against their greatest fighter and won."

"You've never fought against Thomas Belson." Red Bear shook his head.

"You're a coward." Sleeping Rabbit shook his head.

"No, I'm afraid, and if you aren't you're a fool." He shot back.

"I'll show you who the fool is!" Sleeping Rabbit drew his tomahawk and Red Bear drew his.

Stone Lion raised his hand to stop them all. "There will be no bloodshed in this sacred place." He had stayed silent as the council spoke. He stood. Red Bear and Sleeping Rabbit took their seat.

Stone Lion continued once order had been restored. "We have been offered two choices subjugation or death, but there is another way." He let the full weight of his gaze set on the council. "The old ways will not save us." He looked at Silent Eagle. "The new ways will not save us." He looked at Bitting Mule. "And their queer democracy will not save us." He looked at Red Bear. "The Ancient Ways will reclaim our land, though." He looked at the blue fire. "All of it."

"You can't mean…" Red Bear looked at the man he had once admired. He knew it was on the table, but to hear a man like him say it was like a blow he was not ready for.

"I mean the powers with which we created stone temples that reached into the sky. The powers that leveled mountains and flooded deserts. I mean the powers that can push the white man into the sea." Stone Lion let the deadly purpose on his face show. "For years the

Demons we called on were silent in these lands, but we hear them speaking again. Even before this council some have reached out to touch it."

"We turned our backs on such powers a thousand years ago." Red Bear shook his head. "We closed the door on those Demons and the cost was far more than even what the white man takes from us." Red Bear was pleading now. "What will be the cost to close them again? That is a door that stays open."

"It is our only option to destroy the Easterners." He scowled at the young man.

"It might destroy us too." Red Bear shot back.

"And if we do nothing our destruction is assured." Stone Lion looked to the crowd. "I wouldn't have asked this a century ago. I wouldn't have asked this yesterday, but there is no option. The white men go to war with themselves. Their attention is divided, and there are those sympathetic to our cause." Rumbling assent ran through the crowd. "Who is opposed to it now. The lesser of two evils."

Red Bear raised his hand so did Silent Eagle, Biting Mule, and a handful of others. It wasn't enough.

Stone Lion continued. "The course is set." He paused. "Come now!" He shouted outside the tent. A woman walked in beautiful as any Red Bear had ever seen. She was naked except for a necklace of skulls that hung around her neck. She was as seductive as any he had seen, yet Red Bear was disgusted by her. "This is the One Who Speaks to Demons." Stone Lion went on. "There is a woman in the South who has assured us of a war to come. This war will make them weak. Then we will strike." He looked to the woman. "Sing for us." He commanded.

She sung then and the wind picked up. He heard crackling and popping. Her singing was haunting and beautiful. She sung with voices not heard in a thousand years, now released back into the world. The wind extinguished the blue flame and all it represented. Red Bear wept then for his wives and family, for his tribe, and his people as a whole. This was how the way of the Three Spirits died.

CPSIA information can be obtained
at www.ICGtesting.com
Printed in the USA
LVHW111105240321
682292LV00001B/1